GW01459536

Palgrave Studies in the Enlightenment, Romanticism and Cultures of Print

Series Editors
Anne K. Mellor
Department of English
University of California Los Angeles
Los Angeles, CA, USA

Clifford Siskin
Department of English
New York University
New York, NY, USA

Palgrave Studies in the Enlightenment, Romanticism and Cultures of Print features work that does not fit comfortably within established boundaries – whether between periods or between disciplines. Uniquely, it combines efforts to engage the power and materiality of print with explorations of gender, race, and class. By attending as well to intersections of literature with the visual arts, medicine, law, and science, the series enables a large-scale rethinking of the origins of modernity.

Editorial Board: Isobel Armstrong, Birkbeck College, University of London, UK; John Bender, Stanford University, USA; Alan Bewell, University of Toronto, Canada; Peter de Bolla, University of Cambridge, UK; Robert Miles, University of Victoria, Canada; Claudia Johnson, Princeton University, USA; Saree Makdisi, UCLA, USA; Felicity A Nussbaum, UCLA, USA; Mary Poovey, New York University, USA; Janet Todd, University of Cambridge, UK.

More information about this series at
http://www.palgrave.com/gp/series/14588

Matthew Sangster

Living as an Author in the Romantic Period

palgrave
macmillan

Matthew Sangster
University of Glasgow
Glasgow, UK

Palgrave Studies in the Enlightenment, Romanticism and Cultures of Print
ISBN 978-3-030-37046-6   ISBN 978-3-030-37047-3   (eBook)
https://doi.org/10.1007/978-3-030-37047-3

© The Editor(s) (if applicable) and The Author(s), under exclusive licence to Springer Nature Switzerland AG 2021
This work is subject to copyright. All rights are solely and exclusively licensed by the Publisher, whether the whole or part of the material is concerned, specifically the rights of translation, reprinting, reuse of illustrations, recitation, broadcasting, reproduction on microfilms or in any other physical way, and transmission or information storage and retrieval, electronic adaptation, computer software, or by similar or dissimilar methodology now known or hereafter developed.
The use of general descriptive names, registered names, trademarks, service marks, etc. in this publication does not imply, even in the absence of a specific statement, that such names are exempt from the relevant protective laws and regulations and therefore free for general use.
The publisher, the authors and the editors are safe to assume that the advice and information in this book are believed to be true and accurate at the date of publication. Neither the publisher nor the authors or the editors give a warranty, expressed or implied, with respect to the material contained herein or for any errors or omissions that may have been made. The publisher remains neutral with regard to jurisdictional claims in published maps and institutional affiliations.

Cover illustration: Peter Barritt / Alamy Stock Photo

This Palgrave Macmillan imprint is published by the registered company Springer Nature Switzerland AG.
The registered company address is: Gewerbestrasse 11, 6330 Cham, Switzerland

Acknowledgements

This book could not have been written without the backing of the Royal Literary Fund (RLF), which provided the funding that supported both my doctoral research and my concurrent work cataloguing the RLF Archive at the British Library. The experience of completing the catalogue has had an enormous positive impact on my thinking about authorship in the early nineteenth century and on my academic approach more broadly. I'd like to thank the RLF Committee and Eileen Gunn, the Fund's Chief Executive, for their ongoing interest and steadfast support over the twelve years I've been working on this project.

This monograph has benefitted enormously from the digital accessibility of excellent editions of many of the authors I examine and from online repositories of periodicals. However, many of my most transformative research experiences have come from working with paper archives, where I've benefitted both from the meticulous cataloguing work of generations of curators and the generosity of current custodians, who've guided me to materials I'd never have thought to look at on my own and have also been very understanding when letting me browse extensively to facilitate chance encounters. I'd particularly like to thank the curators and staff at the following institutions for their assistance and insights: New York Public Library (especially Elizabeth Denlinger and Charles Carter), the National Library of Scotland (especially Rachel Beattie and Kirsty McHugh) and the Special Collections Department at the University of Reading. I remain hugely indebted to Jamie Andrews and all my other former colleagues at the British Library, particularly Chris Beckett, Rachel Foss, Kathryn

Johnson, Helen Melody, Rachel Stockdale, William Stockting and Zoë Wilcox, for their help and advice.

While I was developing this project as a doctoral thesis, my supervisor, Judith Hawley, provided invaluable guidance and trenchant criticism to keep me on course; I'm profoundly grateful for her many contributions. I'm also grateful for the helpful feedback and encouragement provided by my advisor, Vicky Greenaway, and my examiners, Andrew Bennett and Gregory Dart. Over its long gestation, this book has benefitted enormously from the wisdom and encouragement of colleagues and friends. Conversations with Kerri Andrews, Jennie Batchelor, Alex Benchimol, Daniel Cook, Jeff Cowton, Sarah Crofton, Jeremy Davies, Zara Dinnen, Chris Donaldson, Elizabeth Eger, Mary Fairclough, David Fallon, Margot Finn, Tim Fulford, Michael Gamer, John Gardner, James Grande, Katie Halsey, Oliver Herford, David Higgins, Felicity James, Jordan Kistler, Nigel Leask, Jon Mee, Anthony Mandal, Anne Mellor, Olivia Murphy, Dahlia Porter, Lynda Pratt, Sharon Ruston, William St Clair, Helen Stark, David Stewart, Will Tattersdill, Jo Taylor, Mark Towsey, Bea Turner, Nicky Watson and Jamie Whitehead have been especially important to my progress.

Writing this in June 2020, after several months locked down at home during the COVID-19 pandemic, has brought home to me again how important talking with others at conferences and seminars has been for my development as a scholar. I'm not going to append a long list here, but I'd like to acknowledge the British Association for Romantic Studies and the North American Society for the Study of Romanticism for their ongoing efforts to facilitate conversations in the field. I'd also like to extend a general thanks to all those I've talked with or listened to at conferences not already named above—it's always an enormous pleasure and privilege to hear about others' new work and to gain different perspectives on my own.

I'm grateful to the following organisations for permission to quote directly from unpublished archival materials: the Royal Literary Fund; the British Library; the National Library of Scotland; the Berg Collection and the Carl H. Pforzheimer Collection of Shelley and His Circle, New York Public Library, Astor, Lenox, and Tilden Foundations; and the University of Reading Special Collections.

A few paragraphs modified in the Introduction and Chapter Four first appeared in my article "'You have not advertised out of it": Samuel Taylor

Coleridge and Francis Jeffrey on Authorship, Networks and Personalities' in *Romanticism and Victorianism on the Net*, 61 (2012). A differently inflected version of elements of Chapter Five was published as 'Adapting to Dissect: Rhetoric and Representation in the Quarterly Reviews in the Romantic Period' in *Romantic Adaptations: Essays in Mediation and Remediation*, ed. Cian Duffy, Peter Howell and Caroline Ruddell (Farnham: Ashgate, 2013), pp. 57–72. The shared material is reproduced here with the permission of the publisher.

28th June 2020   Matthew Sangster

Contents

Preface: The Life of the Author   1

Introduction: What Was an Author in the Romantic Period?   13

Chapter One: Publishers, Book Production and Profits   51

Chapter Two: Sociable Alignments   83

Chapter Three: Succeeding in 'the Worst Trade'   121

Chapter Four: The Working Writer   177

Chapter Five: The Oligarchs of Literature: Authority and
the Quarterly Reviews   233

Chapter Six: Refashioning Authorship's Purview   273

Coda: Print Proliferation and the Invention of the Artist   317

Bibliography   335

Index   355

Note on Abbreviations and Attributions

As this book ranges widely rather than focusing intensively on a small body of works, references for books, periodicals and online resources are given fully in the notes for the sake of clarity. However, extensive use has been made of certain manuscript repositories, which are abbreviated as follows:

BL	British Library, London
NLS	National Library of Scotland, Edinburgh
NYPL Berg	Henry W. and Albert A. Berg Collection of English and American Literature, New York Public Library
NYPL Pforzheimer	Carl H. Pforzheimer Collection of Shelley and His Circle, New York Public Library
URSC	University of Reading, Special Collections

I have made particularly heavy use of the Archive of the Royal Literary Fund, held at the British Library (Loan 96 RLF). When referring to parts of this archive, I have generally omitted 'BL' and provided the title and the full number for the relevant series, file or item as given in the online catalogue, compiled while completing this study (the catalogue entries can be accessed using http://searcharchives.bl.uk).

Following standard conventions, I have abbreviated the *Oxford English Dictionary* as *OED* and the *Oxford Dictionary of National Biography* as *ODNB*. In both cases, I have worked from the online versions (www.oed.com and www.oxforddnb.com).

To aid the identification of periodicals at a time when the easiest means of access are digital, I have given enough relevant information clearly to identify a specific issue, generally adding, for example, the month of publication for monthlies or the season for quarterlies. When referring to Romantic-period Reviews, I have given the running title for longer articles where the journal itself provides one; for all relevant reviews, I have given a page range to indicate their scope. I have capitalised 'Review' when referring to periodicals (as opposed to articles) to avoid confusion between containers and contents.

Unless otherwise indicated, authorship attributions for articles in the *Edinburgh Review* are taken from the *Wellesley Index to Victorian Periodicals, 1824–1900* (originally edited by Walter Houghton; now maintained online at http://wellesley.chadwyck.com) and those for the *Quarterly Review* from *The Quarterly Review Archive*, ed. Jonathan Cutmore, *Romantic Circles*, 2005, https://romantic-circles.org/reference/qr/.

All URLs were checked and were functional on 28th June 2020 unless otherwise noted. DOIs or equivalents have been preferred where available.

Preface: The Life of the Author

At the beginning of the twentieth century, existing as an author in Britain was a profoundly different prospect to what it had been at the beginning of the nineteenth. The vast expansion of the reading public, the availability of cheap print and the post-Romantic ideal of the literary work as high art had combined to make authorship viable as both a relatively respectable profession and a heightened quasi-religious vocation. In contrast to previous centuries, a significant body of living writers could prosper through the direct sales of their literary productions, although doing so was by no means easy or inevitable. For most authors, writing was not like being a lawyer, a bank clerk or a doctor. They operated within systems of training, judgement and preferment that were often tenuous, capricious and insecure. However, a developed infrastructure of publishers, distributors and periodical venues provided Edwardian authors with a plethora of visible routes into print, holding out a fulfillable promise of potential prosperity. Authors were increasingly represented by agents and had banded together to assert collective authority through organisations such as the Society of Authors (founded in 1884), a revivified Royal Society of Literature (founded in 1820, but of limited effectiveness until the late nineteenth century), the National Union of Journalists (founded in 1907) and English PEN (founded slightly later in 1921). While not all authorship was securely professional, the idea of professional authorship was an established cultural paradigm rendered socially through networks and materially through

© The Author(s) 2021

M. Sangster, *Living as an Author in the Romantic Period*, Palgrave Studies in the Enlightenment, Romanticism and Cultures of Print, https://doi.org/10.1007/978-3-030-37047-3_1

libraries, bookshops, institutions and a continuous burgeoning of media forms and objects.

Over the course of the nineteenth century, proliferating institutions (both material and conceptual) had also acted to reify a canon of great authors deemed suitable to be taught in an expanding system of schools and universities. Publishers had responded by putting the works of these writers into the hands of millions of readers. As a consequence, a refined literary realm had opened up within which writers could position themselves as rubbing shoulders with a lineage of exalted historical peers. This shifting pantheon served as an aspiration and a means of legitimation for ambitious living authors. As T.S. Eliot put it in 'Tradition and the Individual Talent', 'No poet, no artist of any art, has his complete meaning alone. His significance, his appreciation is the appreciation of his relation to the dead poets and artists.' Eliot goes on to contend that 'what happens when a new work of art is created is something that happens simultaneously to all the works of art which preceded it.'[1] Twentieth-century literary writers could be seen as existing both within their own times and in spaces contiguous with an ever-present literary past. Their significance within this galaxy of predecessors was variously located in their personal identities (as in Eliot's first statement) and ascribed directly to their works (as in his second). In this discourse, authors were no longer seen solely as people like their readers, but as individuals of unusual abilities and distinction who many should read, but few could be.

The widespread acceptance of the Romantic notion of the transcendent artwork served to create a concatenation of anxieties about the extent to which the facts of authors' lives mattered. Eliot's claims and those like them carried the strand of early-nineteenth-century thinking that had disassociated artistic genius and moral virtue towards its logical conclusion, in which quality was determined solely in relation to aesthetics, rather than being influenced by authors' projected characters, as was common in earlier environments. In a very different manner, but with some similar effects, the notion of professionalised authorship provided a means by which authors could be valued as members of a skilled class, rather than exclusively based on their individual merits. Both professional and aesthetic characterisations of authorship thus provided possibilities for de-emphasising the personal qualities of individual writers. However, the

---

[1] T.S. Eliot, 'Tradition and the Individual Talent', in *The Sacred Wood* (London: Methuen, 1920), pp. 42–53 (p. 44).

considerable rewards that authors could reap from seeking personal fame meant that while professionalism and artistry were often invoked as means of legitimation, many authors nevertheless persisted in using their art to keep themselves in the picture. This created a series of strange and often contradictory discourses in which authors and critics denied that writers necessarily haunted their works while simultaneously inscribing aspects of authors' identities (and critics' subjectivities) as valuable contexts for literary creation and curation. While the consensus within the coalescing discipline of literature was that authors' works were detachable from and more significant than authors' lives, biographical discourses proved enduringly difficult to banish.

A representative articulation of this difficulty can be found in Jorge Luis Borges' short story 'Borges and I', a work that showcases its composer's enviable talent for exploring complex ideas with brevity, clarity and elegance. Its narrative describes the author who Borges both is and is not, playing on contrasts and consonances:

> I like hourglasses, maps, eighteenth-century typography, the taste of coffee and the prose of Stevenson; he shares these preferences, but in a vain way that turns them into the attributes of an actor. It would be an exaggeration to say that ours is a hostile relationship; I live, let myself go on living, so that Borges may contrive his literature, and this literature justifies me. It is no effort for me to confess that he has achieved some valid pages, but those pages cannot save me, perhaps because what is good belongs to no one, not even to him, but rather to the language and to tradition. Besides, I am destined to perish, definitively, and only some instant of myself can survive in him. Little by little, I am giving over everything to him, though I am quite aware of his perverse custom of falsifying and magnifying things.[2]

This passage evokes a peculiar tension between Borges-as-man and Borges-as-author, the author translating the man's preferences and self into something that the man can no longer wholly own, which justifies him while erasing great swathes of his being, although—crucially—not quite everything. The story concludes, 'I do not know which of us has written this page.'[3] This could be read as implying that for the reader the story's words are irrevocably those of Borges the author, with Borges the man being

---

[2] Jorge Luis Borges, 'Borges and I', in *Labyrinths* (London: Penguin, 2000), pp. 282–3 (p. 282).
[3] Borges, p. 283.

irredeemably occluded in the moment of writing. However, the story also tantalises its readers' biographical impulses through its genial, melancholy I-narration and through providing specificities that purport to be authentic instants of Borges' self. The story turns on the tension between the intellectual argument it makes about the absolute sacrifices required by authorship and the affective grace with which it conjures its narrator, who purports to be real through his tastes, style and sentiments even as he denies the possibility of his continuing existence. Borges' conjured selves occupy a complex spectrum from fallible, negligible man to transcendent language and tradition. It is impossible to eliminate a Borgesian identity from this story, but it is also impossible to construct the story as an utterance allowing an unmediated connection with another person. Borges thus asserts an elegant and protective form of complexity while ensuring that the credit for articulating this complexity remains attached to his name.

While authors like Borges played creatively with ambiguous shiftings between biographical, aesthetic and professional identities, several important traditions of twentieth-century scholarship took decisive stances against writers seeking to linger within and around their works, arguing that authorial intentions should be eliminated as axes of interpretation. Practical Criticism and the New Criticism focused attention tightly on the text, regarding biographical facts as unsophisticated intrusions. Theorists too sought to clear away subjective messiness. In 'The Death of the Author', Roland Barthes contended polemically that literature is properly understood to be 'that neutral, composite, oblique space where our subject slips away, the negative where all identity is lost, starting with the very identity of the body writing'.[4] In such a formulation, biographical identifications become dangerous and limiting impositions. Barthes' essay argues for the power and autonomy of the interpreting theorist, pushing for a kind of criticism that throws off any authority claims based on the cultural traces that authors leave. For Barthes, attempting to discern such traces comprises a search for 'a single "theological" meaning', one that must inevitably close down many of the possibilities of critical discourse and subordinate the reader to the writer's authority.[5]

---

[4] Roland Barthes, 'The Death of the Author', in *Image Music Text*, trans. Stephen Heath (London: Fontana, 1977), pp. 142–8 (p. 142).

[5] Barthes, p. 146.

To understand the implications of Eliot, Borges and Barthes' positionings, it is crucial to recognise that their characterisations and arguments are all fundamentally post-Romantic. Their stances assume as prerequisites relatively recent models of art and authorship that were theorised and promoted by oppositional cliques in the first quarter of the nineteenth century, but which were only widely accepted in Britain in subsequent decades. Andrew Bennett has eloquently shown how the writings of the poets who came to be seen as the major voices of the Romantic period were shaped by obsessive attention to their posthumous reputations.[6] Borges' flirtations with his own erasure cleverly activate this Romantic artistic tradition. Similarly, Barthes' essay can be placed as the culmination of a movement with its roots in Romanticism's amplification of literature as aesthetics. This amplification went hand-in-hand with a conceptual retreat from the idea that literary texts might be functional or sociable. The beginnings of this process can be traced, among other places, in the claims made by William Wordsworth in the preface to *Lyrical Ballads* and elsewhere about the transcendent nature of the Poet and in the later ambivalent acceptance and promotion of such claims in second-wave Romantic-period periodicals such as *Blackwood's Edinburgh Magazine*.[7] This strain of proto-Romantic thought sought to delineate a defined disciplinary field for the practice of literature as art, a space commensurate with the one that Eliot imagines in 'Tradition and the Individual Talent'. Within this field, authors could operate without being subject to political and moral control, but also without genuinely threatening the status quo. Modern ideas of authorship focused around professionalism on one hand and aesthetics on the other are in many respects defence mechanisms developed by Romantic-period writers to shield themselves from political conflict by providing theoretically depersonalised means of legitimating the value of writing. Aesthetics and professionalism both played key roles in disjoining unambiguous connections between authors' personal

---

[6] Andrew Bennett, *Romantic Poets and the Culture of Posterity* (Cambridge: Cambridge University Press, 1999). Bennett's book has chapters on Wordsworth, Coleridge, Keats, Shelley and Byron; Blake's obscurity in his own time serves, along with his atypical views and practices, to set him outside Bennett's purview. For an excellent account of Blake's eventual entry into the Romantic canon, see H.J. Jackson, *Those Who Write for Immortality: Romantic Reputations and the Dream of Lasting Fame* (New Haven & London: Yale University Press, 2015), pp. 168–89.

[7] For more on this, see David Higgins, *Romantic Genius and the Literary Magazine: Biography, Celebrity, Politics* (London: Routledge, 2005).

opinions and the sentiments expressed in their writings. This served the interests of writers keen to avoid politicised attacks by carving out distinct systems of valuation, but also the interests of elites eager to contain the impact of writing within discourses separate from those of political and social action.

The disciplinary emergence of a narrower sense of literature during the second quarter of the nineteenth century was successful in aesthetically exalting authors and in buffering their potentially revolutionary impacts. However, it failed fully to sunder the link between authors' lives and works. Instead, creating a desirable new specialism triggered an intense interest in the people who were seen as excelling in it, resulting in a range of biographical approaches that both glamorised authors' excesses and domesticated their peculiarities.[8] Denying that authors' lives and attitudes could be read straightforwardly out of their works created a series of new modes of interpretation dedicated to exploring the complexities of the interactions between life and art. While these modes were often disapproved of by authors and institutional arbiters, they possessed significant popular appeal. Many post-Romantic critics and aesthetic techniques have sought to point away from the author, but canny and curious readers have often been inclined to ask who is doing the pointing, and why.

An aspect of authorship that practicing writers commonly wish to elide is its messy financial dimension. The idea of writing principally for money has a long history of negative connotations. In the eighteenth century, getting paid for writing was seen as ungentlemanly and potentially corrupt or corrupting; later, it was perceived to be a cruder motivator than artistic achievement, which largely replaced notions of taste while replicating many of their underlying assumptions. Both these perceptions were results of privileged classes seeking to value writing in manners that benefitted their own productions while limiting the influence of working writers. There are other pragmatic reasons why authors have not generally been forthcoming about their financial affairs. Chief among these is the fact that the direct financial rewards of authorship have often been relatively meagre. It is far more attractive to sell oneself as an inspired artist than an impoverished one. It is also easier to build up an idea of oneself as being brilliant if one possesses good connections and plentiful leisure time. While we might like to think that aesthetic modes of valuation float above

---

[8] See Julian North, *The Domestication of Genius: Biography and the Romantic Poet* (Oxford: Oxford University Press, 2009).

petty social concerns, they are in fact deeply entangled with both social capital and actual capital. For much of history, poor authors have been valorised only in very particular circumstances, and these circumstances have often greatly limited the value ascribed to their achievements.

While authors' financial motivations are frequently passed over, financial factors are only part of a larger spectrum of motivations that the post-Romantic discipline of literature commonly neglects. The greatest gains that living authors can reap from their works are often social, and many of the principal justifications for writing relate to its social functions. The financial value attributed to writing ultimately obtains from perceptions of its social value, whether that be through its providing entertainment, its role in the dissemination of knowledge or its capacity to refine and promote individuals and ideologies. Despite their pretence to the contrary, aesthetic modes of valuation are also irredeemably social, seeking to channel writing's influence into a discrete cultural space within which its practitioners and critics are socially elevated and its potentially disruptive energies restrained. For the purposes of pedagogy and systematisation, literary studies commonly aligns with post-Romantic paradigms by framing writing as a professional or an artistic practice. Both framings allow a set of rhetorical norms to be brought to bear, allowing for institutionalised patterns of judgement to be developed and employed. However, in practice there are myriad specific and idiosyncratic factors that might lead any given author to write. A brief and partial list might include the desire to construct networks, to advocate for ideological positions, to foster friendships, to pursue rivalries, to put oneself forward for posts, to seek public approbation, to counter opprobrium, to gain the respect of peers and authorities, to explain oneself, to protect one's allies, to fulfil a social commitment, to display an affiliation, to garner credit for an innovation, to respond to current social and political events, to display personal expertise, or to divert and delight. For living authors, writings are pronouncements that shape fundamentally the ways in which individuals and society see them. Authorship is not just about building enduring artistic legacies, transmitting knowledge or delivering a product. It is also a means of promoting and inscribing living selves, financially, socially and culturally. It is these oft-neglected contingent processes that this book seeks to recover and examine.

Prefacing *Distinction*, his book on the impurity of taste, Pierre Bourdieu writes that his work 'transgresses one of the fundamental taboos of the intellectual world, in relating intellectual products and producers to the social conditions of their existence'.[9] Critics devoted to post-Romantic models of literary art might accuse this book of a similar kind of transgression. Biographically-focused criticism has an ambivalent reputation, in large part due to the erroneous tendency to see it as a form that seeks definitive explanations of works in the lives of their authors. Resistance to biographical readings was at its sharpest in the middle of the twentieth century, when Michel Foucault claimed it was 'a very familiar thesis that the task of criticism is not to reestablish the ties between an author and his work or to reconstitute an author's thought and experience [...] [rather,] criticism should concern itself with the structures of a work, its architectonic forms, which are studied for their intrinsic and internal relationships.'[10] However, as Foucault and subsequent strands of historicist and sociological criticism have established, this formalist perspective deliberately neglects many of the complex manners in which authors and cultures function. Jeffrey Cox has rightly contended that 'a literary work is both a product and producer of a web of human relations'.[11] While studying these human relations does not exhaust what a literary work might mean for its first audiences or for later ones, it can play a powerful role in tracing motivations, receptions and rewards over shorter and longer terms. Approaches along these lines stress that writing is a contingent practice that necessarily responds to local pressures. In doing so, such approaches can help us to address the crucial question of what authors and societies get from reading and writing.

To contextualise the study of Romantic-period authorship that follows, I want to close this preface by setting out three overarching reasons why I believe that studying authors' lives can be immensely valuable. The first of these reasons is a pragmatic one. Despite institutional pressures to the contrary, it is patently obvious that for readers across history the lives of authors have been inscribed pervasively as contexts. It is no coincidence that authorial images and profiles are such common paratexts, or that author interviews, memoirs, anecdotes, biographies and biopics are extremely popular forms. When we discuss works, it is rhetorically

---

[9] Pierre Bourdieu, 'Preface to the English-Language Edition', in *Distinction: A Social Critique of the Judgement of Taste*, trans. Richard Nice (London: Routledge, 2010), pp. xiii–xvi (p. xv).

[10] Michel Foucault, 'What is an Author?', trans. Joseph V. Harari, in *Modern Criticism and Theory: A Reader*, ed. David Lodge (Harlow: Longman, 1988), pp. 197–210 (p. 198).

[11] Jeffrey N. Cox, *Poetry and Politics in the Cockney School* (Cambridge: Cambridge University Press, 1998), p. 14.

conventional and relatively uncontroversial to refer their effects as achievements of their writers. Whether we consider it acceptable to enjoy or learn from something vests partly in its creator's cultural identity: witness, for example, the recurrent discussions on whether Knut Hamsun's support for the Nazis should place his *Hunger* beyond the pale, or the similar debates on Richard Wagner's anti-Semitism. Whole industries are built around managing the reputations of authors, as hundreds of author-focused societies and writer's house museums attest. Where we do not possess biographical facts, we are prepared to reward those who can create plausible reconstructions. Consider the obsessive interest in Byron's sexuality shown in fiction and biography, or the manifold attempts to build Shakespeare's life from scanty evidence, as well as the countervailing attempts to make that life irrelevant and claim that the plays were authored by another man, one whose story supposedly more properly fits their attributes. Authors may make their works, but they are remade themselves in culture: often partly in their works' image, but seldom wholly so. The linkage between works and lives is complicated, multivalent and at times limiting and destructive. Regardless, it still fundamentally underpins the ways in which twenty-first century readers assimilate what we read into our wider cultural understandings. Critics might sometimes wish that authors' names functioned as taxonomic labels that could be easily curated, but in practice authorship operates through complex networks involving writers, works, publishers, critics, audiences, institutions, forms, canons and lineages. Sociality has always been a major reason why people write, and our cultures continue to reflect this.

A second important reason for examining the lives of authors is that they serve as a potent register of historical change. Being an author has not always meant the same thing, and modern notions of authorship would be surprising—or even alien—to authors of the eighteenth or early nineteenth centuries. In his essay 'The Field of Cultural Production' and elsewhere, Bourdieu posits the idea of a defined 'literary and artistic field' within which works and their producers compete for different kinds of capital, opposing the popular and economically bountiful with the radical and aesthetically daring.[12] This model is one that works well for late-nineteenth-century France, the milieu from which Bourdieu draws the

---

[12] Pierre Bourdieu, 'The Field of Cultural Production, or: The Economic World Reversed', trans. Richard Nice, in *The Field of Cultural Production*, ed. Randall Johnson (London: Polity Press, 1993), pp. 29–73 (p. 37).

lion's share of his examples, but it functions less well for many earlier cultural environments. Bourdieu describes a situation in which the literary and artistic field 'is contained within the field of power [...] while possessing a relative autonomy with respect to it, especially as regards its economic and political principles of hierachization'.[13] One of the main contentions of this study is that a discrete space within which literary works were perceived as operating relatively autonomously from wider economic and political circumstances was only opened up in Britain during the 1820s and 1830s. This occurred as a result of the conflicted twin developments of Romantic ideologies and technologies of mass production and circulation. Before this point, influential authors were largely coterminous with the social elite and its priorities. The degrees of separation between writers and their readers were relatively few. Nearly all literary works were expensive products with relatively small circulations. The limited potential for direct literary profits and the absence of the professionalising influence of modern disciplinary systems meant that authors commonly understood their works as advertisements for themselves. They did not write principally for the sake of art or to address market niches in the manner that Bourdieu's model imagines; rather, they sought to build reputations that would bring them personal, financial and social rewards from relatively small cadres of elite auditors. Recovering evidence of such practices can help us better to understand how and why people wrote as they did. In addition, examining archived and documented histories can throw light on the ways in which modern literary writing remains a practice embedded in networks and coteries. While online communities, prize-giving institutions and creative writing departments operate differently to early-nineteenth-century literary circles, they nevertheless shape culture through sociable and contingent means that criticism has often been slow to acknowledge.[14] Many of the interactions and practices this book discusses will be disconcertingly familiar to readers involved in contemporary academia, within which networks and publications often operate on similar scales to those of the late eighteenth century.

---

[13] Bourdieu, 'Field of Cultural Production', pp. 37–8.

[14] Although there are notable exceptions, such as Mark McGurl's excellent *The Program Era: Postwar Fiction and the Rise of Creative Writing* (Cambridge, MA: Harvard University Press, 2009) and James F. English's *The Economy of Prestige: Prizes, Awards, and the Circulation of Cultural Value* (Cambridge, MA: Harvard University Press, 2008).

A third major advantage of examining authors' lives is that this can show us how and why certain writers have been allowed to speak and endure while others have been silenced or pushed into obscurity. The reasons for this often have much to do with doctrines of taste and the social mechanics of status. A major problem with the implicit claim to disinterestedness made by post-Romantic aesthetics is that when we scrutinise the writers established as being paramount, their literary standing often maps closely onto systems of social privilege. The most celebrated writers within the Romantic period were affluent and well-connected men, and the poets now seen as its guiding spirits were only slightly less privileged as a group. Working-class writers were tightly constrained in what and how they could write, and while several female writers achieved widespread critical and popular acclaim, they were often judged by standards that framed their works as necessarily inferior, leading to their being systematically undercompensated. In the longer term, institutional processes of canon formation have tended to eliminate underprivileged writers from the picture. Examining the ways in which the mechanics of authorship intersect with writers' lives allows us to map the inequalities that muffled the voices of substantial sections of the writing nation. It also provides opportunities to understand marginalised authors better through framing their works within the contexts of the systems and social circumstances that restricted them.

I have laid out these three reasons across separate paragraphs for the sake of clarity. In practice, of course, the pragmatics of sociable authorship, the specificities of historical circumstances and the mechanics of respect and regulation are tightly interwoven issues that will be explored in a more holistic fashion in what that follows. However, I feel it important at the outset to make a serious claim for the historical, literary and ethical potential of such considerations. Neglecting the lives of authors dangerously occludes the extent to which our views of literature are the products of authorial, critical and institutional self-fashionings that have influenced both how society has recognised and rewarded writers and the ways in which writing itself has been understood, assessed and valued. This is not to say that we should never read texts as independent pieces of art, but rather to assert that this should be recognised as one reading strategy among many, and a relatively recent phenomenon in historical terms. Scrutinising literature and history through the lens of authorship can serve to reveal sometimes uncomfortable truths about literary writing's entanglements with circuits of capital, structures of power and systems of exclusion. However, it also lets us appreciate the care and artistry that authors have employed in making themselves both through and alongside their published writings. Examining feedback loops between texts and their creators should be a means for understanding more about both, rather than a mode that sets limits on either. While texts can never be people, the ways in which they continue to people our minds should not be underestimated. If to be a critic or a reader is to live in an empire of signs, one of the responsibilities inherent in the role must lie in recognising that these can be interpreted as life signs, as well as mirrors.

Introduction: What Was an Author in the Romantic Period?

The preceding preface laid out reasons why I believe that records of authors' lives are valuable subjects for critical study, both for their own sakes and for the interpretative possibilities they open up. It also indicated why the Romantic period provides particularly fertile ground for studying literary authorship and requires careful interpretation to avoid the imposition of modern preconceptions. The most familiar contemporary paradigms of authorship—authors operating as artists, as professionals, or as both—were nascent in certain Romantic-period works and lives, but were fully reified only in the mid- to late nineteenth century and have been significantly reconfigured during the twentieth and twenty-first centuries. In order to strip away anachronistic notions regarding aesthetic and professional reasons for writing, this body of this book employs new archival evidence to recover the interlinked social and economic factors that determined the conditions for literary production and innovation in a period stretching from the 1790s to the 1820s. Its chapters trace the limited financial rewards offered by the publishing industry; examine the crucial roles played by affiliation and networking in ensuring literary success; delineate the contexts that allowed certain prominent figures to prosper by writing; uncover the struggles of working authors; map the influence of the powerful quarterly Reviews; and consider the ways in which certain major figures built networks that allowed them to reconfigure the possibilities of literary authorship. However, to frame these considerations, it is important first to establish what authorship meant in Romantic-period

© The Author(s) 2021   13
M. Sangster, *Living as an Author in the Romantic Period*, Palgrave
Studies in the Enlightenment, Romanticism and Cultures of Print,
https://doi.org/10.1007/978-3-030-37047-3_2

contexts. This will be the major work of this introduction, which will analyse the age's conflicted attitudes before establishing positions regarding received notions of Romantic genius and the chronological specificities of the late eighteenth and early nineteenth centuries.

My Book, Myself

The most significant differences between modern approaches to texts and those prevalent in the Romantic period relate to the attribution of meaning. While in modern discourse we allow for a conceptual division between what a text expresses and its author's real opinions, in the late eighteenth and early nineteenth centuries, literary works were commonly read more straightforwardly as their writers' voices. Books existed in tight metonymic relationships with their authors. Those by living writers were commonly seen as aspects of beings who could be encountered, befriended or opposed. This mode of apprehension reflected the status of writing within a literate class that was kept relatively small by economic factors and within which professionalising discourses that placed buffers between texts and authors had yet to take hold. In this highly politicised environment, intention was a basic assumption, rather than a fallacy.[1] As Gregory Dart puts it, the early nineteenth century 'thought of itself as "an age of personality": no period either before or since seems to have been so entirely predisposed to correlate the fate of nations and the dynamics of personal character.'[2] Writers were often read precisely because of who they were, and readers' responses to books were highly mediated by their knowledge of authors. Anonymous publication was common in large part because acknowledged works were regularly employed to impugn authors' reputations.[3] To write under one's own name was to submit oneself for judgement, a prospect that many writers found distinctly unnerving. Mary Brunton, contemplating the publication of her first novel *Self-Control*, wrote to a friend in terms that make this very clear: 'To be pointed at—to be noticed and

---

[1] William K. Wimsatt and Monroe C. Beardsley, 'The Intentional Fallacy', *Sewanee Review*, 54 (Summer 1946), 468–88.

[2] Gregory Dart, 'Hazlitt and Biography', *Cambridge Quarterly*, 29:4 (2000), 338–48 (p. 338).

[3] Only about thirty-five percent of novels in the late eighteenth century directly named their authors on their title pages—see Peter Garside, 'Authorship', in *The Oxford History of the Novel in English Volume 2: English and British Fiction 1750–1820*, ed. Peter Garside and Karen O'Brien (Oxford: Oxford University Press, 2015), pp. 29–53 (p. 39).

commented upon—to be suspected of literary airs—to be shunned as literary women are, by the more unpretending of my own sex; and abhorred, as literary women are, by the more pretending of the other! [...] I would sooner exhibit as a rope-dancer'.[4] To write was necessarily to self-fashion, and such self-fashioning could be ruthlessly contested by others seeking to exert control over culture and society.

Excellent evidence of this propensity for treating books as extensions of their authors can be found by examining the marginal annotations that readers left behind. As H.J. Jackson has shown, annotators commonly addressed books as if they were people, particularly when they were at their most impassioned and engaged:

> In unguarded moments, or under the strong impression that the book was talking to them, readers talked back to their books. All the little gestures of approval, like [Samuel Taylor] Coleridge's "Right!" and "Excellent!" could be understood in this way, as could their opposites. Companionship does not mean automatic agreement. An even plainer sign is the direct address "you."[5]

Jackson proceeds to give numerous examples of this habit. One of the most compelling is her account of William Blake's marginal arguments with the President of the Royal Academy, Sir Joshua Reynolds. In the front of his copy of Reynolds' *Works*, Blake added an inscription stating that 'This Man was Hired to Depress Art This is the Opinion of Will Blake my Proofs of this Opinion are given in the following Notes'.[6] Blake read Reynolds' book as evidencing his bête noire's hated self, which led him wilfully to misread parts with which he might otherwise have agreed. As Jackson writes, 'when Blake grudgingly expresses admiration for an idea or expression in the text, he tends to turn it into a complaint that Reynolds is contradicting himself, thereby proving that he is weak and wanting in self-knowledge'.[7] In Blake's annotations, the good things about Reynolds'

---

[4] Mary Brunton to Mrs Izett, 30 August 1810, quoted in Alexander Brunton, 'Memoir', prefixed to Mary Brunton, *Emmeline, with Some Other Pieces* (Edinburgh: Manners and Miller, 1819), p. xxxvi.

[5] H.J. Jackson, *Romantic Readers: The Evidence of Marginalia* (New Haven: Yale University Press, 2005), p. 124.

[6] Blake's annotation to the frontispiece of the first volume of *The Works of Sir Joshua Reynolds*, 3 vols (London: Cadell and Davies, 1798), BL C.45.e.18–20. Reproduced in Jackson, p. 155.

[7] Jackson, *Romantic Readers*, p. 167.

book become evidence of Reynolds' personal duplicity. By writing himself into Reynolds' *Works*, Blake encounters and resists his adversary, opposing Reynolds' subjectivity with his own. Jackson contends that annotations allowed Blake to '*publish* his quarrel with the author as the book circulated', noting that the lending of annotated works was common.[8] Annotators such as Blake thus established their styles and identities through dialogue with the printed identities of others. The dissemination of such self-definitions could be a crucial means of establishing a reputation by asserting one's own valuable particularity.

Robert Southey indulged in similar—if more anxious and public—self-fashioning while editing the *Remains of Henry Kirke White* (itself a title that indicates the assumed consonance between a book's contents and its author's body). While his ostensible purpose is to account for Henry Kirke White's life, Southey regularly slips himself into the narrative. Discussing his subject's reaction to a ferocious critique, he opines that '[a]n author is proof against reviewing, when, like myself, he has been reviewed above seventy times', boasting both of the attention he has drawn and of the success of his own self-definitions, which he claims have outweighed any single review.[9] In addressing White, Southey evokes his own privileged position, writing that it is his 'fortune to lay before the world some account of one [...] whose virtues were as admirable as his genius.'[10] In the economy Southey establishes, White's effusions are valued as means of memorialising his personal attributes, and his recalled virtues serve in turn as guarantees of his works' value. Southey seeks repeatedly to implicate himself in this feedback loop through describing White's appreciation of their friendship and through recounting incidents such as his finding 'a sonnet addressed to myself' among White's unpublished papers.[11] However, Southey also takes considerable pains to distinguish his own opinions from his subject's where the latter might prove to be controversial:

---

[8] Jackson, *Romantic Readers*, p. 169.

[9] *The Remains of Henry Kirke White; with an Account of his Life*, ed. Robert Southey, 2 vols (London: Vernor, Hood, and Sharpe; Longman, Hurst, Rees, and Orme; J. Dighton, T. Barret, and J. Nicholson, Cambridge; and W. Dunn and S. Tupman, Nottingham, 1807), I, 23.

[10] *Remains*, I, 1.

[11] *Remains*, I, 53.

Of his fervent piety, his letters, his prayers, and his hymns, will afford ample and interesting proofs. I must be permitted to say, that my own views of the religion of Jesus Christ differ essentially from the system of belief which he had adopted; but, having said this, it is indeed my anxious wish to do full justice to piety so fervent.[12]

While Southey is keen to claim that White's faith allowed him to 'keep watch over his heart' and 'correct the few symptoms, which it ever displayed, of human imperfection', he nonetheless feels obliged to differentiate his own religious position, aware that he is implicated in the texts he edits and must control as far as possible the ways in which they can be read back onto him.

Even those writers most closely involved with theorising proto-Romantic aesthetics were conscious that their contemporaries often read their works as evidencing their personalities and predilections. Coleridge, for example, was deeply aware of the extent to which he was read into and out of his writings, as shown in a series of letters he wrote in 1808 to Francis Jeffrey, the influential editor of the *Edinburgh Review*. After complaining in the first of these letters that Jeffrey had been 'perhaps rather unwarrant[ab]ly, severe' on his 'morals and understanding' in print, Coleridge went on to 'intreat—for the sake of man-kind—an honorable review of Mr Clarkson's History of the Abolition of the Slave Trade.—I know the man—and if you knew him you, I am sure, would revere him—and your reverence of him, as an agent, would almost supersede all Judgment of him as a mere literary man.'[13] Coleridge thus contends that Thomas Clarkson should not be read cruelly or crudely as an author, as this represents only a subordinate part of his social existence. He worries that by publishing, Clarkson has opened himself up to having his self negatively reconstructed through the lens of his prose. Earlier in the letter, Coleridge also expresses this anxiety with regard to his own work, assuring Jeffrey that 'If you knew me, you would yourself smile at some of the charges, which, I am told, you have burthened on me.' While these two interlinked statements both assert the inadequate nature of readings that

---

[12] *Remains*, I, 58.
[13] Samuel Taylor Coleridge to Francis Jeffrey, 23 May 1808, NYPL Berg 211218B A331. Printed as Letter 710 in *Collected Letters of Samuel Taylor Coleridge*, ed. Earl Leslie Griggs, 6 vols (Oxford: Clarendon Press, 1956–71), III, 116–7. The texts given here and for the following letter are my transcriptions, which differ from Griggs' in their representation of Coleridge's punctuation and by including deletions that Griggs silently omits.

view texts as definitive summations of their authors, Coleridge neverthe-less recognises that *ad hominem* forms of reading were extremely common and had considerable social and cultural power. While Coleridge thought Jeffrey severe to censure him as part of a Lake School, the continuing cur-rency of this marker speaks to the enduring influence of such rhetorical couplings.

In a second letter, written a couple of months later, Coleridge clarified how he saw himself positioned with respect to public opinion:

> severe & long continued bodily disease exacerbated by disappointment in the great Hope of my Life had rendered me insensible to blame and praise even to a faulty degree, unless they proceeded from the one or two who love me. The entrance-passage to my Heart is choked up with heavy lumber—& I am thus barricadoed ~~myself~~ against attacks, which, doubtless, I should otherwise have felt as keenly as most men. Instead of censuring a certain quantum of irritability respecting the reception of published composition, I rather envy it—it becomes ludicrous then only, when it is disavowed, and the opposite Temper pretended to/. The ass's Skin is almost scourge-proof—while the Elephant's thrills under the movements of every fly, that runs over it.[14]

Reviews, then, cannot hurt Coleridge, or so he says. Misreading is what he expects, except from a few close to him. In his denial, though, he seeks to fascinate and impress through the aptness of his language, the mystery of his great disappointment, the unspecified nature of his unfortunate illness and the evocation of his living body. Coleridge thus seeks to perform a new version of himself for Jeffrey (and for Jeffrey's private and public audiences), portraying himself as an individual with uncommon powers, uncommon problems and an uncommon ability to resist the blandish-ments of society. Here nascent Romantic subjectivity blends with a recog-nition that its time has not yet come. Coleridge recognises, and indeed contends, that he represents a deviation from the common view of author-ship, framing a stronger articulation of writerly independence than society is currently prepared to accept. His triangulations between pragmatic and performative positions speak to his desire to anchor himself as a respect-able and distinctive author within his contemporary milieu while

---

[14] Samuel Taylor Coleridge to Francis Jeffrey, 20 July 1808, NYPL Berg 211210 B A332. Letter 712 in Griggs (III, 118–9).

simultaneously working to rewrite the rules by which authors are judged in manners that favour his own ideals of genius.[15]

As the tenor of these examples indicates, the period's tendency towards *ad hominem* readings combined with ongoing social and cultural strife to create an extremely anxious and rancorous literary environment. Richard Cronin has described the late 1810s and early 1820s as 'a period constituted not, as some have suggested, by the doctrine of sympathy that its leading writers held in common but by the antagonisms that divided them'.[16] This description might easily be extended back as far as the 1790s, when new and devastatingly effective modes of personal attack were pioneered by forces seeking to contain potentially revolutionary energies.[17] Attackers would sometimes disingenuously deny that they manipulated the characters of their victims. John Gibson Lockhart, traducing Leigh Hunt in the late 1810s, stated that 'When I charged you with depraved morality, obscenity, and indecency, I spoke not of Leigh Hunt as a man. I deny the fact,—I have no reason to doubt that your private character is respectable; but I judged you from your works.'[18] However, Lockhart's whole article is predicated on the intrinsic sociality of writing. He attributes his reply to 'common civility', censuring Hunt's rudeness. He asserts that his article was but 'the first paragraph of [Hunt's] indictment', the opening statement in a trial before 'the impartial jury of your country'. He repeatedly personifies Hunt—as an expeller of 'foaming exclamations', as a 'testy person', as possessing excessive 'personal vanity', as a man with 'a partiality for indecent subjects', as a 'poet vastly inferior to Wordsworth, Byron and Moore'.[19] Hunt's writing is read as a social process, mapped onto networks and hierarchies and rhetorically brought under the authority of institutions. Literature here is not seen as something apart; instead, texts and their authors are shown to be powerfully and suggestively interchangeable. In the most extreme cases, such as the article that Byron

---

[15] I examine this complex interaction between Coleridge and Jeffrey at greater length in '"You have not advertised out of it": Samuel Taylor Coleridge and Francis Jeffrey on Authorship, Networks and Personalities', *Romanticism and Victorianism on the Net*, 61 (April 2012), https://doi.org/10.7202/1018602ar.

[16] Richard Cronin, *Paper Pellets: British Literary Culture after Waterloo* (Oxford: Oxford University Press, 2010), p. 13.

[17] I discuss the development of such discourses in more detail in Chapter Five.

[18] [John Gibson Lockhart], 'Letter from Z. To Mr. Leigh Hunt', *Blackwood's Edinburgh Magazine*, 10 (January 1818), 414–7 (p. 416).

[19] [Lockhart], pp. 414–5.

called the 'homicide review of J. Keats', printed attacks were imagined to be capable of literally killing authors.[20] While writing in the early nineteenth century could be a powerful mode of self-assertion, it was also accurately seen as a source of immense personal vulnerability. Making oneself in print could lead to a shattered reputation, compromised financial affairs and, in certain vexed cases, the loss of life itself. The trope of the garret-bound writer starving due to neglect or calumny reflects the reality of a period in which the cultural power of writing was both intimately tied up with personhood and stringently policed by vested interests that could severely curtail what less fortunate authors could gain from their works.

THE MIRAGE OF PROFESSIONALISM

While writing was a high-stakes proposition in reputational terms, this did not prevent increasing numbers of men and women from seeking to build careers through authorship. These individuals were drawn in by the wealth, influence and social cachet of high-profile successes and by the glorification of writing engendered through institutions of education and the periodical press, both of which were becoming increasingly accessible. However, while a few writers, mostly socially advantaged gentlemen, were able to make their fortunes and reputations through writing, for most aspirants, the realities of literary production proved disappointing. Rather than being showered with wealth by publishers, most authors received at best modest payments, seldom sufficient to serve as a sole means of support. Rather than receiving plaudits, their works were generally passed over by a censorious and hierarchal print culture controlled by reviewers more concerned with propagating their own authority than with disinterestedly valuing knowledge or praising art. The ideal of authorial success towards which a considerable number of talented men and women aimed usually proved to be a mirage. As David Williams lamented when explaining why he had founded a Literary Fund to address the plights of authors, those who believed that they could live comfortably by the pen were generally 'soon and miserably undeceived'.[21]

---

[20] Byron to John Murray, 7 August 1821, in *Byron's Letters and Journals*, ed. Leslie A. Marchand, 12 vols (London: John Murray, 1973–94), VIII, 173.

[21] David Williams, *Claims of Literature: The Origin, Motives, Objects, and Transactions, of the Society for the Establishment of a Literary Fund* (London: William Miller, 1802), p. 62. I discuss the Literary Fund in detail in Chapter Four.

It was partly to warn away potential scribblers that Isaac D'Israeli published his 1812 miscellany *Calamities of Authors*, in which he scrutinised
the many pitfalls of literary lives by drawing on examples ranging from the
age of Elizabeth through to his early nineteenth-century contemporaries,
a chronological span he modelled principally in terms of its unfortunate
continuities. From the outset, D'Israeli takes pains to contradict the
impression that constituting oneself as an author leads to a life of comfort
and respectability:

> The title of AUTHOR still retains its seduction among our youth, and is con-
> secrated by ages. Yet what affectionate parent would consent to see his son
> devote himself to his pen as a profession? The studies of a true Author insu-
> late him in society, exacting daily labours; yet he will receive but little
> encouragement, and less remuneration. It will be found that the most suc-
> cessful Author can obtain no equivalent for the labours of his life [...]
> Authors themselves never discover this melancholy truth till they have
> yielded to an impulse, and adopted a profession, too late in life to resist the
> one, or abandon the other. Whoever labours without hope, a painful state to
> which Authors are at length reduced, may surely be placed among the most
> injured class in the community. Most Authors close their lives in apathy or
> despair, and too many live by means which few of them would not blush to
> describe.[22]

Throughout *Calamities* D'Israeli stresses that living by the pen is a risky
and precarious form of existence. He does not dispute the achievements of
writers such as Alexander Pope and Samuel Johnson, who were able to
acquire fame, influence and significant payments through their writings.[23]
Rather, he seeks to counteract the cultural centrality of such starry careers
by marshalling a whole host of less fortunate authors: men and women
who produced valuable work but who nevertheless ended their lives
impoverished, unrecognised or prematurely. D'Israeli is often an enthusiastic proponent of the marginalised writers he examines, using the term
'genius' liberally to describe many of them. However, he contends that
brilliance and innovation have never guaranteed either fortune or esteem.

---

[22] Isaac D'Israeli, *Calamities of Authors; including some Inquiries Respecting their Moral
and Literary Characters*, 2 vols (London: John Murray, 1812), I, viii–ix.

[23] In practice, of course, these authors asserted their claims in vexed dialogue with patrons
and with others who sought control over written discourses; see Dustin Griffin, *Literary
Patronage in England 1650–1800* (Cambridge: Cambridge University Press, 1996),
pp. 123–54, 220–45.

Indeed, he argues that novel works are likely to be met with critical distrust and popular incomprehension, a claim that chimes with William Wordsworth's slightly later assertion that 'every author, as far as he is great and at the same time *original*, has had the task of *creating* the taste by which he is to be enjoyed: so has it been, so will it continue to be.'[24] Wordsworth, of course, could afford to wait (albeit impatiently) for recognition due to his non-literary incomes. Had the pen been his sole source of support, he would have been a very poor man; in 1835 he estimated that over forty years of publishing had earned him 'not above £1000'.[25] Poor remuneration for all but sensations meant that destitution and being forced to produce hack work were common authorial fates. D'Israeli reserves considerable scorn for authors who compromised their principles by accepting money to promote factions, describing them as 'polluters of the press, who have turned a vestal into a prostitute; a grotesque race of famished buffoons or laughing assassins'.[26] Of all the writers he depicts, though, only these clients, together with a few great names mentioned fleetingly, are described as being able to realise a significant income. D'Israeli had the leisure to discourse on literary misfortune only because he was financially independent, having inherited at the age of twenty-five the considerable fortune of his maternal grandmother, Esther Shiprut.[27] Those without such means of support were likely to find that dedicating oneself to authorship also meant becoming impoverished, maligned and embittered.

The contents of this book will demonstrate that D'Israeli's gloom was largely justified. While the productions of authors could potentially bring honour to their creators, authorship did not in itself constitute a respectable or stable profession. In part, D'Israeli's formulations prefigure later snobbish divisions between creators of literary art and authors of

---

[24] William Wordsworth, 'Essay, Supplementary to the Preface' (1815), in *The Prose Works of William Wordsworth*, ed. W.J.B. Owen and Jane Worthington Smyser, 3 vols (Oxford: Clarendon Press, 1974), III, 55–107 (p. 80).

[25] Quoted in J.W. Saunders' classic study of authorship, *The Profession of English Letters* (London: Routledge and Kegan Paul, 1964), p. 171. Saunders is probably drawing on Thomas Moore's journal entry for 20 February 1835—he would have been using Lord John Russell's edition (*Memoirs, Journal, and Correspondence of Thomas Moore*, ed. Lord John Russell, 8 vols (London: Longman, 1853–56); the anecdote appears on p. 70 of Volume VII), but the most convenient modern source is *The Journal of Thomas Moore*, ed. Wilfred S. Dowden, 6 vols (Newark: University of Delaware Press, 1983–91), IV, 1659–60.

[26] D'Israeli, *Calamities*, I, 3.

[27] James Ogden, *Isaac D'Israeli* (Oxford: Clarendon Press, 1969), p. 8.

mass-market fiction. However, in later versions of authorship, both identities became to some extent viable and acceptable. In the early nineteenth century, the privilege of valuing writing was jealously guarded by social elites. This militated against the acceptance of both solid professional practices and exalted artistic claims. While some critical accounts have traced the roots of authorly professionalism in the eighteenth century, this professionalism was usually more rhetoric than reality. As Betty Schellenberg has it, '[t]he term "professional" is often used in literary histories without explicit definition, but by implication simply to denote writing for financial remuneration, in opposition to the sorts of cultural and material rewards offered by coterie writing for manuscript circulation and publishing as part of a patronage system.'[28] Schellenberg is right to resist both a purely financial view of professional activity and the binary which she evokes. Even in modern literary culture, patronage and coteries are entangled in complex ways with professionalism and with the securing of financial rewards, and this was certainly the case in the late eighteenth century. However, I would contend that for an activity to establish itself as genuinely professional, a critical mass of practitioners must be able to support themselves financially and establish themselves socially both individually and as a group by virtue of their participating in it. In D'Israeli's age, authorship did not answer to this description. Unlike 'the three great Professions of Divinity, Law and Physick', whose burgeoning adherents Joseph Addison worried over in 1711, authors lacked a defined area of shared expertise and a strong group identity.[29] Each of the established professions 'was built around access to a specialist corpus of professional knowledge'.[30] Authors, by contrast, were valued for their individual particularities rather than for having mastered a generic skill set. Publishing books did not require 'prolonged training and a formal qualification'; nor did it mandate affiliation with a cohesive community of other writers.[31] Authors' practices were diverse, fractious and idiosyncratic, and they were poorly positioned to lobby collaboratively. Penelope Corfield argues of the professions that

[28] Betty A. Schellenberg, *The Professionalization of Women Writers in Eighteenth-Century Britain* (Cambridge: Cambridge University Press, 2005), p. 13.

[29] *The Spectator*, No. 21 (24 March 1711), [p. 41].

[30] Penelope J. Corfield, *Power and the Professions in Britain 1700–1850* (London: Routledge, 1995), p. 20.

[31] *OED*.

the position[s] of different groups varied according to their sense of collective identity or otherwise and also according to their bargaining power. And that in turn depended upon the interaction of supply with the state of effective demand for professional services, whether that was generated by the state, by other institutions, by individual consumers, or by all these.[32]

The collective identity of authors was weak, their bargaining power as a group was rarely asserted and demand for their productions was tightly constrained because literary works were generally marketed and priced as luxury items. Consequently, the idea of professional authorship was viewed with suspicion. It was better, if one had the means, to be a gentleman who wrote, as Coleridge asserted when he advised in *Biographia Literaria* that aspirant authors should 'Let literature be an honourable augmentation to your arms; but not constitute the coat, or fill the escutcheon!'[33]

This did not prevent some authors from agitating for a respectable professional status. Schellenberg contends that during the latter half of the eighteenth century some writers sought to assert 'the professional's claim to offer a certain specialised set of skills to meet a defined need of society at large and to be deserving of a certain status and economic rewards as a result'. She adds that '[t]his movement is evidenced in the development of institutions such as the critical reviews and the Royal Literary Fund, and in the increasing typology and hierarchization of forms of authorship, and in the self-consciousness of growing prestige most famously expressed by Samuel Johnson and eagerly responded to [...] by the young Frances Burney.'[34] As this study will demonstrate, however, by the early nineteenth century such developments had failed to establish an environment within which a significant body of aspiring writers could achieve prosperity or command respect by working as authors. Reviews in the late 1790s, the 1800s and the 1810s were less conducive to the construction of authorly professionalism than the earlier periodicals that Schellenberg examines, operating a kind of selective, personalised criticism motivated primarily by extra-literary factors. The Literary Fund (tellingly, the right to add 'Royal' to its title was not granted until 1842) was striking in that its committee and subscribers included only a handful of men who made their livings as authors. David Williams persevered with the Fund because he was

---

[32] Corfield, p. 179.

[33] *The Collected Works of Samuel Taylor Coleridge*, gen ed. Kathleen Coburn, 14 vols (Princeton, NJ: Princeton University Press, 1969–93), VII.i, 229.

[34] Schellenberg, p. 13.

convinced that valuable writerly achievements were inadequately recognised, but the Fund's success at countering this lack of recognition was distinctly limited.[35] Literary hierarchies were instituted during this period, but many of those at the top were distinguished precisely because they were not professional authors. Lord Byron paraded his aristocracy, Samuel Rogers relied on his personal wealth and Francis Jeffrey and Walter Scott established themselves as lawyers before turning to literature. As Schellenberg and other critics such as Brian Goldberg have shown, writers certainly 'measured themselves against their audiences, and against other professionals', but in doing so, they often expressed intense anxieties about the value and status of their labour.[36] A very small number of writers secured significant financial returns from writing, but those who did were usually underwritten by incomes other than their publishing profits. Authors commonly addressed elites who might support them through increasingly diverse forms of patronage, but in most cases the audiences for literary works were not numerous enough to sustain a career through direct sales.

For these reasons among others, the idea of authorship occupied a precarious position. As Dustin Griffin writes:

> One of the ironies of literary history is that it was probably the combination of the hard-pressed humble eighteenth-century 'authors by profession' with the successful gentleman-authors—who made up a relatively small proportion of the authors of the day but kept alive the idea that the true author was animated by genius and the goal of literary fame—that set the stage for the appearance, by the mid-nineteenth century, of the talented 'man [or woman] of letters' who might lead a well-rewarded life, and might aspire to be regarded as the equivalent of the members of the honourable learned professions.[37]

I would quibble with the assertion that the man or woman of letters combined authorship-by-profession and the demands of art writing in any kind of stable manner, but concur with Griffin in dating the emergence of

---

[35] I discuss this in detail in Chapter Four.

[36] Brian Goldberg, *The Lake Poets and Professional Identity* (Cambridge: Cambridge University Press, 2007), p. 4.

[37] Dustin Griffin, 'The Rise of the Professional Author', in *The Cambridge History of the Book in Britain Volume V: 1695–1830*, ed. Michael F. Suarez and Michael L. Turner (Cambridge: Cambridge University Press, 2009), pp. 132–45 (p. 145).

a respectable and widely recognised body of professional literary writers to the mid-nineteenth century. As Clifford Siskin notes, in 1831 only 400 census respondents classed themselves as authors, compared with 13,000 in 1901. Siskin traces in the decades leading up to the second quarter of the nineteenth century the formation of the consensus that allowed for this expansion, contending that 'Victorian professionalism had to be written up, word by word, before it became "real" and widespread.'[38] The professionalising rhetoric that critics have traced in eighteenth-century sources and the transformations of language that scholars including Thomas Pfau and Robin Valenza have read in Wordsworth and Coleridge principally comprise this contentious writing-up, rather than reflecting a settled reality.[39] It is also important to note that the fallout from the French Revolution severely disrupted earlier eighteenth-century attempts to constitute authorship as a reputable practice. Paul Keen has identified in the 1790s 'two critical transitions: a shift in focus from literature to authors, and a redefinition of politics as a struggle for professional distinction (the status of author) rather than for national agency (revolution, government reform, the rights of man)'.[40] The 1790s saw the creation of an increasingly combative literary environment in which authors struggling for individual distinction often did so by condemning other writers. This struggle kept the value of authorship under destabilising and sceptical scrutiny. While new, more respectable paradigms that helped to shield writers from personal attacks eventually emerged, it was not really until the 1820s that burgeoning markets and new institutions allowed effective commercial and aesthetic challenges to be mounted against older models in which writing perceived to be worthwhile was principally the preserve of the privileged.

[38] Clifford Siskin, *The Work of Writing: Literature and Social Change in Britain 1700–1830* (Baltimore: Johns Hopkins University Press, 1998), p. 108.

[39] Thomas Pfau, *Wordsworth's Professionalism: Form, Class and the Logic of Early Romantic Cultural Production* (Stanford: Stanford University Press, 1997); Robin Valenza, *Literature, Language, and the Rise of the Intellectual Disciplines in Britain, 1680–1820* (Cambridge: Cambridge University Press, 2009).

[40] Paul Keen, *The Crisis of Literature in the 1790s: Print Culture and the Public Sphere* (Cambridge: Cambridge University Press, 1999), p. 8.

SHAMING AUTHORIAL LABOUR

A key indication of authorship's low inherent cachet is the ease with which attempts at forging identities focused around literature were mocked by writers who operated primarily as gentlemen. In *Beppo*, Byron derides the idea of constituting oneself principally as an author:

> One hates an author that's *all author*, fellows
>   In foolscap uniforms turned up with ink,
> So very anxious, clever, fine, and jealous,
>   One don't know what to say to them, or think,
> Unless to puff them with a pair of bellows;
>   Of coxcombry's worst coxcombs e'en the pink
> Are preferable to these shreds of paper,
> These unquenched snuffings of the midnight taper.
>
> Of these same we see several, and of others,
>   Men of the world, who know the world like men,
> S[co]tt, R[oger]s, M[oo]re, and all the better brothers,
>   Who think of something else besides the pen;
> But for the children of the 'mighty mother's,'
>   The would-be wits and can't-be gentlemen,
> I leave them to their daily 'tea is ready,'
> Smug coterie, and literary lady.[41]

Byron here suggests a different continuity to that which D'Israeli considers. While D'Israeli sees authorship as enduringly unprofitable, Byron, in figuring the persistence of the Grub Street hack and the bluestocking's sycophant, represents all-author authorship as enduringly déclassé. The continuity is stressed by his recalling the 'Mighty Mother'—the goddess Dulness—from Pope's four-book *Dunciad*, a text that also served as a model for William Gifford's attacks on the Della Cruscan poets in the *Baviad* and *Maeviad* and for Byron's own mocking survey of the literary scene in *English Bards and Scotch Reviewers*.[42] In all these works, authors

---

[41] *Beppo: a Venetian Story*, stanzas 75 and 76 (ll. 593–608), in *Byron: The Complete Poetical Works*, ed. Jerome J. McGann, 7 vols (Oxford: Oxford University Press, 1980–93), IV, 152–3.

[42] 'The Mighty Mother, and her Son, who brings/The Smithfield Muses to the ear of Kings/I sing.' From *The Dunciad, in Four Books*, I, lines 1–3, in *The Poems of Alexander Pope Volume V: The Dunciad*, ed. James Sutherland, 2nd edn (London: Methuen & Co., 1953), pp. 267–8.

are portrayed as ridiculous failures, their overriding focus on inky matters the antithesis of the diverse accomplishments required of gentleman. For Byron, the best writing came from well-connected masculine circles, not from bookish obsession, inky-fingered diligence or feminised salon culture.

It is easy to take umbrage at Byron's dismissal of hard-working would-be professionals, particularly when considering his privileged status and the ways in which such assertions fed into his own profitable self-fashioning.[43] However, the prejudices he expresses were not untypical and reflected the reality that many of the highest-profile writers of the early nineteenth century did not depend on their literary earnings. The writers Byron lists as 'know[ing] the world like men' were three of the biggest-selling, best-connected and most acclaimed authors of the period. Of the three, only Thomas Moore relied principally on his pen, and his success was largely contingent on his having access to the elite circles in which he promoted his poetry, performed his hugely profitable *Irish Melodies* and made the contacts that allowed him to publish lucrative biographical writings during the 1820s and 1830s. Walter Scott was established comfortably before he ever published, having acquired a very substantial income through his family, his legal practice, his marriage and the patronage of the Duke of Buccleuch.[44] Samuel Rogers, author of *The Pleasures of Memory* and a pivotal figure in literary society, had a significant interest in his family's profitable bank. After his father's death in 1793, he 'found himself possessed of £5000 a year'.[45] This pleasant discovery granted him the financial muscle to publish and control his own works: a rare and potent privilege. Many other respected authors lived off smaller private incomes, and patronage remained invaluable for writers without independent means. A few writers were supported directly by the state—Robert Southey and Thomas Campbell were both awarded government pensions of £200 a year, Campbell in his late twenties and Southey in his early thirties.[46] Direct and indirect support from wealthy individuals also remained a

---

[43] See Jerome Christensen, *Lord Byron's Strength: Romantic Writing and Commercial Society* (Baltimore: Johns Hopkins University Press, 1993) and Tom Mole, *Byron's Romantic Celebrity: Industrial Culture and the Hermeneutic of Intimacy* (Basingstoke: Palgrave Macmillan, 2007) for accounts of Byron's canny manipulation of his aristocratic credentials and collusions with his publishers and audiences. See also the final section of Chapter Six.

[44] I discuss Moore further in Chapter Three and Scott in Chapter Six.

[45] Richard Garnett, 'Rogers, Samuel (1763–1855)', rev. Paul Baines, *ODNB*, https://doi.org/10.1093/ref:odnb/23997.

[46] Geoffrey Carnall, 'Campbell, Thomas (1777–1844)', *ODNB*, https://doi.org/10.1093/ref:odnb/4534; Geoffrey Carnall, 'Southey, Robert (1774–1843)', *ODNB*, https://doi.org/10.1093/ref:odnb/26056.

factor. Examples include William Hayley's support for William Blake and Charlotte Smith; Tom and Josiah Wedgwood's providing Samuel Taylor Coleridge with an annuity of £150; and Sir William Lowther's securing for Wordsworth the position of Distributor of Stamps for Westmorland, Whitehaven and the Penrith District of Cumberland after registering the poet's discomfort at the idea of straightforward payments.[47]

Such incomes, and the connections that acquiring them entailed, granted their holders the freedom to pursue literary writing in ways denied to authors who could not avoid appealing to a limited market. As William St Clair's ground-breaking work has shown, while at the end of the eighteenth century a larger potential readership existed than a hundred years previously, new literary works by contemporary writers were still well beyond the means of most working men and women.[48] Small editions of five hundred or a thousand copies required a high capital outlay from their publishers and offered a relatively limited return, usually turning a profit only after about 60% of an edition sold through at full price, a circumstance that was far from inevitable.[49] Savings from printing more copies were minor, and when combined with the cost of storing unsold stock, this meant that publishers were unwilling to gamble on longer runs until technological innovations brought costs down during the 1820s. This kept prices high, editions small, audiences limited and authors who depended on their works for their income generally poor. Writers who needed money were often forced to work at an extremely high speed. Generally this impeded their quality of life, necessitating borrowing, thrift and writing for long periods in poor light and circumstances. Byron's 'midnight taper' was burnt at the cost of the eyesight of more than a few.[50] The usual recourses of those who required a steady income were the production of large volumes of periodical and newspaper journalism; composing novels in popular genres such as the gothic; or authoring textbooks and functional non-fiction. Such low-status work seldom brought literary fame, social plaudits or vast payments.

---

[47] Vivienne W. Painting, 'Hayley, William (1745–1820)', *ODNB*, https://doi.org/10.1093/ref:odnb/12769; Richard Holmes, *Coleridge: Early Visions* (London: Penguin, 1990), pp. 176–8; Juliet Barker, *Wordsworth: A Life* (London: Viking, 2000), pp. 438, 440–1, 448–9.

[48] William St Clair, *The Reading Nation in the Romantic Period* (Cambridge: Cambridge University Press, 2004); see especially pp. 193–6.

[49] I examine the practices of the publishing industry in detail in Chapter One.

[50] See my discussion of Robert Heron in Chapter Four.

The low status of authorship was reinforced by aggressive forms of gatekeeping that figured authorial labour as a mindless, proliferating contagion. A typical example is William Gifford's attack on Robert Merry (Della Crusca) in *The Baviad*:

> Lo, DELLA CRUSCA! In his closet pent,
> He toils to give the crude conception vent.
> Abortive thoughts that right and wrong confound,
> Truth sacrific'd to letters, sense to sound;
> False glare, incongruous images, combine,
> And noise and nonsense clatter through the line.[51]

In Gifford's satire, Merry's toil creates only sickness and disorder. His work is portrayed as overabundant to the point of incoherence, lacking the clarifying structure of an established form or a guiding intelligence. In criticising literary labour, Gifford was on shaky ground. A son of poor parents orphaned at an early age, he had been sent to sea as a child for a time. He was removed from schooling and apprenticed to a shoemaker before his juvenile poetry caught the attention of the surgeon William Cookesley.[52] Cookesley's interest propelled Gifford to Oxford, where he acquired the skills that led to his embarking on a translation of Juvenal and receiving sustained patronage from Lord Richard Grosvenor. In *The Baviad*, however, he shields himself from counteraccusations by lacing his poem with scholarly notes that emphasise his classical erudition and university education. Rather than positioning himself as a working author, Gifford assumes the mantle of the cultured gentleman in order to censure the popular success of the Della Cruscans in a largely successful attempt to destroy their reputations and profitability. Robert Merry eventually had to move to the United States; Jon Mee writes that his 'hand was forced by financial necessity compounded by the political context after the Two Acts had passed into law'.[53]

Gifford's *Baviad* is particularly interesting as it was the launchpad for a successful critical career that would see him become the editor of the

---

[51] William Gifford, *The Baviad*, Book II, lines 39–44, from *The Baviad, and Maeviad*, new edn (London: J. Wright, 1797), pp. 12–14.

[52] See *British Satire 1785–1840: Volume 4: Gifford and the Della Cruscans*, ed. John Strachen (London: Pickering and Chatto, 2003), pp. xiv–xvi.

[53] Jon Mee, *Print, Publicity, and Popular Radicalism in the 1790s: The Laurel of Liberty* (Cambridge: Cambridge University Press, 2016), p. 129.

influential *Anti-Jacobin* between 1797 and 1798 and of the more enduring *Quarterly Review* from 1809. In both publications, Gifford penned
and endorsed virulent attacks on radical authors. The excitement provoked by the accusatory *ad hominem* mode he employed made that mode
a key tool for all factions in an increasingly politicised reviewing culture.
Gifford's Whiggish opposite number, Francis Jeffrey of the *Edinburgh
Review*, used very similar language to *The Baviad* when damning Thomas
Moore's *Epistles, Odes, and Other Poems* (1806), portraying Moore's effusions as compulsive and impure:

> he labours with a perseverance at once ludicrous and detestable. He may be
> seen in every page running round the paltry circle of his seductions with
> incredible zeal and anxiety, and stimulating his jaded fancy for new images
> of impurity, with as much melancholy industry as ever outcast of the muses
> hunted for epithets or metre.[54]

Like Byron's 'would-be wits and can't-be gentlemen', Moore is rhetorically made all-author, a ridiculous and unworthy obsessive exposed by the
gaze of his stern and civic-minded judge. By diagnosing corruption in
others, auditors like Jeffrey bolstered their own claims to discernment and
moral probity. This tactic remained common in later decades. In *The Spirit
of the Age* (1825), William Hazlitt calls Gifford 'a critic of the last age', but
he belies this characterisation by using Gifford's own methods, describing
his bête noire as being

> possessed of that sort of learning which is likely to result from an over-
> anxious desire to supply the want of the first rudiments of education: that
> sort of wit which is the offspring of ill-humour or bodily pain: that sort of
> sense which arises from a spirit of contradiction and a disposition to cavil at
> and dispute the opinions of others: and that sort of reputation which is the
> consequence of bowing to established authority and ministerial influence.[55]

Hazlitt's tit-for-tat essay enacts a rhetorical victory over Gifford just as *The
Baviad* enacts one over the Della Cruscans, but in both works the idea of
the working author loses out. This cycle of denigration was rarely broken
within the period's rancorous print culture. In its review of Hazlitt's book,

---

[54] [Francis Jeffrey], 'Moore's *Poems*', *Edinburgh Review*, 8 (July 1806), 456–65 (p. 457).
[55] William Hazlitt, 'Mr. Gifford', in *The Spirit of the Age*, in *The Complete Works of William
Hazlitt*, ed. P.P. Howe, 21 vols (London: J.M. Dent, 1930–34), XI, 114–26 (p. 117).

Blackwood's Edinburgh Magazine attacked him in very similar terms: 'He seems to live in the very lowest society, for he has for years absolutely *been on the Press.*'[56] As Richard Cronin remarks, this 'leaves one wondering where the writers for *Blackwood's* imagined they had been'.[57] One might answer that the key position in this discourse was to be on the attack, focusing on the failings of others while assuming a posture of superiority oneself, forestalling questions regarding one's own position by asserting a presence in 'better circles'.[58] Nevertheless, spectacular rhetoric could not magic away the parlous economic realities of authorship or the advantages of wealth. On his deathbed, Hazlitt dictated a heart-breaking note to the prosperous Jeffrey: 'Dear sir, I am dying; can you send me 10*l.*, and so consummate your many kindnesses to me?'[59] Jeffrey sent £50, the last of a number of donations to a writer he admired, but one that makes clear that talent could only modestly alleviate the stark and extreme inequalities that existed in society in general and which strongly influenced who got to profit from literary production.

At the beginning of the nineteenth century, then, being condemned as an author rather than recognised as someone of consequence who wrote could severely limit what one could achieve. Retractions and regressions from the freedoms of the eighteenth century had particular consequences for women, whose position in literary society worsened significantly. As Elizabeth Eger has argued, the largely positive reception enjoyed by the Bluestocking circle was a fleeting phenomenon; subsequently, 'the cultural anxiety caused by women's very success in the public sphere of letters caused a new generation [...] to displace women from their positions of power.'[60] The high profiles of female radicals after the French Revolution lent political urgency to this conservative reaction. A major tool in the displacement of women was the aggressive and widely read criticism propagated by the anti-Revolutionary press and the party quarterlies. The masculine circles that controlled these new Reviews generally either

[56] 'Works of the First Importance', *Blackwood's Edinburgh Magazine*, 17 (March 1825), 362–5 (p. 362).

[57] Richard Cronin, *Paper Pellets: British Literary Culture after Waterloo* (Oxford: Oxford University Press, 2010), p. 137.

[58] 'Works of the First Importance', p. 362.

[59] Quoted in Duncan Wu, *William Hazlitt: The First Modern Man* (Oxford: Oxford University Press, 2008), p. 429.

[60] Elizabeth Eger, *Bluestockings: Women of Reason from Enlightenment to Romanticism* (Basingstoke: Palgrave Macmillan, 2010), p. 209.

neglected or patronised women and often lambasted female writers who ventured into political discourse, as happened when Anna Laetitia Barbauld published *Eighteen Hundred and Eleven*, her bold vision of England's eventual ruin. The notorious anonymous review in the *Quarterly* now attributed to John Wilson Croker charged her with having 'wandered from the course in which she was respectable and useful' and facetiously belittled her efforts: 'we had hoped, indeed, that the empire might have been saved without the intervention of a lady author.'[61] The sting here is in 'author' as well as 'lady': both denote classes unfit to influence affairs of state. Croker deplores Barbauld's political interventions and denies that she has any facility for operating in masculine modes: 'we must take the liberty of warning her to desist from satire, which indeed is satire on herself alone.'[62] In taking such liberties, Croker both indicated and exercised the strength arrogated by the anonymous periodical reviewer, placing Barbauld, as William Keach puts it, 'outside both the "conjugal family" and the "public sphere"'.[63] The impact of this review has often been overstated. As E.J. Clery has recently demonstrated, by the time Croker published his diatribe, Barbauld's poem had already played a significant role in achieving the political ends it sought.[64] Nevertheless, the limited circulation and mixed reputation of *Eighteen Hundred and Eleven* both attest to reviews' pervasive influence and to their cumulative efficacy in formulating the standards by which culture was judged. Barbauld published no further visionary interventions.

The reviewers' power was by no means absolute. As the nineteenth century progressed and new markets began to open up, some very popular writers were able to make light of periodical attacks. Lady Morgan (née Sydney Owenson) was a pioneer in sensationally appealing to wide readerships. She developed her talent for performative self-display in elite circles and in print, and later used this talent to bait her reviewers as a promotional strategy.[65] Croker reviewed her novel *The Wild Irish Girl* (1806)

---

[61] [John Wilson Croker], 'Mrs. Barbauld's *Eighteen Hundred and Eleven*', *Quarterly Review*, 7 (June 1812), 309–13 (p. 309).

[62] [Croker], 'Mrs. Barbauld's *Eighteen Hundred and Eleven*', p. 313.

[63] William Keach, 'A Regency Prophecy and the End of Anna Barbauld's Career', *Studies in Romanticism*, 33 (Winter 1994), 569–77 (p. 571).

[64] E.J. Clery, *Eighteen Hundred and Eleven: Poetry, Protest and Economic Crisis* (Cambridge: Cambridge University Press, 2017).

[65] For Sydney Owenson's high-society performances, see Natasha Tessone, 'Displaying Ireland: Sydney Owenson and the Politics of Spectacular Antiquarianism', *Éire-Ireland*, 37 (Fall/Winter 2002), 169–86.

and her study *France* (1817) extremely negatively, but the virulent nature of his attacks ended up boosting her sales.[66] Morgan issued spirited responses to Croker in pamphlets and caricatured him as the odious Conway Townsend Crawley, 'with his brogue and effrontery', in her novel *Florence Macarthy* (1818).[67] By the time he came to review Morgan's *Italy* in 1821, Croker refused to print any excerpts, writing that '[b]uried in the lead of her ponderous quartos, the corruption is inoffensive—any examination would only serve to let the effluvia escape, and in some degree endanger the public health.'[68] Instead he reviewed her book's advertisements, arguing that she was attempting to draw interest to her languishing works based on their ability to '*put all the race of intolerant critics* into a STATE of FURY'.[69] Secure in her position, Morgan was confident in asserting her worth in financial terms, writing that 'the *price* given for my last *venture* from Italy is the best answer to those who endeavoured to undervalue the cargo'.[70] The innovative populist publisher Henry Colburn had made her 'a dashing offer of two thousand pounds' for the book and was more than happy with the transaction, writing to *The Times* that

> I am ready to prove, that five hundred copies of this work were sold on the first day of publication; that more copies have been disposed of during the last month, and since the appearance of the 'Quarterly Review,' than in any preceding one since the day of publication; that a new edition is in preparation; that two editions, amounting to 4000 copies, have been printed at Paris, and another in Belgium […] I shall be most happy to receive from the author another work of equal interest, on the same terms.[71]

---

[66] Ina Ferris gives an excellent account of Croker's reviews and the ways in which 'the critical terms in which [Morgan] was cast locate her within the negative paradigm of female reading' in *The Achievement of Literary Authority: Gender, History, and the Waverley Novels* (Ithaca: Cornell University Press, 1991), pp. 45–52 (p. 46).

[67] Sydney, Lady Morgan, *Florence Macarthy: An Irish Tale*, 4 vols (London: Henry Colburn, 1819), III, 133.

[68] [John Wilson Croker], 'Lady Morgan's *Italy*', *Quarterly Review*, 25 (July 1821), 529–34 (p. 529).

[69] [Croker], 'Lady Morgan's *Italy*', p. 532.

[70] Quoted in [Croker], 'Lady Morgan's *Italy*', p. 534.

[71] Quoted in William John Fitzpatrick, *Lady Morgan: Her Career, Literary and Personal* (London; Charles J. Skeet, 1860), pp. 206, 224.

As the potential audiences for literary writing expanded, popular admiration had the potential to serve as a shield against critical malignity. Devoted readers could affirm a writer's value in ways that critics found difficult to counteract without employing the risky (although often effective) strategy of belittling the abilities of those readers. However, while acquiring large readerships became easier as the century progressed, these were exceptions rather than the rule. Those with the privileges of a Lady Morgan were few and far between. Most authors could only aspire to such popularity.

Instead, grim failures were common, as attested by the extensive records of the Literary Fund, which received applications from nearly 700 distressed authors between 1790 and 1830, including 247 individuals now considered important enough to be included in the *Oxford Dictionary of National Biography*.[72] Writers often protested their embarrassment at having to apply, but apply they did, and in large numbers, testament to the fleeting nature of literary rewards. Common in these letters are the fates of writers like William Henry Hall 'an unfortunate, and it may be added, undone gentleman, who was once, by his literary productions an ornament to society, but whose bodily afflictions and whose poverty have driven him to the last state of human sorrow and wretchedness, in an obscure garret, on a dying bed'.[73] Lady Frances Chambers wrote in 1802 on behalf of Charlotte Lennox, author of the *Female Quixote*, 'who is in great distress for the common necessaries of life & is too ill & now too old to assist herself in any way.'[74] The young Thomas Love Peacock was profoundly depressed by the failure of his early works, causing his friend Edward Hookham to write that

I have been most intimately acquainted with Mr Peacock for six years & not unfrequently during that period I have had but too just reason to dread that the fate of Chatterton might be that of Peacock. This inference I have drawn not only from the distressed state of mind in which I have seen him, but

---

[72] Numbers compiled from an expanded version of my catalogue of the Literary Fund Archive, integrated into the British Library catalogue: http://searcharchives.bl.uk.

[73] William Hall to the Committee of the Literary Fund, 11 January 1808, Loan 96 RLF 1/74/3.

[74] Lady Frances Chambers to David Williams, 20 January 1802, Loan 96 RLF 1/12/8.

likewise from the tone of despondency which breathes throughout many of his letters to me.[75]

William Jerdan—the editor and part-owner of the *Literary Gazette* and a Literary Fund committee member from 1817—spent a good part of his four-volume *Autobiography* bemoaning the inconsistencies of his own relatively successful career, stressing the uncertainties that plagued even well-connected authors. In one of a number of tragic examples from his work for the Fund, he describes how he

> found, in a single apartment, a broker's man in possession of an execution for rent, a dead child of two or three years of age on a rug in a corner, a living mother and a living baby on the semblance of a bed, covered with a horse-cloth, on the floor, and the "Literary Man," who had really written some creditable productions, sitting stupefied, like an impersonation of Apathy, on a broken chair.[76]

Jerdan also quotes Charles Lamb's exclamation to the Quaker poet Bernard Barton on hearing that Barton was thinking of leaving his bank position in favour of the realm of letters: 'Throw yourself rather, my dear sir, from the Tarpeian Rock, slap down headlong upon iron spikes.'[77] To weigh against the Morgans, Scotts and Byrons who profitably asserted authorial selves are hundreds for whom dreams of making a reputation as an author curdled into nightmares of poverty, neglect, opprobrium and despair.

ROMANTICISM AND RETROSPECTION

The dismal picture painted above suggests a radically different image of the author to that propagated by the poets from whom the Romantic period now ostensibly takes its name. The 'Big Six' writers positioned as paramount during the twentieth century (William Wordsworth, Samuel Taylor Coleridge, William Blake, Lord Byron, Percy Shelley and John

---

[75] Edward Thomas Hookham to the Committee of the Literary Fund, 20 May 1812, Loan 96 RLF 1/274/4; see also Nicholas A. Joukovsky, 'Peacock Before *Headlong Hall*: A New Look at his Early Years', *Keats-Shelley Memorial Bulletin*, 36 (1985), 1–40.

[76] William Jerdan, *The Autobiography of William Jerdan*, 4 vols (London: Arthur Hall, Virtue & Co., 1852–53), IV, 38.

[77] Jerdan, IV, 42.

Keats) have come down to us as magnificently authorly: synonymous with poetry, achievement and timeless virtue. Wordsworth in particular made himself through his relentless self-presentations the paragon of a kind of writing that claimed a transcendent value detached from the operations of the market and the judgements of contemporaries. While Wordsworth is perhaps the most extreme case, the self-fashioning rhetoric of all the canonical Romantics tends to talk down to the importance of popularity and profession. Literary culture as it emerged over the course of the nineteenth century found it politically and economically useful to collude with these self-presentations, hailing the poets as geniuses, avatars of their age, *sui generis*. Even now, these six writers remain dominant figures. Along with Jane Austen, they are the most common subjects for articles, chapters and books dealing with the period. Their fame is supported by dedicated journals and societies and buttressed by a longstanding institutionalised consensus that makes them nearly automatic inclusions on syllabi and in anthologies.

However, it is important to recognise that prior to the 1820s, success in Romantic terms was a nascent, conflicted and little-recognised formulation. Most of the writers living through what we now call the Romantic period would not have thought of themselves as living through anything of the kind. In the words of Michael Gamer, the term is 'misleading because it posits as representative writers who literally do not represent the range of writing of these decades.'[78] Peter T. Murphy writes similarly that the conventional model of Romanticism 'quite simply excludes all of the most popular poets of the period, with the exception of Byron.'[79] In a table of sales of literary works in the first quarter of the nineteenth century, Wordsworth and Coleridge would be placed relatively low, Keats and Shelley lower and Blake would hardly figure (at least as a poet; he was relatively well known as a commercial illustrator). Of the six, only Byron was the recipient of widespread acclaim, although revelations about his personal life made him more divisive (if not less popular) later in his career. Blake was scarcely commented on as an author in print; Wordsworth and Coleridge both received a large number of conflicted and negative reviews;

---

[78] Michael Gamer, *Romanticism and the Gothic* (Cambridge: Cambridge University Press, 2000), p. 5.

[79] Peter T. Murphy, 'Climbing Parnassus, & Falling Off', in *At the Limits of Romanticism: Essays in Cultural, Feminist and Materialist Criticism*, ed. Mary A. Favret and Nicola J. Watson (Bloomington: University of Indiana Press, 1994), pp. 40–58 (p. 40).

and Keats and Shelley, while not actually killed by critics' pens, were nevertheless severely compromised in the eyes of many by vitriolic responses to their works and lives.

Rather than being garlanded by their contemporaries, five of the six major Romantics achieved their prominence due to processes of canonisation that they set in motion through incorporating self-justificatory theories into their works. The belated but wholehearted acceptance of these arguments has inevitably coloured critical depictions of the time in which they struggled. Jerome McGann's influential thesis in *The Romantic Ideology* is that criticism of Romantic-period authors is often marred by 'an uncritical absorption in Romanticism's own self-representations.'[80] Clifford Siskin writes similarly that 'almost all our literary histories of the late eighteenth and early nineteenth centuries are themselves Romantic. Like the texts they propose to interpret, they tell tales of lyrical development.'[81] Since the values of Romanticism ground the definitions of literary value from which professional academic discourse has developed, the poets benefit from being rooted at the heart of the canon. As Mary Poovey has argued, the modern genre of the literary work emerged during the Romantic period as authors including Coleridge and Wordsworth worked to 'devise a model of value that could challenge the market evaluation registered by *popularity* or *demand*'.[82] Poovey is far from alone in figuring the Romantics as creating new conceptions of literary value in order to oppose their contemporaries' more pragmatic systematisations. Andrew Bennett has subtly and exactingly drawn out the ways in which the canonical poets inflected their poetry towards a posthumous audience, reconfiguring contemporary neglect as a condition for future appreciation.[83] Lucy Newlyn has ranged over an astonishing variety of material in considering how the Romantics anxiously constructed both ideal and fearsome readers in reaction to the contemporary audiences they

---

[80] Jerome J. McGann, *The Romantic Ideology: A Critical Investigation* (Chicago: University of Chicago Press, 1983), p. 1.

[81] Clifford Siskin, *The Historicity of Romantic Discourse* (Oxford: Oxford University Press, 1988), p. 170.

[82] Mary Poovey, *Genres of the Credit Economy: Mediating Value in Eighteenth- and Nineteenth-Century Britain* (Chicago: University of Chicago Press, 2008), p. 286.

[83] Andrew Bennett, *Romantic Poets and the Culture of Posterity* (Cambridge: Cambridge University Press, 1999).

perceived.[84] The coda to this study will follow Poovey, Newlyn and Bennett in considering how the Romantics reacted against prevailing commercial, critical and social assumptions, creating distinctive aesthetic arguments for the value of their works. However, the main body of this book will seek to tell stories that Romanticisation has overwritten, decentring the canonical poets in favour of exploring more fully the modes of valuation they reacted against. It will also highlight the extent to which the Romantics' ability to construct longer-term reputations was predicated on their connections and non-literary incomes. With the exception of Blake, the canonical Romantics occupied positions of relative privilege. I say this not to denigrate them or to mark them out as somehow phony, but rather to contest the claims to universality that Romantic poetry often seems to make. In fact, Romantic poems represent very particular experiences, and we teach and read them as the ultimate representations of their age at the expense of hundreds of other writers and perspectives.

Many Romantic-period authors have, of course, already been reclaimed by critics in recent decades. In particular, a huge amount of valuable work has been done to recover the works of leading female writers, including Charlotte Smith, Ann Radcliffe, Anna Laetitia Barbauld, Maria Edgeworth, Lady Morgan, Mary Shelley, Felicia Hemans and Letitia Elizabeth Landon. While they were often forced to bow to or struggle against the gendered assumptions of their male contemporaries, many of these exceptional women nevertheless enjoyed contemporary popularity far greater than that accorded to the Big Six (Byron again excepted). However, the reversal of this situation in posterity puts critics wishing to speak for the merits of these authors in a difficult position. The main way into the period for modern readers is through Romanticism, but setting women writers against the canonical Romantics can make it seem as if Romantic poetry was the major force oppressing women, rather than social institutions and ideological preconceptions with which the canonical poets were to a greater or lesser extent complicit. Anne Mellor writes that canonical Romantic poetry 'subtly denies the value of female difference. Positive feminine characteristics—sensibility, compassion, maternal love—are metaphorically appropriated by the male poet, while attributes of difference—independence, intelligence, willpower, aggressive action—are denigrated.'[85]

---

[84] Lucy Newlyn, *Reading, Writing, and Romanticism: The Anxiety of Reception* (Oxford: Oxford University Press, 2000).

[85] Anne K. Mellor, *Romanticism and Gender* (London: Routledge, 1993), p. 29.

While this offers a cogent analysis of the ways in which Romantic ideologies have retrospectively silenced women's voices, it is not as helpful for explaining the ways that women writers were excluded in their own time. Mellor argues that 'feminine Romanticism, like masculine Romanticism, was a reformist bourgeois movement' dedicated to bringing about, in Mary Wollstonecraft's words, 'a revolution in female manners'.[86] This ascribes an uneasy common motive to a very diverse group, creating a parallel female Romantic canon that, like the male one, excludes many of the texts Mellor's posited revolution was reacting against. As Marlon Ross has it, 'romanticist critics have made women writers of the period an extension of male romanticism [...] allowing us to keep intact the idea that romanticism can describe the whole period by equating the male romantic poets with all the literature of the time'.[87] Defining women writers as secondary Romantics blurs them into a tradition that many of them strongly opposed, occluding the circumstances and expectations that shaped their works and successes.

Mellor's conclusions on 'feminine Romanticism' for me sell short the works she adroitly explicates by simplifying her previously stated position on the diversity of authorial selves:

> I am not suggesting that male Romantic writers constructed one kind of self and female Romantic writers another. Rather, I am arguing against Foucault that there is no such thing as "*the* Romantic self" or "*the* Modern self," but only differing modes of subjectivity which can be shared by male and female writers alike, and even by the same person in the course of a long and variegated life.[88]

This seems to me to be a very productive way of looking at the period, seeing it as one in which new types of self-expression were becoming possible while recognising that these were adopted by different writers to different degrees at different times. This is a model with which dissimilar works can fruitfully be examined while avoiding deadening Romantic totalisations. While this study does not pretend exhaustively to analyse the ways in which any class of authors wrote in the early nineteenth century, it will attempt to represent the diversity of authorial methods and motives

---

[86] Mellor, p. 212; see also the wider context, pp. 209–12.

[87] Marlon B. Ross, *The Contours of Masculine Desire: Romanticism and the Rise of Women's Poetry* (Oxford: Oxford University Press, 1989), p. 5.

[88] Mellor, p. 168.

through stressing the sociable nature of authorship and making clear the means by which writers were judged before the propagation of Romantic ideologies. Returning to the early nineteenth century's own systems of valuation will bring to light aspects of authorship that both Romantic and counter-Romantic ideologies have occluded.

Change Over Time

Considering the last decade of the eighteenth century and the first three of the nineteenth as a discrete Romantic period often causes us both to neglect the discontinuities within those decades and to exaggerate the differences between them and those that preceded and succeeded them. It is a canard that the Romantic period began with a world-changing revolutionary upheaval, but in Britain reactionary forces were largely successful in preventing the kind of decisive break that radicals sought, ensuring continuity in many aspects of public life. Nevertheless, the outlook for authors in the late 1820s differed considerably from that of the early 1790s. James Chandler, following Claude Lévi-Strauss, has described the Romantic period as a 'hot chronology', during which 'numerous events appear as differential elements.'[89] Authors registered a strong awareness of their specific historical circumstances and often responded to very narrow windows of opportunity. Rendering the period as a homogenous whole impedes appreciations of such circumstances and their effects on the contents and forms of literary works.

Attempting to build up a picture of literary life that is faithful to historical specificities will be an ongoing process throughout this study, but it will be useful at the outset to outline some of the most consequential changes. I would not wish to put too much emphasis on these; as Stephen Behrendt has warned, the desire for 'neatness and cleanliness' can lead to scholarship that 'ignores the discontinuities, the dissonances, the failure to "fit" that characterizes real life no less than the real literary landscapes of Romantic-era Britain'.[90] However, by sketching out large-scale shifts in the environments within which all writers worked, a superstructure can be

---

[89] James Chandler, *England in 1819: The Politics of Literary Culture and the Case for Romantic Historicism* (Chicago: University of Chicago Press, 1998), p. 67.

[90] Stephen C. Behrendt, *British Women Poets and the Romantic Writing Community* (Baltimore: Johns Hopkins University Press, 2009), p. 5.

provided that will be refined and complicated in the detailed case studies that follow.

While the discussions percolating through the relatively open society of the 1780s reached their apogee in the years immediately after the French Revolution, even before the declaration of the long war with France, literary society was moving towards becoming a culture dominated by conservative fears and institutions. While retrospectively it is clear that a rich and transformative revolutionary literature was produced during the 1790s, many texts now considered canonical were either successfully traduced by mainstream publications or ignored altogether. After the furious circulations of the early 1790s, conservative forces worked relatively effectively to suppress a number of the more progressive traditions from earlier in the eighteenth century. The failures of numerous attempts to secure equal rights for Dissenters and Catholics, the Treason Trials of 1794, the passing of the Gagging Acts (the Treason Act and the Seditious Meetings Act) in 1795, the imprisonment of Leigh Hunt in 1813, the prosecution of William Hone in 1817 and the two suspensions of *habeas corpus* in 1793 and 1817 are all examples of the ways in which the establishment worked to censure authors and discourses that it considered dangerous.[91] The state was a useful source of direct and indirect patronage for writers and informally controlled a ferocious propaganda engine. To hazard a confrontation was to risk imprisonment, transportation or obloquy severe enough to scupper any chance of profiting by the pen. As the governments elected in the period prove, state conservatism was often supported by public opinion, or at least by the opinions of the affluent men who comprised a disproportionately influential sector of the reading public.

In some respects, literary writers were protected from the full force of the state's concerned scrutiny. While pamphlets and cheap productions could circulate widely among the populace, the high prices commanded by new literary and philosophical works kept them out of the hands of the masses. In William Godwin's account, the Prime Minister William Pitt dismissed concerns about the *Enquiry Concerning Political Justice* (1793) by arguing that 'a three guinea book could never do harm among those

---

[91] John Barrell explores the implications of many of these events in *Imagining the King's Death: Figurative Treason, Fantasies of Regicide, 1794–1796* (Oxford: Oxford University Press, 2000).

who had not three shillings to spare.'[92] However, while such books were not seen as dangers on the scale of Thomas Paine's *Rights of Man* (1791–1792), they were still subject to damaging censure. George Canning established the *Anti-Jacobin* in 1797 with the express purpose of 'detecting falsehood,—and rectifying error,—by correcting misrepresentation, and exposing malignity'.[93] This was done partly through vitriolic satire that reached its zenith in the poem 'New Morality' in the final issue. In the poem, and in James Gillray's accompanying cartoon, literary innovators including Coleridge, Southey, Godwin, Charles Lamb and Thomas Holcroft were savagely pilloried. Through assaults like this, literary progressivism came to be associated with dangerous radicalism. While liberal and Dissenting magazines and newspapers fought back against such character assassinations, these publications lacked the ability to unsay the curses that could destroy reputations and lives. Although the 1794 treason charges brought against Holcroft were dropped, his formerly successful career foundered. As he wrote in 1799: 'My income has always been the produce of my labour; and that produce has been so reduced, by the animosity of party spirit, that I find myself obliged to sell my effects for the payment of my debts, that I may leave the kingdom till party spirit shall subside.'[94] To be a radical and a writer was thus to take a considerable risk, and the incentives to toe the line were real and significant. This contributed to the 'narratives of withdrawal' that critics have identified in the late 1790s, with the formal and informal discouragement of political debate leading to increasing disciplinary specialisation and the development of smaller, tighter and more contentious literary groupings. As Jon Mee writes, '[l]iterary ideas of conversation were increasingly either domesticated or displaced into ideas of higher forms of communion', although these shifts 'must also be weighed against the continuation of the wider context of ongoing talk about literature, politics and other issues that continued in an array of places, including bookshops, clubs, and in the home'.[95] As the eighteenth century became the

---

[92] Quoted in William St Clair, *The Godwins and the Shelleys: The Biography of a Family* (London & Boston: Faber and Faber, 1989), p. 85. St Clair notes that Pitt misrepresented the price of *Political Justice*, which was actually £1.16s.

[93] 'Prospectus', *Anti-Jacobin; or, Weekly Examiner*, 1 (20 November 1797), 1–10 (p. 2).

[94] Thomas Holcroft, *The Life of Thomas Holcroft*, continued by William Hazlitt, ed. Elbridge Colby, 2 vols (London: Constable & Co., 1925), II, 248.

[95] Jon Mee, *Conversable Worlds: Literature, Contention, and Community 1762 to 1830* (Oxford: Oxford University Press, 2011), pp. 27, 133.

nineteenth, literary culture circulated in increasingly private and mediated spaces. However, this was not solely limiting. Harriet Guest has explored the manners in which the control exerted over public discussions led a number of female writers successfully to 'represent domesticity as the site from which an oppositional political discourse [could] be articulated'.[96] This desire to write into being defined spaces for literary practice contributed to the development of notions of artistry that still influence culture today.

The success of the *Edinburgh Review* (launched in 1802) was a supreme expression of the powerful attraction of regulating and defining authors. On first consideration, it would be logical to assume that the Whiggish *Edinburgh* would have served to counteract the conservative strain in literary culture, but in fact the *Edinburgh* was generally doctrinaire when it came to literary works, inveighing against new styles and lax morals. That its editors had noted the success of the vicious *Anti-Jacobin* style was evident in their keenness to censure, a tendency on full display in Jeffrey's 1807 attack on James Montgomery:

> We took compassion on Mr Montgomery on his first appearance; conceiving him to be some slender youth of seventeen, intoxicated with weak tea, and the praises of sentimental Ensigns and other provincial literati, and tempted in that situation, to commit a feeble outrage on the public, of which the recollection would be a sufficient punishment. A third edition, however, is too alarming to be passed over in silence...[97]

Here Jeffrey asserts the *Edinburgh's* centrality to the country's literary life, identifying its role as that of judging those who would 'outrage' the public and placing it as a corrective to the follies of popular taste. The large readerships that the *Edinburgh* and the *Quarterly* obtained meant that their controlling cliques enjoyed enormous influence, which they exercised through censure and omission.[98] While the selectivity of the quarterlies was partly a symptom of textual proliferation, it was also ideologically motivated. Selectivity, and the priorities of those doing the selecting, led to more structured hierarchies of genres and practitioners in which

---

[96] Harriet Guest, *Small Change: Women, Learning, Patriotism, 1750–1810* (Chicago: University of Chicago Press, 2000), p. 18.

[97] [Francis Jeffrey], 'Montgomery's *Poems*', *Edinburgh Review*, 9 (January 1807), 347–54 (p. 347).

[98] I give detailed information on the quarterlies' circulations in Chapter Five.

gentlemanly male authorship was further privileged over female and lower-class writing. The writers praised in the Reviews during the first fifteen years of the nineteenth century were not necessarily bestsellers and did not necessarily sell well after they were reviewed. Indeed, the quarterlies often defined their values in opposition to a spectral mass market, as in the *Quarterly's* assertion that 'the temperament which disposes the soul to take fire at the beauties of poetry, must, in every state, be limited to a very small number'.[99] What the positive attention of the quarterlies did confer, though, was a far-reaching recognition of a writer's respectability. Such social currency was crucial for authors seeking to establish their importance through writing.

In the 1810s, a combination of factors including increasing book prices, the emergence of several strong new voices and the growing volume and complexity of periodical discourse created a literary environment uniquely conducive to the popular success of narrative poems.[100] The 1810s were the heyday of the quarterlies, with both the *Edinburgh* and the *Quarterly* reaching their peak circulations.[101] It was also the decade in which resistance to the quarterlies brought to prominence a new generation of monthly and weekly magazines, including Leigh Hunt's *Examiner* (commenced in 1808) at the radical end of the political spectrum and *Blackwood's Edinburgh Magazine* (1817) at the conservative end. Many of these periodicals paid considerable attention to poetry, especially after Byron became a phenomenon. Byron's success, made possible through a combination of establishment privilege and print proliferation, epitomised a transformation of celebrity, which became 'no longer something you had, but something you were.'[102] His sensational poetics focused attention on the poet as an exotic social novelty, and many other writers capitalised on his success through imitating his strategies. Walter Scott, though, cannily ceded the mantle of most popular versifier to his younger contemporary and succeeded in establishing the novel as a form that would eventually eclipse

---

[99] [Horace Twiss?], 'Moore's *Irish Melodies*', *Quarterly Review*, 7 (June 1812), 374–82 (p. 376).

[100] The increase in the costs of books and book production was part of a larger pattern of price inflation between 1800 and 1820 (see John Burnett, *A History of the Cost of Living* (London: Penguin, 1969), pp. 198–202), but also resulted from circumstances specific to the book trade, as I discuss in Chapter One.

[101] St Clair, *Reading Nation*, p. 573.

[102] Mole, *Byron's Romantic Celebrity*, p. xii.

poetry, first in terms of sales and eventually in terms of artistic relevance and prestige.

In the 1820s and early 1830s, the widespread adoption of technologies including the steam-driven printing press, the Fourdrinier papermaking machine and the stereotyping process drastically brought down the costs of book production and made economies of scale first viable and then desirable.[103] This led to the development of pioneering low-cost editions, often initially produced by pirate publishers, as for Byron's *Don Juan*, or offshore, as in Galignani's Paris editions of poets' complete works. These practices were eventually taken up by the British publishing mainstream, resulting in the cheap editions of Scott produced by Robert Cadell and popular uniform series such as Richard Bentley's Standard Novels (commenced in 1831). Along with the development of formats such as the gift annual and the proliferation of genuinely cheap periodicals, these editions made contemporary literature an affordable prospect for the majority for the first time, paving the way for true mass literature and for genuinely profitable and professional authorship. The interests mediating print culture greatly multiplied, reducing the ability of any one individual or institution to lead public opinion. Even so, literary writing remained uncertain and tenuous as a career, with newer authors competing with the authority of older poets whose print-cultural moment had finally arrived. The profusion of print brought to a head concerns about valuing works in an increasingly profligate culture and this, combined with their works' increased accessibility, gradually brought to the fore those poets who had most effectively fashioned unique authorial selves, Wordsworth, Coleridge, Shelley and Keats chief among them. Crucially, as David Higgins has put it, 'the idealised image of the Romantic genius was largely produced and popularised by the culture that it supposedly transcended'.[104]

*   *   *

The body of this study falls into three main sections, which develop the ideas sketched out in this introduction with reference to examples drawn

---

[103] James Raven, *The Business of Books: Booksellers and the English Book Trade* (New Haven: Yale University Press, 2007), pp. 325–6.

[104] David Higgins, 'Celebrity, Politics and the Rhetoric of Genius', in *Romanticism and Celebrity Culture, 1750–1850*, ed. Tom Mole (Cambridge: Cambridge University Press, 2009), pp. 41–59 (p. 43).

in large part from underutilised archival sources. Chapters One and Two examine writing as a financial and social activity, using publisher's archives to trace the limited potential for direct literary earnings before employing letters and circulations to explore authorship's enormous social potential. Chapters Three and Four consider authorial careers, looking at the circumstances and advantages that allowed a few writers to prosper while paying due attention to the enormous difficulties faced by most who sought to profit by the pen. Chapters Five and Six look at the ways in which powerful networks that were constituted around the quarterly Reviews and a few particularly well-connected writers reconfigured literary culture in manners that eventually brought it beyond the compass of individual mediators.

Chapter One considers authors' negotiations with the book trade, using evidence from the Longman and Murray archives to explore the contracts that authors signed, consider the processes of production and payment that governed their works and examine the ways in which publishers interacted with each other. As William St Clair, James Raven and numerous other book historians have demonstrated, publishing in the early nineteenth century was a costly, uncertain and ultimately conservative business. Using a range of examples both famous and obscure, this chapter breaks down the structure of the publishing industry from the author's perspective, demonstrating the restricted profits that could be derived by most writers from direct sales.

Chapter Two answers the obvious question raised by the first chapter's analysis: if writers could not live by their publishing profits, how did they hope to benefit from their works? It reiterates that the primary reasons why authors wrote were social, with financial, reputational and personal benefits arising from the ways in which authorship was performed within social matrices. The chapter opens by examining the importance of groups and networks, considering the ways in which such communities were created, constituted and inflected. It then moves on to examine the porous boundaries between public and private circulations, using a fraught exchange between Elizabeth Hamilton and Mary Hays as its key example. Subsequently, it looks at the distinct and personal discourses of privilege that writers constructed in their letters, focusing particularly on Leigh Hunt and the Shelleys. Finally, it concludes by investigating the positions occupied by female writers in the collaborative formation of social systems of legitimation.

Chapters Three and Four build on Chapters One and Two by examining the ways in which authors worked to construct viable careers through writing, with varying degrees of success. Chapter Three considers the social advantages that allowed three writers to secure substantial reputations and incomes. Robert Southey established himself with the aid of funds from friends and family. After garnering contacts and recognition, he moved from conceiving of his labours as being principally poetic to producing profitable political and historical works. Thomas Moore unsuccessfully sought patronage and tried several different modes of literary activity before his sociable talents and facility with lyrics and satire brought him prosperity and renown. Finally, Felicia Hemans worked closely with local and national networks, with institutions and with new modes and forms in order to build a prominent literary career, although inequalities of expectation meant that the returns she was able to realise were sharply limited when compared with those of Southey and Moore.

In literary histories, the successes of a few renowned authors often overwrite the conflicted and complex working lives of less fortunate writers. Chapter Four examines disappointed literary ambitions by employing the extensive archive of the Royal Literary Fund. It first considers the difficulties faced by the Fund's founder, David Williams, and his compatriots as they sought to assist writers of literary merit, examining the Fund's thwarted attempts to instil in society a greater appreciation of the value of authors. It then considers three exemplary case studies: the miscellaneous writer Robert Heron, the gothic novelist Eliza Parsons and the labouring-class poet Robert Bloomfield. By situating these writers within the wider contexts of the Literary Fund's applicants, the chapter assesses the neglected majority who found authorship and its attendant fashions parlous, destructive and fickle.

Chapters Five and Six turn to the larger forces that reconfigured literary culture and the roles of authorship as the period progressed. Chapter Five looks at the *Edinburgh Review* and the *Quarterly Review*, contending that their conductors were pioneers in successfully professionalising literary activity. It examines the ways in which the quarterlies propagated their authority, arguing that they dominated conceptions of literature by bringing a carefully selected range of writers and works before the public to be endorsed or censured. The quarterlies' principal concerns were political, but their literary reviews provided an excellent forum for advancing social agendas, denigrating rivals and building influence.

Chapter Six looks at three prominent authors who worked in concert with interlocking networks to reconfigure the circumstances of reading and writing. It begins by examining Hannah More, arguing that her works played a major and underacknowledged role in shaping British culture and introducing new reading audiences to the pleasures of narrative. Walter Scott, unquestionably the most popular contemporary writer of the early nineteenth century, made huge sums of money through his rapport with readers, in doing so opening up new markets and forging a convincing paradigm of literary professionalism that later writers could and did follow. Byron followed Scott into the popular imagination, but counterpointed him by using judiciously managed self-presentations to create an oppositional space for alienated genius. A brief coda picks up on this opposition between Byron and Scott to consider how the canonical Romantic poets came to prominence by resisting their contemporary circumstances through creating tenets that positioned what became Romanticism as the dominant form of being literary.

*　*　*

Authorship in the Romantic period was both ferociously contested and in transition. The seeds for the Romantic model of the poet-genius and the Victorian model of the respectable professional writer were beginning to germinate, but they did not sprout or bloom until the second quarter of the nineteenth century. The nature of authorship was the subject of many competing discourses, but it remained intensely social and personal, with eighteenth-century models persisting despite attempts to establish radical new modes. Being accepted as a writer has always been a complicated social negotiation, and never more so than in the antagonistic literary environments that prevailed between the opening shots of the French Revolution and the passing of the Reform Bill. In writing itself, authors have a powerful tool for bringing others to acknowledge their merits, but authors' assertions are often disputed, reconfigured and ignored. A career in writing, like the process, is often messier than later summations acknowledge. In looking again at chances and circumstances, this study seeks to highlight both the contingency of success and the politics of omission. If literary authors are now beings that we value, it is important to remain aware of the preconceptions that govern who got—and who gets—to be one.

Chapter One: Publishers, Book Production and Profits

At the beginning of the nineteenth century, there was a considerable disjunction between the sense among the educated young that authorship was a career that could be pursued in similar ways to medicine or the law and the fact that for the vast majority of authors, literary profits proved to be at best a helpful secondary income. The mass reading public conjured fearfully by poets and political commentators was a chimerical one for nearly all living writers. Until the late 1820s, the prices of contemporary literary volumes were, for the most part, prohibitively high; as Richard Altick has it, '[d]uring the first quarter of the nineteenth century [...] new books were more expensive than ever before.'[1] Consequently, novels and volumes of poetry were usually sold to relatively small and elite audiences. The direct profits of such sales were insufficient to sustain more than a handful of the most popular authors.

One of the major tasks this book will undertake is to draw out the social and economic consequences of the divergence between idealising (and paranoid) conceptions of the power of writing and the grim realities of many writers' lives. The chapters that follow will establish the crucial importance of sociability before considering the ways in which authors

---

[1] Richard D. Altick, *The English Common Reader* (Chicago: University of Chicago Press, 1957), p. 260.

© The Author(s) 2021   51

M. Sangster, *Living as an Author in the Romantic Period*, Palgrave Studies in the Enlightenment, Romanticism and Cultures of Print, https://doi.org/10.1007/978-3-030-37047-3_3

attempted to build careers and renegotiate the terms that governed literary culture. To contextualise these interpretations, this opening chapter explores the implications of book trade norms for those seeking to profit by the pen, using archival evidence to show the sharp limitations placed on most authors by the technologies, infrastructures and social practices that governed publication and circulation.

THE PRICE OF LITERATURE

The prevailing publishing model at the beginning of the nineteenth century was long-established and largely conservative. As James Raven writes,

> the basic organisation of the mid-eighteenth-century book trade, with its technological basis in the hand-operated printing press, was still in place by the 1810s. For those publishing, the technical printing process had changed little, the same limited editions were produced, and the same constraints of large initial overheads, warehousing, and printing costs acted upon the small and large operator alike.[2]

Although the number of printers and booksellers continued to rise between the 1790s and the 1810s, most publishers were unable or unwilling to employ new technologies to reduce costs and make literary writing more accessible. In fact, production costs rose considerably during the long war with France, as the hostilities prevented the importing of consignments of rags essential to the paper-making process, leading to a peak in manufacturing costs during the early 1810s.[3] It was only during the 1820s and 1830s that mass production technologies developed in previous decades began to bring costs and prices down significantly. In the 1820s, publishers began to make extensive use of Friedrich Koenig's steam-driven printing presses, which by 1818 had developed to the point where they could produce five times as many impressions per hour as the best Stanhope hand-driven presses could manage.[4] The use of stereotyping, a process for creating plates from which new editions could be printed swiftly and cheaply without the need to assemble type, became far more common. Producing

---

[2] James Raven, *The Business of Books: Booksellers and the English Book Trade* (New Haven: Yale University Press, 2007), p. 227.

[3] Paper costs increased by over fifty percent between 1797 and 1810; see Lee Erickson, *The Economy of Literary Form: English Literature and the Industrialisation of Publishing, 1800–1850* (Baltimore: Johns Hopkins Press, 1996), p. 20.

[4] Hans Bolza, 'Friedrich Koenig und die Erfindung der Druckmaschine', *Technikgeschichte*, 34 (1967), 79–89.

stereotype plates allowed publishers to respond more flexibly and economically to demand, although high initial costs meant that such plates were viable principally for works expected to sell in large numbers over a considerable period.[5] The widespread adoption of the Fourdrinier papermaking machine brought down the cost of paper, which had previously been the highest single cost in most book production processes.[6] Alongside these technological innovations, developments in literary formats such as the packaging of works in gift annuals like *The Keepsake* (1828–1857), the printing of mass-market editions of novels and experiments with cheap periodicals paved the way for literature to reach new and extensive reading publics. As David McKitterick cautiously puts it, 'by about 1830 some of the major changes in manufacture, materials, market demands and economic possibilities had become sufficiently widespread for it to be possible to claim that a revolution of some kind had been effected.'[7] This was not as obvious a revolution as many of the other great shifts in communications media, but nevertheless it was one with profound and far-reaching consequences. These changes caused a boom first in periodicals and then in the novel, propelling both forms into the lives of substantial publics and creating a range of lucrative opportunities for writers.[8] The cumulative effect of these technological, formal and social shifts was to make living by the pen a challenging but plausible career choice in the 1830s, at least for those with the skills necessary to cater for magazine audiences and the ability to write fast and flexibly. A growing cadre of writers began successfully to exploit the possibilities of mass print, inventing and discovering new means by which authorship could be made into a respectable career. Their innovations, combined with continuing technological, institutional and educational expansion, created the fecund print culture of Victoria's reign, a culture starkly different from the earlier nineteenth century in its extent and its commanding cultural and intellectual paradigms.

However, these developments existed only as encouraging or worrying future prospects for most of the authors discussed in this study. Writers publishing at the turn of the nineteenth century faced many of the same

---

[5] William St Clair, *The Reading Nation in the Romantic Period* (Cambridge: Cambridge University Press, 2004), pp. 100–1.

[6] Raven, p. 310.

[7] David McKitterick, 'Introduction' to *The Cambridge History of the Book in Britain Volume VI: 1830–1914*, ed. David McKitterick (Cambridge: Cambridge University Press, 2009), pp. 1–74 (p. 3).

[8] See Erickson, *Economy of Literary Form*, pp. 71–104, 142–70.

difficulties as their brethren writing fifty or a hundred years earlier. Numerous scholarly accounts have made it clear precisely how limited the opportunities for literary profits were in the eighteenth century. While Brean Hammond has established that the theatre offered 'a precarious living for a small number of people and a potentially good living for a few', he writes that '[w]ith respect to the publication of other literary genres [...] it was far more difficult for authors to reap direct rewards from their labours.'[9] Cheryl Turner accurately describes the experience of writing for money for most eighteenth-century women as 'a continual struggle against the prospect of poverty'.[10] Publishers, like academic publishers in the early twenty-first century, generally aimed to sell small editions of high-priced copies, targeting well-heeled buyers along with clubs, libraries and institutions. Reprinting books with established reputations was a far safer prospect than speculating on new writing. With untested authors, publishers looked to minimise their potential losses and to make small profits on editions that sold through while securing occasional windfalls from runaway successes. High capital overheads meant that it was critical for publishers accurately to estimate edition sizes to avoid large losses. The relatively small scale of the book market meant that the vast majority of publishers were required to be generalists, with the kinds of works that modern readers would describe as literary comprising potentially prestigious but risky parts of broader lists that also included religious, educational and instructional works, all of which vastly outsold novels and poems.[11] While some new literary works sold well, a great many books failed to sell through small standard editions of 500 or 1000 copies. This meant that literature was not a commodity for which publishers could afford to pay too much on spec. The effects of this high-cost, low-sales model were particularly pronounced for multi-volume novels, where book clubs, circulating libraries and periodical serialisations were major modes of consumption for all but the wealthy. For a new novel to run to a second

---

[9] Brean S. Hammond, *Professional Imaginative Writing in England, 1670–1740: 'Hackney for Bread'* (Oxford: Clarendon Press, 1997), pp. 61, 69.

[10] Cheryl Turner, *Living by the Pen: Women Writers in the Eighteenth Century* (London: Routledge, 1992), p. 116.

[11] For an overview, see Michael F. Suarez, 'Towards a Bibliometric Analysis of the Surviving Record', in *The Cambridge History of the Book in Britain Volume 5: 1695–1830*, ed. Michael F. Suarez and Michael L. Turner (Cambridge: Cambridge University Press, 2009), pp. 39–65, especially pp. 45–50. See also my analysis of collaborative publication in the last section of this chapter.

edition in book form was a relatively rare occurrence. However, even for single-volume poems or verse collections—octavo editions of which generally sold for between a quarter and a third of the price of a three-volume novel—significant sales figures were exceptions rather than the rule.

Calculating equivalent values across two centuries is a nigh-on impossible task given the shifts in relative worth and the drastic changes in technologies and lifestyles in the intervening period, but it will be helpful to give some indications of the relative expense of books in the early nineteenth century. Details of middle-class incomes can provide a useful yardstick, with the proviso that the middle class at the turn of the nineteenth century was still relatively small, with the vast majority earning considerably less. Richard Holmes draws on a talk by William St Clair on Treasury tax figures to suggest that 'a skilled worker such as a printer earned approximately £90 a year, while a gentleman with a small house and a servant in London could live comfortably on £200 a year.'[12] Edward Copeland, examining the yearly incomes discussed in female-authored novels, writes that '[w]ith £200 the tone of contemporary witnesses shifts from martyrdom and heroic self-denial to one of grudging admission among some authors that such a competence might just achieve gentility', although he notes that £400 or £500 a year was portrayed as being the level needed to comfortably maintain a house and servants.[13] St Clair himself, drawing on Naval List figures issued after the end of the war with France, suggests a standard of £5 a week as 'a reasonable but not extravagant income for members of the upper- or upper-middle classes.'[14] In 1797 Coleridge calculated his expenses to be around £100 a year (probably an optimistically low figure) and in January 1798 Josiah and Thomas Wedgwood provided him with an annuity of £150, which was supposed to be sufficient to allow him to live independently.[15] Labouring wages were much lower; additionally, as Margot Finn notes, servants and labourers often 'received much of their wage payments in kind—in the form of lodging, board, clothing and credit with their master's tradesmen', thus severely constraining their ability to purchase expensive consumer goods like books.[16]

---

[12] Richard Holmes, *Coleridge: Early Visions* (London: Penguin, 1990), p. 176.

[13] Edward Copeland, *Women Writing about Money: Women's Fiction in England, 1790–1820* (Cambridge: Cambridge University Press, 1995), p. 28; wider context pp. 22–33.

[14] St Clair, p. 194.

[15] Holmes, pp. 176–8.

[16] Margot C. Finn, *The Character of Credit: Personal Debt in English Culture, 1740–1914* (Cambridge: Cambridge University Press, 2003), p. 76.

The expense of literature can be extrapolated from these figures through comparing them with the price of Walter Scott's *Waverley*, which cost 21 shillings for three volumes in paper wrappers.[17] This represents a little over 1/200th of the gentlemanly income Holmes and Copeland cite above, or a little over 1/250th of St Clair's suggested standard for the reasonably wealthy. In the UK in April 2017, median gross annual pay for those with full-time jobs was £28,758.[18] If we take £20 as a reasonable price for a modern hardback novel, this would represent a little under 1/1400th of that yearly income, making the novel by Scott somewhere between five-and-a-half and seven times as expensive expressed as a proportion of income. This very rough comparison suggests that the equivalent of the cost of a Scott novel in 2017 terms might be somewhere in the region of £110 to £140. This figure is consonant with other modes of estimation. In her biography of William Jerdan, Susan Matoff quotes correspondence from the Office of National Statistics that suggests that 'as a rule of thumb, prices today are about eighty times those of the nineteenth century.'[19] The relative expense of books can also be indicated by comparison with renting property. In 1817, the Irish poet and songwriter Thomas Moore rented Sloperton Cottage, near Bromham in Wiltshire, furnished, for £40 a year, giving up an expensive house in Hornsey, which had cost him £90 a year. A previous residence at Mayfield Cottage near Ashbourne in Derbyshire had set him back merely £20 per annum.[20] You would be hard-pressed to find a house in Britain today with an annual rent less than ninety times the cost of a new hardback novel (£1800), let alone less than twenty times the cost (£400). New books in the early nineteenth century thus retained their long-standing status as expensive luxury items. Booksellers in the

---

[17] St Clair, p. 636. Scott's success allowed the prices of respectable novels, including his own, to creep up further; he set a standard of 31s.6d with *Kenilworth* in 1821 (cf. Altick, p. 263).

[18] Office of National Statistics, 'Annual Survey of Hours and Earnings: 2017 provisional and 2016 revised results', 26 October 2017, https://www.ons.gov.uk/employmentandlabourmarket/peopleinwork/earningsandworkinghours/bulletins/annualsurveyofhoursandearnings/2017provisionaland2016revisedresults.

[19] Susan Matoff, *Conflicted Life: William Jerdan, 1782–1869: London Editor, Author and Critic* (Brighton: Sussex Academic Press, 2011), p. xii.

[20] Prices cited in Linda Kelly, *Ireland's Minstrel: A Life of Tom Moore: Poet, Patriot and Byron's Friend* (London & New York; I.B. Tauris, 2006), pp. 138–9, 106.

period can helpfully be understood as purveyors of high-priced speciali-ties. While publishers could make reasonable profits from selling numer-ous different books, the writers of those books could not generally live on the sums that they were paid for their works.

Not everyone knew this. Some authors begun writing due to delusions about the potential profits that they could reap, while others wrote because they lacked acceptable alternative means of making money. However, many authors set pen to paper with less directly financial objectives in mind, seeking to promote themselves and their ideas through their writ-ing, to garner influence or to establish networks of affiliation. Publication could serve as a helpful—although sometimes not wholly desirable—route to achieving these ends.

PUBLISHING ARRANGEMENTS: WILLIAM HERBERT'S *HELGA*

In 1815, the Reverend William Herbert, Rector of Spofforth in the West Riding of Yorkshire, approached John Murray seeking to publish his narrative poem *Helga*. This was Herbert's first book-length literary production, but he had distinguished himself previously by pursuing a number of other careers. The third son of Henry Herbert, first Earl of Carnarvon, he was educated at Eton and Oxford and prior to his ordination in 1814 he had worked as a bar-rister and served twice as an MP.[21] During the 1800s he had become a noted translator of Latin and (more unusually) Icelandic works, and in this role he merits a brief mention in Byron's *English Bards and Scotch Reviewers*:

> HERBERT shall wield THOR'S hammer, and sometimes
> In gratitude thou'lt praise his rugged rhymes.[22]

The 'thou' in this couplet is Francis Jeffrey, the editor of the *Edinburgh Review*; at this point in the poem, Jeffrey is being addressed by 'Caledonia's Goddess', who is laying out his future as a critical potentate. As Byron notes, Herbert's connections with the gentlemanly circle that conducted the *Edinburgh* meant that he had the potential to accrue favours that

---

[21] B.D. Jackson, 'Herbert, William (1778–1847)', rev. Richard Smail, *ODNB*, https://doi.org/10.1093/ref:odnb/13063.

[22] Byron, *English Bards and Scotch Reviewers*, lines 510–11, in *Byron: The Complete Poetical Works*, ed. Jerome J. McGann, 7 vols (Oxford: Oxford University Press, 1980–93), I, 245.

would allow him to wield considerable influence. He was thus a man who Murray was obliged to take seriously.

While Herbert's Scandinavian subject matter was novel, the contents of the volume he presented are in many respects quite conventional. *Helga* tells the story of a conflict for the hand of its eponymous heroine between the Danish warrior Angantyr and her father's loyal retainer Hialmar, who she loves and assists. In the poem's second canto, Helga travels to 'Hell' to discover how Hialmar should defeat Angantyr and elicits the following prophecy from its denizens:

> "Deep-bosom'd in the northern fells
> "A pigmy race immortal dwells,
> "Whose skilful hands can forge the steel
> "With many a wonderous muttered spell.
> "If bold Hialmar's might can gain
> "A falchion from their lone domain,
> "Nor stone, nor iron shall withstand
> "The dint of such a gifted brand;
> "Its edge shall drink Angantyr's blood,
> "And life's tide issue with the flood.
> "Victorious, at night's silent hour,
> "The chief shall reach fair Helga's bower."[23]

As is often the case in Scandinavian legends, the fulfilment of this prophecy is even more doom-laden than a cursory reading would indicate. Helga is haunted by her hellish descent and remains in seclusion while Hialmar uses the intelligence she has gathered to acquire the enchanted sword. Unfortunately, while the sword allows Hialmar to slay Angantyr as promised, he is fatally wounded in the duel and reaches Helga's bower only as corpse. Helga perishes in turn when she sees his body. In addition to the main poem, Herbert's volume also contains copious antiquarian notes and two shorter poems, 'The Song of the Vala' and 'Brynhilda', both 'freely imitated' from their source material.[24]

In his introduction, Herbert states that he hopes *Helga* will make his Scandinavian interests more accessible by presenting them in a form that will be 'pleasing to the reader'. He claims that his poem contains 'a faithful

---

[23]William Herbert, *Helga: a Poem in Seven Cantos* (London: John Murray, 1815), pp. 47–48 (Canto II, lines 714–25).

[24]Herbert, p. 273.

picture of the manners and superstitions of the period which it represents', but also asserts that he has 'attempted to give it the coloring of poetry, and to temper with chaster ornaments the rude wildness of Scaldic fiction.'[25] As the quotation above demonstrates, the central poem is written in tetrameter couplets, at times clumsily but generally with a reasonable level of fluency. The text is spiced with some artful archaisms but is clearly following models that Scott had established for versifying and promoting Scottish history and employing modes that Byron had popularised in his Eastern tales. While the arrogated styles of these two poets clash at times with the aesthetics of Herbert's Scandinavian material, his borrowings make it clear that he had a keen eye trained on the tastes of the reading public and was seeking to marry his established talents with proven popular forms and an unexceptionable moral position. It would be easy to assume that in following the two most commercially successful poets of his age, Herbert was seeking to profit financially, but economically, he was already comfortably set up. Although a significant payment from Murray would have been an advantage, the greatest potential reward he could garner from his poem was a burnished reputation, and the greatest potential risk was reputational damage.

Murray evidently thought Herbert's work worth publishing, the transaction of enough moment for him to record in his selective letter book and Herbert important enough to offer a range of financial options. It is this offer of various arrangements, illuminating the most common publishing practices in the period, that makes Herbert's book particularly interesting in the context of this study. On 28 January 1815 Murray submitted the following 'proposals' to Herbert for publishing *Helga*:

1. I will publish it at your own cost & sell it entirely upon your own account
2. I will publish it at my own cost & Risque & give you one Half of the profits
3. I will give you Two Hundred Guineas for the Copyright.[26]

The first arrangement Murray suggests, that of publishing at Herbert's expense, does not at first glance appear profitable for Murray except in

---

[25] Herbert, pp. iv, v–vi.

[26] John Murray to William Herbert, 28 January 1815, from John Murray Letter Book, 2 Apr 1808–13 Mar 1843, NLS Ms.41909, fol. 25ʳ (outgoing side).

terms of his associating himself with Herbert, particularly as Murray would have had to bear the considerable costs of printing and paper, only reclaiming the money later in the process. However, publishers usually charged a commission for such services—generally 10% on sales—so they would still profit as long that the writer concerned paid their debts if the book sold poorly.[27] This was not always the case. Percy Shelley's second novel, *St. Irvyne; or, The Rosicrucian: A Romance*, was published under this arrangement by John Joseph Stockdale in 1811. Shelley had blithely asserted that such a novel was 'a thing which almost *mechanically* sells to circulating libraries.'[28] Shelley was disappointed in his expectations, and evidently so was Stockdale, as he complained in 1827 that he had never received the £300 Shelley owed him for the novel's production.[29] Publishing on commission was a method commonly employed by wealthy writers who wanted to control their texts and by those who could not publish in any other way and were either confident of their potential or desperate to see themselves in print. It carried a considerable risk for authors, as they were liable for the costs should their works not sell. Such costs could be very substantial, as indicated by the £300 that Stockdale claimed Shelley owed him. For writers against whom debts could be more easily enforced, such a bill might conceivably lead to bankruptcy or incarceration.

In some circumstances, publishing on one's own account could be very effective. The wealthy banker-poet Samuel Rogers chose to fund the publication of almost all of his literary works and achieved several notable successes. *The Pleasures of Memory* (1792), an elegant and polished moral poem on eighteenth-century lines, went through four editions in its first year and was reprinted frequently, selling 22,350 copies between 1801 and 1816.[30] Rogers' later long poem, *Italy*, published in two parts in 1822 and 1828, was initially considered a failure, selling poorly and attracting little positive criticism. However, Rogers was able to leverage his social and financial assets to make the poem a triumph. He destroyed the unsold copies, extensively revised the text and reprinted the poem in a lavish edition with plates from illustrations by artists including Thomas Stothard, Samuel Prout and J.M.W. Turner. This new edition and a similarly

---

[27] St Clair, p. 165.

[28] Shelley to Stockdale, 14 November 1810, in *The Letters of Percy Bysshe Shelley*, ed. Frederick L. Jones, 2 vols (Oxford: Clarendon Press, 1964), I, 20.

[29] *Letters of Percy Bysshe Shelley*, I, 130n.

[30] St Clair, p. 632.

luxurious edition of Roger's *Poems* published in 1834 were both critically and commercially successful, more than making back the colossal sum of £7000 that Rogers spent on their production.[31] As that enormous figure indicates, though, Rogers could only pursue such a course due to his vast personal wealth. The luxuries sewed into the fabrics of his books served in themselves as notices that he was a gentleman of consequence. Rogers' cause was also aided by his unparalleled network of personal connections, with a plethora of literary and artistic acquaintances who attended his famous breakfasts willingly assisting in enhancing his works and their reputations. In doing so, they were often paying back financial and social aid that Rogers had previously granted. Rogers never needed to write for money and could spend as much as necessary to meet his ends, a rare and enviable position that led to many considering him one of the leading poets of his age. Byron placed him above all but Scott in the 'triangular "Gradus ad Parnassum"' penned into his 1813 journal.[32]

For authors who were less well connected or more controversial, publishing at one's own expense could be dangerously ineffectual. In addition to *St Irvyne*, a number of Shelley's mature works were published under such arrangements, including *Alastor* (1816) and *The Revolt of Islam* (1818). In analysing the detailed costs for the latter, St Clair concludes that Shelley was almost certainly overcharged, quoting a printer's employee who stated that 'the Paper and Printing are equally bad but it was done as cheaply as possible.'[33] The considerable expense was only an inconvenience to a man as wealthy as Shelley, but because the poem lacked the advocacy of an attractive presentation and an interested commercial agent, it was left to Shelley's friends to attempt to drum up sales and positive reviews. For authors, publishing a book on account was a financial risk that was compounded by the work's being disadvantaged in the marketplace and the Reviews through its lacking a publisher's unequivocal backing. While the arrangement offered authors the highest potential earnings, few writers were in a position fully to exploit that potential.

The second arrangement that Murray proposed to Herbert—that he would bear the costs of publication and split any net profits evenly—was a

---

[31] Richard Garnett, 'Rogers, Samuel (1763–1855)', rev. Paul Baines, *ODNB*, https://doi.org/10.1093/ref:odnb/23997.

[32] *Byron's Letters and Journals*, ed. Leslie Marchand, 13 vols (Cambridge, MA: Harvard University Press, 1973–1994), III, 220. See also Peter T. Murphy, 'Climbing Parnassus, & Falling Off', in *At the Limits of Romanticism*, ed. Mary A. Favret and Nicola J. Watson (Bloomington: University of Indiana Press, 1994), pp. 40–58.

[33] St Clair, p. 508.

common one, widely used both for new authors whose market prospects were not established and by sensible established authors who wished to secure ongoing incomes from their works. The large capital investment required to manufacture and print the book was provided by the publisher and the author did not stand to lose money if the work sold poorly. As with publishing at one's own expense, writers were reliant on their publishers for fair costings. These were not always provided—St Clair notes wryly that 'the accounts which Murray prepared for Austen, in calculating her share of the profits of *Emma*, are as fictional as the novel.'[34] In addition, if a publication failed to make back its declared costs, the writer would end up with little in return for their hard work. This was not an uncommon occurrence. In 1821, Longman & Co. wrote to William Godwin stating that 'As we have little or no demand for the "Lives of the Phillips's" it is our intention to include the remainder in a sale which we shall make to the trade in a few days. When all are sold we shall unfortunately be minus of the expenses.'[35] Godwin's *Lives of Edward and John Phillips, Nephews and Pupils of Milton* had been printed in 250 lavish quarto copies in May 1815, of which 146 were eventually sold at full price, 130 of those prior to June 1816.[36] Twenty-one further copies were 'delivered', or provided gratuitously to Godwin and his friends and to Reviews including the *Quarterly*, the *Eclectic* and the *Monthly*. The book was sold at the high price of 30 shillings, producing a gross profit of £219, but since the total costs for the work's production and promotion were £252.5s.9d, its account ended in deficit. Longmans offered Godwin the remaining copies at remainder prices, but nevertheless all that Godwin received for his labour were his initial presentation copies and the sixty-eight copies that he bought for £17 six years after the book's publication. This meagre return was of little assistance in combatting his continuing financial woes.

The other problem with half-profits arrangements was that even for profitable books there could be a long delay between a work's publication

---

[34] St Clair, p. 164.

[35] Longman & Co. to William Godwin, 9 April 1821, Longman Outletter Book 24 July 1820–31 December 1825, transcribed Michael Bott, URSC MS 1393 Part I.101, letter 117A.

[36] Figures from Longman Divide Ledger D1 1807–1828, URSC MS 1393 Part I.2, fol. 222 and Divide Ledger D2 1818–1866, URSC MS 1393 Part I.3, fol. 200.

and its author receiving any money. Longmans, for example, disbursed half-profits payments for most works each June. Robert Southey's popular epic *Roderick, the Last of the Goths* was first published in September 1814. The initial quarto edition sold out quickly and the octavo second edition also sold extremely well, so Southey received a substantial payment of £272.14s.2d in June 1815, nine months after the poem's first publication.[37] In itself, nine months is already a relatively significant amount of time—a span that would require the author of a half-profits work either to be financially comfortable or to have good credit—but nine months was also a comparatively short delay. Wordsworth's *Excursion*, published in a five-hundred-copy quarto run by Longmans in August 1814, sold 291 copies by June 1815 at the substantial price of 30 shillings a copy.[38] However, the expense of raw materials and the luxurious volume's high printing costs meant that even with just under 60% of the edition sold, Longman did not consider the profits significant enough to make a payment to Wordsworth. It was only in June 1816, twenty-two months after the poem's publication and after the sale of a further forty copies, that Wordsworth received his first payment: £68.15s.10d. Such delays were frustrating but ultimately acceptable for authors like Wordsworth, who had other incomes and could afford to take the long view. For authors who needed money to supply their immediate needs, the deferred and uncertain payments offered by half-profits arrangements were often extremely unappealing.

An attractive alternative arrangement for such authors was the third on Murray's list: the sale of the author's copyright to the publisher. A publisher who purchased the copyright of a work purchased with it the ability to print that work any number of times and retain all the profits from doing so. In return, the author received guaranteed money up front, either immediately or in the form of post-dated bills, as was the case for Byron's *Corsair*. Murray wrote to that poem's designated beneficiary, Robert Charles Dallas, in January 1814 that he had 'the pleasure of inclosing 3 bills at 2, 4 & 6 mo[ths]. payable at my Bankers, amounting to five Hundred Guineas for the Copy-right'.[39] For authors who needed immediate payments, who wanted little to do with the publishing industry or who sought large speculative advances, selling copyrights was a tempting option. However, if a work was

---

[37] Longman Divide Ledger D1, fol. 60.
[38] Longman Divide Ledger D1, fol. 102.
[39] John Murray to R.C. Dallas, 6 January 1814, from Murray Letter Book, NLS Ms.41909, fol. 21ᵛ (outgoing side).

successful, the author would have no legal recourse to claim further remuneration. On some occasions, publishers would make additional payments for further editions, either out of generosity or to please a successful writer whose services they hoped to retain. The arrangements for Southey's *Life of Nelson* included explicit provision for such a payment, Southey writing to Murray in 1813 that, '[t]his evening I have received your draft for one hundred guineas,—for the copy-right of the Life of Nelson. I thank you for it, & I thank you also for your promise of a similar sum, in case a second edition of the work should be printed.'[40] Southey was fortunate in that he was a privileged part of Murray's publishing business due to his prominence in the *Quarterly Review*, and thus Murray, who had suggested that he work up the biography from a review article, was disposed to be generous.[41] The payment to Dallas, who Murray did not much like, did not represent good value for *The Corsair*, but knowing that Byron had no desire to engage in financial wrangling, Murray offered the same as he had paid for the first two cantos of *Childe Harold's Pilgrimage*. Murray went on to make enormous sums on both poems; his ledgers record net profits of £2513.0s.10d for six editions of *Childe Harold* and an even more impressive £3660.8s.9d for 29,500 copies of *The Corsair*.[42] Under half-profits arrangements, the two works combined would have returned over £3000 to Dallas, rather than a thousand guineas.

However, the enormous successes of Byron's works were atypical. For many authors, selling their copyrights was a relatively good option. Copyright payments from a reputable publisher could often be somewhat higher than the expected half-profits return on a first edition. Murray's large payment for *Childe Harold* would have left him facing a considerable loss if the quarto edition had failed. Publishers did on occasion take advantage of poor writers by offering them very low sums in the knowledge that they had little choice but to accept, but even so, this was guaranteed money that could be used to feed children and keep debtors from the door rather than a hazy prospect of future profits. The problem with selling copyrights was a longer-term one. While authors who published successful works under half-profits arrangements could receive continuing payments to underpin their finances, writers

[40] Robert Southey to John Murray, 7 April 1813, in Letters from Southey 1813–1818, NLS Ms.42551.

[41] I discuss Southey's relationship with Murray further in Chapter Three.

[42] Copies Ledger A of the publisher John Murray, 1803–1819, NLS Ms.42724, pp. 97, 57.

who sold their copyrights had to keep writing, and write faster when the money ran out. Conversely, buying copyrights could be very good for publishers if they proved to be valuable. The ability to exploit enduringly valuable copyrights underpinned the finances of most of the major publishing houses, with shares in such copyrights acting as a trade currency and a means of spreading risk, as I shall discuss shortly.

With any of these methods of publication—although most commonly for half-profits arrangements—a subscription list could be compiled. For uncertain prospects, publishers might require that the author and their supporters secure a certain number of subscribers. While subscription editions played a relatively small part in the book trade as a whole, they could serve as an important tool for launching new authors (and, more rarely, for garnering substantial profits for established writers, as was the case with the expensive fifth edition of Charlotte Smith's *Elegiac Sonnets*).[43] Subscription lists were also used as promotional tools for fashionable or charitable publications, with a prominent peer or dignitary heading a list that others would join in the spirit of 'emulative snobbery'.[44] The ways that subscription mitigated risk made it an attractive prospect for publishers, with lists allowing them to map the relatively small social networks of consumers for their products and calibrate their print runs accordingly. Subscription-like practices were also employed within the book trade, with publishers setting up private lists through which other booksellers would agree to buy a certain number of copies of a book on its publication in return for a discount.[45]

For his *Helga*, Herbert eventually chose a slightly different arrangement, also relatively common in the period. In March 1815, Murray wrote to him that 'I will give you 150 Gns. for permission to print 2000 Copies of your poem Helga with Notes, in 8vo to form a Volume similar to Childe Harold.'[46] Herbert thus accepted a slightly smaller payment in order to retain his copyright in case the poem was successful. However, unfortunately for Herbert, the comparison between *Helga* and *Childe Harold*

---

[43] See Michael Gamer, 'Subscription Reprinting: The Third and Fifth Elegiac Sonnets', in *Romanticism, Self-Canonization, and the Business of Poetry* (Cambridge: Cambridge University Press, 2017), pp. 54–90.

[44] Raven, p. 275.

[45] For examples, see John Murray's Subscription Lists (NLS Ms.42808-50) and my discussion of *Calamities of Authors* below.

[46] John Murray to William Herbert, 13 March 1815, from Letter Book, NLS Ms.41909, fol. 25ʳ (outgoing side).

proved to be a misleading piece of flattery on Murray's part. The publisher cautiously printed 1000 copies, rather than the 2000 he had made an offer for. The cost was £345.7s.6d, for expenses including printing, paper, the payment to Herbert and advertising.[47] Murray's caution proved to be justified, as the critical response to the volume was tepid. The *Edinburgh Review* was ambivalent, complaining that '[i]nstead of relying on his own powers, which were not likely to fail him, he has sworn, that no creature shall be admitted within his runic circle, unless he can give it a family likeness to some prototype in Walter Scott and Lord Byron. Under this management, the gigantic forms of Scandinavia have been made to combine in a pretty, modern, melting, love-story.'[48] Such analysis from a publication that Herbert wrote for did not serve to encourage the poem's sales. Murray made a total of £197.4s from the copies that he printed. He initially sold copies for eight shillings, but by December 1817 he was disposing of copies for a shilling each and in January 1818 he sold off the final forty-two copies for a total of £2.2s, or 6d a copy. The account for *Helga* closes with Murray £148.3s.6d out-of-pocket. *Helga* was by no means an abject failure—Herbert went on to publish a series of poetic tales with Murray, forming part of a portfolio of accomplishments that led to his being dubbed 'one of the most learned and accomplished persons of his age' in his *Gentleman's Magazine* obituary.[49] However, the financial circumstances of publishing meant that his accepting a lump sum for *Helga* proved to be prudent. A half-profits arrangement would have made him nothing and publishing the edition at his own risk would have left him indebted to his publisher.

THE COSTS OF PRODUCTION: ISAAC D'ISRAELI'S
CALAMITIES OF AUTHORS

As the losses Murray incurred from *Helga* imply, the high costs of printing and paper meant that publishers had to take care in selecting what to publish and in calculating print runs. A clear example of such a calculation can be drawn from Murray's estimate book, in which he costed one of the touchstones of my introduction, Isaac D'Israeli's miscellany of miseries *Calamities of Authors*. Murray printed an edition of a thousand copies and

---

[47] Copies Ledger B of the publisher John Murray, NLS Ms.42725, p. 114.

[48] [Francis Palgrave], 'Herbert's *Helga*', *Edinburgh Review*, 25 (June 1815), 146–68 (p. 166).

[49] 'Obituary—Hon. and Very Rev. W. Herbert', *Gentleman's Magazine*, New Series, 28 (October 1847), 425–6 (p. 426).

made two estimates of the costs. The second of these estimates provides evidence of a somewhat vexed printing process:

Printing 43 sheets at 51 shillings = £110.18s.6d
Extra for Index, contents & very long notes = £3.13s.6d
Overrunning, correcting & adding to first 5 sheets = £2.12s.6d
Corrections in other parts of work = £5.15s.6d[50]

The total cost for printing that Murray gives, with a further fifteen-shilling tweak included, is £123.15s. The paper for the book was an even greater expense. Murray estimated that *Calamities* would require eighty-eight reams of paper at thirty-seven shillings a ream, a total cost of £162.16s. Murray added to these costs £23.9s for advertising; this included provision for printed advertisements but also sundry related costs such as providing copies to periodical reviewers and key influencers. These costs could vary widely, but the figure that Murray decided on in his estimate was chosen to make the overall total a neat £310, a sum somewhat higher than Murray's earlier estimate due to the costs of the corrections and additional paper. To counteract the increased expenses, Murray tweaked the sale price of the two volumes up from 9s.6d in the first estimate to 10s.6d in the second; this sufficed to make the total expected profits £2 higher in the second estimate. The estimated profit for the book in Murray's revised working is £215, based on the sale of the full thousand copies. No copyright payment to D'Israeli is listed, so the most likely form of recompense would have been a half-profits arrangement; these were commonly employed for D'Israeli's productions.[51] If the edition sold through completely, as Murray's estimate assumes, it would have yielded to each party a little over £100.

For *Calamities* Murray's estimate thus shows him making a profit of about 35% on his initial investment after splitting the profits with D'Israeli and provided that the edition sold through at full price. However, it is interesting to note the potentially significant costs that Murray's estimate does not include. He does not list costs for his time, for the time of his employees, for maintaining his premises or for communicating with his printers, agents and other booksellers. He also gives no indication of the

[50] Details from Estimate Book of the publisher John Murray, NLS Ms.42720, pp. 84–85.

[51] For examples, see the entry for *Quarrels of Authors* (1814) in Murray Copies Ledger A, NLS Ms.42724, p. 65, and the entry for *Curiosities of Literature* (6th edition; 1817) in Murray Copies Ledger B, NLS Ms.42725, p. 50.

cost of warehousing, which, in Raven's words, 'together with stock insurance could swallow up to a quarter of the gross returns on a publication.'[52]
This last oversight was a significant one; Raven goes on describe how
Murray suffered enormous losses in the 1820s due to overprinting, which
eventually forced him to remainder large parts of his inventory.

For a fairly typical book like *Calamities*, then, a publisher in the 1810s
had to put down a great deal of money up front, stood to make no profit
until 60% or so of the edition was sold and could lose in the worst case sce-
nario far more money than he stood to gain in the best case (at least without
laying out further money for more editions). In the event, *Calamities* was
fairly successful. Murray's subscription book lists 377 advance sales to fifty-
six other booksellers, each ordering between two and fifty copies.[53] His
1812 Stock Book indicates that he disposed of copies briskly after publication through sales in his shop and further sales to other booksellers (William
Blackwood, his Edinburgh partner, took fifty copies in May and a further
twenty-four in August).[54] D'Israeli bought thirty-three copies on top of his
fourteen gratis copies (presumably to give as presents), and a number of
copies were sent to major periodicals for their consideration (the *Monthly
Magazine* is specified, and seven other copies are listed as having gone to the
Reviews). Copies also went to influential writers, pressmen and trade figures, including the publisher John Nichols; the poet Thomas Campbell; the
writers George Dyer and Alexander Chalmers; and the editor James Perry.[55]
Such promotions paid off—in his 1813 Stock Book Murray notes that only
seventy-one copies remained on hand.[56] However, unlike D'Israeli's most
successful productions, *Curiosities of Literature* and *The Literary Character*,
Calamities did not merit further editions. Evidently, Murray thought it a
modest rather than a runaway success and he and D'Israeli did not think
that they would profit significantly by a second edition.

While *Calamities* itself was a cheerfully profitable production, the
details of Murray's estimate help to demonstrate how the book trade's
high capital costs and unreliable returns made publishers, in Raven's

---

[52] Raven, p. 304.

[53] Subscriptions Lists of the publisher John Murray (Sales Book), 1812–1817, NLS
Ms.42809, fols. 12ʳ–13ᵛ.

[54] John Murray Stock Book 02 (1812), NLS Ms.42778. Murray's Stock Books are not
foliated, but their indexes mean that figures are easy to locate.

[55] John Murray Copies Day Book 02 (September 1811–February 1817), NLS
Ms.42887, p. 16.

[56] John Murray Stock Book 04 (1813), NLS Ms.42780.

words, 'peculiarly vulnerable to failure.'[57] Lee Erickson states arrestingly that 'typically 70 percent of all publications lost money'; while he frustratingly cites no specific evidence to back up this claim, it does not seem implausible.[58] The payments publishers made to authors must therefore be considered in the context of the considerable risks they were taking. While copyright payments for very successful works might seem in retrospect to be ridiculously low, they often represented reasonable remuneration based on usual levels of sales. While half-profits publications could return relatively little to the author, and that with a considerable delay, the prospect of 50% of the net profits compares quite favourably with modern royalty arrangements, where for many books 10% of gross sales might be a reasonable figure. Although publishers were certainly not above profiting by writerly credulousness, the status of books as luxury goods was a far more significant factor in authorship's limited financial returns. Poor remuneration cannot principally be attributed to publishers' sharp practices; instead, we must look to the limited audiences that authors were addressing, as well as to the natures of those addresses.

The Life of a Successful Book: James Montgomery's *The World before the Flood*

To give a better sense of the circumscribed potential for literary profits in the early nineteenth century, I will now examine the sales history of one of the period's most successful poems: James Montgomery's *The World before the Flood* (1813). While this religious epic is likely to be unfamiliar to most modern readers, in the 1810s and 1820s, Montgomery's works vastly outsold those of now-canonical poets such as Wordsworth, Coleridge and Keats. Born in 1771 to Moravian parents in Ayrshire, Montgomery was a prolific writer from an early age, working as a baker's apprentice and in a general store while failing to get his early verses published.[59] In 1792 he was appointed clerk and bookkeeper in the office of the *Sheffield Register*, to which he became a regular contributor. When the *Register* closed after Joseph Gales, its editor, fled to America to escape prosecution, Montgomery became the editor of a successful successor paper, the *Sheffield Iris*.

---

[57] Raven, p. 294.

[58] Erickson, p. 89.

[59] G. Tolley, 'Montgomery, James (1771–1854)', *ODNB*, https://doi.org/10.1093/ref:odnb/19070.

Montgomery pursued a less radical line than Gales, but nevertheless he was prosecuted for sedition in 1795 and again for malicious libel in 1796 (for reporting that the militia had fired on a riotous crowd). For these offences, he served terms in prison in York of three and six months respectively. However, the publication of the *Iris* continued, Montgomery remaining its editor until he sold the paper in 1825. He also set up as a publisher and printer, which made him a comfortable income. He became a man of substance in Sheffield, serving on boards, joining numerous societies and acting as a mainspring of support for missionary initiatives in the city. However, his wider reputation rested on the hymns he published, many of which are still standard in modern hymnals, and on his poetry, which has persisted rather less well.

Montgomery's first long poem, *The Ocean* (1805), attracted little attention, but his follow-up, *The Wanderer of Switzerland, and Other Poems* (1806) ran through three editions in six months. The *Edinburgh Review* was profoundly and showily unimpressed with Montgomery, calling him 'very weakly, very finical, and very affected.'[60] However, other writers disagreed. The collection was praised by Byron as being 'worth more than a thousand Lyrical Ballads.'[61] Southey was also an advocate, authoring reviews in the *Quarterly* that opposed the *Edinburgh's* harsh judgements.[62] While reviewer reactions to his volume discouraged Montgomery, the book continued to sell well, and his subsequent poem on the slave trade was well received. This response gave him the confidence to undertake a biblical epic expressly inspired by *Paradise Lost*.

The World before the Flood is an accomplished but peculiar work, telling the story of a last pocket of 'patriarchs' led by Enoch, who face the all-conquering armies of the 'Giant-monarch.' Opening with the return of the self-exiled musician Javan to the patriarchs' camp, the poem combines its Miltonic models with extravagant pastoral. It also mixes in an initially intriguing love story, although this romantic narrative is overwhelmed in the middle cantos by a series of retellings of earlier biblical events. The poem finally concludes with a spectacular confrontation between the captive

[60] [Francis Jeffrey], 'Montgomery's *Poems*', *Edinburgh Review*, 9 (January 1807), 347–54 (p. 347). This review is considered in more detail in Chapter Five.

[61] *Byron: The Complete Poetical Works*, I, 407.

[62] [Robert Southey], 'Montgomery's *Poems*', *Quarterly Review*, 6 (December 1811), 405–19 and 'Montgomery's *World before the Flood*', *Quarterly Review*, 11 (April 1814), 78–87.

patriarchs and their oppressors, culminating in an impressive divine intervention that scatters the conquering army and allows the faithful to escape.

In his preface, Montgomery defends building a complex fiction on scanty scriptural material, contending that 'Fiction though it be, it is the fiction that represents Truth; and that *is* Truth,—Truth in the essence, though not in the name; Truth in the spirit, though not in the letter.'[63] This might seem to mark out the territory for a dryly pious poem, but in fact Montgomery's verse is lushly descriptive, blending biblical allusions with skilful landscape writing. Montgomery also employs contemporary narrative vogues such as the brooding, outcast hero:

> As years enlarged his form, in moody hours,
> His mind betray'd its weakness with its powers;
> Alike his fairest hopes and strangest fears
> Were nursed in silence, or divulged with tears;
> The fulness of his heart repress'd his tongue,
> Though none might rival Javan when he sung.[64]

Like Herbert, Montgomery had obviously been paying attention to the tormented protagonists of Eastern tales and gothic fictions, but in his poem, he inverts the common model, redeeming Javan and subsuming him into the pastoral world of the patriarchs. This redemptive religious message is expressed using revelatory rather than didactic rhetoric, relying mainly on affect for its impact. Montgomery's treatment of biblical figures is often more akin to novels of sentiment than to parables. For example, in the following passage, Enoch describes Eve's reaction to the death of Adam:

> "Eve's faithful arm still clasp'd her lifeless Spouse;
> Gently I shook it from her trance to rouse;
> She gave no answer; motionless and cold,
> It fell like clay from my relaxing hold;
> Alarm'd, I lifted up the locks of grey
> That hid her cheek; her soul had pass'd away:
> A beauteous corse she graced her partner's side,
> Love bound their lives, and Death could not divide.

---

[63] James Montgomery, *The World before the Flood, with Other Occasional Pieces* (London: Longman, Hurst, Rees, Orme, and Brown, 1813), pp. x–xi.

[64] *World before the Flood*, Canto I, p. 13.

"Trembling astonishment of grief we felt,
Till Nature's sympathies began to melt;
We wept in stillness through the long dark night:
—And O how welcome was the morning light!"[65]

While the diction here is Miltonic, its elevation is counterpointed both by restricting the depicted reactions to human ones and through the deliberate simplicity of the key couplets. God, with the exception of his intervention at the end of the poem, is kept in the background. Instead, the characters are comforted by an almost Wordsworthian Nature, albeit one whose language wanders a considerable distance from that of 'a man speaking to men.'[66] While less formally innovative and more overtly religious than the canonical Romantics, Montgomery shared with them the key influence of Milton and the ability successfully to hybridise Miltonic verse with contemporary forms and preoccupations.

In combining a religious subject with sentiment and romantic heroism, Montgomery evidently judged the tastes of contemporary readers accurately. Longmans initially printed a cautious octavo edition of 1000 copies, priced at eight shillings. The fact that this first edition was an octavo, rather than a lavish quarto like those that housed the first editions of poems like Southey's *Roderick* and Wordsworth's *Excursion*, might serve to indicate that Longmans saw Montgomery as a poet unlikely to appeal to the highest levels of society, perhaps bespeaking the enduring effects of the *Edinburgh's* chastisement. Nevertheless, *The World before the Flood* swiftly found enthusiastic consumers. The first edition was released in April 1813 and all but 159 copies had been sold or distributed by the time Longmans took stock that June. The book was reprinted in a larger edition of 1500 in September 1813, and this edition, priced at six shillings, also sold very fast, necessitating a further reprint the following June. The poem remained in print at the same price until 1837, its sales dropping off relatively slowly. Montgomery—already a recognised writer and one who was reasonably comfortable financially—had sensibly published the work under a half-profits arrangement. The profits he reaped were quite considerable, as the following table demonstrates:[67]

---

[65] *World before the Flood*, Canto IV, pp. 77–78.

[66] William Wordsworth [and Samuel Taylor Coleridge], *Lyrical Ballads, with Pastoral and Other Poems*, 3rd edn, 2 vols (London: Longman & Rees 1802), I, xxviii.

[67] Figures compiled from Longman Divide Ledger D1 1807–1828, URSC MS 1393 Part I.2, fol. 222, Divide Ledger D2 1818–1866, URSC MS 1393, Part I.3, fols. 113, 309, and Divide Ledger D3 1828–1867, URSC MS 1393, Part I.4, fol. 227.

Date	Copies sold[68]	Monies to Montgomery	Editions
June 1813	813	£109.1s.5d	1st—April 1813 (1000 8vo)
June 1814	1657	£143.8s.8d	2nd—September 1813 (1500 8vo)
June 1815	1181	£91.8s.1d	3rd—June 1814 (1500 8vo)
June 1816	687	£44.2s.0d	4th—November 1815 (1500 8vo)
June 1817	483	£54.16s.1d	
June 1818	392	£55.3s.0d	
June 1819	418	£31.0s.9d	5th—January 1819 (1500 8vo)
June 1820	415	£22.5s.6d	
June 1821	354	£52.13s.11d	
June 1822	305	£44.3s.11d	
June 1823	341	£15.6s.4d	6th—November 1822 (1000 8vo)
June 1824	320	£14.1s.4d	
June 1825	350	£51.16s.9d	
June 1826[69]	181	£26.11s.7d	7th—January 1826 (1000 8vo)
June 1827	409	£18.10s.10d	
June 1828	362	£53.10s.6d	
June 1829	217	£32.5s.11d	8th—February 1829 (1000 8vo)
June 1830	225	£0.0s.0d	
June 1831	198	£23.0s.0d	
June 1832	99	£14.15s.2d	
June 1833	130	£19.5s.3d	
June 1834	106	£15.8s.2d	
June 1835	100	£14.16s.7d	
June 1836	92	£13.12s.6d	
June 1837	37	£5.11s.0d	

The Longman ledgers show that a successful poem like *The World before the Flood* could have a very substantial shelf life. While nearly a quarter of the poem's total sales were in the first fourteen months, it took another

[68] These figures exclude copies marked as 'delivered'. These included complementary copies of each edition given to Montgomery for personal use and to present to friends, as well as copies delivered to the Reviews and to influential figures—Southey is named as a recipient of a first-edition copy. Deliveries were highest for the first edition (twenty-eight copies); they dropped to twelve copies for most of the later editions. In total, 128 copies were delivered over the course of the eight editions.

[69] The figures for this year only account for the sales of the remaining copies of the 6th edition; in fact, copies of the 7th were probably sold prior to this payment, but these are accounted for by Longmans in 1827.

four years for the second quarter of the total to be sold and after that point sales declined relatively slowly. By contrast with the fairly smooth curve for the sales, the yearly profits paid to Montgomery could be quite volatile. He got nothing from each edition until it broke even, but after that point he received a string of relatively large payments as the remaining copies produced profits. This meant that the payments in the 1820s and 1830s often bore only a distant relation to the yearly sales. For example, the 409 copies sold in 1827 returned to Montgomery only £18.10s.10d, while the 362 copies sold in 1828 returned £53.10s.6d, almost three times as much. Such fluctuations did not manifest when editions of *The World before the Flood* sold out within a year, but once sales slowed, there were a number of years during which the profits were meagre and one year (1830) when a new edition failing to break even in its first year meant that Montgomery received nothing at all.

Over the poem's twenty-four-year lifespan in single-volume octavo, Montgomery made a total of £971.15s.3d. He also reaped additional profits in later years after *The World before the Flood* was incorporated into his *Poetical Works*. While these profits are very significant, the lengthy period over which they were returned must be considered. The highest yearly payment to Montgomery fell considerably short of the sum of £250 suggested by St Clair as a comfortable gentlemanly income, and the average amount returned was £42, less than a fifth of St Clair's figure. The volatility of the payments must also be taken into account. An author who depended solely on the income from successful half-profits books would have to be assiduous or fortunate to avoid years in which reprintings or slow sales resulted in a drastically reduced income. A final major consideration is the level of popularity required to produce such returns. In a table prepared by Benjamin Colbert of the top-selling poems published by Longmans in the early nineteenth century, only four poets—Scott, Robert Bloomfield, Moore and Southey—produced works that outsold *The World before the Flood*.[70] Expanding across the trade would add a few more names to this list (including Byron, Samuel Rogers and Thomas Campbell) but it seems safe to name Montgomery as one of the best-selling contemporary poets of his time. That an author as successful as Montgomery, publishing using the most prudent arrangement commonly available, could sustain from a highly profitable poem a return of

---

[70] Benjamin Colbert, 'Popular Romanticism?: Publishing, Readership and the Making of Literary History' in *Authorship, Commerce and the Public*, ed. E.J. Clery, Caroline Franklin and Peter Garside (Basingstoke: Palgrave Macmillan, 2002), pp. 153–68 (p. 155). Bloomfield's appearance on this list is a little misleading, as during the period of his greatest success, from which the figures in the table are compiled, he was not published by Longmans, but by Vernor and Hood.

less than £1000 over a twenty-four-year period indicates the considerable challenges that authors seeking to live by the pen faced in attempting to conjure stable incomes. Montgomery's poetry added to his prosperity both materially and through raising his profile, but direct profits from sales of his books were by no means sufficient to serve as his principal means of support.

CO-OPERATION AND COLLABORATION IN THE BOOK TRADE

Having covered elements of publishing processes from contracts through printing to sales, it remains only to comment briefly on the close co-operation between publishers and the consequences of this co-operation for authors. Much can be shown using one revealing communication: a letter from John Murray to William Blackwood written on New Year's Day 1817. Blackwood had set up as a bookseller in 1804 and had been Murray's agent in Edinburgh since 1811, but at the time the letter was written, he was increasingly focusing on publishing and distributing works under his own imprint.[71] In 1816 he had achieved a coup by securing the rights to co-publish Walter Scott's *Tales of my Landlord* with Murray and in April 1817 he would launch the *Edinburgh Monthly Magazine*, which after rebranding and reorganisation later that year became the influential and controversial *Blackwood's Edinburgh Magazine*. The business relationship between Blackwood and Murray was thus undergoing significant changes, and this put their personal relationship under considerable strain.

Murray opens by stating that Blackwood's previous communication had 'overflowed [his] Cup of bearance' and he vacillates throughout the letter between attempting to heal the rift he identifies and reasserting his sense that he has been wronged.[72] While doing this, he offers Blackwood advice about how to run his business. The most substantive sections are those in which Murray discusses how his firm and Blackwood's should co-operate in order to maximise their profits:

> I will venture to tell you what you must not do—you must not as in a recent instance calculate upon gaining £10 more or less by keeping the whole of one little Volume to yourself—but estimate to what an extent of publication you may proceed by dividing your risque & the very increased profits which

---

[71] Peter Garside, 'Publishing 1800–1830', in *The Edinburgh History of the Book in Scotland Volume 3: Ambition and Industry 1800–1880*, ed. Bill Bell (Edinburgh: Edinburgh University Press, 2007), pp. 79–90 (pp. 83–4).

[72] John Murray to William Blackwood, 1 January 1817 [misdated 1816], from Murray Letter Book, NLS Ms.41909, fols. 28ʳ–29ᵛ (outgoing side) (fol. 28ʳ).

may arise thereby by commanding the whole range of the English Market. Constable is so fully aware of the importance of creating a powerful interest in a Bookseller here that he has not in any instance engaged in a Book which he has not offered a share to a London publisher [...] It is not the profit of this little Volume if it sell that should be thought of but what must be gained in a large scale by the additional Capital divided risque & moral certainty of extensive success.[73]

Murray thus contends that Blackwood's tendency to try and maintain exclusive control risks isolating him in terms of his accessing capital from the trade and of the markets that his works can reach. While Murray is more than a little hypocritical in this letter, since he jealously protected some of his biggest-selling books, including Byron's works, his advice on co-operation is reasonable. Even Longmans, the largest publisher in the period in terms of titles produced, employed agent firms to distribute their books and regularly co-operated and co-published with other houses.[74] Smaller houses were even more reliant on contacts and agents, which were of particular importance for accessing distant markets—as mentioned, Blackwood had previously been the agent for Murray titles in Edinburgh and both Longmans and Murray had partnered with Archibald Constable in the 1800s to distribute the *Edinburgh Review* in London. Dividing and assigning publications kept trade relations amicable, with the major publishers all benefiting from being part of a carefully-controlled environment. In his letter, Murray commends to Blackwood Constable's policy of co-publishing the Waverley novels with a London firm, writing that 'I may mention to you that he never does interfere with the sale in <u>England</u> or partners would be cutting each others <u>Throats</u> at once and we would easily sell our share in Scotland.'[75] Forbearance like Constable's kept business equitable and individual fiefdoms intact, removing the need for competitive price-cutting or similar measures. Constable's policy also allowed him to share the burden of Scott's considerable copyright payments and the costs of printing the massive editions that the Waverley novels ran to.

By operating as a cartel, publishers could keep prices stable, pool their capital and spread their risk. Murray writes to Blackwood that

> these are things which may be deemed evils at first sight, but they will be found to produce commensurate advantages in the liberal & extensive deal-

---

[73] Murray to Blackwood, fols. 28ᵛ–29ʳ.

[74] Longmans' market share and participation in consortia are both detailed in Asa Briggs, *A History of Longmans and their Books 1724–1990: Longevity in Publishing* (London and Delaware: British Library and Oak Knoll Press, 2008), pp. 143–5.

[75] Murray to Blackwood, fol. 29ʳ.

ing for which you ought now to be preparing yourself and at any rate I beg leave to both refer & to defer—to the plan of those who have the most extensive as well as respectable dealings in our trade.[76]

As Murray's statement indicates, these practices were deep-rooted. While a new bookseller might feel that financially co-operating with the establishment was disadvantageous, to go against them was a risky strategy. Those operating outside such arrangements found themselves cut out of trade sales of books and copyright shares and had to compete with the pooled influence of the major houses. The larger publishers formed a heavily interconnected community that made efforts where possible to look after its own and that could co-operate in cutting out undesirable competitors.

Occasionally, such entanglements could become problematic. During the crash of 1826, the collapse of Hurst, Robinson & Co. also brought down Constable, for whom Hurst, Robinson & Co. served as a London agent; the printer James Ballantyne, whose finances were intimately intertwined with Constable's; and Walter Scott, an investor in both the Scottish firms. Other London firms were also severely affected. John Sutherland, while arguing that 'the British book trade as a whole seems to have weathered the 1826 storm quite serenely', quotes figures that indicate that Longmans' entanglements with Hurst, Robinson & Co. forced them to write off £40,000 of debt.[77] Such levels of entwinement bespeak the strength of the culture of co-operation (or connivance) in early-nineteenth-century publishing. However, in normal operating conditions, such co-operation had numerous advantages. The publishing industry's interlaced finances can be traced in firms' copyright ledgers, which record complex transactions involving fractions of the copyrights owned or exercised by the trade. These copyrights run the gamut of genres and make clear the relative diminutiveness of literary production runs compared to the real big sellers: religious and educational works. Such works could be split into very small shares. Longmans' copyright ledgers record that in 1802 the firm owned shares of 1/24th and 1/16th in Graglia's '*Italien Dictionary*'.[78] Longmans later acquired further shares in Graglia's book: a 1/32nd share from John Harris for £15 in 1819 and a 1/64th share from George Whittaker for £13 in 1826. As these prices show, the dictionary remained a valuable property for decades after its initial publication in 1795. The

---

[76] Murray to Blackwood, fol. 29ʳ.

[77] John Sutherland, 'The British Book Trade and the Crash of 1826', *The Library*, 6th Series, 9 (June 1987), 148–61 (pp. 159, 161).

[78] Longman Copyright Ledger no. 3 1794–1827, URSC MS 1393 Part I.279 and Longman Copyright Ledger no. 4 1797–1842, URSC MS 1393 Part I.280. The ledgers are unfoliated, but are arranged alphabetically, so these figures are easy to locate.

Longman copyright ledgers record editions of 3000 in February 1802, 5000 in November 1807, 4000 in January 1815, 5000 in December 1818, 5000 in April 1822, 6000 in February 1826, 6000 in September 1829, 4000 in January 1834, 4000 in February 1837 and 4000 in October 1840. If a complete list, this would indicate that the book actually became increasingly popular twenty years after its publication, probably in order to meet the institutional needs of the expanding education system. The 46,000 copies printed over forty years realised a substantial, albeit long-term, profit for the publishers who owned shares. Even more impressive sales figures were racked up by the most commonly used educational works, such as Lindley Murray's *English Grammar*. This book was first published in 1795 and Longmans' ledgers record it being reprinted at least yearly between 1809 and 1829 in editions of 10,000 copies or more. It continued to be reprinted regularly until the 1870s.[79] The *English Grammar* was only one of Murray's astonishingly successful educational books, which also included his *English Exercises* (1797), his *English Reader* (1799) and a number of new editions and sequels to all three books, as well as popular religious works. Together these books sold millions of copies, both in Britain and in the United States, although the latter's buccaneering copyright practices prevented British publishers from competing effectively in that market. The valuable copyrights for Murray's oeuvre provided the publishers who bought shares in them with a secure underlying source of income from which the high initial costs of publishing new works could be met.

After 1774, older works had become fair game for any publisher to reprint. The House of Lords ruling in the case of *Donaldson v. Beckett* had denied that publishers could hold copyright perpetually, upholding the provisions of the 1710 Statute of Anne, which limited copyright to short terms (before 1842, fourteen years, with one renewal possible if the author still lived).[80] Nevertheless, the publishing establishment often regulated the production of theoretically out-of-copyright works through adhering to the old divisions. Longmans' ledgers show that shares in Samuel Johnson's *Lives of the Poets* existed in denominations as small as 1/200th and record

[79] See the Longman Copyright Ledgers and Ingrid Tieken-Boon van Ostade, 'Murray, Lindley (1745–1826)', *ODNB*, https://doi.org/10.1093/ref:odnb/19640.

[80] See Mark Rose, *Authors and Owners: The Invention of Copyright* (Cambridge, MA: Harvard University Press, 1993).

that the work was printed regularly and co-operatively after the official copyright in it had expired—an 1820 edition lists no fewer than eighteen publishers in its colophon.[81] Longmans also held fractions of most of Johnson's other works, as well as Milton's *Paradise Lost*, James Thomson's *The Seasons*, Adam Smith's *Wealth of Nations*, Laurence Sterne's *Tristram Shandy* and a huge host of other books. The entries for these works in Longmans' copyright ledgers extend well into the nineteenth century, indicating that the benefits of co-operation were significant enough to make holding to old arrangements and paying for fractions of notional copyrights a sensible practice for much of the Georgian era.

While publishers had regular spats, communications between the houses ensured that grievances were not left to fester. For example, Longman & Co. addressed the following letter to Murray in April 1831:

> Dear Sir
> We were not a little surprised yesterday to learn that some of your recently published works were on sale by Mr Tegg at a ~~price~~ considerably depreciated price: for instance Moore's Byron 2 Vols (of which we purchased 8 sets at your late sale & have 5 of them now remaining) for £2.2.0; Irving's Columbus & Granada of both of which we have considerable stocks; one at 9/= & the other at 16/=; which latter cost us 15/= & 26/= P Copy.
> Had we the least idea that these books (& perhaps others) would have been thus early thrown into the market, we certainly should not have purchased to the extent ~~of having the chance of having the books we now have left by subject to a loss:~~ & we did which had by ~~your~~ this depreciation subjected us to a considerable loss. Under these circumstances we suppose that you will not allow us to be loosers upon books so lately purchased <u>at your sale terms</u> of you.[82]

While Longman's irritation at being undercut by the remainder specialist Thomas Tegg with Murray's connivance is understandable, it is telling that the firm bothered to address this letter to Murray to try and resolve the situation. Presumably they would not have done so without expecting a response. A draft of a similar sort of letter in the Murray Archive records Murray's fury

---

[81] Samuel Johnson, *The Lives of the English Poets*, 2 vols (London: Printed for F. C and J. Rivington; J. Nunn; Cadell and Davies; Longman, Hurst, Rees, Orme, and Brown; G. & W.B. Whittaker; J. Richardson; J. Walker; Newman and Co.; Lackington and Co.; Black, Kingsbury, Parbury, and Allen; J. Black and Son; Sherwood, Neely and Jones; Baldwin, Cradock, and Joy; J. Robinson; E. Edwards; Simpkin and Marshall; R. Scholey; and G. Cowie, 1820).

[82] Longman & Co. to John Murray, 22 April 1831, from Longman Outletter Book January 1826–May 1837, transcribed Michael Bott, URSC MS 1393 Part I.102, letter 167D.

at what he believed to be a deliberate accounting error by a clerk at Longmans designed to swindle him out of his small profit for distributing copies of the *Edinburgh Review*. A subsequent note describes how Thomas Norton Longman called personally to resolve the issue; after 'warm discussions' the matter was smoothed over.[83] Both these communications highlight the importance of personal connections within the trade. The publishers, wishing to be seen as respectable and anxious to maintain their cartel, operated with a sense of fair play that tamed cutthroat commercial competition.[84] Their close connections also allowed for easy collaboration. In 1805, for example, Murray wrote to Longman & Co. on their co-publication of the scandalous *Secret History of the Court and Cabinet of St. Cloud*:

> I propose with your concurrence to omit the improprieties complained of in the Life of Talleyrand, & if you'll do me the favour to send the corrected Copy—I will read it with all the Care and Expedition which circumstances require or will Permit & will return it to Gillett. I enclose a curious Passage which when know will materially increase the Public attention to our Book, and as you have some influence in the Morning Post perhaps you will take the trouble to cause its immediate inclusion & it may be paid for or not as they determine.[85]

Murray's willingness to cut the work demonstrates how the labour of producing a book could be spread among the firms according to the priorities of those with an interest, leading to a consensus on how best to present the material to the public (although in this case it is possible that Longmans might have been prepared to risk a more scandalous text than the sober Murray was prepared to countenance). The letter also exhibits the ways in which publishers would pool and leverage their contacts to promote books. This will be discussed further in later chapters, but suffice for now to say that the larger publishers each maintained a portfolio of interests in influential newspapers and periodicals, so amicable relations between them could assist with placing effective advertisements and securing good reviews (or 'puffs').

It is easy to infer from these examples that individual authors approaching the fairly collegiate body of publishers were often at a considerable

---

[83] John Murray to Thomas Norton Longman, 21 August 1807, from John Murray Letter Book, March 1803–11 September 1823, NLS Ms.41908, fols. 75ᵛ–77ʳ. (fol. 76ᵛ).

[84] There were, of course, some notable exceptions, including Tegg, whose phenomenally successful business in cheap remainders regularly had the more respectable publishers grinding their teeth.

[85] John Murray to Messrs Longman, Hurst, Rees & Orme, 15 November 1805, from Murray Letter Book, NLS Ms.41908, fols. 31ᵛ–32ʳ.

disadvantage. The highest advances in modern publishing are generally produced by auctions in which an author's agent persuades multiple competing editors to bid against each other. Romantic-period authors did not have literary agents and the only major auctions in publishing were within the trade.[86] Lacking the ability to make publishers compete, authors would generally get similar sorts of offers wherever they chose to take their books. One of David Williams' ambitions for the Literary Fund was to address this imbalance so that authors might exert pressure as a class.[87] Had this come to pass, authors might have collectively influenced the practices of the hidebound publishing establishment. As it was, though, it was not until the late nineteenth century that the Society of Authors and the first literary agencies were established. Romantic-period writers, unlike publishers, did not generally see each other as professional associates, and thus they usually faced the cartelised publishing industry as lone individuals, or at best with the support of personal friends.

The one advantage that some authors did possess when negotiating with publishers was recognised status, which they could use to pull rank on their literary paymasters. However, this was not an unproblematic strategy, as Thomas Moore found when he attempted it with John Murray during the debate regarding the fate of Byron's memoirs. In the heated discussions, Moore, believing that Murray had insulted him, responded, 'Hard words, Mr Murray, but if you chuse to take the privileges of a gentleman, I am ready to accord them to you.'[88] The privilege Moore offered was the right to duel, and his offer deliberately invoked his gentlemanly status to belittle Murray, who had either to accept the challenge and risk being shot or concede Moore's superior status, with the accompanying assumptions about probity and critical judgement.[89] However, as well as privileges, gentleman had hazily defined but constraining responsibilities.

---

[86] Walter Scott, who had the Ballantyne brothers as proto-agents and who successfully played opposing publishing houses off against each other for profit, was a major exception, as I discuss in Chapter Six. As Dustin Griffin notes, Alexander Pope successfully triggered a bidding war for his Homer, but this was a one-off occurrence ('The Rise of the Professional Author', in *The Cambridge History of the Book in Britain Volume 5*, pp. 132–45 (p. 141)).

[87] Discussed in detail in Chapter Four.

[88] *The Journal of Thomas Moore*, ed. Wilfred S. Dowden, 6 vols (Newark: University of Delaware Press, 1983–1991), VI, 2442 (entry for 17 May 1824).

[89] Duels and their implications form the unifying thread in Richard Cronin's *Paper Pellets: British Literary Culture after Waterloo* (Oxford: Oxford University Press, 2010); I discuss Cronin's book elsewhere in this chapter and study.

In his account of the confrontation, John Cam Hobhouse depicts Murray accomplishing an elegant inversion of Moore's line of attack:

> I do not care whose the MSS are—here am I as a tradesman—I do not care a farthing about having your money, or whether I ever get it or not—but such regard have I for Lord Byron's honour and fame that I am willing and determined to destroy these MSS which have been read by Mr Gifford, who says they would render Lord Byron's name eternally infamous. It is very hard that I as a tradesman should be willing to make a sacrifice that you as a gentleman will *not* consent to!![90]

Through this statement Murray rhetorically makes himself more gentlemanly than a gentleman, calling on Gifford's authority to reassert the propriety of destroying the memoirs and implicitly pegging Moore as an acquisitive false friend. The loose definitions of gentlemanly conduct left rhetors considerable room both for exhorting gentleman not to violate an invoked code of behaviour and for denying their enemies gentlemanly status by asserting their poor conduct. Commercial matters were not supposed to be high on a gentleman's list of priorities, and since the ownership of the memoirs was in large part a question of money, Murray adroitly disarmed Moore by asserting that he, a tradesman, was able to rise above pecuniary concerns.

The limited profits that could be garnered from most works and the potential for significant losses inherent in catering to a relatively small and capricious elite thus encouraged the publishing industry to operate with a kind of collaborative and protective conservatism during the late eighteenth and early nineteenth centuries. This stance was rarely challenged. While publishers commonly enjoyed friendly and productive relations with individual writers, authors as a body were not well placed to dictate the terms by which their works were produced due to their lacking the kinds of mutually applicable incentives that bound together those who printed, marketed and sold their productions. This situation also meant that information on potential publishing profits was not widely available. Consequently, scores of promising writers took up their pens without realising the true scale of the challenges they faced in attempting to realise direct financial returns. However, there were numerous other benefits that authors could accrue from circulating evidence of their opinions and talents. If this chapter has made publishing look like a raw deal for Romantic-period writers, this is because the market comprised only a fraction of the picture.

[90] John Cam Hobhouse, *Hobhouse's Diary*, ed. Peter Cochran (from British Library Additional Manuscript 56548), http://petercochran.files.wordpress.com/2009/12/33-1824.pdf, p. 52.

Chapter Two: Sociable Alignments

While the relatively small audiences for literary works in the late eighteenth and early nineteenth centuries meant that the direct profits authors could expect from sales were limited, writers wrote knowing they addressed reachable individuals from whom they could seek affirmation, affiliation and status. Rather than operating within conventions defined by an institutionalised realm of art or a capital-driven market, authors were aware that their writings addressed interlinked social networks that largely determined the meanings of and rewards for cultural work. By evoking themselves and shaping others through their written and personal interactions, adroit authors could influence the agendas that defined socio-political hierarchies and established the criteria for cultural success. An author's most straightforward path to advancement was to associate themselves with one or more powerful pre-existing groupings, but discontented authors who had the time and privileges necessary to build up influence could construct new systems of social validation in concert with contemporaries. Many of these systems had limited or local appeals, but a few were able eventually to achieve wider currency, through doing so redefining the nature of literary practice.

What differentiated the Romantic-period literary scene from the earlier decades of the eighteenth century was not so much its character or absolute scale, but rather its divisions and intensity. The cohesive egalitarianism that Anne Goldgar and others have identified in eighteenth-century notions of the Republic of Letters was always an ideal that concealed more

© The Author(s) 2021
M. Sangster, *Living as an Author in the Romantic Period*, Palgrave
Studies in the Enlightenment, Romanticism and Cultures of Print,
https://doi.org/10.1007/978-3-030-37047-3_4

vexed realities.[1] However, by the late 1790s the idea of the unified and unifying value of literary writing had been comprehensively undermined by the conflicting ideologies of fissile and heterogeneous groupings that reflected the divisions and uncertainties of an age of political, military and moral strife. Romantic-period authors found it very difficult to locate themselves as disinterested observers, as this was itself a cultural position associated with radicalism and revolution. Taking such a stance would often see an author brought forcibly into the paranoid politics of the periodical press, whether they wished to be or not. Knowing how difficult it was to stay above the fray, canny writers worked to align themselves favourably in relation to a complex and shifting array of competing ideological groupings. Those who did not align themselves were aligned and positioned by others, and even those who did take stances of their own were subject to having their positions critiqued and forcibly recontextualised. The ways in which authors constructed, validated and undermined each other to a great extent determined what could be gained by writing. While sociable interactions could conjure shared democratic visions, they could also serve to mark divisions and assert the pains of irreconcilable differences. The cultural space within which literary authority could profitably be propagated was relatively limited. As a result, it was keenly and often acrimoniously contested.

FRIENDS, GROUPS AND NETWORKS

This book is hardly alone in insisting on the importance of examining social relations. In recent years, numerous scholars have re-examined Romantic-period authors in the contexts of coteries and communities.[2] A key progenitor of this trend was Gillian Russell and Clara Tuite's 2002 collection *Romantic Sociability*, the introduction to which opens by

---

[1] Anne Goldgar, *Impolite Learning: Conduct and Community in the Republic of Letters, 1680–1750* (New Haven: Yale University Press 1995), p. 3.

[2] Important contributions include Stephen C. Behrendt's *British Women Poets and the Romantic Writing Community* (Baltimore: Johns Hopkins University Press, 2009), Susan J. Wolfson's *Romantic Interactions: Social Being and the Turns of Literary Action* (Baltimore: Johns Hopkins University Press, 2010), Jon Mee's *Conversable Worlds: Literature, Contention and Community 1762 to 1830* (Oxford: Oxford University Press, 2011) and Tim Fulford's *Romantic Poetry and Literary Coteries: The Dialect of the Tribe* (Basingstoke: Palgrave Macmillan, 2015). Particular attention has been paid to Leigh Hunt and his circle in works including Jeffrey N. Cox's *Poetry and Politics in the Cockney School* (Cambridge: Cambridge University Press, 1998) and Nicholas Roe's *Fiery Heart: The First Life of Leigh Hunt* (London: Pimlico, 2005); Daisy Hay's *Young Romantics* (London: Bloomsbury, 2010) covers Hunt's circle for a more general readership.

discussing the 'Immortal Dinner' held the artist Benjamin Robert Haydon to celebrate progress on his epic painting *Christ's Entry into Jerusalem*. This intensely self-conscious meal was attended by William Wordsworth, John Keats, Charles Lamb and Wordsworth's cousin Thomas Monkhouse; the party was later joined by the doctor and explorer John Ritchie and—awkwardly for Wordsworth—by John Kingston, deputy comptroller of the Stamp Office and Wordsworth's immediate superior in government service. The discussions and interactions on this deeply performative occasion were at the centre of webs touching on many of the major ideological and social issues of the age.[3] The Immortal Dinner was not simply a pleasurable meeting of cultured friends. It was also a self-consciously resistant production that brought together a young aspirant, a frustrated would-be reformer of art, an eminence who was in his own eyes unjustly neglected and a talented yet conflicted clerk-author to make what Haydon tellingly dubbed 'a night worthy of the Elizabethan age'.[4]

Russell and Tuite rightly assert that literary studies should pay greater attention to the implications of events like the Immortal Dinner in order to counterpoint the discipline's 'considerable ideological investment in canonical genres and forms such as the lyric, as well as in a narrow text-based definition of the public sphere'. They contend that critics 'need to recover the significance of sociability, not simply for biographical studies of Romantic writers or in order to contextualise their work, but as a kind of text in its own right, a form of cultural work […] which was a fundamental part of the self-definition of Romantic writers and artists.'[5] As is probably evident, I wholeheartedly agree with Russell and Tuite's position. I would, however, wish to modify their argument insofar as it identifies sociability as specifically a Romantic project. Meaningful sociability was by no means the sole preserve of the writers and artists we now class as Romantic, nor was it a characteristically Romantic form. In many respects, sociability played a more restricted ideological role in nascent Romantic modes of artistry than it did in the older forms with which they competed and the dominant contemporary paradigms with which they uneasily co-existed. One of the reasons why examining Romantic-period sociability seems novel in the twenty-first century is because Romantic

---

[3] For a deft exploration, see Penelope Hughes-Hallett's *The Immortal Dinner* (London: Viking, 2000).

[4] *Life of Benjamin Robert Haydon, Historical Painter, from his Autobiography and Journals*, ed. Tom Taylor, 2nd edn, 3 vols (London: Longman, Brown, Green and Longmans, 1853) I, 356–7.

[5] Gillian Russell and Clara Tuite, 'Introducing Romantic Sociability', in *Romantic Sociability: Social Networks and Literary Culture in Britain, 1770–1840*, ed. Gillian Russell and Clara Tuite (Cambridge: Cambridge University Press, 2002), pp. 1–23 (p. 4).

lenses were constructed in part to downplay the ways in which now-canonical poets lost out to more adroit contemporaries when they sought to reap immediate social rewards through writing.

The careful management of reputations and affiliations was necessary for almost all artists and authors in the late eighteenth and early nineteenth centuries. One of the first things that budding writers did was seek out the company of other writers, both in person and through writings and paratexts. Astute authors were aware that writing alone could only accomplish so much and that friends could serve as crucial sources of inspiration, promotion and validation. This is true of now-forgotten scribes and the most canonical figures. In Edinburgh, the aspiring author Robert Heron sought out Thomas Blacklock and Hugh Blair as potential mentors.[6] John Keats was taken under the wing of Leigh Hunt; Letitia Landon launched her career by working closely with William Jerdan; and the conservative writers for *Blackwood's Edinburgh Magazine* sought—and often obtained—the approbation of Walter Scott. The seeds of connections whose implications still resonate were sown when Coleridge and Southey planned Pantisocracy and produced poetry together in the early years of the 1790s; this led via further associations to the queasily collaborative *Lyrical Ballads* and to the lifelong written relationships that tied the Lakers together (whether they liked it or not).

Accounts of literary affiliation often focus on the collaborative creation of oppositional ideologies by small, tight-knit communities. In the 1810s, Leigh Hunt's circle linked writers in formations close and distinctive enough to draw sustained and highly critical attacks on their purported philosophies, which were seen as threats by both the Tory establishment and periodical oligarchs. This hostility was by no means unprovoked; as Jeffrey Cox puts it

> the Hunt circle pursued a coterie mode of literary production that resisted at the concrete point of the literary work the subordination of culture to [the] private and privatizing enterprise that they also attacked in the context of that work; faced with an increased sense of the author's isolation in relation to a distant public of purchasers, they sought to forge a collective literary practice and to communicate that communal sensibility through even their printed works.[7]

Part of the threat such groups represented was their potential for shifting the terms governing literary culture. Cox depicts Hunt's Cockney

---

[6] I discuss Robert Heron at length in Chapter Four.

[7] Jeffrey N. Cox, *Poetry and Politics in the Cockney School* (Cambridge: Cambridge University Press, 1998), p. 62.

School as working to oppose the juridical aggression of the quarterlies by constructing a web of public and private texts that validated each other, seeking to create 'a reconfigured social space built upon a new – Cockney – cultural literacy'.[8] Hunt and his associates established their own worth through positioning themselves as opponents of a system that they implicitly and explicitly denigrated through creating alternative critical criteria. Such groups sought became their own judges—as Lucy Newlyn contends, 'Not only did the existence of coteries allow writers to circulate their work before it appeared in print (thus delaying and pre-empting its public reception), it also helped them discover common aims, intentions, and prejudices; a shared and inevitably exclusive language; and strongly cohesive loyalties.'[9] By making themselves into a canon through cross-referencing, anthologising, reviewing and publishing, the Hunt circle and similar groupings sought to constitute new value systems that bypassed and threatened the hierarchy-crafting authorities behind the establishment periodicals.

However, the intrinsic interest of famous oppositional groupings like the Lakers and the Hunt circle should not occlude the fact that the practice of self-conscious association was employed highly effectively by establishment writers. Authors who supported the government made adroit use of publications like the *Anti-Jacobin* and the *Quarterly* to enact complex processes of networking and recruitment.[10] Neither should writers be defined uncomplicatedly as holding to single allegiances or methodologies. Cox asserts that by 'studying a group rather than individual writers, we see literary and other intellectual work not as unique isolated objects but as the products of forces of both affiliation and cultural warfare'.[11] The obvious follow-on would be to say that while studying a group brings out the social purposes of its members' works, there is a risk that unless a broader range of contexts are brought into play, groups' unique activities may be mistaken for common ones, and vice versa. Cox is by no mean unaware of this—to give just one example, he draws illuminatingly on Margaret Ezell's work on seventeenth-century manuscript culture to stress the antecedents of the Hunt circle's modes of circulating writings.[12] Nevertheless, the relatively tight foci of works such as Cox's book and the individual essays in Russell and Tuite's volume leave open a number of questions about the extent to which particular groupings in the period

---

[8] Cox, p. 12.

[9] Lucy Newlyn, *Reading, Writing and Romanticism: The Anxiety of Reception* (Oxford: Oxford University Press, 2000), p. 24.

[10] I discuss this further in the final section of Chapter Five.

[11] Cox, p. 12.

[12] Cox, p. 64.

adhered to widespread or general practices. As this volume's case studies will demonstrate, conducting comparative work reveals a great deal of crossover between influential networks and their practices. A picture of sociability in the period would more closely resemble an interconnected web than a swarm of closed bubbles. Successful writers were usually simultaneously and sequentially members of numerous different communities, friendship groups, clubs, salons, associations and institutions. Nor were these groupings closed off from readers at large. For most authors, the 'distant public of purchasers' that Cox alludes to was neither that large nor that distant, but instead consisted of individuals at one, two or three degrees of separation. Many of those who could afford to buy books also wrote them, or moved in the same circles as their writers.

Groups in literary society were often frangible and unstable, open both to scrutiny and to malevolent imaginative reconfiguration. In attempting to destroy the carefully fostered reputation of the Cockney School, *Blackwood's* circle of young Tories sought to promote their opposing group reputation through attacking men they figured as upstart demagogues assuming dignities to which they were not entitled. *Blackwood's* reviewers often picked up on laudatory statements by weaker group members and used these to attack those who were praised. John Gibson Lockhart, writing as Z., opened his initial attack on Hunt's circle with some poor lines by the relatively peripheral Cornelius Webb.[13] These lines claimed cultural authority for the Cockneys by linking together 'Chaucer, Spenser, Shakspeare, Milton' with 'HUNT, and KEATS,/the Muses' son of promise'. Lockhart employed Webb's evoked connections to link and undermine the group's lynchpins, using Webb's hyperbole to exemplify Hunt's 'extravagant pretensions' and 'exquisitely bad taste'.[14]

In a similar fashion, strong group members could be rhetorically excluded to weaken the group as a whole and to advance alternative agendas. At first blush, Percy Shelley would seem to be an obvious target for *Blackwood's* writers, but in fact, as has long been recognised, he received kinder treatment from them than from any of the other major periodicals, bar Hunt's own *Examiner*. In his 1940 biography, Newman Ivey White goes so far as to identify a systematic campaign to encourage Shelley to triumph by 'abandoning his vices'.[15] This campaign reached its height in 1819 when *Blackwood's* sought out a copy of the three-year-old *Alastor* in order to appreciate Shelley's progress and denounce the ways in which he

---

[13] Cox, p. 19.

[14] [John Gibson Lockhart], 'On the Cockney School of Poetry. No. I', *Blackwood's Edinburgh Magazine*, 2 (October 1817), 38–41 (p. 38).

[15] Newman Ivey White, *Shelley*, 2 vols (New York: Alfred A Knopf, 1940), II, 160.

had been 'infamously and stupidly treated in the Quarterly Review'.[16] *Blackwood's* argues that the *Quarterly's* cavils showed it to be out of touch with the ways that right-thinking Britons saw poetic brilliance after Byron:

> There is, we firmly believe, a strong love of genius in the people of this country, and they are willing to pardon its possessor much extravagance and error—nay, even more serious transgressions. Let both Mr Shelley and his critic think of that—let it encourage the one to walk onwards to his bright destiny, without turning into dark or doubtful or wicked ways—let it teach the other to feel a proper sense of his own insignificance, and to be ashamed, in the midst of his own weaknesses and deficiencies and meanness, to aggravate the faults of the highly-gifted, and to gloat with a sinful satisfaction on the real or imaginary debasement of genius and intellect.[17]

By setting the creative genius above the critical reviewer, *Blackwood's* reverses the dynamic that the older quarterlies sought to propagate, a process that separated its mode of operation from those of its precursors, successfully portraying their methods as outmoded. By bringing Shelley into its own grouping, *Blackwood's* played a crucial role in overturning the *Quarterly* coterie's scorn, successfully configuring its own contributors as the ones who could discern cultural value. Imaginative reclassifications of this kind played a major role in paving the way for the wider acceptance of Romantic genius during the 1820s and 1830s: a point I will return to in the coda.

Blackwood's' praise of Shelley was also consistent with the class concerns expressed in the Cockney School attacks. In the articles, Hunt is dubbed the 'King of the Cockneys' and his associates converted into the 'youthful nobility of Cockaigne'.[18] By making Hunt the meritless king of a delusory kingdom, Lockhart ties the group together under Hunt and mocks their collective pretensions, origins and abilities. However, his satire also encodes his underlying concern about the claims of plebeian writers. As Gregory Dart puts it, the Blackwoodsmen were concerned about the 'blurring of social boundaries' evident in Cockney writing and 'the coming into prominence of an identifiably metropolitan sensibility' that could undercut their traditionally-grounded and self-consciously provincial aesthetic.[19] This anxiety is evident in Lockhart's directing Keats 'back to the

---

[16] 'Alastor; or, the Spirit of Solitude', *Blackwood's*, 6 (November 1819), 148–54 (p. 153).

[17] 'Alastor; or, the Spirit of Solitude', p. 154.

[18] [Lockhart], 'Letter from Z. to Leigh Hunt, King of the Cockneys', *Blackwood's*, 3 (May 1818), 196–201 (p. 196).

[19] Gregory Dart, 'The Cockney Moment', *Cambridge Quarterly*, 32:3 (2003), 203–23 (p. 205).

shop [...] back to "plasters, pills, and ointment boxes"', attempting to shame his socially mobile competition into suburban anonymity.[20] As the son of a wealthy baronet, Shelley was not a true Cockney in *Blackwood's* eyes, so he could safely be cut off from the group to avoid troubling Z.'s narrative of low-born, unrefined upstarts. This allowed him to be pressed into service as one of a collection of genius-poets with which *Blackwood's* challenged the tastes of its quarterly opponents. The 'strong love of genius' that *Blackwood's* evokes thus conveniently serves to legitimate the existing social hierarchies its contributors were predisposed to defend, providing licence for the privileged that was denied to the population at large.

As the impact of *Blackwood's* manipulations shows, groupings provided authors who successfully conjured authority with powerful means for shifting discourses regarding their vocations. When authors interacted with others in society, they could, if they chose, place themselves as representing the tenuous profession of authorship, or play—and thus further define—roles like the poet or the novelist. In doing so, they created themselves as writers while simultaneously altering to a small extent the social consensus regarding what it meant to write. The Immortal Dinner provides an excellent example of such collaborative artistic mythmaking. Writing in his diary afterwards, Haydon expressed his considerable pride in the event he had created:

> There was something interesting in seeing Wordsworth sitting, & Keats & Lamb, & my Picture of Christ's entry towering up behind them, occasionally brightened by the gleams of flame that sparkled from the fire, & hearing the voice of Wordsworth repeating Milton with an intonation like the funeral bell of St Paul's & the music of Handel mingling, & then Lamb's wit came sparking in between, & Keats's rich fancy of Satyrs & Fauns & doves & white clouds, wound up the stream of conversation.[21]

As this passage makes clear, Haydon was gratified in his expectation that his writerly friends would act appropriately. Wordsworth makes himself Miltonic through his recitation; Lamb, free of the East India Company office, teases and provokes, validated by laughter; the young Keats is given the freedom to play with poetic images, to feel his way into his vocation by seeking reactions from more established practitioners. In some ways, Haydon's guests become more powerfully authorial in performance than

[20] [Lockhart], 'The Cockney School of Poetry. No. IV', *Blackwood's*, 3 (August 1818), 519–24 (p. 524).

[21] *The Diary of Benjamin Robert Haydon*, ed. Willard Bissell Pope, 5 vols (Cambridge, MA: Harvard University Press, 1960–63), II, 176.

on the page, provoked into stronger expressions of selfhood by the acceptance and admiration of their peers. Crucially, this transformation is effected in and through the eyes and testimony of Haydon, whose account of a private event makes it available as a lasting memory. As his proprietorial tone indicates, Haydon himself took something away from this process, his pleasure in his guests' talents coming in part from recognising how those talents reflected upon him.

The Immortal Dinner was one part of a series of creative social transactions in which Wordsworth, Keats and Haydon collaboratively inscribed their significance as worthwhile artists. Some of these transactions were considerably more public than the dinner itself. The unfinished canvas of *Christ's Entry* that loomed over Haydon's guests was, as Russell and Tuite argue, designed to act as 'a heroic vindication and, indeed, sanctification of the capacity of men of genius to transcend the age'.[22] By juxtaposing Keats, Wordsworth, Lamb and Hazlitt with Isaac Newton and Voltaire as spectators watching Jesus' triumph, the painting makes an unmistakable claim for their greatness. Haydon's assertion on his friends' behalf also served to reinforce his own self-aggrandising through advertising his affiliation with men whom he hailed as geniuses. Similar reciprocal processes of definition can be observed in three slightly earlier sonnets by Keats and Wordsworth. These poems all make grand claims for Haydon—and by extension for their authors—but they also display an uneasiness about public responses to artistic works and selves, through doing so making clear their own importance as acts of performative recognition. Keats' earliest sonnet 'Addressed to Haydon' concludes, 'Unnumbered souls breathe out a still applause,/Proud to behold him in his country's eye.'[23] Still applause is, of course, a rather cold comfort until Keats translates its absent sound into present words, and the poem turns in part on this tentativeness. The line reads like an excuse for Haydon's quiet reception, an anxious assertion that public silence should be taken as assent or awe rather than indifference. When Keats writes that Haydon's great purpose 'ought to frighten into hooded shame/A money mong'ring, pitiable brood', his 'ought' hedges significantly. In a perfect world, Haydon's 'steadfast genius' would be recognised, but in a world where Hunt's hated money-getters will not be shamed when they are supposed to be, Haydon's recognition must come in the form of his friend's halting poetry. In the end, the sonnet makes an imaginative claim that can only carry the unquestioned

---

[22] Russell and Tuite, p. 2.
[23] 'Addressed to Haydon', in *Keats' Poetry and Prose*, ed. Jeffrey N. Cox (New York: W.W. Norton, 2009), p. 56.

support of the poet making it. It cannot fully stretch beyond friendly circles to take in others less familiar.

Keats' second, more famous, sonnet to Haydon, takes a different tack, affecting to bring before the 'nations' a company of men whose greatnesses are validated by their connections to the past, to the sublime and to a nature vaster in scope than the human communities it succours:

> GREAT spirits now on earth are sojourning;
>   He of the cloud, the cataract, the lake,
>   Who on Helvellyn's summit, wide awake,
> Catches his freshness from Archangel's wing:
> He of the rose, the violet, the spring,
>   The social smile, the chain for Freedom's sake:
>   And lo!–whose steadfastness would never take
> A meaner sound than Raphael's whispering.
> And other spirits there are standing apart
>   Upon the forehead of the age to come;
> These, these will give the world another heart,
>   And other pulses. Hear ye not the hum
> Of mighty workings?—
>   Listen awhile, ye nations, and be dumb.[24]

This poem avoids the problem of public reception by placing its subjects amongst unquestionable verities rather than within society. It makes a more secure claim than Keats' previous attempt by putting the onus on the reader to recognise which artists are being referred to and by asserting that the transformations they will bring are irresistible and already under way. The withholding of proper names flatters the informed reader (who proves Keats' point by recognising the people he is praising) while challenging the uninformed reader to listen harder. The implication that Hunt is sufficiently clued from flowers, sociability and imprisonment and Haydon from the connection to Raphael shows how widely known such preoccupations were assumed to be among those attuned to literary matters. The history of Keats' poem vindicates this assumption, as in addition to acting as an appeal to wider society, it represented an act of affiliation that achieved its desired effect by paving the way for Keats to connect with Wordsworth. Haydon acted as an editor and go-between, transmitting the sonnet to the older poet and arranging several meetings between the

---

[24] 'Addressed to the Same', in *Keats' Poetry and Prose*, p. 56.

two.[25] As well as setting out Keats' beliefs and associations in high words, the poem served successfully as a literary calling card.

Wordsworth's sonnet to Haydon takes a slightly different tack to Keats' poems. Where the younger poet admires greatness, Wordsworth—characteristically—implicates himself in it. By beginning 'High is our calling, Friend!', Wordsworth leagues himself and Haydon as equivalents.[26] He is keen to valorise their artistic occupations, stating that creative art 'Demands the service of a mind and heart,/Though sensitive, yet, in their weakest part,/Heroically fashioned'. However, as the poem progresses, a more interesting strain emerges, stressing the difficulty of vocations that require the pair 'to infuse/Faith in the whispers of the lonely Muse,/While the whole world seems adverse to desert'. Wordsworth makes suffering due to public indifference into a trial that guarantees real artistry, encouraging Haydon to persevere regardless of critical or societal reactions, secure in the knowledge that a qualified fellow practitioner respects and understands what he is doing. As an accomplished work itself, the poem enacts the triumph over adversity it describes and through this performance seeks to prove the struggle worthwhile. This was not so critical when the poem remained a privately circulated communication, but its publication in *The Champion* on 1 April 1816 made this private leaguing into a public statement, serving to promote Haydon and Wordsworth through and alongside a congenial shared view of art. Supposedly private communications could easily slip into more public forums both through formal publication and through the period's astonishingly catty and effective gossip networks. The self-definitions of writers and artists were refined in collaboration and then sent out into wider society to inspire and shape others into supporting or opposing present cultural orthodoxies.

CHARACTER IN PEN AND IN PRINT: ELIZABETH HAMILTON VERSUS MARY HAYS

Thus far, this chapter has focused on some relatively absolute and stagy examples of performed affiliations, in part because these are the most straightforward means of laying out contours. However, many acts of self-fashioning were more subtle and equivocal. Some such acts are irrevocably lost—for example, 200 years on, we can never know exactly how authors

---

[25] Andrew Motion, *Keats* (London: Faber & Faber, 1997), pp. 129, 142. Haydon cut 'in a distant Mart' from the end of the penultimate line in Keats' draft to leave the effective pause that graces the final version.

[26] William Wordsworth, 'To R.B. [B.R.] Haydon, Esq.', in *Shorter Poems, 1807–1820*, ed. Carl H. Ketcham (Ithaca: Cornell University Press, 1989), p. 174.

made themselves in conversations that went unrecorded. However, more provisional and experimental gestures of affiliation and identity-formation often survive in correspondence. Letters were a particularly important form for self-fashioning: both private and shareable, intimate yet performative, acting, as Clare Brant has contended, as 'inscribed, contested, altered outline[s]' of writers' social characters and interactions.[27] The discussions that follow all demonstrate how letters could act as potent catalysts for the inscription of authorial selves. The final elements of the chapter discuss how correspondences focused around Leigh Hunt, the Shelleys, Matilda Betham and Jane Porter opposed opprobrium and neglect through network-based reconfigurations and creativity. Before turning to these more positive models, though, I will first reinforce the difficulties and risks of establishing a public presence through writing by examining the vexed interactions between personal relations, literary production and perceptions of betrayal.

On 13 March 1797, Elizabeth Hamilton wrote an indignant letter to her erstwhile friend Mary Hays regarding a mixed review that Hays had written of Hamilton's first novel, *Translation of the Letters of a Hindoo Rajah*, which had been published the previous year. In her letter, Hamilton vented her anger at what she saw as her former confidant's cruelty and duplicity, expressing incredulity at Hays' claims regarding the fairness of her actions:

> You assert the "purity of your intentions." I am afraid I am not sufficiently versed in the new nomenclature of virtues thoroughly to understand your meaning. In my old fashioned way of thinking purity of intentions comprehends <u>candour</u> and <u>sincerity</u>, and is altogether incompatible with every shade or degree of <u>Treachery</u> or <u>Malevolence</u>. In the case which you have <u>forced</u> upon my recollection there is no need of any appeal to the recording Angel in search of the inspiring Motive.—<u>The Action Speaks for itself</u>.[28]

Hamilton's letter makes it clear that she expected Hays to keep faith with private amities rather than attempt objective candour in her public pronouncements (although Hamilton's sarcastically noting a 'new nomenclature' bespeaks a certain anxiety about the currency of this opinion). For Hamilton, Hays' betrayal makes her almost a criminal, 'motive' having

---

[27] Clare Brant, *Eighteenth-Century Letters and British Culture* (Basingstoke: Palgrave Macmillan, 2006), p. 27.

[28] Elizabeth Hamilton to Mary Hays, 13 March 1797, NYPL Pforzheimer Misc Ms. 2210. Printed in *The Correspondence of Mary Hays (1779–1843), British Novelist*, ed. Marilyn L. Brooks (Lampeter: Edwin Mellen Press, 2004), pp. 313–5.

begun to slip into its modern legally-inflected definition by this time.[29] Her reference to the recording angel hints at hellish consequences for Hays' self-evidently malicious action.

Having rhetorically damned Hays, Hamilton goes on to assert her book's innocence, describing it as 'containing <u>no</u> Accusations against any sect or party' and 'throwing out <u>no</u> Aspersions upon any character'. This assertion is interesting in that while Hamilton denies that her book's 'innocent raillery' offers Hays any cause for public objection, she implies that a political or overtly satirical work might justify a dissenting friend's published censure. However, believing as she does that her novel does not fall within the categories of works that might be criticised with propriety, Hamilton positions Hays' attack as emotionally irresponsible and irrevocably personal. She expresses mournful surprise that while Hays had 'in confidence confessed how severely you had felt the slight animadversions that had been made upon your first performance in one of the reviews', she had nevertheless not scrupled in her own reviewing: 'with the smile of friendship upon your face, did you <u>Voluntarily</u> offer yourself as the instrument of inflicting similar pains upon the Mind of your unsuspecting friend'. Hamilton also recognised that Hays' review represented a threat to more than just her feelings, depicting it vividly as a form of character assassination: 'You, in the dark, and with a muffled dagger aimed the blow which was to fix, as far as it is in the power of a review to fix, the fame, and character of the person you saluted as a friend!' Hamilton argues that by not 'fairly' presenting her arguments, Hays aimed to establish her own unflattering interpretation of Hamilton's capabilities as definitive in public discourse. Hamilton's concern was not unreasonable; as Gary Kelly writes, commenting on Hays' own traducing by Charles Lloyd, 'the danger of being misread and misrepresented, textually and personally, had [...] increased greatly by the late 1790s'.[30] For female authors, writing represented one of a fairly limited range of socially-acceptable modes for engaging with public matters. Kelly asserts that *Hindoo Rajah* 'gave [Hamilton] a public and even political identity without sacrificing her feminine and domestic one'.[31] Hamilton's letter confirms that she saw her books as constituting acts of speech that were irrevocably hers. Hays' public interpretations threatened to destabilise Hamilton's textual self, potentially compromising the social influence she sought to construct and exert. While Hamilton's letter is not without its gothic flourishes, her feelings of

---

[29] *OED*.

[30] Gary Kelly, *Women, Writing and Revolution, 1790–1827* (Oxford: Clarendon Press, 1993), p. 125.

[31] Kelly, p. 143.

betrayal and her sense of the damage that a false friend's social reconfigurations could do should be taken seriously.

By the later standards of the quarterlies or *Blackwood's*, Hays' offending review for the *Analytical* is fairly tame, if somewhat condescending. At the outset, she grants that 'we have received entertainment from the perusal of this lively and amusing little work' and she allows that the novel's sixty-page preliminary dissertation displays 'considerable knowledge of Indian affairs'.[32] However, contrary to Hamilton's prefatory assertion that British rule on the subcontinent is seen universally as a 'happy change', Hays believes that many readers will be 'inclined to believe' that 'these injured people have merely *changed masters*.'[33] She also evokes suspicions regarding the novel's dedication to Warren Hastings, the recently acquitted former governor-general of Bengal, writing that Hamilton's dedication 'will be adjudged by the reader, either as just, or the grateful language of private obligation and friendship, according to his own preconceived opinions on the subject'.[34] Hays here ostensibly offers protection to Hamilton by extending a choice of two positive interpretations, but this blatant railroading hints at less generous readings that might be advanced. In fact, Hamilton's sense of private obligation to Hastings is made very clear in the full text of the dedication, which thanks him for his patronage of 'Shanscrit, and Persian literature' and for being 'the honoured patron and friend' of Hamilton's 'beloved, and much lamented brother', Charles.[35] Hays' discussing Hamilton's 'private' connection with Hastings highlights the extent to which literary writing was assumed to be tied up with politics and political circles. In this respect, Hays' review accords with Hamilton's letter in portraying a society in which print necessarily acted on the social relationships between authors and their subjects.

Hays' criticisms come through most strongly in her final summary paragraph, in which her comments on the novel slip into personal condemnations. She takes strident issue with what she sees as the novel's dogmatism, writing that Hamilton 'sometimes betrays a spirit not perfectly consistent with the mildness and simplicity of the religion of Jesus: railing is substituted for reasoning, and a frightful picture is held up of the adversaries of revelation, in which truth and soberness are sacrificed […] to *undue*

---

[32] [Mary Hays], 'Hamilton's *Letters of a Hindoo Rajah*', *Analytical Review*, 24 (October 1796), 429–31 (p. 429).

[33] [Hays], '*Hindoo Rajah*', p. 429.

[34] [Hays], '*Hindoo Rajah*', p. 429.

[35] Eliza Hamilton, *Translation of the Letters of a Hindoo Rajah* (London: G.G. and J. Robinson, 1796), [unnumbered leaf at beginning of volume]. See also Pam Perkins, 'Hamilton, Elizabeth (1756?–1816)', *ODNB*, https://doi.org/10.1093/ref:odnb/12062.

alarm.[36] While Hamilton believed that her book 'merely raised a laugh at some self-evident absurdities', Hays saw it as slipping into reactionary propaganda. She also claimed that it sought to work on its reader's emotions, rather than appealing to sense: 'Candid and calm discussion, not *abuse*, is the proper method of making rational converts'. Hays' progressive politics and Jacobin sympathies are evident in her opposing Hamilton's muscular Christian expressions. She makes Hamilton sound shrill and fanatical, but in doing so she betrays her own affiliations through her Godwinian advocacy of rational argument. There is an irony here, of course, in Hays' massive misstatement of the public taste. For writers of the period, calumny proved to be a far more effective means than Godwinian logic for entertaining readers into sympathy with just or unjust causes. The kinds of rational and sober discussion that Hays and the Dissenting *Analytical* sought to promote came under increasing pressure in the late 1790s, as Hamilton's eventual print response to Hays' review demonstrates.

As well as censuring Hamilton's attitudes, Hays also contends that she is 'still less successful, and equally illiberal, in her attack upon moral philosophy and metaphysical enquiry, in which little knowledge and great assumption are manifested'.[37] That these attributed flaws are read as failings in Hamilton rather than in her book again demonstrates how written texts were seen as being interchangeable with their authors. Hays' suggestion that Hamilton should have focused on 'fashionable follies' is one that Hamilton found particularly infuriating, especially as she detected in the claim evidence of Hays' own personal attachments:

> it is a strange sort of compliment you pay your friend Mᵣ Godwin, in taking it for granted that he has made a Monopoly of all the absurdity, and extravagance, in the world [...] Ignorant as I am, and ignorant <u>as to the world you have declared me to be</u>, I could point out to your perusal volumes upon volumes where you might see, in the regions of Metaphysicks fancy has taken as bold a flight—and that in the rage for systematising Authors of at least as distinguished an eminence have laid themselves open to ridicule.[38]

Hamilton's defence is somewhat shaky here, as Mr Vapour in her novel echoes William Godwin's *Enquiry Concerning Political Justice* quite specifically.[39] Hamilton attempts to keep the moral high ground by attacking Hays' condescension, but Godwin's notoriety made a defence based on a lack of

---

[36] [Hays], '*Hindoo Rajah*', p. 431.
[37] [Hays], '*Hindoo Rajah*', p. 431.
[38] Hamilton to Hays, 13 March 1797.
[39] Discussed by Brooks in *Correspondence of Mary Hays*, p. 314.

specificity a sketchy kind of plea. While Hamilton claims that Hays was the one who brought personal character into play, Hays' review implies this was not the way she saw it. As such, both the review and the letter provide telling examples of the ways in which supposedly innocent or rational writings could be read by those that disagreed with them as indulging in unprovoked personal abuse. The exchange reveals the ease with which writing slipped between politics and people, and from public ideals to supposedly private lives. Despite their friendship, Hamilton represented a threat to the agenda that Hays wished to advance, and publicly curbing her served to protect that agenda. For Hamilton, Hays' action represented a public betrayal of their private amities, a politicised manoeuvre that threatened Hamilton's ability to express herself as an author by denying her intellectual agency. This was not something that Hamilton was willing to countenance. In her claim that 'it was not I who sought this contest', it is possible to see Hamilton attempting pre-emptively to justify responding to Hays in a manner that took full advantage of the blurred divisions between personal and public discourse.

Hamilton's published rejoinder to Hays in her 1800 novel *Memoirs of Modern Philosophers* was to portray her erstwhile friend in a character named Bridgetina Botherim (one might think the name alone revenge enough). Hamilton was not subtle, and the consonances with Hays were immediately noted by reviewers. Bridgetina is gloatingly described by the *Anti-Jacobin Review* as 'one of those young ladies, who, disregarding all the old-fashioned female excellencies by which the women of this country have been so eminently distinguished, has devoted herself to the study of Godwinian and Wolstonecraftian philosophy'.[40] In constructing Bridgetina, Hamilton quotes extensively from Godwin's writings and from Hays' novel *Memoirs of Emma Courtney* (1796), helpfully providing footnotes that refer readers to the relevant passages in the originals.[41] *Emma Courtney* was a fruitful source for *ad feminam* satire. Hays' novel is defiantly autobiographical, contains near-verbatim reproductions of some highly personal correspondence, is often stylistically overwrought and was socially

---

[40] '*Memoirs of Modern Philosophers*' (first part), *Anti-Jacobin Review*, 7 (September 1800), 39–46 (p. 39).

[41] The first of many references to Godwin is to his necessitarianism, Mr Myope 'judiciously' observing that a tart 'could never have been so nicely sweetened, *if Alexander the Great had not set fire to the palace of Persepolis.*' For this, Hamilton footnotes *Political Justice* 'vol. i. p. 161.' (Elizabeth Hamilton, *Memoirs of Modern Philosophers*, ed. Claire Grogan (Peterborough, Ontario: Broadview Press, 2000), p. 40). Later references direct the reader to Godwin's *Enquirer* and *Caleb Williams*. Specific notes for Hays are less common and begin later. The earliest directs the reader to 'See Emma Courtney, a philosophical novel; to which Miss Botherim seems indebted for some of her finest thoughts' (p. 175). Several further direct references and numerous allusions follow.

controversial. On its release, it was reviewed positively by sympathetic Dissenting journals. The *Analytical Review*, despite some cavils about its plausibility, called it 'the vehicle of much good sense and liberal principle'.[42] The *Monthly Review* also gave it a largely laudatory notice, but cautioned presciently that the book contained 'sentiments that are open to attack'.[43] As the 1790s became ever more censorious, Hays' novel came increasingly to represent a point of ideological and personal vulnerability that was highly congenial to those who wished to oppose the ideals she espoused.

In her own novel, Hamilton was able to take full advantage of Hays' candour in a depiction that Claire Grogan describes as 'bitingly cruel' and that the *Critical Review* characterised at the time as 'grossly and farcically overcharged'.[44] Bridgetina is short, ugly and prone to wearing attire described as outlandish and ridiculous. She is unable to converse effectively, speaking largely in quotations that Hamilton explicitly appropriates for her own purposes. By marooning Hays' and Godwin's words in the mouths of the credulous Bridgetina and the scruple-free seducer Vallaton, Hamilton makes these words both preposterous and pernicious. Godwin comes off better than Hays; while his philosophies are shown to be impracticable, and dangerous when misinterpreted, many of the more considered characters admire his ambitions and the character most analogous to him, Mr Myope, is an enthusiast rather than an imbecile. By contrast, Bridgetina is hypocritical, self-obsessed, incapable of thinking independently and romantically undesirable. Not content with social and mental humiliations, Hamilton also has Bridgetina fall into open sewers (twice) and sees her physically accosted by pickpockets, streetwalkers, watchmen and an 'obstreperous and unmanageable' herd of pigs.[45]

The multi-part appreciation of the novel in the *Anti-Jacobin Review*, running to sixteen pages over two issues, smirked that Hamilton had constructed 'an excellent imitation of that vicious and detestable stuff which has issued from the pen of M—y H—s. Indeed the whole character of Bridgetina so strongly resembles that of this impassioned Godwinian, that it is impossible to be mistaken.'[46] That the review names the subject of the satire is worth noting, as is the fact that the *Anti-Jacobin Review* took the

---

[42] 'Miss Hays's *Memoirs of Emma Courtney*', *Analytical Review*, 25 (February 1797), 174–8 (p. 174).

[43] '*Miss* Hays's *Memoirs of* Emma Courtney', *Monthly Review*, 2nd series, 22 (April 1797), 443–9 (p. 449).

[44] Claire Grogan, 'Introduction' to Hamilton, *Modern Philosophers*, pp. 9–26 (p. 19); '*Memoirs of Modern Philosophers*', *Critical Review*, new series, 29 (July 1800), 311–3 (p. 311).

[45] Hamilton, *Modern Philosophers*, p. 157.

[46] '*Memoirs of Modern Philosophers*' (second part), *Anti-Jacobin Review*, 7 (December 1800), 369–76 (p. 371).

opportunity to discuss the real-life events that informed both *Emma Courtney* and Hamilton's parody. Before an extensive quotation, the *Anti-Jacobin Review* writes of the subject of Bridgetina's admiration, Henry Sydney, that 'Like Mr F—d he declines all her advances; and she, in imitation of M—y H—s, writes to him the following philosophical love letter.'[47] 'Mr F—d' is William Frend, the Unitarian author and academic whose rejection of Hays was a major factor in occasioning *Emma Courtney*.[48] In her introduction to Hays' novel, Eleanor Ty goes so far as to assert that '[s]ince many of the letters to Godwin are replicated *verbatim* in *Emma Courtney*, we can assume that many of the letters Emma writes to Augustus were originally Hays's love letters to Frend.'[49] Whether or not this is the case, it is certainly true that in satirising the letters in *Emma Courtney*, Hamilton also mocks the close relatives that Hays addressed privately. Hamilton thus unpicks Hays' attempted fictionalisation, and the *Anti-Jacobin Review* finishes this process by bringing Hays' private connections explicitly before the public in order to rejoice in Hamilton's travesty. In Hamilton's versioning, Hays' serious reflections and emotions are made into vapid and ridiculous self-regard. Asked whether it is 'possible that Henry Sidney can really have engaged your affections', Bridgetina replies

> it is not only possible, but literally and demonstrably true. The history of my sensations are equally interesting and instructive. You will there see, how sensation generates interest, interest generates passions, passions generate powers; and sensations, passions, powers, all working together, produce associations, and habits, and ideas, and sensibilities. O Julia! Julia! what a heart-moving history is mine.[50]

Hamilton follows this passage by noting that on hearing this it was 'almost impossible even for Julia to refrain from laughing'. In her preface to *Emma Courtney*, Hays wrote that her book was 'calculated to operate as a *warning*, rather than as an example'.[51] In Hamilton's version, all such caveats are removed, so Bridgetina's philosophy, rather than flowing from properly-contextualised notions of sensibility and utility, is made to express selfishness and pigheaded stupidity. The *Anti-Jacobin Review* brings this full circle by refracting Bridgetina and Henry Sydney back onto Hays and

---

[47] '*Memoirs of Modern Philosophers*' (second part), *Anti-Jacobin Review*, p. 374.

[48] Marilyn L. Brooks, 'Hays, Mary (1759–1843)', *ODNB*, https://doi.org/10.1093/ref:odnb/37525.

[49] 'Introduction' to Mary Hays, *Memoirs of Emma Courtney*, ed. Eleanor Ty (Oxford: Oxford University Press, 2009), pp. viii–xxxvii (p. xiv).

[50] Hamilton, *Modern Philosophers*, p. 174.

[51] Hays, *Emma Courtney*, p. 4.

Frend. It saw Hamilton's recasting as displaying 'an admirable exposition of Godwinian principles', dispensing with the characters with 'all due poetical justice'.[52]

By meting out poetical—or novelistic—justice, Hamilton overwrote Hays' preferred modes of being and writing in manners that encompassed her creative works, her person and her associates. Hays' attempts to promote '[c]alm and candid discussion' of philosophical and affective principles proved to be no match for novelistic richness or for the combination of curiosity and censoriousness that characterised literary life in the late 1790s and the 1800s. As Hamilton's biographer Elizabeth Benger wrote: 'The popularity of *The Modern Philosophers* was a passport to fame and distinction; and Miss Hamilton consequently found herself admired by the celebrated and the fashionable, and an object of curiosity and interest to the public.'[53] Hays' career, by contrast, went into a decline, her social authority compromised by her earlier honesty and by the increasing conservatism of the culture in which she sought to work.

I have dwelt on this exchange at length because it demonstrates the extraordinary extent to which authors were beholden to their contemporaries' constructions of their characters. It might be protested that Hays is a poor example, as *Emma Courtney* does rather invite this sort of reading. However, it is simple to cite other instances of the ease with which personal actions became public currency. In a tightly interconnected literary milieu, knowledge of the affairs of others was a potent form of social capital. Personal lives served both as subjects for the gossip that helped constitute groups of writers as communities and as material for authors keen to sell a work based on a scandalous connection to a figure who was already popular or notorious. John William Polidori's *The Vampyre* (1819), published under Byron's name and featuring a Byronic nobleman as the titular villain, is an obvious example, as is Caroline Lamb's *Glenarvon* (1816), from whose thinly veiled Byron substitute Polidori took his central character's name. Other examples of potent depictions drawing on personal knowledge are easy to cite: William Gifford's *Baviad* (1791) and *Maviad* (1795); the parodies in the *Anti-Jacobin* (1797–1798); Richard Polwhele's *The Unsex'd Females* (1798); Byron's *English Bards and Scotch Reviewers* (1809) and *Vision of Judgment* (1822); James and Horace Smith's *Rejected Addresses* (1812); the various iterations of Hunt's *The Feast of the Poets* (printed in *The Reflector* in 1811; revised and published as a book in 1814);

---

[52] *Anti-Jacobin Review*, 7 (December 1800), p. 375.

[53] Elizabeth Benger, *Memoirs of the Late Mrs. Elizabeth Hamilton*, 2 vols (London: Longman, Hurst, Rees, Orme, and Brown, 1818), I, 132.

Blackwood's 'Chaldee Manuscript' (1817) and 'Noctes Ambrosianae' (1822–1835); Thomas Love Peacock's *Nightmare Abbey* (1818); John Gibson Lockhart's *Peter's Letters to his Kinsfolk* (1819); Percy Shelley's 'Julian and Maddalo' (completed in 1819; first published in 1824); John Hamilton Reynolds' 'The Pilgrimage of Living Poets to the Stream of Castaly' (1816) and *The Press* (1822); Robert Montgomery's *The Age Reviewed* (1827); much of Peter Pindar's work; and so on. In achieving social prominence through publishing, writers surrendered control over aspects of their characters, which could be taken up and refashioned by others in numerous different manners. In an environment in which scandal remained a valuable currency, entrusting one's secrets to writers or writings could end up being a costly reputational proposition. As Hamilton's success with *Memoirs of Modern Philosophers* shows, writers' own depictions of themselves did not necessarily remain the dominant ones.

Relational Self-Fashioning: Leigh Hunt's Correspondence

Towards the end of her letter to Hays, Hamilton writes of the importance of her personal network for her sense of well-being: 'In the little circle of friends by whom I should wish to see myself surrounded I hope <u>the light</u> will <u>always shine</u> of <u>sound judgement</u> and <u>unsophisticating truth</u>.'[54] Hamilton makes it clear that the opinions of trusted associates played a critical role in defining the nature of her works and authorship. The public support of private friends could directly influence works' wider receptions, as Southey hoped when he wrote in an 1808 letter, 'Puff me, Coleridge! if you love me, puff me! Puff a couple of hundreds into my pocket!'[55] However, private partiality did not necessarily need to be published for it to be of use to authors. While a network of well-connected partisans might propel an author to success, more local and intimate circles could also provide valuable encouragement, advice and validation, as Jane Austen discovered when she solicited critical responses from her friends after *Mansfield Park* failed to attract reviewers' attention. These responses served to reassure her that she was read and provided her with a spectrum of views that helped shape her later works. The novel's heroine, Fanny

---

[54] Hamilton to Hays, 13 Mar 1797.

[55] Robert Southey to Samuel Taylor Coleridge, 12 February 1808, Letter 1427 in the *Collected Letters of Robert Southey: A Romantic Circles Electronic Edition*, gen. eds. Lynda Pratt, Tim Fulford and Ian Packer, *Romantic Circles*, 2009–, https://romantic-circles.org/editions/southey_letters/Part_Three/HTML/letterEEd.26.1427.html.

Price, inspired both fondness and frustration; she was variously described as 'delightful', 'liked', 'disliked', unbearable, 'insipid' and 'natural'.[56] Mary Cooke noted that she 'Admired Fanny in general; but thought she ought to have been more determined on overcoming her own feelings'; John Plumptre felt 'the want of some character more striking & interesting to the generality of Readers, than Fanny was likely to be'.[57] Austen evidently found such opinions useful—presumably, she would not have repeated the procedure for *Emma* had she not found it productive, and it seems reasonable to see Emma herself as an attempt to write a more active and striking heroine than Fanny, addressing some of the concerns her respondents raised.[58]

Correspondents let authors see their writings—and, by extension, the selves they were presenting—through different eyes in some cases and echoed pleasingly back in others. Both these responses could serve to encourage and enable. Private reactions, both direct and indirect, helped authors to redefine and modify the impressions they gave, either broadly or for specific addressees. In our modern literary culture, after the rise of a true mass reading audience, the role of writing for communicating ideas and selves to close associates is easy to overlook, but even today writers write for those they know as well as for wider publics, seeking to cultivate affinities and empathy. In the early nineteenth century, when any given individual constituted a far larger proportion of a literary writer's potential audience and when stark income inequalities and systems such as that of clerical preferment meant that the extent to which an individual reader might aid a writer varied extremely widely, writing for a very small reading audience could be extremely effective, as the number of antiquarian churchmen who published only until they acquired good livings indicates. There are, however, less cynical reasons for writing for a very particular audience, including emotional support, the creation of alternative systems of valuation and the development of personalities through mutual exchange. It is to this process of negotiated self-creation that this chapter now turns, using Leigh Hunt as its primary example.

Reviewing *The Revolt of Islam*, John Taylor Coleridge wrote that while Shelley lacked Hunt's 'bustling vulgarity', 'ludicrous affectations' and 'factious flippancy', for either man it was true that 'like a speculator in

---

[56] 'Opinions of *Mansfield Park*' in Jane Austen, *Later Manuscripts*, ed. Janet Todd and Linda Bree (Cambridge: Cambridge University Press, 2008), pp. 230–2.

[57] 'Opinions of *Mansfield Park*', pp. 232, 233.

[58] 'Opinions of *Emma*' in Jane Austen, *Later Manuscripts*, pp. 235–9.

trade, he would be rich without capital and without delay'.[59] While this is obviously an interested view, in some respects Coleridge is quite insightful about how Hunt had to operate. Becoming 'rich without capital' was in a very real sense the financial and social challenge that he faced. While not from a wholly deprived background, Hunt did not attend university, was not trained to a profession and derived the vast majority of his income from his pen. He could not easily succeed in the patrician paradigm that Coleridge implicitly defends in his review; instead, he was forced to create new ways of being an author, both through his outspoken liberalism in the *Examiner* and through the cultivation of his circle and its distinctive modes. Jon Mee argues that what was consistent across Hunt's 'loose and often shifting groups' was 'the ability to reproduce the idea of culture as a form of amiable exchange in which readers could easily join.'[60] Where the closed authoritarian discourses of the quarterlies sought to emphasise the power and professionalism of their critics and readers, Hunt sought to converse and refine, employing a vision of amiability in order to build his status and reify through dialogue new forms of literary identity that transcended establishment paradigms.

In March 1817, Hunt addressed a brief note to Lord Holland, the doyen of Whig high society. Its express purpose was to thank Holland for a revised edition of the peer's *Account of the Life and Writings of Lope Felix de Vega Carpio*, which contained a newly added account of another Spanish dramatist, Guillen de Castro:

> My Lord,
> I have been most unwarrantably negligent in delaying to acknowledge the receipt of a new edition of Lope de Vega, which, I presume, by what appears on a blank leaf, the bookseller sent me by your Lordship's direction. I have been waiting from day to day, in the expectation of begging your acceptance, of a new edition of a little work of my own; but the printing has been so slow, that I am really ashamed of putting off my acknowledgements any longer, & must beg your Lordship not to think them the less sincere, or indeed eager, for making their appearance so late. The Lope de Vega is an old acquaintance; but of Guillen de Castro I knew nothing but by name, though often tempted to try & look into Spanish poetry,—poetry indeed, in any language, being something I can almost as little help getting into, as a clump of green trees. Guillen however did not begin with treating me very

---

[59] [John Taylor Coleridge], 'Shelley's *Revolt of Islam*', *Quarterly Review*, 21 (April 1819), 460–71 (p. 469).

[60] Mee, *Conversable Worlds*, p. 248.

luxuriously; your Lordship's account of him having fairly kept me two hours awake the other night, in bed, unable to cease thinking of the filial gallantry of the Cid. It appears to me, I confess, infinitely finer than in Corneille.

Will your Lordship allow me to take this opportunity of repeating, in private, what I have sometimes indulged myself with expressing elsewhere? The name of Lord Holland has always presented to my mind that mixture of the genial & intellectual, which render respect affectionate; & it is with this feeling that I have the honour to be,

My Lord,

Your most obliged & obed[t]. humble serv[t].

Leigh Hunt.[61]

Hunt is considerably more formal in this letter than when writing to those he considered close friends (where he sometimes tripped himself up by being a little too familiar, offending the prickly Byron by omitting his title).[62] Nevertheless, this letter presents a personal narrative of passionate response, showing the gift of literature as being gratefully received and expressing a wish that the gift-giving might be made mutual. However, there are also more powerful claims being asserted. Hunt hints that the social gulf between himself and Holland can be negotiated through an equivalent exchange of works, just as the individuals in Hunt's circles bound themselves together by exchanging books, dedications and sonnets. Hunt also makes distinctive claims for his own importance by portraying himself as a reader and an aesthete: a man unable to resist literature and nature, familiar with de Vega and Corneille, and enraptured into sleeplessness by the story of the Cid. These responses claim a kind of superiority of sensitivity, a claim reinforced by Hunt's description of the complex resonances created in him by Holland's name. Even the acknowledged lateness of his response could be read as an assertion of artistic status, his preoccupation with literature causing the claims of the quotidian present to lose their urgency. Hunt's literary life in this letter to a lord is figured as a genteel and leisurely one—almost, in fact, aristocratic. In this letter Hunt is not a frantic producer of copy, 'bruised & overwhelmed by the quantity

---

[61] Leigh Hunt to Lord Holland, 3 March 1817, NYPL Pforzheimer LH 0256. Also printed in Eleanor M. Gates, *Leigh Hunt: A Life in Letters; Together with Some Correspondence of William Hazlitt* (Essex, CT: Falls River Publications, 1988), pp. 80–1.

[62] See Hunt's awkward letter to Lord Byron dated 13 Feb 1822, NYPL Pforzheimer LH 0258.

I write', as he is in less guarded letters to intimates like Shelley.[63] Instead, he makes himself like the peer he addresses: a passionate admirer of writing and an influential connector. The frustrations occasioned by slow printers add a touch of professional reality to the ideas that Hunt seeks to sell to Holland: the idea of himself as a sensitive, worthwhile and respectable friend and the idea of authorship as a skilled and valuable occupation. The eventual establishment of the value of writing as an expression of genius theoretically unbound by the existing social order has its roots in exchanges such as this, in which literary authority and more established forms of social authority could be depicted as being different yet equivalent.

Hunt was similarly preoccupied with conjuring himself and his friends in his letters to Percy and Mary Shelley, but with closer associates, he was more familiar and creative. In these letters the power of writing is regularly celebrated, as when Hunt evokes his words' ability to bring his self to the Shelleys:

> Whenever I write to you, I seem to be transported to your presence. I dart out of the window like a bird, dash into a southwestern current of air, skim over the cool waters, hurry over the basking lands, rise like a lark over the mountains, fling like a swallow into the vallies, skin again, pant for breath—there's Leghorn—eccomi!—how d'ye do?[64]

This opening echoes tropes from Shelley's own poetry. Later in the letter, Hunt praises Shelley's 'Lines Written Among the Euganean Hills', and his language here mirrors the winds, birds and vistas of that poem, although Hunt's more grounded style ties the flight down at either end through the references to his Hampstead window and his bursting in on the Shelleys' own 'windless bower' with a cheeky greeting.[65] The lark Hunt makes himself interestingly prefigures Shelley's 'To a Skylark', in which the bird becomes a poet who 'Pourest thy full heart/In profuse strains of unpremeditated art'.[66] By this I do not mean to suggest that Hunt's effusion directly inspired Shelley's poem, but rather that playing with the established lyric trope connecting birds and poets formed a small part of the friends' shared personal vocabulary. In writing to the Shelleys, Hunt travels to them imaginatively both in the narrative of his journey and in employing a lexicon of mutually beloved images that are shared and

[63] Hunt to Percy Bysshe Shelley, 3 November 1820, NYPL Pforzheimer LH 0030.

[64] Hunt to Percy and Mary Shelley, August 1819, NYPL Pforzheimer LH 0025; also in Gates, p. 99, in which the date is tentatively given as the 23rd.

[65] 'Lines Written Among the Euganean Hills', line 344, in *Shelley's Poetry and Prose*, ed. Donald H. Reiman and Neil Fraistat, 2nd edn (New York: W.W. Norton, 2002), p. 118.

[66] 'To A Skylark', lines 4–5, *Shelley's Poetry and Prose*, p. 304.

reconfigured by all participants in the exchange. While the imagined journey is fanciful, the closeness created through this echoing is more tangible,
a written affirmation of their shared ambitions.

The building of this shared language and ethos pervades even the most
personal matters, as shown in the letter Hunt wrote after receiving news of
the death of the Shelleys' young son:

> He was a fine little fellow,—was William; & for my part, I cannot conceive,
> that young intellectual spirit which set thinking out of his eye, & seemed to
> comprehend so much in his smile, can perish like the house it inhabited. I
> do not know that a soul is born with us; but we seem, to me, to <u>attain</u> to a
> soul, some later, some earlier; & when we have got that, there is a look in
> our eye, a sympathy in our cheerfulness, & a yearning & grave beauty in our
> thoughtfulness, that seems to say—Our mortal dress may fall off when it
> will:—our trunk & our leaves may go:—we have shot up our blossom into
> an immortal air. This is poetry, you will see, & not argument; but then there
> comes upon me another fancy, which would fain persuade me, that poetry is
> the argument of a higher sphere. Do you smile at me? Do you too, Marina,
> smile at me? Well, then,—I have done something at any rate.[67]

This letter's movement from the sorrow of loss to metaphysical speculations might initially seem jarring, but the allusions Hunt makes carried
particular resonances for the group. William is described in two of his
father's favourite words as an 'intellectual spirit'. In a previous letter, Hunt
had admired the respect paid to the 'Spirit of Intellectual Beauty' by the
Greek tragedians through their 'lurking impatience & irreligion against
their own plot[s]' and their 'yearning after every sphere of beauty, moral
& physical'.[68] This earlier letter responded to Shelley's own 'Hymn to
Intellectual Beauty', which sceptically reworks aspects of Wordsworth's
Immortality ode. Hunt's response to William's death is indebted to the
language and mood of Wordsworth's poem, but contends that rather than
being immanent, as the older poet contended, the soul descends like
Shelley's own spirit of beauty. In his hymn, Shelley writes of his unsuccessful childhood search for gothic inspiration before describing a true revelation catalysed by the spirit: 'Sudden, thy shadow fell on me;/I shrieked,
and clasped my hand in ecstasy!'[69] In arguing that William precociously
exhibited both an intellectual spirit and the sympathy that Shelley ascribed
to its operation, Hunt equates the son with his father and becoming a real

---

[67] Hunt to Percy Shelley, [8?] July 1819, NYPL Pforzheimer LH 0023. Printed in
Gates, p. 96.

[68] Hunt to Mary Shelley, 9 March 1819, NYPL Pforzheimer LH 0022.

[69] 'Hymn to Intellectual Beauty', lines 59–60, *Shelley's Poetry and Prose*, p. 95.

person with thinking like their mutual conception of the poet. Hunt's attempt to comfort Shelley affirms a shared belief in the value of their vocations by boldly asserting that William, young as he was, had also manifested this belief. In this communal discourse, poetry is seen not as a process or a genre, but as a superior manner of being, a manner that promises a kind of beautifully evoked—if ill-defined—immortality. By arguing that poetry is 'the argument of a higher sphere', Hunt makes it a replacement for religion as a medium for explaining calamities, validating the sorts of literary perceptions that his circles' exchanges were writing into being. He is a little uncertain about pushing the value of life so far into literature, aware that he might come across as unfeeling through bringing up aesthetics in response to a very real bereavement. Hedging against this, he tempers his statements by gently burlesquing his fanciful nature in the passage's final lines, portraying himself as deliberately overreaching in his claims for poetry while still holding out the prospect of their being true. Faced with death, Hunt turns towards a shared textual pantheon to produce comfort, while remaining emotionally astute enough to realise that he can only gesture towards consolation. He wrote to Mary shortly afterwards, 'I wish in truth I knew how to amuze you just now.'[70]

Hunt's literary claims were not all so exalted; indeed, he was often more comfortable discussing the quotidian aspects of pen-pushing. Attempting to amuse Mary in a later letter, Hunt plays imaginatively with writing's physicality:

> I will tell you, Marina, what I meant by "gigantic paragraphs":—short letters written in large characters. Count the number of words in one of my letters, & in one of yours, & see which has the greater. Thus you write a long letter, it is true, but not a full one. The characters I write in are like the devils in Pandemonium, who shrunk themselves to pigmies that they might all get in;—yours are the leaders of them in secret conclave,—mightier, but not so numerous.[71]

Hunt here takes Mary lightly to task for short-changing him as a correspondent, but in doing so, he makes a series of claims about writing and being writerly. His diabolic comparisons display a shared delight in figurative language and playfully echo the opinions of the Hunt circle's conservative opponents, who, as Kim Wheatley has noted, tended to configure

---

[70] Hunt to Mary Shelley, 25–27 July 1819, NYPL Pforzheimer LH 0024.
[71] Hunt to Mary Shelley, 12 September 1819, NYPL Pforzheimer LH 0027.

radicals as 'Satanic rebels against orthodoxy'.[72] Writing here becomes its writer, and while Hunt is happy to rank Mary's might above his own, he nevertheless chides her for closing herself off behind large, secretive characters while his own letters cram words—and therefore self—into whatever space is available.[73] For Hunt, such generous individual expression was of immense importance. Later in the same letter, he writes that he has been reading the *Meditations* of Marcus Antonius and has found in him a powerful argument for entangling art and friendship:

> He advises people who wish to rejoice themselves, to call to mind the several virtues or gifts of those they are acquainted with,—as the industry of this person, the good nature of that, &c. So you see, you are to beatify yourself any time at a moment's notice by reflecting on Shelley's ardour of benevolence, Marianne's paper-cutting, or my performance of a Venetian ballad,—on any thing, in short, great or small, which is pleasurable and belongs to your friends. But the notion is beautiful, is it not?

In Marcus Antonius, Hunt finds a precedent for his faith in the ability of creative groupings to sustain their members. Artistry is not only a means of expression for the artist, but also for their friends: a source of strength both aesthetic and personal. By encouraging Mary to see herself as part of a circle of talented individuals, Hunt offers to her the consolations of art and friendship, or rather of the one expressed through the other, both being, in his formulation, inextricably intertwined.

Hunt also encouraged the Shelleys in more pragmatic ways by updating them on the progress of their publications, often painting sunny pictures of their British reception. On the publication of *The Cenci*, he wrote that 'Shelley's tragedy is out & flourishing. I receive, both as his friend & representative, congratulations on all sides, upon the dedication, the preface & the drama.' He described the poem rapturously as 'a true, stately, & yet affectionate mixture of poetry, & philosophy, & human nature, & horror, & all-redeeming sweetness of intention' and noted his promotion of this view in the *Examiner:* 'I gave a brief notice of it two or three weeks ago, announcing this longer one, which will just precede, I hope, the second

---

[72] Kim Wheatley, *Shelley and his Readers: Beyond Paranoid Politics* (Columbia, MO: University of Missouri Press, 1999), p. 2.

[73] Hunt's last lines often shrink considerably to keep the letter on a single sheet of paper, probably partially as postal costs for letters were calculated based on the number of sheets as well as the distance travelled. Such costs, generally paid by the recipient, were fairly significant, so many letter-writers got into the habit of restricting themselves to single sheets. A useful account of historical postal costs can be found on the website of the Great Britain Philatelic Society: http://www.gbps.org.uk/information/rates/inland/index.php.

edition.'[74] For Shelley, physically removed from the literary scene in Britain, Hunt acted as a crucial promoter: of sales, in print and of Shelley's confidence in his own work. This supportive relationship was reciprocal. Hunt often expressed pleasure on receiving compliments and continued to convey his appreciation for Shelley's 'overwhelmingly generous gift of £1400', a payment made in 1818 to help Hunt settle his debts.[75] Hunt's letters regularly stress his gratitude by laying out plans to improve his financial situation through literary work:

> How you delight me with what you say of the Indicator! I hope you will like the succeeding papers as well. I have now already completed a volume, & I speculate upon writing three at least, if my health will hold out,—three years in all, being the time for which I have given up what I told you to my creditors.[76]

Contrariwise, Hunt shared his frustrations with Shelley when his aspirations were thwarted. While Hunt was far more successful at getting his work to readers than the Shelleys were, his prominence meant that he was commonly the target of attacks on their shared aspirations. In his letters, he leagues himself and the Shelleys as part of an aggrieved opposition to a perfidious establishment. Writing in 1821, he complains that illness and worry have made him 'thin & gaunt', that the *Examiner* 'has been lamentably falling off', that his family are unwell and that his brother is imprisoned. He attributes these calamities to his paper's honesty: 'we could not have been treated with more spite & revenge, in some respects, if we had been Jesus himself come upon earth again, unknown to his would-be Christians.'[77] Hunt makes this potentially blasphemous comparison secure in the knowledge that his atheistic friends will allow him the liberty. As long as Hunt and the Shelleys have each other, they are in certain respects market- and critic-proof, their works assured of at least a few appreciators to justify their continuing to write.

The role of Shelley's best sounding-board was one that Hunt actively sought. He continued to evoke and defend the special status of their interactions long after his friend's untimely death. In a later querulous letter to Mary Shelley, he objected to her characterisation of her husband as having '"possessed a quality of mind which <u>experience</u> has shewn you <u>no other human being</u> as possessing, in more than a <u>very slight</u>

---

[74] Hunt to Percy and Mary Shelley, 6 April 1820, NYPL Pforzheimer LH 0031.
[75] Roe, *Fiery Heart*, p. 311.
[76] Hunt to Percy Shelley, 23 August 1820, NYPL Pforzheimer LH 0032.
[77] Hunt to Percy and Mary Shelley, 10 July 1821, NYPL Pforzheimer LH 0035.

degree,"—"underlined"".[78] He argued that he too was unworldly and that his continuing difficulties (exemplified—although not in his account—by his having twice applied to the Literary Fund during the 1830s) revealed that he, like Shelley, had written for goals other than contemporary wealth and fame.[79] That unworldliness could be considered an attractive trait later in Hunt's life is a testament to the transformations his circle wrought. Discourses refined through private sociability could thus break out to wider audiences. While Hunt himself was not the most significant beneficiary of this transformation, in part due to presentational missteps he made while under intense financial pressure in the late 1820s, the types of oppositional authorship he championed became and remain his circle's potent legacy in the mainstream.

WOMEN, NETWORKING AND AUDIENCES

Arguing against viewing women's literary activities separately from those of men, Stephen Behrendt writes that 'while gender undeniably played a considerable part in the literary and cultural politics of the period, it is an error to assume [...] that the activities of men and women were therefore wholly delineated and separated on the basis of notions about the "separate spheres" that have become commonplace in twentieth-century criticism and theory.' Rather, he contends, 'there were in fact both overlapping and competing (or alternative) spheres'.[80] Examining women's correspondence networks bears this out this assertion, but also makes clear that while letters could conjure situations of equal exchange, these did not always translate into action. As women were often barred by custom and resources from many of the physical and conceptual spaces within which men socialised and promoted themselves, they often found the associative powers of letters to be particularly important. However, the fruitful relationships conjured and promised in letters were not always successfully translated into more public arenas.

Some of the possibilities and tensions inherent in women's authoring themselves through correspondence can be drawn out from a multiform missive sent in 1810 by Matilda Betham to the eccentric scholar George Dyer, a man who would later support her applications to the Literary Fund.[81] Betham's sociability and literary talents had allowed her to establish

---

[78] Leigh Hunt to Mary Shelley, 25 June [?], NYPL Pforzheimer LH 0016.

[79] See Mr Leigh Hunt (full name: James Henry Leigh Hunt), Loan 96 RLF 1/734. For more on the Literary Fund, see Chapter Four.

[80] Behrendt, p. 8.

[81] Miss Matilda Betham (or Mary Matilda Betham), Loan 96 RLF 1/361.

herself as a welcome presence in numerous companies. Her first collection, *Elegies, and Other Smaller Poems,* published in 1797, received an encouraging notice in the *Monthly Review,* which rated her talents as being 'beyond the common sphere of merit.'[82] This relative success led Betham to travel to London and attempt to earn a living by the pen. 'Many people have thought me naturally a singular and perhaps imprudent person because I rhymed and ventured into the world as an artist,' she wrote, 'but I belonged to a large family, and dreaded dependence.'[83] She was successful in building a network of literary supporters; as Paula R. Feldman writes, 'she was the close friend of Robert Southey and Charles and Mary Lamb and knew John Opie, Frances Holcroft, Hannah More, Anna Letitia Barbauld, Germaine de Staël and Samuel Taylor Coleridge'.[84] In 1802, the last of these compared her to Sappho and assured her that 'the fair, wild Offspring of thy Genius [...] Have found a little Home within *my* Heart.'[85] While she worked at writing, Betham supplemented her literary income by giving readings from Shakespeare and painting miniatures. In 1804, she published a *Biographical Dictionary of the Celebrated Women of Every Age and Country.* It was reviewed sparsely, but the *British Critic* praised its 'authenticity' and pronounced it satisfying and interesting.[86] In the opinion of the *Critical Review,* her 1808 volume of *Poems* showed 'the clearest marks of being written by a person of elegant genius, and of a warm and generous heart.'[87]

By 1810, then, Betham was an accomplished and relatively well-connected writer, if not a commercially successful one (her affluent relatives continued to provide funds to support her). Her letter to Dyer shows her comfortably at home in literary society: 'I have seen the Holcrofts, Mrs Montagu & Mr Lamb. Miss Lamb did not return to town with him.'[88] Dyer, a close friend of the Lambs, would have known that this tactful reference to Mary signified her having been confined in an asylum due to a

---

[82] '*Elegies and other Small Poems*', *Monthly Review,* 2nd series, 26 (May 1798), 92–4 (p. 92).

[83] Quoted in her niece Matilda Betham-Edwards' *Six Life Studies of Famous Women* (London: Griffith & Farran, 1880), p. 235. Originally from her privately-printed autobiographical book *Crow-Quill Flights,* pages of which survive in the Literary Fund Archive (Loan 96 RLF 1/361/15).

[84] Paula R. Feldman, *British Women Poets of the Romantic Era: An Anthology* (Baltimore: Johns Hopkins University Press, 1997), p. 91.

[85] Samuel Taylor Coleridge, 'To Matilda Betham, from a Stranger', lines 8 and 11, in *The Collected Works of Samuel Taylor Coleridge,* gen ed. Kathleen Coburn, 14 vols (Princeton, NJ: Princeton University Press, 1969–1993), I.ii, 727.

[86] *British Critic,* 24 (August 1804), p. 212.

[87] 'Betham's *Poems*', *Critical Review,* new series, 14 (July 1808), 273–77 (p. 274).

[88] Matilda Betham to George Dyer, 20 August 1810, NYPL Pforzheimer Misc. Ms. 3616h.

recurrence of her debilitating mental illness. The inclusion of such personal information indicates the extent to which networks of authors were constituted as friendship groups rather than professional circles, although of course such friendships were often capitalised on for the purposes of writerly advancement. Betham confirms the importance of personal sociability in an added postscript:

> Since I wrote the above a large party of us have been down to Purfleet to a ball on board my brother's ship—and Mr Lamb, though he did not dance was one, and very much contributed to [making] the passage there & back (in the latter we were becalmed & were from 9 in the morning till 8 at night returning) pleasant to us all. We wished you to have been with us—for it was the prettiest night I ever saw.

Betham goes on to describe the party—the glowing 'Chinese lanterns', the 'handsome orchestra', the flags festooning the deck, the baffled Chinese sailors 'who in their best attire, and with countenances full of surprise and pleasure beheld us all dancing and seemed mightily amused.' Through this description, she draws Dyer into the party that he was unable to attend, giving him something of the occasion and of herself by sharing her perspective. In describing Lamb's presence and good humour, she reassures Dyer that Lamb is being cared for and is bearing up despite his trying circumstances. In Betham's friendships, as in those of many of her contemporaries, writing was an aspect of a broader conviviality, serving to communicate affection as well as profundities. It is a mistake to read writerly friendships solely as bookish endeavours; when writers assisted and bonded with each other, the reasons did not exclusively relate to their literary priorities. One valuable benefit of examining convivial letters like Betham's is the ways in which they flesh out our senses of writers as individuals motivated by numerous different connections and anxieties. For its writer, writing is never a closed process of creation; rather, it is woven into the tapestry of living. While we can only access the written remnants of relationships, we must take it as read that there was more to them than what survives in text.

While the body of Betham's letter to Dyer is concerned with personal matters, poetry is also in play. At the end of the initial letter, Betham writes that '[m]y friend has been copying out the rhymes you scolded me about & I have revised them for your service.' These rhymes comprise a draft entitled 'Fancy fettered' on the letter's second leaf. Since this draft version has to my knowledge never been printed, it is given here in full:

O! blame me not that I do restrain
   Thy wandering footsteps! Thus thy wings confine!
   'Tis the decree of Fate, it is not mine,
   For I would let thee Fancy widely stray
   Would follow gladly, tend thee on thy way
  And never of thy vagaries complain;
  Never thy wild and sportive flights disdain
Though reasonless those graceful moods may be,
They still, alas! Are passing sweet to me!

Then pity me who am compelled to bind
   This murmuring captive; her who ever strove,
   By little playful arts to win my love;
   And ever inoffending, ever bright,
   Danc'd in my view and pleased me to delight.
  She scattered showers of lilacs on my mind,
  For O! so fair, so fresh and so refined,
Her childlike offerings, without thorns to pain,
Without one canker'd wound, or earthly stain.

O! darling! as, at duty's call I twine
   Those fetters round thee, they are wet with tears,
   For the sweet playmate of my early years
   I cannot thus afflict, nor thus resign,
   My equal liberty and not repine
  For I would make thee, infant as thou art,
  Queen of my hopes, my leisure and my heart
But that affection, venerable cause,
I linked with Duty's unrelenting laws.

She blames me that I let thy sports offend
   Old Time, and lay thy snare within his path
   To make him falter, as it often hath;
   But O! I love him not, he holds his breath
   And hurries on, and is in league with Death,
  To make the path through which my footsteps bend,
  Late rich in all that rural scenes attend,
A gloomy desert; and I droop and die,
Beneath the gaze of his dull, threatening eye.[89]

---

[89] Matilda Betham to George Dyer, 20 August 1810, NYPL Pforzheimer Misc. Ms. 3616h.

This poem examines the tension between self-indulgent but truthful self-expression and the pressure to conform to societal norms, a tension inherent in the creation of socialised, communicative poetry. Being a respectable author in this poem is depicted as a process of self-restraint, not one of gushing forth. However, the poem remains ambivalent about the value of enslaving (feminine) Fancy at the behest of supposedly more mature impulses (a feminine Duty, but one operating at the behest of a masculine Time). By complaining of the need for restraint, Betham creates a space to enumerate Fancy's charms, making surrendering to her seem a far more attractive prospect than a life under the aegis of Duty. This places the poem itself in a peculiar position—it implies that writing dutifully requires the resignation of childhood impulses and liberty, but through portraying this, the poem has it both ways, gaining credit both for the beauty of fancy and for its resignation to social norms. By placing the poem initially within the context of a private letter, Betham tests out these complex sentiments and obliquely addresses Dyer on the sacrifices she makes. By asking Dyer's opinion, she ensures that he will read her verses and thus better understand his friend—or, at least, the poetic persona she projects. Perhaps in its original context the poem also expressed the hope that Dyer would be able to help Betham negotiate the problems it depicts, serving as a practical psychological confession as well as a more general pronouncement.

Betham and her circle obviously valued these lines, as they appeared in print in two different forms. The *Edinburgh Annual Register*, a publication with which her friend Southey was heavily involved, published them with minor alterations and many additional exclamation marks in its 1812 volume.[90] A revised version was also published in *The Lay of Marie* (1816), Betham's long poem on Marie de France, in which the lines comprise one of the first songs that the eponymous heroine plays for the court that constrains her.[91] The *Lay* itself is interesting in that a number of Betham's friends were heavily involved in its composition and production. In May 1814, Southey, at Betham's instigation, had suggested that her most lucrative literary prospects would be to 'adapt some of our old plays to the stage' or 'to versify some popular tale; better still, to manufacture one with a melodrama or grand spectacle for the stage.'[92] Southey's advice drew on familiar precedents. Coleridge had recently completed his most financially

[90] Matilda Betham, 'The Fettering of Fancy', *The Edinburgh Annual Register* (1812), pp. 24–5. The punctuation changes move the poem closer towards the stereotype of the breathless feminine effusion—an interesting mediation on the part of the editors.

[91] Matilda Betham, *The Lay of Marie* (London: Rowland Hunter, 1816), pp. 14–15.

[92] Robert Southey to Matilda Betham, 15 May 1814, in *A House of Letters*, ed. Ernest Betham (London: Jarrold & Sons, 1905), p. 146.

successful production—his play *Remorse*—and Southey himself specialised in spectacular poetry both original and adapted, although his works were long-term prospects in terms of their financial and reputational returns.[93] Perhaps tellingly, Southey's letter concludes by slipping from advice to invitation: 'These are things which may be talked over at leisure when you come to us; we shall all rejoice to see you, and it is very likely that among my books you may find something which will suit your purpose.' This might be read in two ways. One would be to see Southey as slipping away from Betham's literary ambitions by placing her company first. The other would be to recognise that even Southey, a man whose love of quietness among his books was notorious, thought that Betham's literary needs might best be met by incorporating them into a broader sociability.

Precisely how Betham read Southey's letter is difficult to determine, but she continued to correspond with him about her productions and to develop her ideas through questionings and circulations. Once Betham set to work on her *Lay*, Southey wrote again advising her to look at Marie de France's originals: 'the writing is not likely to be difficult [...] but I dare say George Dyer would lend you his eyes if your own should be puzzled.'[94] He shrewdly suggested that including the original lays would ensure that Betham's book had 'an antiquarian value'. Betham took up this suggestion and included a great deal of ancillary material in the volume.[95] Her book was thus to some extent co-authored by her circle. She consulted Dyer, discussed plans and drafts with Southey and asked Lamb to help see the poem through the press. Feldman describes Lamb as having 'made some substantive, though not always helpful changes', basing her assertion on the following passage from an 1816 letter:[96]

> I will go thro' the Poem, unless you should feel more safe by doing it yourself. In fact a second person looking over a proof is liable to let pass any thing that sounds plausible. The act of looking it over seeming to require only an attention to the words that they have the proper component letters, one scarce thinks then (or but half) of the sense.—You will find one line I have ventured to alter in 3ᵈ sheet. You have made hope & yoke rhime, which I find intolerable. Every body can see & carp at a bad rhime or no rhime. It strikes as slovenly, like bad spelling.[97]

---

[93] On *Remorse*, see Richard Holmes, *Coleridge: Darker Reflections* (London: Flamingo, 1999), pp. 335–8. On Southey, see Chapter Three.

[94] Southey to Betham, 30 May 1814, in *A House of Letters*, p. 147.

[95] Connections might be drawn here with William Herbert's *Helga*, discussed in Chapter One.

[96] Feldman, p. 92.

[97] Charles Lamb to Matilda Betham, [1816], in *A House of Letters*, p. 162.

Feldman implies from Lamb's line alteration that he ran roughshod over Betham's original, but read in the context of the full passage, Lamb's modifications come across rather differently. He takes up the poem at Betham's request, limits his attention principally to proofing and makes the one alteration that he explicitly mentions based on a conviction that the line as it stands would reflect badly on his friend. Lamb was a man whose taste and talents were respected, and asking friends for editorial assistance was not uncommon—Byron commented on Hunt's *Story of Rimini* (1816), Gifford made suggestions on Byron's works at his request and John Clare's published works were constructed in (not unproblematic) consultations with numerous acquaintances, most prominently his publisher, John Taylor.[98] In giving her poem into Lamb's hands, Betham invited him at least implicitly to refine and improve her text and thus to help her achieve the success she sought.

There is, however, something more in Feldman's claim about the nature of Lamb's editorial interventions. Lamb describes himself as taking his task very seriously, but his other commitments frequently interfered, and he later felt compelled to drop the project as his 'distrest state of mind' was impeding his performance. 'The blunders I have already overlooked,' he wrote, 'have weighed upon me almost insufferably.'[99] Of course, while the blunders weighed upon Lamb, they also presumably weighed upon Betham's poem. Lamb apologised for this in a later letter:

> I have drawn you into a scrape and am ashamed, but I know no remedy. My unwellness must be my apology. God bless you (tho' He curse the India House, and fire it *to the ground*), and may no unkind error creep into 'Marie.' May all its readers like it as well as I do, and everybody about you like its kind author no worse![100]

Having a network of friends to assist in preparing works was invaluable for an author, but the status of these friends as friends rather than professionals meant that they could not be held to account in the same way that someone doing a job could be (at least, by someone with sufficient status). Betham's friends were in some senses her competitors and had their own careers to consider, as Lamb's letter makes clear. Betham was a woman who other writers were glad to know and whose presence they valued; in her old age, a young admirer stated that he 'would rather talk to Matilda Betham than to

---

[98] Roe, *Fiery Heart*, pp. 243–44; Fiona McCarthy, *Byron: Life and Legend* (London: John Murray, 2002), p. 149; Jonathan Bate, *John Clare: A Biography* (London: Picador, 2004), discussed at numerous points, but particularly pp. 203–7.

[99] Lamb to Betham, 1 June 1816, in *A House of Letters*, p. 164.

[100] *A House of Letters*, pp. 165–6.

the most beautiful young woman in the world.'[101] Her friends were happy to assist her, but there were also practical limits to their level of investment in the works as opposed to the writer. Southey's slip from advice to invitation in the letter cited earlier perhaps indicates that friends keen for her company valued Betham's conversation above her verse and might have been kind in their professed assessments of her works while declining to promote them amongst their other friends. Read in this light, Lamb's 'may all its readers like it as well as I do' acquires a kind of dangerous ambiguity. This is, of course, an unprovable and possibly unjustified speculation. Nevertheless, it serves to make the point that while sociability was a powerful mode of validation, it could also be a slippery and potentially delusive one. It is easy to lie to maintain the good opinions of those we care about or whose approbation we seek; doubtless, as in any period, many insincere compliments smoothed the functioning of early nineteenth-century literary society.

Many of Betham's principal correspondents were male (although she maintained a lifelong friendship with Charlotte Jerningham, Lady Bedingfield, and exchanged letters with Sara Coleridge, Edith Southey and Mary Lamb). To provide a contrast, it therefore seems apposite to conclude this examination of the slips of sociability by looking at a letter connecting two female writers: Jane Porter and Mary Cockle. Porter was a popular and well-established writer of historical romances, most famously *Thaddeus of Warsaw* (1803) and *The Scottish Chiefs* (1810).[102] Cockle was (and remains) more obscure. J.R. de J. Jackson states that she 'was governess to the Misses Fitzclarence' (the illegitimate children of the Duke of Clarence (later William IV) and the actress Dorothea Jordan) and that she 'contributed to *The Iris* and *The Keepsake* annuals'.[103] She published a number of educational books in the 1800s, including *The Juvenile Journal* and *Important Studies for the Female Sex, in reference to Modern Manners.* In 1810, she published *Lines on the Lamented Death of Sir John Moore*, which she followed up in 1812 with *Simple Minstrelsy*, a collection consisting principally of familiar poems addressed to friends. In 1814, she published *National Triumphs*, a long patriotic poem celebrating British victories in the Napoleonic Wars; reviewing this, the *Anti-Jacobin Review* described her as 'a Lady whose talents and genius have ever been directed to the promotion of virtue'.[104] She also produced a number of shorter

---

[101] Betham-Edwards, p. 300.

[102] See St Clair, pp. 630–1.

[103] J.R. de J. Jackson, *Romantic Poetry by Women: A Bibliography, 1770–1835* (Oxford: Clarendon Press, 1993), p. 64. Recently expanded and placed online: https://jacksonbibliography.library.utoronto.ca/.

[104] 'National Triumphs', *Anti-Jacobin Review*, 46 (June 1814), 553–61 (p. 553).

poetic pamphlets: pious elegies on the deaths of Princess Charlotte and George III, and, in 1817, two disapproving poems on Byron, which damned his morals while admiring his talents, bemoaning his ability to '*charm* the fancy–but *corrupt the heart*'.[105] By September 1820, Cockle was governess to the daughter of 'Mr. & Mrs. Pearson' at 'Unthank Hall' and it was to this address that Porter sent a newsy letter.

Porter's letter is particularly interesting in its depicting a distinctive female network of literary sociability:

> I was staying with Mrs. Hort, where I had the pleasure of seeing Mrs. Opie very often.—She spoke to me of you, with high encomium of your talents, and told me Miss. More was a friend of hers.—Just before I went to Brighton Mrs. Opie and I went to a Literary Dinner at Mr Longmans Hampstead villa, and found it very pleasant. The Hospitality of our modern Maecenas, was as splendid as anything that ever groaned on Roman tables; and the guests who encircled it, were worthy of the host. His amiable wife was at the head of the board; and, besides some few ladies, of no earthly names of note, (so if you please we may suppose them the nine heavenly sisters, in mortal disguise!) we had Mrs. Marcet, Miss. Aikin, &. &. Gentlemen of the Muse, without number! And, on the whole, everything went off as gaily as wisely;—for, I own, I anticipated some Dullness, in a circle of so much profundity. However I was most agreeably disappointed.[106]

This letter extends to Cockle the presences of other sympathetic female writers—in this passage, Porter names Amelia Opie, Hannah More, Jane Marcet and Lucy Aikin; later in the letter she mentions her sister, Anna Maria. In Porter's descriptions, these women constitute authoritative sources of legitimation, by contrast with the male writers at Longman's dinner, who are lightly dismissed as a numberless mass. Even Longman himself is abstracted as a 'modern Maecenas', made to seem grand but less immediately interesting than the ladies present. The encouraging praise placed at the head of the letter is Opie's, with the prospect of the formidable More's held out by association. Porter's humorous dismissal of the ladies of no earthly name makes it clear that it is specifically a network of female writers in which she wishes to include Cockle. This shared privileging of the achievements of other female authors is amplified when Porter later writes that '[n]either Miss Pamela FitzGerald, nor myself, have forgotten your wish for a scrap of Mde. De Genlis hand-writing'. Pamela FitzGerald was the wife of the Irish patriot Lord Edward FitzGerald and

---

[105] Mary E. Cockle, *Reply to Lord Byron's "Fare Thee Well"* (Newcastle: S. Hodgson, 1817), p. 7.

[106] Jane Porter to Mrs Cockle, 24 September 1819, NYPL Pforzheimer Misc. Ms. 3930.

the adopted daughter of Stéphanie Félicité Ducrest de St-Aubin, comtesse de Genlis, a famed harpist and wit who produced a body of educational writings and novels that were extremely popular in Britain; these were probably the source of Cockle's interest. That Cockle wished to collect this keepsake and that Porter was happy to collude in this indicates the totemic value that successful female writers could have for their contemporaries.

Jacqueline Pearson has contended that 'novel-reading [...] gave women readers a series of potent images to deal with their anxieties about, or even fight for their rights to, literary authority.'[107] Porter's letter demonstrates that women writers, as well as their works, could serve directly as exemplars and inspirations. It also suggests that such interpretations were fostered and promoted through circles who sought each other out, read together, socialised with each other and collaborated in admiring interlocking canons of female writers. While women's access to public forums, institutional authority and gentlemanly networks was limited and their works were often maligned or neglected by these formations, letters like Porter's show that masculine neglect in no way precluded networks of female authors and readers from articulating potent discourses of their own, writing into being resistant criteria for determining social and literary value. The female reading public, often described by male authors as being passive and undiscerning, was in fact a network of active correspondents that could exert considerable influence over authors' careers, both in concert with male writers and through opposing them.

Such social interactions serve to show that while the rhetorics of emerging institutions like the quarterly Reviews affected total control over the sphere of literary opinion, recognition as a worthwhile author could in practice be sought through a wide range of different networks and affiliations. Since the literary marketplace did not support many different gradations of commercial success for most authors, these social methods of validation were crucial in determining the worth of writing. The tight-knit nature of literary society meant—for the relatively privileged, at least—that connections and friendships with other writers were both fairly easy to establish and freighted with powerful affective potential. The economic, cultural and personal relationships sustained through such associations had profound implications for the ways in which writers were valued, both within intimate and influential circles and, through collaboration and dissemination, by the expanding literary public.

---

[107] Jacqueline Pearson, *Women's Reading in Britain 1750–1835: A Dangerous Recreation* (Cambridge: Cambridge University Press, 1999), p. 218.

Chapter Three: Succeeding in 'the Worst Trade'

Having considered the limited scope for direct literary profits and the powerful positive and negative affordances of sociable connections in the previous two chapters, it now seems appropriate to examine how a small number of authors were able to build potent literary reputations by paying keen attention to their culture's systems of affiliation and distinction. This chapter explores the circumstances of three of the most prominent poets of the early nineteenth century, all of whom managed to build relatively profitable careers through writing promiscuously and working socially to establish the value of their works and selves. However, all three possessed uncommon advantages. While Robert Southey, Thomas Moore and Felicia Hemans were each the products of unique circumstances, they shared access to networks of influence that let them accrue the time and opportunities necessary to benefit seriously from authorship. I will detail these networks more fully in what follows, but to summarise briefly: in Southey's case, they included his extended family; the friends he made at Westminster and Oxford; radical and intellectual circles in Bristol; the other Lake poets and their associates; John Murray's authors; and the Tory establishment. While at Trinity College Dublin, Moore made connections that brought him into contact with Whiggish aristocrats and literati whose combined influence did a great deal to promote and shape him. Hemans benefitted from the patronage of well-to-do figures in Liverpool

© The Author(s) 2021

M. Sangster, *Living as an Author in the Romantic Period*, Palgrave Studies in the Enlightenment, Romanticism and Cultures of Print, https://doi.org/10.1007/978-3-030-37047-3_5

and the northwest for her initial launch and was keenly aware of the opportunities opened up by new forms of publication, her connections at the English universities, her friends in Edinburgh, rising literary institutions, similarly inclined contemporaries, distinctive female networks and the new reading audiences of the 1820s. While all three authors were highly accomplished, talent alone was nowhere near enough to guarantee a living from literature. Consequently, they had to manage their self-fashionings carefully within the contexts of the rancorous periodical culture, contentious political headwinds and gendered expectations. They also had to remain alert to contemporary circumstances and narrow windows of opportunity. Most writers of the age could appeal eloquently to eternal verities, but only the fleet-footed could strike chords through seeming uniquely timely.

ROBERT SOUTHEY: ENTIRE MAN OF LETTERS?

Robert Southey is a poet who has only recently received renewed critical attention after a long eclipse.[1] His modern advocates have been keen to assert his importance by invoking Byron's description of him as 'the only existing entire man of letters.'[2] However, many accounts have dialled down the significance of the 'only existing' in that characterisation, seeing Southey as ushering in a significant change in literary society. Michael

---

[1] Important scholarly contributions include the meticulous new editions of Southey's poetry comprising *Poetical Works 1793–1810*, gen ed. Lynda Pratt, 5 vols (London: Pickering & Chatto, 2004) and *Later Poetical Works, 1811–1838*, gen. eds. Tim Fulford and Lynda Pratt, 4 vols (London: Pickering & Chatto, 2012); W.A. Speck's excellent biography, *Robert Southey: Entire Man of Letters* (New Haven: Yale University Press, 2006); a significant essay collection, *Robert Southey and the Contexts of English Romanticism*, ed. Lynda Pratt (Aldershot: Ashgate, 2006); and the *Collected Letters of Robert Southey: A Romantic Circles Electronic Edition*, gen. eds. Lynda Pratt, Tim Fulford and Ian Packer, *Romantic Circles*, 2009–, https://romantic-circles.org/editions/southey_letters. The *Collected Letters* will be abbreviated as *CLRS* in the following notes. A fuller survey of the state of Southey scholarship can be found in Tim Fulford and Matthew Sangster, 'Introduction—Southeyan Correspondences', *Romanticism on the Net*, 68–9 (Spring–Fall 2017), https://doi.org/10.7202/1070618ar.

[2] For a time, this quotation featured prominently on the website for the *Collected Letters* project (http://www.nottingham.ac.uk/crc/robert-southey/index.php [accessed 12 Feb 2010]) and it provides the subtitle for W.A. Speck's biography. Both cite from *Robert Southey: The Critical Heritage*, ed. Lionel Madden (London: Routledge & Kegan Paul, 1972), p. 157; Madden himself cites from Byron's journal entry for 22 November 1813 (using R.E. Prothero's edition).

Gamer writes that '[t]he manner in which he conducted his career [...] signals a new era of professional writing—one characterized neither by patronage, nor by venture capitalism, but rather by careful planning and a determination to eliminate unwanted contingencies and turns of fortune.'[3] Having established that 'new forms of professionalism are partially based on the management of risk', Brian Goldberg argues that in Southey's preferred paradigm '[a] poet's encounter with the marketplace would, ideally, be profitable, but an ideology of vocational solidarity would also serve as a new source of status and affiliation transcending birth.'[4] These are fair descriptions of Southey's aspirations, but both critics occlude to some extent the auspicious circumstances that allowed him partly to realise them. By the 1810s, the period on which Gamer's discussion focuses, Southey was able to earn significant sums by carefully husbanding the revenue streams his works provided. However, significant support from friends, family and the government had been instrumental in allowing him to build his reputation to a point where his writing could return substantial profits. While he may have wished for vocational solidarity, this was not strongly evident in the early stages of his writing life, when he relied heavily on the older, more selective and affective grouping practices inherent in coterie writing.[5] He built a relatively secure professional identity for himself, but he did so on a foundation comprised of pre-existing networks of sociable connections, rather than through constructing with other authors a shared model that could easily be duplicated. As late as 1837, in the letter to Charlotte Brontë often rebuked for attempting to check her ambitions, Southey represented his own circumstances as both particular and fortunate: 'I, who have made literature my profession, and devoted my life to it [...] think myself nevertheless bound in duty to caution every young man who applies as an aspirant to me for encouragement and advice, against taking so perilous a course.'[6] While he knew authorship had

---

[3] Michael Gamer, 'Laureate Policy', *The Wordsworth Circle*, 42 (Winter 2011), 42–7 (p. 42).

[4] Brian Goldberg, *The Lake Poets and Professional Identity* (Cambridge: Cambridge University Press, 2007), pp. 21, 194.

[5] See the introduction and the first two chapters of Tim Fulford's *Romantic Poetry and Literary Coteries: The Dialect of the Tribe* (Basingstoke: Palgrave Macmillan, 2015).

[6] Robert Southey to [Charlotte Brontë], March 1837, in *Life and Correspondence of the Late Robert Southey*, ed. Charles Cuthbert Southey, 6 vols (London: Longman, Brown, Green, and Longmans, 1849–50), VI, 328.

worked to his own advantage, Southey was under no illusions that it was a stable career that others might safely bank on pursuing.

Southey's father was a linen draper whose financial circumstances were often shaky and who finally went bankrupt in 1792.[7] While Southey was young, his prosperous relatives helped to support and educate him. Until he reached the age of seven, he lived for the majority of the time with his mother's half-sister, Elizabeth Tyler, in Bath. After an early education at a series of small schools, his uncle Herbert Hill paid his fees for Westminster School, hoping to prepare him for a clerical career. Southey entered Westminster at the age of fourteen and was expelled in his final year for writing an article attacking corporal punishment in a student magazine called *The Flagellant*, which he produced with a group of close friends who would later prove instrumental in facilitating his literary career. Despite his expulsion, he was able to attend university at Oxford, matriculating at Balliol College (his second choice) in November 1792, supported financially by his uncle, his aunt and friends he had made at Westminster. He remained at Oxford until late 1794, often discontent, making a brief resolution to study medicine, aware that his republican sympathies meant that securing a politically dependent appointment was unlikely. In 1794, change came to Southey in the form of Coleridge and their combined scheme to found an egalitarian settlement in America. Inspired, Southey spent most of 1795 in the West Country, collaborating with Coleridge and promoting their scheme, supported partly by his relatives, partly by some small profits from early literary works such as *The Fall of Robespierre* (1794) and *Joan of Arc* (1796), and partly by earnings from schemes such as the public lectures he and Coleridge arranged in Bristol. During this period, money was tight, particularly after Elizabeth Tyler cut off her nephew on hearing of his pantisocratic plans and his engagement to Edith Fricker, a seamstress. When Herbert Hill suggested that he pay for Southey to visit him in Portugal, Southey was therefore happy to oblige. However, he secretly married Edith before leaving Bristol in November 1795, making his commitment to her clear. A year earlier, Southey had written to his brother that 'money is a huge evil with which we shall not have long to encounter', but, despite continuing aid from his relatives, his earnings at this time were not enough to sustain even relatively modest schemes, let

---

[7] My principal source for biographical evidence is Speck unless otherwise indicated.

alone pantisocracy.[8] His being able to operate as a writer was heavily dependent on his being underwritten by family and friends.

Southey's situation improved considerably in 1797, again due to an intervention resulting from a sociable connection. His Westminster contemporary and lifelong friend Charles Watkin Williams Wynn committed to granting him an annuity of '£160 for life, payable quarterly on the 20 of Jan, April, July and October'.[9] Wynn hoped that this money would help Southey fulfil his potential; he thought that a legal career might be a good option for his compatriot, although in practice Southey only gestured in this direction. However, the Wynn annuity was crucial for Southey's developing a literary profile, providing the greater part of his income while he established his reputation. Despite its being a generous sum—not far short of a gentlemanly competence in itself—it was not sufficient to meet Southey's family's needs. Southey's most recent biographer, W.A. Speck, writes that in late 1797

> he was reduced to asking [Joseph] Cottle to lend him ten pounds, explaining that 'my expenses this quarter have exceeded my income'. He was so hard up that he took on a prodigious amount of literary work, reviewing for the *Critical Review* and publishing poems in the *Morning Post*. The *Critical Review* paid him 'at the low rate of three guineas a sheet', though he admitted that 'my work was not worth more. It brought me from £50 to £100 yearly, a very acceptable addition to my straightened income.' 'In 1798 [Daniel] Stuart offered me a guinea a week to supply verses for the *Morning Post*', he was to recall many years later: 'that offer was very acceptable to me & all the pieces which bear date from that time to 1800, when I went for the second time to Portugal, were written under that engagement. About 60 lines a week I thought a fair discharge.'[10]

Even early in his career, Southey was not (and could not be, and perhaps did not wish to be) purely a poet. Instead, he pursued poetry in parallel with a career as a pen-for-hire, heavily subsidised by the Wynn annuity. He relied on his connections with periodicals and composed in a range of modes, including journalism, translation (sometimes unattributed) and travel writing, the latter in the form of his *Letters Written during a Short*

---

[8] Robert Southey to Thomas Southey, 12 October [1794], Letter 106 in *CLRS*, https://romantic-circles.org/editions/southey_letters/Part_One/HTML/letterEEd.26.106.html.

[9] Speck, p. 68.

[10] Speck, p. 71.

Residence in Spain and Portugal (1797), the opportunity for which arose from his uncle's largesse. He continued to work on both lyric and epic poems, the former going to the *Morning Post* to secure small but immediate financial gains, the latter representing his main hope for literary glory. Southey thus faced the same challenges as many aspirant writers—only by continuing to write extensively could he make moderate sums from the publishers. However, Southey had fall-back options unavailable to less well-connected authors. For example, when he travelled to Portugal for the second time in 1800, he received £100 from Peter Elmsley, a Westminster friend who had also helped support his education at Oxford.[11] The ability to solicit a gift of this size, a sum greater than the yearly incomes of many tradesmen, gave Southey a cushion that less fortunate writers lacked. While his pen was the focus of his long-term ambitions, it was selling the image of himself as a productive, valuable and interesting individual to his intimate acquaintances that paid the bulk of Southey's expenses in his twenties. In this respect, we might think of his letters from this period as being ultimately his most remunerative writings, laying the groundwork for the rest of his career.

The income he secured from his family and friends gave Southey a window in which he was able to acquire the contacts and expertise necessary to establish himself without falling too far into debt. In the 1800s, he began to leverage his knowledge, connections and accumulated writings to build a formidable reputation from his new rural base at Greta Hall, where he would work for the best part of the next forty years. His yearly rent, negotiated initially by Coleridge, was £42, a sum that could easily be met out of the Wynn annuity.[12] The relative isolation of the Lakes and the support of his growing family meant that he could pour his attention into a range of literary occupations. As Gamer argues, his main goal was strategically to secure himself against financial failure: 'Rather than writing exclusively in a few given genres [...] Southey diversified, working on multiple projects in a given day on the assumption that each piece of writing might produce a small but consistent stream of income.'[13] He continued to produce a great deal of journalism while he completed *Madoc* (1805), *The Curse of Kehama* (1810) and numerous shorter poems. He undertook

---

[11] Speck, p. 83; Christopher Collard, 'Elmsley, Peter (1774–1825)', *ODNB*, https://doi.org/10.1093/ref:odnb/8737.

[12] Richard Holmes, *Coleridge: Early Visions* (London: Penguin, 1990), p. 278.

[13] Gamer, p. 45.

paid translation work drawing on his Iberian expertise, including a version of Vasco de Lobeira's *Amadis of Gaul*, which was published in 1803 and for which he received £100 for the copyright. He also produced a corrected version of *Palmerin of England* (1807) and his *Chronicle of the Cid* (1808), a complex fusion of several source texts.[14] His enduringly successful *Letters from England* (1807) was another production influenced by his Iberian experiences, which allowed him to assume the guise of a Spaniard, Don Manuel Alvarez Espriella, in order to examine and critique British idiosyncrasies. Although his long-cherished desire to write a history of Portugal was never fully realised, the research he conducted for this project informed a number of other works, notably his *History of Brazil*, the first volume of which was published in 1810. His range of incomes, both earned and secured through patronage, meant that had enough leisure to work on behalf of the family of Henry Kirke White; he edited the poet's *Remains* for publication in 1807, sustaining an interest that had its roots in his work with Joseph Cottle on a posthumous edition of Thomas Chatterton for the benefit the poet's sister.[15] The Henry Kirke White volume was enormously popular—it sold through its first 750-copy edition within a year, was reprinted in larger 1500-copy editions in each of the subsequent three years, and continued to be frequently reprinted after that.[16] That Southey took the time to produce such a work is indicative both of his relative affluence and of his gentlemanly commitment to patronising and promoting good writing by those in less fortunate positions than his own. Projects like the White edition made potent statements to his contemporaries about his good character, influence and credit.

By this point, Southey was able to sustain his family in relative comfort, but he never produced an original sensation that sold quickly to a sizable audience. His epic poems provided him with initially disappointing financial returns—as he wrote to his friend William Taylor in 1806, '"Madoc" is ~~going~~ doing well in all but sale. If you do not know the current value of epic poetry at the present time I can help you to a pretty just estimate. My profits on this poem in the course of twelvemonths amount precisely to

[14] William St Clair, *The Reading Nation in the Romantic Period* (Cambridge: Cambridge University Press, 2004), p. 654.

[15] For more on Southey's engagement with Chatterton's family and with Chatterton's implications for literary men, see Nick Groom, 'Love and Madness: Southey Editing Chatterton', in *Robert Southey and the Contexts of English Romanticism*, pp. 19–35, and Goldberg, pp. 193–214.

[16] St Clair, p. 654.

three pounds, seventeen shillings, & one penny.'[17] He went on jealously to compare his earnings with those of Walter Scott. Southey's letter protests a little too much—the fact that *Madoc* returned any profits at all after the first year meant that it was not a true failure in terms of sales, having sold enough to allow Longmans to recoup their costs. The profits that Southey reaped in subsequent years from the two-guinea quarto were significant, and during the 1810s and 1820s, continuing sales justified several further editions.[18] While the returns that Southey received from his epics were slower than he might have wished, the prudent half-profits arrangements under which they were published meant that he received ongoing remuneration. Collectively, his epics also played a major role in making his reputation as a poet and a scholar, comprising a profitable back catalogue that laid the foundations for his future clout and prosperity.

Nevertheless, during the 1800s, Southey's finances continued to be underpinned by funds sourced by Charles Wynn. In 1807, the original annuity was replaced by a government pension of £200 a year that Wynn procured while serving as part of the Ministry of All the Talents. This income allowed Southey to use parts of his portfolio of literary revenues to guard against unexpected disasters. In 1809, he took out a £1000 life insurance policy to provide for his family in the event of his early death. Tellingly, Speck writes that 'when doing so he had to declare his profession, and found that poet, historian and reviewer were not acceptable legal terms, so had to describe himself as Gentleman'.[19] When Southey was appointed Poet Laureate in 1813, he used his yearly salary to pay the premium on another £3000 policy, hedging against his death in a move that Gamer reads as characteristic:

> whatever the difficulties in reconciling premiums and policies to higher notions of poetic service and fame, Southey never ceases to convert both sets of terms into a single currency, if only to assist him in arriving at the best long-term business decision [...] Robert Southey the writer might die at any time, but Southey Incorporated—consisting not just of his wife and children

[17] Robert Southey to William Taylor [fragment], [c. 23–25 April 1806], Letter 1177 in *CLRS*, https://romantic-circles.org/editions/southey_letters/Part_Three/HTML/letter-EEd.26.1177.html.
[18] St Clair, p. 653.
[19] Speck, p. 136.

but also his two sisters-in-law and their progeny—might continue, as planned, with confident assurance.[20]

Gamer here clarifies one of the reasons why Southey sits uncomfortably within later Romantic models of poetic genius. Unlike Wordsworth or Coleridge in their more militant moods, Southey did not really argue for a conceptual separation between the inspired poet and the crassnesses of market society. Instead, he saw his career as an endeavour that must produce both economic and reputational currency and that provided situations in which one might be leveraged to secure the other. As Gamer puts it, he was 'a poet who wrote poetry *before* breakfast in order not to impinge on the scheduled hours after breakfast devoted to writing books and articles that paid.'[21] Southey's success in this project reveals a good deal about the lack of currency of Romantic ideologies within what has come to be termed the Romantic period. While Wordsworth and Coleridge won out in the eyes of posterity, during the 1800s and 1810s, Southey's works were far more lucrative and enjoyed considerably larger readerships. Wordsworth and Coleridge sought to change the rules that governed authorship, but Southey was a far more effective operator within the systems current at the time.

Southey's audiences and remuneration were both hugely increased by his connection with John Murray's *Quarterly Review*. Southey had refused an offer to write for the *Edinburgh* in 1807, antagonised by its politics and by Francis Jeffrey's attacks on the Lake School.[22] The *Edinburgh*'s minimum remuneration of ten guineas a sheet would have been welcome—it was more than three times what the *Critical* paid him. However, by sticking to his principles, Southey made himself an ideal candidate to write for Murray's opposing publication. Scott, a key mover in the new enterprise, consequently recruited Southey for the first issue. Southey's spirited, popular and often aggressive reviews played a major role in defining the *Quarterly*. The *Quarterly Review Archive* attributes fifty-six articles wholly or partly to Southey between 1809 and 1824, indicating that he wrote almost as many articles in that period as there were issues.[23] At times, he

---

[20] Gamer, pp. 46–7.

[21] Gamer, p. 45.

[22] I discuss Jeffrey's responses to Southey in Chapter Five.

[23] See the *Quarterly Review Archive*, ed. Jonathan Cutmore, *Romantic Circles*, 2005, https://romantic-circles.org/reference/qr/index/01.html.

clashed with Murray and with the *Quarterly's* editor, William Gifford, who regularly modified his contributions. In his first article, on the Baptists, Gifford 'excised any indication of indifference to theological orthodoxy, and Southey was furious when he saw how cruelly his article had been mutilated.'[24] However, the sting was lessened by his receiving £21.13s for his work, 'better pay than I ever yet received for any former occupation', as he noted in a letter to his uncle.[25] As Southey's importance to the *Quarterly* became apparent, Murray began to offer him '100£ per piece', pay that Southey rightly considered 'very liberal'.[26] As his views became more closely aligned with those of his Tory associates, he was entrusted with key articles, allowed considerable latitude in what he chose to review and permitted to call on Murray for the books he needed to prepare his critiques—a considerable bonus for a noted bibliophile.

Southey also accrued several other reputational benefits from his association with Murray's journal, benefits augured by the first issue containing a glowing review by Scott of his *Chronicle of the Cid*.[27] On some occasions, Southey was able directly to select his reviewers. *Roderick, the Last of the Goths* (1814) was assessed by his school friend Grosvenor Charles Bedford. When Murray expressed doubts about this, Gifford wrote to him that 'Bedford was not selected by me […] He was fixed upon by Southey'. Having received Bedford's copy, Gifford felt it impolitic greatly to change it, despite his own reservations, writing that 'the difficulty with me is Southey. He entertains a very high opinion of his friend's talents, as he shewed by employing him & he has seen & approved the critique […] he is after all the sheet anchor of the Revw & should not be lightly hurt.'[28] Southey's connection with the *Quarterly* thus gave him considerable power to shape the ways in which he was perceived by others while also allowing him to dispense literary patronage to friends and fam-

---

[24] Geoffrey Carnall, 'Southey, Robert (1774–1843)', *ODNB*, https://doi.org/10.1093/ref:odnb/26056.

[25] Robert Southey to Herbert Hill, 8 March 1809. Letter 1596 in *CLRS*, https://romantic-circles.org/editions/southey_letters/Part_Three/HTML/letterEEd.26.1596.html.

[26] Rates discussed in Robert Southey to John Murray, 7 October 1818, in Letters from Southey 1813–1818, NLS Ms.42551, but instituted earlier—see Southey to Murray, 17 Nov 1816 (in the same folder).

[27] [Walter Scott], 'Chronicle of the Cid', *Quarterly Review*, 1 (February 1809), 134–53.

[28] William Gifford to John Murray, letters dated [1814] and 28 January 1815, *Quarterly Review Archive*, ed. Jonathan Cutmore, *Romantic Circles*, 2005, https://romantic-circles.org/reference/qr/index/25.html.

ily. Both quarterly Reviews falsely affected to be above puffing, but for their key associates they offered unprecedented opportunities for shaping receptions and reputations.[29]

The opportunities that the *Quarterly* presented came at a fortunate time for Southey, as he had grown tired of producing poetry. Writing to Gifford on the publication of *Roderick*, he described himself as 'poor enough to need its success,—but far too proud to feel either disappointment or mortification at its failure.' He no longer felt fully engaged with the processes of poetic creation: 'My bolt is shot, at my age the faculties of the mind are mature, & tho' not yet tending upon decay, I suspect in myself a lack of enterprize which would not have been felt a few years ago.'[30] David Craig has described how later in his career Southey enjoyed poetry 'more as a private hobby than a public vocation', preferring to take up cudgels as a periodical moralist to earn his income.[31] In a complementary essay, Mark Storey has traced numerous iterations of Southey's complaints against poetry, making clear his concern that its composition excited him 'more than it is desirable to be excited.'[32] For Southey, there was something uncomfortably revealing about the emotional aspects of versifying, and this led him increasingly to spend his time on endeavours that were more obviously profitable and less challenging to his subjectivity. Storey traces his movement, against the grain of later disciplinary developments, from writing verse that at its best manifests a 'quiet, public intimacy' to producing grander histories. This, Southey contended, was based on 'a conviction in my own mind that I shall ultimately hold a higher place

---

[29] See also Chapter Five and Coleridge's approaches to Jeffrey regarding reviewing Thomas Clarkson in the *Edinburgh*, discussed in my article '"You have not advertised out of it": Samuel Taylor Coleridge and Francis Jeffrey on Authorship, Networks and Personalities', *Romanticism and Victorianism on the Net*, 61 (April 2012), https://doi.org/10.7202/1018602ar. Publishers often successfully solicited reviewers for favoured authors. Longmans, 'deeply interested in the success of Moore's Lalla Rookh', wrote to the Reverend William Shepherd suggesting that he write for the *Quarterly* 'a pretty full review of the work', assuring him that 'we shall be most happy to remunerate you liberally'. See Longmans to William Shepherd, 17 November 1817, Longman Outletter Book, 8 July 1816–26 May 1818, transcribed Michael Bott, URSC 1393 Part I.100, Letter 173.

[30] Robert Southey to William Gifford, 25 November 1814, extracted in John Murray Letter Book, 2 April 1808–13 March 1843, NLS Ms. 41909, fol. 3ᵛ (incoming side).

[31] David M. Craig, 'Subservient Talents? Robert Southey as Public Moralist', in *Robert Southey and the Contexts of English Romanticism*, pp. 101–14 (p. 103).

[32] Mark Storey, '"Bob Southey!—Poet Laureate": Public and Private in Southey's Poems of 1816', in *Robert Southey and the Contexts of English Romanticism*, pp. 87–100 (p. 90).

among historians [...] than among poets.'[33] However, Southey's view of poetry was from an early stage deeply historical. David Fairer writes that he was 'acutely conscious of the many tracings and retracings of literary history, and he continued to associate the formation of his own character with the character of the nation's poetry.'[34] It is not a huge leap from the fanciful but carefully-constructed poetic histories in Southey's epics to his later historical writing, and it is one that publishers' inducements and Southey's increasing mastery of political and historical contexts made very attractive.

Southey's transitions from newspaper verse to politicised *Quarterly* reviewing and from epics to histories worked out very well for Murray, who published most of Southey's later prose works, effectively poaching his productivity from Longmans, who published his poetry. Southey's later books were regularly developed from ideas rehearsed in his *Quarterly* articles, often at Murray's instigation or with his encouragement. One of Southey's most enduring productions had its kernel in a review he wrote attacking an old rival, James Stanier Clarke. Southey had described Clarke's *Progress of Maritime Discovery* (1803) as a 'national disgrace' in the *Annual Review*; Clarke had responded by savaging *Madoc* in the *Monthly*.[35] Southey struck again by rubbishing Clarke's *Nelson* (1809) in the *Quarterly* and Murray, sensing an opportunity, was keen to see the review expanded, writing to Southey that he felt that Nelson's life was

> so noble a subject for you, in every respect, that I wish it to receive all your care, and a good portion of what Turner calls the "prime" of your mind [...] I wish it to be made such a book as will become the heroic text of every midshipman in the navy.—& the association of Nelson and Southey will not I think be ungrateful to you—if it be worth your attention in this way, I am disposed to think that it will enable me to trebble the sum I first offered as a slight remuneration [...] you will of course omit totally all criticism on Clarke &c. &—I wish to make the price of the volume—one Dollar![36]

[33] Storey, pp. 100, 91.

[34] David Fairer, 'Southey's Literary History', in *Robert Southey and the Contexts of English Romanticism*, pp. 1–17 (p. 17).

[35] Speck, p. 106, 137.

[36] John Murray to Robert Southey, 28 October 1811, in Murray Letter Book, NLS Ms. 41909, fol. 17ʳ (outgoing side).

Murray here demonstrates a number of strategies for persuading Southey—flattering him, appealing to his patriotism in time of war, speaking of his own large ambitions for the work, offering financial inducements and hinting at his willingness to adopt a pricing scheme that might produce further profits. He slips in his instruction about Clarke in the middle of a sentence, deemphasising it to forestall Southey's potential objections. Murray thus played on Southey's desire to accumulate connections, prestige and income, selling Southey his own sense of the benefits the book would provide. His canny calculations were correct—the book sold in large quantities and has remained in print almost continuously since its publication. The *Life of Nelson* was the first of several historical works that Southey produced for Murray. In 1813, having consulted with Gifford, Murray offered Southey a thousand guineas for a work on the Peninsular War 'a subject in every way worthy of you, & one upon which we both feel that you should raise up as one of the pillars of your Fame.' He agreed to provide the best 'portraits, plans & views' if the text 'be finished before we begin to print.'[37] Southey agreed to this plan and poured a great deal of time into the work, although unfortunately for both parties, Murray's hint about rewards for speed went unheeded. Southey's painstaking research for this long, bookish project meant that it emerged belatedly in three volumes between 1823 and 1832, to mixed reviews.

The influence that Murray and the *Quarterly* had on Southey's writing practices made him uncomfortable at various points during the relationship. He expressed his discontent to Murray in October 1818, contending that

> the price which I receive for my writings is by no means a matter of indifference to me, but it can make no difference in the manner of my writing. The same diligence, the same desire,—& the same power (whatever that may be) were brought to the task when you paid me ten guineas per sheet, as when you raised it to 100£ per piece. This last is a great price, & it is very convenient for me to receive it. But I will tell you with that frankness which you have always found in my correspondence & conversation that I suspect my time might be more profitably employed (as I am sure it might be more worthily) than writing for your Journal even at that price.[38]

---

[37] John Murray to Robert Southey, 16 July 1813, in Letters from Southey 1813–1818, NLS Ms.42551.

[38] Robert Southey to John Murray, 7 October 1818, in Letters from Southey 1813–1818, NLS Ms.42551.

At this moment and at other times, Southey sought anxiously to assert his independence by claiming that the lavish payments Murray offered had no effect on what he chose to write while also, contrariwise, arguing that he should cut back on his *Quarterly* work because it might not be the most profitable use of his time. As this contradiction implies, his assessment of his *Quarterly* work as poor value was principally rhetorical, ostensibly designed to remind Murray of his importance, but also covertly expressing his discomfort at the balance of power between the two men. Southey was deeply conflicted about his reliance on Murray, complaining a great deal about him in his private correspondence. In 1816, he noted to Grosvenor Bedford that 'Lord Byron calls him the Grand Murray' and he took to doing so himself, describing Murray facetiously as 'the very grandest personage among mankind, now that there is no longer a Grand Mogul'.[39] In 1818, he came up with a new title, 'Murraymagne', opining that 'so great a man deserves to have his greatness incorporated with his name like Charlemagne'.[40] However, even when Southey declared in exasperation that Murray's letters were 'as coxcombical as need he be, as booksellerish as can be', he found 'mixed with all this [...] good sense.'[41] In pursuing a career as a writer, Southey had come to be pragmatic, and while he sought to maintain his gentlemanly superiority over his publisher in front of his friends, he recognised both the value of Murray's expertise and the mutual benefits that resulted from their connection, which endured despite Southey's occasional performative qualms. When Murray wrote to John Gibson Lockhart in April 1829, worried about declining circulation, his main hope for boosting the sales of the next issue was that 'chance might cast upon an interesting article, or two from Sir Walter, & Southey' and he listed two Southey articles in his prospective contents list.[42] Southey

[39] Robert Southey to Grosvenor Charles Bedford, 31 August 1816, Letter 2833 in *CLRS*, https://romantic-circles.org/editions/southey_letters/Part_Five/HTML/letter-EEd.26.2833.html; Robert Southey to Herbert Hill, 18 September 1818, Letter 3195 in *CLRS*, https://romantic-circles.org/editions/southey_letters/Part_Five/HTML/letter-EEd.26.3195.html.

[40] Robert Southey to Henry Herbert Southey, 7 February 1818, Letter 3074 in *CLRS*, https://romantic-circles.org/editions/southey_letters/Part_Five/HTML/letter-EEd.26.3074.html.

[41] Robert Southey to Grosvenor Charles Bedford, 3 February 1815, Letter 2548 in *CLRS*, https://romantic-circles.org/editions/southey_letters/Part_Four/HTML/letter-EEd.26.2548.html.

[42] John Murray to John Gibson Lockhart, 3 April 1829, in Murray Letter Book, NLS Ms. 41909, fols. 42ʳ–43ʳ (outgoing side).

continued reviewing for the *Quarterly* well into the 1830s, his concerns lulled by Murray's generosity and the influence that reviewing allowed him to wield.

In his later career, Southey kept up a constant stream of book-length productions, principally in prose rather than in verse. These included his *Life of Wesley* (1820), his long-planned and profitable *Book of the Church* (1824) and his biographical writings for editions of John Bunyan's *Pilgrim's Progress* (1830) and William Cowper's *Works* (1835–1836). In such productions, he positioned himself as a critical commentator on religious and political issues and indulged his ongoing interest in curating Britain's literary heritage while writing himself into it. Perhaps his strangest late production to modern eyes was *Sir Thomas More, or, Colloquies on the Progress and Prospects of Society* (1829), a series of dialogues in which the shade of More debates with Montesinos, a version of the younger Southey. In these dialogues, the Laureate reprimanded his own youthful utopianism while decrying exploitative manufacturing practices, arguing that workers' financial and cultural poverty must be alleviated within the system to which Southey was habituated in order to prevent damaging class warfare.[43] Thomas Babington Macaulay, reviewing the book in the *Edinburgh Review* 'observed with great regret the strange infatuation which leads the Poet-laureate to abandon those departments of literature in which he might excel, and to lecture the public on sciences of which he has still the very alphabet to learn.'[44] By contrast, the leading article in the *Quarterly* puffed the work as 'a beautiful book, full of poetry and feeling' and argued that Southey was entirely correct to 'point out [...] the gangrene which is creeping through the land, and the quickening spirit which alone can stay its progress.'[45] This division is indicative of the view of Southey that his reviews and histories had promoted: that of his being 'the most powerful literary supporter of the Tories in the present day'.[46] However, Macaulay's comment is also symptomatic of the shift in the 1820s away from the sociable literary world in which Southey had shaped his career as a talented generalist. As Philip Connell has shown, Macaulay judged Southey 'ignorant of the true principles of economic science' and

---

[43] For a fuller exploration, see Philip Connell, *Romanticism, Economics, and the Question of 'Culture'* (Oxford: Oxford University Press, 2001), pp. 258–65.

[44] [Thomas Babington Macaulay], 'Southey's *Colloquies on Society*', *Edinburgh Review*, 50 (January 1830), 528–65 (p. 528).

[45] 'Southey's *Colloquies*', *Quarterly Review*, 41 (July 1829), 1–27 (pp. 1, 25).

[46] William Lowther, Viscount Lowther, quoted in Speck, p. 284.

thus insufficiently qualified to comment on matters that were properly the preserve of specialists in the increasingly professional discipline of political economy.[47] Ironically, the poetry that Southey had largely left behind now served to define him, while his having moved away from it left him a transitional figure, caught between an emergent literary professionalism manifested in the younger generation of periodical writers and novelists and the countervailing paradigm of Romantic poetic genius. The diverse abilities that had allowed Southey to prosper in the 1800s and 1810s thus came to count against him in the context of the segmented and institutionalised literary culture that emerged during the second quarter of the nineteenth century.

However, this is not to say that Southey's works had no enduring influence. As Raymond Williams noted, his ideas played crucial roles in the formations of nineteenth-century conservatism, the Young England movement and the notion that culture could successfully oppose industrial alienation.[48] By the 1830s, Southey was one of the establishment's most notable grey eminences and a prominent public intellectual. His exertions received their crowning temporal recognition in 1835 when Robert Peel offered him a baronetcy, which Southey cannily refused 'on the grounds that he could not sustain the dignity of the title'.[49] This caused Peel to replace his initial offer with a £300-a-year pension. Southey took advantage of this new source of income by ceasing to review. He subsequently used his time to work on his cherished incomplete histories and his fascinating and digressive novel/miscellany/philosophy-of-life *The Doctor, &c.* until his writing was finally halted by the failure of his mind in 1839.

When Southey wrote to John Murray in 1812 about reviewing D'Israeli's *Calamities of Authors*, he included a sunny examination of his own literary life to contrast with D'Israeli's grim vignettes. While he considered literature generally to be 'the worst trade to which a man can possibly betake himself', he asserted that he had 'never regretted [his] choice':

> The usual censure ridicule & even calumnies which it has drawn upon me never gave me a moments pain,—but on the other hand literature has given me friends among the best & wisest & most celebrated of my contemporaries it has given me distinction,—if I live twenty years longer I do not

[47] Connell, p. 9.
[48] Raymond Williams, *Culture and Society 1780–1950* (London: Penguin, 1961), p. 40.
[49] Quoted in Speck, p. 229.

doubt that it will give me fortune, & if it pleases God to take me before my family are provided for, I doubt as little that in my names & in my works they will find a provision.[50]

Southey puffs himself a little in this letter, as he was accustomed to do, but his prognosis was largely accurate. Although he glosses over the considerable advantages that he gained from his connections during the early years of his literary career—stating that literature had given him friends while not acknowledging that his friends had also given him the ability to pursue literature—he was right to assert that by the 1810s he had built a profile sufficient to support both his own family and Coleridge's. However, even the most successful literary careers could be dangerously unstable. Southey worked hard to achieve his profile, but his finances were stretched at times even after he had secured numerous income streams. When his son Herbert died in 1816, he had to ask Grosvenor Bedford to pay the funeral expenses, and as late as 1827 disruptions to his periodical incomes could leave him 'desperately short of money'.[51] It took a combination of literary connections, patronage incomes, understanding friends and accrued value to his publishers to create Southey's particular brand of professionalism, and it was just that: an inimitable and somewhat unstable brand, not a formula that Southey could easily pass on to the many aspiring authors who wrote to him asking how they could best pursue literary careers.[52]

Lynda Pratt has argued that after his death '[Southey's] reputation was entangled [...] in both the complex web of family feuds and the politics of romantic literary criticism', causing his works to fall 'into textual disrepair and critical ignominy.'[53] While he hoped that his long poems and histories would guarantee his immortality, the increasing prominence of lyric poetry and developments in historiographic practices during the nineteenth century meant that, in H.J. Jackson's words, 'both his intense desire for literary immortality and his program for achieving it [...] proved in the long

---

[50] Robert Southey to John Murray, 14 August 1812, in Letters from Southey, 1808–1812, NLS Ms.42550. Letter 2135 in *CLRS*.

[51] Speck, pp. 167, 203.

[52] As previously mentioned, the most famous of these was Charlotte Brontë, but see also Dennis Low's accounts of Southey's mentoring Caroline Bowles, Maria Gowen Brooks and others in *The Literary Protégées of the Lake Poets* (Aldershot: Ashgate, 2006).

[53] Lynda Pratt, 'Family Misfortunes?: The Posthumous Editing of Robert Southey', in *Robert Southey and the Contexts of English Romanticism*, pp. 219–38 (p. 238).

run to be counterproductive.'[54] Southey built his career as a necessarily diverse writer, subsidising his poetry and histories through piecework, periodical journalism, editing, fixed-rate translation and social commentary. Unfortunately for his posthumous reputation, the breadth of his literary experience counted for little once time had stripped away the immediate relevance of his political works and seen much of his non-fiction superseded. The care that he took in planning his working life worked against him when the paradigms that his fellow Lakers had promoted were taken up. Neither uncomplicatedly professional nor securely Romantic, he became and remains an uncomfortable prospect for later systems of being writerly. For this reason, among many others, he is a crucial figure for understanding the scope and nature of early-nineteenth-century print culture, as the rich veins of interest and opinion being recovered in the ongoing twenty-first-century republications of his writings demonstrate.

THOMAS MOORE AND SOCIABLE AUTHORSHIP

In terms of the sources of his income, Thomas Moore has a rather better claim to having lived purely by the pen than Southey does, although this was by no means his intention. He operated in a manner that differed considerably from Southey's, relying to an even greater extent on cultivating powerful connections and a personal myth. While Southey structured his working life by corresponding carefully from his library at Keswick, Moore operated as a metropolitan man of fashion. Sociable, affable and somewhat chaotic, his career was based more on his keen eye for opportunities than on long-term planning, although he could be a patient and assiduous worker both in his poetry and his relationships with others.

Moore's modern critical stock is relatively low. In *England in 1819*, James Chandler asserts that 'there may well be no British writer of the period who has fallen so dramatically in reputation'; tellingly, he uses Moore as 'a kind of "mediocre hero" of the sort we find in the new historical novels of the post-Waterloo period'.[55] Moore has, however, been the subject of two substantial biographies in recent years, and a rising number of new studies and articles convincingly locate him at the centre

---

[54] H.J. Jackson, *Those Who Write for Immortality: Romantic Reputations and the Dream of Lasting Fame* (New Haven & London: Yale University Press, 2015), p. 59.

[55] James Chandler, *England in 1819* (Chicago: University of Chicago Press, 1998), pp. 267, xvii.

of the period's political and literary world, seeing him as a key mediator and disseminator of national and cultural identities.[56] These kinds of attention respond to the nature of Moore's existence as an author, high-lighting the associations and the love of company that were major con-tributors to his prosperity.

A couple of brief characterisations will help to demonstrate Moore's particular manner of being writerly. His biographer Ronan Kelly quotes an anecdote of Edmund Gosse's that comprises a story Gosse had been told by Richard Henry Horne:

> Horne met Moore one evening at the Leigh Hunts', Wordsworth being also present. Moore sang some of his own songs at Mrs Hunt's piano, and was much complimented. Wordsworth was asked if he also did not admire these songs, and he replied: 'Oh! yes, my friend Mr. Moore has written a great deal of agreeable verse, although we should hardly call it *poetry*, should we, Mr Moore?' to which the bard of Erin, sparkling with good nature, answered, 'No! Indeed, Mr. Wordsworth, of course not!' without exhibiting the slight-est resentment.[57]

This meeting, supposed to have taken place in 1835, was a gathering of an older literary generation at a time when Wordsworth's critical star was in the ascendant (not before time, in his own opinion). Moore, a beloved figure by this point in his career, is depicted as performing with typical grace, both literally on Marianne Hunt's piano and socially in terms of his response to Wordsworth's rude dismissal. In this anecdote, Moore is a man eager to please, a man who brightens up a party in a manner that contrasts markedly with Wordsworth's sublime social awkwardness. He

---

[56] The biographies are Linda Kelly's *Ireland's Minstrel: A Life of Thomas Moore: Poet, Patriot and Byron's Friend* (London: I.B. Tauris, 2006) and Ronan Kelly's *Bard of Erin: The Life of Thomas Moore* (London: Penguin, 2009); these are my points of reference for biographical details unless other works are cited. Mohammed Sharafuddin's *Islam and Romantic Orientalism* (London: I.B. Tauris, 1994) discusses representations of the Orient in Moore's *Lalla Rookh*. Leith Davis's *Music, Postcolonialism, and Gender: The Construction of Irish National Identity, 1724–1874* (Notre Dame, IN: University of Notre Dame Press, 2006) considers Moore's patri-otic works and his formative role in the creation of modern Irish identities. Jane Moore has published fascinating articles on Moore as patriot, humourist and traveller, as well as an excel-lent edition of his satires. Interesting new perspectives on Moore, including accounts of pio-neering digital projects, can be found in Francesca Benatti, Sean Ryder and Justin Tonra (eds.), *Thomas Moore: Texts, Contexts, Hypertext* (Oxford: Peter Lang, 2013).

[57] Ronan Kelly, p. 513.

asserts himself through finding an appropriate place within society from which to present his works, not through promoting himself as a haughty, obdurate genius.

In *The Spirit of the Age* (1825), Hazlitt opined that Moore tended to write 'the poetry of the bath, of the toilette, of the saloon, of the fashionable world; not the poetry of nature, of the heart, or of human life.'[58] Like Gosse's anecdote, Hazlitt depicts Moore as Wordsworth's opposite, seeing the nature of the poet reflected in his verse's fashionable affability:

> Mr. Moore is in private life an amiable and estimable man. The embellished and voluptuous style of his poetry, his unpretending origin and his *mignon* figure, soon introduced him to the notice of the great, and his gaiety, his wit, his good-humour, and many agreeable accomplishments fixed him there, the darling of his friends and the idol of fashion.[59]

Lest this assessment be thought wholly positive, Hazlitt adds that Moore was perhaps too 'accustomed to the society of Whig Lords', too 'enchanted with the smile of beauty'. In questioning Moore's conduct, he asks, '[b]ecause he is genteel and sarcastic, may not others be paradoxical and argumentative?'[60] For the prickly Hazlitt, as for later readers searching for radical spirits, Moore's willingness to accommodate can sometimes be off-putting. The care he took in making himself pleasing to contemporary reading audiences and to high society meant that as literary preferences changed and that society slipped away, aspects of his works lost their pertinency. Nevertheless, dismissing him occludes both the centrality his works to the literary culture of his age and the very real zest, interest and bite of many of his productions.

Like Southey, Moore was the son of a tradesman. He was educated in Dublin's leading grammar school by Samuel Whyte, who encouraged his theatrical and literary interests, providing exactly the sort of belletristic education that the founder of the Literary Fund, David Williams, thought potentially deceptive and dangerous.[61] Moore's family were Catholics; consequently, he was only able to enter Trinity College Dublin in 1795

---

[58] William Hazlitt, 'Mr. T. Moore—Mr. Leigh Hunt', in *The Spirit of the Age*, in *The Complete Works of William Hazlitt*, ed. P.P. Howe, 21 vols (London: J.M. Dent, 1930–34), XI, 169–78 (p. 170).

[59] Hazlitt, XI, 175.

[60] Hazlitt, XI, 175, 176.

[61] I discuss Williams' view on literary education in Chapter Four.

due to the war with France, which had occasioned the lifting of discriminatory penal laws in order to ease tensions within the British Isles. At Trinity, Moore acquired sound groundings in classical languages and patriotic politics before taking his degree in the spring of 1799. While he was recognised as an accomplished young man, he was not as fortunate as Southey and did not make friends who were prepared to support him financially. Like Southey, the Inns of Court were seen as a viable professional destination, and with much scrimping, his family saved enough to pay for his entry into the Middle Temple. However, rather than seriously pursuing his legal studies, Moore used his metropolitan position to write and network. An early London acquaintance, Joseph Atkinson, a politician and amateur dramatist, engineered Moore's introduction to Francis Rawdon, the Earl of Moira, an influential Whig magnate. Moira's closeness with the Prince of Wales was expected to bear fruit, but it was a costly association, exacerbated by the fact that Moira was 'habitually extravagant, generous, and hospitable, and spent beyond his large income.'[62] Moore's long-term financial hopes of the man who became his first patron came to little, but he was able to exploit the connection to get permission to dedicate his first book, the *Odes of Anacreon* (1800), to the Prince of Wales, who headed an impressive sixteen-page subscription list that also included 'two dukes, sixteen earls, nine viscounts and a descending array of lesser nobility.'[63] Moore's publisher, John Stockdale of Piccadilly, was unwilling to make an advance payment to an unknown writer and left much of the work of selling the book to its author. Fortunately, Moore proved to be an extremely able self-promoter. The *Anacreon* volume, initially published as a handsome quarto with generously spaced text and copious learned notes, was an immediate success.

In the *Odes*, Moore contains sensuous poetry within a dense farrago of narratorial masks and scholarly notes, a form of paratextual play that he employed frequently during his later career. In his introductory remarks, he argues that Anacreon's soul 'speaks so unequivocally through his odes' that 'we find him there the elegant voluptuary, diffusing the seductive charm of sentiment over passions and propensities at which rigid morality

---

[62] Roland Thorne, 'Hastings, Francis Rawdon (1754–1826)', *ODNB*, https://doi.org/10.1093/ref:odnb/12568.

[63] Linda Kelly, p. 37.

might frown.'[64] This statement says as much about Moore as it does about Anacreon, Moore having expertly folded his own poetic persona into the ancient poet's, as he also does in his elegant translation of Anacreon's 'Ode XXII':

> THE Phrygian Rock, that braves the storm,
> Was once a weeping matron's form—
> And Progne, hapless, frantic maid,
> Is now a swallow in the shade.
> Oh! that a mirror's form was mine,
> To sparkle with that smile divine;
> And like my heart then I should be,
> Reflecting thee, and only thee!
> Or were I love, the robe which flows
> O'er every charm that secret glows,
> In many a lucid fold to swim,
> And cling and grow to every limb!
> Oh! could I, as the streamlet's wave,
> Thy warmly-mellowing beauties lave,
> Or float as perfume on thine hair,
> And breathe my soul in fragrance there!
> I wish I were the zone, that lies
> Warm to thy breast, and feels it's sighs;
> Or like the envious pearls that show
> So faintly round that neck of snow,
> Yes—I would be a happy gem,
> Like them to hang, to fade like them;
> What more would thy Anacreon be?
> Oh! Any thing that touches thee.
> Nay, sandals for those airy feet—
> Thus to be press'd by thee were sweet![65]

This ode exemplifies Moore's early strengths as a poet—an easy and fluent way with line and rhythm, a richness of language combined with clarity of expression, and a suggestiveness quite outré for his increasingly conservative age. By contrast with the lush verse, many of his notes are ostensibly starchy—in the introduction, he quotes an extensive list of editions and

---

[64] Thomas Moore, *Odes of Anacreon, translated into English verse, with Notes* (London: John Stockdale, 1800), pp. 10–11.
[65] Moore, *Anacreon*, pp. 92–6.

translations he has consulted and in the body of the book more than half of each page is regularly taken up with citations and samples of poetry influenced by Anacreon. However, some notes define a more lyrical agenda. Moore part-rebuts John Ogilvie's accusation that 'Ode XXII' 'is meer sport and wantonness' by asserting 'it is the wantonness however of a very graceful Muse', playing off Ogilvie to position the poems as beautiful and daring.[66] The Provost of Trinity, John Kearney, who read the paraphrases when they were submitted for a competition, remarked that '[t]he young people will like it', and in his notes Moore often seems to be appealing to a high-spirited audience by winking through his academic mask.[67] He glosses 'zone' in 'Ode XXII' as 'a ribband, or band, called by the Romans fascia and strophium, which the women wore for the purpose of restraining the exuberance of the bosom', running the technical explanation into a half-lush, half-prudish definition which seems far more in sympathy with the lush side.[68] Invoking the motif of the zone again in a defence that applies just as well to his own methods as to his source's, Moore writes that 'our poet was amiable; his morality was relaxed, but not abandoned; and virtue, with her zone loosened, may be an emblem of the character of Anacreon.'[69] He thus attempts a delicate balancing act, positioning himself as morally relaxed enough to be novel while not being quite indecent enough to deserve censure. This strategy was relatively successful for the *Odes* and for his subsequent *Poetical Works of the Late Thomas Little Esq.* (1801), in which he published more obviously risqué original material masked by a Chatterton-like deceased persona and employing paratextual techniques that Justin Tonra has accurately described as displaying 'overlapping irony and sincerity'.[70] Both books sold well and brought him acclaim.

The most significant advantage that Moore gained from his early publications was his entry into Whiggish high society, a set he associated with for the rest of his life and which did a great deal to assist him both financially and in reputational terms. However, establishing himself in this select milieu was expensive. In a letter to his mother, he wrote that before

[66] Moore, *Anacreon*, p. 92. Ogilvie's opinion was expressed in his 'Essay on the Lyric Poetry of the Ancients' printed with his *Poems on Several Subjects* (London: G. Keith, 1762).

[67] Quoted in Linda Kelly, p. 37.

[68] Moore, *Anacreon*, p. 95.

[69] Moore, *Anacreon*, p. 11.

[70] Justin Tonra, 'Masks of Refinement: Pseudonym, Paratext, and Authorship in the Early Poetry of Thomas Moore', *European Romantic Review*, 25:5 (2014), 551–73 (p. 566).

his introduction to the Prince of Wales he had needed to acquire a new coat, which he got 'in a very economical plan, by giving two guineas and an *old coat*, whereas the usual price of a coat here is near four pounds'.[71] He noted in the same letter that he was still in debt to another tailor. The costs of living and being seen in London meant that the payments Moore received for his works were quickly depleted, a situation not helped by his limited financial acumen. Contrary to Chandler's assertion that he was 'a shrewd entrepreneur', Linda Kelly gives the following bald précis of Moore's early dealings with the book trade:[72]

> From the first he seems to have been a hopeless businessman. He had sold the copyright of *Anacreon* in order to repay a debt of £70 to his friend [Thomas] Hume for the expenses involved in launching it; since the poems […] ran into nine editions, he was certainly the loser by the bargain. He had transferred to a new publisher, James Carpenter, for the poems of Thomas Little, and having been encouraged to draw on him for expenses was dismayed to find himself in debt for £60. The publisher obligingly suggested that he should clear it by selling him the copyright of Little's poems, which Moore, in his innocence, was happy to do. Carpenter admitted some years later that he was still making £200 a year on the poems.[73]

Considered retrospectively, Moore's decisions look rather foolish. However, in context, they represent part of a reasoned strategy. Rather than accruing a series of ongoing half-profits arrangements, as Southey did, Moore sold his copyrights for short-term gains in order to promote himself to those who might provide him with a sinecure or position that would keep him secure in the long term. Instead of trying to be any kind of businessman, Moore was seeking to establish himself as a bright young talent for whom a suitable post should be found. He sought ready cash from his publisher in order to maintain his credit and creditability until one of his patrons was able to act on his behalf. This was not necessarily a foolish strategy; numerous writers successfully leveraged their reputations to gain administrative or clerical appointments. However, in Moore's case, things did not work out quite as well as he had hoped. His expectations were raised in 1803 when Moira acquired for him a potentially lucrative post as registrar to the Naval Prize Court in Bermuda. Moore uprooted

---

[71] Linda Kelly, p. 39.
[72] Chandler, p. 268.
[73] Linda Kelly, p. 46.

himself, took loans and sold many of his possessions in order to fund his journey. Unfortunately, by the time he assumed the post, French maritime commerce had largely been extinguished and Moore's profits from commissions on prizes were almost non-existent, as were his duties. He duly appointed a deputy and returned to England in April 1804 via the United States and Canada, taking the opportunity while travelling to perform and gather materials for topical and topographical verse. Disappointed in his immediate hopes for a lucrative place, he struggled to make ends meet throughout the 1800s, relying on friends and on payments for the copyrights of works and poems contributed (often anonymously) to the newspapers.

In the middle of the decade, Moore's prospects were thrown into doubt by attacks on the morality of his productions. In December 1802, Coleridge refused to contribute to an anthology that included a poem by Moore, grouping his work with Matthew Lewis's *The Monk* and arguing that Moore's and Lewis's names were 'those of men, who have sold provocatives to vulgar Debauchees, & vicious School boys'.[74] Coleridge's private communications were indicative of a censorious reaction against Moore that found potent public expression in Francis Jeffrey's review of *Epistles, Odes, and Other Poems* (1806). While allowing that Moore's works possessed 'a singular sweetness and melody of versification', Jeffrey pronounced him 'the most licentious of modern versifiers.'[75] He painted Moore as a foul-minded voluptuary: 'he takes care to intimate to us, in every page, that the raptures which he celebrates do not spring from the excesses of an innocent love, or the extravagances of a romantic attachment; but are the unhallowed fruits of cheap and vulgar prostitution'. He twisted the knife further by contending that not only was Moore a sybaritic sensualist, he was not even a particularly good one: 'to us, indeed, the perpetual kissing, and twining, and panting of these amorous persons, is rather ludicrous than seductive'.[76] Despite the absurdities he traced, Jeffrey worried that Moore might lead less-educated readers—particularly women—astray.[77] He portrayed his own review as a means of protecting such readers by damning Moore to social disgrace.

---

[74] Coleridge to Mary Robinson, 27 December 1802, in *Collected Letters of Samuel Taylor Coleridge*, ed. Earl Leslie Griggs, 6 vols (Oxford: Clarendon Press, 1956), II, 905.

[75] [Francis Jeffrey], 'Moore's *Poems*', *Edinburgh Review*, 8 (July 1806), 456–65 (p. 456).

[76] [Jeffrey], p. 458.

[77] I return to this review in my examination of the *Edinburgh's* institutional authority in Chapter Five.

This character-traducing appraisal led the hot-headed Moore to challenge Jeffrey to a duel. Unfortunately, rather than demonstrating Moore's honour, the subsequent meeting further damaged his reputation. As Byron put it, 'In 1806, Messrs. JEFFREY and MOORE, met at Chalk Farm. The duel was prevented by the interference of the Magistracy; and, on examination, the balls of the pistols, like the courage of the combatants, were found to have evaporated.'[78] Accusations about 'LITTLE'S leadless pistol' were not to Moore's liking, and the farcical nature of the encounter continued to dog him. His standing as 'Anacreon Moore' was tainted by accusations of immorality and buffoonery.

Moore sought to remedy this situation by beginning to work in new forms and media, developing his talents for occasional and national poetry. While his early publishing decisions did not always prove lucrative, Chandler's characterising him as a shrewd entrepreneur is correct in that he was a man with a good eye for opportunities and 'an extraordinary capacity to win friends and influence people'.[79] Even though they had duelled, Jeffrey later became a close friend, as did Byron, who Moore also challenged. Richard Cronin has argued that challenges in the early nineteenth century often expressed a queasy mixture of antagonism and approbation; once honour was satisfied or anger had faded, they could function as introductions.[80] Moore was an expert at negotiating such potentially fraught situations and turning them to his advantage. His ability to get key influencers on side by employing his personal charm was crucial to his establishing a profitable public character.

Moore's ability to configure his reputation favourably is amply demonstrated in a letter he wrote to his friend Lady Barbara Donegall in 1808. He begins by asserting that he 'allow[ed] the good people of Dublin to think (as indeed I have told them) that it was the toss-up of a ten-penny token which decided me against going to London, yet to you I must give some better signs and tokens of rationality and account for my change of mind in somewhat a more serious manner'.[81] He claims that he does not

---

[78] Byron, *English Bards and Scotch Reviewers*, footnote to line 467, in *Byron: The Complete Poetical Works*, ed. Jerome J. McGann, 7 vols (Oxford: Oxford University Press, 1980–93), I, 407.

[79] Chandler, p. 272.

[80] Richard Cronin, *Paper Pellets: British Literary Culture after Waterloo* (Oxford: Oxford University Press, 2010), p. 230.

[81] Thomas Moore to Lady Donegall, 29 April [1808], transcribed Michael Bott, URSC MS 1393 Part II.26B, 1/Part 1/138. All further quotations in this paragraph and the next are from the same letter unless otherwise indicated.

care how 'light and inconsiderate' he may seem to the world, before admitting that he does in fact care inasmuch as that he goes out of the way to promote that image, letting Dubliners believe that he is blithe, flighty and—by implication—successful. In the closed circles in which he expects the letter to circulate, however, he recognises that his marketable image as an airy wit is not conducive to conducting business or forging friendships. He conjures it and casts it aside to demonstrate to Lady Donegall that she has been taken into his confidence. He also enjoins her to share this confidence among their mutual friends, 'not forgetting our trusty and well-beloved [Samuel] Rogers.' Moore moves among a connected elite. Aware that his words will circulate, he is careful to spin a personal performance for his supporters alongside a less particular one for the wider public.

Moore states that his motivations for going to London would have been '<u>pleasure</u> and <u>ambition</u>.' He uses the first of these motives to flatter his patron: 'the <u>strongest</u> attraction that my Epicureanism would have in London at present is the pleasure of being near you, with you & about you'. He takes care to connect his second motive with Lady Donegall's interest in the welfare of their shared homeland. At this point in his career, Moore was busy preparing *Corruption* and *Intolerance*, two anonymously published attacks on England's treatment of the Irish:

> We hear you talk of Britain's glorious rights,
> As weeping slaves, that under hatches lie,
> Hear those on deck extol the sun and sky![82]

Moore thus responded to Jeffrey's attack by addressing serious and patriotic issues. This repositioning was carefully deliberated; in his letter he writes that 'by republishing those last poems with my name, together with one or two more of the same nature which I have written, I <u>might</u> catch the eye of some of our patriotic politicians and thus be enabled to serve both <u>myself</u> and the <u>principles</u> which I cherish'. While Moore plays at bravery by asserting that acknowledging such opinions might damage his reputation, in fact, as he implies, there were plenty of Whiggish grandees to whom such sentiments would have been highly congenial. His desire to reframe himself for such figures demonstrates the quandary in which he found himself: his previous poetry collections had made him popular, but

---

[82] [Thomas Moore], *Corruption and Intolerance* (London: J. Carpenter, 1808), pp. 2–3.

they had brought him no continuing income and their ascribed notoriety had marred his reputation and with it his hopes of patronage. He was additionally disadvantaged in that he lacked the money necessary to move comfortably in society in order to re-establish his good name. In his letter, he expressed his frustration at this situation in a spritely analogy:

> many of the reasons why Austria should not go to war were the very reasons why I should not go to London—an <u>exhausted treasury, dilapidated resources</u>, the necessity of seeking subsidies from those who would fleece me well for it in turn, ~~when they could get an opportunity~~, the unprepared state of my <u>Capital</u> &c.&c.—"I have here a home, where I can live at but little expence, and I have a summer's leisure before me to prepare something for the next campaign, which may enable me to look <u>down</u> upon my enemies without <u>entirely looking</u> up to my friends—for, let one say what one will, <u>looking up</u> too long is tiresome, let the object be ever so grand or lovely, (whether) the Statue of Venus or the Cupola of St. Paul's"—Such were my reflections, while I waited for the answer to a letter which I had written to Carpenter, sounding him upon the kind of assistance which he would be willing to give me & suggesting that as it was entirely <u>for his interest</u> that I should go over, (to get the work through the Press which I left in his hands) I thought he ought at least to defray my expences—His answer was so niggardly and so chilling, that it instantly awaked me to the folly of trusting myself again in London without some means of <u>commanding</u> a supply; and I resolved to employ this Summer in making wings for myself ~~to~~ against winter to carry me completely out of the mud

There is an element of demonstrative gentlemanly snobbery in Moore's reference to his publisher—while Carpenter indisputably underpaid him for his poetry, it still seems a little unreasonable of Moore to expect subsidies for the considerable expense of the London season. However, without money, Moore could not mend his reputation by appearing as a gentleman and he did not wish to attenuate his friendships or prospects by explicitly asking for support. Of course, Moore's request that his letter be circulated to the wealthy Rogers could well imply that he had not entirely given up on the idea of going to London if a generous benefactor could be found. The masterful display of Moore's abilities and charm in his Austria analogy and his attack on the 'niggardly' tradesman certainly invite wealthy readers to consider remedying the injustice of his exclusion from the capital's expensive delights.

In the event, Moore finally secured his income neither through his satires nor through high-society patronage, nor even strictly through poetry, although all these things contributed to his receiving what turned out to be an extremely profitable opportunity from the music publishers William and James Power. The first volume of the *Irish Melodies*, a collaboration in which Moore provided lyrics for arrangements of Irish tunes collected by Sir John Stevenson, was published in 1808. Although Moore short-sightedly sold his copyright in the volume for £50, its extraordinary success, driven in part by Moore's playing the songs at society gatherings, enabled him to enter into a more profitable arrangement that assured his prosperity. In March 1811, Moore and James Power signed an agreement that provided 'the said Thomas Moore an Annuity of Five Hundred pounds per annum' in return for producing each year a further number of the *Melodies* or a similar production and 'at the least four Ballads songs or pieces or compositions equivalent or tantamount thereto'.[83] Moore thus got in Power what he had wanted from Carpenter—a publisher who would supply him with a regular income that would allow him to move in society and provide for his new wife and the family he was expecting. For his part, Power was pleased to have secured a profitable series, as well as the implicit understanding that Moore would use his glamour and influence in Whig circles in order to promote the *Melodies*.

After signing the 1811 agreement, Moore was comfortably established financially, allowing him the leisure to develop his reputation further. As the 1810s progressed, he produced a series of sprightly satires, including *Intercepted Letters; or, The Twopenny Post-Bag* (1813), *The Fudge Family in Paris* (1818) and a string of shorter pieces published in the *Morning Chronicle*, the *Examiner* and other papers and journals.[84] In these new satires, he shifted away from the Juvenalian disgust of *Corruption* and *Intolerance*, writing in a later introduction that he 'found that lighter form of weapon, to which I afterwards betook myself, not only more easy to wield, but, from its very lightness, perhaps more sure to reach its mark.'[85] He acknowledged explicitly that his 'unembittered spirit' was advantageous since it allowed his targets to 'refer to and quote' his barbs 'with a

---

[83] Deed of Covenant between Thomas Moore and James Power, 6 Mar 1811, URSC MS 1393 Part II.26B, 2/1.

[84] Moore's satiric output is collected and contextualised in *British Satire 1785–1840: Volume 5: The Satires of Thomas Moore*, ed. Jane Moore (London: Pickering and Chatto, 2003).

[85] *The Poetical Works of Thomas Moore*, 10 vols (London: Longman, Orme, Brown, Green, & Longmans, 1840–41), III, vi.

degree of good-humour' rather than taking offence.[86] His books turned up in the houses of the ministers they satirised, who took care to make it known that that they did not mind 'the humorous and laughing things', as Lord Castlereagh, one of the main targets of the *Fudge Family*, described them.[87] Such circulations served to increase Moore's fame and to enmesh him firmly within political and literary networks. He was able to act as a crucial conduit between the privileged and a wider community of middle-class readers, conveying information and scandal in a humorous mode that entertained and informed the reading public without alienating the taste-makers it both needled and flattered.

As well as diversifying his satire, Moore continued to expand the range of his publications, contributing two articles to the *Edinburgh* with Jeffrey's encouragement and working on a long, carefully researched oriental poem designed to demonstrate his literary abilities and knowledge. For this new work, Moore disentangled himself from Carpenter, who had offered him £2000 for the copyright (as had John Murray informally, at Byron's urging). His friend James Perry, the editor of the *Morning Chronicle*, suggested that Moore should publish with Longmans and helped him to negotiate an extremely lucrative contract. Having found out that the greatest single sum paid for a poem previously had been 3000 guineas (paid to Scott for *Rokeby*), Perry determined that his friend deserved the same, and Longmans were induced to agree (although the sum was later reduced to a still-princely £3000). Longmans also offered Moore the prospect of better treatment, a prospect that was borne out when both the head of the firm, Thomas Norton Longman, and a senior partner, Owen Rees, proved to be faithful friends during Moore's later financial difficulties.

Unusually, both the first and second editions of Moore's *Lalla Rookh* (1817) were luxurious two-guinea quartos, a format that indicated Longmans' high expectations. The poem was an immediate sensation. Jeffrey's fulsome thirty-five-page *Edinburgh* review found Moore's sensuousness far more acceptable when it was displaced to the orient:

> The beauteous forms, the dazzling splendours, the breathing odours of the East, seem at last to have found a kindred poet in that Green Isle of the West; whose Genius has long been suspected to be derived from a warmer

[86] *Poetical Works of Thomas Moore*, III, vii.
[87] Ronan Kelly, pp. 238, 311.

crime, and now wantons and luxuriates in those voluptuous regions, as if it felt that it had at length regained its native element.[88]

However, Jeffrey did not think the poem faultless; or insomuch as he did, he thought this in itself a fault. He recorded the rapturous reactions of Moore's admirers, who claimed that 'you cannot open this book without finding a cluster of beauties in every page', but suggested that although he found Moore's ornamentation in itself 'truly and exquisitely beautiful', the poet was 'decidedly too lavish of his gems and sweets'.[89] This was a relatively minor cavil within the wider contexts of Jeffrey's review, but others judged Moore's opulent poetry more harshly. The *Eclectic Review* accurately pinned the poem as an object of fashion, arguing that 'Mr. Moore's pretty little gilded gondola is the gayest thing in the world for a Vauxhall regatta, or a Venetian carnival, but [...] it could not hope to live in the heave and swell of the mighty ocean'.[90] However, most reviewers responded to Moore's superlatives with their own. Notably, the nascent *Blackwood's* gushed that after *Lalla Rookh* 'it was universally acknowledged throughout Britain, that the star of Moore's genius, which had long been seen shining on the horizon, had now reached its altitude in heaven, and burnt with uneclipsed glory among its surrounding luminaries.'[91] *Blackwood's* also explicitly laid to rest Jeffrey's 1806 accusations, writing that 'it is long since Mr Moore has redeemed himself—nobly redeemed himself, and become the eloquent and inspired champion of virtue, liberty, and truth.'[92] *Lalla Rookh* was a triumph, completing Moore's critical rehabilitation. It was also an enormous commercial success. After the two quarto editions, it ran through twelve octavo editions totalling 18,000 copies between 1817 and 1827, before being tranched down to duodecimo and continuing to sell throughout the nineteenth century. It was also pirated by William Dugdale, another significant testament to its popularity.[93] Nor was *Lalla Rookh* the only product in its range. Plates by Richard Westall and sheets of its songs were sold alongside the book itself, and it

---

[88] [Francis Jeffrey], 'Moore's *Lalla Rookh*', *Edinburgh Review*, 29 (November 1817), 1–35 (p. 1).

[89] [Jeffrey], 'Moore's *Lalla Rookh*', pp. 2, 3.

[90] 'Moore's *Lalla Rookh*', *Eclectic Review*, 8 (October 1817), p. 341.

[91] 'Review.—*Lalla Rookh*' (second part), *Blackwood's Edinburgh Magazine*, 1 (August 1817), 503–10 (p. 503).

[92] 'Review.—*Lalla Rookh*' (first part), *Blackwood's*, 1 (June 1817), 279–85 (p. 279).

[93] St Clair, pp. 619–20.

spawned a considerable number of visual and theatrical interpretations; Chateaubriand described a lavish *tableau vivant* staged in Berlin and featuring the grand Duchess of Russia as Lalla Rookh as '"the most splendid & tasteful thing" he had ever seen'.[94] *Lalla Rookh* succeeded spectacularly in tapping the trend for Eastern tales and in playing on Moore's celebrity, driving both to new heights.

Sadly for Moore, the success of *Lalla Rookh* represented in many respects the peak of his literary career. In 1818, Moira's patronage finally began to affect his finances. Unfortunately, this was in a hugely detrimental manner, as it was discovered that the deputy Moore had appointed to oversee his post in Bermuda had absconded, leaving him responsible for debts of over £6000. Since he had no hope of paying such a huge sum, he was forced to flee to avoid imprisonment. Longmans were granted power of attorney and assiduously pleaded Moore's case with his creditors.[95] Their mediation was assisted by a very considerable donation from Henry Petty-Fitzmaurice, the Marquess of Lansdowne, whose seat at Bowood was near Moore's home, Sloperton Cottage, and who had previously given Moore the run of his library. After Moore had spent three discontented years on the continent, the majority of these with his family in tow, his advocates eventually secured an agreement that his creditors would accept. Nevertheless, Moore's finances remained precarious. The post in which Moore had originally invested his hopes thus ultimately came close to destroying his authorial career, which had transcended its original role as a means of self-promotion and become in Moore's particular case the underpinning of his social and financial existence.

Seeking to address his pecuniary problems, Moore, like Southey, sought lucrative contracts for works touching on recent history: in his case, biographies. His huge network of contacts, his cosy relationships with publishers and his talent for writing works that tantalised the public without offending those implicated made him well-suited for pursuing such projects. His life of the playwright and Whig politician Richard Brinsley Sheridan (published in 1825) earned him £1000 from Longmans, but this large sum was dwarfed by the four thousand guineas that Murray paid for his *Life of Byron* (1832).[96] By this point, though, Moore was by in debt to

---

[94] Ronan Kelly, p. 297.

[95] The document, dated 13 September 1819, survives (URSC MS 1393 Part II.26B, 2/5).

[96] See Copies Ledger B of the publisher John Murray, NLS.42725, p. 228. It is telling that over £3000 of the *Life of Byron* advance went directly to Longmans, presumably covering money they had advanced to Moore.

both Longmans and Murray. Interest payments on this borrowing and the costs of conducting necessary research took considerable bites out of his profits. However, he still had his annuity for his continuing work on the *Irish Melodies* and his reputation allowed him to command extremely high fees for newspaper contributions—*The Times* paid him '£400 in 1826 and 1827, and £200 thereafter'.[97] During this period, Moore was still in his pomp: in tune with the market, widely respected for his talents and able comfortably to support his family and write as he chose. *The Loves of the Angels* (1822), in which three fallen angels describe their love for mortal women, and the strident Irish nationalism of his *Memoirs of Captain Rock* (1824) could have given ample fuel for the Tory press to destroy the reputation of a less well-established writer, even in the more liberal climate of the 1820s. As it was, Moore was able to weather temporary storms. He was safely ensconced in the literary pantheon and acclaimed as a national treasure in Ireland, a fact that stood him in good stead as both Catholic emancipation and parliamentary reform approached.

As it turned out, Moore eventually required the kind attention of his liberal friends, as the shaky foundations of his prosperity were made sharply apparent when the publication of the *Irish Melodies* ceased in 1834. Moore had initiated a split with James Power, the *Melodies'* publisher, on discovering in 1832 that Power had been taking unauthorised payments out of Moore's annuity to pay a new composer, Henry Bishop, since Sir John Stevenson had left the project in 1818. These deductions meant that rather than running a surplus with Power, as he had expected, Moore owed him £500. Having not noticed the deductions for quite some time and having entangled his financial affairs with Power's by frequently borrowing from him, Moore was in a poor situation to protest against Power's abuse of his trust. The resulting legal battle left Moore having to write a further number of the *Melodies* and release the copyrights for his songs to Power in return for a final payment of £350.[98] After the termination of the Power annuity, which had underpinned his finances for twenty-three years, Moore was left potentially facing a hard life of hackwork. Unlike Southey, he had sold most of his copyrights, and while he could collect and reissue his verse, he had neither a series of half-profits arrangements nor a long-

---

[97] Geoffrey Carnall, 'Moore, Thomas (1779–1852)', *ODNB*, https://doi.org/10.1093/ref:odnb/19150.

[98] Linda Kelly, p. 221.

term periodical connection to fall back on. However, in this difficult moment, he was again fortunate in his associations. After the Whigs won re-election in 1835, Lord Lansdowne and Lord John Russell pulled strings on his behalf and Moore, like Southey, was awarded a pension of £300 a year. While for Southey an increased government pension represented a helpful augmentation to his existing income, Moore's pension was desperately needed and comprised his main source of support through many of his remaining seventeen years.

This is not to say that Southey's proto-professionalism was an unambiguously better mode of proceeding than Moore's more sociable literary manner. While Southey published a large number of notable works, Moore's great successes were far more popular, driven by his undoubted talents as a writer, self-promoter and self-fashioner. Like Southey, Moore's career encompassed changing paradigms. He took expert advantage of these by positioning himself as a bridge between privileged networks and expanding middle-class readerships. By cultivating his celebrity using his high society contacts and cannily shaping his publications, Moore brought literary innovations, society satires and patriotic effusions to large and appreciative audiences. However, his exertions were still insufficient to guarantee a permanently comfortable living from literary profits. While problems resulting from patronage and contracts were not all foreseeable, they demonstrate the extent to which even the most successful writers could be exposed to financial risk. Moore's career is a salutary reminder that in the early nineteenth century social capital was the key resource on which financial and cultural capital remained contingent. Moore's talents were considerable, but it was his connections that brought them to notice, and it was ultimately personal friendships rather than direct sales that secured him in his later years.

Felicia Hemans and the Poetry of Exchange

Neither Southey nor Moore was born into circumstances as privileged as those enjoyed (albeit ambivalently) by writers like Scott, Percy Shelley and Byron. However, they nevertheless established themselves as capable gentlemen in the eyes of their contemporaries, in doing so partaking of a plethora of social advantages usually denied to female writers and those of lower status. The potential for literary success was often restricted for those who lacked established social advantages by what Ian Duncan has called 'the patronizing and professionalizing ethos' that dominated literary production in the early nineteenth century.[99] In a rigorously policed culture, the cards were stacked against women and labouring-class writers to an even greater extent than in the eighteenth century. It is striking that two of the most prominent female poets of the Romantic period (Anna Laetitia Barbauld and Charlotte Smith) produced the greater part of their works before 1800, while another two (Letitia Elizabeth Landon and Felicia Hemans) launched the main phases of their careers in the 1810s and 1820s. Barbauld and Smith both established themselves successfully before the retreats of the later 1790s led to an eclipse of liberal Dissenting periodicals and a shift towards a masculinised and exclusionary reviewing culture. Landon principally flourished along with the proliferation of new magazines and annuals during the 1820s, when access to increasingly diverse readerships assisted her in pioneering new modes of celebrity, productivity and criticism. Hemans' career, which began somewhat earlier than Landon's, was predicated in part on new reading audiences, but it also intersected with both older social formations and evolving institutional paradigms. She proved to be an immensely canny operator, comfortable both in communicating with established elites and in navigating the opportunities presented by emerging societies, formats and publishers.

However, while Hemans negotiated the changing literary culture of her age more adroitly than Moore or Southey in many respects, the credit she received was starkly limited by stereotypes about the nature and value of women's writing. Opening a largely positive review of Hemans in the *Edinburgh* in 1829, Jeffrey grandly asserted that 'Women, we fear, cannot do everything; nor even everything they attempt'.[100] When he got to the subjects he believed to be suitable for female authors, the considerable force of his condescension was in full flow:

Their proper and natural business is the practical regulation of private life, in all its bearings, affections, and concerns; and the questions with which they have to deal in that most important department, though often of the utmost difficulty and nicety, involve, for the most part, but few elements; and may generally be better described as delicate than intricate;—requiring for their solution rather a quick tact and fine perception than a patient or laborious

[99] Ian Duncan, *Scott's Shadow: The Novel in Romantic Edinburgh* (Princeton, NJ: Princeton University Press, 2007), p. 43.

[100] [Francis Jeffrey], 'Felicia Hemans' [review of *Records of Woman* and the second edition of *The Forest Sanctuary*], *Edinburgh Review*, 50 (October 1829), 32–47 (p. 32).

examination. For the same reason, they rarely succeed in long works, even on subjects the best suited to their genius; their natural training rendering them equally averse to long doubt and long labour.

Discourses like this make it apparent that women working outwith the confines of carefully circumscribed forms and genres would find it extremely difficult to get a fair hearing. When Jeffrey finally reaches his principal subject, he states that 'we think the poetry of Mrs Hemans a fine exemplification of Female Poetry'.[101] The caveat here speaks volumes. While Jeffrey reads Hemans' verse with some sensitivity, he nevertheless feels it necessary to box her up first, confining her to a space enclosed from the wider fields roamed over by the 'rougher and more ambitious sex.'[102]

Nor was Jeffrey alone in articulating this position, which can be heard even from those purporting to be Hemans' staunchest advocates. Opening his *Memorials of Mrs. Hemans*, her erstwhile collaborator Henry Fothergill Chorley cites Hemans' close friend Maria Jane Jewsbury on the difficulties faced by female authors, before objecting to the currency of Jewsbury's characterisation:

> "If"—to quote one who wrote eloquently in defence of, and apology for, her own sex—"we still secretly dread and dislike female talent, it is not for the reason generally supposed—because it may tend to obscure our own regal honours; but because it interferes with our implanted and imbibed ideas of domestic life and womanly duty." But this prejudice (let us not inquire whether or not it may have been based upon experience) is fading rapidly away. With the increase of female authorship, a change has taken place in the position of the authors. Our gifted women must feel themselves less alone in the world than was formerly their case; they have therefore daily less and less cause to despise its ordinances—to claim toleration for eccentricity of habits as well as latitude of opinion; and thus they are winning day by day, in addition to the justice of head commanded by their high and varied powers, the justice of heart which is so eminently their due.[103]

While Chorley asserts blithely that Jewsbury describes a waning prejudice, his reaction makes it apparent that if anything the opposite was the case.

---

[101] [Jeffrey], 'Felicia Hemans', p. 34.

[102] [Jeffrey], 'Felicia Hemans', p. 32.

[103] Henry Fothergill Chorley, *Memorials of Mrs. Hemans*, 2 vols (London: Saunders and Otley, 1836), I, 7–8.

His discussion advocates conventional domesticity and correlates conform-ing to this with the increased comfort felt by female authors. In his scorn-ing female deviance and using a perceived reduction in claims for toleration as an index of female contentment, it seems likely that Chorley is register-ing increasingly effective social policing, rather than increasing happiness. His bracketed demurral to enquire about Jewsbury and Hemans' lived experiences indicates a desire to sweep the real problems that women faced under the carpet. It is also evident that Chorley thought women should be the ones doing the sweeping, an attitude he shared with many other male observers. In the preface to his 'Extempore Effusion Upon the Death of James Hogg', in which Hemans is described as 'that holy Spirit,/Sweet as the spring, as ocean deep', Wordsworth nevertheless calls her 'a spoilt child of the world' and laments that her 'most unfortunate' education had left her 'totally ignorant of housewifery', meaning that she 'could as easily have managed the spear of Minerva as her needle.'[104]

Such constraining attitudes had tangible knock-on effects on women's earning power and on the social capital they could accrue. Despite her high reputation, a clear discrepancy can be seen between Hemans' profits and those of Southey and Moore. Paula R. Feldman's estimate, compiled scrupulously from the Murray and Blackwood Archives and factoring in Hemans' other known income streams, establishes that her 'career earn-ings could not have been less than about £3000' (the precise total Feldman gives is £2988.17s.6d, but she makes a strong case that this is likely to be short of the mark).[105] Three thousand pounds is an impressive sum, but also one that equates Hemans' total career profits with the handsome pay-ment that Moore received for a single poem (*Lalla Rookh*), or with the sum his *Irish Melodies* annuity paid over its first six years. Similarly, Hemans' aggregated literary earnings are equivalent to between half and two thirds of the likely total that Southey received for his *Quarterly* review contribu-tions, or to fifteen years of the £200-a-year government pension he was

---

[104] William Wordsworth, 'Extempore Effusion Upon the Death of James Hogg', as pre-sented in *Felicia Hemans: Selected Poems, Letters, Reception Materials*, ed. Susan Wolfson (Princeton, NJ: Princeton University Press, 2000), pp. 576–9 (pp. 578, 576–7).

[105] Paula R. Feldman, 'The Poet and the Profits: Felicia Hemans and the Literary Marketplace', *Keats-Shelley Journal*, 46 (1997), 148–76 (pp. 175, 151). A modified version was printed under the same title in *Women's Poetry, Late Romantic to Late Victorian: Gender and Genre, 1830–1900*, ed. Isobel Armstrong and Virginia Blain (Basingstoke: Palgrave Macmillan, 1999), pp. 71–101; I use the earlier text here as it contains some pertinent details omitted from the later publication.

paid between 1807 (when it replaced his substantial annuity from Charles Wynn) and 1835 (when it was upgraded by Robert Peel, who provided one-off assistance to the dying Hemans from the secretive Royal Bounty Fund in the same year). The fact that Hemans' traceable literary earnings can be equated with fractions of the career incomes of older male poets shows that the expanding markets she addressed were not lucrative to the extent that they could negate the advantages conferred by masculine social privilege. Hemans was popular as a writer, and her poems popular as an oeuvre, but no single volume achieved the kind of sensational success that Moore enjoyed with *Lalla Rookh* or that Byron and Scott achieved with numerous poems. She sold approximately 18,000 volumes during her lifetime, a total that compares favourably with Wordsworth or Coleridge, but which is somewhat lower than poets like Thomas Campbell, Samuel Rogers or James Montgomery.[106] However, once nearly four hundred poetical contributions made to magazines and annuals are factored in, it becomes apparent that Hemans produced more and received much less in recompense than her male contemporaries, in terms of direct payments, social recognition, establishment support and meaningful patronage.[107]

These contexts serve to make what Hemans achieved all the more impressive. She had to build her reputation carefully, negotiating long-standing social prejudices without the benefit of sudden fame bestowed by a spectacular debut or a barnstorming early volume. She accomplished this through employing her adroit and productive pen in private correspondences that built a formidable network of support. When discussing Hemans' profits, Feldman characterises her achievement principally in terms of her 'shrewd business acumen'. She concludes by contending that 'the case of Felicia Hemans demonstrates that a professional woman author, insisting on writing poetry exclusively, by the 1820s and 1830s could be an economically viable entity, who could maintain a comfortable middle-class existence through literary labor alone.'[108] However, Hemans' economic viability was substantially determined by factors beyond the laws of supply and demand. Many of her accomplishments arose from recognising how she might benefit from social opportunities; as Feldman rightly acknowledges, 'good fortune and well-placed friends [also played] their

---

[106] Feldman, p. 176.

[107] Nanora Sweet, 'Hemans [*née* Browne], Felicia Dorothea (1793–1835)', *ODNB*, https://doi.org/10.1093/ref:odnb/12888.

[108] Feldman, p. 176.

parts in helping [Hemans] to increase her income'.[109] Describing Hemans' position as that of a comfortable professional therefore seems a mischaracterisation. There was no widely accepted paradigm for female literary professionalism, so Hemans had to triangulate very carefully to position her poetry favourably for influential cliques and periodical arbiters as well as emerging readerships. Her correspondence makes it clear that this work was not always congenial; her career was slow to take off, and while she sustained it for a considerable period, she ended her life as an applicant to the Literary Fund after isolating ill health caused her income to dip seriously in the early 1830s.[110]

Discussing the qualities of Hemans' verse, Nanora Sweet and Julie Melnyk suggest helpfully that 'Hemans's active career can be divided into three periods: *early*, public and largely occasional poetry; *middle*, more intimate and haunting lyric poems; and *late*, experiments towards a new, scriptural polity.'[111] As well as reflecting Hemans' changing priorities, these phases reflect shifts in the literary environment, being cognate with movements from a poetic economy based on impressing key influencers to one focused on marketing one's self more broadly as a unique mind. However, making such distinctions risks masking important continuities in Hemans' practice. While her subjects changed over the course of her career, she remained an eminently social poet, in dialogue with popular concerns and with changing notions of literary value, as well as with a cosmopolitan cultural tradition that took in a wide swathe of European productions. The sociability and currency of her verse were sometimes denigrated by those seeking to exalt a rarefied notion of literature. In his preface to the 'Extempore Effusion', Wordsworth remarked sniffily that 'Mrs. Hemans was unfortunate as a poetess in being obliged to write for money, and that so frequently and so much, that she was compelled to look out for subjects wherever she could find them, and to write as expeditiously as possible.'[112] Hemans herself wrote in a late letter excerpted frequently in posthumous accounts that 'It has ever been one of my regrets [...] that the constant necessity of providing sums of money to meet the exigencies of the boys' education has obliged me to waste my mind in

---

[109] Feldman, p. 159.

[110] Mrs Felicia Dorothea Hemans, Loan 96 RLF 1/825.

[111] Nanora Sweet and Julie Melnyk, 'Introduction' to *Felicia Hemans: Reimagining Poetry in the Nineteenth Century* (Basingstoke: Palgrave, 2001), pp. 1–15 (pp. 4–5).

[112] Wordsworth, 'Extempore Effusion', p. 576.

what I consider mere desultory effusions'.[113] However, such denigrations undersell the effectiveness of the sociable verse that Hemans composed, which, while perhaps lacking the purity and comprehensiveness that she affected to aspire to, achieves powerful and subtle effects of its own. Concluding an article on Hemans' contributions to annuals, Laura Mandell writes that 'The goal of a gift-book aesthetic, of what I've been calling 'productive consumption', as Hemans formulates it [...] is to envision and BE art that is expendable, art that stimulates feeling about losses of living realities, and returns the consumer to those realities, offering detachment from the work of art itself.'[114] Similarly, Andrew Stauffer locates the mode of reading that Hemans encourages at 'an intersection of the conventional and the personally specific'.[115] Both these responses envisage a kind of poetry that is less dictatorial than stereotypical high Romantic modes, stimulating its reader through shared associations rather than the forceful imposition of its writer's vision. Many of Hemans' works speak to a communal culture, evoking historical and contemporary incidents to generate mutually recognisable affects, allowing her to work collaboratively with her readers.[116] While her mature verse is recognisably hers, it commonly makes itself available for possession by others, scorning forms of subjectivity that exalt the writer while implicitly abasing the reader and instead preferring modes that focus on sharable sentiments and relatable narratives.

The roots of Hemans' modes of operation can be seen in some of her earliest literary interactions. Her family circumstances were somewhat straightened due to the wartime disruption of her family's business

---

[113] Hemans to Rose Lawrence, 13 February 1835, in *Selected Poems, Letters, Reception Materials*, p. 521; as Wolfson notes, this was included in [Harriet Mary Hughes], 'Memoir of the Life and Writings of Felicia Hemans, by her Sister', in *The Works of Mrs Hemans*, 6 vols (Edinburgh and London: William Blackwood and Thomas Cadell, 1839), I, 1–317 (pp. 296–7) and in Chorley, II, 257.

[114] Laura Mandell, 'Hemans and the Gift-Book Aesthetic', *Cardiff Corvey: Reading the Romantic Text*, 6 (June 2001), 1–12 (p. 9), http://www.romtext.org.uk/articles/cc06_n01/.

[115] Andrew Stauffer, 'Hemans by the Book', *European Romantic Review*, 22:3 (2011), 373–80 (p. 378).

[116] Chad Edgar discusses Hemans collaborating with her readers in the production of poetic series in 'Felicia Hemans and the Shifting Field of Romanticism', in *Felicia Hemans: Reimagining Poetry in the Nineteenth Century*, ed. Nanora Sweet and Julie Melnyk (Basingstoke: Palgrave, 2001), pp. 124–34 (p. 125).

importing wine, which led to 'paternal absence and financial hardship'.[117] However, she was also exposed to international and cosmopolitan influences through the Liverpool circles with which she was connected and through her wide-ranging reading. Her father served as Tuscan and imperial consul in the port city until he emigrated to Canada in 1806, and at home she 'learned French, Italian, Spanish, Portuguese, German, drawing, and music', as well as receiving tuition in Latin.[118] Her first volume, *Poems*, emerged in 1808 thanks to the combined offices of a family acquaintance, Matthew Nicholson, and a 'surprised and delighted' William Roscoe, who used his influence to place the collection with his publishers, Cadell and Davies. Roscoe was also instrumental in securing a list of 978 subscribers. As with Moore's *Anacreon*, this list was headed by the collection's dedicatee, the Prince of Wales. It drew in both aristocratic names and a wide range of people located principally in the northwest and Ireland (Hemans' father's homeland). A significant proportion of the subscribers were women, with male subscribers often implicitly marked as fathers or brothers to wives and groups of sisters; these groups include four Miss Cotters, five Miss Foulkes and five Miss Oliphants.[119] Some sense of this audience is apparent in the poems themselves. In the first piece in the volume, which is addressed to Viscountess Kirkwall, Hemans writes that 'I will not sigh to gain the poet's bays;/Or soar with Genius on the wing of fire,/If gentle bosoms prize my artless lays'.[120] Within the volume, Kirkwall was also directly credited with ensuring the collection's publication, the advertisement stating that the poems' appearance was due to her 'kind and condescending favour'.[121] While male patrons interceded with publishers behind the scenes, it was a female patron who performed the public work of introducing the result.

The contents of *Poems* run a gamut of established subjects. The volume includes poems to Fancy, Hope, God and the moon; verses on the weather and seasons; and addresses to family members and friends. There are several hymns, a number of locodescriptive pieces and quite a few effusions on fairies. However, the collection also includes more obviously public

[117] Barbara D. Taylor, 'Felicia Hemans and *The Domestic Affections, and Other Poems*, or Mrs Browne's Publishing Project', *Women's Writing*, 21:1 (2014), 9–24 (p. 10).

[118] Nanora Sweet, 'Hemans [*née* Browne], Felicia Dorothea (1793–1835)', *ODNB*, https://doi.org/10.1093/ref:odnb/12888.

[119] Felicia Dorothea Browne, *Poems* (London: Cadell and Davies, 1808), pp. xii, xiii, xxi.

[120] Browne, *Poems*, p. 1.

[121] Browne, *Poems*, p. vii.

poems, addressing subjects such as Admiral Nelson, Shakespeare, Robert Burns, patriotism and the Welsh bards. A few of its inclusions, such as 'The Spartan Mother and her Son', which touches on the relationship between military valour and familial relations, gesture towards subjects that Hemans would make her own as her career progressed. The collection also features poems in French and translations, manifestations of the wider interests that Hemans' education and patrons had opened up. As Diego Saglia put it while writing on Hemans' liberalism, 'Roscoe's local political and cultural activities had national resonance through his connections with Holland House (Roscoe was Lord Holland's regular correspondent between 1797 and 1829), as well as an international dimension because of the links between the Liverpool group and Madame de Staël's circle of Coppet.'[122] Such connections had a continuing influence on Hemans' career and poetry. It is apparent from an 1808 letter to her aunt that Hemans first read Germaine de Staël's *Corinne*, with its strident genius-heroine, soon after its publication, when she was fourteen or fifteen. It proved to be an enduring influence, providing her with epigraphs for poems including 'The Widow of Crescentius' (1819), 'The Grave of a Poetess' (1827) and 'A Parting Song' (1828), as well as serving as direct inspiration for 'Corinne at the Capitol' (1827) and indirect inspiration for a number of her later collections and self-presentations.[123] She also admired another of Roscoe's connections, Jean Charles Léonard de Sismondi, a key member of de Staël's circle. Hemans set an epigraph from Sismondi's *History of the Italian Republics* beneath de Staël at the head of 'The Widow of Crescentius'. She published lyrics in support of the forms of Italian republicanism he advocated in the *New Monthly Magazine* and commended his works in warm terms to Jewsbury.[124] Hemans' intellectual ambitions and talents eventually allowed her to become a significant proponent and interpreter of continental culture, even though she never herself left the British Isles. As the *Quarterly Review* noted, the poems she

---

[122] Diego Saglia, '"Freedom's Charter'd Air": The Voices of Liberalism in Felicia Hemans's *The Vespers of Palermo*', *Nineteenth-Century Literature*, 58:3 (2003), 326–67 (p. 340).

[123] Felicia Hemans to her aunt, 19 December 1808, in *Selected Poems, Letters, Reception Materials*, p. 475. All poems as given in the same volume: 'The Widow of Crescentius', pp. 70–89; 'The Grave of a Poetess', pp. 403–4; 'A Parting Song', p. 425; 'Corinne at the Capitol', pp. 460–1.

[124] Hemans to Maria Jane Jewsbury, mid-1826, in *Selected Poems, Letters, Reception Materials*, pp. 491–3 (p. 492).

translated as her career progressed '[embraced] almost every language in which the Muse has found a tongue in Europe.'[125]

Like Leigh Hunt, who published a collection of *Juvenilia* in 1800 containing poems he wrote between the ages of twelve and sixteen, Hemans was explicitly launched as a prodigy, albeit an even more precocious one. Her first volume's advertisement assured its readers that the poems were 'genuine productions of a young lady, written between the age of eight and thirteen years'. This source of 'additional interest' is flagged at the feet of some of the early poems, where an age at the time of composition is given.[126] However, while the list of subscribers was substantial, Hemans' early work had limited success in breaking out to a national audience. Anna Laetitia Barbauld, writing anonymously in the *Monthly Review*, called for the volume to receive an 'indulgent reception', but thought much of what it contained 'extremely jejune'. Nevertheless, she opined that if the author would 'content herself for some years with reading instead of writing, we should open any future work from her pen with the expectation of pleasure.'[127] Other reviews in national publications, including the *Annual Review* and the *Poetical Register*, concurred that Hemans still had some way to go.

For her initial volumes, Hemans was thus principally encouraged by and speaking to local circles. Such environments could be powerful catalysts for later fame, but parochial patronage relationships were rarely completely comfortable. As Barbara D. Taylor has shown, the correspondence between Hemans, her mother and Matthew Nicholson displays 'the complicated politics of [a] middle-class family struggling to maintain its home and respectability in the middle of financial instability'.[128] This was made particularly complex when it became apparent that Nicholson (born 1746) had developed an emotional attachment to Hemans (born 1793), which required careful epistolary handling once her marriage became a settled prospect. Nevertheless, the correspondence did a great deal to shape

---

[125] [John Taylor Coleridge], 'Mrs. Hemans's *Poems*', *Quarterly Review*, 24 (October 1820), 130–9 (p. 133). The attribution is from the *Quarterly Review Archive*, which provides substantial evidence that an older attribution to William Gifford is likely to be inaccurate.

[126] Browne, *Poems*, p. vii.

[127] [Anna Laetitia Barbauld], review of *Poems*, by Felicia Dorothea Browne, *Monthly Review*, 2nd series, 60 (November 1809), 323. Attribution from Duncan Wu via *Selected Poems, Letters, Reception Materials*, p. 525.

[128] Taylor, 'Felicia Hemans and *The Domestic Affections*', p. 22.

Hemans' sense of herself as a poet. Her letters to Nicholson discuss shared reading interests, including works by Scott, Campbell, Roscoe, Reginald Heber, Jane Porter and Joshua Reynolds. Nor were these abstract discussions—Hemans was already connected with Roscoe and Heber and would later collaborate with Scott and Campbell. She was keen to draw on Nicholson's experience in order to expand her knowledge and build her reputation, asking in an 1812 letter whether he or Roscoe could 'recommend any poem in French, Italian or Spanish, which you think would be desirable [as a translation]'.[129] Nicholson actively made suggestions about the forms he thought suitable for Hemans, writing to her mother in December 1809 that 'perhaps [Hemans] will think it best to avoid arousing the passions by declamation and to persevere in interesting descriptions and undisputed Morals and in captivating appeals to the heart and affections'.[130] Taylor sees this view guiding the composition of many of the poems in Hemans' 1812 *The Domestic Affections, and Other Poems*, for which Nicholson, with Hemans' mother's connivance, took charge of publication. While this volume failed to break through to a wider public or garner significant profits, it allowed Hemans to continue developing her abilities, laying the groundwork for the networks of people and knowledge that would underpin her later career.

With Hemans' marriage, her publishing temporarily ceased, but the habits of reading and writing that had been inculcated in familial and local circles continued, allowing her to build up a considerable body of work by the time she re-entered the public sphere. Her second wave of publications showed a keen awareness of the contemporary scene: in approaching Walter Scott with a poem that he published in the *Edinburgh Annual Register* for 1815, she chose his own *Waverley* as her subject. Her pitching towards national and international concerns was evident in her topical poem *The Restoration of the Works of Art to Italy*, which emerged through the offices of John Murray in 1816, earning Hemans £70 for its copyright. While, as Feldman has shown, this poem returned profits to Murray very slowly, it was successful in launching Hemans onto the national stage. The *Augustan Review* wrote that 'The name of [Felicia Hemans] has

[129] Felicia Hemans to Matthew Nicholson, 12 March 1812, in *Selected Poems, Letters, Reception Materials*, p. 479.

[130] Matthew Nicholson to Mrs Felicity Dorothea Browne, 7 December 1809, in Francis Nicholson, 'Correspondence between Mrs Hemans and Matthew Nicholson, an early member of this Society', *Manchester Memories*, 54.9 (1910), 1–39 (p. 18).

hitherto been unknown to us; and we hail the auspicious rising of a new star in the galaxy of living luminaries. The poem is excellent, and all the accessaries are good.'[131] The *Monthly Review* called the poem a 'classical and elegant' production and the *British Critic* thought it demonstrated that Hemans was 'possessed of a powerful imagination and of a commanding mind'.[132] Reviewers' praise was not entirely unalloyed. The *British Critic* opined that Hemans 'rises too often into the turgid', and while the *Gentleman's Magazine* thought her work 'nervous, elegant, and classically correct', it also implied that the primary motivation for purchasing the poem would be either chivalry or charity: 'should we induce any of our readers to become purchasers of the entire Poem, we have reason to believe they would be rendering an acceptable service to a highly cultivated female.'[133]

As well as bringing Hemans into the wider circulations of national periodical culture, her new publications allowed her to strike up a working relationship with Murray that brought her a number of benefits. Like Southey, she was not shy in calling on him for the volumes she needed to take part in wider conversations:

> I received the books safely, but as I find that the Quarterly review and Dallaway's History of Statuary contain all the information I wanted on the Elgin Marbl[es] I return the others on that subject, as well as Forsyth['s] Italy, which I had seen before—I shall be much obliged if you will send me instead of them, Hoare['s] Epoch of the Arts; Schlegel on dramatic literature, eith[er] in French or English; the tragedy of Bertram; Coleridg[e's] Christabel and Mad. De Stael, sur la litterature ancienne et modern[.][134]

In requesting these publications from Murray, Hemans demonstrated her desire to assimilate prominent contemporary cultural touchstones. She also sought to use Murray as a barometer for current trends, although his

---

[131] Review of *The Restoration of the Works of Art to Italy* and *The Tears of the Artists*, *The Augustan Review*, 3 (July 1816), 29–33 (p. 30).

[132] Review of *The Restoration of the Works of Art to Italy*, *Monthly Review*, 2nd series, 82 (March 1817), 325–6 (p. 325); Review of *The Restoration of the Works of Art to Italy*, *British Critic*, 6 (new series) (September 1816), 311–3 (p. 311).

[133] Review of *The Restoration of the Works of Art to Italy*, *British Critic*, p. 313; Review of *The Restoration of the Works of Art to Italy*, *Gentleman's Magazine*, 86 (July 1816), 53–4 (p. 53).

[134] Hemans to John Murray, 2 June 1816, NLS Ms.40544, p. 90. I am grateful to Paula Feldman for depositing her transcriptions of Hemans' letters to Murray in the NLS.

input was not always timely. In 1817, after sending him *Modern Greece*, she wrote (perhaps archly) that, 'Had I been more fully aware of the very limited taste for the Arts which you inform me is displayed by the Public, I should certainly have applied myself to some other subject; but from having seen so many works advertised on Sculpture, Painting, &c. I was naturally led to imagine the contrary'.[135] As with her earlier patrons, Hemans was keen to seek Murray's advice on building her reputation, writing that she would 'be much favoured by your suggesting to me any subject, or style of writing, likely to be popular'. However, despite such positionings, Hemans was far from a passive recipient in her exchanges with her publisher. She was clear in her negotiations about what she might do to assist her works' circulation, asserting that 'As I have several friends at both Universities, and one in particular of great interest and high literary reputation at Cambridge, I cannot but think that the present work, if published, would be well received there and at Oxford,—and I could easily procure their exertions, even were it to appear without my name.'

Hemans had secured the contacts she alludes to in part through family and friends, but her connections were also cemented through private sociable verse. One of her most charming early poems, 'Epitaph on Mr. W—, a Celebrated Mineralogist', was never printed during her lifetime, but was a personal gift to her friend Charles Pleydell Neale Wilton, the mineralogist of the title. In the poem, Hemans displays a talent for dextrous facetiousness very different from the tones she generally employed in her public verse:

> Weep not, good reader! he is truly blest
> Amidst chalcedony and quartz to rest—
> Weep not for him! but envied be his doom,
> Whose tomb, though small, for all he loved had room:—
> And, O ye rocks!—schist, gneiss, whate'er ye be,
> Ye varied strata, names too hard for me,
> Sing, "Oh, be joyful!" for your direst foe,
> By death's fell hammer, is at length laid low.
> Ne'er on your spoils again shall—riot,
> Clear up your cloudy brows, and rest in quiet!
> He sleeps—no longer planning hostile actions,—
> As cold as any of his petrifactions;
> Enshrined in specimens of every hue,

---

[135] Hemans to John Murray, 26 February 1817, NLS Ms.40544, p. 92.

Too tranquil e'en to dream, ye rocks, of you. (ll. 25–38)[136]

In his *Memorials*, in which he includes this poem, Chorley is keen to celebrate Hemans' playful wit and sense of humour, but he is also explicit about the reasons why these elements of her personality had been held back, writing that 'Mrs. Hemans was wisely unwilling to risk the chance of being confounded with the heartless and satirical, whose laughter comes of disappointment and bitterness, not elasticity of temper'.[137] Chorley makes it clear that Hemans' public performances were constrained by gendered expectations, but he also shows how her private interactions revealed another side of her personality that served to endear her to those she laughed with. This is not to say that Hemans cynically planned to act in this manner, but rather to assert that one of the reasons her acquaintances were keen to act on her behalf was the pleasure they took in her company. While Wilton the mineralogist was a student at Cambridge when Hemans wrote his epitaph, rather than the man of 'great interest and high literary reputation' she mentioned to Murray, in the tightly networked and relatively circumscribed literary world of the later 1810s, friends in any well-connected town could be considerable assets. An important contributing factor to Hemans' success was her employing her talents for sociability to make herself someone for whom others were happy to act.

A combination of carefully-considered public poetry and thoughtful private connections served Hemans well in establishing a substantial reputation during the 1810s. A key sign of her success was an 1820 article in the *Quarterly Review* attributed to John Taylor Coleridge, which covered five of Hemans' productions for Murray in fulsome terms. While the *Quarterly* was Murray's own journal, and never wholly disinterested where his authors were concerned, Coleridge's review nevertheless indicated the considerable status that Hemans had accrued. He sought to position Hemans as an exceptional individual 'in whom talent and learning have not produced the ill effects of often attributed to them; her faculties seem to sit meekly on her, at least we can trace no ill humour or affectation, no misanthropic gloom, no querulous discontent; she is always pure in

---

[136] Hemans, 'Epitaph on Mr. W—, a Celebrated Mineralogist', in *Selected Poems, Letters, Reception Materials*, pp. 16–17 (p. 17).

[137] Chorley, I, 244.

thought and expression, cheerful, affectionate, and pious.'[138] Both womanly and accomplished, Hemans is held up by Coleridge as a paradigmatic modern poet who is still continuously improving: he concludes by writing that 'in our opinion all her poems are elegant and pure in thought and language; her later poems are of higher promise, they are vigorous, picturesque, and pathetic.'[139]

As we have seen, Hemans was keen to seek advice from her friends about types of writing that might help to establish her reputation, and as she achieved a higher profile, she extended this receptivity to public pronouncements on her works. Stephen Behrendt has argued that she used statements like Coleridge's to narrow in on kinds of verse from which she was most likely to benefit:

> Felicia Hemans listened [...] and in reformulating her works to perform ever more effectively a particular aesthetic and emotive function for her readers she likewise reformulated herself. No more was she the fresh and easily Romanticized young woman—Felicia Dorothea Browne—whose poetic productions with their coolly classical style and polish had seemed 'certainly not [from] a female pen'. After 1820 she became ever more that 'Mrs Hemans' whose very name bespoke a compliant domesticity that belied the reality of her marital circumstances.[140]

Behrendt credits Hemans with 'considerable pragmatism' in reshaping her reputation, making deliberate choices designed to raise her profile. However, he is also keen to assert that Hemans was able to incorporate complex subtexts into verse designed to appeal to wide audiences. In this, he concurs with Feldman, who while addressing one of Hemans' later collections contends that '[t]hough *Records of Woman* is a strong feminist work, its ironies and subversion were subtle, for Hemans literally could not afford to alienate any major segment of her buying public.'[141] Feldman's evocation of segments is important here. By the later 1820s,

---

[138] [John Taylor Coleridge], 'Mrs. Hemans's *Poems*', *Quarterly Review*, 24 (October 1820), 130–9 (pp. 130–1). The review covers *The Restoration of the Works of Art to Italy, Tales and Historic Scenes, Translations from Camoens and Other Poets, The Sceptic* and *Stanzas to the Memory of the Late King*.

[139] [Coleridge], 'Mrs. Hemans's *Poems*', p. 139.

[140] Stephen C. Behrendt, '"Certainly not a Female Pen": Felicia Hemans's Early Public Reception', in *Felicia Hemans: Reimagining Poetry in the Nineteenth Century*, pp. 95–114 (p. 109).

[141] Feldman, pp. 167–8.

the reading public was far from monolithic. Hemans took advantage of this by writing verse with multiple levels of appeal. Listening to reviewers, close friends, creative acquaintances and the conversations of the culture at large was crucial for allowing her successfully to situate her verse.

In the late 1810s and the early 1820s, Hemans was particularly sensitive to new opportunities. Her relationship with Murray was providing clear dividends in terms of reputation and connections, but the financial benefits were rather less impressive. The slow sales of *The Restoration of the Works of Art to Italy* had led him to offer half-profits arrangements for future works, which mandated considerable delays in Hemans' receiving payments. In the years from 1816 to 1821, her earnings from her books averaged about £53, demonstrating that cleaving to Murray's publication model alone was not sufficient to realise a significant income.[142] Hemans appears to have responded to this by taking advantage of institutional opportunities and through building a larger network of literary friends who could keep her abreast of new possibilities. One means she employed for diversifying her channels of communication was entering carefully-designed poems into competitions. She had worked on prize themes in her early collections, writing 'The Statue of the Dying Gladiator' (published in *The Domestic Affections*) on the subject assigned to Oxford undergraduates competing for the 1810 Newdigate Prize.[143] The fluency that she had developed in writing to such themes made her a formidable competitor. In 1819, her *Wallace's Invocation to Bruce* won first prize 'against fifty-seven competitors' in a competition funded by 'A Native of Edinburgh, and Member of the Highland Society of London'.[144] When published by William Blackwood, it attracted positive notices from two of his periodicals, the *Edinburgh Monthly Review* and *Blackwood's Edinburgh Magazine*. These appreciations served to burnish Hemans' reputation and catalyse a series of useful connections in Scotland. While the *Edinburgh Monthly Review* was relatively short-lived, John Wilson's enduring admiration allowed Hemans to develop a lucrative association with Blackwood as a publisher and with *Blackwood's* itself, which provided a profitable venue for her shorter poetry in the 1820s and 1830s. In 1831, Hemans asked

---

[142] Derived from Feldman, p. 150.

[143] See Grant F. Scott, 'Felicia Hemans and Romantic Ekphrasis', in *Felicia Hemans: Reimagining Poetry in the Nineteenth Century*, pp. 36–54 (p. 38).

[144] 'Prize Poem, by Mrs. Hemans', *Edinburgh Monthly Review*, 2:11 (November 1819), 574–81 (p. 575); 'Advertisement' in Felicia Hemans, *Wallace's Invocation to Bruce: A Poem* (Edinburgh and London: William Blackwood and Cadell & Davies, 1819), p. 5.

Blackwood for a fee of two guineas a page for her contributions; after taking advice from Wilson, Blackwood replied that 'Though 2 guineas a page is so much higher than what I pay even to my most gifted friend, I will not grudge it to you, as I look forward to your bringing out another volume in which these can be inserted.'[145] *Wallace's Invocation to Bruce* can thus be read as Hemans' entrée into Edinburgh's literary networks, allowing her successfully to strengthen her alignment with a major publishing centre at a time when it was reaching its cultural apogee.

Hemans was also the author of *Dartmoor*, the Royal Society of Literature's inaugural (and, as it turned out, only) prize poem. While the RSL made provision in various advertisements and charters for 'distinguished female writers', its founders were men and its main ongoing form of institutional patronage was exclusively available to selected male authors.[146] As RSL associates, ten men—including Samuel Taylor Coleridge, Thomas Robert Malthus and Hemans' erstwhile patron William Roscoe—were paid one hundred guineas each a year for doing very little.[147] Nevertheless, Hemans was able to profit considerably from the Society's competition, which used an anonymised submission process that allowed her to compete on equal terms. Barbara Taylor has described Hemans' entry as 'part of a calculation to widen her literary networks at a point where her regular publisher, John Murray, became less willing to print her new work.'[148] While Hemans' association with a somewhat controversial Society was not without risk, her calculation was in the main successful. The fifty-guinea prize she received was a substantial benefit, and her entry introduced her to important friends including William Jones (who would negotiate the publication of *The Forest Sanctuary*) and William Jerdan (who subsequently reviewed her works very positively in the *Literary Gazette*). Prize-facilitated connections also brought Hemans into the circle of contributors to the *New Monthly Magazine*, which from 1823 'published at least one of her poems every month', providing along with *Blackwood's* a second reliable source of periodical income during the

---

[145] William Blackwood to Felicia Hemans, 26 September 1831, William Blackwood Magazine Letter Book Apr 1830–Nov 1832, NLS MS 30312, p. 234.

[146] 'Royal Society of Literature', *Gentleman's Magazine*, 90 (November 1820), p. 444.

[147] See Matthew Sangster, 'British Institutions, Literary Production and National Glory in the Romantic Period', *POETICA*, 82 (2014), 39–57.

[148] Barbara D. Taylor, 'The Search for a Space: A Note on Felicia Hemans and the Royal Society', in *Felicia Hemans: Reimagining Poetry in the Nineteenth Century*, pp. 115–23 (p. 121).

1820s.[149] As Linda H. Peterson has shown, Hemans' strong relationships with monthly magazines allowed her to test out new ideas and publish much of her poetry twice in order to 'increase the profits and circulation of her verse'.[150] While not all of Hemans' institutional interventions were as eye-catching as her victory with *Dartmoor*, more modest works like the *Selection of Welsh Melodies* she prepared with John Parry for the Cymmrodorion Society in 1822 also played roles in incrementally advertising her name and diversifying her income and reputation.[151] By cannily employing the entry points available to her, Hemans was able to reduce her reliance on any individual publication venue, allowing her to place her works in a range of apposite locations and secure approbation from writers and institutions across the cultural spectrum.

However, Hemans was only imperfectly successful in her work for the institution that remained the most profitable venue that a Romantic-period writer could access: the theatre. By the early 1820s, she had acquired sufficient kudos to get her play *The Vespers of Palermo* produced at Covent Garden. In this, she was encouraged by the clergyman-poet Reginald Heber, who had first read her poetry in 1811 and was, in Chorley's words, 'the first literary character of any distinction, with whom she became familiarly acquainted'.[152] Hemans was also assisted by one of her Oxford connections, Henry Hart Milman, who has secured a considerable dramatic success of his own with his tragedy *Fazio*. Writing to Milman in 1821, Hemans expressed some trepidation about venturing onto the stage, while also asserting that the support of her friends was crucial in persuading her to persevere: 'I begin almost to shudder at my own presumption, and if it were not for the kind encouragement I have received from you and Mr. Reginald Heber, should be much more anxiously occupied in searching for any outlet of escape, than in attempting to overcome the difficulties which seem to obstruct my onward path.'[153]

---

[149] Taylor, 'The Search for a Space', p. 121.

[150] Linda H. Peterson, 'Nineteenth-Century Women Poets and Periodical Spaces: Letitia Landon and Felicia Hemans', *Victorian Periodicals Review*, 9:3 (Fall 2016), 396–414 (p. 402).

[151] See Elizabeth Edwards, '"Lonely and Voiceless Your Halls Must Remain": Romantic-Era National Song and Felicia Hemans's *Welsh Melodies* (1822)', *Journal for Eighteenth-Century Studies*, 38 (March 2015), 83–97.

[152] Chorley, I, 55.

[153] Hemans to Henry Hart Milman, 21 October 1821, in Chorley, I, 68–70 (p. 69).

The Vespers of Palermo was not a triumph on its debut. The reviewer for the *Morning Post* wrote that 'In many of the scenes we were pleased with the lofty and appropriate language put into the mouths of the *Dramatis Personae*, but there is a want of situation, which is a defect not easily atoned for in a drama, and the characters are not very felicitously imagined.' The *Post* thought Procida and Raymond's meeting in the first act 'very effective' and the end of the third act 'exceedingly good', but found the play in general uneven and noted that consequently 'the audience manifested considerable displeasure before the curtain fell.' '[G]eneral expressions of disapprobation' forestalled a second London performance.[154] When John Murray published the play, the *Monthly Review* identified it swiftly as one of Hemans' weaker publications.[155] However, despite its failure to add another string to Hemans' increasingly distinctive bow, it is clear that she profited in a considerable number of ways from her dramatic attempt. While the play did not make it to a third night (traditionally the first conducted for the author's benefit), it attracted a copyright payment of two hundred guineas from Murray and sold well. Even a failed tragedy was still a marker of distinction, with a play's staging a clear sign of the approval of powerful influencers. Perhaps more importantly, her play's development reinforced a series of connections through which Hemans' reputation would continue to grow and which bolstered her confidence in her literary abilities. Writing to Milman after *Vespers*' first performance, Hemans admitted that 'It is difficult to part with the hopes of three years without some painful feelings, but your kind letter has been of more service than I can attempt to describe'.[156] Such personal validations were rewards that could matter a great deal to authors. Chorley notes that 'Mrs. Hemans never spoke of her tragedy without gratefully recurring to the kindness and sympathy shown her during its progress and upon its failure.'[157]

While many of Hemans' connections were with male writers, she took special care in the 1820s to connect with other female authors, accessing the more 'egalitarian and collaborative models of reading' that Lucy Newlyn has detected in women's networks.[158] She greatly admired Mary Russell Mitford, to whom she introduced herself in a fulsome letter of

---

[154] 'The Theatres', *Morning Post*, 13 December 1823, p. 3.

[155] Review of *The Vespers of Palermo*, *Monthly Review*, 2nd series, 102 (October 1823), pp. 177–81.

[156] Hemans to Henry Hart Milman, 16 December 1823, in Chorley, I, 75–7 (p. 75).

[157] Chorley, I, 78.

[158] Lucy Newlyn, *Reading, Writing and Romanticism: The Anxiety of Reception* (Oxford: Oxford University Press, 2000), p. 253.

appreciation, contending that Mitford was a kind of writer who could not be read 'without feeling as if we really *had* looked with them upon the scenes they bring before us, and as if such communion had almost given us a claim to something more than mere intercourse between author and "gentle reader."'[159] Hemans' approach occasioned a considerable correspondence that ended only in her last year, when she desired as her health failed that Mitford 'should be told of the delight which her country scenes and sketches had given'.[160] As previously mentioned, Hemans was close friends with Maria Jane Jewsbury, forming a union that Chorley characterises as being 'as honourable as it was profitable to both parties'.[161] Jewsbury and Hemans shared favourite works, collaborated on verse annuals and served each other as powerful sources of encouragement. Hemans also worked with Joanna Baillie, who thought her 'a woman of high genius, and respectable in every way'.[162] Hemans gladly contributed to the *Collection of Poems, Chiefly Manuscript, and From Living Authors* that Baillie compiled in 1823 for the benefit of a friend. Although she thought that many of the poems in the resulting volume were 'inferior to what may be expected from the high names of the authors', Hemans expressed a strongly favourable opinion of Baillie's own works, particularly admiring the 'gentle fortitude, and deep self-devoting affection in the women whom she portrays.'[163] She corresponded extensively with Baillie, exchanging books and securing Baillie's permission to dedicate *Records of Women* to her. For her part, Baillie made a major intervention on behalf of Hemans' play, persuading Walter Scott to secure a second production in Edinburgh. Responding to Baillie's request, Scott wrote, 'To hear is to obey—and the enclosed line will show that the Siddons are agreeable to act Miss Hemans drama'.[164] While Scott was keen that his interventions be kept secret, he nevertheless told Baillie, 'I have great pleasure […] in serving Miss Heman[s] both on account of her own merit and because of your

[159] Hemans to Mary Russell Mitford, 6 June 1827, in Chorley, I, 151–4 (p. 152).

[160] Chorley, II, 350.

[161] Chorley, I, 172.

[162] Joanna Baillie to Walter Scott, 1 July 1823, in *Selected Poems, Letters, Reception Materials*, p. 542.

[163] Hemans to Miss [?], 15 May 1823, in Chorley, I, 95–7 (p. 96).

[164] Walter Scott to Joanna Baillie, 9 February 1824, in *The Letters of Sir Walter Scott*, ed. Sir Herbert Grierson, transcribed Takero Sato, 12 vols, *Walter Scott Digital Archive*, Edinburgh University Library, http://www.walterscott.lib.ed.ac.uk/etexts/etexts/letters.html, VIII, 173–4.

patronage'.[165] The Edinburgh production of *Vespers* in April 1824 was considerably better received than the Covent Garden version, taking the edge off Hemans' disappointment at her play's initial reception and boosting its public reputation.

This diversification of her connections and publication venues allowed Hemans to pursue a profitable literary career during the later 1820s. Feldman's estimates show her making an average of around £250 a year between 1825 and 1830—a respectable income touching towards that of an affluent gentleman.[166] However, her fame did not come without strings attached. As Chorley makes clear, the visitors who came to see the noted poetess could at times be trying:

> The frequent and unwelcome invasions of her privacy [...] were often as comical as they were annoying. The hyperbolical compliments which were paid to her must have raised a smile on a Fakir's face. I have heard her requested to read aloud, that the visitor "might carry away an impression of the sweetness of her tones." I have been present when another eccentric guest, upon her characterising some favourite poem as happily as was her wont, clapped her hands as at a theatre, and exclaimed, "O Mrs. Hemans! *do* say that again, that I may put it down and remember it!" The subjects suggested to her as themes for her poems were motley enough to help out the contriver of a pantomime. What wonder, then, that when she could no longer keep aloof from those who could not understand her, she would vent her weariness in some whimsical complaint, or epithet, or *soubriquet*?[167]

While Hemans' verse succeeded in part due to its sociability and sensitivity, the connections this made came with tacit commitments to perform in manners that were not always agreeable, particularly once Hemans moved from Wales to the vicinity of Liverpool after the death of her mother, making herself more easily accessible. Chorley writes that 'from every corner of England and America, offers of service, letters of introduction, crowded upon her; literary engagements were pressed upon her from the divinity treatise to the fairy tale'.[168] Such irritations and impositions were rapidly becoming part of the business of poetry in an age of proliferating print and transport technologies, and while the demands on Hemans were often

---

[165] *Letters of Sir Walter Scott*, VIII, 174.
[166] Feldman, p. 150.
[167] Chorley, I, 244–5.
[168] Chorley, I, 212, 214, 210–11.

galling, they were also a testament to the success of her project to write herself into the networks of literary culture.

Felicia Hemans, then, was a poet who worked all the angles. From a young age, she laboured to build her reputation through local networks and friends. Once established as a Murray author, she demonstrated a range of diverse talents through occupying forms suggested by her own inclinations, her cosmopolitan engagements and her wide reading. However, the profits from this enterprise were not sufficient to allow her to rest on her laurels. Consequently, she explored further opportunities, employing new periodicals and institutions to further her reputation and secure a portfolio of connections from which she might seek to profit. By the mid-1820s, her poetry appeared across numerous respectable venues in forms that linked it both with leading authors and with a gallery of contemporaries who Hemans admired. *Records of Women*, Hemans' most successful collection, is often read as being quintessentially hers, but its paratexts take pains to map it tightly into a wider culture spanning histories, national traditions and continents. Epigraphs embed fragments from Byron, Ippolito Pindemonte, Jewsbury, Friedrich Schiller, Baillie, Torquato Tasso, Coleridge, James Fenimore Cooper, Milman, Samuel Rogers, Scott, Landon, William Curran Bryant and Bernard Barton. While for some of her poems, Hemans set her own verse at the head, for others, she reached out to acknowledge inspirations, ground emotions and connect sentiments. Rather than insisting on her uniqueness in isolation, Hemans conjured herself as a key node in a sprawling network. It was this facility for connections that allowed her to succeed in a competitive literary culture whose preconceptions made it doubly difficult for women to receive a fair hearing.

Chapter Four: The Working Writer

The previous chapter discussed three writers who managed to build some-what stable careers through assiduous labour, cultivating networks and employing canny representational strategies. However, these authors were rare exceptions. Hundreds of men and women sought to use their literary talents to draw attention during the Romantic period, and most of them failed, or were only modestly or briefly successful. The writers who achieved fame commonly began from positions of relative privilege that they leveraged persistently to bring themselves to notice. Less fortunate authors faced difficult struggles for limited rewards on a playing field that was a long way from level.

Mapping the careers of such aspirants can be difficult due both to the relative scarcity of testimonies from the disadvantaged and to the distortions in the testimonies that do survive. When discussing what they did, writers tended to place a high value on writing in an attempt to reify that value. The class-inflected binary that set accomplished, leisured, high-status writing against the drudgeries of authorial labour often served to discourage financial revelations.[1] The desire to talk up the importance of their works and the social incentives for projecting an aura of personal success meant that writers' pronouncements regularly concealed their unexpectedly scanty incomes. Such biases have skewed our accounts of

---

[1] I discuss the denigration of authorial labour in the Introduction.

© The Author(s) 2021

M. Sangster, *Living as an Author in the Romantic Period*, Palgrave Studies in the Enlightenment, Romanticism and Cultures of Print, https://doi.org/10.1007/978-3-030-37047-3_6

Romantic-period authorship, occluding the real circumstances of the troubled majority who attempted to carve out literary reputations.

There were, of course, exceptional moments when certain authors discussed their situations relatively frankly. For example, Charlotte Smith writes with considerable candour in the preface to the second volume of her *Elegiac Sonnets*, detailing her reluctance at being pressed to address her 'pecuniary inconveniences' by gathering subscriptions, but nevertheless establishing the necessity of accepting payments in order to provide for her children.[2] She also censures the impatience of those who cavilled at the volume's delays, people she depicts as worrying unreasonably about half-guineas they had added to 'a sum, which no contrivance, no success, was likely to make equal to one year of the income I ought to possess.'[3] On a more upbeat note, in 1820, the editorial persona of *Blackwood's Edinburgh Magazine*, Christopher North, made provocatively extravagant claims about his periodical's success, crowing that 'OUR SALE IS PRODIGIOUS—AND WE ARE ABSOLUTELY COINING MONEY.'[4] It is telling that the individual author writing in the 1790s is far less sanguine about the prospects for literary profits than the member of a collective writing twenty-three years later. This reflects both the changing nature of the literary market and the considerable power possessed by the networked actors behind successful periodicals. A restricted market favours those who can band together to muster the social authority to distort it. While authors who successfully affiliated themselves with influential connectors could sometimes garner decent rewards, lone individuals could produce a considerable quantity of popular or well-respected work over a long period of time and still end up facing destitution or debtors' prison.

Not all those who displayed an awareness of the social conditions of authorship were happy with this situation, or with the binary that opposed polite achievement and hackish obsession. One of authorship's most persistent advocates was David Williams—philosopher, Dissenting minister, educationalist and man of letters. Williams was a passionate believer in the dissemination of knowledge and was deeply troubled both conceptually and personally by the poor financial and social returns that authors received

---

[2] Charlotte Smith, *Elegiac Sonnets, and Other Poems: Volume II* (London: Cadell and Davies, 1797), p. ii.

[3] Smith, p. v.

[4] [John Wilson], 'An Hour's Tete-a-Tete with the Public', *Blackwood's Edinburgh Magazine*, 8 (October 1820), 80–105 (p. 80).

for their labours. In 1790, Williams acted on his discontent by establishing the Literary Fund, a charitable organisation to assist struggling writers and advocate for the value of authorship. The Fund has operated continuously since its foundation; it was awarded its charter in 1818 and was granted the right to add 'Royal' to its name in 1842.[5] The older parts of its archive are deposited on loan at the British Library, where the papers held include minute books, annual reports, administrative documents and details about finances and fundraising. However, the heart of the archive is a series of case files covering over 3650 writers who first applied to the Fund between 1790 and 1939. Nearly seven hundred of these files relate to authors who applied before 1830 and the majority of these contain letters in which writers describe the circumstances that led them to place their cases before the Fund's Committee. Both quantitatively and qualitatively, these cases paint a grim picture of authors' prospects.

The main body of this chapter will use examples from the Literary Fund archives to show how the cards were stacked against working writers, focusing on the fates of three individuals recognised by their peers as possessing the right stuff: an extremely productive miscellaneous writer of acknowledged talent; one of the most popular female novelists of the 1790s; and the author of one of the period's best-selling poems. The fact that these writers experienced impoverishment, rejection, illness, confinement and—in at least one case—early death shows the extent of the difficulties facing those who sought to live by the pen. Before turning to these cases, though, it will first be useful to examine the circumstances that led to the Literary Fund's establishment, considering the philosophies of its founders and the challenges that it faced in getting off the ground, challenges that in themselves provide strong evidence of the conflicted and problematic status of the working writer.

THE FOUNDATION AND PHILOSOPHIES OF THE LITERARY FUND

The first volume of the Literary Fund's minute books opens with a summary of David Williams' arguments for the value of writing:

> Men of genius [...] are the greatest benefactors of every community; and their cases known, they should never be suffered to experience distress. It is

---

[5] Details of the modern Fund can be found on its website, http://www.rlf.org.uk.

distress, or the apprehension of distress, that perverts talents and produces their crimes.

To reclaim them, punishment is generally applied, but punishment is a precarious and odious instrument; justice and recompence are the true and certain means to obtain their services.

Neglect and menace produce repugnance and hostility; rewards and the prospects of consolation in misery and old age, would produce prodigies of Zeal and exertion.[6]

Williams was painfully aware that many writers who had produced works of recognised value were, in Isaac D'Israeli's words, 'good enough to be praised, but not to sell'.[7] Both Williams and D'Israeli bemoaned the fact that innovative productions were often met with incomprehension. However, Williams pushed his argument further than D'Israeli did. He saw impoverished writers not as a series of individual melancholy cases, but as victims of a large-scale social injustice. While in *Calamities of Authors* D'Israeli portrayed the miseries of writers as being regrettable but some-how inevitable, Williams believed passionately that authors' calamities could be legislated against. Removing the threat of pecuniary distress from authors would, he asserted, allow the world to benefit from an out-pouring of superior intellectual work.

This assertion was in keeping with Williams' larger philosophical proj-ect, through which, as James Dybikowski asserts, '[t]he theme of the pri-macy of intellectual liberty runs as a seamless web'.[8] In his earlier years, Williams believed that a liberal society should be founded on free presses through which thriving communities of writers could communicate with-out being threatened either politically or financially. He was thus in line with what Paul Keen has described as '[t]he Enlightenment ideal of litera-ture as a means of generating and diffusing new ideas'. This eighteenth-century constitution of the Republic of Letters, as Keen notes, 'collapsed partly under the weight of the overtly political stresses' following the

---

[6] London, British Library, Archive of the Royal Literary Fund, Royal Literary Fund Minute Book—Volume 1, Loan 96 RLF 2/1/1. William's 'Account of the Institution' is on unnum-bered pages at the opening of the volume. Following references to the Royal Literary Fund (RLF) Archive in this chapter give the manuscript name and reference only.

[7] Isaac D'Israeli, *Calamities of Authors; including some Inquiries Respecting their Moral and Literary Characters*, 2 vols (London: John Murray, 1812), I, 205.

[8] J. Dybikowski, *On Burning Ground: An Examination of the Ideas, Projects and Life of David Williams* (Oxford: Voltaire Foundation, 1993), p. 229.

French Revolution.[9] As this chapter will demonstrate, this collapse is discernible both in Williams' own thought and in the Literary Fund's early institutional history. Over the course of its first fifteen years, the Fund moved from pursuing a wide-ranging and relatively radical agenda to defining for itself a more conservative and limited purview.

Williams' ambitions for aiding authors can be traced as far back as 1773, when he presented his first proposal for an institution to assist writers to the Club of Thirteen, a debating society he had formed with his friend Benjamin Franklin. Franklin and Williams became acquainted after Franklin had expressed admiration for Williams' deist *Essays on Public Worship, Patriotism, and Projects of Reformation* and they maintained a lively dialogue throughout Franklin's residency in England. Other members of the Club included Colonel Richard Dawson, the Lieutenant Governor of the Isle of Man; the pottery and porcelain manufacturers Josiah Wedgwood and Thomas Bentley; the scientific instrument maker John Whitehurst; the architect and painter James Stuart; the botanist Daniel Solander; the educationalist Thomas Day; and the songwriter and soldier Captain Thomas Morris.[10] In pitching his scheme to this eclectic, well-connected company, Williams was keen to stress that his proposal was not simply to establish an aid-dispensing charity, but rather to create an institution with a wider social and moral remit that would verify the value of authors' intellectual labour. Tellingly, the other members of the club agreed that such a scheme would be virtuous, but doubted whether subscribers could be found to aid such an ill-defined group as distressed 'men of genius'. Franklin opined that were Williams to undertake such an institution, it would 'be honourable to him', but warned that it would 'require so much time, perseverance and patience, that the Anvil may wear out the hammer'.[11]

Franklin's caution was justified, as the first full meeting of the Literary Fund's committee did not take place for a further seventeen years. Williams' time in the 1770s was taken up with religious, historical and political writings and with running a school.[12] He also worked on another

---

[9] Paul Keen, *The Crisis of Literature in the 1790s* (Cambridge: Cambridge University Press, 1999), p. 75.

[10] Nigel Cross, *The Common Writer: Life in Nineteenth-Century Grub Street* (Cambridge: Cambridge University Press, 1985), p. 8.

[11] Royal Literary Fund Minute Book—Volume One, Loan 96 RLF 2/1/1.

[12] Cross, *Common Writer*, pp. 9–10. For more on Williams' wider contexts, see Dybikowski and Whitney R.D. Jones, *David Williams: The Anvil & the Hammer* (Cardiff: University of Wales Press, 1986).

of the Club's projects, his *Liturgy on the Universal Principles of Religion and Morality*, which drew favourable notices from Jean-Jacques Rousseau, Voltaire and Frederick the Great and was credited as a major influence on religious practices in post-Revolutionary France.[13] However, Williams never wholly gave up on his liberal literary plan. After the conclusion of the American War of Independence, he arranged audiences with the philosopher Adam Smith; the politicians William Pitt, Charles James Fox and Edmund Burke; and the President of the Royal Society, Joseph Banks, to discuss the idea. Unfortunately for Williams, none of these luminaries would consent to patronise a fund to aid authors. Pitt, Banks and Smith expressed some interest, but would not commit their time or resources. Fox received Williams in a state of disarray and referred him swiftly on to Burke. The meeting with Burke was particularly unsuccessful—in Williams' words, his intimidating interlocutor 'looked fiercely in my face and said: "Authors, writers, scribblers are the pests of the country, and I will not be troubled with them."'[14] Williams, 'infected' with Burke's fury, responded, 'Who and what are you to use such language? If you had not been a man of letters, you would have been a bogtrotter.'[15] The meeting did not recover.

Burke's lordly dismissal is usefully indicative of the ingrained attitudes that hindered Williams' attempts to advance his scheme. In their exchange, Burke argued that authors as a class were beneath his notice, while Williams contended that it was the existence of the category of author that had allowed Burke to reach his current position. Both these assertions are significant. Williams was correct that Burke brought himself to notice by writing. However, Burke's political career and influence were predicated on his having formed a specific public identity rather than his being identified generically as an author. To succeed in a society within which literature was predominantly the preserve of a small and tightly interconnected elite meant becoming known as a specific self rather than as a representative of a somewhat disreputable trade. The fact that a few literary individuals were valued—rather than authors as a class—meant that Williams faced an uphill struggle in promoting the interests of anonymous writers, as his

---

[13] David Williams, 'The Missions of David Williams and James Tilly Matthews to England', *English Historical Review*, 53 (October 1938), 651–68 (p. 652).

[14] David Williams, *Incidents in My Own Life Which Have Been Thought of Some Importance*, ed. Peter France (Brighton: University of Sussex Library Press, 1980), p. 45.

[15] Williams, *Incidents*, p. 46.

own impulse to approach eminent exemplars indicates. Even publishers were not sanguine about authors' attractiveness. When Williams approached 'an aged and experienced bookseller, on the means of removing the difficulties in his way', he elicited the following response: 'Good God! Sir, no body will meddle with authors.'[16]

Discouraged, Williams subsequently dropped his idea for a time, only resuming his scheme in 1787 when Floyer Sydenham, an acquaintance of his, died as a result of his inability to pay a small bill for provisions. Sydenham was a noted scholar of Greek whose writings had achieved positive critical notices but whose subscriber numbers had failed to match up to his expectations, forcing him to contract debts that placed him in the circumstances that led to his demise.[17] Surviving sources are unclear on whether he died in debtors' prison or whether he committed suicide before he was incarcerated.[18] Whatever its cause, his untimely death reawakened Williams' resolve. Having failed to secure the interest of an influential patron, he decided to press ahead with the Fund in partnership with a small group of clubbable friends.

The Fund's eight original subscribers included three doctors, Hugh Downman, Thomas Dale and Alexander Johnson; the architect Robert Mitchell; the portraitist John Francis Rigaud; the patent medicine entrepreneur Isaac Swainson; the businessman Alexander Blair; and James Martin, a banker and the long-serving MP for Tewkesbury.[19] Downman was a poet, having produced among other works a long didactic poem entitled *Infancy, or, The Management of Children* (1774) and Dale was 'a good linguist and classical scholar', but none of the initial subscribers lived principally by writing.[20] Williams' project to help authors was thus realised through the offices of men aligned with more stable and established roles and professions. These men were evidently willing to accept Williams'

[16] David Williams, *Claims of Literature: The Origin, Motives, Objects, and Transactions, of the Society for the Establishment of a Literary Fund* (London: William Miller, 1802), p. 102.

[17] E. I. Carlyle, 'Sydenham, Floyer (1710–1787)', rev. Anna Chahoud, *ODNB*, https://doi.org/10.1093/ref:odnb/26861.

[18] In the papers of the Literary Fund and writings by Williams, Sydenham is always referred to as having died 'in consequence of an arrest for a small debt' or something similar (Williams, *Incidents*, p. 47).

[19] Cross, *Common Writer*, p. 13.

[20] Alick Cameron, 'Downman, Hugh (1740–1809)', *ODNB*, https://doi.org/10.1093/ref:odnb/7983; G.S. Boulger, 'Dale, Thomas (1748/9–1816)', rev. Kaye Bagshaw, *ODNB*, https://doi.org/10.1093/ref:odnb/7018.

argument that writing's true value went unrecognised by markets or existing institutions. They were also willing to sacrifice their time and money
to attempt to remedy this situation. As the initial group expanded, men
whose livelihoods were more closely involved with literature joined the
Fund's Committee, including the fashionable farceur and journalist
Edward Topham and the booksellers Lockyer Davis and Edward Brooke.[21]
Of particular importance was the tireless support of John Nichols, inheri-
tor of William Bowyer's prosperous printing house, editor of the
Gentleman's Magazine and a respected and well-connected antiquarian
who was also the Deputy of Farringdon Ward and a close friend of the
radical politician John Wilkes.[22] While the book trade began to associate
itself with the Fund at a fairly early stage, in the first years of its existence
the organisation was funded neither by established aristocratic patrons nor
by successful writers seeking to assist their less fortunate compatriots.
Instead, the Fund's foundation was a testament to the growing resources
of an increasingly professional middle class that had excess capital to invest
in charitable causes and enough of an investment in the value of writing to
wish to better the lots of its producers. The Literary Fund, like the book
club and the subscription library, allowed its subscribers to pool their
resources in order to access and influence literary culture in manners previously reserved for the wealthy.[23] In line with Williams' vision, the Fund
operated under democratic principles, with confidential applications and a
decision-making process modelled on Parliament. Through these measures, it sought (albeit with limited success) to mitigate the compromising
sense of obligation created by more traditional patronage arrangements.

However, the Fund's launch was not a smooth process, and setting its
finances on an even footing necessitated innovations and compromises.
The nascent Committee advertised in various London newspapers in order
to attract subscribers. Early notices were fairly unassuming, stating that 'a
small number of Gentlemen [...] have formed the outlines of an Institution

---

[21] Cross, *Common Writer*, pp. 16–17. See also the RLF Annual Reports, which contain full
subscriber lists, the earliest dating from 1792 (Loan 96 RLF 3) and the Minute Books, which
contain lists of members present at each meeting (Loan 96 RLF 2).

[22] Julian Pooley and Robin Myers, 'Nichols family (*per. c.*1760–1939)', *ODNB*, https://
doi.org/10.1093/ref:odnb/63494.

[23] On book clubs, see Ina Ferris, *Book-Men, Book Clubs, and the Romantic Literary Sphere*
(Basingstoke: Palgrave Macmillan, 2015). On subscription libraries, see Mark Towsey and
Kyle Roberts (eds.), *Before the Public Library: Reading, Community, and Identity in the
Atlantic World, 1650–1850* (Leiden and Boston: Brill, 2017).

to relieve and support Genius and Learning in sickness, in age, and at the termination of life; and to preserve from distress the widows and orphans of those who have any claims on the Public, from their Literary industry or merit.'[24] This advertisement omits any real reference to the wider social objectives that Williams espoused, restricting the Fund's purview to the practical alleviation of suffering. Such modest messages met with a limited response. The Committee subsequently shifted to a more assertive line, stating that the Fund's goal was

> to withdraw those apprehensions of extreme poverty, and those desponding views of futurity, which lead Genius and Talent from the path of Virtue, prostitute them to pernicious factions, and convert the Liberty of the Press into a detestable and unsufferable license.[25]

In this formulation, subscribers would not merely aid struggling writers, but would also protect the population at large from the insidious effects of unscrupulous (and potentially revolutionary) writings. This advertisement appeals to anyone with pretensions to being a cultured citizen, selling writers as key influencers who should be nurtured and valued in order to encourage them to work towards the creation of a better society.

Despite this change from restrained sentiment to bullishness, for two years the Fund's advertisements only produced enough income to defray the costs of their production and print a proposed constitution. As he came to recognise, the problem that Williams faced was that 'in the Literary Fund, he could produce no symbols of misery; no actual specimens and scenes to engage that compassion and humanity on which he was obliged to place its first reliance.'[26] Since the Fund was committed to aiding its applicants confidentially, it could not bring the grateful recipients of its charity before donors to attest to the efficacy of its aid, as was the common practice of organisations like the Foundling Hospital or the Magdalen Hospital for the Reception of Penitent Prostitutes. Neither, as Williams' fraught meetings had proved, could it rely on the class position of authors or on the social capital of those extolled as men of genius in order to attract support. As a result, the Committee experimented with

---

[24] 'Literary Fund', *The World*, 24 May 1788, p. [1]. Reprinted in several other papers.

[25] 'Literary Fund', *St James's Chronicle or the British Evening Post*, 25–27 May 1790, p. [1]. Reprinted later in various papers, often with the subscription list appended—see for example 'Literary Fund', *The World*, 26 August 1790, p. [4].

[26] Royal Literary Fund Minute Book—Volume 1, Loan 96 RLF 2/1/1.

several forms of public promotion. In 1792, they staged a fundraising amateur production of *Richard III*, featuring committee member Thomas Morris in the leading role.[27] While the *Morning Chronicle* wrote delicately that the production was 'infinitely more correct than we had a right to expect from Gentlemen unpractised in the art', the sociable appeal of theatrical performances did not appear to represent a sustainable solution to the Fund's cash-flow problems.[28]

The ingenious fundraising solution eventually devised by John Nichols carefully avoided making explicit cases for the individuals the Committee sought to aid, instead employing social performativity to draw contributors together under the twin signs of entertainment and ideals. In 1793, the Fund held its first Anniversary Dinner, inviting eminent political, social and literary figures who drew in other paying parties in their wake. These dignitaries and gentlemen were wined, dined and toasted while being told of the good work the Fund was doing in a generalised manner. Subsequently, they were encouraged to donate, subscribe or increase their existing contributions. The dinners quickly became major events in the London calendar, allowing the Fund to build its profile through leveraging its members' social capital. Early gatherings were chaired by men closely involved with the Society, including Sir Joseph Andrews, Thomas Williams and Sir James Bland Burges, but as the Fund became increasingly connected to the establishment during its second decade, more senior noblemen were enlisted to address the company, including the Duke of Somerset, the Earl of Chichester and the Duke of Kent.[29] Attendance grew rapidly. Eighty-six men dined in 1794, the first year for which numbers survive, but 160 were present in 1797 and 250 in 1799, a scale that was sustained or improved upon in the first years of the nineteenth century.[30] The tavern bill for the 1800 dinner, which is representative of the general run, records that 314 diners got through 294 bottles of port and 69 bottles of sherry along with considerable quantities of other alcoholic beverages.[31] Rhetorical gestures,

---

[27] Preparations for the theatricals are detailed in Royal Literary Fund Minute Book—Volume 1, Loan 96 RLF 2/1/1, pp. 15, 20, 27, 35.

[28] 'Benefit of the Literary Fund', *Morning Chronicle*, 17 April 1792, p. [3].

[29] The Anniversary Dinner Documents (Loan 96 RLF 4) are the principal source of information about this aspect of the Fund's work. The RLF's Annual Reports (Loan 96 RLF 3) are a good supplementary source.

[30] Figures taken from folders for respective years in Loan 96 RLF 4/1.

[31] Tavern Bill, in the folder for 1800, in Anniversary Dinners 1793–1820, Loan 96 RLF 4/1.   ·

public performances and carefully deployed booze thus served to bring in resources that allowed the Fund to provide discreet aid to established authors and less prominent figures. By the turn of the century, the Committee had heard almost one hundred cases and provided money to writers including the increasingly infirm Charlotte Lennox, the exiled Chateaubriand and the young Samuel Taylor Coleridge.[32]

However, while the dinners were successful fundraising occasions, they did little to advance Williams' broader goal of advocating for authors as a class. The tension between the dinners' celebrations and Williams' wide-ranging critiques of social attitudes to writing are embodied in *Claims of Literature*, a book of prose and verse that the Committee voted to prepare in 1801 to celebrate the first ten years of the Fund's existence. When *Claims of Literature* was printed in 1802, it epitomised a struggle that had developed within the Fund's Committee regarding its activities and purview. The verse portion of *Claims* included celebratory odes written for the dinners by Committee members including D'Israeli; the lawyer William Boscawen; the former politician and current Poet Laureate Henry James Pye; and the staunch Hanoverian and patriot William Thomas Fitzgerald. While these writers were all relatively respectable gentlemen, their poetry did not meet with universal acclaim. Pye's Laureateship was a political reward and his verse was routinely mocked. Fitzgerald is now remembered mainly as a victim of satires, including James and Horace Smith's 'Loyal Effusions' (in their *Rejected Addresses*) and Byron's *English Bards and Scotch Reviewers*, which opens, 'Still must I hear?—shall hoarse Fitzgerald bawl/His creaking couplets in a tavern hall,/And I not sing?'.[33] As Byron's verse indicates, the poems printed in *Claims* were written to be recited to soused and appreciative audiences in order to provoke donations. For this purpose, they were effective, but on the page they are not particularly inspiring. They generally contain a plethora of muses and graces, allusions to the fates of writers like Thomas Chatterton and Thomas Otway and a great deal of bombast about how the work of the Literary

---

[32] RLF Case Files: Mrs Charlotte Lennox, Loan 96 RLF 1/12; Monsieur le Vicomte François Auguste de Chateaubriand, Loan 96 RLF 1/75; Mr Samuel Taylor Coleridge, Loan 96 RLF 1/41.

[33] James and Horace Smith, *Rejected Addresses: Or, The New Theatrum Poetarum* (London: John Miller, 1812), pp. 1–4; George Gordon, Lord Byron, *English Bards and Scotch Reviewers*, lines 1–2, in *Byron: The Complete Poetical Works*, ed. Jerome J. McGann, 7 vols (Oxford: Oxford University Press, 1980–93), I, 229.

Fund will bring further glory to ever-glorious Britain. Fitzgerald's contribution for 1799 begins

> Is there a sight the heart can hold more dear
> Than what Humanity contemplates here?
> Pure's the delight that animates the breast,
> To see you throng to succour the distress'd.
> Manes of Butler, Otway, Dryden, rise!
> Behold an object grateful to your eyes:
> England, at last atoning for her crime—
> England, that starved the witty and sublime!
> With contrite feeling opes her ample store,
> And bids the Sons of Genius starve no more.[34]

Fitzgerald continues by arguing that the Literary Fund is a manifestation of a decent English concern with liberty, which he contrasts with the tyranny and destruction unleashed by the 'Gallic Daemon, hated by the wise', before concluding with an encomium to Williams (eliding—perhaps awkwardly, perhaps tactfully—the well-publicised Revolutionary sympathies that Williams had displayed earlier in the 1790s, when he was closely involved with the Legislative Assembly in Paris before the outbreak of war).[35] Fitzgerald's lines show how the Fund's officers found ways to align its mission with an emerging interest in the lives of distressed geniuses: the same interest to which D'Israeli would later cater in *Calamities*. He gestures towards Whiggish progressivism through describing the Fund as righting historic wrongs, but he also ties the Fund's mission to his own virulent patriotism. Fitzgerald's bombastic yearly performances were often picked out as high points of the Fund's dinners in newspaper reports; an encomium in the *Annual Biography and Obituary* for 1830 records that '[t]he spirit [his recitations] infused into the company, and the consequent benefit to the funds of the institution, were generally acknowledged.'[36] However, his rhetoric also highlights the ways in which Williams' expansive vision for the Fund was tempered by the involvement of more conservative figures, who became financially crucial once it became clear that the

---

[34] William Thomas Fitzgerald, 'An Address to the Company Assembled at Freemasons' Hall, on the Anniversary of the Literary Fund, May 2, 1799', in *Claims*, pp. 216–19 (p. 216).

[35] *Claims*, p. 218.

[36] *The Annual Biography and Obituary, 1830*, Vol. 14 (London: Longman, Rees, Orme, Brown, and Green, 1830), p. 314.

Anniversary Dinners were going to be the Fund's primary source of new revenue. This is not to say that such men were useless to the Fund except as purses. Fitzgerald in particular emerges from the archive as a kindly and considerate advocate for numerous struggling authors. Byron's begrudging him his annual chance to posture was a little cruel. Nevertheless, the lordly liberal poet was accurate in skewering the Fund as an organisation increasingly identified with the establishment.

However, *Claims of Literature* is a book of two halves, and Williams' opening prose section contrasts markedly with the second half's grandiloquent verse. As the Fund's founder, Williams was asked to write a report on its achievements. However, he ended up taking a rather different route, contending that because the Fund's work had to remain confidential in order to protect its applicants, he could not produce a conventional history. Instead, he sought to explain why the Fund existed in the first place, employing more than a hundred pages to construct an account that consisted, by his own admission, 'more of argument than narrative'.[37] As Dybikowski has contended, Williams uses his section of *Claims* to 'situate the Fund in a larger picture which it by itself was powerless to change'.[38] In contrast to the self-congratulatory poetry, which figured the Fund as an achieved success, Williams believed that the Fund would necessarily fail unless energy was exerted to change the social conditions and intellectual presumptions that determined the conditions of authorship. His section of *Claims* was a means of advocating for such changes.

Williams begins his argument with a consideration of genius: 'the actuating principle of all these arts; the origin of all the distinctions of man from other animals, and the source of all his peculiar happiness.'[39] Genius, in Williams' formulation, is inherently inventive, inherently self-justifying and its products are inherently useful. He is clear that there are different kinds of genius—a philosopher is not required to put novel ideas into novel prose, and a poet is not expected to create new thoughts as well as new expressions. For Williams, a genius is simply someone who enriches society by originating and spreading new knowledge or new techniques. He takes pains to stress that he believes that such innovations confer ongoing benefits that are almost inevitably undervalued:

---

[37] *Claims*, p. 7.
[38] Dybikowski, p. 242.
[39] *Claims*, p. 11.

MEN OF GENIUS, instead of being unproductive, as intimated by a popular writer, are the most productive of all the classes of mankind. Their inventions not only fix and realise themselves in some subject, and for some time, but they direct the mode of storing and setting in motion future industry; and instead of perishing in the performance, they are renovated in every renewed action of a similar nature, and endure for ever in some permanent habit, regulating the conduct, shortening the labour, and multiplying the comforts, of mankind.[40]

In taking a jab at Adam Smith (the 'popular writer' of the first line), Williams seeks to debunk Smith's characterisation of men of letters in the second book of *The Wealth of Nations*. In his treatise, Smith asserted that authorship 'produces nothing which could afterwards purchase or procure an equal quantity of labour', placing authorial labour in a category of works that '[perish] in the very instant of [their] production'.[41] In *Claims*, Williams agrees that the constitution of society makes the first of Smith's assertions accurate, but contends that rather than perishing as they are produced, literary works continue to live after their initial creation, exerting an extended web of influence through reiteration, imitation and development. This argument strikingly prefigures parts of Martin Heidegger's argument in 'The Origin of the Work of Art', which claims that works of art are reborn or reoccur whenever new eyes consider them.[42] However, Williams did not make his argument through the medium of aesthetics, a discourse unavailable to him in its modern form. Instead, he hybridised Smith's political economy with eighteenth-century theories of genius, which, as Zeynep Tenger and Paul Trolander have contended, 'argued that the productive forces of society were, or ought to be, organized according to the distribution of natural or acquired intellectual powers'.[43] In such formulations, genius was not associated with 'creative imagination and emotional spontaneity' so much as with 'judgement, learning and

---

[40] *Claims*, pp. 22–3.

[41] Adam Smith, *An Enquiry into the Nature and Causes of the Wealth of Nations*, gen. eds. R.H. Campbell and A.S. Skinner, textual ed. W.B. Todd, 2 vols (Oxford: Clarendon Press, 1976), I, 331.

[42] See Martin Heidegger, 'The Origin of the Work of Art', in *Basic Writings* (London: Routledge, 1993), pp. 143–209 (particularly the third section, 'Truth and Art').

[43] Zeynep Tenger and Paul Trolander, 'Genius versus Capital: Eighteenth-Century Theories of Genius and Adam Smith's *Wealth of Nations*', *Modern Language Quarterly*, 55 (June 1994), 169–89 (p. 170).

artful restraints.'[44] By contrast with later Romantic configurations, Williams' genius was a social agent whose productions both arose from and pragmatically contributed to society and its institutions.

Williams' central claim was that authors deserved remuneration equivalent to the benefits produced by their works. He contended that developments in knowledge are incremental, that each increment is indispensable and that incremental social and cultural progress arises in large part from writerly productions. This being the case, he saw men of genius as being grossly undercompensated:

> Is it wonderful men of genius become exasperated and turbulent, when they find an equitable distribution allowed in every province but that of literature? The state derives immense advantages from what may be called the incorporation of the common stock of the knowledge of the country, on which every capitalist and every adventurer may draw at his pleasure. Great portions of this stock are furnished by persons who linger out their lives in obscurity and want.[45]

For Williams, the gross misevaluation of intellectual property should represent a major financial disincentive to its production. His view as to why literary production was undervalued was grounded partly in literature's lacking collective voices that could advocate for its producers. He contended that in more developed disciplines, such as medicine, divinity and the law, 'the difficulty of ascertaining a standard, induced genius and learning to call in auxiliaries, to prevent the necessity of perpetual evaluations, by the privileges of PROFESSIONS, and the institution of ORDERS and CORPORATIONS.'[46] Without similar powerful institutions to represent their interests, authors' works were inevitably valued by and placed in the service of more organised groupings. Because authorship was wrongly perceived to be a secondary achievement and an individual good rather than a serious social contribution, the achievements of authors could easily be neglected and misdirected.

Williams developed his argument further through examining the reasons why authorship could seem to be a viable career choice when so many of its adherents ended up financially disappointed. His explanation for this

---

[44] M.H. Abrams, *The Mirror and the Lamp: Romantic Theory and the Critical Tradition* (Oxford: Oxford University Press, 1971), p. 21.

[45] *Claims*, pp. 46–7.

[46] *Claims*, p. 43.

was also institutionally inflected. Williams believed that schools and academies inculcated unrealistic expectations in their pupils, frequently damaging rather than aiding the objects of their attentions:

> "Give them an education," says ignorant and charitable Opulence, pointing at the squalid offspring of the famishing poor. WISDOM would say of the greater number, "Give them nutricious food, and certain elementary instructions, and inure their bodies to labour." They are all immured in hospitals and schools, deprived of bodily exercise, and fed sparingly, but disciplined into a wretched species of LITERATURE, which they are instructed to believe is a PATENT for riches and honours. With bodies rendered unfit for labour, with sedentary habits, a passion for reading, and an expectation of being provided for and distinguished, they enter the world.
>
> In these circumstances, the best disposed may have the fewest chances. They who are early susceptible of servility and intrigue, succeed in various directions; but when the professions are supplied, the surplus produce of many charitable institutions in Great Britain, is an endless succession of petty scholars, whose misery is the opprobrium of modern literature.[47]

This argument complicates Williams' earlier assertions by arguing that a surfeit of scholars is possible, although the two arguments can be reconciled by considering the excess as being problematic only because the rewards for learning are insufficient. It would also be possible to consider these scholars as falling outside the group of geniuses that Williams wished to make independent, although this contradicts his assertions about the value of talents. As Jennie Batchelor puts it, 'learning', 'labour' and 'utility' have key secondary positions in Williams' 'intellectual division of labour'.[48] Regardless, the idea that large numbers of men are being over-educated creates an interesting tension in Williams' argument, as the same schools that produce unnecessary educated men are presumably also the places where the ideas of 'men of genius' are received, taught and valued. For Williams, though, as for other contemporary commentators, a little learning is a dangerous thing, producing 'SICKLY SPAWN' in 'the male and female pupils of the CIRCULATING LIBRARIES'.[49] While Williams valued writing, *Claims* by no means advocates for universal writerly suffrage. At this

---

[47] *Claims*, pp. 73–4.

[48] Jennie Batchelor, *Women's Work: Labour, Gender, Authorship, 1750–1830* (Manchester: Manchester University Press, 2010), pp. 154–5.

[49] *Claims*, pp. 98–9.

late stage in his career, Williams' main wish was for a professionalisation of knowledge work that would provide support for a reasonable number of worthy writers. He was happy for the state to take a hand in this, hoping that 'the truths exemplified by [the Literary Fund], might induce an enlightened legislature, to form a LITERARY JURISPRUDENCE, to allot to GENIUS, in all its exertions, an equitable portion, present and eventual, of the effects of those exertions'.[50] This is emphatically not a market-based model, but one that requires elites to promulgate the value of writing, measuring its impacts and employing its insights for the good of a wider public that would not necessarily be required to understand why certain writings were to be valued. In Williams' system, authors specifically, rather than the populace in general, were to be elevated. Rather than disposing of the mediations that determined the rewards for writing, he sought means to guarantee that worthy writers would profit from their ideas. However, he failed to elaborate on how the government might cover the inevitable costs or act to formalise existing provision from systems such as the Civil List and the secretive Royal Bounty Fund (the latter, ironically, founded by Burke).

Despite its moderating some of Williams' earlier radical positions, *Claims of Literature* caused a serious clash with a fellow committee member, the former politician and minor poet Sir James Bland Burges. Burges, as Dybikowski notes, was part of an increasingly large conservative grouping within the Fund. In the late 1790s he had collaborated with William Boscawen in getting friends appointed to the Committee, proceeding carefully 'for fear of alarming the Democrats & creating a schism before the Institution is quite in a settled state.'[51] Believing Williams' part of *Claims* to be an unacceptable attempt to politicise the Fund's work, Burges resigned when the publication went ahead. For his part, Williams wrote that Burges had 'endeavoured to pervert [the Fund] by mingling religious and political enquiries with the cases of the unfortunate claimants'.[52] Ultimately, both men's fears about politicisation proved to be unfounded. *Claims* was the last major expression of Williams' desire to restructure society in order to assist authors. In some ways, its ideals date from earlier decades, seeking to reconstruct or replace a vision of the

---

[50] *Claims*, p. 126.

[51] William Boscawen to James Bland Burges, 12 April 1798, quoted in Dybikowski, p. 240. Original: Oxford, Bodleian Library, Bland Burges Deposit 22/14.

[52] Williams, *Incidents*, pp. 51–2.

Republic of Letters that had been largely discredited by conservative crackdowns on radical activities in the public sphere. While the Fund as it developed retained some of the characteristics of a bourgeois organisation, it added prominent aristocrats to its subscription lists during the 1800s, with pride of place given to the Prince of Wales, who in 1806 provided the money for a house to serve as the Fund's headquarters.[53] While Williams had envisioned the Fund as being more than an instrument for distributing charity, he was forced by flattery, economics and circumstances to scale back his ambitions. The established Fund was a broad church and was generally scrupulous in distributing its bounty without fear or favour. However, rather than transforming the character of authorship, its impact was limited to the often-temporary mitigation of individual writers' trying circumstances, as the following exemplary cases make clear.

ROBERT HERON: 'THE CASE OF A MAN OF LETTERS, OF REGULAR EDUCATION, LIVING BY HONEST LITERARY INDUSTRY'

In *Calamities of Authors*, D'Israeli quotes the greater part of a despairing letter from Robert Heron to the Literary Fund under the heading given in the subtitle above. He does so in order to furnish his readers with a cautionary tale by depicting 'the fate of one, who [...] with a pertinacity of industry, not common, having undergone regular studies, and not without talents, not very injudiciously deemed that the life of a man of letters could provide for the simple wants of a philosopher.'[54] Two hundred years later, Robert Heron's account can still serve as a telling example of the many directions that a literary life could take in the Romantic period without proving to be stable or profitable. Despite the vast quantity of work that Heron produced and the diverse activities in which he participated, he was ultimately unable to secure a reasonable livelihood:

> "Ever since I was eleven years of age I have mingled with my studies the labour of teaching or of writing, to support and educate myself.

---

[53] Royal Literary Fund Annual Reports Vol. I, Loan 96 RLF 3/1. See also the Administrative Documents: Loan 96 RLF 5/1/6—Message from the Prince of Wales respecting a House; Loan 96 RLF 5/7—House, 1805–1872. The house eventually decided upon was 36 Gerrard Street.

[54] D'Israeli, I, 218.

"During about twenty years, while I was in constant or occasional attendance at the University of Edinburgh, I taught and assisted young persons, at all periods, in the course of education; from the Alphabet to the highest branches of Science and Literature.

"I read a course of Lectures on the Law of Nature, the Law of Nations; the Jewish, the Grecian, the Roman, and the Canon Law; and then on the Feudal Law; and on the several forms of Municipal Jurisprudence established in Modern Europe. I printed a Syllabus of these Lectures, which was approved. They were intended as introductory to the professional study of Law, and to assist gentlemen who did not study it professionally, in the understanding of History.

"I translated Fourcroy's Chemistry twice, from both the second and the third editions of the original; Fourcroy's Philosophy of Chemistry; Savary's Travels in Greece; Dumourier's Letters; Gessner's Idylls in part; an abstract of Zimmerman on Solitude, and a great diversity of smaller pieces.

"I wrote a Journey through the Western Parts of Scotland, which has passed through two editions; a History of Scotland, in six volumes 8vo.; a Topographical Account of Scotland, which has been several times reprinted; a number of communications in the Edinburgh Magazine; many Prefaces and Critiques; a Memoir of the Life of Burns the Poet which suggested and promoted the subscription for his family; has been many times reprinted, and formed the basis of Dr. Currie's Life of him, as I learned by a letter from the doctor to one of his friends; a variety of *Jeux d'Esprit* in verse and prose; and many abridgments of large works.

"In the beginning of 1799 I was encouraged to come to London. Here I have written a great multiplicity of articles in almost every branch of science and literature; my education at Edinburgh having comprehended them all. The London Review, the Agricultural Magazine, the Anti-jacobin Review, the Monthly Magazine, the Universal Magazine, the Public Characters, the Annual Necrology, with several other periodical works, contain many of my communications. In such of those publications as have been reviewed, I can show that my anonymous pieces have been distinguished with very high praise. I have written also a short system of Chemistry, in one volume 8vo.—and I published a few weeks since a small work called "Comforts of Life," of which the first edition was sold in one week, and the second edition is now in rapid sale.

"In the Newspapers—the Oracle, the Porcupine when it existed, the General Evening Post, the Morning Post, the British Press, the Courier, &c., I have published many Reports of Debates in Parliament, and, I believe, a greater variety of light fugitive pieces than I know to have been written by any one other person.

"I have written also a variety of compositions in the Latin and the French languages, in favour of which I have been honoured with the testimonies of liberal approbation.

"I have invariably written to serve the cause of religion, morality, pious Christian education, and good order, in the most direct manner. I have considered what I have written as mere trifles; and have incessantly studied to qualify myself for something better. I can prove that I have, for many years, read and written, one day with another, from twelve to sixteen hours a day. As a human being, I have not been free from follies and errors. But the tenor of my life has been temperate, laborious, humble, quiet, and, to the utmost of my power, beneficent. I can prove the general tenor of my writings to have been candid, and ever adapted to exhibit the most favourable views of the abilities, dispositions, and exertions of others.

"For these last ten months I have been brought to the very extremity of bodily and pecuniary distress.

"I shudder at the thought of perishing in a gaol.

    92, Chancery-lane,

    Feb. 2, 1807.   (In confinement)."[55]

This extensive catalogue makes it clear how heterogeneous a literary career necessarily was for many who lacked private means. Heron was not simply a theologian, a journalist, a legal author, a biographer, a travel writer, a belletrist, an educator or a historian—in the twenty or so years during which he pursued his literary occupations, he had to be all these things and more. His litany does not even present a comprehensive view of his endeavours, omitting, among other things, his *New and Complete System of Universal Geography*; his work on Sir John Sinclair's *Statistical Account of Scotland*; his contributions to the *Encyclopaedia Britannica*; his edition of the letters of Junius; and his disastrous attempt to launch himself as a dramatist with the comedy *St Kilda in Edinburgh; or, News from Camperdown*, a play that Robert Chambers' *Biographical Dictionary of Eminent Scotsmen* describes as being 'devoid of every thing like interest' and 'violating in many parts the common rules of decency'.[56] The play was heckled off the stage at its first and only performance; a note in John Russell's copy claims that after a sarcastic jibe from the young Henry

---

[55] D'Israeli, I, 219–24. Original: Robert Heron to the Committee of the Literary Fund, 2 February 1807, Loan 96 RLF 1/196/1.

[56] Robert Chambers, *A Biographical Dictionary of Eminent Scotsmen*, 4 vols (Glasgow: Blackie and Son, 1835), III, 46; T.F. Henderson, 'Heron, Robert (1764–1807)', rev. H.C.G. Matthew, *ODNB*, https://doi.org/10.1093/ref:odnb/13090.

Brougham, 'no more of the play was heard without roars of laughter—and the Curtain was dropt'.[57] While Heron's career subsequently floundered, the more privileged Brougham went on to become one of the principal movers in the *Edinburgh Review* and ended his political career as Lord Chancellor.

It is striking to compare Heron's heterogeneous activities with those of canonical Romantics like Byron and Wordsworth or gentlemanly poets like Samuel Rogers. Their relatively comfortable circumstances meant that these men were able to publish verse volumes almost exclusively, albeit buttressed by formidable correspondences. Heron's multifarious productions highlight the division between those who necessarily wrote for money and those who had the leisure to direct their writing towards cultivating social status or pursuing personal agendas. As Heron admits when he writes in his letter that he 'studied to qualify [him]self for something better', he did not see his vast output as being particularly valued or valuable. Throughout his writing life, he supplemented his earnings from the 'mere trifles' that he produced through preaching, teaching, lecturing, editing and writing for periodicals. Heron was in many ways ideally suited to this kind of work. He was well educated, could compose swiftly and had connections that were sufficient to secure him contracts and assignments. To remain financially solvent, though, he had to use all these advantages. He could not simply work in privileged forms, nor could he just translate, or write on Scottish subjects, or produce journalism. Indeed, by the time he wrote to the Literary Fund, doing all these things together could not keep him from the mercies of his creditors. In appealing to the Committee, Heron aligns himself convincingly with assiduous talent rather than lofty genius, presenting himself as an earnest, moral and hardworking scholar undone by circumstances beyond his control. His shudder at the prospect of death in debtors' prison stresses the gravity of his situation.

So, how did Heron come to write this desperate letter? Born in 1764, he was brought up in relatively humble circumstances. His father, John Heron, was a weaver and he was tutored by his mother, a relative of the philologist Alexander Murray, until the age of nine.[58] Educationally

---

[57] [Robert Heron], *St Kilda in Edinburgh; or News from Camperdown. A Comic Drama, in Two Acts; with a Critical Preface: to which is added An Account of a Famous Ass-Race* (Edinburgh: [no publisher given], 1798). Russell's copy: NLS Ry.IV.f.28 (note opposite title page).

[58] Biographical sources on Heron are sparse; this summary principally draws on the *ODNB*, Chambers and Catherine Carswell, 'Robert Heron: a Study in Failure', *Scots Magazine*, 18 (1932–33), 37–48.

precocious, he excelled once he started to pursue formal education and was made master of the parochial school at Kelton at the age of fourteen. With the income from this appointment, and with some assistance from his relatives, he was able to enter the University of Edinburgh two years later as a student of divinity. To make ends meet, he taught and produced magazine articles and other miscellaneous work for various Edinburgh booksellers. In 1789 he published his first full book, a substantially-prefaced edition of James Thomson's much-admired panoramic poem *The Seasons*. At this time, he enjoyed several advantageous connections, becoming a friend of the blind poet and author Thomas Blacklock and being for a time being employed as an assistant to Hugh Blair—rhetorician, pioneering critic and author of two hugely influential books: his *Sermons* and his *Lectures on Rhetoric and Belles Lettres*. Through Blacklock, Heron came to know Robert Burns during the 1780s. He was thus well placed to take advantage of posthumous interest in Burns by publishing biographical articles in the *Monthly Magazine*; these were collected in an octavo volume in 1797.

As these contacts with respected writers indicate, Heron had ambitions beyond hackwork, and he was deeply anxious that his talents be recognised. After the calamitous failure of *St Kilda in Edinburgh*, he swiftly published the play with a long justificatory preface, which he ill-advisedly opened by quoting from *Tristram Shandy*:

> The learned Bishop HALL, tells us, in one of his Decades, at the end of his Divine Art of Meditation, "That it is an abominable thing for a man to commend himself;"—and I really think, it is so.
>
> And yet, on the other hand, when a thing is executed in a masterly kind of fashion, which thing is not likely to be found out;—I think, it is fully as abominable, that a man should lose the honour of it.
>
> This is precisely my situation.[59]

By ripping this passage from the convivial contexts of its parent work, where it justifies Tristram's 'master-stroke[s] of digressive skill', Heron converts its playful ironies into uncomfortable arrogance.[60] This effect is further compounded when Heron quotes a famous line from Jonathan Swift's *Thoughts on Various Subjects, Moral and Diverting*: 'WHEN A TRUE

[59] [Heron], *St Kilda*, p. [i].
[60] Laurence Sterne, *The Life and Opinions of Tristram Shandy, Gent.*, ed. Howard Anderson (New York: W.W. Norton, 1980), p. 51 (Volume I, Chapter XXII).

GENIUS appears in the world, you may know him by this sign,—that the DUNCES are all in confederacy against him.'[61] Heron thus employed the idea of the misvalued writer to summarily (and erroneously) dismiss the *'malignity, intoxication* and *pert blockheadism'* of his critics, who he believed sought 'not the mere damnation of the piece; but the UTTER RUIN of its author'.[62] The problem, of course, remained that however much Heron spurned his detractors, his lack of income and limited social prominence meant that he was reliant on others' approbation to be able to work as he wished. His preface displays an acute social anxiety, vacillating from asking 'who among all my contemporaries can, within the same quantity of writing, produce a greater number of original thoughts?' to worrying that he had 'hitherto done nothing to entitle me to that rank in literature, to which every man who cultivates the arts ought to aspire'.[63] He dismisses *St Kilda* as a trifle at the outset, but it becomes uncomfortably clear during the course of a defence longer than the play itself that he had pinned his hopes of fame upon it. Without social recognition to secure sales, patronage, a clerical living or a profession, Heron could never become a Sterne or a Swift. Instead, he was forced to continue working on projects for which the booksellers would guarantee payments. Rather than being something to conjure with, his name was—at best—confined to small text below his many titles.

Robert Chambers' disapproving account of Heron, written during the 1830s, turns on the trope of his vanity, portraying him as 'another striking instance of the impossibility of shielding genius from poverty and disgrace when blinded by passion, or perverted by eccentricity'.[64] Contemporary evidence beyond the *St Kilda* preface can be mustered to buttress this view. In Burns' 1789 epistle to Dr Blacklock, Heron is by no means portrayed as a sober-minded careerist:

> The *Ill-thief* blaw the *Heron* south!
> And never drink be near his drouth!
> He tald mysel, by word o' mouth,
>   He'd tak my letter;
> I lippen'd to the chiel in trouth,
>   And bade nae better.—

[61] [Heron], *St Kilda*, p. [ii].
[62] [Heron], *St Kilda*, pp. 4, 6.
[63] [Heron], *St Kilda*, p. 22.
[64] Chambers, III, 50.

> But aiblins honest Master Heron
> Had at the time some dainty *Fair One*,
> To ware his theologic care on,
>   And holy study:
> And, tired o' *Sauls* to waste his lear on,
>   E'en tried the body.——[65]

In these stanzas Heron is painted as an engaging presence, a man able easily to convince Burns of his trustworthiness and charm the 'dainty fair one' with his religious erudition. However, he is also shown to be unreliable and immoral. He is blown south by the 'Ill-thief' (Devil) and uses his spiritual learning to effect a temporal seduction, leading to his failure to deliver Burns' letter. Heron himself would not have found this damning portrait entirely unfair. A 1930s article by Catherine Carswell—pointedly entitled 'Robert Heron: a Study in Failure'—reveals that the journal he kept between 1789 and 1798 contains numerous passages of ferocious self-censure; in 1789, for example, he described himself as 'indolent, passionate, foolish, vain and regardless of truth.'[66]

Heron was thus by no means perfect, even by his own measure. However, it is interesting to note that the ascription of his fate to his moral character was a relatively late development in the limited literature on his life. There are telling discrepancies between the accounts published by D'Israeli in 1812 and Chambers in the 1830s. D'Israeli sentimentalised Heron's fate in order to bolster his argument that talented authors often ended their days unrewarded, unrecognised and prematurely. As he put it, 'O, ye populace of scribblers! before ye are driven to a garret, and your eyes are filled with constant tears, pause—recollect that few of you possess the learning or the abilities of HERON; shudder at all this secret agony and silent perdition!'[67] By contrast, Chambers used Heron as an example of extravagance and folly. In his first version of Heron's story, printed in *Chambers' Edinburgh Journal,* he states that while Heron's life is not an example of 'positive virtue and good conduct', it nevertheless forms 'an entertaining article, and cannot fail to have a good effect *negatively,* as

---

[65] Robert Burns, '[To Dr Blacklock]', lines 7–18, in *The Poems and Songs of Robert Burns,* ed. James Kinsley, 3 vols (Oxford: Clarendon Press, 1968), I, 490.

[66] Manuscript 'Journal of my conduct', quoted in Carswell, p. 43.

[67] D'Israeli, I, 225.

showing the uselessness of talent when it is not guided by prudence'.[68] While D'Israeli blamed Heron's fate on systemic and social failings of the kind Williams identified, Chambers read it as amusing evidence of Heron's turpitude.

Chambers' portrayal is not wholly unjustified, but his account fails to recognise the extent of the differences between Heron's Edinburgh of the 1780s and 1790s and Chambers' in the 1820s and 1830s. Chambers built his reputation through writing works such as his *Illustrations of the Author of Waverley* (1822) and *Traditions of Edinburgh* (1824).[69] As their titles suggest, these books drew on the large readerships galvanised by Walter Scott's popular productions. *Chambers's Edinburgh Journal*, his landmark publication, was a pioneering cheap weekly paper, which within three months of its first appearance in February 1832 was selling 30,000 copies an issue. Chambers thus catered professionally to an emerging mass market, and it was to this large new audience that he damned Heron. However, 'author-by-profession' in Heron's age remained a synonym for a hack, and the desirable model was the gentleman. Remembering this throws a different light on the behaviours that Chambers condemns. Evidencing Heron's improvidence, Chambers writes that he exhibited an 'extravagant desire of supporting a style of living which nothing but a liberal and certain income would admit of'.[70] From Chambers' perspective, this looks like a foolish inability to identify one's proper class; from Heron's perspective, such a way of living would have comprised a social performance that, like his preface, strained towards a more respectable status. Chambers records that 'Wishing to be thought an independent man of fortune, [Heron] would carry his folly so far as at times to keep a pair of horses, with a groom in livery.'[71] Chambers reads this as evidence of Heron's hubris, but fails to take into account that maintaining a respectable façade was crucial for those who wished to interact profitably with tastemakers and patrons. Heron's high-stakes, high-status performance was in many ways canny. As Margot Finn has discussed, eighteenth-century novels accurately depict the fact that 'trade credit was not determined by known quantities of

---

[68] 'Biographical Sketches: Robert Heron', *Chambers's Edinburgh Journal*, 2 (20 July 1833), p. 198–9 (p. 198).

[69] Sondra Miley Cooney, 'Chambers, Robert (1802–1871)', *ODNB*, https://doi.org/10.1093/ref:odnb/5079.

[70] Chambers, III, 46.

[71] Chambers, III, 47.

capital but by perceived qualities of character.'[72] Finn also argues that those who recorded their thoughts at the time 'agreed that a fundamental nexus obtained between personal character and personal credit', going on to contend that 'the inherent fluidity of these systems of identity, meaning and exchange thwarted the construction of stable interpretations of consumer characters.'[73] By acting as a gentleman, Heron could access the finances to live temporarily as a gentleman and could mix in gentlemanly society in order to seek the kind of validation and recognition that he attempted to solicit in the preface to his failed play. This approach was by no means unusual or ill-advised. As I have discussed, Thomas Moore's success was to a large extent mediated by social performance, and the Lake Poets all promoted themselves through circles of gentlemanly contacts before bartering their connections into larger incomes.

Unfortunately for Heron, credit-supported performances could not be maintained indefinitely. He was imprisoned for debt quite early in his career, in 1793. To regain his freedom, he contracted to produce a six-volume *History of Scotland* between 1794 and 1799, from which his creditors received most of the proceeds. Having completed this enormous task—and following the disappointment of *St Kilda*—he moved to London in 1799, seeking a new start. In London he improved his prospects through writing for and editing periodicals. In a letter to his parents, he reported that

> My whole income, earned by full sixteen hours a-day of close application to reading, writing, observation, and study, is but very little more than three hundred pounds a year. But this is sufficient to my wants, and is earned in a manner which I know to be the most useful and honourable—that is, by teaching beneficial truths, and discountenancing vice and folly more effectually and more extensively than I could in any other way.[74]

It might be suspect to read too much into Heron's pieties considering their context, but it is interesting that he justifies his work not by the profits he derives but through the moral and intellectual influence he claims to wield. He is careful to frame himself as writing for 'honourable' and gentlemanly ends, thus performing or internalising the values of the class with

---

[72] Margot C. Finn, *The Character of Credit: Personal Debt in English Culture, 1740–1914* (Cambridge: Cambridge University Press, 2003), p. 47.

[73] Finn, pp. 102–3.

[74] Quoted in Chambers, III, 47.

which he wishes to be identified. If accurate, Heron's £300 a year would have matched his professed morals, comprising a relatively comfortable gentlemanly income. However, Heron does not exaggerate the effort he expended to realise these returns. He writes wistfully that 'were I able to execute more literary labour I might readily obtain more money'. Since he already claimed to be working sixteen-hour days, it is hard to see how he might have achieved this. As we can infer from the interactions we know about and the types of works he produced that Heron generally sold his copyrights and productions for a single fee, he had to write on, and keep writing. This took a considerable physical toll. Chambers records that Heron 'would betake himself to his work, as an enthusiast in every thing, confining himself for weeks to his chamber, dressed only in his shirt and morning gown, and commonly with a green veil over his eyes, which were weak, and inflamed by such fits of ill regulated study.'[75] When writers complained about being broken by literary work, they were not necessarily exaggerating. The damage that Heron did to his eyes can be compared with other cases in the Literary Fund's archive where writers such as the compiler of language textbooks Louis Du Mitand, the poet Edmund Henry White and the legal writer Robert Matthew Annesley became blind in part due to their literary exertions.[76]

As Heron's case shows, writing for money was a dangerous balancing act at the best of times. Remaining financially, socially and physically healthy was a complex operation, and it only took a small disruption to bring everything crashing disastrously down. The circumstances that led to Heron's incarceration in 1807 are given in the first part of his letter to the Literary Fund, which D'Israeli omits but which remains preserved in the archive. In 1806 *The Fame*, a newspaper founded by Heron, failed. At the same time, he lost his position as the editor of a government-backed French newspaper as a result of the nation's straitened finances and did not receive back payments of his salary. He was also suffering from 'rheumatism, asthma and spasms in [his] stomach'.[77] Combined, these misfortunes left him unable to meet his obligations. His resulting confinement as

[75] Chambers, III, 48.

[76] RLF Case Files: Monsieur Louis Huguenin Du Mitand, and Mademoiselle Jane Du Mitand, his daughter, Loan 96 RLF 1/63; Mr Robert Matthew Annesley, and Mrs Martha Annesley, his widow, Loan 96 RLF 1/964; Mr Edmund Henry White, and Mrs Elizabeth Martha White, his widow, Loan 96 RLF 1/1299.

[77] Robert Heron to the Committee of the Literary Fund, 2 February 1807, Loan 96 RLF 1/196/1.

a debtor worsened his health, which in turn reduced his ability to exercise his talents and write his way out of debt as he had done previously. In these circumstances, he appealed to the Literary Fund as a last resort. Several sources erroneously claim that Heron received no response to his application.[78] In fact, the committee provided a grant of twenty pounds—not extravagant, but fairly standard for the Fund at a time when its own means were still relatively limited. Heron wrote back expressing his gratitude, but the money was insufficient to clear his debts. In D'Israeli's words, 'About three months after, HERON sunk under a fever, and perished amid the walls of Newgate.'[79] He was forty-three years old.

Heron's career was a long way from that of a comfortable professional. After failing in his attempts to present himself as a gentlemanly writer, his authorial income was strung together from numerous sources. He was enormously productive, securing at times windows of relative prosperity, but his inability to continue to profit from his past works meant that he constantly needed to find new assignments. When he could not, no secure fall-back was available to him. The Fund, D'Israeli and Chambers all agreed that Heron's works had value, but in a confined literary marketplace, his writing could not realise returns sufficient to prevent his early and impecunious death. In his preface to *St Kilda*, he asked 'is it then a *crime* in the eyes of the Public [...] to have, in the want of other means, honestly striven to derive from the humble productions of my literary labour, the scanty means which I require to enable me to indulge in that literary life which alone I love?'[80] It might be answered that while it was not precisely a crime, literary labour often mitigated against the kinds of respect that Heron sought. When constituted as work rather than as a polite accomplishment, literature, even for the zealous, often proved to be a poor prospect. Had he been born, like Robert Chambers, in 1802, the story might have been very different, but in the 1790s and 1800s, productivity could mitigate damagingly against both financial and social recognition.

---

[78] Carswell and, at the time of initial composition, the *ODNB*, although the latter has now been corrected.

[79] D'Israeli, I, 225.

[80] [Heron], *St Kilda*, p. 21.

ELIZA PARSONS: 'COMPELLED BY DIRE NECESSITY TO BECOME AN AUTHOR'

In Jane Austen's *Northanger Abbey*, Catherine Morland, the somewhat credulous heroine, bonds with the flighty Isabella Thorpe over their shared enjoyment of Ann Radcliffe's popular novel *The Mysteries of Udolpho*. Consequently, Isabella proposes that they read 'ten or twelve more [novels] of the same kind' and provides a list of suitable suggestions: '*Castle of Wolfenbach, Clermont, Mysterious Warnings, Necromancer of the Black Forest, Midnight Bell, Orphan of the Rhine,* and *Horrid Mysteries.*' Catherine wishes to be assured that these books are 'all horrid'; Isabella replies that she is 'quite sure; for a particular friend [...] one of the sweetest creatures in the world, has read every one of them.'[81]

This exchange lampoons uncritical consumption generally and the reading of gothic novels in particular. Gothic was the most prominent form of genre fiction in the 1790s, with canny publishers and writers working assiduously to sate the demand produced by the post-Revolutionary upsurge of interest in shocking and dramatic works. Such fictions explored forms developed in precursors like Horace Walpole's *The Castle of Otranto* (1764), Clara Reeve's *The Old English Baron* (1778) and the works that Wordsworth impugned in the preface to *Lyrical Ballads* as 'sickly and stupid German Tragedies.'[82] William Lane's Minerva Press was particularly associated with this movement, operating as the premier purveyor of mass-market gothic fiction. It was Lane who published six of the seven novels on Isabella Thorpe's list, or 'those scanty intellectual viands of the whole female reading public', as Charles Lamb later described them, retrospectively denying their popularity among both genders.[83]

---

[81] Jane Austen, *Northanger Abbey*, ed. Barbara M. Benedict and Deirdre Le Faye (Cambridge: Cambridge University Press, 2006), p. 33.

[82] William Wordsworth [and Samuel Taylor Coleridge], *Lyrical Ballads, with Other Poems*, 2nd edn, 2 vols (London: Longman & Rees, 1800 [actually published January 1801]), p. xix. Academic interest in the gothic has exploded since the publication of initial modern studies such as David Punter's *The Literature of Terror* (London: Longman, 1980; revised in two volumes 1996). Particularly formative works include E.J. Clery's *The Rise of Supernatural Fiction, 1762–1800* (Cambridge: Cambridge University Press, 1995), Robert Miles' *Gothic Writing 1750–1820: A Genealogy* (London: Routledge, 1993) and Michael Gamer's analysis of gothic's reception history and its troubled entanglements with its ostensible opponents in *Romanticism and the Gothic* (Cambridge: Cambridge University Press, 2000).

[83] Elia [Charles Lamb], 'Popular Fallacies', *New Monthly Magazine*, 16 (January 1826), 519–20 (p. 520). Gamer convincingly challenges the accuracy of depicting the gothic as the

Two of the 'horrid' novels in the *Northanger Abbey* list—*The Castle of Wolfenbach* (1793) and *The Mysterious Warning* (1796)—were written by Eliza Parsons, an author driven by her circumstances to become an adept deployer of gothic and sentimental tropes. The following paragraph, taken from an 1803 letter to Thomas Dale, who was serving as one of the Literary Fund's registrars, details the conditions that caused her to take up novel writing:

> I was born to affluence & married a respectable Turpentine Merchant with every prospect of happiness. A Sudden & Unexpected reverse of fortune Originating from the American War & its Subsequent Effects robbed us of a Considerable fortune, & while Struggling with these Misfortunes, a dreadful fire broke out in our Manufactory at Bowbridge and Completed our ruin. My Husband's Spirits Sank under his troubles, he languished 3 years under a paralytic affliction, when a second stroke terminated his existence.–I was left with eight children Wholly Unprovided for—their existence depended Upon me, but the resources for a well educated female Without Money are very few & after Several fruitless Efforts, I was compelled by dire necessity to become an Author[.][84]

In this account, Parsons makes clear authorship's relatively unattractive status, but also signals its position as one of the few economic recourses available to a respectable widow with children to provide for. Parsons was fifty-one in 1790 when Thomas Hookham published her first novel, the epistolary, Richardsonian *History of Miss Meredith*, by subscription. Over the next decade-and-a-half she turned her hand to further sentimental works and honed her skill with adroit social comedy, but her most successful novels were Minerva Press gothics. Parsons' work rate for Lane was prodigious—she completed nine novels totalling thirty-one volumes between 1791 and 1797, when she switched publishers to Longmans, and she continued to write until the mid-1800s, switching publishers again in 1799. She was in many respects exceptionally gifted; by Peter Garside's reckoning, she was the fourth-most-productive author of novels between 1750 and 1819, publishing eighteen confidently attributed titles, as well

---

domain of female readers with reference to library records marshalled by Paul Kaufman and Jan Fergus (*Romanticism and the Gothic*, pp. 38–40).

[84] Eliza Parsons to Thomas Dale, 30 May 1803, Loan 96 RLF 1/21/13.

as a translation of August Lafontaine and a farce, *The Intrigues of a Morning*, which was performed at Covent Garden.[85]

However, Parsons' impressive work rate was necessary to achieve even a scanty living. William Lane was reputed to be fairly generous with his payments to authors. Dorothy Blakey writes that '[p]rices somewhat above the average level [£5–£20] were at least offered by the Minerva' and the (somewhat suspicious) evidence of the firm's advertisements suggests 'an average of approximately thirty pounds'.[86] Nigel Cross suggests that Lane paid Parsons, one of his leading authors, a slightly higher figure of around £40 for each of her copyrights.[87] However, Lane's supposed generosity was relative. While his risks were not insignificant, when a book sold well, as it seems Parsons' did, Lane, as the copyright owner, would profit greatly. Lane was also able to garner additional income through his role as a pioneering supplier of circulating libraries, selling prospective proprietors bulk collections of volumes from his own press. Lane's success in the circulating library trade was a significant advantage for him, but it was more problematic for his authors. Because so many readers borrowed expensive novels rather than purchasing them, only the most popular works could drum up the level of demand necessary to mandate multiple editions. While a considerable number of Parsons' fellow Minerva Press novelists—including Maria Hunter, Eliza Norman, Elizabeth Helme, Regina Maria Roche and Selina Davenport—ended up applying to the Literary Fund, Lane's estate was valued at 'something under £17,500' after his death.[88] Lacking better alternatives, Parsons was compelled to accept Lane's terms, but she was painfully aware that 'as Necessity always obliges me to sell the Copy Rights, my Advantages are trifling [compared] to what the Publisher gains.'[89] Parsons' income stream from her literary earnings was accordingly both episodic and slight. Even supplemented by

---

[85] Peter Garside, 'Authorship', in *The Oxford History of the Novel in English Volume 2: English and British Fiction 1750–1820*, ed. Peter Garside and Karen O'Brien, (Oxford: Oxford University Press, 2015), pp. 29–53 (p. 33).

[86] Dorothy Blakey, *The Minerva Press, 1790–1820* (London: Bibliographical Society, 1939), pp. 73, 74.

[87] Cross, *Common Writer*, p. 170.

[88] RLF Case Files: Mrs Maria Hunter, Loan 96 RLF 1/25; Mrs Eliza Norman, Loan 96 RLF 1/36; Mrs Elizabeth Helme, Loan 96 RLF 1/97; Mrs Regina Maria Roche, Loan 96 RLF 1/590; Mrs Selina Davenport, Loan 96 RLF 1/1247. William Lane's wealth at death as given in Blakey, p. 23.

[89] Eliza Parsons to Thomas Dale, 7 July 1796, Loan 96 RLF 1/21/8.

a £40-per-annum second income from her position as a seamstress in the Royal Household, it was only by writing a three- or four-volume novel every eight months that Parsons could expect to earn around £100 a year, and this sum was scarcely sufficient to meet her needs. Accidents, or any interruption to either of her income streams, could be disastrous.

Parsons first applied to the Literary Fund in December 1792 after 'a dreadful fall' left her suffering from 'a Compound Fracture of the worst kind':

> [I was] obliged unavoidably to Contract Debts which now threaten me Impending Evil within a few Days. Still confined to my Room, my leg on a pillow, Splinters of Bones continually working thro' which keeps me in extreme Tortures, I have been nevertheless obliged to Struggle with Pain and try to write.[90]

Here, as in many of her other letters, Parsons appropriates—albeit not without some knowing irony—the tropes of the sentimental protagonists of her gothic narratives. She depicts herself as a woman suffering as a result of unprovoked afflictions, but also as someone who has made the best of a bad lot while struggling to maintain her modesty and her moral authority in the face of a censorious world. In framing herself as a worthy recipient of generosity, Parsons displays the ease with which literary techniques could be transferred from the contexts of novels into the world of social interactions. At the same time, she was also, as Jennie Batchelor has demonstrated, 'an adept ventriloquist of the emergent discourse of literary professionalism'.[91] While she was unable to sustain a secure income through writing, she knew how to position herself as someone who should be able to. In her letters she carefully locates herself as an underappreciated cog in Lane's industry and as someone sympathetic to the discourses regarding authorship that Williams sought to propagate, arguing in a 1796 letter that difficulties 'blunt the edge of Genius' while aligning herself with the 'unrecognised victims' of society's misvaluation of literature.[92] Parsons' letters established that she was hard-working, talented, afflicted by unfortunate personal setbacks and disadvantaged by systemic factors. The 'feeling and Benevolent hearts' of the Fund's Committee were

---

[90] Eliza Parsons to Thomas Dale, 17 December 1792, Loan 96 RLF 1/21/1.
[91] Batchelor, *Women's Work*, p. 166.
[92] Parsons to Dale, 7 July 1796, Loan 96 RLF 1/21/8.

evidently swayed by these carefully asserted claims, as they were persuaded to come to her rescue on five occasions, providing grants that were relatively substantial by their early standards.[93]

Parsons' 1792 accident was the first of several misfortunes that caused significant disruptions in her writing life. In 1796 she was forced to apply to the Fund because the Civil List, which provided the other part of her income, was 'in the Seventh Quarter of Arrears' due to the war with France. Consequently, she had been driven to the 'Mortifying necessity' of fleeing her home to avoid her creditors.[94] On receiving this application, and on the receipt of two further applications in 1798 and 1799, the gentlemen of the Committee were able to provide Parsons with enough support to address her immediate problems.[95] However, the Fund's grants could not address the underlying insecurity of Parsons' finances. In May 1803 she wrote to Dale that she had 'experienced the loss of liberty and every attendant Mortification'. In the previous year, her debts had been called in at a time when she was unable to locate sufficient funds:

> All the Money I had or could raise which would have paid more that 5S. in the Pound I offered to my Creditor which was refused, and the Consequence was that being arrested, every Guinea of that little all I would have gladly given to him, was expended in law charges & in procuring the rules of the King's Bench Prison as a less dreadful & less expensive confinement than within the Walls. In these Melancholy Circumstances I have to write works of fancy for my daily Subsistence[.][96]

Parsons' debts, as these examples demonstrate, were potentially socially as well as financially ruinous. As authorship did not confer respectability, Parsons had to take great care in managing her middle-class reputation. She wrote in an earlier letter that she had 'struggled thro' innumerable difficulties to persevere in my Employment & preserve a decent appearance knowing the Illiberality of the world ridicules and Contemns an Unfortunate poor Author.'[97] As a woman, her access to the social arenas in which respectability could be performed was more restricted than Heron's. This was one reason why she took extreme care in advertising

---

[93] Eliza Parsons to Thomas Dale, 18 December 1792, Loan 96 RLF 1/21/2.
[94] Parsons to Dale, 7 July 1796, Loan 96 RLF 1/21/8.
[95] See Loan 96 RLF 1/21/10a-12.
[96] Parsons to Dale, 30 May 1803, Loan 96 RLF 1/21/13.
[97] Parsons to Dale, 7 July 1796, Loan 96 RLF 1/21/8.

her reputable affiliations though prefacing and dedicating her works.[98] Access to credit was dependent firstly on connections—by far the easiest sources were friendly acquaintances—and secondly on being able to present an impression of affluence and good character. Parsons' express wish in writing was to provide decent employments for her children. This she accomplished: her literary profits and her carefully maintained social status allowed her sons to follow (sadly fatal) military and naval careers and permitted her surviving daughters to teach or pursue needlecraft before their marriages.[99] However, maintaining the reputation and finances to secure these positions for her offspring was draining, requiring that Parsons perform continuously both in print and in person. Even her eventual arrest failed to lift the burden of social performance, as she had to exert herself in order to pay back her creditors and obtain her release. She was also required to make additional payments for permission to house herself within the rules of the King's Bench (a demarcated district close to the prison) rather than within the walls of the gaol itself. Failing to make these payments would have amplified her problems and compromised her own sense of worth. As she wrote of her jailers, 'poverty is the worst crime in their opinion who keeps these rules, & if not regular in my payments I shall soon be turned out to make room for those who can pay & be thrown among a set of low profligate beings I shudder to think of.'[100]

In pitching to the Literary Fund in the 1790s and 1800s, Parsons did not claim that her works were great achievements, either intellectually or proto-aesthetically. However, she did move a little from the position she had taken in the preface to her first novel, in which she hoped that having written to support her children would 'shield MISS MEREDITH from every shaft of criticism.'[101] Sensible of the Literary Fund's desire to back writers of merit, she wrote to Dale that she was 'compelled to Avail myself of the fashion of the times and write Novels, which I trust tho' perhaps deficient in Wit and Spirit, are at least Moral and tend to Amend the Heart.'[102] This

---

[98] For more details of Parson's paratextual art and artifice, see Karen Morton, *A Life Marketed as Fiction: An Analysis of the Works of Eliza Parsons* (Kansas City: Valancourt Books, 2011), pp. 60–92.

[99] 'Introduction' to Eliza Parsons, *The Castle of Wolfenbach*, ed. Diane Long Hoeveler (Kansas City: Valancourt Books, 2006), p. viii.

[100] Parsons to Dale, 30 May 1803, Loan 96 RLF 1/21/13.

[101] Eliza Parsons, *The History of Miss Meredith*, 2 vols (London: Thomas Hookham, 1790), I, vi.

[102] Parsons to Dale, 17 Dec 1792, Loan 96 RLF 1/21/1.

is an argument sustained in her books, which, as Batchelor notes, 'present their author as her readers' moral benefactor'.[103] Parsons commonly writes herself as an instructor in the codes of acceptable and righteous conduct, mirroring the kinds of performance necessary in her real-world social interactions while also occasionally criticising the hypocrisies of such performances. In *The Castle of Wolfenbach*, the central character, Matilda, is a quintessential gothic heroine—kind, a little credulous, oft-fainting—who for reasons of principle refuses both to disclaim the paternal authority vested in her lecherous uncle and to contemplate marrying above her station (both of these refusals conveniently serve to drive forward the plot). Parsons contrasts a series of doubles with Matilda, including the saintly Mother Magdalene, who explains to Matilda that she took holy orders after her father (like Parsons' husband) lost his money through misfortunate business ventures, leading to a trail of further calamities and betrayals. Mother Magdalene's story is one of several episodes in *Wolfenbach* during which Parsons explores the terrible contingency of financial success and notes the error of equating wealth with moral value. Parsons is not sanguine on the general tendency of society to right wrongs, as is made clear in a speech by the Count de Bouville, Matilda's love interest:

> there ought not to be any poor, that is, I mean beggars, in England, such immense sums are raised for their support, such resources for industry, and so many hospitals for the sick and aged, that, if proper management was observed, none need complain of cold or hunger; yet in my life I never saw so many painful and disgusting objects as there are in the streets and environs of London.[104]

Despite her novels' compliance with gothic formulae and with Protestant notions regarding rewards for virtue and punishments for vice, Parsons manages to work in cutting commentary on society's failure correctly to value talents. Her characters are generally rewarded only through the intervention of merciful and exceptional benefactors and her novels stress both the difficulties of dealing with calamities and the atypical and personal nature of acts of kindness. She expressed similar convictions in a letter to the politician William Windham in 1794, writing that 'in this world of prejudice the garb and supplications of Poverty generally excite

---

[103] Jennie Batchelor, '"The Claims of Literature": Women Applicants to the Royal Literary Fund', *Women's Writing*, 12:3 (2005), 505–21 (p. 513).

[104] Parsons, *Wolfenbach*, p. 58.

Contempt or Cold useless pity.'[105] This clear-eyed understanding of class bigotries served Parsons well in her own attempts to stay afloat. However, her circumstances meant that her clever objections were poorly placed for serious recognition.

Parsons' works did draw considerable attention. She was among the most frequently reviewed authors of the late eighteenth century and her periodical auditors appreciated many aspects of her work.[106] In the *Monthly Review*, William Enfield praised *Miss Meredith* as a work in which '[a] natural and interesting tale is related in neat and unaffected language; and the moral which it inculcates, is the reverse of those romantic notions, which most novels have a tendency to inspire.'[107] However, reviewers' praise was often tempered by their tendency to read Parsons' novels as representatives of a large group of generic and suspicious productions. The *Critical Review*, despite appreciating aspects of *Wolfenbach*, wrote that '[w]e do not pretend to give this novel as one of the first order, or even of the second'.[108] The *Literary Journal* observed of *Murray House* (1804), that '[t]his novel, compared to others of the same sort, may be considered a *tolerable* publication.'[109] By using forms known to be popular, Parsons opened her works up to snobbish dismissals, making it unlikely that her payments from her publishers would ever be supplemented by rewards resulting from critical or social recognition.

For many auditors, Parsons' novels were also compromised by the circumstances of their production. Reviewers often complained that they showed signs of hasty composition. The *Critical Review*, considering *The Mysterious Warning*, opined that

the novels of Mrs Parsons would be more interesting, if her plans had more unity: when the principal narrative is frequently broken in upon by different

---

[105] Eliza Parsons to William Windham, 14 May 1794, BL Additional Manuscript 37914.

[106] Ann R. Hawkins counts nineteen of her titles as having been reviewed, behind only Charlotte Smith among female authors. See Hawkins and Stephanie Eckroth, 'General Introduction' to *Romantic Women Writers Reviewed*, 9 vols (London: Pickering & Chatto, 2010–13), I, xvi.

[107] [William Enfield], *Monthly Review*, 2nd series, 3 (September 1790), p. 90. Attribution from *The English Novel 1770–1829: A Bibliographical Survey of Prose Fiction Published in the British Isles*, ed. Peter Garside, James Raven and Rainer Schöwerling, 2 vols (Oxford: Oxford University Press, 2000) I, 513. This review and those following are helpfully collected in Morton (pp. 254–81).

[108] '*Castle of Wolfenbach*', *Critical Review*, new series, 10 (Jan 1794), 49–52 (p. 50).

[109] *Literary Journal*, 3 (June 1804), 609–10 (p. 609).

stories, however entertaining in themselves, attention flags, the mind experiences a kind of disappointment, loses the connection, proceeds languidly and is not easily reanimated.[110]

Often the first volumes of her works were preferred to the later ones. In the *Monthly Review* of *Ellen and Julia* (1793) the critic wrote that '[i]n the first volume the story is diversified with many striking incidents, but, through a greater part of the second, the writer's invention appears to flag.'[111] The *English Review* found *Lucy* (1794) 'sufficiently interesting throughout the first volume' but complained that 'it dwindles into a mere farrago of wonderful and improbable adventures.'[112] *The Voluntary Exile* (1795) was almost universally identified as being 'faulty from its want of unity'.[113] The *British Critic*, writing on *An Old Friend with a New Face* (1797), observes 'as the critic did to Sir Fretful Plagiary, there is a *falling off* in the last volume.'[114] Parsons' grammar was also frequently attacked as her reviewers sought to demonstrate their own superior educations.[115] Such critical standards, which valued the polish of slow composition and the discerning display of individual accomplishments, stacked the deck against working writers who needed to publish regularly to survive.

Surveying Parsons' career, Dorothy Blakey writes that 'there seems reason to suspect that Mrs Parsons wrote 'horrid' books for profit, and expressed her real self in topical satire.'[116] This statement echoes similar claims made by her contemporaries and by modern critics including Devendra Varma and Diane Long Hoeveler.[117] All of these writers imply that Parsons might have been able to write novels that were more successful by critical or aesthetic standards had she not had to rush to procure the next copyright payment. Her career in this respect provides a revealing contrast with Ann Radcliffe's. Like Parsons, Radcliffe published her first novel with Thomas Hookham. However, Radcliffe had a prudent husband,

---

[110] *Critical Review*, new series, 16 (April 1796), p. 474.

[111] *Monthly Review*, 2nd series, 14 (August 1794), p. 465.

[112] '*Lucy; a Novel*', *English Review*, 24 (July 1794), 62–3 (p. 63).

[113] 'Mrs. Parson's *Voluntary Exile*', *Analytical Review*, 21 (March 1795), 296–9 (p. 296).

[114] *British Critic*, 11 (May 1798), p. 562.

[115] For examples see the *Analytical* review referred to above and the *British Critic's* review of *The Voluntary Exile*, which lists oversights 'which admit no excuse' (6 Aug 1795, p. 190).

[116] Blakey, p. 60.

[117] See Devendra P. Varma 'Introduction' to Eliza Parsons, *The Mysterious Warning: A German Tale* (London: Folio Press, 1968), p. xi and Hoeveler, 'Introduction' to Parsons, *Wolfenbach*, p. viii.

did not need to provide for children and did not have to deal with pressing debts. She was therefore able to write her later novels at a fairly leisurely pace, fine-tuning her narratives so that they might achieve remarkable—rather than generic—levels of success. Three years passed between the publications of *The Romance of the Forest* and *The Mysteries of Udolpho* and three more between *Udolpho* and *The Italian*. Radcliffe was paid significant amounts for these later works. After three novels with Hookham, she changed publishers for *Udolpho*; an extant copy of the contract records that she received £500 for the copyright, more than twelve times what Parsons could expect to receive for one of her works.[118] Radcliffe changed publishers again for *The Italian*, again receiving a significant payment. Her earliest biographer, Thomas Noon Talfourd, speculated that, as with Parsons, money was a reason why Radcliffe wrote and also believed that a sufficiency was one of the reasons why she stopped writing: 'At first the sums she received, though not necessary, were welcome; but, as her pecuniary resources became more ample, she was without sufficient excitement to begin on an extended romance.'[119] For Radcliffe, money from writing was useful, but not needful. She did not have to write at speed in order to survive, as Parsons did, and, perhaps partly as a result, she was able to garner profits and plaudits in ways that Parsons could not.

With regard to her avowed goal of supporting her family, Parsons' literary career can be considered a success. Although four of her eight children predeceased her, four married daughters whose school fees she had paid and whose careers as teachers and mantua-makers she had launched survived after her death in 1811.[120] This was not an ending as unambiguously happy as one she might have composed under duress, but it bespeaks her dedication in the face of publishing conventions that were not conducive to producing the kind of steady income she required. However, the testimonies preserved in her letters to the Literary Fund make it clear that her successes were achieved at considerable personal cost and the responses of

[118] Deborah D. Rogers, *Ann Radcliffe: A Bio-Bibliography* (Westport, CT: Greenwood Press, 1996), p. 106.

[119] Thomas Noon Talfourd, 'Memoir of the Life and Writings of Mrs. Radcliffe', prefixed to Ann Radcliffe, *Gaston de Blondeville, or the Court of Henry III Keeping Festival in Ardenne: a Romance & St Albans Abbey: a Metrical Tale*, 2 vols (Philadelphia: H.C. Carey and I. Lea, 1826), I, 57.

[120] Parsons gives some details of her children's careers in her letter to William Windham. Details of her surviving daughters from Elizabeth Lee, 'Parsons, Eliza (1739–1811)', rev. Rebecca Mills, *ODNB*, https://doi.org/10.1093/ref:odnb/21455.

her reviewers show that her works were compromised in the eyes of many of her contemporaries through being marked by the social and economic conditions of their composition. It is perhaps no coincidence that, as Nigel Cross has remarked, 'Of the five women novelists active between 1780 and 1815 whose work is at all well-known today—Fanny Burney, Mrs Inchbald, Ann Radcliffe, Maria Edgeworth and Jane Austen—only Mrs Inchbald lacked private means, but she was a beauty, which was nearly as good since it led to a stage career rather than governessing or needle-work.' Cross goes on to contend that '[m]ost women simply did not have the leisure to cultivate their talents; they had to dash off fiction at piece rates just to keep a roof over their heads'.[121] While Cross fails to acknowledge the extent to which he perpetuates the prejudices that have seen women's writing repeatedly sidelined in systems of literary valuation, it is hard to argue from a perspective shaped by modern aesthetic expectations that all of Parsons' books are consistently brilliant reads. Her works contain moments of genuinely delightful comedy, sharp insight and pungent critique, as well as many surprising elegances and pleasures, but it nevertheless seems likely that Eliza Parsons was prevented from reaching her full potential by the unfortunate conditions that necessitated her turning to the pen. For her, authorship was a last resort, and its manifesting as such both textually and paratextually militated against her achieving the kind of socially-mediated success that might have solved her enduring financial problems. The fact that Parsons spent much of her literary career lacking a room of her own in a literal as well as a metaphorical sense provides a clear example of the interlinked feedback loops that kept working writers trapped in parlous social, critical and financial circumstances.

Patronage and Fashion: Robert Bloomfield as the Farmer's Boy

David Williams had a low opinion of the patrons of literature. Their vagaries were one of his principal justifications for establishing the Literary Fund. In *Claims*, he writes that

> I have hardly ever conversed with an English Mecænas, who did not imagine men of genius and learning should be poor, because poverty impels exertion. The fruits of dire necessity, and of literary leisure, are, however,

---

[121] Cross, *Common Writer*, p. 172.

> extremely different. But those patrons have been generally collectors of
> books from vanity, half-learned, demi-connoisseurs, open to gross flattery
> on account either of birth, fortune, or other circumstances, which neither
> bestow, nor exclude, talents, virtue, or merit.[122]

Williams' attack belittles the character of patronage, but locates it implicitly as an important part of the current literary scene. In this, he agrees
with more modern critics. As Dustin Griffin has argued, the Whiggish
view that the patronage system declined after 1755—with Samuel
Johnson's letter chiding Lord Chesterfield being the symbolic turning
point—is profoundly inaccurate.[123] In fact, direct and indirect patronage
persisted well into the nineteenth century as a major contributor to
authors' incomes, as can be seen from the careers discussed in the previous
chapter and from the cases of Parsons and Heron, who both held posts
acquired through their connections: Parsons at court, Heron writing for a
government publication. By the end of the eighteenth century, patronage
networks had diversified to include influential editors, newly prosperous
professionals, certain well-to-do publishers, a few wealthy authors and
institutions such as the Literary Fund itself. At a time when an author's
gains from selling the copyright of a novel could be as little as £5 or £10,
wealthy patrons who could provide or secure enduring three-figure
incomes for favourites necessarily remained a hugely significant shaping
force in literary culture. As well as providing direct financial support,
patrons played major roles in the promotion of authors. Parsons' first
novel, dedicated to the Marchioness of Salisbury, boasted a substantial list
of eminent subscribers, including the Prince of Wales, the Dukes of York
and Gloucester, Elizabeth Montagu and Horace Walpole.[124] This implied
that Parsons' fiction was a commodity that important people valued and
helped to establish her appeal to the reading audiences that sustained her
parlous career and led eventually to her works' cameo appearance in
Northanger Abbey.

   While patronage relationships could be subject to the problems that
Williams describes, they could also be beneficial to both sides. Several of
the canonical Romantics were sustained for large parts of their careers by

---

[122] Williams, *Claims*, pp. 79–80.

[123] Dustin Griffin, *Literary Patronage in England 1650–1800* (Cambridge: Cambridge
University Press, 1996), pp. 246–8.

[124] Parsons, *Miss Meredith*, I, i-25. List also printed in full in Morton, pp. 243–53.

incomes facilitated by patrons. In 1813, when Wordsworth was in financial difficulties, he was assisted by Samuel Rogers in making an appeal to Sir William Lowther, Lord Lonsdale, which elicited an offer of one hundred pounds a year. On registering Wordsworth's qualms about accepting this money, Lonsdale instead acquired for him a well-remunerated official position: Distributor of Stamps for Westmorland and the Penrith area of Cumberland. Wordsworth held this post for nearly thirty years, eventually passing it on to his son.[125] In some cases, poets did not scruple about accepting money directly—for much of his adult life, Coleridge was partly supported by an annuity provided by the brothers Tom and Josiah Wedgwood, and William Blake secured financial support for a time from the generous didactic poet William Hayley. These patronage relationships sometimes resulted in substantial collaborations. Tom Wedgwood and Coleridge were friends who travelled together, shared ideas and corresponded on personal and philosophical matters.[126] Blake produced engravings for a number of Hayley's works, including his *Life of Cowper* (1803–1804), and Hayley wrote a series of ballads for Blake to illustrate and profit from.[127] Although the Blake-Hayley relationship became strained due to differences in temperament between the radical artisan and his gentlemanly supporter, even after Blake returned from Felpham to London, Hayley provided money and a barrister to assist him in successfully opposing sedition charges. Hayley also continued to help Blake gain commissions. Wordsworth's relationships with his patrons were less dependent on artistic exchanges, but he gratefully dedicated *The Excursion* (1814) to Lord Lonsdale and was on friendly terms with him and with his other major patron, Sir George Beaumont, visiting both men regularly.

However, before they acquired patrons, these three writers were already to some extent established—Wordsworth and Coleridge as poets and gentlemen, Blake as an engraver and artist. Robert Bloomfield, by contrast, was reliant on patronage for his initial introduction. This entailed a fraught set of dynamics that damaged his long-term prospects by creating disabling expectations of dependency. Writers from labouring backgrounds had to contend with a high level of reflexive snobbery from more

[125] Juliet Barker, *Wordsworth: A Life* (London: Viking, 2000), pp. 438, 440–1, 448–9.

[126] See Richard Holmes, *Coleridge: Early Visions* (London: Penguin, 1989), pp. 174–80, 336–7, 359.

[127] Vivienne W. Painting, 'Hayley, William (1745–1820)', *ODNB*, https://doi.org/10.1093/ref:odnb/12769.

privileged authors. In *English Bards and Scotch Reviewers* (1809), Byron gives the following satirical description of Bloomfield's career trajectory:

> When some brisk youth, the tenant of a stall,
> Employs a pen less pointed than his awl,
> Leaves his snug shop, forsakes his store of shoes,
> St. Crispin quits, and cobbles for the muse,
> Heavens! how the vulgar stare! how crowds applaud!
> How ladies read! and Literati laud!
> If chance some wicked wag should pass his jest,
> 'Tis sheer ill-nature—don't the world know best?
> Genius must guide when wits admire the rhyme,
> And CAPEL LOFFT declares 'tis quite sublime.
> Hear, then, ye happy sons of needless trade!
> Swains! quit the plough, resign the useless spade[.][128]

Byron was keen to defend poetry as a gentlemanly prerogative; consequently, he mocked the idea that verse could be produced by artisan labourers in the same manner as trade goods. However, his satire is somewhat defensive, seeking both to belittle the substantial successes achieved by artisan writers and to head off any imputation that his own writing might be considered as crudely commercial. Byron's concern was by no means unique. Coleridge was similarly worried about what he characterised as lower-class intrusions, opining cynically in an 1811 lecture that 'in these times, if a man fail as a tailor, or a shoemaker, and can read and write correctly (for spelling is still of some consequence) he becomes an author.'[129] Both men were defending a model of literature as an upper- and middle-class accomplishment, where it functioned as a social tool and a marker of distinction. However, as Scott's epics and novels and Byron's own later works proved, it was becoming possible to write works that would operate more like fashionable consumer goods than exclusive luxuries. Nor were Scott and Byron the pioneers in addressing broader audiences through verse. Before either of them published a bestselling poem, Bloomfield had produced one of the great popular successes of the Romantic period.

---

[128] Lord Byron, *English Bards and Scotch Reviewers*, lines 765–76, in *Byron: The Complete Poetical Works*, I, 253.

[129] *The Collected Works of Samuel Taylor Coleridge*, gen ed. Kathleen Coburn, 16 vols (Princeton, NJ: Princeton University Press, 1969–1993), V.ii, 463.

Bloomfield was launched after his brother George sent the manuscript of his poem *The Farmer's Boy* to Capel Lofft, a Suffolk gentleman described facetiously by Byron as 'a kind of gratis Accoucheur to those who wish to be delivered of rhyme, but do not know how to bring it forth.'[130] In Bloomfield's case, Lofft's help was invaluable. Finding the poem to be 'very pleasing and characteristic', he secured Bloomfield a publishing contract and drew his protégée to the attention of a number of influential figures.[131] Particularly important was Augustus Henry Fitzroy, the third Duke of Grafton, a well-connected Whig and former prime minister. Impressed by Bloomfield's work and personal conduct—tellingly, both were of importance—Grafton committed to pay him an annuity of fifteen pounds; he also supported Bloomfield's publications and provided him with books.[132] However, while Grafton's support was liberal in some respects, it was noticeably calibrated to Bloomfield's perceived status. Bloomfield's annuity was only a tenth of that awarded by the Wedgwoods to Coleridge, an early sign of the preconceptions that would place severe limits on the social mobility that Bloomfield could achieve through writing.

Once brought to attention, Bloomfield achieved success swiftly and sweepingly. His publisher, Vernor and Hood, published *The Farmer's Boy* under a slightly confused and disadvantageous half-profits arrangement that also seems to have claimed a half-share of Bloomfield's copyright in the poem.[133] *The Farmer's Boy* proceeded to sell over 26,100 copies in the first two-and-three-quarter years after its publication and continued to sell in large quantities in subsequent years.[134] Its sequels, *Rural Tales, Ballads, and Songs* (1802) and *Wild Flowers; or, Pastoral and Local Poetry* (1806),

---

[130] Byron, footnote to *English Bards*, in *Byron: The Complete Poetical Works*, I, 414.

[131] Capel Lofft, 'Preface' to Robert Bloomfield, *The Farmer's Boy: a Rural Poem* (London: Vernor and Hood, 1800), p. i. For a biographical account of Lofft, see Simon J. White, *Robert Bloomfield, Romanticism and the Poetry of Community* (Aldershot: Ashgate, 2007) pp. 84–5.

[132] Robert Bloomfield to Capel Lofft, 5 March 1800, letter 23 in *The Letters of Robert Bloomfield and his Circle*, ed. Tim Fulford and Linda Pratt, *Romantic Circles Electronic Editions*, 2009, https://romantic-circles.org/editions/bloomfield_letters/. Further references to this edition will abbreviate the title to *LRBC*.

[133] For a full account of the poem's publication history, see B.C. Bloomfield, 'The Publication of *The Farmer's Boy* by Robert Bloomfield', *The Library*, 6th Series, 15 (June 1993), 75–94. Details of the copyright arrangements are given in a letter from Thomas Hood quoted on p. 81.

[134] B.C. Bloomfield, p. 83.

although not as sensationally successful as Bloomfield's first book, also did relatively well. William St Clair estimates that Bloomfield's later works sold 'at least 46,500' copies between 1803 and 1826.[135] As well as being commercially successful, Bloomfield received gratifying plaudits in the press. Robert Southey wrote in the *Critical Review* that in *The Farmer's Boy* 'we were delighted to meet with excellence that we had not expected'.[136] He went on to garnish significant extracts from *Rural Tales* with praise. However, he also made a prescient point about the dangers Bloomfield faced, noting that 'to acquire reputation has ever been easier than to preserve it. Mr. Bloomfield's poems will now be compared with what he formerly produced; and the Farmer's Boy is his most dangerous rival.'[137]

The Farmer's Boy was rendered additionally threatening for Bloomfield as one of the hidden costs associated with patronage was his surrendering a degree of control over his presentation within his texts. Lofft edited *The Farmer's Boy* and added a contextualising preface to the first edition. Its readers therefore encountered a detailed narrative of Bloomfield's upbringing before they read a line of his verse. The first-edition preface was relatively shrewd and benign. Following a strategy similar to those employed in launching previous working-class prodigies such as James Woodhouse and Mary Leapor, Lofft stressed Bloomfield's struggle to acquire literacy and his aptitude for literary pursuits, but also his modesty and amiability, making readers aware that Bloomfield was a moral and non-threatening writer, not a potentially dangerous demagogue.[138] Initially, Lofft did not overplay his own role in Bloomfield's success, although he did signal his gentlemanly accomplishments by asserting that his contribution had been 'to revise the MS. making occasionally corrections with respect to Orthography, and sometimes in grammatical construction'.[139]

The poem's success gave Lofft motivation and occasion for further interference, with unfortunate consequences for Bloomfield. In Simon White's view, Lofft 'believed his position as patron or editor to be threatened', and this anxiety manifested in profuse textual additions to later

---

[135] William St Clair, *The Reading Nation in the Romantic Period* (Cambridge: Cambridge University Press, 2004), p. 582.

[136] [Robert Southey], 'Bloomfield's *Rural Tales*', Critical Review, new series, 35 (May 1802), 67–75 (p. 67).

[137] [Southey], 'Bloomfield's Rural *Tales*', p. 68.

[138] See White, pp. 86–7.

[139] Lofft, 'Preface' to *The Farmer's Boy*, p. xv.

printings of the poem.[140] He added a seven-page supplement to the preface in the second edition of *The Farmer's Boy*. In the third, he inserted a sonnet and a twenty-five-page critical appendix, which he expanded further in the fourth edition. This later material was more proprietorial than the initial preface, attempting to impose Lofft's views on Bloomfield's verse. At points, Lofft depicted Bloomfield as a comic figure, diminishing the poet in order to assert his own superiority and influence.[141] He also succumbed to the temptation to write about himself, at times hugely inappropriately, using parts of the appendix to protest against his dismissal as a magistrate.

Such domineering interventions both damaged and discomforted Bloomfield. His publisher, Thomas Hood, made it clear prior to the publication of *Rural Tales* in 1802 that he wanted the notes and preface Lofft had written to be dropped. Lofft considered this request 'the height of absurdity' and accused Bloomfield of being Hood's unwitting pawn.[142] Despite his discomfort, Bloomfield felt that he had little choice but to side with his increasingly problematic benefactor. He wrote to Hood that should Lofft's additions be omitted

> To the Duke of Grafton and many other friends it will be utterly impossible for me to escape the charge of the blackest baseness and ingratitude: for who of them will have patience, to hear my defence? Or take the pains to acquire information? My character will sink rapidly[.][143]

The notes remained, but both Hood and Bloomfield were right to have been concerned about them. While the volume was otherwise well reviewed, the *Poetical Register* remarked that Lofft's 'impertinence of commentary cannot be too severely reprobated' and the critic for the *Anti-Jacobin Review* '[could not] help smiling at the self-importance of

---

[140] White, p. 86.

[141] Fully detailed in White, pp. 89–100.

[142] Capel Lofft to Robert Bloomfield, 24 October 1801, letter 59 in *LRBC*, https://romantic-circles.org/editions/bloomfield_letters/HTML/letterEEd.25.59.html.

[143] Robert Bloomfield to Thomas Hood, undated [? late October 1801], letter 64 in *LRBC*, https://romantic-circles.org/editions/bloomfield_letters/HTML/letterEEd.25.64.html.

the man, who, throughout the volume, has tacked his criticism to the end of each piece.'[144]

Bloomfield's class and initial framing thus made aspects of his career contingent on the opinions of gentlemanly and aristocratic parties who sought to shape his public persona for their own ends. This left Bloomfield feeling, in the words of Tim Fulford and Debbie Lee, that 'his muse (that is to say, his expression of his unique self in verse) was tainted by his patrons' appropriation of his words in their own causes.'[145] Fulford and Lee partly attribute Bloomfield's declining publication rate to anxieties about these usurpations, although, as White has convincingly argued, in his later works Bloomfield took principled stands that allowed him to produce poetry of which he remained proud.[146] These later works, though, reached considerably smaller audiences than *The Farmer's Boy*, leaving Bloomfield principally defined by his first appearance.

In terms of direct literary profits, Bloomfield was astonishingly successful. B.C. Bloomfield has estimated that Bloomfield made around £4000 from *The Farmer's Boy* over the course of his lifetime.[147] After factoring in the Grafton annuity and the payments that Bloomfield received for his other volumes, it initially seems hard to credit his later poverty. His average income post-1800 could be estimated as being at least £250 a year—a reasonably gentlemanly figure. However, this income was not uniform, and circumstances placed extraordinary demands on Bloomfield and his finances. The interest aroused by his poetry necessitated the exhibition of his talents and person at the houses of his patrons. He could not gracefully refuse such engagements, which could be costly in themselves, which he often found trying and which left him with less time for cobbling or for his side-line in constructing Aeolian harps, activities that had supported him in various forms since the early 1780s. These social demands, combined with recurrent illness and an increasing confidence in his literary work, led him largely to abandon his old trades. His confidence in his talents was not unjustified, but while the profits from *The Farmer's Boy* were significant,

---

[144] *Poetical Register*, 2 (January 1803), 426–7 (p. 427); *Anti-Jacobin Review*, 11 (Apr 1802), 394–6 (p. 394).

[145] Tim Fulford and Debbie Lee, 'The Vaccine Rose: Patronage, Pastoralism and Public Health', in *Robert Bloomfield: Lyric, Class and the Romantic Canon*, ed. Simon White, John Goodridge and Bridget Keegan (Lewisburg: Bucknell University Press, 2006), pp. 142–58 (p. 146).

[146] This argument is made particularly strongly in discussions of Bloomfield's final collection, *May Day with the Muses* (1822)—see White, pp. 122–36.

[147] B.C. Bloomfield, p. 93.

they were not consistent. In 1801, he had to ask his publishers for an advance payment to tide him over. In 1802, the Duke of Grafton, seeking to provide him with a more stable income, secured him a place as under-sealer to the King's Bench court. Bloomfield did not find the responsibilities congenial, writing to his brother on the day before he left the position that 'another 4 months such as I have past might perhaps indeed drive me mad'.[148] By this time, though, the profits from his poem had begun to make their way to him; consequently, he prospered during the rest of the 1800s, although his income was at times taxed by his generosity. He supported his mother through her final illness and after her death in December 1803 he bought the title to her cottage for his stepfather and gave considerable sums to his brothers. While he lived fairly comfortably, he was not able to save a great deal or to invest to secure a permanent income beyond the small Grafton annuity.

In the 1810s, Bloomfield's financial situation grievously worsened, in part due to the extent to which he had been expected to surrender control over his publications. The death of Thomas Hood in 1811 left Bloomfield's publishers in the hands of a partner named Sharpe, and by April 1812 the firm's losses had brought it close to bankruptcy. To raise funds, Sharpe sold his share of Bloomfield's copyrights to another bookseller for £509 and disposed of his remaining copies of Bloomfield's works for credit, neglecting to pass any of the profits on to Bloomfield himself and placing his regular income in abeyance.[149] Bloomfield was not fond of Benjamin Crosby, the publisher who acquired the largest share of Vernor, Hood and Sharpe's copyrights, and when he negotiated new terms with him in 1814 he believed that he 'obtained about half the sum [...] their chance is worth', although it is possible that he overvalued his declining stock.[150] His prospects deteriorated further when Crosby also went bankrupt, leaving his copyrights divided among a number of booksellers. Reprints of Bloomfield's earlier works realised increasingly small returns and half of these diminishing profits went to a portfolio of publishers who often had no interest in his current status or his new productions.[151] Attempting to

---

[148] Robert Bloomfield to George Bloomfield, 27 May 1803, letter 109 in *LRBC*, https://romantic-circles.org/editions/bloomfield_letters/HTML/letterEEd.25.109.html.

[149] Jonathan Lawson, *Robert Bloomfield* (Boston: G.K. Hall & Co., 1980), p. 39.

[150] B.C. Bloomfield, p. 86.

[151] For an idea of the diminished but not negligible returns during Bloomfield's late career, see the table detailing costs and profits given in Robert Baldwin to Robert Bloomfield, 5 April 1821, letter 350 in *LRBC*, https://romantic-circles.org/editions/bloomfield_letters/HTML/letterEEd.25.350.html.

sort out these tangled affairs cost Bloomfield further time and money, and repeated journeys to London did his fragile health little good.

Bloomfield also found it difficult to gain traction for reinventing himself in changing circumstances. He was valued initially, as the Duke of Grafton put it to Capel Lofft, as a 'real untaught genius'.[152] By 1800, this was an established tradition with its own restrictive conventions. As Peter Denney puts it, 'the laboring-class poet was expected by the polite to conform to a model of exemplary private virtue, diligent, dutiful, and suitably distanced from what were perceived to be the vulgar elements of collective plebeian life.'[153] Bloomfield's ability to represent himself was thus constrained by an image built as much by his patrons and by existing conventions as by the qualities of his own self-presentations. Ian Haywood has argued that even modern readings of *The Farmer's Boy* succumb to some of these conventions: 'the prevailing pastoralization (indeed, pasteurization) of the poem reveals a curious critical tendency to evade or minimize the poem's striking evocations of violence, terror, and guilt.'[154] Readers recognised and responded to Bloomfield's novel evocations within a limiting tradition of patronised rural writing, seeing in his poetry the things they wanted to see rather than what Bloomfield hoped to present. This was especially awkward for Bloomfield because, as Tim Fulford has written, '[d]espite his self-characterization in his poems as "Giles" the "farmer's boy," Bloomfield was, when he wrote, a Londoner working in one of the capital's hundreds of cramped workshops.'[155] He was thus expected to fill a role within which he did not comfortably fit.

---

[152] Quoted in a letter from Capel Lofft to George Bloomfield, 1 March 1800, letter 21 in *LRBC*, https://romantic-circles.org/editions/bloomfield_letters/HTML/letterEEd.25.21.html.

[153] Peter Denney, 'The Talk of the Tap-Room: Bloomfield, Politics, and Popular Culture', in *Robert Bloomfield: The Inestimable Blessing of Letters*, ed. John Goodridge and Bridget Keegan, *Romantic Circles Praxis*, January 2012, https://romantic-circles.org/praxis/bloomfield/HTML/praxis.2011.denney.html, paragraph 1.

[154] Ian Haywood, 'The Infection of Robert Bloomfield: Terrorizing *The Farmer's Boy*', in *Robert Bloomfield: The Inestimable Blessing of Letters*, https://romantic-circles.org/praxis/bloomfield/HTML/praxis.2011.haywood.html, paragraph 1.

[155] Tim Fulford, 'Bloomfield in His Letters: The Social World of a London Shoemaker Turned Suffolk Poet', in *Robert Bloomfield: The Inestimable Blessing of Letters*, https://romantic-circles.org/praxis/bloomfield/HTML/praxis.2011.fulford.html, paragraph 3.

As a result, and as Southey had predicted, Bloomfield found it increasingly difficult to interest patrons and the public in his later productions. His initial rush of fashionable success had worn out his novelty. This made it difficult for him to reposition himself to pursue new kinds of writing. The demand for his presence at literary gatherings dried up, and in any case his attending such events became impractical after his worsening finances necessitated his leaving London for a cheaper abode in Shefford. When the third Duke of Grafton died in March 1811, Bloomfield heard nothing from his successor for months. It was only after two letters and more than a year that the fourth Duke eventually responded to Bloomfield's entreaties by paying the arrears of the annuity and arranging for its continuation.[156] In 1817, when Bloomfield's friends were attempting to raise desperately needed money to assist him, Wordsworth wrote ruefully to Benjamin Haydon from the Duke's seat: 'This Spot, and its neighbourhood are the scene of the Farmer's Boy; from this bond of connection something was expected from the noble Duke, nor was that expectation wholly fruitless—for he has given five Pounds!!!'[157]

This grudging ducal pittance played a small part in a major operation undertaken by Bloomfield's friends to set his finances on an even footing. Bloomfield was fortunate in that unlike Heron or Parsons he had a significant body of influential supporters and contacts, the most essential resource for succeeding in literary society. Southey advised Bloomfield on how best to order his finances and raise money from the book trade. Rogers also provided advice and assistance. In 1816, Sir Samuel Egerton Brydges organised a subscription effort, writing in the testimonial that 'one who admires the moral worth of [Bloomfield's] character, as well as his writings, is willing to contribute his share of active friendship on this occasion' in order to raise a sum of money 'which may secure independence and comfort to himself and his family during the remainder of his own sickly existence.'[158] As the tone of this intervention makes clear,

---

[156] Robert Bloomfield to the 4th Duke of Grafton, 7 September 1811 and 7 April 1812, letters 271 and 274 in *LRBC*, https://romantic-circles.org/editions/bloomfield_letters/HTML/letterEEd.25.271.html and https://romantic-circles.org/editions/bloomfield_letters/HTML/letterEEd.25.274.html.

[157] William Wordsworth to Benjamin Haydon, 20 January 1817, letter 307 in *LRBC*, https://romantic-circles.org/editions/bloomfield_letters/HTML/letterEEd.25.307.html.

[158] Appeal of Sir Samuel Egerton Brydges on behalf of Robert Bloomfield, 15 September 1816, letter 303 in *LRBC*, https://romantic-circles.org/editions/bloomfield_letters/HTML/letterEEd.25.303.html.

Bloomfield remained someone on whose behalf more socially eminent figures felt empowered to act. Unfortunately for Bloomfield, while Brydges'
plan cleared his immediate debts, it did not raise enough to purchase the
proposed annuity. In 1818, Anne Pye wrote to the Literary Fund that
'Robert Bloomfield, the Author of the Farmer's Boy &c.—is now in circumstances of the greatest embarrassment, having lost the sight of one
eye, & the other is at times so much affected that he can neither see to
read nor write, from which most unfortunate event he is rendered totally
unable to support himself & family'.[159] The Literary Fund granted
Bloomfield £40, a substantial sum by their standards. Bloomfield was
grateful, but was also careful to stress that he was not directly involved in
the application, asking Walter Pye to communicate his 'sincere thanks in
any form you please to Mr Fitzgerald and all who may have thus nobly
distinguished an absent man without his personal solicitation or written
statement of circumstances.'[160] A further application to the Literary Fund
was made in 1822, and another on behalf of Hannah Bloomfield after her
father's death in 1823, when Bloomfield's family had to auction his books
and household effects to settle his outstanding debts. The Fund responded
to both applications with further grants. With such support, Bloomfield
avoided the debtors' prisons that had claimed Heron and—temporarily—
Parsons, but only by inviting, against his inclinations, further patronisa-
tion from others.

Like Parsons and Heron, Bloomfield was socially compromised by his
illiquidity. However, his greater public profile and additional reliance on
patronage meant that the consequences were even more disabling. Because
he was poor, potential patrons assumed that others who had previously
supported him must have found him wanting. In his later years, his activities were carefully scrutinised for signs of moral laxity. In 1821, this was
explicitly brought to his attention by Thomas Lloyd Baker, his companion
on a Wye tour in happier times:

> it has been remarked that for some time past *neither yourself* nor *any of your
> family* have been in the habit of attending *any place of worship whatsoever*. It
> has also been observed that you are in the habit of reading some periodical
> works which are very hostile to the government of this country. Perhaps
> from these two circumstances coupled together has originated the idea that

[159] Anne Pye to the Committee of the Literary Fund, Nov 1818, Loan 96 RLF 1/382/2.
[160] Robert Bloomfield to Walter Pye, 17 Nov 1818, Loan 96 RLF 1/382/3.

you have imbibed both Deistical & Republican principles […] These considerations have induced many of your friends & patrons *upon principle* to withhold from you their accustomed protection & assistance, thinking that by doing as they had done, & as they still wish to do, they should be giving countenance to a dangerous man.[161]

In his response to Lloyd Baker, Bloomfield made it clear that he resented the intrusion into his private affairs. He stressed that his patronage income was not precisely 'accustomed', regular payments being limited to the Grafton annuity and a smaller, short-term one from a Mrs Andrews Sharp. He also pointed out that when the subscription had been raised for him, 'many worthy hands assisted; the Earl of Lonsdale, Mr Rogers, Lord Holland, and people of the most opposite opinions.' More bullishly, he wrote that when he was first 'brought before the public', he had determined that he '*never would in public writing or intimate correspondence enter into disputation or disquisition on the two grand subjects which keep the world in agitation, Religion and politics.*' 'I have kept my word or vow,' he asserted, 'and you will find that I can keep it.'[162]

Bloomfield's response to Lloyd Baker rightfully defends his conduct, but it also shows that he felt he compelled to disavow his political agency in order to operate in polite society. While Bloomfield felt constrained from airing his political views, this constraint did not extend to those with an interest in his celebrity. As Denney writes, '[t]hroughout his career, [Bloomfield's] work and public image were appropriated to serve a political cause by people of a radical as well as a conservative persuasion, and this must have reinforced the poet's sense that politics was utterly incompatible with the independence he so much wanted to preserve.'[163] While politicians like William Windham and writers like William Cobbett employed Bloomfield for political ends, he could not express his own politics without risking censure from patrons and institutions that praised him only so long as he wrote from a position that posed no threat to them.[164]

[161] Thomas John Lloyd Baker to Robert Bloomfield, 23 May 1821, letter 351 in *LRBC*, https://romantic-circles.org/editions/bloomfield_letters/HTML/letterEEd.25.351.html.

[162] Robert Bloomfield to Thomas John Lloyd Baker, 25 May 1821, letter 352 in *LRBC*, https://romantic-circles.org/editions/bloomfield_letters/HTML/letterEEd.25.352.html.

[163] Denney, paragraph 27.

[164] Denney, paragraphs 22–6.

In a notice marking Bloomfield's death in 1823, the *Monthly Magazine* published a damning assault on his achievements and on the propriety of working-class writers seeking to publish:

> His ambition [...] was disappointed; and, for some years, he was in a state of mental depression, which, it is stated, rendered his death consolatory to his connections. Under these circumstances, and they are such as constantly attend genius without pecuniary independence, the editor of this Magazine is not ashamed of the advice which he gave Bloomfield at his outset. The world would have lost nothing by the non-appearance of the Farmer's Boy, as it then existed in Bloomfield's original manuscript, and the poet would have enjoyed the comforts of an industrious life, enhanced by his love of the Muses.[165]

Bloomfield's brother George was understandably infuriated by this article. In a letter to Joseph Weston, the editor of Bloomfield's *Remains*, he took great pains to rebut its charges. He described the extent to which '[a]ll the comforts myself and brothers enjoyed, evidently sprung from the success of Robert', pointing out that at times Bloomfield was supporting relatives numbering in the high twenties.[166] George was also angered by the article's '*inference*, that the *poor* man of talents should not dare to enter the fields of literature, but leave them to the men of "*pecuniary indepen-dence*."' Bearing in mind Bloomfield's substantial achievements, George was justified in rejecting the article's insulting insinuations. However, the *Monthly* was largely correct in asserting that financial independence and a certain level of social status were necessary for an author to exert a reason-able level of control over his or her destiny. Bloomfield's literary produc-tions were enduringly successful. By B.C. Bloomfield's 'considerable under-estimate', around 283,000 volumes containing *The Farmer's Boy* were sold during the nineteenth century.[167] In Bloomfield's lifetime, though, he was patronised in both senses. When considering his career, it becomes clear that the credit that he could gain for his literary talent was sharply circumscribed by social expectations that continue to shape the manners in which he is (and is not) read.

---

[165] 'Died', *Monthly Magazine*, 56 (Sep 1823), 181–3 (p. 183).

[166] George Bloomfield to Joseph Weston, 9 June 1824, letter 389 in *LRBC*, https://romantic-circles.org/editions/bloomfield_letters/HTML/letterEEd.25.389.html.

[167] B.C. Bloomfield, p. 92.

SOUTHEY'S CRITIQUE AND THE PROFESSION OF AUTHORSHIP

Looking at the careers of Heron, Parsons and Bloomfield makes it clear that D'Israeli and Williams were both right when they argued that achieving profitable recognition was a serious problem for those who had been told that they could better their situations through writing. Prejudicial assumptions concerning labour, class, genre and gender all played important roles in limiting the financial and social profits that most writers could reap. As its interventions in these three cases reveal, the Literary Fund was to some extent effective in reaching the disadvantaged. However, its subsidiary role in these three stories and the responses it provoked from its critics both demonstrate that the Fund's ability to effect positive change was relatively restricted.

On the publication of *Calamities of Authors*, Robert Southey, not yet Poet Laureate but still a well-established, solvent and respected writer, wrote to John Murray to propose that he 'give wings to [D'Israeli's] work' by reviewing it for the *Quarterly*. He was also keen to use the opportunity to 'say something upon the absurd purposes of the Literary Fund, with its despicable ostentation of patronage'.[168] Southey's account of *Calamities* in the resulting review was largely positive. He agreed that D'Israeli was right to attempt to 'enforce a truth which may save many a one from a life of dependence, disappointment, and wretchedness'.[169] However, he expressed uncertainty about whether many of D'Israeli's calamities were genuinely specific to authors. He asserted that while writing carried health risks, these were hardly comparable to the potential hazards faced in more active professions: 'Sailors and night-coachmen are short lived for want of due sleep: he who lives, night as well as day, in his study among the dead, converses usually longer with the living also, than those men of hard lives and iron temperament.'[170] He extended this observation to argue that many of the problems that D'Israeli attributed to authorship resulted from wider social conditions or unrelated mental characteristics.

Southey had his own agenda in attempting to disassociate authorship and dysfunction. His own position as a trusted and influential commentator rested partly on his having successfully promoted himself as a talented

---

[168] Robert Southey to John Murray, 14 August 1812, in Letters from Southey, 1808–1812, NLS Ms.42550.

[169] [Robert Southey], 'D'Israeli's *Calamities of Authors*', *Quarterly Review*, 7 (September 1812), 93–114 (p. 109).

[170] [Southey], 'D'Israeli's *Calamities*', p. 99.

professional gentleman. Therefore, when he described Heron as 'a poor miserable laborious man, who has the strongest claim upon our compassion for the wretchedness of his fate, but who has no claim for anything further', Southey was carefully distancing the ranks of 'proper' literary men like himself from those who wrote and failed. While he admitted that authorship was generally 'a very unprofitable profession', he remained self-interestedly determined that it be recognised as a respectable career for select adherents.[171] This proprietorial attitude also informed his response to Williams' attempt to alleviate the problems of distressed writers:

> We have, it is true, a literary fund for the relief of distressed authors, the members of which dole out their alms in sums of five, ten and twenty pounds, (never, we believe, exceeding the latter sum), dine together in public once a year, write verses in praise of their own benevolence, and recite them themselves. Nothing can be more evident, than that such liberality is as useless to literature as it is pitiful in itself.[172]

Like Williams, Southey deplored the excesses of patrons, but, unlike Williams, he saw the worst excesses of patronage exemplified in the Fund itself. He found these excesses particularly offensive as he believed that the grants the Fund's Committee offered were often woefully insufficient. While a writer taken up by a traditional wealthy patron might expect substantial support, the Fund, with its limited income and numerous applicants, could usually only offer a stay of execution. As Southey put it

> The Literary Fund provides no present employment for the hungry and willing labourer, and holds out no hope for the future; a first donation operates against a second claim; a second or third becomes a bar to any further bounty, and the learned mendicant who leans upon the broken reed is abandoned by it in prison, or turned over to the parish or the hospital at last.[173]

Southey treated the Literary Fund harshly, but he also had a point. The Fund certainly helped a considerable number of people. Of the nearly seven hundred authors who applied between 1790 and 1830, the Fund provided about 85% with much-needed relief, many of them on several

---

[171] [Southey], 'D'Israeli's *Calamities*', p. 101.
[172] [Southey], 'D'Israeli's *Calamities*', p. 112.
[173] [Southey], 'D'Israeli's *Calamities*', p. 113.

occasions.[174] Without the interest drawn by the self-congratulatory dinners that Southey deplored, the Fund would have had very little money with which to aid its applicants. Even with the dinners, though, the aid that the 'joint-stock-patronage-company' could disburse was spread among so many writers that the value of individual grants was often insufficient (as in Heron's case) or only enough to address immediate problems (as in Parsons').[175] The work the Fund did was well-intentioned and valuable, but it did not stimulate a revolution in the status of literary production. As Williams had feared, the scale of the problem was too vast and the vested interests seeking to keep authorship a limited, high-class accomplishment too ingrained. The Fund could not single-handedly engender the kind of respectability that served to stabilise a profession. As Penelope Corfield has written, in the early nineteenth century 'it proved insuperably difficult to translate literary freedom into the trappings of formal professionalism.'[176] For the unfortunate, for the poorly connected and for many female and lower-class writers, the vision of independence through literary success proved to be a dangerous illusion. While many aspirant writers assumed they could build steady and respectable careers as authors, they generally discovered that the supposedly liberating power of writing was channelled by vested interests in manners that meant its emancipatory potential was distressingly limited.

---

[174] Statistics drawn from my catalogue data for the RLF Case Files (Loan 96 RLF 1).

[175] [Southey], 'D'Israeli's *Calamities*', p. 113.

[176] Penelope J. Corfield, *Power and the Professions in Britain 1700–1850* (London: Routledge, 1995), p. 185.

Chapter Five: The Oligarchs of Literature: Authority and the Quarterly Reviews

In many respects, the first literary writers to muster genuinely professional modes of authority were the conductors of the *Edinburgh Review* and the *Quarterly Review*. By pooling and channelling influence, the coteries behind these periodicals amassed both sociocultural power and considerable, reliable financial dividends. Their scathing, juridical criticisms dominated the works of individual authors who they profited by depicting as slipshod and morally fallible. During the 1800s and 1810s, key reviewers eclipsed the vast majority of those that they reviewed in terms of readerships, remuneration and influence. The previous chapters have touched on the clout of the quarterlies in discussing specific writers; this chapter will build on these allusions by examining how the quarterlies redefined previous reviewing practices, rewarding those who wrote for them and propagating potent and far-reaching discourses of conservative authority.

New Criticism?

Henry Cockburn, in his 1852 *Life of Lord Jeffrey*, wrote that his friend's most notable achievement, the *Edinburgh Review*, represented 'an entire and instant change of every thing that the public had been accustomed to in that sort of composition', adding that on its emergence '[t]he old

© The Author(s) 2021
M. Sangster, *Living as an Author in the Romantic Period*, Palgrave Studies in the Enlightenment, Romanticism and Cultures of Print, https://doi.org/10.1007/978-3-030-37047-3_7

periodical opiates were extinguished at once.'[1] Cockburn was being some-what extravagant, but his account tallies with those of other contempo-raries in envisaging the emergence of the *Edinburgh* as an event that transformed criticism and authorship. Where previous journals had cata-logued, nurtured and responded to literary culture, the *Edinburgh* sought to shape and dominate it, leveraging critical authority for political gain. Its voice was, for a time, uniquely commanding; as William Hazlitt put it,

> The persons who wrote in this Review seemed 'to have their hands full of truths,' and now and then, in a fit of spleen or gaiety, let some of them fly; and while this practice continued, it was impossible to say that the Monarchy or the Hierarchy was safe. [...] The principles were by no means decidedly hostile to existing institutions: but the spirit was that of fair and free discus-sion; a field was open to argument and wit; every question was tried upon its own ostensible merits, and there was no foul play. The tone was that of a studied impartiality (which many called *trimming*) or of a skeptical indifference.[2]

Hazlitt figures the *Edinburgh* reviewers as a potent new pantheon whose emergence served to put the established order on the back foot. Like Cockburn's account, Hazlitt's is hyperbolic and at points downright dis-ingenuous. In particular, his assertion that the *Edinburgh's* spirit was one of 'free and fair discussion' would have come as a surprise to many of the authors the Review subjected to debilitating attacks. Furious responses from aggrieved writers were numerous enough five years after the *Edinburgh* commenced to fill John Ring's *Beauties of the 'Edinburgh Review', alias the Stinkpot of Literature*. Ring gives his target's chief beau-ties as 'calumny and detraction' and claimed (not without cause) that it 'makes war on the whole host of authors; and mangles them without mercy, for the sake of amusing the public.'[3]

As Ring recognised, the professional authority the *Edinburgh's* critics wielded was achieved at least partly at the expense of those they reviewed. The *Edinburgh* self-consciously asserted its pre-eminence through felicity

---

[1] Henry Cockburn, *Life of Lord Jeffrey: with a Selection from his Correspondence*, 2 vols (Edinburgh: Adam and Charles Black, 1852), I, 131.

[2] William Hazlitt, 'Mr. Jeffrey', in *The Spirit of the Age*, in *The Complete Works of William Hazlitt*, ed. P.P. Howe, 21 vols (London: J.M. Dent, 1930–34), XI, 126–34 (pp. 126–7).

[3] John Ring, *The Beauties of the 'Edinburgh Review', alias the Stinkpot of Literature* (London: H.D. Symonds and John Hatchard, 1807), p. 2.

of style, frequent censure, careful editing and flaunting insider knowledge. As Francis Jeffrey put it when setting out his editorial principles in a letter to Charles Koenig:

> To be learned and right is no doubt the first requisite—but to be ingenious and original and discursive is perhaps something more than the second in a publication which can only do good by remaining popular—and cannot be popular without other attractions than those of mere truth and correctness.[4]

As Jeffrey makes clear, the *Edinburgh's* conductors understood that its authority was built on its success as a performance. Specifically, the *Edinburgh* performed entertaining judgements laid down by a brilliant, anonymised (but knowable) voice against named, fallible, amateurish defendants.

Hazlitt was accurate in depicting establishment nervousness regarding the *Edinburgh*. In 1807, John Murray, only recently made undisputed head of his father's publishing house and keen to make both profits and his mark, wrote a worried letter to George Canning, who had become Foreign Secretary earlier that year and who had previously successfully barracked Whiggish and radical opponents in the *Anti-Jacobin*. Murray described the *Edinburgh* as being 'written with such unquestionable talent, that it has already attained an extent of circulation not equalled by any similar publication.'[5] Worried by the dissemination of principles he considered 'radically bad', he suggested that 'some means, equally popular, ought to be adopted to counteract their dangerous tendency.' The publication Murray founded, the *Quarterly Review*, followed the trail that the *Edinburgh's* clique had blazed by creating its own authoritative critical voice designed to produce and perpetuate popularity and clout. Its success in doing so was demonstrated by the responses it provoked from its opponents, such as Percy Bysshe Shelley's admission that the *Quarterly* was 'a dreadful preponderance against the cause of improvement' or Hazlitt's

---

[4] Francis Jeffrey to Charles Koenig, 20 January 1806, BL Additional Manuscript 32439, fol. 235, as reprinted in John Clive, *Scotch Reviewers: The 'Edinburgh Review' 1802–1815* (London: Faber & Faber, 1957), p. 54.

[5] John Murray to the R⁺ Hon. G.C. (George Canning), 25 September 1807, from John Murray Letter Book, 2 April 1808–13 March 1843, NLS Ms.41909, fols. 17ᵛ–18ʳ (outgoing side) (fol. 17ᵛ).

furiously describing it as 'one foul blotch of servility, intolerance, false-hood, spite, and ill-manners'.[6]

It is important to stress that while the quarterlies were inherently political publications, they were not simply mouthpieces for opposing parliamentary factions. Walter Scott perceptively drew out the subtleties in an 1808 letter to the editor of the nascent *Quarterly*, William Gifford:

> It would certainly not be advisable that the work should at its outset assume exclusively a political character. On the contrary the articles upon science and miscellaneous literature ought to be such as may challenge comparison with the best of contemporary reviews. But as the real reason for instituting the publication is the disgusting and deleterious doctrine with which the most popular of these periodical works disgraces its pages it is essential to consider how opposite & sounder principles can be most advantageously brought forward.[7]

Scott here makes explicit one of the key manners in which the quarterlies operated—having established their authority through their superior reviewing, they exercised that authority to win what Mark Schoenfield has termed the 'war of representation' by inducing readers to accept their political pronouncements and world views.[8] Their editors thus had a strong incentive to make sure that all published reviews played a part in propagating a sense of their journals' brilliance and rigour. To achieve this, Jeffrey and Gifford exercised tight editorial controls, freely 'finessing' contributors' copy to make it 'palatable': in Scott's words, converting 'an unmarketable commodity into one which from its general effect and spirit is not likely to disgrace those among which it is placed.'[9] This editorial convoking allowed the quarterlies to forge powerful and unified anonymised voices. By using these voices to enact dominance over the spheres

[6] Shelley to Thomas Love Peacock, 25 February 1819, in *The Letters of Percy Bysshe Shelley*, ed. Frederick L. Jones, 2 vols. (Oxford: Oxford University Press, 1964), II, 81; Hazlitt, 'Mr. Jeffrey', XI, 127.

[7] Walter Scott to William Gifford, 25 October 1808, in *The Letters of Sir Walter Scott*, ed. Sir Herbert Grierson, transcribed Takero Sato, 12 vols, located at *The Walter Scott Digital Archive*, Edinburgh University Library, http://www.walterscott.lib.ed.ac.uk/etexts/etexts/letters.html, II, 105.

[8] Mark Schoenfield, *British Periodicals and Romantic Identity: The "Literary Lower Empire"* (New York: Palgrave Macmillan, 2009), p. 85. See also the wider context (pp. 84–99) and Schoenfield's earlier section on Lord Chancellor Eldon's concern about the press's shaping political discourse through the ways it chose to represent it (pp. 38–47).

[9] *Letters of Sir Walter Scott*, II, 104.

of culture, science and letters, they purchased credibility and respect that made their political articles into potent interventions. As Jon Klancher has it, '[n]o discourse was so immediately identified with power in the nineteenth century as that of the great party quarterlies', which 'carved between them what seemed to be the universe of political thought.'[10]

Both quarterlies vastly outsold their competition in the first twenty years of the nineteenth century. The *Edinburgh*, launched in October 1802, achieved ubiquity first, but from 1809 the *Quarterly* swiftly made up for lost time, becoming the *Edinburgh's* equal opponent, somewhat different in its processes of selection but employing similar kinds of rhetoric and circulating to a similarly wide audience. The *Quarterly's* sales peaked at around 14,000 in the late 1810s, a figure slightly higher than the *Edinburgh's* peak of around 13,000 copies earlier in the decade.[11] By comparison, William St Clair quotes sources giving 4000 copies as a circulation figure for *Blackwood's Edinburgh Magazine* in the late 1810s— although he notes that its most successful numbers could sell a great deal more—and cites an account from 1813 listing a circulation of 4500 copies for the *Monthly Magazine* and 2000 each for the *Critical Review*, the *Anti-Jacobin Review* and the *British Critic*.[12] However, these figures only tell part of the story. As Jeffrey wrote to Thomas Moore in 1814, '[w]e print now nearly 13,000 copies and may reckon I suppose modestly on three or four readers of the popular articles in each copy—no prose preachers I believe have so large an audience.'[13] Jeffrey highlights habits of sharing and circulation that allowed texts to reach readerships far in excess of their print runs. These habits compounded the quarterlies' advantages over their competition, bringing each number before a considerable percentage of the enfranchised reading public.

It is difficult accurately to estimate the size of the reading nation in the Romantic period. A figure commonly given is a purported estimate by Edmund Burke that towards the end of the eighteenth century there were around 80,000 book readers. This figure is usually cited from A.S. Collins'

[10] Jon P. Klancher, *The Making of English Reading Audiences, 1790–1832* (Madison: University of Wisconsin Press, 1987), p. 69.

[11] William St Clair, *The Reading Nation in the Romantic Period* (Cambridge: Cambridge University Press, 2004), p. 573. Number-by-number figures can be found in the Murray and Longman archives.

[12] St Clair, pp. 573–4.

[13] Francis Jeffrey to Thomas Moore, 14 September 1814, transcribed Michael Bott, URSC MS 1393 Part II.26B, 1/Part 1/299.

1928 *Profession of Letters*, although it also appears in the preface to the first volume of Charles Knight's *Penny Magazine*, printed in 1832.[14] Knight's preface goes on to show the massive expansion that had taken place by the time he commenced his work: 'In the present year', he wrote, 'it has been shown by the sale of the 'Penny Magazine,' that there are two hundred thousand *purchasers* of one periodical work. It may be fairly calculated that the number of readers of that single work amounts to a million.' The *Penny Magazine*'s vast circulation demonstrates the great strides in printing technology that had been made by the 1830s. Charles Henry Timperley's *Dictionary of Printers and Printing* (1839) gives a telling comparison: 'from two sets of plates, by machines made by Applegath and Cowper, the same quantity of press work may be performed in ten days, as would take two men, by the old mode [...] more than five calendar months.'[15] This goes some way towards explaining why the *Edinburgh* and the *Quarterly* waned after the 1810s, eclipsed by cheaper and more diverse competition that served to enfranchise new classes of readers. It also, however, implies that while the reading public grew during the early nineteenth century, before the developments of the 1820s, the number able to access new works and the periodicals that reviewed them was nowhere near Knight's million *Penny Magazine* readers. In an 1812 review of George Crabbe, Jeffrey estimated that 'there probably are not less than two hundred thousand persons who read for amusement or instruction among the middling classes of society. In the higher classes, there are not as many as twenty thousand.'[16] Based on these figures, it seems fair to say that the *Edinburgh* and the *Quarterly* reached a seldom-equalled fraction of those who were able to afford new literary works.

The extent to which the *Edinburgh* and the *Quarterly* reconfigured literary culture has not always been fully recognised in modern studies. Klancher's   incisive   account   of   the   fragmentation   of   periodical

---

[14]A.S. Collins, *The Profession of Letters: A Study of the Relation of Author to Patron, Publisher, and Public, 1780–1832* (London: Routledge, 1928), p. 29; 'Preface' to *The Penny Magazine of the Society for the Diffusion of Useful Knowledge, Volumes 1–2*, ed. Charles Knight (London: Charles Knight, 1832), p. iii. Richard Altick notes the *Penny Magazine* reference and states that his efforts to find the figure in Burke's writings were 'fruitless' (*The English Common Reader* (Chicago: University of Chicago Press, 1957), p. 49).

[15]Charles Henry Timperley, *A Dictionary of Printers and Printing: with the Progress of Literature; Ancient and Modern* (London: H. Johnson, 1839), p. 920.

[16][Francis Jeffrey], 'Crabbe's *Tales*', *Edinburgh Review*, 20 (November 1812), 277–305 (p. 280).

audiences—the touchstone for much valuable recent work—considers the quarterlies as part of a chapter on the formation of self-consciously middle-class readerships. However, in doing so he to some extent occludes their formative roles and their particular heightened statuses. He lists the 'most significant journals' in the field of cultivating middle-class identities as 'the *Edinburgh Review* (1802), the *Examiner* (1808), the *Quarterly Review* (1809), the *New Monthly Magazine* (1814), *Blackwood's Edinburgh Magazine* (1817), the *London Magazine* (1821), the *Westminster Review* (1824), the *Athenaeum* (1828), *Fraser's Magazine* (1830), the *Metropolitan* (1831).'[17] The dates in this list and the figures cited previously demonstrate that considering these periodicals as peers glosses over significant differences in sizes of readerships and circumstances of production. With the exception of the weekly *Examiner*, it was not until the late 1810s and the 1820s that the quarterlies faced major challengers to their hegemony when a second wave of revamped monthlies began to react against them. Competition from publications seeking to address general readerships also developed a lot later—of the four periodicals Klancher names in opening his chapter on mass audiences, *The Mirror of Literature, Amusement, and Instruction* was established in 1822, *The Hive* ran from 1822 until 1824 and the *Penny Magazine* and *Chambers's Edinburgh Journal* did not begin circulating until 1832.[18] While radical publications such as William Cobbett's *Political Register* (priced at two pence from November 1816) and Thomas Wooler's *Black Dwarf* (established in 1817) achieved very high circulation figures earlier in the century, their audiences largely consisted of those who were kept out of the exclusive scene the quarterlies sought to regulate by high prices and cultural gatekeeping.[19]

What I wish to do, then, is posit an additional stage in Klancher's model, between the eclipse of the old periodicals in the late 1790s and the emergence of distinct mass and middle-class audiences in the third decade of the nineteenth century. As David Stewart contends, as late as 1825, '[m]agazines [...] created much of their perplexing effect by acknowledging the mixed nature of an audience they could not securely divide into

---

[17] Klancher, p. 50.
[18] Klancher, p. 77.
[19] Altick, pp. 325–6.

separate groups.'[20] A number of recent studies have brought out the richness and diversity of magazine culture in the late 1810s and 1820s, the period in which 'genius first became widely discussed and represented' in the works of the writers we now associate most strongly with Romantic periodical writing—Charles Lamb, Hazlitt, Leigh Hunt, Thomas De Quincey and Thomas Carlyle—as well as in articles by many less famous names.[21] I shall return to these important developments in the coda, but I would like to emphasise that the 'spectacle of multiplicity' these publications presented emerged in opposition to contexts that the quarterly colossi had determined.[22] While in certain respects the quarterlies were harbingers of a new age of mass print production, they were also the bastions of a literary world within which relatively small groups of elites sought to control the meanings of diverse written discourses, the regulation of which they believed to be their rightful responsibility and purview.

ENLIGHTENMENT VS. *THE ANTI-JACOBIN*

To explain the transformations that the quarterlies wrought is best accomplished by first discussing the periodicals they eclipsed. The earliest British periodicals were the proceedings of learned societies, but at the beginning of the eighteenth century writers began to use the form to imagine and address a wider public. Joseph Addison and Richard Steele explicitly intended that the *Spectator* would open up the literary world. In a famous and much-discussed declaration, their persona asserted that 'I shall be ambitious to have it said of me, that I have brought Philosophy out of the Closets and Libraries, Schools and Colleges, to dwell in Clubs and Assemblies, at Tea-Tables, and in Coffee-Houses.'[23] Many other early periodicals were similarly explicit in seeking to make intellectual culture accessible to a wider (although still far-from-universal) readership. When the first general magazines and Reviews were 'initiated by bookseller-

---

[20] David Stewart, *Romantic Magazines and Metropolitan Literary Culture* (Basingstoke: Palgrave Macmillan, 2011), p. 206.

[21] David Higgins, *Romantic Genius and the Literary Magazine: Biography, Celebrity, Politics* (London: Routledge, 2005), p. 150. Other works focusing principally on this later period include Mark Parker's *Literary Magazines and British Romanticism* (Cambridge: Cambridge University Press, 2000), which focuses on the period 1820–1834, and Stewart's book, the introduction to which gives a date range of 1815–1825.

[22] Stewart, p. 10.

[23] *The Spectator*, No. 10 (12 March 1711), [p. 19].

publisher-distributors', their reviews were, in Marilyn Butler's words, 'plainly aimed not at selling the individual book [...] but at creating and developing an audience for "literary intelligence."'[24] The principal duties of the early reviewer were to set out the contents of the book under consideration and place these in contexts that non-specialist auditors could understand. The synoptic method employed to accomplish these duties allowed readers of periodicals like the *Monthly Review* (established in 1749) and the *Critical Review* (1756) to keep abreast of developments across a wide range of fields without having to acquire either comprehensive knowledge or a large number of expensive new books.

Such Reviews affected and largely practiced enlightened egalitarianism. While women and lower-class writers were often condescended to, the Reviews' pretensions to inclusiveness ensured that their works were at least noticed. As I have discussed, Eliza Parsons' Minerva Press gothics were reviewed extensively and in many respects even-handedly. The *Critical's* four-page account of *The Castle of Wolfenbach* (1793) quoted expansively, and while the review claimed that 'there is no fine writing in these volumes' and was happy to point out 'vulgarisms', it also stressed that the novel was a moral publication and that it had 'sufficient interest to be read with pleasure'.[25] The *British Critic* was more impressed; its brief review concluded that *Wolfenbach* was 'more interesting than the general run of modern novels' and 'abound[ed] with interesting, though improbable situations.'[26] Despite their snobbishness, Parsons' reviewers allowed her merits and gave her works opportunities to speak directly to readers through summary and direct quotation.

Even works that might have been seen to be morally dubious were generally reviewed appreciatively and sensitively. A good example would be William Beckford's oriental fantasia *Vathek* (1786), a work originally written in French and translated into English by Beckford's former tutor, Samuel Henley. The *Critical's* review cannily noted that 'the disguise of a translator of an invisible original, is now suspected' and pointed out slightly suspiciously that the work displays 'the acute turns of modern composition, so easily learned in the school of Voltaire.'[27] Nevertheless, its

---

[24] Marilyn Butler, 'Culture's Medium: The Role of the Review', in *The Cambridge Companion to British Romanticism*, ed. Stuart Curran (Cambridge: Cambridge University Press, 1993), pp. 120–47 (p. 131).

[25] '*Castle of Wolfenbach*', *Critical Review*, new series, 10 (January 1794), 49–52 (p. 50).

[26] *British Critic*, 3 (February 1794), 199–200 (pp. 199–200).

[27] '*The History of the Caliph Vathek*', *Critical Review*, 62 (July 1786), 37–42 (pp. 39, 38).

praise was relatively unreserved, although it did skip over some of *Vathek's* more gruesome scenes, instead making much of the scholarship displayed in the notes (added to the novel by Henley). The *Gentleman's Magazine* 'earnestly recommend[ed] "Vathek" to every class of readers; for the morality of the design, and the excellence of the execution entitle it to universal attention'.[28] The *English Review* (a publication revealingly sub-titled '*an abstract of English and foreign literature*') did comment suspiciously on *Vathek's* principles, but in a way that interestingly restated its own commitment to the active pursuit of knowledge:

> The moral which is here conveyed, that ignorance, childishness, and the want of ambition, are the sources of human happiness, though agreeable to the strain of eastern fiction, is inconsistent with true philosophy, and with the nature of man. The punishments of vice, and the pains of gratified curiosity, ought never to have been confounded. Although the *tree of knowledge* was once forbidden, in the present condition of humanity it is the *tree of life*.[29]

This extract explicitly supports Butler's argument that Reviews were invested in fostering a reading public that valued bookish knowledge. In service to this ideal, the eighteenth-century reviewer was more a cataloguer than a judge—the qualities of the work took centre stage, and reviewers generally clarified, commented and categorised rather than presenting partisan opinions or promoting their own ideas. Klancher has stressed the collaborative appearance of eighteenth-century periodicals, particularly the printing of correspondence and the letter-like aspects of reviews, arguing that such practices let them manifest 'an *enjoined* rather than a self-confirming discourse, a community of reading and writing and not a projection on the public.'[30] The idea that the readers of journals could easily become their writers created a sense of equality and equivalency, with composers and auditors imaginatively united in the interested pursuit of knowledge. This played a crucial part in the process of making print seem safe to new readers; as Clifford Siskin has it, 'writing induced a fundamental change in readers—leading them to behave as writers—which, in turn, induced more writing.'[31] Eighteenth-century periodicals

---

[28] *Gentleman's Magazine*, 56 (July 1786), 593–4 (p. 594).

[29] '*The History of the Caliph Vathek*', *English Review*, 8 (September 1786), 180–4 (p. 184).

[30] Klancher, p. 22.

[31] Clifford Siskin, *The Work of Writing: Literature and Social Change in Britain 1700–1830* (Baltimore: Johns Hopkins University Press, 1998), p. 4.

were a key avenue for the proliferation both of authorship and of the idea that producing books could be a valuable occupation.

In the pressurised environment of the 1790s, though, reviewers' priorities began to change. As Paul Keen writes,

> Beyond the continuing goal of encouraging the diffusion of learning [...] reviews were now required to perform the more conservative task of preserving the coherence of the republic of letters as a unique cultural domain (and therefore upholding the claims for the social distinction of authors) by taming those political and cultural pressures which threatened to erode literature's unique social function.[32]

Keen argues that Reviews attempted to accomplish this new regulatory role by systematising literary production, by selecting and castigating their subjects and by trying to ensure their own permanence. These new tendencies were often most apparent in the periodicals that were founded in opposition to the older Reviews. The reasons for this were partly political. As Butler has noted, 'all four owner-editors of the journals dealing seriously with literary matters in 1790—the *Monthly Review*, the *Critical Review*, the *English Review* and the *Analytical Review*—were Dissenters.'[33] The eighteenth-century periodical itself had a Dissenting cast—rational, independently minded and with a wide purview that more closely resembled the broad curricula of the Scottish universities and the Dissenting academies than the staid offerings of Oxford and Cambridge. The conductors of the Dissenting journals, eager to secure full political rights for their brethren, ensured that their periodicals keenly supported the repeal of acts restricting non-Anglican involvement in politics and education. After reformist hopes were dashed by the outbreak of war in 1793, 'the journals' continued support for liberal causes, including peace with France, became all the more counter-cultural and elicited a powerful backlash against literary culture from about 1796.'[34] This backlash took the form both of active repression—for example, the jailing of Joseph Johnson, the doyen of radical publishers, for publishing seditious works in 1798—and of a satirical reconfiguring and politicisation of the literary world through *ad hominem* attacks in publications typified by the *Anti-Jacobin*.

---

[32] Paul Keen, *The Crisis of Literature in the 1790s: Print Culture and the Public Sphere* (Cambridge: Cambridge University Press, 1999), p. 117.

[33] Butler, p. 130.

[34] Butler, p. 130.

A weekly journal, the *Anti-Jacobin* was founded by George Canning, at the outset of what would become a stellar political career, and edited by William Gifford, who later edited the *Quarterly*. It had a fairly short run between November 1797 and July 1798, but was kept in the public mind by its successor journal, *The Anti-Jacobin Review and Magazine* (published from 1798), and by the reprinting of key materials in book form. Parts of its contents were made available both as a relatively expensive two-volume work (in quarto and octavo) and in a smaller, cheaper volume entitled *The Beauties of the Anti-Jacobin*. This title displays a certain level of irony, as the poems that make up over half the volume are generally ferocious parodies, written in supposed pro-Revolutionary Jacobin voices and expressing radical sentiments in ways that comprehensively undermine them. A good, if blunt, example is 'The Jacobin', first published in April 1798, which adapts its form from radical poems by Robert Southey:

> I Am a hearty Jacobin,
> Who own no God, and dread no Sin,
> Ready to dash thro' thick and thin
> > For freedom:
>
> And when the teachers of Chalk Farm
> Gave Ministers so much alarm,
> And preach'd that Kings do only harm,
> > I fee'd 'em.
>
> By Bedford's cut I've trim'd my locks,
> And coal-black is my Knowledge-box,
> Callous to all, except hard knocks
> > Of thumpers;
>
> My eye a noble fierceness boasts,
> My voice is hollow as a ghost's,
> My throat oft wash'd by factious toasts
> > In bumpers.
>
> Whatever is in France, is right;
> Terror and blood are my delight;
> Parties with us do not excite
> > Enough rage.

Our boasted Laws I hate and curse,
Bad from the first, by age grown worse,
I pant and sigh for univers-
                            al suffrage.

Wakefield I love—adore Horne Tooke,
With pride on Jones and Thelwall look,
And hope that they, by hook or crook,
                            Will prosper.

But they deserve the worst of ills,
And all th' abuse of all our quills,
Who form'd of strong and *gagging bills*
                            A cross pair.

Extinct since then each Speaker's fire,
And silent ev'ry daring lyre
Dum-founded they whom I would hire
                            To lecture.

Tied up, alas! is every tongue
On which conviction nightly hung,
And Thelwall looks, though yet but young,
                            A Spectre.

Huzza! the French will soon invade,
And we shall drive a roaring trade;
To us will ev'ry Gallic blade
                            Be welcome;

And surely no more joyful sound
To Corresponders can be found;
Unless Marat should through the ground
                            From Hell come.[35]

Here, as in much of the *Anti-Jacobin's* verse, the fictive Jacobin is made to damn himself and others, explicitly naming and implicitly shaming key radical figures while encoding evidence of his faction's defeat in his

---

[35] 'The Jacobin', from *The Beauties of the Anti-Jacobin*, ed. William Gifford (London: C. Chapple, 1799), pp. 205–6.

ostensible celebration of its values. The *Anti-Jacobin's* writers openly crowed at the cleverness of this strategy; a note to this poem comments archly that in the third-to-last stanza '[t]hese words, of *conviction* and *hanging*, have so ominous a sound, it is rather odd that they were chosen.' This not-so-subtle threat was the final element in the first published version; the two even blunter final stanzas were added in the *Beauties* volume to drive home the point.[36] The *Beauties* volume also extended the poem's introductory note to add a claim that this example of radical Sapphics was taken 'from a roll of miscellaneous papers dropped in the park by some Jacobin.' It is evident that the more distant readers of a relatively cheap book could not be trusted to appreciate the poem's ironies from the less obvious setup used in the periodical version. The *Anti-Jacobin's* parodies achieved a wide circulation; reviewing Southey in the first issue of the *Edinburgh*, Jeffrey noted that 'the melancholy fate of his English Sapphics, we believe, is but too generally known.'[37]

Such rabble-rousing reconfigurations were characteristic of the *Anti-Jacobin's* professed interest in acting as a corrective to the nation's periodical culture, which it figured as foolish, subversive and dangerous. As Gifford put it in the introduction to the *Beauties* volume,

> There is nothing in which the enemies of the constitution have so much the advantage of its friends as in their strict adherence to each other and their *judicious* management of *the Press* […] that fatal engine which has done more than the sword, the musquet, or the cannon, for the extension of anarchy, and the destruction of the social world.[38]

The *Anti-Jacobin* set itself up (disingenuously) as a resistance movement, fighting for truth in a high-stakes battle against seditious and mendacious adversaries. In its paranoid discourse, the idea that all additions to knowledge are valuable became suspect and outmoded. Gifford's prospectus makes it very clear that in a time of partisan and international conflict, disinterested appreciation was not a mode that he and his associates could countenance:

---

[36] 'The Jacobin', *Anti-Jacobin*, 2 (9 April 1798), 133–5.

[37] [Francis Jeffrey], 'Southey's *Thalaba*', *Edinburgh Review*, 1 (October 1802), 63–83 (p. 72).

[38] 'Advertisement', *The Beauties of the Anti-Jacobin*, pp. iv–v.

We avow ourselves to be *partial* to the COUNTRY *in which we live*, notwith-standing the daily panegyricks which we read and hear on the superior vir-tues and endowments of its rival and hostile neighbours. We are *prejudiced* in favour of *her* Establishments, civil and religious; though without claiming for either that ideal perfection, which modern philosophy professes to dis-cover in the more luminous systems which are arising on all sides of us.[39]

Such rhetoric positions those who affect unprejudiced discourse as dan-gerous and irresponsible malcontents. The *Anti-Jacobin* accepts that writ-ers influence political processes, but turns this against liberal authors by arguing that their writings reveal them to be 'ignorant, and designing, and false, and wicked, and turbulent, and anarchical—various in their language, but united in their plans, and steadily pursuing through hatred and con-tempt, the destruction of their Country.'[40] The weekly's concluding shot in its final issue—the poem 'New Morality'—named many of its targets, binding together Thomas Paine, William Godwin, Thomas Holcroft and the Literary Fund's founder David Williams as 'creeping creatures, ven-omous and low'. It also included among those enjoined to 'praise Lepaux' Samuel Taylor Coleridge, Southey, Lamb, the *Morning Chronicle* and the *Morning Post*, Joseph Priestley, John Thelwall and Gilbert Wakefield.[41] Leading poets, Dissenters and papers were thus explicitly leagued with France against England, cast as threats to be contained and condemned. Such attacks on individual authors and on writers as a group undermined the inclusive, knowledge-promoting methodology propagated by the older Reviews. The *Anti-Jacobin* was one of a wave of publications that articulated a new sense of the periodical writer as a stern judge whose duty was to bring feckless authors into line. As Gifford put it, 'We reverence LAW,—We acknowledge USAGE,—We look even upon PRESCRIPTION without hatred or horror.'[42] While Derek Roper has rightly stressed that reviewers for early periodicals were often eminently qualified, their low rates of pay and the quantities of work that key reviewers undertook pro-vided ammunition for rousing the Grub Street-inspired spectre of careless hackery, facilitating accusations of blithe overproduction and of puffing

---

[39] 'Prospectus', *Anti-Jacobin*, 1 (20 November 1797), 1–10 (pp. 3–4).
[40] '[Untitled]', *Anti-Jacobin*, 2 (9 July 1798), 615–23 (p. 622).
[41] 'New Morality', *Anti-Jacobin*, 2 (9 July 1798), 623–40 (pp. 635–6).
[42] 'Prospectus', *Anti-Jacobin*, p. 6.

with the 'mere cant of Authorship.'[43] The *Anti-Jacobin* and similar works played on this by making writers and writing the objects of necessary suspicion, closing down inclusive Enlightenment discourse in response to the perceived threat of unbounded and politicised literature. It was not for nothing that the *Anti-Jacobin's* successor, the *Anti-Jacobin Review*, subtitled itself the '*Monthly, Political, and Literary Censor*'.

THE *EDINBURGH'S* METHODOLOGY

The *Edinburgh Review* thus emerged in a climate in which older styles of periodical writing were figured as politically and socially questionable. The bright, ambitious young men who formed the *Edinburgh's* initial circle of contributors were keen to avoid being seen as either tradesmen or subversives. Francis Jeffrey, Francis Horner and Henry Brougham had trained as lawyers and Sydney Smith, the *de facto* editor of the first three numbers, was an unbeneficed clergyman. They all knew the social advantages granted by respectable professional identities, and a key element in the *Edinburgh's* success was its working to establish the critic as a professional role: the skilled arbiter of the literary realm, a writer at the very least the equal of the poet or the historian, and decidedly superior to the novelist. As Mark Schoenfield has argued, pitches for this position are made in the *Edinburgh's* very first number, in which economic articles by Jeffrey and Horner stress the regulatory and professional character of the periodical, emphasising its ability to 'influence the flow of other commodities within the marketplace of ideas' and promoting its central role in 'constitut[ing] a culture of knowledge.'[44]

Both quarterlies made widely accepted claims that they should occupy privileged supervisory positions. These were based in part on the respectability and integrity of their contributors. Hazlitt wrote of the *Edinburgh Review* that 'the pre-eminence it claims is from an acknowledged superiority of talent and information, and literary attainment'.[45] Explaining the value of the *Quarterly* to the American émigré John Bristed, Murray also drew on the discourse of acknowledged talent, although his approach was snobbier: 'the writers are all gentlemen of the first rank & talents & indeed

---

[43] See Derek Roper, *Reviewing before the 'Edinburgh': 1788–1802* (London: Methuen & Co, 1978), p. 30; *Anti-Jacobin*, 2 (9 July 1798), p. 615.

[44] Schoenfield, p. 73.

[45] Hazlitt, 'Mr Jeffrey', XI, 128.

nothing but the greatest ~~talent~~ ability will enable a man to write a review which is to compress the information of a folio in the compass of a few pages & to render them interesting.'[46] Both these formulations posit quarterly reviewers as acknowledged betters in terms of their abilities and moral probity. Quarterly critics as a group were in this respect pioneers in the literary field in asserting the 'control of intangible expertise' that Penelope Corfield has pegged as being crucial to the formation of a powerful and stable professional identity.[47]

Within their reviews, the quarterly reviewers' key method was enacting rhetorical triumphs over the works and authors they examined. However, they also employed extra-textual strategies to promote their authority and respectability, as Scott highlighted while advising Gifford on the *Quarterly*:

> The extensive reputation and circulation of the *Edinburgh Review* is chiefly owing to two circumstances. First that it is entirely uninfluenced by the Booksellers who have contrived to make most of the other reviews mere vehicles for advertising & puffing off their own publications or running down those of their rivals. Secondly the very handsome recompence which the Editor not only holds forth to his regular assistants but actually forces on those whose rank & fortune make it a matter of indifference to them.[48]

The circumstances that Scott describes allowed the *Edinburgh* to assert its dominance in financial terms that also contributed to an appearance of superior objectivity (although this appearance of disinterestedness was in many respects an elaborate textual illusion). The *Edinburgh* began by paying its contributors ten guineas per sheet. This was more than three times the three-guinea rate that Southey was paid for his work on the *Critical Review* and twice the rate that the *Monthly Review* paid.[49] Its conductors raised this rate to fifteen guineas in 1808 and to twenty-five in 1812. Key movers were paid even more generously. As editor, Jeffrey earned £300 in

---

[46] John Murray to John Bristed, 8 June 1810, from John Murray Letter Book, March 1803–11 September 1823, NLS Ms.41908, fols. 148ᵛ–149ᵛ (fol. 149ʳ).

[47] Penelope J. Corfield, *Power and the Professions in Britain 1700–1850* (London: Routledge, 1995), p. 18.

[48] Scott to Gifford, 25 October 1808, in *The Letters of Sir Walter*, II, 102–3.

[49] See my discussion of Southey's early career in Chapter Three; Ina Ferris, 'The Debut of *The Edinburgh Review*, 1802', *BRANCH: Britain, Representation and Nineteenth-Century History*, ed. Dino Franco Felluga, http://www.branchcollective. org/?ps_articles=ina-ferris-the-debut-of-the-edinburgh-review-1802.

the early years of the Review, but in 1809 he negotiated a share of the profits for the original contributors that saw him earning over £3000 a year by the 1820s.[50] The *Quarterly* endeavoured to offer similar rates-per-sheet from the outset and paid its most valuable contributors, like Southey, considerably more.

The *Edinburgh's* other major innovation, as Scott notes, was the provision of a fee to everyone who wrote for it, regardless of their wealth, status or objections. This neatly sidestepped the stigma of paid employment for contributors who felt they should be above such things while also raising the status of the Review by attracting prominent figures. Its high rates of pay meant that when the *Edinburgh* employed the discourse of professionals censuring amateurs, this was often grounded in the economic realities. Until it was matched by the *Quarterly*, the *Edinburgh* was by far the highest-paying periodical venue and was able to cherry-pick its contributors. The later normalisation of similar rates of pay had enormous consequences for writers. While it took a couple of decades before there was enough demand to sustain a reasonable number of high-paying magazines, the adoption of *Edinburgh*-like remuneration models by the publications founded in the late 1810s and the 1820s ushered in a period during which a substantial number of writers could finally earn a living wage by the pen.

These strategies all helped to recast the quarterly critic as a well-paid and respectable professional, rather than a poor hireling, a diffident amateur or someone very much like his or her readers.[51] This marked a decisive break from the inclusive methodologies of earlier journals. Clifford Siskin has described the *Edinburgh* as 'the first fully *professional* review', 'doubly exclusive' in its contributors and content.[52] Klancher writes that 'public knowledge of ample payments to contributors signalled the distancing of the audience. No longer a society of readers and writers, the journal represented itself as an institution blending writer, editor and publisher in what could only appear to be an essentially authorless text.'[53] I would modify this by noting that while the quarterlies affected authorless-

---

[50] Figures given in William Christie, *The Edinburgh Review in the Literary Culture of Romantic Britain: Mammoth and Megalonyx* (London: Pickering & Chatto, 2009), pp. 35–6.

[51] The *Edinburgh's* contributors were almost exclusively male, another break from earlier periodicals, which employed a considerable number of women among their reviewers.

[52] Siskin, p. 224.

[53] Klancher, p. 51.

ness, the social cachet of their known contributors was one of their selling points. Group voices served to shield individual reviewers and let the quarterlies' editors channel multiple intelligences into a united front, but their rhetorical authority was bolstered by the fact that it was known that many of those who contributed were respectable and influential. While Byron suspected (wrongly) that Jeffrey was his Scotch reviewer, his counterblast took in a large group: 'Athenian Aberdeen', 'HERBERT', 'Smug SYDNEY', 'classic HALLAM', 'SCOTT', 'paltry PILLANS', 'blundering BROUGHAM' (the real culprit) and 'gay Thalia's luckless votary, LAMBE'.[54] Even satirically configured, the size of this company bespeaks a considerable public knowledge of the figures behind the *Edinburgh*, their personal reputations both reinforced by and reinforcing its critiques.

Unlike previous periodicals, the *Edinburgh* selected what it would cover very carefully. Its convenors declared in the advertisement to the first issue that they would 'confine their notice, in a very great degree, to works that have either attained, or deserve, a certain portion of celebrity.'[55] This argument justified omissions by implicitly dismissing the works that the Review's controllers chose not to assess. By moving away from an encyclopaedic model, the *Edinburgh* gave itself room to define a range of disciplines that it considered important, chief among them 'the specialisms for which Scottish universities were famous, especially the natural sciences, moral philosophy and political economy.'[56] Political works were also prominently featured—the *Edinburgh* would review quite flimsy pamphlets if doing so afforded it an opportunity to influence public opinion. Interestingly, the *Edinburgh's* coverage of poetry and novels was comparatively sparse—in the order that it inculcated, imaginative writings occupied a slightly dubious position, as its often critical reviews attest. The *Quarterly*, perhaps in opposition to the *Edinburgh's* scholarly foci, was keener to engage with literature, although its coverage could be equally scathing.

As Ina Ferris has pointed out, a key factor in the *Edinburgh's* declared policy was 'the *social* ground ("celebrity"—either attained or deserved) of the selection'. She goes on to clarify that '[t]he interest of the early

---

[54] Byron, *English Bards and Scotch Reviewers*, lines 509, 510, 512, 513, 514, 515, 524 and 516, in *Byron: The Complete Poetical Works*, ed. Jerome J. McGann, 7 vols (Oxford: Oxford University Press, 1980–93), I, 245.
[55] 'Advertisement', *Edinburgh Review*, 1 (October 1802), [2–3] (p. [2]).
[56] Butler, p. 131.

Edinburgh reviewers […] lay less in what was being written than in what was—or should be—read.'[57] The *Edinburgh* established itself as a publication noticing all important writers, but also one that reserved for itself the ability to determine whether or not their prominence was deserved. For the *Edinburgh*, books were inevitably social and politicised objects, and it was through interrogating the ways that they represented their authors' views and imagining how educated and uneducated readers might respond to them that its critics sought to shape proper literature and—by extension—contemporary society and politics. The *Edinburgh* corrected authors not only for their own sakes, but also in order to correct the tastes of the reading public, to whom the *Edinburgh* represented itself as an indispensable arbiter.

Within individual reviews, the *Edinburgh's* critics enacted a major shift in the balance between description and criticism, allowing works less space to speak for themselves and taking more time to comment upon and censure their authors. This can be seen by comparing two different reviews that Jeffrey wrote assessing Southey's *Thalaba the Destroyer* (1801). In the first issue of the *Edinburgh*, Jeffrey used Southey as an excuse to take on the whole field of modern poetry, positioning the *Edinburgh* with respect to radicalism, aesthetics and the Lake Poets, a sect he wrote into being to oppose. By contrast, Jeffrey's concurrent review in the *Monthly* largely followed the old style, moving swiftly into plot summary, extract and commentary. He concluded the *Monthly* review with the following relatively humble opinions:

> On the whole, we conceive that this work contains more and ample proofs of the author's genius and capacity for poetical impressions, than any of his former publications: but at the same time, we are sorry to observe that it affords no indications of his advancement towards a more correct taste or more manly style of composition. Together with much that must please readers of every description, it contains not a little that will offend those whose suffrages Mr. Southey should be most ambitious of securing.[58]

The measured style Jeffrey assumes here affects to offer an impartial, balanced assessment, praising Southey's improvements while lightly rebuking

---

[57] Ina Ferris, *The Achievement of Literary Authority: Gender, History, and the Waverley Novels* (Ithaca: Cornell University Press, 1991), p. 25.

[58] [Francis Jeffrey], 'Southey's *Thalaba the Destroyer*', *Monthly Review*, 2nd series, 39 (November 1802), 240–51 (p. 251).

his poetry for displaying faulty taste and a dubious style. Jeffrey ascribes the failures he detects principally to Southey's composition—Southey himself is advised to write more carefully in future, but the review clearly holds out the prospect of his progressing to produce better work.

By contrast, the final paragraph of the *Edinburgh* review focuses squarely on Southey himself. His errors are explicitly depicted as errors of character rather than of style, and are attributed to his entanglement with the suspicious new school that Jeffrey castigates:

> All the productions of this author, it appears to us, bear very distinctly the impression of an amiable mind, a cultivated fancy, and a perverted taste [...] He is often puerile, diffuse, and artificial, and seems to have but little acquaintance with those chaster and severer graces, by whom the epic muse would be most suitably attended. His faults are always aggravated, and often created, by his partiality for the peculiar manner of that new school of poetry, of which he is a faithful disciple, and to the glory of which, he has sacrificed greater talents and acquisitions, than can be boasted by any of his associates.[59]

The first sentence here is a classic Jeffrey sting, two compliments undercut by a concluding condemnation. Southey's abilities are made to seem childish and poorly developed and his poetry is denied the chasteness and severity that characterise Jeffrey's own prose. This serves to position Southey as a writer distinctly inferior to his judge, who can detect his errors and do what he cannot. Where the *Monthly* mainly describes the work, the *Edinburgh* censures the man, making sweeping statements of truth in a self-consciously worked and controversial style that performed the authority the *Edinburgh* reviewers hoped to assert.

While the *Edinburgh's* reviewers were accepted by their contemporaries as experts, in fact their expertise was often more rhetorical than technical. As William Christie has argued, '[t]he Review attests to their argumentative competence in an important range of areas, but it is precisely this, and not an expertise in a specific area, that represents their critical strength.'[60] It was reviewers' cutting, controversy-courting writing, rather than their arcane wisdom, that bought readers flocking to the *Edinburgh*. As Jeffrey had recognised, the reading nation wanted to be entertained into agreement, and readers proved to be more than willing to accept the *Edinburgh's*

---

[59] [Jeffrey], 'Southey's *Thalaba*', *Edinburgh Review*, p. 83.
[60] Christie, pp. 36–7.

exciting new reviewing model, validating its claims to superiority. In the face of the *Edinburgh's* competition, the existing periodicals wilted. As Roper puts it, the longstanding Reviews 'continued to attract good contributors and print good articles', but they failed to 'take their share of the growth' in reading audiences.[61] Scott wrote in 1808 that prior to the *Edinburgh*, Reviews 'gave a dawdling, maudlin sort of applause to everything that reached even mediocrity', adding approvingly that '[t]he Edinburgh folks squeezed into their sauce plenty of acid, and were popular from novelty as well as from merit.'[62] The *Edinburgh* thus succeeded in overwriting older reviewing models and inaugurating a new era of powerful, respected critics who were well aware of the advantages they could accrue through judicious censure.

DISCIPLINING AUTHORS AND READERS

As previous chapters have intimated, both quarterlies were generally morally and aesthetically conservative when it came to literature, and they were not slow to stick in the boot. Reviewing Thomas Campbell's *Gertrude of Wyoming* (1809) in the *Quarterly's* second issue, Scott helpfully lays out the some of the modes by which gleeful and aggressive reframings could be accomplished:

> [A]ccording to the modern canons of criticism, the Reviewer is expected to shew his immense superiority to the Author reviewed, and at the same time to relieve the tediousness of narration by turning the epic, dramatic, moral story before him into quaint and lively burlesque. We had accordingly prepared materials for caricaturing Gertrude of Wyoming, in which the irresistible Spanish pantaloons of her lover were not forgotten, Albert was regularly distinguished as old Jonathan, the provincial troops were called Yankie-doodles, and the sombre character of the Oneyda chief was relieved by various sly allusions to 'blankets, strouds, stinkubus, and wampum.' And having thus clearly demonstrated to Mr. Campbell and to the reader that the whole effect of his poem was as completely at our mercy as the house which a child has painfully built with a pack of cards, we proposed to pat him on the head

[61] Roper, p. 27.
[62] Walter Scott to George Ellis, 18 Nov 1808, in *Letters of Sir Walter Scott*, II, 128.

with a few slight compliments on the ingenuity of his puny architecture, and dismiss him with a sugar-plum as a very promising child indeed.[63]

Scott conjures this practice in order to make a case for the new *Quarterly* against the arrogant *Edinburgh*, moving on to state that the beauty of Campbell's work prevented him from following through with this standard spoofing strategy. Despite Scott's disavowal, however, the *Quarterly* was generally just as quick as the *Edinburgh* to employ rhetoric in order to assert its critics' superiority. By sketching out the *Edinburgh's* purported line before he refutes it in his examination of Campbell, Scott gets to have things both ways, displaying his jokes and then censuring his opponents for their cruelty. Reviewers in this period were both combatants seeking to assert power and rhetors looking to entertain their readers into sympathy. The prize that they competed for was cultural capital, which could be parlayed into social and political influence both for reviewers themselves and for the periodical institutions that they represented. Appreciations in such an environment were always qualified.

Scott was correct in asserting that even the much-admired Campbell could not wholly escape correction at the *Edinburgh's* hands. While Jeffrey's review of *Gertrude of Wyoming* is appreciative, he takes time to note that 'the narrative is extremely obscure and imperfect' and asserts that the poem's greatest fault 'is the occasional constraint and obscurity of the diction, proceeding apparently from too laborious an effort at emphasis or condensation.'[64] By pointing out the ways in which Campbell falls short, Jeffrey plays up his own ability to conceive of better works, building his own authority by limiting Campbell's. Jeffrey's final page pushes this further by imagining Campbell to be a man bedevilled by doubt: 'It seems to us, as if the natural force and boldness of his ideas were habitually checked by a certain fastidious timidity, and an anxiety about the minor graces of correct and chastened composition.'[65] Campbell is thus depicted as a man in desperate need of the *Edinburgh's* praise. As well as correcting the work, Jeffrey suggests that his judicious criticism might serve to correct Campbell's character:

[63] [Walter Scott], '*Gertrude of Wyoming*', *Quarterly Review* 1 (May 1809), 241–58 (p. 254).

[64] [Francis Jeffrey], 'Campbell's *Gertrude of Wyoming*', *Edinburgh Review*, 14 (April 1809), 1–19 (p. 16).

[65] 'Campbell's *Gertrude of Wyoming*', p. 19.

We wish any praises or exhortations of ours had the power to give him confidence in his own great talents; and hope earnestly, that he will now meet
with such encouragement, as may set him above all restraints that proceed
from apprehension, and induce him to give free scope to that genius, of
which we are persuaded that the world has hitherto seen rather the grace
than the richness.[66]

The *Edinburgh* here presents itself as a necessary catalyst for perfect poetry,
its applause a prerequisite for greatness. Even when reviewing those it
acclaimed, the *Edinburgh* tended to reserve the highest position for itself.

The *Edinburgh* sought to establish its elite credentials from its first
number, and once they were established, it sought jealously to maintain
them. As Andrea Bradley writes, 'because it require[d] a sure footing for
the establishment of its position as a critical center, the periodical reveals a
near obsession with authority of all kinds—aesthetic, financial, social,
legal, but above all cultural authority.'[67] This can be demonstrated by
returning to Jeffrey's review of Southey's *Thalaba*, in which he positions
his Review on the centre ground by rejecting Wordsworth's attempts to
claim for poetry the language of common men. The *Edinburgh* may have
been published liveried in the buff and blue of Charles James Fox, but it
was not and could not afford to be perceived as being on the side of
revolution. As Robert Miles has it, '[t]hough a liberal, Jeffrey, as a Whig,
detested the levelling impulse of the Jacobins; and he detected Jacobinism
in poems such as "The Thorn" because they implicitly endorsed a "democratic subject".'[68] Jeffrey refuted Wordsworth's troubling claims for ordinary language by arguing that social classes differ fundamentally in the
ways that they feel: 'The love, or grief, or indignation of an enlightened
and refined character, is not only expressed in a different language, but is
itself a different emotion from the love, or grief, or anger of a clown, a
tradesman, or a market-wench. The things themselves are radically and
obviously distinct'.[69] In Jeffrey's formulation, Wordsworth's practice is
both an imposition on the lower classes and a pointless and potentially
dangerous constraint. For Jeffrey, poetry is essentially the preserve of the

[66] 'Campbell's *Gertrude of Wyoming*', p. 19.

[67] Andrea Bradley, 'Correcting Mrs Opie's Powers: The *Edinburgh* Review of Amelia
Opie's *Poems* (1802)', in *Romantic Periodicals and Print Culture*, ed. Kim Wheatley
(London: Frank Cass, 2003), pp. 41–61 (p. 55).

[68] Robert Miles, *Romantic Misfits* (Basingstoke: Palgrave Macmillan, 2008), p. 82.

[69] [Jeffrey], 'Southey's *Thalaba*', *Edinburgh Review*, p. 66.

cultured men to whom he principally addresses himself. If others wish to write it, they must acquire the kind of discerning language that Jeffrey himself sells: 'In serious poetry, a man of the middling or lower orders *must necessarily* lay aside a great deal of his ordinary language; he must avoid errors in grammar and orthography; and steer clear of the cant of particular professions, and of every impropriety that is ludicrous or disgusting: nay, he must speak in good verse, and observe all the graces in prosody and collocation.'[70] Jeffrey's man must do this so as not to threaten the existing class order, but also in order to be subject to the type of criticism that Jeffrey hopes to found his career on. The *Edinburgh* sought to build its hegemony by monopolising and limiting the language of cultural discourse, enforcing a social barrier to accessing literary culture just as high prices enforced an economic one. Wordsworth and Southey could be configured as direct threats to this scheme and could therefore be rhetorically shut out in order to promote it. To accomplish this, Jeffrey rhetorically leagued the Lakers with radical demagogues while positioning the *Edinburgh* in a moderate position, remarking that '[w]ealth is just as valid an excuse for one class of vices, as indigence is for the other.'[71] By rejecting those unable to afford expensive quarterlies and those depicted as perversely championing their language and rights, the *Edinburgh* defined the boundaries of the cultural, social and political realm over which it staked its claim.

I touched on Jeffrey's slashing review of Thomas Moore's 1806 volume in Chapter Three, but will now examine it in more detail in order to draw out the ways in which Jeffrey conjures Moore as a threat in order to emphasise the *Edinburgh's* importance. The review opens with a long sentence that builds Moore up in the manner of a gothic villain, ringingly concluding that he is 'the most poetical of those who, in our times, have devoted their talents to the propagation of immorality.'[72] After damning Moore's book, Jeffrey asserts that the *Edinburgh* could 'trample it down by one short movement of contempt and indignation', but adds that he will prolong his analysis as he is aware that Moore is 'abetted by patrons who are entitled to a more respectful remonstrance, and by admirers who may require a more extended exposition of their dangers'.[73] By revealing

---

[70] [Jeffrey], 'Southey's *Thalaba*', p. 67.
[71] [Jeffrey], 'Southey's *Thalaba*', p. 72.
[72] [Francis Jeffrey], 'Moore's *Poems*', *Edinburgh Review*, 8 (July 1806), 456–65 (p. 456).
[73] [Jeffrey], 'Moore's *Poems*', p. 456.

that he knows of Moore's many Whiggish connections, he hints at levels of access that he denies to his readers, asserting the *Edinburgh's* central and accountable place in public discourse. He tempts his readers to read on by teasing the sensational nature of Moore's work, encouraging them to anticipate the enjoyment that will ensue from seeing it contained and neutralised.

After this initial lambasting, Jeffrey calms briefly to consider who exactly is threatened by the corruption he accuses Moore of wishing to unleash. He is quick to assert that 'our sex, we are afraid, is seldom so pure as to leave them much to learn from publications of this description.'[74] The 'our' here could be read as connoting the collective masculine voice of the *Edinburgh*, but could also be an 'our' uniting the reviewer with his male readers through evoking a kind of experience rhetorically bemoaned but implicitly celebrated insomuch as it places those who have it beyond the reach of Moore's corrupting schemes. This is by contrast with fragile women, who Jeffrey simultaneously sublimates and belittles in ways that foreshadow conservative Victorian gender divisions:

> [I]f they should ever cease to be the pure, the delicate, and timid creatures that they are now—if they should cease to overawe profligacy, and to win and to shame men into decency, fidelity, and love of unfulfilled virtue—it is easy to see that this influence, which has hitherto been exerted to strengthen and refine our society, will operate entirely to its corruption and debasement; that domestic happiness and private honour will be extinguished, and public spirit and national industry most probably annihilated along with them.[75]

The revolution-evoking collapse Jeffrey envisages if women were to be so foolish as to read Thomas Moore indicates his lack of trust in feminine probity and critical power. In Jeffrey's review, the idea of writing as a dangerous technology lives on, but the dangers are restricted to genders and classes that he depicts as being weak and credulous. For cultured male *Edinburgh* readers, reading Moore is unproblematic as they will be equipped to recognise his perversity, or, at worst, will be restrained by their virtuous womenfolk.

Jeffrey's portraying women as intellectually vacuous, easily moved to excess and in perpetual need of male guardianship has obvious

---

[74] [Jeffrey], 'Moore's *Poems*', p. 458.
[75] [Jeffrey], 'Moore's *Poems*', p. 460.

consequences for his appreciations of female writers. A key part of the *Edinburgh's* constructing a safe reading nation was its restricting that nation's reading to books written by those of whom it approved. Women were rarely among these writers. When it deigned to review their works, it was, in Stuart Curran's words, 'uniformly supercilious and virtually dismissive'.[76] As indicated in my earlier discussion of Hemans, reviewers generally assessed women's writing positively only when it was located in defined and denigrated genres. The attitudes of the exclusively male cliques who controlled the quarterlies were thus a major bar to women achieving literary recognition.

Jeffrey's Moore review also makes large claims for the political potential of writing. He argues that in contemporary Britain 'all parts of the mass, act and react upon each other with a powerful and unintermitted agency; and if the head be once infected, the corruption will spread irresistibly through the whole body.'[77] By this logic, ideas expressed in costly literary works are dangerous because their price will not necessarily bar their circulation. Influencing elite readers will make it easy to influence less informed consumers through periodical circulation and due to lower-class readers' propensity for imitating the higher classes. This mistrustful configuration has a great deal in common with the reasoning that the *Anti-Jacobin* advanced when it contended that writers and writing should be controlled. Aware that the *Edinburgh* could potentially be implicated in transmitting Mooreish infections from the head of the body politic to the rest, Jeffrey reassures his readers by employing the rhetoric of his other profession, asserting that he will 'put the law in force against this delinquent, since he has not only indicated a disposition to do mischief, but seems unfortunately to have found an opportunity.'[78] Kim Wheatley has described such formulations as a form of period-specific paranoid politics in which 'both Tory and Whig reviewers translate their intense partisanship into a vocabulary of moral absolutism' and 'pin the blame for actual or potential social unrest on one person or a small band of conspirators.'[79] The idea of the Review protecting society against scribbling plotters was

[76] Stuart Curran, 'Woman and the *Edinburgh Review*', in *British Romanticism and the Edinburgh Review*, ed. Massimiliano Demata and Duncan Wu (Basingstoke: Palgrave Macmillan, 2002), pp. 195–208 (p. 195).

[77] [Jeffrey], 'Moore's *Poems*', p. 460.

[78] [Jeffrey], 'Moore's *Poems*', p. 460.

[79] Kim Wheatley, *Shelley and his Readers: Beyond Paranoid Politics* (Columbia, MO: University of Missouri Press, 1999), p. 2.

hugely useful in establishing reviewers' importance. If publications such as Moore's were powerful enough to do vast harm, then such writings were obviously worthy of the depth of scrutiny that the quarterlies brought to them. If the power of writing was regularly abused, the quarterlies were doubly valuable as guardians against immorality and social disorder. The forms of rhetoric employed in accusatory criticism are also naturally dramatic and engaging; as Wheatley succinctly puts it, 'persecution is fun!'[80] By censuring fervidly, Jeffrey entertained his readers into acknowledging his importance as a doughty analyst of culture and a moral guide to literature. Readers' acceptance of such claims made the quarterlies' critiques exceptionally potent, as Moore and other authors discovered to their cost.

While Jeffrey's review of Moore at least allows him a little talent, all that James Montgomery is permitted is 'the merit of smooth versification, blameless morality, and a sort of sickly affectation of delicacy and fine feelings, which is apt to impose on the amiable part of the young and illiterate.'[81] He is reviewed explicitly to counteract his popularity. Jeffrey seeks to pass off his latest work as a fad, asserting that 'in less than three years nobody will know the name of the Wanderer of Switzerland'.[82] The certainty of Montgomery's eclipse is attributed to the badness of his readers—'young, half-educated women, sickly tradesmen, and enamoured apprentices'.[83] Jeffrey's polite auditors are invited to sneer at underprivileged and ailing plebeian book-lovers, who are depicted as being unable to view critically in the manner of the *Edinburgh* and its readers. Derogatory references to lower-class publics continue in the disapproving comments that adorn the article's quotations, which repeatedly associate Montgomery's verse with the excesses of the popular theatre. Part of *The Wanderer of Switzerland* 'appears to us like the singing of a bad pantomime.' Of Montgomery's style, Jeffrey writes that '[i]ts chief ornaments are ejaculations and points of admiration; and, indeed, we must do Mr Montgomery the justice to say, that he is on no occasion sparing of his ohs and ahs.' One of Montgomery's verses is described as being 'as tawdry and vile as the tarnished finery of a strolling actress.'[84] Just as the classes he writes for are figured as being stupid and sickly, so is Montgomery himself,

---

[80] Wheatley, p. 4.

[81] [Francis Jeffrey], 'Montgomery's *Poems*', *Edinburgh Review*, 9 (January 1807), 347–54 (p. 347).

[82] [Jeffrey], 'Montgomery's *Poems*', p. 347.

[83] [Jeffrey], 'Montgomery's *Poems*', p. 348.

[84] [Jeffrey], 'Montgomery's *Poems*', pp. 349, 351, 352.

as the corruptions in his verse are ascribed to corruption in his mind. Jeffrey employs a particularly insulting analogy to drive this home:

> Medical writers inform us, that spasms and convulsions are usually produced by debility; and we have generally observed, that the more feeble a writer's genius is, the more violent and terrific are the distortions into which he throws himself. There is a certain cold extravagance, which is symptomatic of extreme dullness; and wild metaphors and startling personifications indicate the natural sterility of the mind which has been forced to bear them. This volume abounds with these sallies of desperate impotence.[85]

Unmanned, unwell, undone and soon to be unread, Montgomery is systematically destroyed for the enjoyment of the *Edinburgh's* audience. Jeffrey's review is very facile and very funny but also deeply cruel. It shows the unpleasant side of the *Edinburgh's* aggregated authority—its willingness to mercilessly bully innocuous authors in order to entertain its readers into confirming its dominion.

Unsurprisingly, this horrible review was not accepted with equanimity by its unfortunate subject. Montgomery wrote to a friend shortly after its publication that

> All that I had suffered from political persecution and personal animosity in the former part of my life seemed manly and generous opposition in comparison with the cowardly yet audacious malignity of this critic, who took advantage of the eminence on which he was placed beyond the reach of retaliation, to curse me like Shimei; to cast stones and dirt at me, because he knew I must from necessity be as passive as David: an injured and insulted author replying to the sarcasms of his unjust judge being as impotent as the trodden worm that turns to the foot that crushes it, but can do no more.[86]

Montgomery's helplessness comes through strongly here—in the face of the *Edinburgh's* metropolitan authority, his own provincial networks are powerless to salve his reputation. However, the knowledge that he had no venue in which to respond did not preclude him from dwelling on it. His biographers recorded that the margins of his copy of the review were

---

[85] [Jeffrey], 'Montgomery's *Poems*', p. 349.

[86] James Montgomery to Daniel Parken, 16 April 1807, as quoted in John Holland and James Everett, *Memoirs of the Life and Writings of James Montgomery*, 7 vols (London: Longman, Brown, Green, and Longmans, 1854–56), II, 142–3.

packed with shorthand notes; when they questioned him, Montgomery admitted that these constituted his 'unpublished defence'.[87] For months after the review's publication, Montgomery's letters show that his 'escape with barely my life in my hand from the tomahawks of the northern banditti' remained a burden on his mind, pushing him towards depression and obsession. 'All the kindness of my friends has been exerted to soothe me for the malice of one cowardly enemy who spat in my face in the dark,' he wrote, 'and yet I feel the venom of his spittle still on my cheek, that burns at the recollection of the indignity.'[88] The metaphor here actualises the livid mark the *Edinburgh* made on Montgomery's reputation, his constantly recalling it a sign of its psychological impact.

The review was considered extreme even by the *Edinburgh's* standards; consequently, Montgomery received sympathy, both covertly and in print. Walter Scott privately communicated his disapprobation and Lucy Aikin published supportive lines in her father's *Athenaeum*, beginning 'DROOP not sweet bard!'[89] While this poem was doubtless well-intentioned, one wonders whether Montgomery drew much comfort from it, as amongst her encouraging rhetoric Aikin makes it clear that the expected reaction to a ferocious *Edinburgh* review was to 'droop', asserts that Montgomery's bays had been 'violated' and implies that the review had rendered him pitiable. By this point, five years into its run, the *Edinburgh's* overbearing authority was a cultural truism.

Perhaps the most notable defences of Montgomery were Southey's reviews of his later works in the *Quarterly*. Southey was a partisan of Montgomery's, writing to John Murray that he had refused to write for the *Edinburgh* 'upon the ground, among others, of the cruel manner of criticism which Jeffray had adopted', stating that Montgomery's case was 'peculiarly cruel and unjust.' Reviewing Montgomery in the *Quarterly* represented for him 'the opportunity of doing justice to one whom I consider as undoubtedly a man of genius'.[90] However, Southey's review of Montgomery's poetry is obliged constantly to refer back to Jeffrey's. Even its positive assertions implicitly or explicitly echo Jeffrey's accusations.

---

[87] Holland and Everett, II, 137.

[88] James Montgomery to Daniel Parken, 28 May 1807, from Holland and Everett, II, 149.

[89] Lucy Aikin, 'To Mr. Montgomery', *Athenaeum*, 1 (April 1807), 399–400 (p. 399).

[90] Robert Southey to John Murray, 12 August 1810, in Letters from Southey 1808–1812, NLS Ms.42550. Letter 1800 in the *Collected Letters of Robert Southey*, gen. eds. Lynda Pratt, Tim Fulford and Ian Packer, *Romantic Circles*, 2009–, https://romantic-circles.org/editions/southey_letters/Part_Four/HTML/letterEEd.26.1800.html.

Southey depicts Montgomery as an independent man with 'no friends among the oligarchs of literature' who was welcomed 'with the applause he deserved' only to be capriciously cast down when 'the master of the new school of criticism thought [it] proper to crush the rising poet.'[91] To demonstrate this crushing, he quotes Jeffrey at considerable length, propagating the *Edinburgh's* opinion even as he attempts to annul it. This effect is exacerbated as Southey is unable or unwilling to offer stringent arguments on Montgomery's behalf. He spends a considerable amount of time admitting that Montgomery's poetry is often flawed, at one point decrying, as Jeffrey had done previously, 'the tinsel and tawdry with which our modern poetry has so long abounded'.[92] He attempts to refute the *Edinburgh* by claiming originality and strength for Montgomery—'a mind overflowing with feelings, but in the highest degree pure and pious'—and through quoting extensively and respectfully, letting Montgomery's verse speak for itself. However, his general assertions compare poorly with Jeffrey's vivid characterisations.[93] Southey's final pages evoke one very specific example of Montgomery's beneficial effects, describing 'a female whom sickness had reconciled to the notes of sorrow' finding 'consolation and delight' in Montgomery's poems, which 'beguiled the weary hours of sickness and pain, and strewed her path to the grave with flowers.'[94] This pathetic example smacks of special pleading in a way in that Jeffrey's juridical style rarely does. Southey's inability to move beyond Jeffrey's mockery reveals that its effects remained pervasive among tastemakers. In a subsequent review of *The World before the Flood*, Southey notes that Montgomery's preface has him coming before the public with 'many apprehensions, and with small hopes.'[95] Southey is anxious to reassure Montgomery and the *Quarterly's* readers that 'there is no reason for this distrust', but it is evident that despite his ongoing commercial success, Montgomery's rejection by the elite circles behind the *Edinburgh* continued to sting.

---

[91] [Robert Southey], 'Montgomery's *Poems*', *Quarterly Review*, 6 (December 1811), 405–19 (p. 412).

[92] [Southey], 'Montgomery's *Poems*', p. 408.

[93] [Southey], 'Montgomery's *Poems*', p. 412.

[94] [Southey], 'Montgomery's *Poems*', p. 417.

[95] [Robert Southey], 'Montgomery's *World before the Flood*', *Quarterly Review*, 11 (April 1814), 78–87 (p. 87).

THE QUARTERLIES AND CANONICAL ROMANTICISM

Montgomery, however, was luckier than some of the canonical Romantics. His poetry was formally approachable and, as Jeffrey disapprovingly implied, safely in tune with middle-class tastes. By comparison, the innovations for which the canonical Romantics were subsequently treasured rendered them strange and off-putting prospects for many contemporary readers. Had the quarterlies been sensitive to their particular merits, they might have served as bridges between these poets and the wider public. However, what later critics would recognise as the aesthetic merits of writers' works were not major factors in the quarterlies' hierarchies of value. Wordsworth, Coleridge and Southey were all victims of the *Edinburgh's* ire, as was Byron initially. Shelley was wholly excluded from its pages while he lived, although Jeffrey must be credited with making some perceptive if tardy remarks on John Keats in the August 1820 issue. The *Quarterly*, founded after the Lake Poets swung towards conservatism, was kinder to the older generation, especially the heavily-involved Southey, although it continued to be somewhat frustrated by their writings. Discussing Wordsworth's defence of his methods in 1815, it huffed that 'if he is not now or should not be hereafter a favourite with the public, he can have no one to blame but himself.'[96] However, the *Quarterly's* critics reserved their sharpest condemnations for the younger poets. Shelley and Keats were both subject to reviews designed to ruin their reputations. The *Quarterly* was keen to ensure that writers it saw as its political opponents would acquire few converts from among its readers.

In the *Quarterly's* April 1819 issue, John Taylor Coleridge published what was ostensibly a review of Shelley's *Laon and Cythna* and its later, partly expurgated, version, *The Revolt of Islam*. In practice, though, this review focused its attack on Shelley himself, condemning and dismissing his poetry at the outset: 'it has not much ribaldry or voluptuousness for prurient imaginations, and no personal scandal for the malicious; and even those on whom it might be expected to act most dangerously by its semblance of enthusiasm, will have stout hearts to proceed beyond the first canto.'[97] By stigmatising the poem as something the *Quarterly's* readers would find unrewarding, Coleridge gave himself latitude to disregard its

---

[96] [William Rowe Lyall?], 'Wordsworth's *White Doe* [and *Poems*]', *Quarterly Review*, 14 (October 1815), 201–25 (p. 225).

[97] [John Taylor Coleridge], 'Shelley's *Revolt of Islam*', *Quarterly Review*, 21 (April 1819), 460–71 (pp. 462–3).

overall structure. Instead, he quotes and reconfigures select parts of the epic to tell a gripping story about Shelley's corruption. *Laon and Cythna* is in effect rewritten as a work of subversive yet incoherent political philosophy from which Coleridge creates a damning portrait of Shelley as an inept but odious gothic seducer—'a young and inexperienced man, imperfectly educated, irregular in his application, and shamefully dissolute in his conduct.' Coleridge has evidently dug into Shelley's background, as his review makes glowering references to Shelley's expulsion from Oxford and to his association with William Godwin.[98] Towards the end of the review, Coleridge affects to hold out a hand to Shelley, hoping that he might perhaps improve himself by turning to the Bible. However, this illusion of forgiveness is shattered in a tailpiece which asserts that after completing the original review Coleridge received *Rosalind and Helen*, a work 'less interesting, less vigorous and chaste in language, less harmonious in versification, and less pure in thought; more rambling and diffuse, more palpably and consciously sophistical, more offensive and vulgar, more unintelligible' than the review's principal subject.[99] In light of this new outrage, Coleridge retracts his earlier comments about the possibility of Shelley's redemption. Instead, *Rosalind and Helen's* badness presents him with a pretext for a less circuitous attack; consequently, he makes it explicit that he has privileged information about Shelley's personal depravity: 'if we might withdraw the veil of private life, and tell what we *now* know about him, it would be indeed a disgusting picture that we should exhibit.'[100] Shelley is left as whatever the *Quarterly's* readers most abhor, his poetry's increasing offensiveness an index of his degeneracy. The review enacts a process of consideration, censure, attempted leniency and finally total condemnation. By its end, Shelley is rhetorically concluded and silenced. Likened to the pursuers of Moses, 'he sinks "like lead" to the bottom.'

Although Coleridge rejects and abhors Shelley, his review does make some effort to engage with his subject's point of view. Shelley's privileged background meant that he had to be shown to be a reprobate 'in spite of the manifest advantages of education and society which his work displays', as the *Monthly Review* put it.[101] By contrast, 'Cockney' Keats could be

---

[98] [Coleridge], 'Shelley's *Revolt of Islam*', pp. 465, 468.

[99] [Coleridge], 'Shelley's *Revolt of Islam*', p. 470.

[100] [Coleridge], 'Shelley's *Revolt of Islam*', p. 471.

[101] '*The Revolt of Islam*', *Monthly Review*, 2nd series, 88 (March 1819), 323–4 (p. 323).

unhesitatingly trashed, as he was in John Wilson Croker's infamous review of *Endymion*. Croker begins by stating explicitly that he has not read three of the four cantos of the poem because the single canto that he had 'painfully toiled' through made absolutely no sense to him.[102] Within the first paragraph, reading Keats becomes a thankless task, his work a Sisyphean burden on its polite auditors. While his 'prototype' Hunt is decried as presumptuous, Keats is depicted as downright irrational, pouring out verse with no regard for sense. Croker asserts that Keats composes by sound alone, creating poetry filled with signs that fail to signify:

> He seems to us to write a line at random, and then he follows not the thought excited by this line, but that suggested by the *rhyme* with which it concludes. There is hardly a complete couplet inclosing a complete idea in the whole book. He wanders from one subject to another, from the association, not of ideas but of sounds, and the work is composed of hemistichs which, it is quite evident, have forced themselves upon the author by the mere force of the catchwords on which they turn.[103]

Having asserted that Keats only focuses on the mechanisms of poetry, Croker goes on to deny that he has any talent even for this, spending the remaining paragraphs of his review taking apart snippets of *Endymion* by attacking their grammar, metre and coinages. Despite its pretence, this attack on Keats is not the result of baffled frustration at his obscurity; rather, it is a conscious attempt to silence him and mock his mentor. By denying Keats meaning, the *Quarterly* buttressed its own.

It is debateable whether Keats' confidence was deeply dented by Croker's attack. He wrote to his brother and sister-in-law that '[e]ven as a Matter of present interest the attempt to crush me in the Quarterly has only brought me more notice.'[104] However, the trope of his being a poet who was 'snuffed out by an Article' had considerable cultural currency.[105] The responsibility for propagating this view lies in large part with Byron

---

[102] [John Wilson Croker], 'Keats's *Endymion*', *Quarterly Review*, 19 (April 1818), 204–8 (p. 204).

[103] [Croker], 'Keats's *Endymion*', p. 206.

[104] *The Letters of John Keats, 1814–1821*, ed. Hyder E. Rollins, 2 vols (Cambridge, MA: Harvard University Press, 1958), I, 394.

[105] Byron, *Don Juan*, Canto XI, line 480, in *Complete Poetical Works*, V, 483. See also the poetic responses to Keats' death analysed by Jeffrey C. Robinson in *Reception and Poetics in Keats: "My Ended Poet"* (New York: St. Martin's Press, 1998).

and Shelley. Shelley was particularly invested in Keats' fate, asserting in the preface to *Adonaïs* that the *Quarterly's* review 'produced the most violent effect on his susceptible mind; the agitation thus originated ended in the rupture of a blood-vessel in the lungs; a rapid consumption ensued, and the succeeding acknowledgements from more candid critics of the true greatness of his powers were ineffectual to heal the wound thus wantonly inflicted.'[106] It is telling that Shelley chooses to target the *Quarterly*, which had attacked his own work most ferociously, rather than *Blackwood's*, whose 'Cockney School' articles had seemingly troubled Keats more. As Duncan Wu records, 'Benjamin Bailey wrote that "Keats attributed his approaching end to the poisonous pen of Lockhart", and Keats apparently told his friend Charles Brown "If I die you must ruin Lockhart."'[107] However, it is perhaps not surprising that Shelley chose to blend his own agendas and travails with Keats'. In a letter to Marianne Hunt, Shelley wrote that in encouraging Keats 'I am aware indeed in part [tha]t I am nourishing a rival who will far surpass [me] and this is an additional motive & will be an added pleasure.'[108] For Shelley, Keats could serve as an aspirational figure, a younger, purer version of himself. By celebrating Keats' transcendent potential, Shelley sought to put them both beyond the purview of their reviewers—Keats explicitly, himself implicitly through association and through asserting his ability to make visible a genius denied by the critics.

Refuting the *Quarterly's* critical hierarchies is clearly part of Shelley's intention in the *Adonaïs* preface:

As to *Endymion*, was it a poem, whatever might be its defects, to be treated contemptuously by those who had celebrated, with various degrees of complacency and panegyric, *Paris*, and *Woman*, and a *Syrian Tale*, and Mrs. Lefanu, and Mr. Barrett, and Mr. Howard Payne, and a long list of the illustrious obscure? Are these the men who in their venal good nature presumed to draw a parallel between the Reverend Mr. Milman and Lord Byron? What gnat did they strain at here, after having swallowed all those

---

[106] Percy Bysshe Shelley, 'Preface' to *Adonaïs*, from *Shelley's Poetry and Prose*, ed. Donald H. Reiman and Neil Fraistat, 2nd edn (New York: W.W. Norton, 2002), p. 410.

[107] Duncan Wu, *William Hazlitt: The First Modern Man* (Oxford: Oxford University Press, 2008), p. 256.

[108] Shelley to Marianne Hunt, 29 October 1820, in *The Letters of Percy Bysshe Shelley*, II, 240.

camels? Against what woman taken in adultery dares the foremost of these literary prostitutes to cast his opprobrious stone?[109]

In this passage, Shelley opposes the *Quarterly* in its own style, depicting its reviewers as ignorant philistines who praise where no merit is to be found and slander without any care for their subjects. Just as reviews of Shelley placed him outside the realm of acceptable and accomplished literature, so Shelley casts down the popular works praised by his accusers, asserting that they could only be appreciated by the venal and complacent. However, Shelley's attempt to position the *Quarterly* as petty is destabilised by his appropriating its own methods, even going so far as to echo its religiously inflected rhetoric. His attempt to deny its authority is also undercut by his account of its disastrous impact on Keats. In seeking to topple the quarterly critic from his judge's chair, Shelley railed alone against a powerful set of mutually-reinforcing opponents, as examining the careers of the authors that he derided will serve to prove.

Adonaïs was privately printed at Pisa in an edition of 250 copies, although, unlike most of Shelley's works, it did sell well enough to justify a second edition. By contrast, Eaton Stannard Barrett's *Woman* was, according to Donald Reiman, 'more popular during his lifetime than any single work by a major or secondary poet then living, including Scott and Byron' and 'reached a seventeenth London edition.'[110] *Woman* was first published in 1810, but, as Barrett wrote in the preface to the heavily-revised 1818 version, after 'the critics abused it', he came to find his original 'obscure, affected, and replete with all those errors which arise from an unformed and ambitious style.'[111] The moral he drew from this was that 'we should listen with deference to those critics, whose judgement differs from our own.'[112] He explicitly worked to bring his poem into line with the *Quarterly's* expressed preferences; his reference to his old 'ambitious style' echoes a review of Henry Hart Milman by John Taylor Coleridge in which 'an ambitious style' is 'loosely defined to be an unnatural and artificial sustainment of the language and imagery, when neither the warmth of the author's mind prompts it, nor the elevation of his thoughts demands

---

[109] Shelley, 'Preface' to *Adonaïs*, p. 410.

[110] Donald H. Reiman, 'Introduction' to Eaton Stannard Barrett, *Woman; Henry Schultze*, facsimile edition (London: Garland, 1979), p. xii.

[111] Eaton Stannard Barrett, *Woman: a Poem* (London: Henry Colburn, 1818), pp. 5, 6.

[112] Barrett, p. 7.

it.'[113] The *Quarterly* scorned such flourishes in favour of a clearer, more traditional poetics—'simplicity in our sense is little other than synonymous with fitness.'[114] Cannily, Barrett assumed the style that the Reviews advocated and took measures to make sure that he was recognised for doing so. The *Quarterly's* positive notice found that the revised version of *Woman* 'evinced both talent and genius'.[115] This effusive response was doubtless in part due to Barrett's having solicited the review from his friend John Taylor Coleridge. The poem's subsequent sales indicate that the *Quarterly's* taste was shared by a large enough fraction of the reading public to make Barrett's careful efforts to conform and self-promote eminently pragmatic.

Another poem on Shelley's list, George Croly's *Paris in 1815*, was praised by John Wilson Croker as 'the work of a powerful and poetic imagination'.[116] By contrast with the 'unmanly brutality of Mr Hobhouse, and the unwomanly brutality of Lady Morgan', Croker finds Croly's treatment of the Bourbon restoration 'beautiful' and imbued with 'deep and real feeling.'[117] The defects he identifies are stylistic. Croly's inversions—'the wretched expedient which [Erasmus] Darwin employed to cover the weakness of his style, and the poverty of his imagination'—are attributed to copying from bad models.[118] Croly's strengths, on the other hand, are granted to be his own, and it is implied that if he takes the *Quarterly's* judicious advice and purges perfidious influences he can expect continuing support as a poet 'who seems to exhibit a union, unhappily too rare, of piety and poetry, of what is right in politics, respectable in morals, correct in taste, and splendid in imagination.'[119] Croly was only too happy to be recognised by the establishment and to play a part in buttressing it. He later wrote a cruelly parodic attack in *Blackwood's* on Shelley's 'unintelligible' *Adonaïs* and the 'Grub Street Empire' of the Cockneys, in which he

---

[113] [John Taylor Coleridge], 'Milman's *Fazio*' [and *Judicium Regale*], *Quarterly Review*, 15 (April 1816), 69–85 (p. 70).

[114] [Coleridge], 'Milman's *Fazio*', p. 71.

[115] [John Taylor Coleridge], '*Woman: a Poem*', *Quarterly Review*, 19 (April 1818), 246–50 (p. 250). For attribution, see Murray Archive letters quoted in Reiman and the *Quarterly Review Archive*, ed. Jonathan Cutmore, *Romantic Circles*, 2005, https://romantic-circles.org/reference/qr/index/37.html.

[116] [John Wilson Croker], '*Paris: a Poem*', *Quarterly Review*, 17 (April 1817), 218–29 (p. 218).

[117] [Croker], '*Paris: a Poem*', pp. 223, 224.

[118] [Croker], '*Paris: a Poem*', p. 229.

[119] [Croker], '*Paris: a Poem*', p. 229.

denigrated their 'Della Cruscan' manners in order to assert the primacy of the conservative style and circle with which he had aligned himself.[120]

The *Quarterly's* support for Henry Hart Milman, Shelley's contemporary at Eton and Oxford, would have been particularly galling for the disappointed elegist of *Adonaïs*. By contrast with Shelley's own, Milman's early career was orthodox and materially successful. He was ordained in 1816, his early poems were published by Murray, his drama *Fazio* was a rousing success, he regularly reviewed for the *Quarterly* during the 1820s and in 1821 he was made Professor of Poetry at Oxford.[121] He was first reviewed by the *Quarterly* in April 1816; John Taylor Coleridge praised his work, albeit with the caveats about his 'ambitious style' discussed above. In 1818, though, his epic *Samor, the Lord of the Bright City*, about the Saxon invasion of England (the titular bright city is Gloucester), attracted Coleridge's censure as well as his praise:

> Samor exhibits all that is affected in language, strange even to solecism in usage, involved in construction and meretricious in ornament [...] Mr. Milman may be, we are sure that he is, gifted with unusual powers, but this fault is a weight, that might over-burthen and keep down the pinions of an eagle: while the clothing of his thought is such as it is now, he can never aspire to the fame of a true poet.[122]

Through this review, the *Quarterly* sought to rebuke and shape Milman, admiring his beauties while offering suggestions as to how he could counteract his 'numerous and important' faults.[123] Coleridge follows the *Quarterly's* general line in taking Milman to task for his failure to adhere to the 'grand simplicity' of Homer, Virgil and Milton, writing that '[t]he true poet never sacrifices accuracy of reasoning or description for the sake of increasing a particular effect.'[124] Milman is thus dismissed as the sort of flashy poet that both quarterlies held in contempt. Despite the possibilities

---

[120] [George Croly], 'Remarks on Shelley's *Adonais*', *Blackwood's Edinburgh Magazine*, 10 (December 1821), 696–700 (p. 697).

[121] H.C.G. Matthew, 'Milman, Henry Hart (1791–1868)', *ODNB*, https://doi.org/10.1093/ref:odnb/18778.

[122] [John Taylor Coleridge], 'Milman's *Samor*', *Quarterly Review*, 19 (July 1818), 328–47 (p. 346).

[123] [Coleridge], 'Milman's *Samor*', p. 345.

[124] [Coleridge], 'Milman's *Samor*', p. 338.

for redemption the review proffers, contemporary letters indicate that Milman took this rejection hard.[125]

In May 1820, however, Milman's *Fall of Jerusalem* received a glowing 28-page *Quarterly* review from Reginald Heber, a clergyman who was later to become 'one of his dearest friends'.[126] While not wholly uncritical, Heber was keen to assure his readers that Milman had overcome his errors, writing that 'the peculiar merits of his earlier efforts are heightened, and their besetting faults, even beyond expectation, corrected'.[127] He thus vindicates the *Quarterly* both for asserting Milman's potential and for seeking to tame his excesses. Milman is compared to Milton and set up to oppose Byron, Heber opining that while 'one of the mightiest spirits of the age has, apparently, devoted himself and his genius to the adornment and extension of evil, we may well be exhilarated by the accession of a new and potent ally to the cause of human virtue and happiness'.[128] This is the comparison to which Shelley explicitly objects in the *Adonaïs* preface. The review probably stuck in his mind particularly as Heber also finds space within it to snub Shelley's own work, writing that 'Mr Shelley alone, since the days of Titus Andronicus and the tragic schoolmaster in Gil Blas, has expected to afford mankind delight by a fac-simile of unmingled wickedness and horror.'[129] Heber's review explicitly leagues Milman with the *Quarterly* against the poets described by Southey as the 'Satanic School.'[130] Though this process of correction and sanctification, the *Quarterly* both established its own ability to improve promising poets and recruited Milman as part of its moral company. In the *Quarterly's* world, authors were either for it or against it, creating an entertaining drama that left little doubt about which side was the side of the angels.

Like the *Anti-Jacobin*, the *Quarterly* sought to use criticism to bolster the government and Anglicanism against perceived threats. However, it did so from an explicit position of strength, promising writers the acclaim of its large audience should they accept its strictures. The *Quarterly* and those it praised enjoyed a symbiotic relationship, together propagating a

---

[125] See the *Quarterly Review Archive*, https://romantic-circles.org/reference/qr/index/38.html.

[126] W.E.H. Lecky, *Historical and Political Essays* (London: Longmans, 1908), p. 255.

[127] [Reginald Heber], 'Milman's *Fall of Jerusalem*', *Quarterly Review*, 23 (May 1820), 198–225 (p. 225).

[128] [Heber], 'Milman's *Fall of Jerusalem*', p. 225.

[129] [Heber], 'Milman's *Fall of Jerusalem*', pp. 201–2.

[130] Robert Southey, 'Preface' to *A Vision of Judgement* (London: Longman, Hurst, Rees, Orme, and Brown, 1821), p. xxi.

hugely influential view of poetry that was largely hostile to what later generations would consider to be the Romantic canon. Its exemplars included
classical authors and the regular, lucid poetry of the eighteenth century.
Among the living poets Byron and Crabbe were cited as models for Croly,
and Milman's best work was compared 'with the pictures drawn by the
magic pencil of Southey in Thalaba and Kehama.'[131] It is possible to detect
a little market-based self-interest here, as the authors in this modern constellation were all heavily involved with Murray, the *Quarterly's* publisher.
However, they were also all established as being relatively popular and
were thus easy to set against obscure and obtuse radicals like Shelley. The
quarterlies could only stray so far in their attempts to shape taste; as John
Clive puts it, '[w]hen the absurdity he ridicules is taken seriously by the
majority, it is only too easy for the critic himself to appear absurd—and to
lose his readers.'[132] Conversely, that which is strange to the majority is easy
prey for the critic seeking to position himself as a leader of public opinion.
The quarterlies were controlled by cliques heavily invested in established
oligarchies of power, and their corporate views both represented these
oligarchies and were key means by which their ranks were swelled.

Writing the introduction to his contributions to the *Edinburgh*, Jeffrey
recalled remonstrating with Scott, who wanted the journal to be less partisan and forthright on national matters. Jeffrey argued in response that
'[t]he Review, in short, has but two legs to stand on. Literature no doubt
is one of them: But its *Right leg* is Politics.'[133] According to this metaphor,
without literature and politics, the *Edinburgh* would fall, but it is also an
institution set over these fields, bearing down upon them. However, as I
have contended throughout this chapter, Jeffrey is disingenuous in figuring literature and politics as separate matters. In fact, they were inextricably intertwined. The quarterlies in their pomp held out the potent prospect
of preferment to those who accepted their aesthetics or who were politically useful to their controllers. Conversely, they had considerable success
in ostracising authors who opposed them, placing such authors in
socially—and sometimes financially—compromising positions. Their popularity and authority made them the most effective public voices seeking
to determine the meanings of texts. Consequently, they played powerful
and wide-ranging roles in shaping the lives and ideologies of those who
sought to promote themselves through writing.

---

[131] [J.T. Coleridge], 'Milman's *Samor*', *Quarterly Review*, p. 339.

[132] Clive, p. 91.

[133] Francis Jeffrey, *Contributions to the Edinburgh Review*, 2nd edn, 3 vols (London:
Longman, Brown, Green and Longmans, 1846), I, xix.

Chapter Six: Refashioning Authorship's Purview

As the last chapter established, the quarterly Reviews were crucial means by which authorship transitioned towards more professional rhetoric, grouping practices and structures of payment. However, the quarterlies were far from the only forces reshaping the conditions of authorship in the late eighteenth and early nineteenth centuries. The relatively small scale of cultural production and its contiguousness with networks of elite authority meant that it was possible for privileged individuals with novel ideas and good connections to catalyse significant cultural change by redefining what reading audiences expected of books and their authors. This chapter considers three writers who had an outsize influence on how authorship and literature were framed in their contemporary moments. The first of these writers, Hannah More, operated on similar terms and with similar priorities to the wielders of elite systemic authority in her age, but her commitment to circulating narratives for moral purposes played a major role in enfranchising and educating a new generation of literary consumers. In his role as the preeminent teller of stories for such readers, Walter Scott began to carve out a more distinct role for literature, in which it served as an arbiter of cultural value and memory. In doing so, the 'Author of *Waverley*' laid the groundwork for a model of authorship centred on productive industry, Protestant values and reconciliation through history. Lord Byron reified the seductive countervailing model: that of the literary

© The Author(s) 2021
M. Sangster, *Living as an Author in the Romantic Period*, Palgrave
Studies in the Enlightenment, Romanticism and Cultures of Print,
https://doi.org/10.1007/978-3-030-37047-3_8

writer as justified rebel, permitted or compelled by genius to flout social conventions and say the formerly unsayable.

Through using these writers as barometers, this chapter will trace movements from the relatively restricted literary culture of the late eighteenth century toward a more expansive field regulated increasingly by specialist institutions and expertise in the second quarter of the nineteenth century. In doing so, it will demonstrate how its subjects served as figureheads and tools for negotiating wider social adjustments as they were propelled forward by the larger networks and groupings with which they were affiliated. As this book has stressed throughout, cultural change did not occur principally as a result of sudden thunderbolts or great individual leaps forward, but through complex mediations between older systems of social privilege and emerging technologies, disciplinary paradigms, coteries and institutions. More, Scott and Byron were well suited to serve as loci for such negotiations, as while each sought to achieve things that were unprecedented, other aspects of their practices and positionings were quite traditional and conservative. Their openness to imaginative appropriation by different schools of thought made them subjects of widespread interest, expanding the ways in which other agents could employ them to think through or specify what literary culture should entail.

HANNAH MORE: INCULCATING THE READING NATION

While she has recently received some much-deserved scholarly attention, Hannah More is no longer really a name to conjure with. In part, this is because her extraordinary success in constructing works that were in tune with the social expectations of her era. Her sensitivity to the concerns of her contemporaries meant that as the priorities of literary culture shifted over the course of the nineteenth century, she was left increasingly out of place. However, during her lifetime, she was recognised almost universally as one of her age's most prominent and effective communicators. The radical journalist William Cobbett, who distributed More's tracts in his youth and who followed her in producing cheap, consciousness-raising print for labouring-class audiences, called her 'as artful, as able, and as useful a scribe as ever drew pen in the cause of the system.'[1] While there is a definite sting in the tail of this compliment, Cobbett nevertheless

---

[1] William Cobbett, 'Letter XIII. To the People of the United States', *Cobbett's Weekly Political Register*, Vol. XXX No. 29 (18 May 1816), 611–28 (p. 616).

recognised that More was supremely talented at writing to achieve power-ful social and material effects. Compelling evidence for Cobbett's claims can be found in the wealth that More accumulated. Despite her extensive charitable and household outgoings, on her death in 1833, she left an estate that her most recent and accomplished biographer, Anne Stott, val-ues at £27,500. The *Oxford Dictionary of National Biography* gives a slightly higher estimate: 'approximately £30,000'.[2] More's remaining wealth at the time of her death was thus nine or ten times what Felicia Hemans made in direct profits over the course of her whole career.[3] It was also substantially more than the lifetime literary incomes of most leading male poets and novelists, excepting only a handful of well-situated indi-viduals such as the two this chapter will move on to discuss. However, Scott and Byron both started building their reputations from situations that were considerably more privileged than More's. For a woman from a respectable but relatively modest family background to secure such a for-tune in large part through writing was a remarkable accomplishment. More's wealth-at-death attests both to the huge audiences that she reached and to the esteem in which she was held by elite contemporaries. The recipients of this wealth, which principally went to around two hundred carefully selected charities, are also helpfully suggestive, reflecting the huge range of groupings with which More worked and in which she felt invested.

A principal reason why More was so successful was her ability to write in manners that were perceived by influential people as being—and which consequently became—socially impactful. While many writers were seen as entertainers, pundits or nuisances, More's friends saw her as a morally seri-ous author whose works had the ability to effect (or forestall) real change. The assumed potency of her writings is shown in the direct appeals that were made to her in the wake of the most serious ideological crisis of her lifetime. As her first biographer William Roberts put it, during the period following the souring of the French Revolution in 1792, when the British establishment lived in fear of distributed Revolutionary philosophies,

---

[2] Anne Stott, *Hannah More: The First Victorian* (Oxford: Oxford University Press, 2003), p. 331; S. J. Skedd, 'More, Hannah (1745–1833)', *ODNB*, https://doi.org/10.1093/ref:odnb/19179.

[3] For Hemans' career, see Chapter Three and Paula R. Feldman, 'The Poet and the Profits: Felicia Hemans and the Literary Marketplace', *Keats-Shelley Journal*, 46 (1997), 148–76.

letters poured in upon Hannah More, by every post, from persons of eminence, earnestly calling upon her to produce some little popular tract, which
might serve as a counteraction to those pernicious writings. The sound part
of the community cast their eyes upon her as one who had shown an intimate
knowledge of human nature, and had studied it successfully in all its variet-
ies, from the highest to the lowest classes, and the clear and lively style of
whose writings had been found so generally attractive.[4]

In discussing More, Roberts is prone at times to exaggeration and to
finessing his material to fit the story of staid evangelical excellence he
wishes to tell, but his assertions here are well supported. More's correspondence and activities during this period demonstrate the impact that
could be realised through the substantial profile she had built up during
the 1770s and 1780s by authoring sprightly satires, moral essays, dramatic
triumphs, abolitionist interventions, publicised pronouncements and private social interactions. The acknowledged potency of her words made
them uniquely valuable to those who agreed with her sentiments, allowing
her to access powerful webs of interest and circulation that in turn served
to amplify her voice and standing.

Importantly, More was able to justify her reputation when called upon,
even when prevented by circumstances from invoking her name to autho-
rise the writings she produced. Responding to the crisis of 1792, she built
ably on her previous interventions in the debates surrounding abolition by
producing an extremely effective pamphlet with considerable dispatch.
Horace Walpole described More's *Village Politics*—purportedly written by
Will Chip, 'a country carpenter'—as 'infinitely superior to anything on the
subject, clearer, better stated and comprehending the whole mass of matter in the shortest compass'.[5] While Walpole was both a friend of More's
and a practiced flatterer, he was also an excellent critic able accurately to
gauge some of the major reasons for her pamphlet's efficacy. As well as
clarity, eloquence, comprehensiveness and brevity, *Village Politics* was
remarkable for alloying establishment views with a recognition of the genuine currency of popular concerns. M.G. Jones describes *Village Politics* as
'Burke for Beginners', but also accurately contends that More's 'respect

---

[4] William Roberts, *Memoirs of the Life and Correspondence of Mrs. Hannah More*, 2nd edn,
4 vols (London: Seeley and Burnside, 1834), II, 345–6.

[5] Horace Walpole to Hannah More, 9 February 1793, in *Horace Walpole's Correspondence*,
gen. ed. W.S. Lewis, 48 vols (New Haven: Yale University Press, 1937–83), XXXI, 380.

and affection for the poor was in marked contrast to [Burke's] contempt'.[6] In describing the pamphlet's strategies, Stott characterises its conservatism as 'ambiguous and paradoxical', pointing out that while it misrepresents the case for revolution, it nevertheless draws from radical discourse the criteria by which it assesses the existing state of Britain, arguing for the crucial importance of 'equal justice, property rights, press freedom [and] social benefits'.[7] These are not all factors that traditional Tories would have considered it important to address. While More was a defender of the established order, she also believed strongly in the emancipatory potential of culture, reading and religion. Some of her pamphlet consists of scare-mongering, but she also presents a positive vision of an improvable Britain. Tom Hod the mason, who initially plays the role of discontented militant in the dialogue, displays this approach by accounting for the arguments put to him using a quintessentially British framework:

> Let me sum up the evidence, as they say at 'sizes—Hem! To cut every man's throat who does not think as I do, or hang him up at a lamppost!—Pretend liberty of conscience, and then banish the parsons only for being conscientious!—Cry out liberty of the press, and hang up the first man who writes his mind!—Lose our poor laws!—Lose one's wife perhaps upon every little tiff!—March without clothes, and fight without victuals!—No trade!—No bible!—No sabbath nor day of rest!—No safety, no comfort, no peace in this world—and no world to come![8]

While in many respects the characterisation of Tom is crude—for much of the dialogue his wild assertions set up his more accomplished partner's rhetorical flourishes—this summation shows More successfully ventriloquising contentions that evoke an improving social contract, one that she herself worked hard to bring into being through her charitable and educational works. Her direct mouthpiece, Jack Anvil, expresses bullish patriotism, but he also recognises that the system as it stands has faults that should be remedied: 'We have as much liberty as can make us happy, and more trade and riches than allows us to be good. We have the best laws in the world, if they were more strictly enforced; and the best religion in the world, if it was but better followed.'[9] This is not a description of utopia,

---

[6] M.G. Jones, *Hannah More* (Cambridge: Cambridge University Press, 1952), p. 134.
[7] Stott, pp. 143, 144.
[8] [Hannah More], *Village Politics* (Manchester: J. Harrop, 1793), p. 15.
[9] [Hannah More], *Village Politics*, p. 16.

but rather an approach that carefully incorporates discourses of discontent within an overarching defence of the existing order. While More was a master of what Robert Hole calls the 'propaganda of integration', her integrations and her propaganda both benefitted from acknowledging the partial legitimacy of critique.[10] *Village Politics* is very clear about its ideological position, but it also makes reasoned attempts to show as well as tell, contending implicitly that certain revolutionary objections should be heard.

While More moaned in her private correspondence that producing the pamphlet was 'a sort of writing repugnant to my nature', it can be seen as an extension of her previous practice.[11] Introducing later editions of her first play, *The Search After Happiness*, More states that it had been composed due to her 'earnest wish to furnish a substitute for the very improper custom, which then prevailed, of allowing plays, and those not always of the purest kind, to be acted by young Ladies in boarding schools.'[12] Much of More's work, including *Village Politics*, operated in a similar way, refashioning popular forms in manners perceived to be more socially acceptable by substantial audiences. More was innovative in identifying modes with the potential to communicate widely and working examples of these to a high degree of polish. Through doing so, she drew credit for producing works that were considered both aesthetically and morally better than their inspirations by the common standards in play when she was writing. Her appropriations have often made later critics uncomfortable, and not without reason. In examining *Village Politics*, Cato Marks has read More's use of language she described as 'vulgar' as a means of silencing the working classes, contending that 'Tom Hod is unable to put forward a counter argument to the status quo; and Jack becomes an inarticulate (according to standard theories of pronunciation) mouthpiece for the upper classes.'[13] One of More's bluestocking correspondents, Frances Boscawen, makes it clear that More's evocation of dialect was not received sensitively in sophisticated London circles. She writes that when

[10] Robert Hole, 'Hannah More on Literature and Propaganda, 1788–1799', *History*, 85 (October 2000), 613–33 (p. 616).

[11] Hannah More to Frances Boscawen, 1793, in Roberts, pp. 378–80 (p. 379).

[12] [Hannah More], *The Search After Happiness: A Pastoral Drama*, 13th edn (London: T. Cadell and W. Davies, 1810), p. 7.

[13] Cato Marks, '"Let poor volk pass": Dialect and Writing the South-West Poor out of Metropolitan Political Life in Hannah More's *Village Politics* (1792)', *Romanticism*, 20:1 (2014), 43–58 (p. 57).

the Bishop of London, Beilby Porteus, performed *Village Politics*, he 'read the delectable dialogue to us, in tones so suitable that he was interrupted continually with our bursts of laughter'.[14] However, both Boscawen and Porteus were keen advocates of More's works precisely because they believed her words communicated effectively across social strata. The inarticulacy of the protagonists according to systems of metropolitan snobbery might in this respect be further evidence of More's craft, reflecting cultural prejudices far more likely to be expressed by the relatively refined than by the purchasers or recipients of her three-penny remedy. The clarity of More's language and opinions across the many modes in which she worked rendered her productions an attractive proposition for those becoming newly familiar with literate culture, while her subtleties flattered those with the existing cultural capital to spot them. More had begun her career as a teacher, and her voice remained one from which her audiences found it very easy to learn, even when they resisted aspects of her message.

This proved to be the case with *Village Politics*, which the grateful establishment battened on to with considerable ardour. Roberts assets dramatically that

> It flew, with a rapidity which may appear incredible to those, whose memories do not reach back to that period into every part of the kingdom. Many thousands were sent by government to Scotland and Ireland. Numerous patriotic persons printed large editions of it at their own expense; and in London only, many hundred thousands were soon circulated.[15]

A wide range of individuals and institutions thus played roles in ensuring that *Village Politics* took flight. Porteus, addressing More as 'Mrs. Chip', wrote that 'If the sale is rapid as the book is good, Mr. Chip will get an immense fortune and completely destroy all equality at once.'[16] Since the Bishop of London was a man with considerable influence, he was well placed to hasten the pamphlet's circulation both directly through the use of church resources and through recommending it to friends, as he did in the performance Boscawen witnessed. The bluestocking hostess Elizabeth Montagu, with whom More had a long and mutually rewarding association, wrote that *Village Politics* was 'allowed to have been the most gener-

---

[14] Frances Boscawen to Hannah More, 1792, in Roberts, II, 350–2 (p. 351).
[15] Roberts, II, 346.
[16] Beilby Porteus to Hannah More, 1792, in Roberts, II, 347–8 (p. 347).

ally approved and universally useful of any thing that has been published in the present exigency of the times.' More concretely, Montagu informed More that she had 'sent many copies to all the counties where I had any correspondence, and had the satisfaction to hear of their most happy effect; particularly in Northumberland, where the worthy parson of my parish found them so useful, that he intended to get a thousand copies printed.'[17] Similarly, Boscawen made it clear that she saw More's work as a uniquely effective panacea:

> Last night a gentleman gave me 'Reasons for Contentment,' by Archdeacon [William] Paley, addressed to the labouring part of the British public. I cast my eyes over it, and though I honour Archdeacon Paley, yet I assured the giver that I would send him the production of one, the minute I got home, who understood the language much better: and accordingly I despatched a little packet of Will Chip, before I sat down at home. You will believe that I have not forgotten to supply Richmond. Our minister and our apothecary are supplied, and the first went to the house of Cambridge and there excited envy, Mr. Cambridge declaring he wished he had written it. Mr. Rivington still dispenses them by thousands, (I hope some go to France) and though he cannot get anything by them, nor the pleasant author, yet both will allow that this is success.[18]

Boscawen here recognises that More's history of educational and charitable work has made her better qualified to intervene than those who moved less habitually between different kinds of communities. Her letter also shows how a social consensus taking in large sections of the Church, social elites, major publishers and key representatives of the bourgeoisie came together behind More's works. However, it is crucial in understanding More's impact to recognise that this privileged consensus encompassed only part of her range. She knew her critics, her publishers and most of the major influencers of her time personally, but she also studied the needs and desires of readers that many authors considered to be beneath their notice. While from a modern perspective she might rightly be accused of condescension, her commitment to demystifying aspects of religion, culture and society allowed and required her to triangulate between elite arbiters and the wider audiences that were slowly but surely opening up to written communications.

---

[17] Elizabeth Montagu to Hannah More, 1792, in Roberts, II, 348–9 (p. 349).
[18] Frances Boscawen to Hannah More, 1792, in Roberts, II, 350–2 (p. 351).

More's talents as chameleon and activist made her an author of unique prominence. Anne K. Mellor has gone so far as to argue that 'one can plausibly say that Hannah More's writings consolidated and disseminated a revolution, not in the overt structure of public government, but, equally important, in the very culture or mores of the English nation.'[19] This, as Mellor admits, is a substantial claim, but one with which I would agree except insofar as it attributes agency solely to More's writings. While it would be wrong to downplay the significance of the texts More produced, her careful management of her identity as their producer was a key contributor to their successes, as evidenced by their slow slipping away from currency after her death. Even more crucially, as the *Village Politics* correspondence demonstrates, More did not achieve her triumphs alone. Her collaborations with the fashionable world, with literary women, with evangelicals and the established church, with national and provincial networks of power, and with publishers were all crucial for projecting her voice in manners that catalysed a cultural shift. To an even greater extent than authors like Southey, Moore and Hemans, More needs to be considered as existing outwith the belatedly defined field of literature in order for her achievements fully to be recognised. While More was a woman of strong principles, her projects were infused with a quality Patricia Demers perceptively calls 'insistent pragmatism'.[20] More did not employ her considerable talents to make abstruse or abstracted literary works; rather, her productions are best seen as dynamic social interventions.

Examining More's social fluency alongside her literary talents makes it possible to see how she balanced these things in self-consciously different manners in different writings and interactions. Such differences have often been registered in critics' responses, but their implications have not always been explicitly explored. For example, M.G. Jones holds More's correspondence in high regard, opining that 'Her letters [...] emerge triumphantly from the biographies. Clear, vivid, informative, free from pose and affectation, they have a refreshing spontaneity, some wit and shrewd judgement of men and affairs.' However, Jones also writes that 'the literary value [of her works], in contrast to that of her letters, is negligible',

---

[19] Anne K. Mellor, *Mothers of the Nation: Women's Political Writing in England, 1780–1830* (Bloomington and Indianapolis: Indiana University Press, 2000), p. 14.

[20] Patricia Demers, *The World of Hannah More* (Lexington: University of Kentucky Press, 1996), p. 11.

although she allows their utility as 'documentaries'.[21] While the value judgements implicit in this division might be disputed, it remains interesting in that it identifies a stark dissonance between the public and the semi-private More. Her performances in her letters to her peers are no less performative than her poems or her dramas, but they perform in intimate, affectionate and often comic manners with which she rarely felt comfortable in her widely circulated writings. From an early stage in her career, More learned carefully how to nuance her voice depending on her audience. In exploring her achievements, it becomes obvious that this ability to vary her style dramatically without losing either her clarity or her identity was crucial to More's singular eminence.

More did not come from a wealthy background. Her father's ambitions to enter the church had been thwarted, leading him to settle near Bristol and work first as an excise officer and then as a schoolmaster at Fishponds, an occupation Stott describes as 'demeaning as well as badly paid'.[22] More's three older sisters ran a school at which she was first a pupil and then a teacher, but while this was a successful venture, it was far from a life of leisured ease. More's ability to write and interact in the manners that brought her success was predicated on a very particular disappointment that nevertheless served to emancipate her from immediate financial concerns. In 1767, More became engaged to a Somerset landowner, William Turner. However, in 1773, the engagement was broken off after six years of hesitations. In recompense for his dithering and the resulting damage to the twenty-eight-year-old More's prospects, More's friends and family secured from Turner an annuity of £200, to be paid quarterly, which they eventually induced More to accept. This was a very significant intervention; as More's sister Patty put it to a family friend, '£200 P Ann is not to be sported with, tis a noble provision'.[23] Virginia Woolf would later claim that 'a woman must have money and a room of her own if she is to write fiction'.[24] While More's writing was far from being exclusively fiction and was written in contexts more defiantly social than those that Woolf invokes, the Turner annuity was nevertheless invaluable for removing the straightforward financial limitations that would have constrained her ability to

[21] M.G. Jones, pp. ix, x.

[22] Stott, p. 4.

[23] Patty More to Ann Gwatkin, 9 December 1773, quoted in Stott, p. 20.

[24] Virginia Woolf, *A Room of One's Own*, in *A Room of One's Own and Three Guineas*, ed. Anna Snaith (Oxford: Oxford University Press, 2015), pp. 1–86 (p. 3).

choose what, how and when she wrote. As Patty affectionately put it, 'this *Poet* of ours is taken care of and may sit down on her large *behind* and *read*, no *devour*, as many books as she pleases.'[25] More herself was deeply aware of the benefits of her financial independence. Writing to her family from London in 1776, she averred that 'It is not possible for anything on earth to be more agreeable to my taste than my present manner of living. I am so much at my ease; have a great many hours at my own disposal, to read my own books and see my own friends; and, whenever I please, may join the most polished and delightful society in the world!'[26] This was not a privilege offered to many, and More took full advantage.

It is no coincidence that it was shortly after the end of her engagement that More began to make serious waves, as free time and secure finances allowed her to embark on a substantial programme of self-development and promotion. The early works with which she made her name have sometimes been dismissed. Robert Hole notes that they were 'well regarded within her circle', but contends that many were 'little more than 'in-jokes' or flattery between friends'.[27] Such views reflect modern prejudices about what literary works should be while failing fully to account either for the limited circles who could access culture in the late eighteenth century or for the roles played by sociality in determining the value of texts. More's early works were as much about building relationships as anything else. Hole backhandedly recognises the importance of such relationships when he asserts that More's tragedy *Percy* succeeded 'due not to its literary or dramatic merit but to the skill and reputation of her friend and patron David Garrick'. However, this claim sells More considerably short. While Garrick's intercession did a great deal to help More get her plays onto the London stage, Garrick did not assist everyone who approached him for aid. His support for More was based both on a genuine admiration for her work and on the personal relationship she assiduously cultivated. As Kerri Andrews rightly puts it, More's facility for 'well-crafted flattery' was a considerable asset that she leveraged to build a formidable constellation of supporters, in which Garrick was only the brightest of many stars.[28]

---

[25] Patty More to Ann Gwatkin, 9 December 1773, quoted in Stott, p. 20.

[26] Hannah More to her family, 1776, in Roberts, I, 78.

[27] Hole, p. 614.

[28] Kerri Andrews, *Ann Yearsley and Hannah More, Patronage and Poetry: The Story of a Literary Relationship* (London: Pickering & Chatto, 2013), p. 9.

Hole's dismissive assessment also underplays the work that More put in to learn how to write a drama that would appeal to a wide audience. *The Search After Happiness*, written for amateur performance in schools, was a considerable success before More was properly introduced in London circles, and served her well as a calling card. *The Inflexible Captive*, performed with Garrick's assistance at the Theatre Royal Bath in 1775, caused a stir in a local context, but the fact that this was trialled in the provinces rather than at one of the major London theatres shows that More's dramatic reputation was carefully husbanded while she developed her craft. Rather than being a freakish one-off, *Percy* completed a trajectory towards success that More judiciously managed, working diligently to discover how plays were judged and who judged them. While Garrick was important, *Percy* was more spectacularly successful than any one patron could have guaranteed, being performed nineteen times at Covent Garden during the 1777–1778 theatrical season, with each performance 'netting more than £200'.[29] More's own profits were very significant—as she wrote to Ann Gwatkin in March 1778,

> The author's nights, sale of the copy, &c. amounted to near six hundred pounds (this is *entre nous*); and as my friend, Mr. Garrick, has been so good as to lay it out for me on the best security, and at five per cent., it makes a decent little addition to my small income. Cadell gave £150,—a very handsome price, with conditional promises. He confesses (a thing not usual) that it has had a very great sale, and that he shall get a good deal of money by it. The first impression was near four thousand, and the second is almost sold. I do not wish to rise on any body's fall; but it has happened rather luckily for Percy, that so many unsuccessful tragedies were brought out this winter.[30]

This passage makes clear that More had a keen sense of the profits that could be made from theatrical writing. Her careful investments—presumably she refers to lucrative and secure 5% stocks issued by the government in part to fund the war with the American colonies—allowed her to add to her annuity from Turner and increase her already significant income in a prudent and sustainable manner while also building the capital reserves that allowed her eventually to make her vast posthumous bequests. More knew that the theatre was not to be relied on, asserting that *Percy* succeeded in part due to the lack of any serious competition from other

---

[29] Stott, p. 40.
[30] Hannah More to Ann Gwatkin, 5 March 1778, in Roberts, I, 139–42 (p. 140).

debuts. Consequently, she took careful advantage of her good fortune to lay the foundations for ongoing prosperity.

However, while the direct profits of *Percy* were far from negligible, it was the social capital that More accumulated through the play's success that she valued most highly and which she took considerable pains to monitor. Despite stating that 'I never think of going' when reporting the seventh night of *Percy* in a letter to her sisters, she was aware the play had benefitted from 'a very brilliant house', remarking happily that 'I have the great good fortune to have the whole town warm in my favour', bar two writers who were 'very ill of the yellow jaundice'. For the ninth night, More's thoughts had obviously changed, as she ventured to the theatre herself and took careful note of the other attendees:

> Lady North [wife of the Prime Minister] did me the honour to take a stage box. I trembled when the speech against the wickedness of going to war was spoken, as I was afraid my lord was in the house, and that speech, though not written with any particular design, is so bold, and always so warmly received, that it frightens me; and I really feel uneasy till it is well over. Mrs. Montagu had a box again; which, as she is so consummate a critic, and is hardly ever seen at a public place, is a great credit to the play. Lady B[oscawen] was there of course; and I am told she has not made an engagement this fortnight, but on condition she should be at liberty to break it for Percy. I was asked to dine at the chancellor's two or three days ago, but happened to be engaged to Mrs. Montagu, with whom I have been a good deal lately. We also spent an agreeable evening together at Dr. [William] Cadogan's, where she and I, being the only two monsters in the creation who never touch a card, (and laughed at enough for it we are) had the fireside to ourselves; and a more elegant and instructive conversation I have seldom enjoyed. I met Mrs. [Hester] Chapone one day at Mrs. Montagu's; she is one of *Percy*'s warmest admirers; and as she does not go to plays, but has formed her judgment in the closet, it is the more flattering.[31]

This account shows how the success of *Percy* opened a series of doors for More, consolidating and expanding her circle of friends and supporters in manners that placed her at the centre of British literary culture. Her theatrical career subsequently faltered: after Garrick's death, her final stage play, *The Fatal Falsehood*, which lacked his support and suffered from More's inattention, made it to a third night at Covent Garden (the first

---

[31] Hannah More to her family, [December] 1777, in Roberts, I, 125–7 (pp. 126–7).

conducted for the author's benefit), but no further. However, More's theatrical engagements had already secured her reputation, allowing her to move on to other projects in a position of considerable strength. Her status as a leading woman of culture was marked by her prominent depiction in Richard Samuel's 1778 painting *Portraits in the Characters of the Muses in the Temple of Apollo* and its 1779 print remediation *The Nine Living Muses of Great Britain*. This clearly signalled her affiliation with a group of remarkable women who, in Elizabeth Eger's words, 'personified the aims of a civilized society' and served as 'cultural standard-bearers of considerable influence.'[32]

Nor was More lax in contributing to the discourses that her Bluestocking friends sought to promote. Her poem *The Bas Bleu; or, Conversation*, written in 1783, celebrates and inscribes the fame of her compatriots even as it works to advance one of their shared projects: promoting the value of dialogue within familiar circles and across societal divisions, particularly those constructed around gender. Addressed to the salonnière Elizabeth Vesey, the poem's elegantly poised quick-fire references position the Bluestockings at the dawn of a new age, having successfully beaten back previous barbarities:

> Long was Society o'er-run
> By Whist, that desolating Hun;
>   Long did Quadrille despotic sit,
> That Vandal of colloquial wit
> And Conversation's setting light
> Lay half-obscur'd in Gothic night.
> At length the mental shades decline,
> Colloquial wit begins to shine;
> Genius prevails, and Conversation
> Emerges into *Reformation*.
> The vanquish'd triple crown to you,
> BOSCAWEN sage, bright MONTAGU,
> Divided, fell;—your cares in haste
> Rescued the ravag'd realms of Taste[.][33]

---

[32] Elizabeth Eger, *Bluestockings: Women of Reason from Enlightenment to Romanticism* (Basingstoke: Palgrave Macmillan, 2010), pp. 3, 5.

[33] Hannah More, *The Bas Bleu; or, Conversation*, in *The Works of Hannah More*, 11 vols (London: T. Cadell, 1830), I, 289–305 (pp. 292–3).

Initially, this poem was circulated relatively circumspectly in manuscript among More's circle, but it quickly broke out into the wider world of the social elite:

> Elizabeth Carter thought it 'delightful'; Fanny Burney longed for a copy of her own—no doubt because [Sir William Weller] Pepys had told her that the silent figure of 'Attention' in the poem was a portrait of herself [...] [Samuel] Johnson described it to Hester Thrale as 'a very great performance'. In his first extant letter to More, written in March 1784, Walpole praised 'the quantity of learning [that] has all the air of negligence instead of that of pedantry'. The king liked it so much that he wanted a copy of his own, and More sat up one night to write it out for him.[34]

The Bas Bleu was finally published in 1786, but as Stott's account shows, by that time it had already done considerable work on More's behalf, further cementing her status as one of the most accomplished poets of her generation and strengthening her network of appreciators. By watching society carefully and reflecting its preoccupations back, filtered through forms and lenses adapted to her needs, More made herself an indispensable presence.

However, as the 1780s wore on, More became dissatisfied with writing works to impress her cultured friends. The first major fruit of her strengthening Evangelical convictions was her protest poem *Slavery*, which she wrote to intervene in the 1788 debates surrounding the Slave Trade Act. She was keenly aware of the importance of timeliness, writing to her sister that 'if it does not come out at the particular moment when the discussion comes on in parliament, it will not be worth a straw'.[35] She also refused to pull her punches in her condemnations. Describing slavers as 'WHITE SAVAGE[s]' was unlikely to have endeared her to some of her Bristolian neighbours.[36] She presented a positive vision of the moral good that legislation leading to abolition would achieve, but this was underpinned by a clear sense that the current state of affairs was buttressed by cruel hypocrisy:

> Shall Britain, where the soul of Freedom reigns,
> Forge chains for others she herself distains?
> Forbid it, Heaven! O let the nations know

---

[34] Stott, p. 64.
[35] Hannah More to her sister, 1788, in Roberts, I, 96–7 (p. 97).
[36] Hannah More, *Slavery: A Poem* (London: T. Cadell, 1788), p. 15 (l. 211).

> The liberty she loves she will bestow;
> Not to herself the glorious gift confin'd
> She spreads the blessing wide as humankind;
> And, scorning narrow views of time and place,
> Bids all be free in earth's extended space.[37]

While More took pains over her poem, she recognised it as part of a larger undertaking. In the March 1788 *Monthly Review*, the review of *Slavery* was preceded and succeeded by accounts of poems on the same subject by John Newell Puddicombe, Ann Yearsley (More's former protégée) and Thomas George Street.[38] While her plays and poems had often benefitted from her alignments with influential groups and networks, *Slavery* was part of a collective endeavour of a kind that would become increasingly important to More as she began to co-ordinate charitable contributions, soothe local egos and gather staff and resources to establish the Mendip Schools.[39] Rather than simply building her own reputation, More increasingly sought to use her literary talents and accrued authority to rewrite wider cultural presumptions.

It was this activist incarnation of More who in the mid-1790s embarked on one of the most remarkable publishing projects of the eighteenth century: the Cheap Repository Tracts. The Cheap Repository was inspired in part by the success of *Village Politics*, but expanded the concept to a multiple-author series eventually totalling over two hundred publications circulated throughout the nation by an immense and complex network of writers, publishers, sellers, subscribers and supporters. Kevin Gilmartin, evoking Wordsworth's claims in prefacing *Lyrical Ballads*, has invited readers to 'consider the Cheap Repository as the most institutionally ambitious, and arguably the most influential, of the many romantic-period efforts to create the taste by which a new literature was to be enjoyed.'[40] However, More went considerably beyond Wordsworth and Coleridge in her efforts not only to refashion taste, but to extend that refashioning beyond her upper- and middle-class sympathisers to people whose previous access to print had been spotty and uncertain. The Repository's published *Plan*, seeking to appeal to the same concerned audiences that had

---

[37] More, *Slavery*, p. 18 (ll. 251–8).
[38] See Articles 25 to 28 in the *Monthly Review*, 78 (March 1788), 245–8.
[39] Stott, pp. 103–25.
[40] Kevin Gilmartin, *Writing Against Revolution: Literary Conservatism in Britain, 1790–1832* (Cambridge: Cambridge University Press, 2007), p. 64.

supported *Village Politics*, stated that its object was 'the circulation of Religious and Useful Knowledge as an antidote to the poison continually flowing through the channel of vulgar and licentious publications'.[41] However, the *Plan* also showed More's influence in recognising that consumers of cheap print were not likely to read or purchase unsweetened bossy instructions:

> BEING well aware, that sermons, catechisms, and other articles of perceptive piety, may be had from the great societies already formed, we shall prefer what is striking to what is merely didactic. Instructive incidents, lives, deaths, remarkable dispensations of Providence, useful narratives, will form a considerable part of the plan; from which will be carefully excluded whatever is enthusiastic, superstitious or absurd.[42]

Like many of her previous works, the Cheap Repository Tracts that More wrote sharpened the existing traits of popular forms and alloyed these with engaging narratives shaped using her talent for clear voicing. More investigated the culture in which she planned to intervene as carefully as she had previously studied the requirements of successful drama or the tastes of her privileged contemporaries. As Gary Kelly has described, the extensive research collection she assembled took in both 'traditional chapbooks [that] accept[ed] gentry hegemony without embracing it', and what she called her 'sans-culotte library': the works of radicals who sought to use cheap literature to advance the cause of social reform along Revolutionary lines.[43] Armed with these materials and with her formidable list of contacts, she marshalled her forces and set to work building a movement.

More's project was successful almost immediately. As Richard Altick recounts, 'In the first six weeks (March 3–April 18, 1795) 300,000 copies were sold at wholesale; by July of the same year, the number had more than doubled; and by March 1796, the total number had reached the staggering figure of 2,000,000.'[44] In a period where most literary works were printed in runs of one or two thousand copies, this was a genuinely vast

---

[41] *A Plan for Establishing by Subscription a Repository of Cheap Publications, on Religious & Moral Subjects* (London: [?John Marshall], 1795), p. 1.

[42] *Plan for Establishing by Subscription a Repository of Cheap Publications*, p. 2.

[43] Gary Kelly, 'Revolution, Reaction, and the Expropriation of Popular Culture: Hannah More's *Cheap Repository*', *Man and Nature*, 6 (1987), 147–59 (pp. 150, 148).

[44] Richard D. Altick, *The English Common Reader: A Social History of the Mass Reading Public 1800–1900* (Chicago: University of Chicago Press, 1957), p. 75.

quantity of printed matter, much of it poetry and fiction. However, the precise nature of its impact remains disputed and hard to measure. Stott, among others, has questioned whether the tracts genuinely reached working-class readers, arguing that testimony as to sales does not prove 'that labourers and maidservants were queuing up to read moralistic little tracts; what it does show is that, like *Village Politics*, the Cheap Repository was a huge hit among the middle classes'.[45] This makes it sound like the tracts had a rather limited influence, but there are numerous reasons to believe that they had a more considerable effect. This first is that the relatively small middle class in the Romantic period had often previously been barred from easy access to modern literature by high prices. The Cheap Repository thus represented a significant opportunity for the middling sort to acquire both cultural capital and new reading habits. The second reason relates to patterns of circulation. While Gary Kelly has claimed that the wholesale pricing of the tracts and the publishing of editions 'on "superior" paper and with finer printing' suggests that 'the tracts appealed more to the middle and upper ranks', he implicitly assumes that the wholesale copies sat idle while the poor rejected what he calls 'a fantasy of social order'.[46] This may have happened in some cases, but records of labouring-class engagements with writing commonly emphasise processes of sharing, reuse and reading aloud that make it likely that the tracts reached even further than the number of copies would suggest. A third indicator of the tracts' success is the string of continuing publications and republications. The figures above are only for the first year of the Cheap Repository, which ran for several further years under More's direction. They do not cover subsequent sales; the collected editions that followed; the versions issued in Ireland, Europe and the United States (where the Cheap Repository was reissued as late as 1851); or repurposing of the tracts in other ventures, including More's own collected works, in which they were included from 1801. While More's formidable organisational skills and social clout might have sufficed to launch the venture, publishers would not have ensured that the tracts enjoyed a sustained print-cultural presence if no one was purchasing and reading them.

The Cheap Repository was often dismissed by later nineteenth-century auditors as propaganda, and this is not without grounds. Recounting the reported reaction of a duke in a letter to her sister, More wrote that 'he said that though he admired the scheme exceedingly, and had a high respect for me, he should not subscribe, because he took it for granted, knowing the character of the lady, that all the doctrines would be on one side. I desired my friend to tell his grace that they certainly would.'[47] However, like *Village Politics*, the tracts emerge as being ideologically complex when considered in the wider contexts of their age. The polarising Revolution debate was not the only driver of change, and while the tracts condemned radicalism, they sought to reconfigure society in other ways. They are too literary, multifarious and diverse to be easily dismissed as simple reiterations of a party line; rather, they reflect the differing agendas of their various writers and inspirations. In particular, those written by More display her own complex sense of an improvable world. As D.W. Bebbington puts it, 'if Hannah More insisted on the duties of the poor, she had already written on the obligations of their superiors': her focus was very much on the 'reciprocal duties' that bound together individuals into an effective society.[48] One of the most radically attractive parts of this conception was the space it opened up for political action by women. In an important reading, Mitzi Myers contends that the tracts were directed towards propagating new kinds of feminine authority: 'Through female influence and moral power, this cultural myth's new woman would educate the young and illiterate, succor the unfortunate, amend the debased popular culture of the lower orders, reorient worldly men of every class, and set the national house in order'.[49] Ideals like this proved to have a surprisingly wide appeal. Edmund Downey, discussing an unpublished letter from More to the Newcastle-based publisher and engraver Ralph Beilby, has indicated that the *Tracts* were successful in 'co-opting the figures and networks associated with radical culture in the late eighteenth century'.[50] Perhaps this was because while the *Tracts* were conservative in their defence of the existing social order, they were liberal in other respects—in their desire to bring new readers into the fold of cul-

---

[47] Hannah More to her sister, 1795, in Roberts, II, 430–1 (p. 430).

[48] D.W. Bebbington, *Evangelicalism in Modern Britain: A History from the 1730s to the 1980s* (London and New York: Routledge, 1993), p. 70.

[49] Mitzi Myers, 'Hannah More's Tracts for the Times: Social Fiction and Female Ideology', in *Fetter'd or Free? British Women Novelists, 1670–1815*, ed. Mary Anne Schofield and Cecilia Macheski (Athens, OH: Ohio University Press, 1986), pp. 264–84 (p. 266).

[50] Edmund Downey, 'An Unpublished Letter from Hannah More to Ralph Beilby: Radical Connections and Popular Periodical Literature', *Notes and Queries*, 61 (December 2014), 504–7 (p. 504).

ture, for example, and in their representations of female subjectivity. As Julia Saunders puts it, reflecting the views of recent scholars who have sought to reclaim More, 'though her opinions locate her amongst the conservatives when compared to radical contemporaries, the implications of her educational and literary practice place her amongst the most progressive writers of her day'.[51] Anti-slavery themes are covered repeatedly in the *Tracts*.[52] They also take considerable care in dispensing useful practical advice—in 'Betty Brown, the St. Giles's Orange Girl', for example, examinations of the dangers of high-interest loans and clear explanations of the value of financial independence sit alongside assertions that all the events of Betty's life had been 'under the direction of a good and a kind Providence'.[53] More was canny in providing negative examples as well as models of virtue—while characters like Black Giles and Tawney Rachel meet bad ends, More gets to have her cake and eat it by laying out entertaining accounts of their illegal exploits before she condemns them to their fates. The tracts approached readers in the guise of an old form, but they promoted a revised social order. By focusing so heavily on narratives in poetry and prose, they also made this social order one in which literary composition had a central place as a mode of knowledge, a desideratum of culture and a positive moral force.

While the Cheap Repository was More's largest-scale cultural intervention, after its cessation, she continued to write works that combined narrative and instruction, perhaps most notably her hugely successful novel *Coelebs in Search of a Wife*. She also continued to leaven her generally conservative works with more progressive proposals. In her *Strictures on the Modern System of Female Education*, for example, she seems to take a sidelong look at her own career while advocating for women's talents:

> But there is one *human* consideration which would perhaps more effectually tend to damp in an aspiring woman the ardours of literary vanity, (I speak not of real genius, though there the remark often applies,) than any which she will derive from motives of humility, or propriety, or religion; which is,

---

[51] Julia Saunders, 'Putting the Reader Right: Reassessing Hannah More's *Cheap Repository Tracts*', *Romanticism on the Net*, 16 (1999), https://doi.org/10.7202/005881ar, paragraph 24.

[52] Detailed in Hole, pp. 619–20.

[53] Hannah More, 'Betty Brown, the St. Giles's Orange Girl', in *Tales for the Common People and other Cheap Repository Tracts*, ed. Clare MacDonald Shaw (Nottingham: Trent Editions, 2002), pp. 53–63 (p. 62).

that in the judgment passed on her performances, she will have to encounter the mortifying circumstance of having her sex always taken into account; and her highest exertions will probably be received with the qualified appro- bation, *that it is really extraordinary for a woman.*[54]

More's writings may not all appeal to modern readers, but she deserves to be recognised as a writer whose wide-ranging achievements were genu- inely extraordinary, with no need for caveats. Demers has claimed that More 'devoted her long career to one overriding cause: galvanizing women of the middle and upper ranks to act, not as domestic ornaments, but as thinking, engaged, and responsible social beings.'[55] This might be extended to cover readers more generally. More has a real claim to be the foremost eighteenth-century writer in terms of opening the field of liter- ary culture to new entrants. Unfortunately for her posthumous reputa- tion, the very success of her writings and the emerging infrastructures that distributed them ensured their eventual obsolescence. The expanded read- ing audience she played a significant role in creating presented a market for which publishers and writers competed in creating new kinds of spe- cialist writing that slowly made More's more general disquisitions seem obsolete. Nevertheless, she deserves considerable credit for her role in carving out a space and an audience that allowed for the creation of the discipline of literature as we understand it today. Without More, there would have been considerably fewer Romantic-period readers trained to admire, value and think critically about narrative as a social and moral force.

WALTER SCOTT: THE WIZARD OF THE NORTH

In *The Spirit of the Age*, William Hazlitt contended that Byron and Scott were the writers

who would carry away the majority of suffrages as the greatest geniuses of the age. The former [Byron] would, perhaps, obtain the preference with the fine gentlemen and ladies (squeamishness apart)—the latter with the critics and the vulgar. We shall treat of them in the same connection, partly on account of their distinguished pre-eminence, and partly because they afford

---

[54] Hannah More, *Strictures on the Modern System of Female Education*, 2nd edn, 2 vols (London: T. Cadell and W. Davies, 1799), II, 13.
[55] Demers, p. 132.

a complete contrast to each other. In their poetry, in their prose, in their politics, and in their tempers, no two men can be more unlike.[56]

The remainder of this chapter will expand on Hazlitt's contrast through contending that the different manners in which Scott and Byron operated were paradigmatic of a developmental division in the increasingly distinctive literary field that emerged from the works of writers like More and her contemporaries. While their spectacular successes were each unique, Scott and Byron's trailblazing careers played major roles in setting the terms that would henceforward govern authorship more widely. They offered, as Hazlitt suggests, two competing models for what being writerly should entail, which might broadly be described as the commercial and professional on the one hand and the artistic or oppositional on the other. However, these new models were not mutually exclusive; nor were they independent of existing conventions. Scott and Byron achieved their dominant positions in large part through leveraging systems of social privilege to create new affordances in a cultural sphere that was becoming increasingly distinct from the general operations of political and financial power without ever becoming wholly separate from them.

Scott's contemporaries were in no doubt about the extent of his influence. Opening an 1838 article examining the female characters in the Waverley novels, Letitia Elizabeth Landon boldly claimed that 'Sir Walter Scott was the Luther of literature. He reformed and he regenerated.'[57] These high claims were echoed by other voices. Hazlitt, despite his distaste for Scott's politics, opined that 'the Author of Waverley is one of the greatest teachers of morality that ever lived, by emancipating the mind from petty, narrow, and bigoted prejudices'.[58] However, Landon's chosen metaphor of Reformation is particularly appropriate in its capturing the sense that Scott had approached a somewhat moribund monoculture and carved out a powerful alternative. The theses Scott implicitly advanced suggested a sharper sense of literature than had previously been current, presenting literary writing as a powerful means for understanding the world, but also one that was distinct from rather than coextensive with

---

[56] William Hazlitt, 'Lord Byron', in *The Spirit of the Age*, in *The Complete Works of William Hazlitt*, ed. P.P. Howe, 21 vols (London: J.M. Dent, 1930–34), XI, 69–78 (p. 69).

[57] The Author of *The Improvisatrice* [Letitia Elizabeth Landon], 'Female Portrait Gallery, from Sir Walter Scott: No. I.—Flora McIvor and Rose Bradwardine', *New Monthly Magazine*, 52 (January 1838), 35–39 (p. 35).

[58] Hazlitt, 'Lord Byron', XI, 71.

straightforward historical writing or with the insights granted by religion, philosophy or political economy. Additionally, as Hazlitt put it, he 'completely got rid of the trammels of authorship; and [tore] off at one rent [...] all the ornaments of fine writing and worn-out sentimentality.'[59] By stripping away many of the previous conventions of sociable writing, Scott opened his works up both to broader audiences—to whom he provided the cipher along with the code—and to those who wanted literature to serve as a mode of truth in itself, with its own unique affordances as a discourse.

Scott was also, as Robert Mayer notes, 'approachable in ways his forebears had not been and his contemporaries were not.'[60] He was an assiduous networker and fixer who has a strong claim to have been the best-connected writer of the early nineteenth century. This openness and connectedness granted him social and financial clout that operated in manners that were mutually reinforcing. The aesthetic and moral changes that Landon and Hazlitt see Scott as catalysing were inextricably linked with his being one of the most brilliant commercial writers in literary history. He was not merely financially successful in himself; he also directly and indirectly inspired a huge range of subsidiary productions, including plays, tours, guidebooks, operas, editions, visual media, merchandise, periodical writings and whole subgenres of novels and poetry. With the possible exception of Byron, he was the best-selling living poet of the Romantic period, selling 17,800 copies of *The Lay of the Last Minstrel* and an even more impressive 29,300 copies of *The Lady of the Lake* in the five years after their respective publications, sales figures that dwarfed those of most of his contemporaries.[61] When he switched to writing novels, he became the nineteenth century's biggest-selling novelist. As William St Clair has it, '[d]uring the romantic period the 'Author of *Waverley*' sold more novels than all the other novelists of the time put together.'[62] This is

---

[59] William Hazlitt, 'Sir Walter Scott', in *The Spirit of the Age*, in *The Complete Works of William Hazlitt*, ed. P.P. Howe, 21 vols (London: J.M. Dent, 1930–34), XI, 57–69 (p. 61).

[60] Robert Mayer, *Walter Scott and Fame: Authors and Readers in the Romantic Age* (Oxford: Oxford University Press, 2017), p. 4.

[61] See Benjamin Colbert, 'Popular Romanticism? Publishing, Readership and the Making of Literary History' in *Authorship, Commerce and the Public*, ed. E.J. Clery, Caroline Franklin and Peter Garside (Basingstoke: Palgrave Macmillan, 2002), pp. 153–68 (p. 155) and William St Clair, *The Reading Nation in the Romantic Period* (Cambridge, Cambridge University Press, 2004), pp. 216–8.

[62] St Clair, p. 221.

a mind-boggling statistic that emphasises both the relatively small size of the market for novels and the scale of Scott's achievement in opening up fiction to new readerships. While most novels sold hundreds of copies, Scott's inevitably sold tens of thousands. As well as saturating the market, his works enjoyed other forms of success. In Ian Duncan's words, 'their claim on the cultural authority of the Enlightenment human sciences, as well as their artistic prowess, helped win them an overwhelming critical prestige; and their author stood at the center of the regional network of Tory patronage'.[63] Scott dominated culture in the 1810s and 1820s. Through doing so, he altered fundamentally the statuses of the novel, Scotland and writing as a profession.

Despite this, Scott claimed to have seen authorship as an unstable source of potential wealth rather than a way to acquire a solid income. It was perhaps in part for this reason that he was able to engage in it speculatively with such success. When considering his career, he contended that he had believed from an early stage that 'literature should be my staff, but not my crutch'.[64] He managed to keep to this dictum in a personal capacity for much of his career, but also made unparalleled interventions in book-trade infrastructure through aggressively leveraging his assets to invest in his printers and publishers. This allowed him fleetingly to monopolise his works' means of production, but it also rendered his household dangerously vulnerable to circumstances beyond his direct control. Scott the author and Scott the man were in tight alignment for large parts of his career, but eventually the demands of the latter combined with a series of unfortunate circumstances to commit the former beyond his very considerable capabilities.

Like More, Scott was able to write to make a reputation, rather than requiring literary profits to meet his basic needs. He established an extremely healthy personal income relatively early in his life through his family, his legal career, seeking patronage and marriage.[65] His father, also

---

[63] Ian Duncan, *Scott's Shadow: The Novel in Romantic Edinburgh* (Princeton, NJ: Princeton University Press, 2007), p. xi.

[64] In the 'Introduction to *The Lay of the Last Minstrel*' from Cadell's 1830 edition of the *Poetical Works*, as quoted in John Gibson Lockhart, *Memoirs of the Life of Sir Walter Scott, Bart.*, 7 vols (Philadelphia: Carey, Lea & Blanchard, 1837–38), I, 249. Lockhart quotes this demurral to downplay the importance of his father-in-law's investments in the book trade, having previously highlighted the respectable incomes I detail in subsequent paragraphs.

[65] Factual information taken from John Sutherland, *The Life of Walter Scott* (Oxford: Blackwell, 1995) unless otherwise attributed.

called Walter Scott, held the title of Writer to the Signet, a senior position in Scotland's legal hierarchy. Scott the elder funded a piecemeal gentlemanly education for his sickly third son, and it was expected that he would end up working in his father's office. However, Scott was an ambitious man, refusing his father's offer of a partnership in 1790 and instead qualifying into the potentially more prestigious role of advocate in 1792. Unfortunately, he was an indifferent performer in the courtroom, making 23 guineas, 55 guineas and £84 in his first three years of practice. He quickly realised that he was not well suited to advocacy, and, as John Sutherland has it, he 'sensibly invested his hopes in what patronage might do for him', cultivating the acquaintances of powerful men including Henry Scott, Duke of Buccleuch; Robert Dundas, the lord advocate; and Robert Macqueen, Lord Braxfield, the lord justice clerk.[66] This course proved prudent—Scott was appointed Sherriff of Selkirkshire in 1799, a position in the gift of Buccleuch, the responsibilities of which were principally handled by a deputy. He held the position until his death in 1832 at an initial salary of £250, later raised to £300. In 1797, he had secured £500 a year through his marriage to Charlotte Carpenter (this surname being an Anglicised version of her original French surname, Charpentier). After his father's death in 1799, he inherited family money and by 1800, before he made any significant profits from his literary endeavours, his household income had reached a very considerable sum: between £1000 and £1500 a year.[67] He later improved his legal income further by politicking with the aid of his patrons for one of the principal clerkships of the Court of Session, agreeing in 1806 to fulfil the duties of an elderly incumbent gratis in return for guaranteed succession to the post. The incumbent, William Home, lived longer than Scott expected, but was induced to retire in January 1812, at which point Scott began to receive the post's salary, £1300 a year at that time, less a sum contributed to his predecessor's pension. By 1812, his non-literary incomes totalled around £2000 a year, a sum ten times the size of Southey's first government pension, four times as much as Moore's *Irish Melodies* annuity and equal to two-thirds of what Hemans is estimated to have made over the course of her whole career. Scott would thus have been a very prosperous man had he never published a single word. His choosing to write was due to the gentlemanly

---

[66] John Sutherland, p. 49.

[67] Edgar Johnson, *Sir Walter Scott: The Great Unknown*, 2 vols (New York: Macmillan, 1970), I, 176.

cachet of composition, the prospect of enhancing his reputation and his genuine investment in culture.

The forms of culture that Scott was particularly interested in were those oriented towards negotiating the value of the past in the present. In one of his snarkier comments on his eminent contemporary, Hazlitt asserts that '[Scott] is just half what the human intellect is capable of being: if you take the universe, and divide it into two parts, he knows all that it *has been*; all that it *is to be* is nothing to him.'[68] However, such sniffiness occludes the scale of Scott's engagement with shaping cultural memory in his present. As Ann Rigney puts it, 'Scott opened up the past as an imaginative resource, inspiring a fashion for history as a key to collective identity'.[69] His pre-eminence in this area was widely recognised at the time. Landon claims that 'Scott's works have done more towards awakening a rational curiosity, than a whole world of catechisms and abridgements would ever have accomplished. History has been read owing to his stimulus.'[70] Scott can be credited with making the past available and comprehensible in manners that respected its multivalent potential, rather than reducing it to political allegory. The painstaking labour this entailed was not something he was required to do, but Scott wanted more than simply to exist comfortably. He was a hard-working—even obsessive—individual. Literary culture in the form of collection, editing and composition provided a means of channelling his energies into forms from which he could profit socially, financially and personally. While he could not master the courtroom, it turned out that the archive, the page and the convivial gathering were well-suited to his organisational talents.

Along with history, Scott was also fascinated by both money and the book trade. His financial and social resources combined with the currency of his works to allow him to indulge these fascinations. Through experimentation and speculation, he was able to spread his reclamations and reconfigurations of the past to hungry audiences with an almost unprecedented level of control. As a gentleman in an established profession, it would have been unseemly for him to be seen to involve himself in business, but he circumvented disapprobation by working clandestinely with James and John Ballantyne, brothers who he knew from his schooldays in

---

[68] Hazlitt, 'Sir Walter Scott', XI, 57.

[69] Ann Rigney, *The Afterlives of Walter Scott: Memory on the Move* (Oxford: Oxford University Press, 2012), p. 4.

[70] [Landon], 'Female Portrait Gallery', p. 36.

Kelso who were also his Masonic brethren. James Ballantyne's Kelso press published Scott's earliest works, *An Apology for Tales of Terror* and the ballad 'The Eve of St John' (both 1799). Ballantyne was also involved with the *Minstrelsy of the Scottish Border* (1802–1803), which was published by a London firm, Cadell and Davies, but printed by Ballantyne at Scott's insistence. After the success of Scott's ballad collections, he persuaded James Ballantyne to move to Edinburgh and loaned him £500 to establish a press there. He also used his legal connections to secure for Ballantyne the lucrative printing contract for the Court of Session. When the success of the *Lay of the Last Minstrel* (1805) stretched the fledgling firm's resources, Scott seized on the opportunity to buy in as a partner, injecting £1500 in return for a third share in the company. Scott's connection to the firm was kept secret from all but a few, partly due to his gentlemanly scruples but also because this allowed him to use his clandestine involvement to generate advantage. When he was considering preparing an edition of Dryden, Scott contacted the editor of a competing edition, Edward Forster, made an agreement to collaborate and then insisted that the printing be done by Ballantyne. Ballantyne quoted a very high price, which, combined with doubts expressed by the edition's London publisher, got Forster ejected from the project and Scott installed in his place.[71]

Another major contributor to Scott's success was the premier figure in Edinburgh's book trade, Archibald Constable. Constable had his eye on Scott from an early stage. He bought significant shares in Scott's early productions and finally secured him in January 1807 by offering a thousand guineas for *Marmion* (1808), more than double the £500 that Longmans had paid for the *Lay of the Last Minstrel.*[72] Constable's careful wooing led to a long and fruitful collaboration, albeit one interrupted by a number of fallings-out. During the poetical phase of his career, Scott generally sold his copyrights, and Constable was happy to profit by this and to let Scott borrow against these payments before works were complete. Constable also found other kinds of employment for the industrious author, arranging for him to compile an edition of the works of Jonathan Swift, for which Constable paid £1500, £500 in advance. This edition, begun in 1808 and finally completed in 1814, was the source of much frustration for Scott and was one of a number of factors that led him to

---

[71] John Sutherland, p. 129.

[72] David Hewitt, 'Constable, Archibald (1774–1827)', *ODNB*, https://doi.org/10.1093/ref:odnb/6101.

turn against Constable. He came to resent his publisher's profits, disliked Constable's partner, Alexander Hunter, and was annoyed by a negative review of *Marmion* in the *Edinburgh*, which Constable owned. Seeking to bring his works' profits into his own hands, he approached John Ballantyne with the idea of setting up a rival publishing company in which Scott himself would secretly hold a half share and the Ballantyne brothers a quarter share each. The first production of John Ballantyne and Co. was Scott's *Lady of the Lake* (1810), which sold through a first edition of two thousand two-guinea quartos within weeks and ran through a succession of cheaper octavo editions at a rapid rate. As John Sutherland writes, 'in return for the copyright Scott "nominally" received 2000 guineas; but his profit-share income was probably around £10,000 in 1810 [...] He had, as he said, "put a nail in Fortune's wheel."'[73]

Another project in which Scott had a hand at this time was the nascent *Quarterly Review*. He wrote at great length to John Murray and William Gifford discussing strategies for ensuring the new periodical's effectiveness, used his connections to secure talented contributors and wrote four articles for the first issue. Prudently, he also made sure that the Ballantynes had a share in it. As a consequence, after 1809, Scott found himself a key mover in one of the major Reviews, meaning that he was able, like Southey, to influence considerations of his own works and the works of others. During this period, he also became the dominant partner in James Ballantyne's printing house, so for a time he had almost total control over all the stages of his works' production: 'he could write his books, publish his books, print his books, sell his books and—if he was daring enough— review (or have friends review) his books in *his* journal.'[74] At this point, Scott seemed to have mastered the literary marketplace. Each stage of the publication process brought money to him, and since the sales of his works were on an almost unprecedented scale for poetry, the amount of money brought in was enormous. It is no coincidence that it was around this time that Scott began to realise his dream of lairdhood by buying the property that would become Abbotsford.

However, this form of mastery was not to remain Scott's for long, in large part because he overreached in estimating the extent to which his readers would wish to follow him in the pursuit of his wider interests. John Ballantyne's firm was dangerously undercapitalised due to

---

[73] John Sutherland, p. 144.
[74] John Sutherland, p. 139.

Scott's substantial demands on its reserves and his insistence on initiating costly projects that realised slow or poor returns, such as a posthumous edition of his friend Anna Seward in three volumes (1810) and a fourteen-volume edition of the Jacobean dramatists Francis Beaumont and John Fletcher (1812). Such weighty productions were pioneering attempts to curate British print culture from an Edinburgh base, but their slow sales left Scott's own works among the few productions on the Ballantyne list that brought in swift and significant profits. The biggest drain on the firm's funds was the *Edinburgh Annual Register*, an attempt at a periodical of record that inevitably appeared late and contained a great deal of undistinguished material rushed off by Scott himself with the aim of filling its two overambitious volumes. By 1812, the *Register* was losing the firm at least £1000 a year.[75] Since John Ballantyne's principal creditor was James Ballantyne's press, it seemed possible that debts could bring down both businesses. Keen to have his most popular author back on side, Constable took on £1300 of John Ballantyne's unsold stock and bought a quarter-share in the copyright of Scott's next poem, *Rokeby*, for £700 to tide the firm over while he investigated its liabilities. To the shock of the partners, he found that the firm would require £4000 to avoid a bankruptcy that would unmask Scott as a profit-hungry investor and force him to resign his clerkship. Scott appealed in desperation to the Duke of Buccleuch, who agreed to stand as guarantor for the sum, allowing the partners to extricate themselves from the ruins of John Ballantyne's firm while leaving James Ballantyne's press and Scott's reputation intact. A great number of unsold volumes were left over; in his later dealings, Scott cannily required that those who wished to publish his novels also covertly took on a quantity of dubious Ballantyne inventory.

However, the collapse of these attempts to curate culture through editing, printing and publication did not discourage Scott. Rather, it spurred him on to experiment with new forms. He was always a pluralist in his interests, and he enjoyed the challenge of mastering new kinds of discourse, acting as a gentleman of many accomplishments even as the specialised knowledge required for each of these accomplishments became increasingly extensive. By 1813, he decided he had been eclipsed as a popular poet by Byron, a prospect he affected to face with relative equanimity. John Gibson Lockhart, his son-in-law and biographer, quotes him as saying 'Byron hits the mark where I don't even pretend to fledge my

[75] Johnson, I, 415.

arrow'.[76] This dismissal was doubtless partly performative, as Scott continued to write verse for some time after Byron's success, but it also reflects his beginning to build upon his earlier dalliances with novel-writing. The romantic narrative of Scott's taking up *Waverley* again after chancing across the manuscript in an old writing desk has been questioned by Peter Garside among others, but it seems likely that Scott did begin a novel in the 1800s and that he returned to the idea after the relative failure of *Rokeby* and the actual failure of John Ballantyne's firm.[77] On its completion, *Waverley* was sold to Constable as an anonymous work (although Constable doubtless knew that Scott was the author). An initial demand of £1000 was met with a cautious counteroffer of £700 before the parties eventually settled on a half-profits arrangement. This tentative initial payment paved the way for Scott to reach whole new levels of financial success.

For Scott's contemporaries, its historical specificity and its masculine evocations made *Waverley* a superior sort of novel. Jeffrey wrote in the *Edinburgh* that it displayed 'a consistency in nature and truth, the want of which may always be detected in the happiest combinations of fancy'.[78] For Jeffrey and other nineteenth-century critics, as Ina Ferris has demonstrated, *Waverley* offered relief from 'the feminised space of modernity' from which they figured earlier novels as springing.[79] By intermixing gently comic and fallibly romantic characters within compelling and serious narratives set at key moments in the historical past, Scott was by no means inventing the wheel, but he was reinventing it in a fashion that employed his talents, historical learning and social sensitivity to exert a powerful influence over his contemporaries. While Scott derided generic subtitles in *Waverley's* first chapter, the Waverley novels were read and marketed as their own special category, and were appropriated as such by critics, who used them to make claims for their own authority over the sphere of novel-writing. Such claims in turn legitimated the Author of *Waverley* as the creator of 'the most remarkable productions of the present age.'[80]

---

[76] Lockhart, III, 239.

[77] Peter Garside, 'Popular Fiction and National Tale: the Hidden Origins of Sir Walter Scott's *Waverley*', *Nineteenth Century Literature*, 46 (June 1991), 30–51.

[78] [Francis Jeffrey], 'Waverley—a Novel', *Edinburgh Review*, 24 (November 1814), 208–43 (p. 208).

[79] Ina Ferris, *The Achievement of Literary Authority: Gender, History, and the Waverley Novels* (Ithaca: Cornell University Press, 1991), p. 94.

[80] [Francis Jeffrey], '*Ivanhoe*', *Edinburgh Review*, 33 (January 1820), 1–54 (p. 2).

Jeffrey's describing Scott's works as 'productions' highlights the fact that, as Kathryn Sutherland has written, 'Scott engages with fiction in accordance with the mixed codes of the economist and the romancer'.[81] Scott accurately saw his massively popular works as operating within a wide-ranging sphere of cultural production, rather than within an exclusive gentlemanly or artistic space. In the 'Author of *Waverley*', he self-consciously created a literary brand with an unprecedentedly wide reach and unparalleled profit-making potential. That Scott enjoyed doing business from behind this mask is evident from the teasing preface he added to the third edition of *Waverley*, in which he 'leaves it to the candour of the public' to decide whether he is 'a writer new to publication' or 'a hackneyed author, who is ashamed of too frequent appearance' or 'a man of a grave profession, to whom the reputation of being a novel-writer might be prejudicial; or [...] a man of fashion, to whom writing of any kind might appear pedantic.'[82] Of course, Scott could be said to have been all of these things, creating an additional pleasure for those in the know, but without that knowledge being in any way required to derive meaning. The Author's mask also allowed Scott to discuss trade without shame, as Sutherland recognises when she describes the 'Author of *Waverley*' as Scott's 'ungentlemanly counterpart and man of business'.[83] Scott's financial views on authorship are incorporated into his novels at various points, including the 'Introductory Epistle' to *The Fortunes of Nigel* (1822), in which he argues—contra Adam Smith and in line with David Williams—that 'a successful author is a productive labourer, and that his works constitute as effectual a part of the public wealth as that which is created by any other manufacture.'[84] As well as being, in Fiona Robertson's words, 'histories of legitimacy in terms both of plot and of declared political orientation', Scott's novels also act textually and contextually to legitimate his own

---

[81] Kathryn Sutherland, 'Fictional Economies: Adam Smith, Walter Scott and the Nineteenth-Century Novel', *ELH: English Literary History*, 54 (Spring 1987), 97–127 (p. 99).

[82] Walter Scott, *Waverley; or 'tis Sixty Years Since*, ed. Claire Lamont (Oxford: Oxford University Press, 1986), p. 344.

[83] Kathryn Sutherland, p. 113.

[84] Walter Scott, 'Introductory Epistle' to *The Fortunes of Nigel*, ed. Frank Jordan (Edinburgh: Edinburgh University Press, 2004), p. 14. Scott's view chimes interestingly with David Williams' response to Smith, discussed in Chapter Four.

critical and commercial stock.[85] In a very real sense, Scott's open-minded curations of texts and selves wrote a stable paradigm of respectable prose authorship into being. As Hazlitt put it, 'It is no wonder that the public repay with lengthened applause and gratitude the pleasure they receive. He writes as fast as they can read, and he does not write himself down. He is always in the public eye, and we do not tire of him. His worst is better than any other person's best.'[86]

From the first, Scott's authorship was more widely known than his trade investments. Jane Austen, by no means a figure at the centre of the literary world, was obviously aware of his activities, writing on *Waverley's* publication that 'Walter Scott has no business to write novels, especially good ones.—It is not fair.—He has Fame and Profit enough as a Poet, and should not be taking the bread out of other people's mouths.'[87] Austen's complaint makes clear the perceived division between poetry as the medium of glory and fiction as that of laborious profit, although before Scott began publishing fiction, this was a dubious distinction, as the largest previous payments for literary works had been for long poems like Moore's *Lalla Rookh* and Scott's own *Rokeby*. Austen also trenchantly highlights the limitations of the reading audience for novels and presciently predicts the scale of Scott's impact. Whether or not Scott actually crushed the careers of his competitors is hard to say. It can certainly be argued that his influence was in large part 'generative', spawning a vast train of imitators, kick-starting a vogue for historical fiction and creating a new market for works on Scottish history and topography that was catered for by men like the young Robert Chambers.[88] His legacy could also be said to have aided other novelists in that the pioneering cheap editions of his works cultivated a hunger for novels among those who were newly able to afford them. What can be said with certainty is that Scott's fiction transformed the field of literary production. It would not be a stretch to implicate him as a major factor in the eclipse of volume-length poetry by the novel during the 1820s and 1830s, with the more approachable form he

---

[85] Fiona Robertson, *Legitimate Histories: Scott, Gothic, and the Authorities of Fiction* (Oxford: Clarendon Press, 1994), p. 12.

[86] Hazlitt, 'Sir Walter Scott', XI, 64.

[87] Jane Austen to Anna Austen, 28 September 1814, in *Jane Austen's Letters*, ed. Deirdre Le Faye, 3rd edn (Oxford: Oxford University Press, 1995), p. 277.

[88] Duncan, p. xi; for scale of impact see also pp. 32–4. For more on Robert Chambers, see the section on Robert Heron in Chapter Four.

refined proving more popular than the coded complexities of sustained poetic language.[89]

From 1814 until 1826, Scott published phenomenally-successful novel after phenomenally-successful novel and made unprecedented sums while doing so. He generally sold the rights to print editions of 10,000 or 12,000 copies for £3000 or (later) £2500. He also drew a second income stream from these editions as they were inevitably printed by James Ballantyne. In 1816, he took advantage of his easy productivity to begin a second novel franchise, *Tales of My Landlord*, offering these new works to William Blackwood in partnership with John Murray in return both for generous remuneration and for Blackwood's taking on £600 of old Ballantyne stock. When this sale seemed temporarily uncertain, Scott used his contacts to make sure he benefited significantly from his new inspiration: '[e]mploying first James [Ballantyne], then John, as his agents, Scott [...] managed to get Constable, Longman, Blackwood, and Murray all hotly bidding for the unknown novelist.'[90] He thus instigated an early rights auction, a rare occurrence until the emergence of well-connected agents at the end of the nineteenth century.[91] Scott spread his works among a network of leading publishers, securing access to their resources, connections and coffers and asserting his own centrality to literary life. This dominance was also enacted in his works. As Kathryn Sutherland argues, '[i]n the rival output of two prolific novelists, and subsequently in the whole team of narrators and editor-historians spawned by the "Author of *Waverley*," and in the *Tales'* sustained Cervantean redactions, Scott discovered the unimpeded exercise of his talents and the consequent increase in their fertility.'[92] Despite his masks, accolades flooded in to the man at the centre, the most notable being the baronetcy awarded to him in 1820, the first of George IV's reign. The great product of the wealth that Scott accumulated was Abbotsford, into which he poured tens of thousands of pounds. His works continued to sell, the capital kept flowing and all seemed well.

---

[89] See Lee Erickson, *The Economy of Literary Form: English Literature and the Industrialisation of Printing 1800–1850* (Baltimore: Johns Hopkins Press, 1996), pp. 146–9, 36–9.

[90] Johnson, I, 550.

[91] For the early history of literary agents, see Mary Ann Gillies, *The Professional Literary Agent in Britain: 1880–1920* (Toronto: University of Toronto Press, 2007).

[92] Kathryn Sutherland, p. 105.

Unfortunately for Scott, while his cultural centrality proved unassailable during his lifetime, his financial prosperity was eventually derailed by his overreaching entanglements in publishing and finance. During the summer of speculation in 1825, Joseph Ogle Robinson of Hurst, Robinson & Co., one of Constable's major London connections, unsuccessfully attempted to corner the hops market. He lost his firm a vast amount of money in the process, leaving it dangerously indebted.[93] When Hurst, Robinson & Co. finally collapsed in January 1826, its fall dragged down Constable and Ballantyne as well. Scott's demands had drained Constable's coffers and the capital resources of both firms were dangerously leveraged. All three points of the production triangle—Scott, Ballantyne and Constable—regularly exchanged 'accommodation bills' with each other. Accommodation bills were essentially paired sets of I.O.U.s repayable on a certain date, each of which could be sold on to raise funds. However, when both parties sold their bills, this left the collective owing twice what either party had borrowed, and both parties were liable for both halves of the bill. Scott was the worst offender in this potentially risky form of borrowing, as he required a vast amount of capital to realise his ambitions for his estate. As a consequence of this, when creditors alarmed by Hurst, Robinson & Co.'s problems started to call in bills that Constable and Ballantyne had backed, the profitable firms were unable to produce the requisite money.

This calamitous turn of events left Scott with four options. The first was to accept the offers of aid that poured in from friends, but this he refused to countenance. He could have declared personal bankruptcy, but that would have endangered his life-rent of Abbotsford, as well as his movables and books, and would probably have resulted in his having to live out the rest of his days in exile on the continent. He could have applied for trade bankruptcy, which would have protected his personal assets and allowed him to negotiate favourable terms, but his gentlemanly scruples precluded this. He was already mortified that his speculations were now known, and he could not accept failure as a tradesman. Instead, he sought to secure the agreement of his creditors for the establishment of a trust into which he would pay all his literary earnings and through which he proposed to pay back the full amount he owed—as he put it in the journal he kept for

---

[93] Simon Eliot, '1825–6: Years of Crisis?', in *The Edinburgh History of the Book in Scotland Volume 3: Ambition and Industry 1800–1880*, ed. Bill Bell (Edinburgh: Edinburgh University Press, 2007), pp. 91–5 (p. 92).

the last six years of his life, 'my own right hand will do it.'[94] Since his liabilities were calculated as £121,000, it might have been expected that his creditors would baulk at Scott's chivalrous intentions, but in fact a general sympathy with his predicament and the proven profitability of his works meant that only one creditor failed to agree to the arrangement, and after this dissenter was paid off by one of Scott's friends, the plan proceeded. James Ballantyne's debt was included in the purview of the trust, preserving his firm, but Scott cut himself off from Constable, leaving his former publisher to die the next year with little to show for his former greatness. Constable's partner, Robert Cadell, escaped relatively unscathed, set up in business again in a matter of months and brought out many further Scott works, including the authoritative Magnum Opus edition of the novels and the pioneering cheap editions that had been one of Constable's most prescient ideas.

The most incredible thing about Scott's enormous debts is that he succeeded in paying them off in full, a powerful testament to the value of the new kinds of cultural capital he had created through his writings. Admittedly, the last payments were made through the sale of the remaining Waverley copyrights to Cadell in 1847, fifteen years after Scott's death, but nevertheless, it remains an impressive achievement. In his lifetime, he reduced his debt from £121,000 to £53,000, making around £10,000 each year for his creditors.[95] During this period, he drew on his other incomes for his own support and lived in relative comfort at Abbotsford. His creditors allowed him to do additional literary work in his own time, so his total earnings were even higher than that £10,000 sum would indicate. While some later Scott novels show indisputable signs of quick composition, the momentum of his brand was considerable, and his works continued to sell in enormous quantities. Scott added to his fiction several vast historical projects—his *Life of Napoleon* (1827–1828), a *History of Scotland* (1829) and his historical works for children, the *Tales of a Grandfather* (published in four series; 1828–1831). These projects drained his energies—after his wife's death he wrote for full days, complained of headaches and was often depressed. He suffered a number of increasingly serious strokes after 1830, finally agreeing to a Mediterranean trip for the

---

[94] *The Journal of Sir Walter Scott*, ed. W.E.K. Anderson (Oxford: Clarendon Press, 1972), p. 65.

[95] *Walter Scott Digital Archive*, Edinburgh University Library, http://www.walterscott.lib.ed.ac.uk/biography/finance.html.

sake of his health in October 1831. On the return journey in May 1832, he suffered a further stroke. He was back in Abbotsford by July, but was suffering, confused and often incoherent. He finally died on September 21st.

In one sense, it is difficult to take Scott's extraordinary career as paradigmatic because it is so out of keeping with any that had come before and with all but a few that came after. His poetic career is easier to contextualise, as while he was fantastically successful as a poet, he was challenged later by Byron, with several other poets—including Rogers, Campbell and Moore—in a similar league in terms of sales. It is his career as a novelist that was unprecedented. It is illuminating to contrast the sales of his novels with Jane Austen's print runs. The probable size of the first edition of *Emma* (1815) was 2000 copies, and it was not reprinted until 1833. *Pride and Prejudice* (1813) did better, requiring three editions, but the third did not sell through and was remaindered.[96] By contrast, any given *Waverley* novel was printed in an initial edition five times the size of *Emma*'s, was kept almost constantly in print and continued to sell in staggering quantities. The bestsellers like *Guy Mannering* (1815), *Rob Roy* (1817) and *Waverley* itself racked up sales of between 40,000 and 50,000 copies between their publication dates and the mid-1830s.[97] In the minds of his contemporaries Scott was *the* novelist. As Kathryn Sutherland has written, he can be seen as being largely responsible for 'the Victorian transformation [...] of Smith's "unproductive entertainers" into profitable producers of social good, and, indirectly, of advancing economic prosperity', serving as the model both for later professional men-of-letters and for writers-as-industries such as Charles Dickens and William Morris.[98]

Scott's career shows that the best way to make money from books in the early nineteenth century was to act as a venture capitalist as well as an author, although his fate demonstrates that this was a risky proposition. However, no other writer was financially and temperamentally placed to follow him down this particular path. The trail he blazed that other writers could follow resulted from his showing how an author could be productive while still being respectable. While the scale of his success was not something that could be duplicated, he established genres of works that could garner reliable profits and created ways of being indisputably bookish while remaining a pillar of polite and commercial society. After Scott

---

[96] St Clair, pp. 578–80.
[97] St Clair, pp. 636–7.
[98] Kathryn Sutherland, p. 123.

and after the *Waverley* novels, a life of authorial labour was no longer regarded as suspiciously as it had been in previous decades. While other factors—including the relaxing of systems of political oppression and the proliferation of new periodicals—contributed to making the 1820s and 1830s a far more congenial environment for working writers, the example of Scott played an enduring role in validating literary production and in showing how the pen could safely and beneficially speak to and for the nation. Scott was not only successful in himself, then, but successful to the extent that he spearheaded the establishment in the public mind of the respectable nineteenth-century literary professional.

LORD BYRON: TRANSCENDING SELF-PROMOTION

Writing shortly after Scott's death, Landon contended that his influence lingered across the reading nation:

> Small need for tribute unto thee,
>   To let the fancy roam—
> To thee, who hast by many a hearth
>   An altar and a home:
> Each little bookshelf where thy works
>   Are carefully enshrined,
> There is thy trophy, there is left
>   Thy heritage of mind.[99]

However, despite the physical and intellectual ubiquity of his works in the 1830s, Scott's critical stock fell slowly but inexorably over the course of the nineteenth century. Suggesting one reasons for this, Ann Rigney has written that as Scott 'incorporated transience into the very principle of historicization, his own obsolescence was part and parcel of his continuing legacy. His being so quickly forgotten was paradoxically a sign of his influence.'[100] The practical aesthetics of Scott's historically-focused writings are certainly one factor in his eclipse, but another is the nature of the paradigm of authorship with which he was associated. Tellingly, Hugh Walpole, defending Scott in 1926, thought that it would be conventional

---

[99] L.E.L. [Letitia Elizabeth Landon], '[On Walter Scott]', in 'Death of Walter Scott', *Literary Gazette*, 29 September 1832, 619–20 (p. 620).
[100] Rigney, p. 4.

to be 'aghast at his material view'.[101] Scott may have served as the acme of professionalised writing, but, as Walpole's statement implies, this was not the form of literary production that became institutionalised as the most valuable. The heritage of Scott's mind lingered, but his modes of self-fashioning proved less attractive than those forged by authors who constructed themselves more self-consciously as being positioned, in Keats' words, 'on the forehead of the age to come'.[102]

If Scott carved out a space for respectable authorship and for forms of literature that evoked and constructed shared histories through narrative, then his most immediate antitype—despite their mutual admiration—might well be said to be Byron, who asserted the privileges of status and genius in composing poetry that focused on outsider figures and proclamations of singularity. Byron's heroes were decidedly not mediocre; instead, they were seen as reflecting their author in their glamourous alienation from the mainstream. As Hazlitt put it, Byron was seen as being 'in a striking degree, the creature of his own will. He holds no communion with his kind; but stands alone, without mate or fellow'.[103] Contrasting Byron with Scott, Hazlitt asserted that

> The object of the one writer is to restore us to truth and nature: the other chiefly thinks how he shall display his own power, or vent his spleen, or astonish the reader either by starting new subjects and trains of speculation, or by expressing old ones in a more striking and emphatic manner than they have been expressed before.[104]

While with Scott the focus was on the work, with Byron, the focus was on the author, but not in the manner of older social texts in which opinions were seen as being relatively transparently expressed. Byron, and those who colluded with him, modelled a form of difference between author and reader that validated the relationship between the two by asserting the author's exceptional character, staging a heightened version of genius for expanding audiences.

---

[101] Hugh Walpole, *Reading: An Essay* (New York and London: Harper & Brothers, 1926), p. 23.

[102] John Keats, 'Addressed to the Same' [B.R. Haydon], in *Keats' Poetry and Prose*, ed. Jeffrey N. Cox (New York: W.W. Norton, 2009), p. 56.

[103] Hazlitt, 'Lord Byron', XI, 69.

[104] Hazlitt, 'Lord Byron', XI, 70.

While this eventually became a common formulation, Byron was the only one among the Big Six canonical Romantic poets who managed to express it in a manner that made him unabashedly popular during the first quarter of the nineteenth century. His success was highly contingent on the ways he and his publishers configured and reconfigured his mixed status as a handsome poetical aristocrat to enchant his readers. As Tom Mole has eloquently demonstrated, Byron operated self-consciously as a potent site of fascination:

> For many of Byron's first readers, buying, reading, reading aloud, lending, borrowing, copying into commonplace books, annotating and discussing Byron's poetry were the central activities among a group of practices aimed at investigating Byron the man in order to know more about him or relate more intimately to him [...] Reading Byron's poems was supplemented by such activities as buying and looking at portraits of Byron, or illustrations in which the Byronic hero was represented as the poet, soliciting introductions to Byron, writing to him, dressing in Byronic fashion, reading newspapers, cartoons or reviews, and falling in love, either with the noble lord or violently, passionately and hopelessly, as his characters were wont to do.[105]

This 'hermeneutic of intimacy' was crucial to Byron's appeal and to his innovative manner of existing as an author. Mole argues that Byron's verse tales acted as 'relays of desire, lenses through which his readers' gazes and desires could pass, centring, finally, on the poet's body as a locus of signification for interior subjective realities.'[106] Jerome Christensen contends similarly that Byron's romances 'simultaneously convey to their consumer that he or she is an intentional subject and instil anxiety about the singularity of that position.'[107] By revealing, concealing and performing his self, Byron tempted readers into engaging with him through imitation, projection and purchase. As Corin Throsby puts it, 'By making the Byronic hero such an uncertain, open—flirtatious—text, Byron invites a response'.[108] Among his contemporaries, these Byronic invitations were highly successful, as the deluge of fan letters preserved in the Murray Archive proves.

---

[105] Tom Mole, *Byron's Romantic Celebrity: Industrial Culture and the Hermeneutic of Intimacy* (Basingstoke: Palgrave Macmillan, 2007), pp. 24–5.

[106] Mole, p. 77.

[107] Jerome Christensen, *Lord Byron's Strength: Romantic Writing and Commercial Society* (Baltimore: Johns Hopkins University Press, 1993), p. 16.

[108] Corin Throsby, 'Flirting with Fame: Byron's Anonymous Female Fans', *The Byron Journal*, 32:2 (2004), 115–23 (p. 117).

If Scott's proto-professional methods of literary production can be seen as supercharged versions of those employed by writers like Southey, then Byron's parade of selves could be seen as indebted in some respects to the sociable methods employed by Moore. However, Byron's status, talents and character combined with the publication methods available to him and the time that he entered the literary scene to make his self-marketing more potent and farther-reaching than his friend's. The secondary merchandise for Moore's *Lalla Rookh* related mainly to the content of poem, but the secondary merchandise that sprung up around Byron's verse related principally to its author: images and accounts of him, speculations about him, continuations in his name and misattributions seeking to draw on his significance. Byron created in tandem with his readers, publishers and auditors a newly glamourous form of equivalency between his person and his productions. The imaginative intimacy conjured between the poet and his audience meant that he largely transcended attempts to manage him through criticism. While conservatives fulminated against his morals, they were telling readers little that they didn't think they already knew and were in many cases reinforcing the transgressive qualities that made Byron and his works attractive in the first place.

By dint of his class and wealth, Byron was not required to court social acceptability among particular networks to accrue social and financial capital. As Hazlitt resentfully wrote, Byron was an 'anomaly in letters and in society, a Noble Poet. It is a double privilege, almost too much for humanity. He has all the pride of birth and genius.'[109] He employed this privilege to bypass pre-existing tastemakers by means of his carefully managed sudden rise. While he valued hobnobbing with the literati and used his influence to promote other writers he admired—Coleridge not the least among them—Byron's fame was not straightforwardly reliant on establishment approbation. His being in a position to start writing was a product of his background, but his success was due principally to the ways in which he pioneered methods of approaching mass readerships through the powerful projection of poetic personality and through the newly realised powers of commerce activated on his behalf by John Murray. Byron's privileged position meant that he could reasonably affect not to care about the opinions of others; his wealth let him travel both physically and in the imaginations of his readers; and the two combined let him set himself above the literary squabbling of his contemporaries as a sublime and fascinating ego,

---

[109] Hazlitt, 'Lord Byron', XI, 77.

both attractive and potentially dangerous (with the potential danger rein-forcing the attraction). Byron's example determined to a large extent what a poet should be for early nineteenth-century audiences, producing one of the key components of the weird and unstable gestalt at the centre of Romanticism. While Scott was the prototype for the productive Victorian man of letters, Byron served as a key model for the feeling literary artist.

Considered financially, Byron's career can be divided into two sections. In the first, he took the long-established aristocratic position and affected to care very little about his literary profits. This attitude meant that Murray did very well out of the poetry written during the years of Byron's London fame.[110] Peter Cochran has disproved the myth that Byron accepted no money for his poems prior to his leaving England in 1816, putting his total earnings at £3850. However, Cochran has also stressed that the pro-cess of financial settlement was 'a complex and convoluted one, involving much posturing and prevarication on Byron's part, and much patience and generosity on Murray's'.[111] The sums involved, while large, were dwarfed by Byron's other assets and his expenditures. When he sold Newstead Abbey to pay his debts, he raised £94,500, but even this was not sufficient. After the sale, he urged his friend Douglas Kinnaird to make renewed efforts to get rid of his Rochdale property to allow him to clear the rest of his liabilities.[112] While Scott speculated on his talents to secure vast sums of money, for Byron, who was already hugely wealthy, the financial value of his works was initially of far less interest than the fact of their popularity. At first, he drew satisfaction from his fame, but subsequently, he found it challenging to break free from Murray's creation of 'a recognisable brand Byron who would answer the demands of a wide readership with mini-mum commercial risk.'[113] His literary power fascinated him, but he became increasingly uncomfortable with the extent to which his position as a focus of others' desires occluded his own subjectivity. Increasingly, what Murray was seeking to sell was not who Byron thought he was.

After 1816, disenchanted by the reaction that forced him into exile, Byron changed direction and began to define a modified version of his authorial self. From this point in his career, as Christensen puts it, 'it

---

[110] See the section on publishing arrangements in Chapter One for further details.

[111] Peter Cochran, 'Did Byron Take Money for his Early Work?', *The Byron Journal*, 31 (2003), 72–6 (p. 76).

[112] Fiona MacCarthy, *Byron: Life and Legend* (London: John Murray, 2002), p. 335.

[113] Mole, pp. 113–4.

becomes important to distinguish between Byronism, the […] speculative machine owned and operated by John Murray, and Lord Byron.'[114] While he remained an assiduous reader of his own reviews, he no longer wrote for acclaim in any uncomplicated sense, but instead played off his awareness of his large audience in taking his self-presentations in darker and more ironic directions. As Shelley astutely and enviously opined, 'he touched a chord to which a million hearts responded, and the coarse music which he produced to please them disciplined him to the perfection which he now approaches'.[115] Byronism provided Byron with a direct connection to a wide audience that he both courted and in some ways despised. This allowed him to develop his poetry confident in the knowledge that it would be read, rather than feeling, as Shelley did, that he was required constantly to reframe himself in order to induce others to notice him.

For his later works, Byron began to negotiate more fiercely. For the third canto of *Childe Harold* and *The Prisoner of Chillon* (1816), Murray had planned to offer fifteen hundred guineas (£1575), although, as he put it in a slightly barbed compliment, 'The Poem is however so much beyond any thing in Modern days that I may be out in my Calculation—it requires an ethereal mind like its Authors to cope with it.'[116] Despite Murray's concern about the ethereality of the standard reader's mind, Kinnaird and Shelley, negotiating on Byron's behalf, were able to talk Murray up to two thousand guineas for the two poems. Murray's combined profits for the first two editions of both poems were a relatively modest £775.11s.6d.[117] Byron haggled similarly carefully for many of his other late productions. He did not precisely need the money—after the death of his mother-in-law in 1822, he had an income of £6000 a year; he gained around £2500 of that from her estate, so even before receiving the inheritance, he was exceptionally well off.[118] However, the money from Murray was a good way of keeping abreast of the value of his works once he was cut off from direct access to English literary society. It also served as a way of asserting both his value to and his independence from his publisher's commoditising agendas.

[114] Christensen, p. 172.

[115] Shelley to John Gisborne, 18 June 1822, in *The Letters of Percy Bysshe Shelley*, ed. Frederick L. Jones, 2 vols (Oxford: Clarendon Press, 1964), II, 436.

[116] Murray to Byron, 20 September 1816, in *The Letters of John Murray to Lord Byron*, ed. Andrew Nicholson (Liverpool: Liverpool University Press, 2007), pp. 176–7.

[117] Murray Copies Ledger B, NLS Ms.42725, p. 132.

[118] MacCarthy, p. 411.

The literary marketplace for Byron was a very different prospect than it was for other authors of his age and for later poets who lived in the shadow of his achievements. The luxury of seeing financial success a way of keeping score was reserved for a few privileged writers. This luxury allowed Byron considerable freedom to develop in directions that would have had grave consequences for an author who was easier socially or financially to restrain. For Byron, success was a stage on which he could perform himself, and his works were received more as performances from a fascinating celebrity than as the products of a respectable gentlemanly pen. While it might be going too far to date the death of the gentleman author exactly to the point when the more attractive models of Scott-like professionalism and transgressive Byronic performance emerged, the influence of both models on subsequent generations was profound and transformative. Byron's titanic fame dragged and glamorised other poets in his wake, contributing to the wave of biographical interest in the 1820s and 1830s that consolidated the idea of the poetic genius and the respectable professional author as the two models for early Victorians seeking to be writerly. Somewhat ironically, Byron's sparking a new interest in the character of the poet also ended up contributing to the belated acceptance of members of the older generation of Lakers, whose contrasts with him in a paradigm in which he was ubiquitous drew new attention from more conservative readers and tastemakers. While Wordsworth and Coleridge laid the intellectual foundations for what would become Romanticism, Byron's glamour, fame and opposition were crucial in galvanising the transformation of the poet from commentator into visionary. In living as he did and being as he was, Byron played a formative role in carving out the ideological space within which the literary artist would subsequently operate.

Coda: Print Proliferation and the Invention of the Artist

In his 'Extempore Effusion Upon the Death of James Hogg', composed in 1834, William Wordsworth mourns Hogg alongside a gallery of recently deceased acquaintances by recalling experiences of their company. In evoking brief memories of Samuel Taylor Coleridge, Walter Scott, George Crabbe, Felicia Hemans and Charles Lamb, Wordsworth brings to mind connections that he depicts as being both stronger and more complex than those of professional association or aesthetic admiration. Personal familiarity is central to the ways in which Wordsworth imagines the literary scene. This has some peculiar consequences; as Janette Currie has observed, Hogg himself, who Wordsworth knew less well and with whom he was less comfortable, is side-lined in a poem in which he is the ostensible subject.[1] Wordsworth paints a literary world in which a company of major authors kept company with one another, a world in which personal associations united the most important among those who wrote. However, the poem's melancholy catalogue gives the sense that this convivial world is slipping away. Wordsworth is one of a decreasing band left 'to hear/A timid voice, that asks in whispers/ "Who next will drop and disappear?"'[2] The poem

---

[1] Janette Currie, 'Re-Visioning James Hogg: The Return of the Subject to Wordsworth's "Extempore Effusion"', *Romantic Textualities: Literature and Print Culture, 1780–1840*, 15 (Winter 2005), http://www.romtext.org.uk/articles/rt15_n01/, 7–28 (pp. 7–8).

[2] William Wordsworth, 'Extempore Effusion on the Death of James Hogg,' lines 26–8, in *Last Poems, 1821–1850*, ed. Jared Curtis (Ithaca: Cornell University Press, 1999), pp. 305–7 (p. 306).

© The Author(s) 2021
M. Sangster, *Living as an Author in the Romantic Period*, Palgrave
Studies in the Enlightenment, Romanticism and Cultures of Print,
https://doi.org/10.1007/978-3-030-37047-3_9

explicitly positions itself at the juncture between two literary eras. What comes next seems at first to be terrifyingly absent. However, the poem itself provides a model for what will replace Coleridge's 'mortal power [...] frozen at its marvellous source' and the body of Lamb, 'vanished from his lonely hearth'.[3] Their selves are replaced by textual representations and their original networks and contexts replaced with Wordsworth's canonising arrangement. This grouping serves to sanctify Wordsworth himself through his being acquainted with the pantheon he sketches. He carefully configures his subjects in such a way as to promote his own particular convictions—it is notable, for example, that Scott is described as 'the Border-minstrel' rather than the Author of *Waverley*: a poet and collector, rather than an all-conquering novelist and brand.[4] This is a company endued with the sublime inherent qualities of Romantic artists, rather than the bibliographic, social or professional trappings of authors. The sociability they enjoyed among themselves is converted into poetic associations that code quintessential connections for posterity, rather than preserving the practical and quotidian aspects of living as an author.

This poem represents in microcosm a number of the crucial shifts that occurred between the late 1810s and the 1830s. These shifts began to establish what the Romantic literary canon would look like during the nineteenth and twentieth centuries and the consensus on English literature that would subsequently be presented through periodicals, uniform series and formal education. The greater part of the preceding study has focused on the first decades of the nineteenth century, an environment within which Romanticism 'constituted an emergent rather than a dominant discourse'.[5] The canonical Romantic poets have often haunted the margins of the previous chapters, as (with the exception of Byron) they did the sociable literary culture of their time, providing perceptive commentaries and telling contrasts, but acting in many respects as strange or radical alternatives to a relatively conservative literary mainstream. In concluding this study, I want briefly to bring them centre stage in order to outline the developments that meant when Wordsworth wrote the 'Extempore Effusion' in the early 1830s, he was in tune with a far wider

---

[3] 'Extempore Effusion', lines 15–16, 20, pp. 305, 306.

[4] 'Extempore Effusion', line 8, p. 305.

[5] Paul Keen, *The Crisis of Literature in the 1790s: Print Culture and the Public Sphere* (Cambridge: Cambridge University Press, 1999), p. 237. As Keen notes, 'In 1817, Coleridge was still able to write of Wordsworth that "His fame belongs to another age".'

reading public than he had been able to reach in previous decades and operating within a culture that had begun to accept arguments about poetry and genius that the quarterlies and the sociable elite had previously resisted.

In the 1800s and 1810s, Wordsworth, Coleridge, Shelley and Keats were painfully aware that their works failed to match up to their most successful contemporaries in terms of sales, profitability and critical acclaim. As Lucy Newlyn puts it, '[f]ar from being oppressed by the burden of the past [...] the Romantic writers were intensely preoccupied with the combined threats of modernity and futurity.'[6] Wordsworth, Coleridge, Shelley and Keats were manifestly not as good at appealing to contemporary audiences as writers like Robert Bloomfield, Charlotte Smith, James Montgomery, Thomas Moore and Matthew Lewis. None of them possessed the wide-ranging kudos enjoyed by Thomas Campbell or, in slightly more vexed manners, by the conveniently deceased Robert Burns. They were not as well-connected as figures like Francis Jeffrey or Samuel Rogers, whose literary credentials both reinforced and were reinforced by their access to wealth, power and media through which they could voice themselves. Certainly, none of them combined financial success, popular appeal, critical acclaim and social influence in the manner that Scott did. The Wizard of the North represented the greatest possible level of success a literary writer could achieve—by comparison, most of Harold Bloom's visionary company occupied relatively marginal positions.

One of the main reasons proliferating markets, networks and readerships troubled the canonical poets was that they remained heavily invested in older practices and systems. Coleridge and Wordsworth were university-educated beneficiaries of established forms of recognition, receiving income from interested friends, legacies and the government. Shelley and Byron were heirs to aristocratic titles and to a long tradition of literary endeavour among the advantaged, although Shelley especially sought to craft a new kind of authorial identity that did not rely explicitly on his fortunate circumstances (though his having the leisure to do so was heavily contingent on his family wealth). Keats was not from a particularly exalted background, but in his short life he lived principally on inherited money. Keats and the Hunt circle also operated as a coterie in manners reminiscent of much earlier writers, employing manuscript circulation and

---

[6] Lucy Newlyn, *Reading, Writing, and Romanticism: The Anxiety of Reception* (Oxford: Oxford University Press, 2000), p. x.

promoting each other's work through private praise as well as public advocacy in periodicals. The poets whose reputations won out in the long run thus often worked from or appropriated privileged gentlemanly positions. However, while they were relatively successful at establishing themselves within the contexts of networking practices that survived the earlier eighteenth century, they had to reckon with the fragmentation and politicisation of the assumptions underpinning these practices during the conflicts of the 1790s. This left them with the dual challenge of validating their works in the eyes of emergent readerships that treated them relatively indifferently and of opposing powerful bands of increasingly professionalised critics who arrogated to themselves the right to determine the values and meanings of literary texts.

That the Romantics were successful in claiming paramount positions in the longer term is futile to deny. They are clearly 'greater' or 'stronger' writers by the literary standards that accreted in their wake than most of their contemporaries. Saying this, though, requires us to consider what excellence entails, and here I would agree with Jerome McGann, Clifford Siskin and many others that the criteria critics use to judge literature today are both intrinsically Romantic and historically contingent.[7] It does not seem implausible that the majority of readers in the early nineteenth century genuinely derived greater enjoyment from poems such as Rogers' *Pleasures of Memory*, Bloomfield's *Farmer's Boy* and Scott's *Lady of the Lake* than from Shelley's *Prometheus Unbound* or Wordsworth's *Excursion*. It also seems condescending to think that they were foolish for doing so. It is grossly reductive to believe that audiences were just waiting for the brilliance of canonical Romanticism to sweep away their trivial distractions. The acceptance of Romanticism in the middle decades of the nineteenth century was a result of major shifts in the ways that poets and poetry were appraised by emerging media and institutions. Acknowledging this aesthetic turn and the ways in which it responded to market discourses and systems of social control lets us see both the Romantic period and Romanticism in more critical and clear-eyed manners.

It is important to recognise that while Romantic ideologies were articulated in opposition to the perceived commercialisation of culture and to aggressive professionalised criticism, they also took inspiration from both

---

[7] See Jerome J. McGann, *The Romantic Ideology* (Chicago: University of Chicago Press, 1983) and Clifford Siskin, *The Historicity of Romantic Discourse* (Oxford: Oxford University Press, 1988).

these things. Newlyn considers Romanticism 'a species of reaction-formation against the new power of reading' by which authors '[sought] to consolidate their diminishing sense of authority through strategies of mystification.'[8] Wordsworth's ideas about the inspired authority of the Poet and Shelley's arguments for acknowledging unacknowledged legislators mirror in certain respects the strategies for the 'maintenance of "mystery"' that Penelope Corfield has identified as crucial in the emergence of more conventional professional identities.[9] As Andrew Bennett has argued, one of the self-fashioning strategies commonly employed by the poets was presenting their works as pioneering, deferring their validation until the arrival of a more hospitable future:

> In order to discriminate the poet from the scribbler or hack, the poem from common, everyday verse, Romantic theories of poetry produce an absolute and non-negotiable opposition between writing which is original, new, revolutionary, writing which breaks from the past and appeals to the future, and writing which is conventional, derivative, a copy or simulation of earlier work, writing which has immediate appeal and an in-built redundancy.[10]

While novelty had been valued previously to a certain extent, in Romantic arguments, it was made paramount. By fetishising the originality of their verse and their experiences, the Romantics attempted to escape both the hierarchies of taste propagated by the periodical oligopolies and the expectations aroused by the circulations of their more commercially minded contemporaries. If the Romantics convinced as original innovators, they were no longer unsuccessful, but rather the developers and keepers of new specialist knowledge. By grounding their claims in heightened aesthetics, Poets with a capital P could successfully position themselves as challenging and outmoding the existing social authority of critics, gentlemen and reading audiences.

Explicit examples of such arguments can be found in the paratexts of *Lyrical Ballads*, particularly its preface, usually credited solely to Wordsworth (as future sentences will credit it for the sake of grammatical convenience), but written with considerable input from Coleridge, who

---

[8] Newlyn, p. 48.

[9] Penelope J. Corfield, *Power and the Professions in Britain 1700–1850* (London: Routledge, 1995), p. 28.

[10] Andrew Bennett, *Romantic Poets and the Culture of Posterity* (Cambridge: Cambridge University Press, 1999), p. 3.

claimed that it '[arose from] the heads of our mutual Conversations'.[11] The preface opens with an assertion that the poetry that follows will inevitably ruffle feathers. In refusing to write verse that will 'gratify certain known habits of association', Wordsworth claims for himself the authority of originality.[12] This chimes with the advertisement to the London copies of the 1798 first edition, in which the poems were framed as 'experiments'.[13] The advertisement also made a bolder claim, asserting that '[i]t is the honourable characteristic of Poetry that its materials are to be found in every subject which can interest the human mind. The evidence of this fact is to be sought, not in the writings of Critics, but in those of Poets themselves.'[14] This statement radically extends the purview of poetry and in doing so makes claims for the poet beyond the explicit assertion that it makes. If poetry may be found in every subject, then the poet moves from being a craftsman assembling conventional elements or a gentleman indulging a talent to being an interpreter of reality, the philosopher of nature that Coleridge hoped Wordsworth would become through writing *The Recluse*. For this to be recognised, though, the relationship between poets, readers and critics had to be substantially redefined. Wordsworth puts the case relatively discreetly, but his argument allows the poet to bypass contemporary critics by implying they have missed the targets he has struck. It also places him above his readers, who have proved incapable of divining his purpose without further explication. The pragmatic need to contextualise his poems is thus converted into a means through which to advance an agenda that privileges the type of particularised Poet that Wordsworth wants to be and the kind of work he produces.

[11]Coleridge to William Sotheby, 13 July 1802, in *Collected Letters of Samuel Taylor Coleridge*, ed. E.L. Griggs, 6 vols (Oxford: Clarendon Press, 1956–71), II, 811. The collaboration is helpfully explored by Adam Sisman in *The Friendship: Wordsworth and Coleridge* (New York: Viking, 2007); see especially pp. 306–13.

[12]William Wordsworth [and Samuel Taylor Coleridge], *Lyrical Ballads, with Other Poems*, 2nd edn, 2 vols (London: Longman & Rees, 1800 [actually published January 1801]), I, ix. This and the following early editions consulted using *Lyrical Ballads: An Electronic Scholarly Edition*, ed. Bruce Graver and Ron Tetreault, *Romantic Circles*, 2003, https://romantic-circles.org/editions/LB/.

[13]Although these claims were somewhat disingenuous, as Mary Jacobus explores in *Tradition and Experiment in Wordsworth's Lyrical Ballads (1798)* (Oxford: Clarendon Press, 1976).

[14][William Wordsworth and Samuel Taylor Coleridge], *Lyrical Ballads, with a Few Other Poems* (London: J. & A. Arch, 1798), p. i.

Other poets employed similar arguments, although often with subtle modifications. For example, Shelley's *Revolt of Islam* is characterised in its preface as 'an experiment on the temper of the public mind as to how far a thirst for a happier condition of moral and political society survives, among the enlightened and refined, the tempests which have shaken the age in which we live.'[15] Shelley's poet is a presumptuous activist, his poem written both to provoke and to condition a response from his readers. While his limited success in reaching wide readerships caused him to vary his strategies, Shelley continued to promote the transcendent power of poetry from different angles as his career proceeded. In the preface to *Prometheus Unbound*, when he writes that '[p]oets, not otherwise than philosophers, painters, sculptors and musicians, are in one sense the creators and in another the creations of their age', Shelley positions artists as shapers dynamically engaged with politics and history, rather than as gentlemen possessed of portfolios of polite accomplishments.[16] Even when disavowing his own authorship, as in the advertisement to *Epipsychidion*, whose supposed author 'died at Florence', Shelley seeks to reify poetic genius by claiming that the poem's narrator's life holds interest 'less on account of the romantic vicissitudes which diversified it, than the ideal tinge which it received from his own character and feelings.'[17]

The formulations that we now group as Romantic thus worked to promote their authors both through making clear their unique and specific virtues and through attempting to legitimate the idea of poets transcending other social and professional discourses. One of the clearest examples of this heightening process is the answer Wordsworth gives when he asks (again using that significant capital) 'What is a Poet?':

He is a man speaking to men: a man, it is true, endued with more lively sensibility, more enthusiasm and tenderness, who has a greater knowledge of human nature, and a more comprehensive soul, than are supposed to be common among mankind; a man pleased with his own passions and volitions, and who rejoices more than other men in the spirit of life that is in him; delighting to contemplate similar volitions and passions as manifested

---

[15] Preface to *Laon and Cyntha/The Revolt of Islam*, in *The Poems of Shelley*, ed. Kelvin Everest and Geoffrey Matthews, 4 vols (Harlow: Longman, 1989–), II, 32.

[16] Preface to *Prometheus Unbound*, in *Shelley's Poetry and Prose*, ed. Donald H. Reiman and Neil Fraistat, 2nd edn (New York: W.W. Norton, 2002), p. 208.

[17] Advertisement to *Epipsychidion*, *Shelley's Poetry and Prose*, p. 392.

in the goings-on of the Universe, and habitually impelled to create them where he does not find them.[18]

While he begins the sentence as an equal, Wordsworth's Poet is quickly refined into a sort of empathic saint who sees more, comprehends more fully and feels better than other men (as many critics have remarked, the discourses of canonical Romanticism as they emerged in the nineteenth century are conspicuously masculine, operating in manners that deliberately seek to sideline female creativity). Crucially, the Wordsworthian Poet is also posited as a man who requires no external validation. His abilities are depicted as being largely inherent. The functioning of his superior consciousness does not require a social context. If others ignore or criticise him, that may lessen them, but does not meaningfully detract from his comforts or achievements.

However, while the poets publicly scorned the conspicuous successes of their contemporaries, comforting themselves with celebrations of their own sensitivities and intimations of future vindication, this did not mean they successfully turned their backs on their age. The Romantics did not give themselves wholly over to Romantic ideologies—indeed, they could not, as these were not yet fully formulated. Only a monstrously confident (and affluent) writer would have been able to devote themselves solely to the prospect of posthumous recognition. It is thus unsurprising that the Romantics, even as they oriented themselves towards what they considered to be better futures, sought to engage with the present in order to bring those futures more swiftly into being. Pragmatic measures the poets undertook to promote themselves are easy to name: Shelley's pamphleteering and prefacing; Keats' networking; Coleridge's lecturing, theorising and periodical publications; Wordsworth's *Convention of Cintra* (1808) and *Guide to the Lakes* (1810; revised editions in 1820, 1822, 1823 and 1835); the dramas that all the poets sought to produce. While the Romantics evoked the prospect of future glory, they also sought to bring this to pass through self-promotion, looking to boost their profiles by trading on their connections and commenting on their contemporary milieu. Their relatively privileged positions ensured that small audiences paid attention, setting the stage for wider recognition when the right conditions obtained.

---

[18] William Wordsworth [and Samuel Taylor Coleridge], *Lyrical Ballads, with Pastoral and Other Poems*, 3rd edn, 2 vols (London: Longman & Rees 1802), I, xxviii.

In finally securing prominence, the Romantics benefitted from three major print-cultural shifts. The first was the promotion of poetic genius in the monthly magazines founded from the late 1810s onwards, which drew on the poets' conceptions to oppose the hegemony of the quarterlies. The second was the vogue in the 1820s and 1830s for authorial biography, a consequence of the interest sparked by periodical responses to Romanticising theories of genius. The third was the proliferation of literary institutions including libraries, literary and philosophical societies, schools and universities, all of which sought to organise, promote and regulate literature for emerging audiences. The common factor that connects these shifts is the importance they placed on writers' evoked identities. It is no coincidence that the Romantics' works created strongly personalised selves to oppose the theoretically anonymous critic and the increasingly unknown and unknowable reader. Not least among their achievements are the intensely figured consciousnesses in their works. As Bennett neatly puts it, 'Romantic poets [...] want to know what we think about them and what we think about them is largely a function of what they think of our thinking.'[19] These three shifts can be understood as stages in a process engendered by this reciprocal scrutiny. The concept of the elevated genius was employed to oppose market-based, professional and gentlemanly valuations that established common socialised standards for literary expertise. Subsequently and consequently, those who claimed the exceptional status of genius became the subjects of biographical attention as critics and audiences attempted to justify or refute their claims. Finally, the accepted exemplars of genius were read back out in an attempt to redefine genius itself, creating the somewhat awkward umbrella of Romanticism.

In his excellent book on the promotion of notions of genius in literary magazines, David Higgins quotes a telling extract by the Tory journalist William Maginn, who argued in 1826—with, as Higgins puts it, 'a degree of ironic hyperbole'—that under the influence of *Blackwood's Edinburgh Magazine*

the whole periodical criticism of Britain underwent a revolution. Principles were laid down and applied to passages from our great living poets. People were encouraged to indulge their emotions, that they might be brought to know their nature. That long icy chill was shook off their fancies and

[19] Bennett, p. 200.

imaginations, and here, too, in Criticism as in Politics, they began to feel, think, and speak, like free men.[20]

Maginn identifies the popularisation of Romantic genius as part of a periodical revolution that has successfully shaken off the stifling authority of the quarterlies and made room for new magazines and voices. The *Edinburgh* and the *Quarterly* sold themselves to a large extent on the brilliance and probity of their reviewers. Other magazines found it difficult to compete with them on their own terms and were forced to find new ways of asserting their interests. *Blackwood's* responded by producing unprecedentedly venomous, personalised and provocative critiques, but also by praising certain writers to the skies, a rare occurrence in the authoritarian quarterlies. In opposing the *Edinburgh*, *Blackwood's* writers paid particular attention to Jeffrey's bête noire, Wordsworth; as Higgins puts it, '[h]is genius was constantly celebrated and he was treated as a profound thinker, worthy of veneration' in passages that often displayed 'religious overtones'.[21] By casting themselves as harbingers of the virtues of strongly personalised poets, *Blackwood's* and other periodicals, including the *London Magazine* (launched in 1820), the *New Monthly Magazine* (relaunched as a literary periodical in 1821) and the *Westminster Review* (published from 1824), took up arms against the quarterlies' hegemony by figuring literary authors and their consciousnesses as objects of intense inherent interest, rather than subjects for politicised regulation and dismissal. The 'young men of strong sensibility and meditative minds' depicted by Coleridge in *Biographia Literaria* as responding to Wordsworth with almost '*religious* fervour' thus succeeded in taking control of channels that the poets themselves had been unable or unwilling to access.[22]

However, periodicals' promotions of individual figures as geniuses was not solely due to their accepting Romantic aesthetic ideologies. It also served the more pragmatic purpose of providing a range of interesting

[20] David Higgins, *Romantic Genius and the Literary Magazine: Biography, Celebrity, Politics* (London: Routledge, 2005), p. 18; [William Maginn [and John Wilson?]], 'Preface', *Blackwood's Edinburgh Magazine*, 19 (January 1826), [i]–xxx (p. xii).

[21] Higgins, p. 93. *Blackwood's* relationship with Wordsworth was complicated by their occasionally publishing attacks and printing biographical material that Wordsworth saw as intrusive (see Higgins, pp. 90–101).

[22] *The Collected Works of Samuel Taylor Coleridge*, gen ed. Kathleen Coburn, 14 vols (Princeton, NJ: Princeton University Press, 1969–93), VII.ii, 9.

figures that reviewers could build up and knock down in order to hold the attention of their readers. In Eric Eisner's terms, the Reviews 'evolved a highly reflexive and self-aware commentary on the personalities of authors, maintained both through discussions of individual works and through surveys of the literary scene, and through a particular delight in gossip about writers (including, of course, fellow periodical writers).'[23] Periodicals thus filled their pages by presenting their readers with a gallery of literary figures who were suitable objects of discussion due to their having obtained or sought falsely to obtain positions that set them apart from the common run. As Higgins puts it

> Authors such as Burns, Coleridge, Scott, Shelley and Wordsworth were often portrayed as fundamentally different from normal people, but also functioned as sites of desire for readers and critics who felt that they too were somehow different from the norm. The fact that, in the case of writers associated with social transgression, this desire existed alongside a degree of fear or repulsion probably only added to its power.[24]

The propagation of Romantic genius thus operated through a kind of queasy symbiosis between the poets and their interpreters. Periodicals brought poets' works before a wider public, but did so by representing and misrepresenting those poets as objects of fascination in themselves. Readers responded to poets' assertions of their exceptional natures with a curiosity that was as much social as it was aesthetic. Along with the conveniently-timed deaths of the younger Romantic generation, this paved the way for a wave of articles that cemented poets as potentially glamourous subjects of interest, but which also subjected their lives and habits to intense scrutiny. Evidence of poetic lives became an increasingly valuable commodity. Writers like William Hazlitt and Thomas De Quincey bolstered their own reputations and made considerable sums of money by giving accounts of their acquaintances with poets. These accounts were not always flattering, but the new generation of post-Byron geniuses were not expected to keep to conventional standards. It was as flawed and antisocial brilliances that the Romantics particularly fascinated. In Julian

---

[23] Eric Eisner, *Nineteenth-Century Poetry and Literary Celebrity* (Basingstoke: Palgrave Macmillan, 2009), p. 11.

[24] Higgins, p. 4.

North's words, '[b]iography was […] the most influential transmitter of the myth of the Romantic poet in the nineteenth century and beyond'.[25]

To give an example: Coleridge holds a prime position at the close of Hazlitt's 1818 lecture 'On the Living Poets', delivered at the Surrey Institution. Hazlitt first talks briefly about Coleridge's work, taking a mostly critical tone—he describes Coleridge's tragedies as 'drawling sentiment, and metaphysical jargon' and dismisses much of his prose as 'dreary trash.'[26] However, his tone changes markedly when he moves on to discuss the man:

> But I may say of him here, that he is the only person I ever knew who answered to the idea of a man of genius. He is the only person from whom I ever learnt any thing. There is only one thing he could learn from me in return, but *that* he has not. He was the first poet I ever knew. His genius at that time had angelic wings, and fed on manna. He talked on for ever; and you wished him to talk on for ever. His thoughts did not seem to come with labour and effort; but as if borne on the gusts of genius, and as if the wings of his imagination lifted him from off his feet. His voice rolled on the ear like the pealing organ, and its sound alone was the music of thought. His mind was clothed with wings; and raised on them, he lifted philosophy to heaven. In his descriptions, you then saw the progress of human happiness and liberty in bright and never-ending succession, like the steps of Jacob's ladder, with airy shapes ascending and descending, and with the voice of God at the top of the ladder. And shall I, who heard him then, listen to him now? Not I! …. That spell is broke; that time is gone for ever; that voice is heard no more: but still the recollection comes rushing by with thoughts of long-past years, and rings in my ears with never-dying sound.[27]

What is striking about this passage is the extent to which Coleridge lives in Hazlitt's memory not for his poetry but for his thoughts, conversation and way of being. Coleridge's brilliance vests in his recollected self, which Hazlitt fashions in such a way as to promote his own talents through skill, contrast and association. Hazlitt's portrayal teases both Coleridge and his audiences, deliberately withholding the 'one thing' that he could have taught Coleridge. He evokes a marvellous Coleridge only to declare him

---

[25] Julian North, *The Domestication of Genius: Biography and the Romantic Poet* (Oxford: Oxford University Press, 2009), p. 3.

[26] William Hazlitt, 'On the Living Poets', in *Lectures on the English Poets* (London: Taylor and Hessey, 1818), pp. 283–331 (pp. 327–8, 329).

[27] Hazlitt, pp. 329–30.

irrevocably lost, granting him a kind of authority based securely in the past and making him a poet through his having existed so strongly as Hazlitt asserts a poet should. This model of genius cannot easily be challenged by textual analysis. Denying it mandates an alternative biographical argument that intensifies the focus on the poet. Privileging such biographical approaches makes poems only one aspect of a poet's extended self, which also comprises social encounters, the memories of friends, letters, pictures, places, scandals, rhetoric and apocrypha.

Not coincidentally, these other elements were subject to profitable manipulations and mediations by other writers. Think of Moore's enormously profitable *Life of Lord Byron* (1832), of Edward John Trelawney's *Adventures of a Younger Son* (1831), of Hunt's *Lord Byron and Some of his Contemporaries* (1828), of the popularity of 'Table Talk' volumes, of De Quincey's controversial articles on Coleridge and Wordsworth, of Thomas Love Peacock's satirical versions of the poets, of Benjamin Disraeli's *Venetia* (1837). For the increasing influence of rhetorics of genius on the poets beginning their careers during the 1820s, think of Letitia Elizabeth Landon's carefully manipulated pseudonymity, the ways in which she played with and reconfigured her femininity and the difficulties that she suffered when the press began to read her love poetry onto her life. L.E.L.'s reception was in many ways more like those accorded to actresses than the receptions previously accorded to authors, a testament to the increasing currency of literary celebrity.[28] Both amused and chagrined, she wrote of the rumours surrounding her person:

> One young lady heard at Scarborough last summer, that I had had two hundred offers; and a gentleman at Leeds brought an account of three hundred and fifty straight from London. It is really very unfortunate that my conquests should so much resemble the passage to the North Pole and Wordsworth's Cuckoo, 'talked of but never seen.'[29]

Authors like Landon were public personalities who were of interest to large popular audiences in ways that their earlier counterparts rarely were.

---

[28] Of course, several successful actresses, including Mary Robinson and Elizabeth Inchbald, bartered their theatrical celebrity into relatively successful literary careers in the late eighteenth century. What had changed was not that celebrities could become authors, but that authors could more easily become celebrities.

[29] Laman Blanchard, *The Life and Literary Remains of L.E.L.*, 2 vols (London: Henry Colburn, 1841), I, 50–1.

In the 1820s, the closed circuits of the older literary scene—with its patrons, its privileged buyers of expensive books, its sociable publishing monopolies and powerful periodical oligarchies—were diminishing in importance. They were making way for a more extensive and various literary culture within which the gulf between writers and readers inevitably widened and within which authors could trade far more usefully and successfully on performing the emerging mysteries of their craft.

The canonical Romantics initially suffered to a certain extent from living during a transitional period in the history of art, artifice and literary production, but they benefitted substantially in the longer term. They were among the last generation to live as part of a relatively small-scale literary milieu that was exclusive, tight-knit and founded on sociable connections. While (Byron excepted) they did not espouse the most popular literary ideals within this culture (and were subject to the blandishments of those who did), they were able successfully to cultivate friendships and networks through which their ideas and reputations could slowly spread. During their lifetimes, new types of literary fame were being formulated, both in concert with and in opposition to the nascent mass reading public. As some of the key originators of what became oppositional aesthetic ideologies, the poets later identified as Romantic were better placed than their more high-profile competitors to take advantage when technologies and expanding audiences splintered sociable authorship into positions identified with commercial professionalism and exalted genius.

A tipping point can be located quite specifically in the late 1820s and early 1830s. Southey's spectral Sir Thomas More remarked in 1829 that '[a]ll classes are now brought within the reach of your current literature […] on the quality of which, according as it may be salubrious or noxious, the health of the public mind depends.'[30] Pioneering cheap editions like Robert Cadell's Collected Edition of the Waverley Novels (printed between 1829 and 1833) and the Standard Novels series launched by Richard Bentley and Henry Colburn in 1831 slashed the prices for prose fiction. In 1834 *Tait's Edinburgh Magazine* remarked that '[t]he expensive quartos and octavos, which used to issue in such swarms from Albemarle Street, and The Row, and from the Edinburgh press in *Constable's* days, have given place to the *Waverley Novels, Lardner's Cyclopaedia, The Edinburgh Cabinet Library,* and some scores more of

---

[30] Robert Southey, *Sir Thomas More: or, Colloquies on the Progress and Prospects of Society,* 2 vols (London: John Murray, 1829), II, 362–3.

similar works, published in monthly parts, at cheap prices.'[31] The article also notes the falls of the quarterlies: 'The *Quarterly Review*, the organ of the wealthy classes of wealthy England, was once as high in circulation as 14,000 and is now understood to have fallen to 9000 or 8000. The *Edinburgh Review* has steadily been sinking from 12,000, to somewhere around 7000 or 6000.' The purpose of *Tait's* article is to lay out its reasons for dramatically dropping its price from half-a-crown to a shilling. Its success when it did so indicated the flourishing of a genuine mass print culture within which the authority of single arbiters was limited.

The Romantics thus achieved controversial prominence just prior to a significant wave of expansion and were being transformed into established greats at a time when huge reductions in the cost of literature and growth in systems of education could take them to unprecedented audiences. Richard Cronin asserts that 'it was in this period that writers first began to flaunt the status of their productions as commodities'.[32] The Romantics were already established as opposing this commercial wave, positioning them to seem like exemplars of a purer and greater age. They also benefitted from (and perhaps in part caused) a collapse in the demand for new poetry. As Lee Erickson has demonstrated, the buoyant market for poetry books that characterised the 1810s peaked around 1820 and then subsided in the face of competition from cheap novels, periodicals and collections of works by already-recognised geniuses. Publishers began to refuse to take on new poets, and by the middle of the century 'there was almost no one but Edward Moxon' publishing them, and he generally did so on the condition that 'the author would have an equal share of the profits and the losses'.[33] The difficulty of publishing poetry collections meant that the Romantics remained among the most modern poets with established presences on bookshop shelves, and they benefitted greatly from the resulting references in schoolbooks, periodicals and popular culture. Their having defied earlier publics placed them as ideal cultural commodities to value and disseminate in an age that both feared and embraced the consequences of mass production.

---

[31] '*Johnstone's Edinburgh Magazine:* The Cheap and Dear Periodicals', *Tait's Edinburgh Magazine*, 4 (January 1834), 490–500 (p. 492).

[32] Richard Cronin, *Romantic Victorians: English Literature, 1824–1840* (Basingstoke: Palgrave, 2002), p. 11.

[33] Lee Erickson, *The Economy of Literary Form: English Literature and the Industrialization of Publishing, 1800–1850* (Baltimore: Johns Hopkins Press, 1996), pp. 38, 37.

The poets were also ambiguously fortunate in their coming to be considered as part of a larger movement. This grouping was formulated partly from the ideologies in their works, but was also grounded in many other contexts—in histories and chronologies, in wider European cultural patterns, in developments in other arts, in popular perceptions, in print culture, in the testimonies of friends and enemies, in philosophy, and—crucially—in retrospect. It is powerfully suggestive that, unlike many previous literary epochs, the Romantic period is not named for its rulers or dates, but for its eventually triumphant opposition. Nevertheless, it is important to remain aware that this naming arose later and that it represents a historical conclusion that was for the poets—and even more so for their contemporaries—by no means the one that seemed inevitable. The widely-propagated version of Romanticism is in many ways delusive. It serves to occlude the particularities of the poets, the vibrant, social, intricately-networked print culture of their period, and the hundreds of other writers who wrote for money, reputation, public praise or private friends. Romanticism can be a useful, if distorting, lens through which to view the Big Six and to examine the things that unite them. It is a fascinating movement in world culture, if one for which precise parameters are extremely difficult to delimit. However, as the definitive summation of several decades of literary culture, society and production, Romanticism is, as I hope this book has shown, a deeply inadequate label.

In the preface, I referred to several scholars, Roland Barthes chief amongst them, who were concerned with delineating theories that allowed the authority of the author to be rhetorically constrained or discounted. Strategies along these lines ease the way for criticism by clearing texts of the awkward specificities of authors' lives. Such professionalised reading techniques can produce brilliant and incisive results, but they do so by adopting a mode of reading seldom practiced outside the confines of the academy and one that ultimately remains personalised through the weight it places on the interpretive powers of the critic. This study has pursued an alternative method, focusing on documenting the practices of authorship by examining how individuals and groups struggled with their historical circumstances to make livings, acquire respect, operate socially and express themselves through writing. Authorship, like literature, can be read in macro in search of general principles, and such readings are invaluable for comprehending its larger implications. However, many of the pleasures of studying authorship lie in the particular and the peculiar, in poignant and irreducible specifics. Just as we respect the complexity and multifariousness of literary works, so too should we recognise and value the distinctive manners in which writers have fashioned their selves and their contemporaries, creating a plethora of conflicting, sublime, networked and quotidian ways of being authorly.

This study has focused on the late eighteenth and early nineteenth centuries, contending that this period was a transitional one during which mainstream authorship slowly moved from being a mode of communication among the privileged to a means of addressing wider publics from the more distanced and alienated positions of the professional wordsmith and the inspired genius. It has stressed that these developments were contingent both on technological and sociological change and on new practices and schools of thought that coalesced in response. It has also emphasised that these changes did not occur smoothly or straightforwardly. Transitions occurred at varying rates for different people in different places. They developed as the result of a composite of diverse individual approaches, mediated by societal and cultural pressures and by intended and unintended consequences. Some fortunate authors flourished within a series of shifting paradigms. The reputations of others fell or rose as they adapted or failed to adapt to new environments. It remained the case that many less socially and financially fortunate writers struggled to profit by their pens. The rules of authorship changed, but they remained the rules for a rigged game, within which existing social advantages could count for a great deal. The rhetoric around writing held out the promise of freedom, but in practice whether a writer was listened to depended a great deal on who they were and how well they manipulated established constraints.

In some respects, it would be convenient for critics if writing could genuinely be judged by a set of disinterested standards. However, it is not the nature of literary communications to submit to timeless verities or fit within unmoving hierarchies. Literary experiences are fundamentally subjective, shaped by past knowledge, present moods, the reactions of others and the wider assumptions of our cultures. Works of literature are more than just feats of art or modes of entertainment. They are also social claims, channelled experiences, commercial products, acts of affiliation and devotion, public and private responses, networked allusions, and witting and unwitting testimonies about the times in which they were written. Considering works as authored and considering those who authored them can help to bring into focus the full range of uses to which writing can be put. It can also lead us to encounter individuals and perspectives that we might otherwise have passed over. At its worst, the idea of authorship can be a deeply exclusionary one. However, at its best, articulating the diversity behind the written experiences we have the privilege of being able to access can radically expand the potential of writing for fulfilling its most important function: allowing us to touch on and assimilate ideas, perspectives and feelings other than our own.

BIBLIOGRAPHY

MANUSCRIPT SOURCES

Edinburgh, National Library of Scotland (NLS), Blackwood Archive.
Edinburgh, National Library of Scotland (NLS), John Murray Archive.
London, British Library (BL), Archive of the Royal Literary Fund, Loan 96 RLF.
London, British Library (BL), Papers of William Windham, Additional Manuscript 37914.
New York Public Library (NYPL), Henry W. and Albert A. Berg Collection of English and American Literature.
New York Public Library (NYPL), Carl H. Pforzheimer Collection of Shelley and His Circle.
Reading, University of Reading, Special Collections (URSC), Longman Archive, URSC 1393.

PERIODICAL SOURCES

Anti-Jacobin
Anti-Jacobin Review
Analytical Review
Athenaeum
Blackwood's Edinburgh Magazine
British Critic
Champion
Cobbett's Weekly Political Register

© The Author(s) 2021   335
M. Sangster, *Living as an Author in the Romantic Period*, Palgrave
Studies in the Enlightenment, Romanticism and Cultures of Print,
https://doi.org/10.1007/978-3-030-37047-3

Critical Review
Eclectic Review
Edinburgh Annual Register
Edinburgh Monthly Review
Edinburgh Review
English Review
Gentleman's Magazine
Literary Gazette
Monthly Magazine
Monthly Review
Morning Chronicle
Morning Post
New Monthly Magazine
Penny Magazine
Poetical Register
Quarterly Review
Spectator
St James's Chronicle, or the British Evening Post
Tait's Edinburgh Magazine
The World

Primary Works

Annual Biography and Obituary, 1830, Vol. 14 (London: Longman, Rees, Orme, Brown, and Green, 1830).

Austen, Jane, *Jane Austen's Letters,* ed. Deirdre Le Faye, 3rd edn (Oxford: Oxford University Press, 1995).

Austen, Jane, *Northanger Abbey*, ed. Barbara M. Benedict and Deirdre Le Faye (Cambridge: Cambridge University Press, 2006).

Austen, Jane, *Later Manuscripts*, ed. Janet Todd and Linda Bree (Cambridge: Cambridge University Press, 2008).

Barbauld, Anna Letitia, *Eighteen Hundred and Eleven: a Poem* (London: Johnson and Co., 1812).

Barrett, Eaton Stannard, *Woman: a Poem* (London: Henry Colburn, 1818).

Barrett, Eaton Stannard, *Woman; Henry Schultze*, facsimile edition, introduction Donald H. Reiman (London: Garland, 1979).

Benger, Elizabeth, *Memoirs of the Late Mrs. Elizabeth Hamilton*, 2 vols (London: Longman, Hurst, Rees, Orme, and Brown, 1818).

Betham, Ernest (ed.), *A House of Letters* (London: Jarrold & Sons, 1905).

Betham, Matilda, *The Lay of Marie* (London: Rowland Hunter, 1816).

Betham-Edwards, Matilda, *Six Life Studies of Famous Women* (London: Griffith & Farran, 1880).

Blanchard, Laman, *The Life and Literary Remains of L.E.L.*, 2 vols (London: Henry Colburn, 1841).

Bloomfield, Robert, *The Letters of Robert Bloomfield and his Circle*, ed. Tim Fulford and Linda Pratt, *Romantic Circles Electronic Editions*, September 2009, https://romantic-circles.org/editions/bloomfield_letters/.

Bloomfield, Robert, *The Farmer's Boy: a Rural Poem* (London: Vernor and Hood, 1800).

Bloomfield, Robert, *Selected Poems*, ed. John Goodridge and John Lucas, rev. edn (Nottingham: Trent Editions, 2007).

Browne, Felicia Dorothea, *Poems* (London: Cadell and Davies, 1808).

Burns, Robert, *The Poems and Songs of Robert Burns*, ed. James Kinsley, 3 vols (Oxford: Clarendon Press, 1968).

Byron, George Gordon, *Byron: The Complete Poetical Works*, ed. Jerome J. McGann, 7 vols (Oxford: Oxford University Press, 1980–93).

Byron, George Gordon, *Byron's Letters and Journals*, ed. Leslie A. Marchand, 12 vols (London: John Murray, 1973–94).

Chambers, Robert, *A Biographical Dictionary of Eminent Scotsmen*, 4 vols (Glasgow: Blackie and Son, 1835).

Chorley, Henry Fothergill, *Memorials of Mrs. Hemans*, 2 vols (London: Saunders and Otley, 1836).

Cockburn, Henry, *Life of Lord Jeffrey: with a Selection from his Correspondence*, 2 vols (Edinburgh: Adam and Charles Black, 1852).

Cockle, Mary E., *Reply to Lord Byron's "Fare Thee Well"* (Newcastle: S. Hodgson, 1817).

Coleridge, Samuel Taylor, *Collected Letters of Samuel Taylor Coleridge,* ed. Earl Leslie Griggs, 6 vols (Oxford: Clarendon Press, 1956–71).

Coleridge, Samuel Taylor, *The Collected Works of Samuel Taylor Coleridge*, gen ed. Kathleen Coburn, 14 vols (Princeton, NJ: Princeton University Press, 1969–93).

Croly, George, *Paris in 1815* (London: John Murray, 1817).

D'Israeli, Isaac, *Calamities of Authors; including some Inquiries Respecting their Moral and Literary Characters* (London: John Murray, 1812).

Feldman, Paula R. (ed.), *British Women Poets of the Romantic Era: An Anthology* (Baltimore: Johns Hopkins University Press, 1997).

Fitzpatrick, William John, *Lady Morgan: Her Career, Literary and Personal* (London; Charles J. Skeet, 1860).

Gifford, William, *The Baviad, and Maeviad,* new edn (London: J. Wright, 1797).

Gifford, William (ed.), *The Beauties of the Anti-Jacobin* (London: C. Chapple, 1799).

Godwin, William, *Lives of Edward and John Phillips, Nephews and Pupils of Milton* (London: Longman, Hurst, Rees, Orme, and Brown, 1815).

Hamilton, Elizabeth, *Memoirs of Modern Philosophers*, ed. Claire Grogan (Peterborough, Ontario: Broadview Press, 2000).

Hamilton, Elizabeth, *Translation of the Letters of a Hindoo Rajah* (London: G.G. and J. Robinson, 1796).

Haydon, Benjamin Robert, *The Diary of Benjamin Robert Haydon*, ed. Willard Bissell Pope, 5 vols (Cambridge, MA: Harvard University Press, 1960–63).

Haydon, Benjamin Robert, *Life of Benjamin Robert Haydon, Historical Painter, from his Autobiography and Journals*, ed. Tom Taylor, 2nd edn, 3 vols (London: Longman, Brown, Green and Longmans, 1853).

Hays, Mary, *The Correspondence of Mary Hays (1779–1843), British Novelist*, ed. Marilyn L. Brooks (Lampeter: Edwin Mellen Press, 2004).

Hays, Mary, *Memoirs of Emma Courtney*, ed. Eleanor Ty (Oxford: Oxford University Press, 2009).

Hazlitt, William, *Lectures on the English Poets* (London: Taylor and Hessey, 1818).

Hazlitt, William, *The Complete Works of William Hazlitt*, ed. P.P. Howe, 21 vols (London: J.M. Dent, 1930–34).

Herbert, William, *Helga: a Poem in Seven Cantos* (London: John Murray, 1815).

Hemans, Felicia, *Felicia Hemans: Selected Poems, Letters, Reception Materials*, ed. Susan Wolfson (Princeton, NJ: Princeton University Press, 2000).

Hemans, Felicia, *Wallace's Invocation to Bruce: A Poem* (Edinburgh and London: William Blackwood and Cadell & Davies, 1819).

[Heron, Robert], *St Kilda in Edinburgh; or News from Camperdown. A Comic Drama, in Two Acts; with a Critical Preface: to which is added An Account of a Famous Ass-Race* (Edinburgh: [no publisher given], 1798).

Hobhouse, John Cam, *Hobhouse's Diary*, ed. Peter Cochran (from British Library Additional Manuscript 56548), http://petercochran.wordpress.com/hobhouses-diary/.

Holcroft, Thomas, *The Life of Thomas Holcroft*, continued by William Hazlitt, ed. Elbridge Colby, 2 vols (London: Constable & Co., 1925).

Holland, John and James Everett, *Memoirs of the Life and Writings of James Montgomery*, 7 vols (London: Longman, Brown, Green, and Longmans, 1854–56).

[Hughes, Harriet Mary], 'Memoir of the Life and Writings of Felicia Hemans, by her Sister', in *The Works of Mrs Hemans*, 6 vols (Edinburgh and London: William Blackwood and Thomas Cadell, 1839), I, 1–317.

Jeffrey, Francis, *Contributions to the Edinburgh Review*, 2nd edn, 3 vols (London: Longman, Brown, Green and Longmans, 1846).

Jerdan, William, *The Autobiography of William Jerdan*, 4 vols (London: Arthur Hall, Virtue & Co., 1852–53).

Johnson, Samuel, *The Lives of the English Poets*, 2 vols (London: Printed for F. C and J. Rivington; J. Nunn; Cadell and Davies; Longman, Hurst, Rees, Orme, and Brown; G. & W.B. Whittaker; J. Richardson; J. Walker; Newman and Co.; Lackington and Co.; Black, Kingsbury, Parbury, and Allen; J. Black and Son;

Sherwood, Neely, and Jones; Baldwin, Cradock, and Joy; J. Robinson; E. Edwards; Simpkin and Marshall; R. Scholey; and G. Cowie, 1820).

Keats, John, *The Letters of John Keats, 1814–1821*, ed. Hyder E. Rollins, 2 vols (Cambridge, MA: Harvard University Press, 1958).

Keats, John, *Keats' Poetry and Prose*, ed. Jeffrey N. Cox (New York: W.W. Norton, 2009).

Knight, Charles (ed.), *The Penny Magazine of the Society for the Diffusion of Useful Knowledge, Volumes 1–2* (London: Charles Knight, 1832).

[Landon, Letitia Elizabeth], *The Improvisatrice; and Other Poems* (London: Hurst, Robinson & Co., 1824).

Lecky, W.E.H., *Historical and Political Essays* (London: Longmans, 1908).

Lockhart, John Gibson, *Memoirs of the Life of Sir Walter Scott, Bart.*, 7 vols (Philadelphia: Carey, Lea & Blanchard, 1837–38).

Milman, Henry Hart, *The Fall of Jerusalem* (London: John Murray, 1820).

Milman, Henry Hart, *Samor, the Lord of the Bright City* (London: John Murray, 1818).

Montgomery, James, *The Wanderer of Switzerland, and Other Poems*, 3rd ed. (London: Longman, Hurst, Rees, and Orme, 1806).

Montgomery, James, *The World before the Flood, with Other Occasional Pieces* (London: Longman, Hurst, Rees, Orme, and Brown, 1813).

Moore, Thomas, *British Satire 1785–1840: Volume 5: The Satires of Thomas Moore*, ed. Jane Moore (London: Pickering and Chatto, 2003).

[Moore, Thomas], *Corruption and Intolerance* (London: J. Carpenter, 1808).

Moore, Thomas, *Lalla Rookh: An Oriental Romance* (London: Longman, Hurst, Rees, Orme, and Brown, 1817).

Moore, Thomas, *The Journal of Thomas Moore*, ed. Wilfred S. Dowden, 6 vols (Newark: University of Delaware Press, 1983–91).

Moore, Thomas, *Memoirs, Journal, and Correspondence of Thomas Moore*, ed. Lord John Russell, 8 vols (London: Longman, 1853–56).

Moore, Thomas, *Odes of Anacreon, translated into English verse, with Notes* (London: John Stockdale, 1800).

Moore, Thomas, *The Poetical Works of Thomas Moore*, 10 vols (London: Longman, Orme, Brown, Green, & Longmans, 1840–41).

More, Hannah, *The Works of Hannah More*, 11 vols (London: T. Cadell, 1830).

[More, Hannah], *The Search After Happiness: A Pastoral Drama*, 13th edn (London: T. Cadell and W. Davies, 1810).

More, Hannah, *Slavery: A Poem* (London: T. Cadell, 1788).

More, Hannah, *Strictures on the Modern System of Female Education*, 2nd edn, 2 vols (London: T. Cadell and W. Davies, 1799).

More, Hannah, *Tales for the Common People and other Cheap Repository Tracts*, ed. Clare MacDonald Shaw (Nottingham: Trent Editions, 2002).

[More, Hannah], *Village Politics* (Manchester: J. Harrop, 1793).

Morgan, Sydney, *Florence Macarthy: An Irish Tale*, 4 vols (London: Henry Colburn, 1819).

Murray, John, *The Letters of John Murray to Lord Byron*, ed. Andrew Nicolson (Liverpool: Liverpool University Press, 2007).

Murray, Lindley, *An English Grammar Comprehending the Principles and Rules of the Language Illustrated by Appropriate Exercises, and a Key to the Exercises*, new edn, 2 vols (York: printed by Thomas Wilson & Son for Longman, Hurst, Rees, and Orme; and Darton and Harvey, London; for Wilson and Son, and R. and W. Spence, York: and for Constable and Co Edinburgh, 1808).

Nicholson, Francis, 'Correspondence between Mrs Hemans and Matthew Nicholson, an early member of this Society', *Manchester Memories*, 54.9 (1910), 1–39.

Ogilvie, John, *Poems on Several Subjects* (London: G. Keith, 1762).

Parsons, Eliza, *The Castle of Wolfenbach*, ed. Diane Long Hoeveler (Kansas City: Valancourt Books, 2006).

Parsons, Eliza, *The History of Miss Meredith*, 2 vols (London: Thomas Hookham, 1790).

Parsons, Eliza, *The Mysterious Warning: A German Tale* (London: Folio Press, 1968).

Plan for Establishing by Subscription a Repository of Cheap Publications, on Religious & Moral Subjects (London: [?John Marshall], 1795).

Pope, Alexander, *The Poems of Alexander Pope Volume V: The Dunciad*, ed. James Sutherland, 2nd edn (London: Methuen & Co., 1953).

Radcliffe, Ann, *The Mysteries of Udolpho*, ed. Bonamy Dobrée, introduction and notes Terry Castle (Oxford: Oxford University Press, 1998).

Ring, John, *The Beauties of the 'Edinburgh Review', alias the Stinkpot of Literature* (London: H.D. Symonds and John Hatchard, 1807).

Roberts, William, *Memoirs of the Life and Correspondence of Mrs. Hannah More*, 2nd edn, 4 vols (London: Seeley and Burnside, 1834).

Rogers, Samuel, *The Pleasures of Memory* (London: T. Cadell, 1792).

Scott, Walter, *The Fortunes of Nigel*, ed. Frank Jordan (Edinburgh: Edinburgh University Press, 2004).

Scott, Walter, *The Journal of Sir Walter Scott*, ed. W.E.K. Anderson (Oxford: Clarendon Press, 1972).

Scott, Walter, *The Letters of Sir Walter Scott*, ed. Sir Herbert Grierson, transcribed Takero Sato, 12 vols, *Walter Scott Digital Archive*, Edinburgh University Library, http://www.walterscott.lib.ed.ac.uk/etexts/etexts/letters.html.

Scott, Walter, *Waverley; or 'tis Sixty Years Since*, ed. Claire Lamont (Oxford: Oxford University Press, 1986).

Shelley, Percy Bysshe, *The Letters of Percy Bysshe Shelley*, ed. Frederick L. Jones, 2 vols (Oxford: Clarendon Press, 1964).

Shelley, Percy Bysshe, *The Poems of Shelley*, ed. Kelvin Everest and Geoffrey Matthews, 4 vols (Harlow: Longman, 1989–).

Shelley, Percy Bysshe, *Shelley's Poetry and Prose*, ed. Donald H. Reiman and Neil Fraistat, 2nd edn (New York: W.W. Norton, 2002).

Smiles, Samuel, *A Publisher and his Friends: Memoir and Correspondence of the late John Murray, with an Account of the Origin and Progress of the House, 1768–1843*, 2 vols (London: John Murray, 1891).

Smith, Adam, *An Enquiry into the Nature and Causes of the Wealth of Nations*, gen. eds. R.H. Campbell and A.S. Skinner, textual ed. W.B. Todd, 2 vols (Oxford: Clarendon Press, 1976).

Smith, James and Horace Smith, *Rejected Addresses; or the New Theatrum Poetarum* (London: John Miller, 1812).

Southey, Robert, *The Book of the Church* (London: John Murray, 1824).

Southey, Robert, *The Collected Letters of Robert Southey*, gen. eds. Lynda Pratt, Tim Fulford and Ian Packer, *Romantic Circles*, 2009–, https://romantic-circles.org/editions/southey_letters/index.html.

Southey, Robert, *Life and Correspondence of the Late Robert Southey*, ed. Charles Cuthbert Southey, 6 vols (London: Longman, Brown, Green, and Longmans, 1849–50).

Southey, Robert, *Poetical Works 1793–1810*, gen ed. Lynda Pratt, 5 vols (London: Pickering & Chatto, 2004).

Southey, Robert, *Later Poetical Works, 1811–1838*, gen. eds. Tim Fulford and Lynda Pratt, 4 vols (London: Pickering & Chatto, 2012).

Southey, Robert, *Sir Thomas More: or, Colloquies on the Progress and Prospects of Society*, 2 vols (London: John Murray, 1829).

Southey, Robert, *A Vision of Judgement* (London: Longman, Hurst, Rees, Orme, and Brown, 1821).

Sterne, Laurence, *The Life and Opinions of Tristram Shandy, Gent.*, ed. Howard Anderson (New York: W.W. Norton, 1980).

Strachen, John (ed.), *British Satire 1785–1840: Volume 4: Gifford and the Della Cruscans* (London: Pickering and Chatto, 2003).

Talfourd, Thomas Noon, 'Memoir of the Life and Writings of Mrs. Radcliffe', prefixed to Ann Radcliffe, *Gaston de Blondeville, or the Court of Henry III Keeping Festival in Ardenne: a Romance & St Albans Abbey: a Metrical Tale*, 2 vols (Philadelphia: H.C. Carey and I. Lea, 1826).

Timperley, Charles Henry, *A Dictionary of Printers and Printing: with the Progress of Literature; Ancient and Modern* (London: H. Johnson, 1839).

Walpole, Horace, *Horace Walpole's Correspondence*, gen. ed. W.S. Lewis, 48 vols (New Haven: Yale University Press, 1937–83).

White, Henry Kirke, *The Remains of Henry Kirke White; with an Account of his Life*, ed. Robert Southey, 2 vols (London: Vernor, Hood, and Sharpe; Longman,

Hurst, Rees, and Orme; J. Dighton, T. Barret, and J. Nicholson, Cambridge; and W. Dunn and S. Tupman, Nottingham, 1807).

Williams, David, *Claims of Literature: The Origin, Motives, Objects, and Transactions, of the Society for the Establishment of a Literary Fund* (London: William Miller, 1802).

Williams, David, *Incidents in My Own Life Which Have Been Thought of Some Importance*, ed. Peter France (Brighton: University of Sussex Library Press, 1980).

Wordsworth, William, *Last Poems, 1821–1850*, ed. Jared Curtis (Ithaca: Cornell University Press, 1999).

Wordsworth, William and Dorothy Wordsworth, *The Letters of William and Dorothy Wordsworth: The Early Years 1787–1805*, ed. Ernest de Selincourt, rev. Chester L. Shaver (Oxford: Clarendon Press 1967).

[Wordsworth, William and Samuel Taylor Coleridge], *Lyrical Ballads, with a Few Other Poems* (London: J. & A. Arch, 1798).

Wordsworth, William [and Samuel Taylor Coleridge], *Lyrical Ballads, with Other Poems*, 2nd edn, 2 vols (London: Longman & Rees, 1800 [actually published January 1801]).

Wordsworth, William [and Samuel Taylor Coleridge], *Lyrical Ballads, with Pastoral and Other Poems*, 3rd edn, 2 vols (London: Longman & Rees, 1802).

Wordsworth, William and Samuel Taylor Coleridge, *Lyrical Ballads: An Electronic Scholarly Edition*, ed. Bruce Graver and Ron Tetreault, *Romantic Circles*, 2003, https://romantic-circles.org/editions/LB/.

Wordsworth, William, *The Prose Works of William Wordsworth*, ed. W.J.B. Owen and Jane Worthington Smyser, 3 vols (Oxford: Clarendon Press, 1974).

Wordsworth, William, *Shorter Poems, 1807–1820*, ed. Carl H. Ketcham (Ithaca: Cornell University Press, 1989).

Secondary Criticism

Abrams, M.H., *The Mirror and the Lamp: Romantic Theory and the Critical Tradition* (Oxford: Oxford University Press, 1971).

Altick, Richard D., *The English Common Reader: A Social History of the Mass Reading Public 1800–1900* (Chicago: University of Chicago Press, 1957).

Andrews, Kerri, *Ann Yearsley and Hannah More, Patronage and Poetry: The Story of a Literary Relationship* (London: Pickering & Chatto, 2013).

Bailey, Elaine, 'Matilda Betham: A New Biography', *The Wordsworth Circle*, 38 (Summer 2007), 143–6.

Barker, Juliet, *Wordsworth: A Life* (London: Viking, 2000).

Barcus, James E. (ed.), *Shelley: The Critical Heritage* (London: Routledge and Kegen, 1975).

Barrell, John, *Imagining the King's Death: Figurative Treason, Fantasies of Regicide, 1794–1796* (Oxford: Oxford University Press, 2000).

Barthes, Roland, 'The Death of the Author', in *Image Music Text*, trans. Stephen Heath (London: Fontana, 1977), pp. 142–8.

Batchelor, Jennie, '"The Claims of Literature": Women Applicants to the Royal Literary Fund', *Women's Writing*, 12:3 (2005), 505–21.

Batchelor, Jennie, *Women's Work: Labour, Gender, Authorship, 1750–1830* (Manchester: Manchester University Press, 2010).

Bate, Jonathan, *John Clare: A Biography* (London: Picador, 2004).

Bebbington, D.W., *Evangelicalism in Modern Britain: A History from the 1730s to the 1980s* (London and New York: Routledge, 1993).

Behrendt, Stephen C., *British Women Poets and the Romantic Writing Community* (Baltimore: Johns Hopkins University Press, 2009).

Behrendt, Stephen C., '"Certainly not a Female Pen": Felicia Hemans's Early Public Reception', in *Felicia Hemans: Reimagining Poetry in the Nineteenth Century*, ed. Nanora Sweet and Julie Melnyk (Basingstoke: Palgrave, 2001), pp. 95–114.

Bell, Bill (ed.), *The Edinburgh History of the Book in Scotland Volume 3: Ambition and Industry 1800–1880* (Edinburgh: Edinburgh University Press, 2007).

Benatti, Francesca, Sean Ryder and Justin Tonra, (eds.), *Thomas Moore: Texts, Contexts, Hypertext* (Oxford: Peter Lang, 2013).

Bennett, Andrew, *The Author* (London: Routledge, 2005).

Bennett, Andrew, *Romantic Poets and the Culture of Posterity* (Cambridge: Cambridge University Press, 1999).

Blakey, Dorothy, *The Minerva Press 1790–1820* (London: Bibliographical Society, 1939).

Bloom, Harold, *The Visionary Company: A Reading of English Romantic Poetry* (New York: Doubleday, 1961).

Bloomfield, B.C., 'The Publication of *The Farmer's Boy* by Robert Bloomfield', *The Library*, 6th Series, 15 (June 1993), 75–94.

Bolza, Hans, 'Friedrich Koenig und die Erfindung der Druckmaschine', *Technikgeschichte* 34 (1967), 79–89.

Bourdieu, Pierre, *Distinction: A Social Critique of the Judgement of Taste*, trans. Richard Nice (London: Routledge, 2010).

Bourdieu, Pierre, 'The Field of Cultural Production, or: The Economic World Reversed', trans. Richard Nice, in *The Field of Cultural Production*, ed. Randall Johnson (London: Polity Press, 1993), pp. 29–73.

Bradley, Andrea, 'Correcting Mrs Opie's Powers: The *Edinburgh* Review of Amelia Opie's *Poems* (1802)' in *Romantic Periodicals and Print Culture*, ed. Kim Wheatley (London: Frank Cass, 2003), pp. 41–61.

Brant, Clare, *Eighteenth-Century Letters and British Culture* (Basingstoke: Palgrave Macmillan, 2006).

Briggs, Asa, *A History of Longmans and their Books 1724–1990: Longevity in Publishing* (London and Delaware: British Library and Oak Knoll Press, 2008).

Brown, Susan, Patricia Clements, and Isobel Grundy (eds.), *Orlando: Women's Writing in the British Isles from the Beginnings to the Present* (Cambridge: Cambridge University Press Online, 2006), http://orlando.cambridge.org/.

Burnett, John, *A History of the Cost of Living* (London: Penguin, 1969).

Butler, Marilyn, 'Culture's Medium: The Role of the Review', in *The Cambridge Companion to British Romanticism*, ed. Stuart Curran (Cambridge: Cambridge University Press, 1993), pp. 120–47.

Butler, Marilyn, *Romantics, Rebels and Reactionaries: English Literature and its Background 1790–1830* (Oxford: Oxford University Press, 1981).

Carswell, Catherine, 'Robert Heron: a Study in Failure', *Scots Magazine*, 18 (1932–33), 37–48.

Chandler, James, *England in 1819: The Politics of Literary Culture and the Case for Romantic Historicism* (Chicago: University of Chicago Press, 1998).

Christensen, Jerome, *Lord Byron's Strength: Romantic Writing and Commercial Society* (Baltimore: Johns Hopkins University Press, 1993).

Christie, William, *The Edinburgh Review in the Literary Culture of Romantic Britain: Mammoth and Megalonyx* (London: Pickering and Chatto, 2009).

Clery, E.J., *Eighteen Hundred and Eleven: Poetry, Protest and Economic Crisis* (Cambridge: Cambridge University Press, 2017).

Clery, E.J., *The Rise of Supernatural Fiction, 1762–1800* (Cambridge: Cambridge University Press, 1995).

Clive, John, *Scotch Reviewers: The 'Edinburgh Review' 1802–1815* (London: Faber & Faber, 1957).

Cochran, Peter, 'Did Byron Take Money for his Early Work?', *The Byron Journal*, 31 (2003), 72–6.

Colbert, Benjamin, 'Popular Romanticism?: Publishing, Readership and the Making of Literary History', in *Authorship, Commerce and the Public*, ed. E.J. Clery, Caroline Franklin and Peter Garside (Basingstoke: Palgrave Macmillan, 2002), pp. 153–68.

Collins, A.S., *The Profession of Letters: A Study of the Relation of Author to Patron, Publisher, and Public, 1780–1832* (London: Routledge, 1928).

Connell, Philip, *Romanticism, Economics, and the Question of 'Culture'* (Oxford: Oxford University Press, 2001).

Copeland, Edward, *Women Writing about Money: Women's Fiction in England, 1790–1820* (Cambridge: Cambridge University Press, 1995).

Corfield, Penelope J., *Power and the Professions in Britain 1700–1850* (London: Routledge, 1995).

Cox, Jeffrey N., *Poetry and Politics in the Cockney School* (Cambridge: Cambridge University Press, 1998).

Craig, David M., 'Subservient Talents? Robert Southey as Public Moralist', in *Robert Southey and the Contexts of English Romanticism*, ed. Lynda Pratt (Aldershot: Ashgate, 2006), pp. 101–14.

Cronin, Richard, *Paper Pellets: British Literary Culture after Waterloo* (Oxford: Oxford University Press, 2010).

Cronin, Richard, *Romantic Victorians: English Literature, 1824–1840* (Basingstoke: Palgrave, 2002).

Cross, Nigel, *The Common Writer: Life in Nineteenth-Century Grub Street* (Cambridge: Cambridge University Press, 1985).

Cross, Nigel, *The Royal Literary Fund 1790–1918: An Introduction to the Fund's History and Archives with an Index of Applicants* (London: World Microfilm Publications, 1984).

Curran, Stuart (ed.), *The Cambridge Companion to British Romanticism* (Cambridge: Cambridge University Press, 1993).

Curran, Stuart, 'Woman and the *Edinburgh Review*', in *British Romanticism and the Edinburgh Review*, ed. Massimiliano Demata and Duncan Wu (Basingstoke: Palgrave Macmillan, 2002), pp. 195–208.

Currie, Janette, 'Re-Visioning James Hogg: The Return of the Subject to Wordsworth's "Extempore Effusion"', *Romantic Textualities: Literature and Print Culture, 1780–1840* (Winter 2005), http://www.romtext.org.uk/articles/rt15_n01/, 7–28.

Cutmore, Jonathan (ed.), *The Quarterly Review Archive*, Romantic Circles, 2005, https://romantic-circles.org/reference/qr/index.html.

Dart, Gregory, 'The Cockney Moment', *Cambridge Quarterly*, 32:3 (2003), 203–23.

Dart, Gregory, 'Hazlitt and Biography', *Cambridge Quarterly*, 29:4 (2000), 338–48.

Davis, Leith, *Music, Postcolonialism, and Gender: The Construction of Irish National Identity, 1724–1874* (Notre Dame, IN: University of Notre Dame Press, 2006).

Demers, Patricia, *The World of Hannah More* (Lexington: University of Kentucky Press, 1996).

Denney, Peter, 'The Talk of the Tap-Room: Bloomfield, Politics, and Popular Culture', in *Robert Bloomfield: The Inestimable Blessing of Letters*, ed. John Goodridge and Bridget Keegan, *Romantic Circles Praxis*, January 2012, https://romantic-circles.org/praxis/bloomfield/HTML/praxis.2011.denney.html.

Donaghue, Frank, *The Fame Machine: Book Reviewing and Eighteenth-Century Literary Careers* (Stanford: Stanford University Press, 1996).

Downey, Edmund, 'An Unpublished Letter from Hannah More to Ralph Beilby: Radical Connections and Popular Periodical Literature', *Notes and Queries*, 61 (December 2014), 504–7.

Duncan, Ian, *Scott's Shadow: The Novel in Romantic Edinburgh* (Princeton, NJ: Princeton University Press, 2007).

Dybikowski, J., *On Burning Ground: An Examination of the Ideas, Projects and Life of David Williams* (Oxford: Voltaire Foundation, 1993).

Edgar, Chad, 'Felicia Hemans and the Shifting Field of Romanticism', in *Felicia Hemans: Reimagining Poetry in the Nineteenth Century*, ed. Nanora Sweet and Julie Melnyk (Basingstoke: Palgrave, 2001), pp. 124–34.

Edwards, Elizabeth, '"Lonely and Voiceless Your Halls Must Remain": Romantic-Era National Song and Felicia Hemans's *Welsh Melodies* (1822)', *Journal for Eighteenth-Century Studies*, 38 (March 2015), 83–97.

Eger, Elizabeth, *Bluestockings: Women of Reason from Enlightenment to Romanticism* (Basingstoke: Palgrave Macmillan, 2010).

Eisner, Eric, *Nineteenth-Century Poetry and Literary Celebrity* (Basingstoke: Palgrave Macmillan, 2009).

Eliot, Simon, '1825–6: Years of Crisis?', in *The Edinburgh History of the Book in Scotland Volume 3: Ambition and Industry 1800–1880*, ed. Bill Bell (Edinburgh: Edinburgh University Press, 2007), pp. 91–5.

Eliot, T.S., 'Tradition and the Individual Talent', in *The Sacred Wood* (London: Methuen, 1920), pp. 42–53.

English, James F., *The Economy of Prestige: Prizes, Awards, and the Circulation of Cultural Value* (Cambridge, MA: Harvard University Press, 2008).

Erickson, Lee, *The Economy of Literary Form: English Literature and the Industrialisation of Printing 1800–1850* (Baltimore: Johns Hopkins Press, 1996).

Fairer, David, 'Southey's Literary History', in *Robert Southey and the Contexts of English Romanticism*, ed. Lynda Pratt (Aldershot: Ashgate, 2006), pp. 1–17.

Favret, Mary A. and Nicola J. Watson (eds.), *At the Limits of Romanticism: Essays in Cultural, Feminist and Materialist Criticism* (Bloomington: University of Indiana Press, 1994).

Feldman, Paula R., 'The Poet and the Profits: Felicia Hemans and the Literary Marketplace', *Keats-Shelley Journal*, 46 (1997), 148–76.

Feldman, Paula R. and Theresa M. Kelley (eds.), *Romantic Women Writers: Voices and Countervoices* (Hanover, NH: University Press of New England, 1995).

Ferris, Ina, *The Achievement of Literary Authority: Gender, History, and the Waverley Novels* (Ithaca: Cornell University Press, 1991).

Ferris, Ina, *Book-Men, Book Clubs, and the Romantic Literary Sphere* (Basingstoke: Palgrave Macmillan, 2015).

Ferris, Ina, 'The Debut of *The Edinburgh Review*, 1802', in *BRANCH: Britain, Representation and Nineteenth-Century History*, ed. Dino Franco Felluga, http://www.branchcollective.org/?ps_articles=ina-ferris-the-debut-of-the-edinburgh-review-1802.

Finn, Margot C., *The Character of Credit: Personal Debt in English Culture, 1740–1914* (Cambridge: Cambridge University Press, 2003).

Foucault, Michel, 'What is an Author?', trans. Joseph V. Harari, in *Modern Criticism and Theory: A Reader*, ed. David Lodge (Harlow: Longman, 1988), pp. 197–210.

Fulford, Tim, 'Bloomfield in His Letters: The Social World of a London Shoemaker Turned Suffolk Poet', in *Robert Bloomfield: The Inestimable Blessing of Letters, Romantic Circles Praxis*, ed. John Goodridge and Bridget Keegan, *Romantic Circles Praxis*, January 2012, https://romantic-circles.org/praxis/bloomfield/HTML/praxis.2011.fulford.html.

Fulford, Tim, *Romantic Poetry and Literary Coteries: The Dialect of the Tribe* (Basingstoke: Palgrave Macmillan, 2015).

Fulford, Tim, *Romanticism and Masculinity: Gender, Politics and Poetics in the Writings of Burke, Coleridge, Cobbett, Wordsworth, De Quincey and Hazlitt* (Basingstoke: Macmillan, 1999).

Fulford, Tim and Debbie Lee, 'The Vaccine Rose: Patronage, Pastoralism and Public Health', in *Robert Bloomfield: Lyric, Class and the Romantic Canon*, ed. Simon White, John Goodridge and Bridget Keegan (Lewisburg: Bucknell University Press, 2006), pp. 142–58.

Fulford, Tim and Matthew Sangster, 'Introduction – Southeyan Correspondences', *Romanticism on the Net*, 68–9 (Spring-Fall 2017), https://doi.org/10.7202/1070618ar.

Gamer, Michael, 'Laureate Policy', *The Wordsworth Circle*, 42 (Winter 2011), 42–7.

Gamer, Michael, *Romanticism and the Gothic* (Cambridge: Cambridge University Press, 2000).

Gamer, Michael, *Romanticism, Self-Canonization, and the Business of Poetry* (Cambridge: Cambridge University Press, 2017).

Garside, Peter, James Raven and Rainer Schöwerling (eds.), *The English Novel 1770–1829: A Bibliographical Survey of Prose Fiction Published in the British Isles*, 2 vols (Oxford: Oxford University Press, 2000).

Garside, Peter, 'Authorship', in *The Oxford History of the Novel in English Volume 2: English and British Fiction 1750–1820*, ed. Peter Garside and Karen O'Brien (Oxford: Oxford University Press, 2015), pp. 29–53.

Garside, Peter, 'Popular Fiction and National Tale: the Hidden Origins of Sir Walter Scott's *Waverley*', *Nineteenth Century Literature*, 46 (June 1991), 30–53.

Garside, Peter, 'Publishing 1800–1830', in *The Edinburgh History of the Book in Scotland Volume 3: Ambition and Industry 1800–1880*, ed. Bill Bell (Edinburgh: Edinburgh University Press, 2007), pp. 79–90.

Gates, Eleanor M., *Leigh Hunt: A Life in Letters; Together with Some Correspondence of William Hazlitt* (Essex, CT: Falls River Publications, 1988).

Gillies, Mary Ann, *The Professional Literary Agent in Britain: 1880–1920* (Toronto: University of Toronto Press, 2007).

Gilmartin, Kevin, *Writing Against Revolution: Literary Conservatism in Britain, 1790–1832* (Cambridge: Cambridge University Press, 2007).

Goldgar, Anne, *Impolite Learning: Conduct and Community in the Republic of Letters, 1680–1750* (New Haven: Yale University Press 1995).

Goldberg, Brian, *The Lake Poets and Professional Identity* (Cambridge: Cambridge University Press, 2007).

Goodridge, John and Bridget Keenan (eds.), *Robert Bloomfield: The Inestimable Blessing of Letters*, Romantic Circles Praxis, January 2012, https://romantic-circles.org/praxis/bloomfield/.

Griffin, Dustin, *Literary Patronage in England 1650–1800* (Cambridge: Cambridge University Press, 1996).

Griffin, Dustin, 'The Rise of the Professional Author', in *The Cambridge History of the Book in Britain Volume 5: 1695–1830*, ed. Michael F. Suarez and Michael L. Turner (Cambridge: Cambridge University Press, 2009), pp. 132–45.

Groom, Nick, 'Love and Madness: Southey Editing Chatterton', in *Robert Southey and the Contexts of English Romanticism*, ed. Lynda Pratt (Aldershot: Ashgate, 2006), pp. 19–36.

Guest, Harriet, *Small Change: Women, Learning, Patriotism, 1750–1810* (Chicago: University of Chicago Press, 2000).

Guillory, John, *Cultural Capital: The Problem of Literary Canon Formation* (Chicago: University of Chicago Press, 1993).

Hammond, Brean S., *Professional Imaginative Writing in England, 1670–1740: 'Hackney for Bread'* (Oxford: Clarendon Press, 1997).

Hawkins, Ann R. and Stephanie Eckroth, *Romantic Women Writers Reviewed*, 9 vols (London: Pickering & Chatto, 2010–13).

Hay, Daisy, *Young Romantics* (London: Bloomsbury, 2010).

Haywood, Ian, 'The Infection of Robert Bloomfield: Terrorizing *The Farmer's Boy*', in *Robert Bloomfield: The Inestimable Blessing of Letters*, ed. John Goodridge and Bridget Keegan, *Romantic Circles Praxis*, January 2012, https://romantic-circles.org/praxis/bloomfield/HTML/praxis.2011.haywood.html.

Heidegger, Martin, 'The Origin of the Work of Art', in *Basic Writings* (London: Routledge, 1993), pp. 143–209.

Higgins, David, 'Celebrity, Politics and the Rhetoric of Genius', in *Romanticism and Celebrity Culture, 1750–1850*, ed. Tom Mole (Cambridge: Cambridge University Press, 2009), pp. 41–59.

Higgins, David, *Romantic Genius and the Literary Magazine: Biography, Celebrity, Politics* (London: Routledge, 2005).

Hole, Robert, 'Hannah More on Literature and Propaganda, 1788–1799', *History*, 85 (October 2000), 613–33.

Holmes, Richard, *Coleridge: Early Visions* (London: Penguin, 1990).

Holmes, Richard, *Coleridge: Darker Reflections* (London: Flamingo, 1999).

Holmes, Richard, *Shelley: The Pursuit* (London: Penguin, 1987).

Hughes-Hallett, Penelope, *The Immortal Dinner* (London: Viking, 2000).

Jackson, H.J., *Romantic Readers: The Evidence of Marginalia* (New Haven: Yale University Press, 2005).

Jackson, H.J., *Those Who Write for Immortality: Romantic Reputations and the Dream of Lasting Fame* (New Haven & London: Yale University Press, 2015).

Jackson, J.R. de J., *Romantic Poetry by Women: A Bibliography, 1770–1835* (Oxford: Clarendon Press, 1993).

Jacobus, Mary, *Tradition and Experiment in Wordsworth's Lyrical Ballads (1798)* (Oxford: Clarendon Press, 1976).

Johnson, Edgar, *Sir Walter Scott: The Great Unknown*, 2 vols (New York: Macmillan, 1970).

Jones, M.G., *Hannah More* (Cambridge: Cambridge University Press, 1952).

Jones, Whitney R.D., *David Williams: The Anvil & the Hammer* (Cardiff: University of Wales Press, 1986).

Joukovsky, Nicholas A., 'Peacock Before *Headlong Hall*: A New Look at his Early Years', *Keats-Shelley Memorial Bulletin*, 36 (1985), 1–40.

Keach, William, 'A Regency Prophecy and the End of Anna Barbauld's Career', *Studies in Romanticism*, 33 (Winter 1994), 569–77.

Keen, Paul, *The Crisis of Literature in the 1790s: Print Culture and the Public Sphere* (Cambridge: Cambridge University Press, 1999).

Kelly, Gary, 'Revolution, Reaction, and the Expropriation of Popular Culture: Hannah More's *Cheap Repository*', *Man and Nature*, 6 (1987), 147–59.

Kelly, Gary, *Women, Writing and Revolution, 1790–1827* (Oxford: Clarendon Press, 1993).

Kelly, Linda, *Ireland's Minstrel: A Life of Tom Moore: Poet, Patriot and Byron's Friend* (London: I.B. Tauris, 2006).

Kelly, Ronan, *Bard of Erin: The Life of Thomas Moore* (London: Penguin, 2009).

Klancher, Jon P., *The Making of English Reading Audiences, 1790–1832* (Madison: University of Wisconsin Press, 1987).

Lawson, Jonathan, *Robert Bloomfield* (Boston: G.K. Hall & Co., 1980).

Low, Dennis, *The Literary Protégées of the Lake Poets* (Aldershot: Ashgate, 2006).

Madden, Lionel (ed.), *Robert Southey: The Critical Heritage* (London: Routledge & Kegan Paul, 1972).

Mandell, Laura, 'Hemans and the Gift-Book Aesthetic', *Cardiff Corvey: Reading the Romantic Text*, 6 (June 2001), 1–12, http://www.romtext.org.uk/articles/cc06_n01/.

Matoff, Susan, *Conflicted Life: William Jerdan, 1782–1869: London Editor, Author and Critic* (Brighton: Sussex Academic Press, 2011).

Mayer, Robert, *Walter Scott and Fame: Authors and Readers in the Romantic Age* (Oxford: Oxford University Press, 2017).

McCalman, Iain (ed.), *An Oxford Companion to the Romantic Age: British Culture 1776–1832* (Oxford: Oxford University Press, 1999).

McCarthy, Fiona, *Byron: Life and Legend* (London: John Murray, 2002).

McGann, Jerome J., *The Romantic Ideology: A Critical Investigation* (Chicago: University of Chicago Press, 1983).

McGurl, Mark, *The Program Era: Postwar Fiction and the Rise of Creative Writing* (Cambridge, MA: Harvard University Press, 2009).

McKitterick, David, 'Introduction' to *The Cambridge History of the Book in Britain Volume VI: 1830–1914*, ed. David McKitterick (Cambridge: Cambridge University Press, 2009), pp. 1–74.

Mee, Jon, *Conversable Worlds: Literature, Contention and Community 1762 to 1830* (Oxford: Oxford University Press, 2011).

Mee, Jon, *Print, Publicity, and Popular Radicalism in the 1790s: The Laurel of Liberty* (Cambridge: Cambridge University Press, 2016).

Mellor, Anne K., *Mothers of the Nation: Women's Political Writing in England, 1780–1830* (Bloomington and Indianapolis: Indiana University Press, 2000).

Mellor, Anne K., *Romanticism and Gender* (London: Routledge, 1993).

Miles, Robert, *Gothic Writing 1750–1820: A Genealogy* (London: Routledge, 1993).

Miles, Robert, *Romantic Misfits* (Basingstoke: Palgrave Macmillan, 2008).

Mole, Tom, *Byron's Romantic Celebrity: Industrial Culture and the Hermeneutic of Intimacy* (Basingstoke: Palgrave Macmillan, 2007).

Mole, Tom (ed.), *Romanticism and Celebrity Culture, 1750–1850* (Cambridge: Cambridge University Press, 2009).

Morton, Karen, *A Life Marketed as Fiction: An Analysis of the Works of Eliza Parsons* (Kansas City: Valancourt Books, 2011).

Motion, Andrew, *Keats* (London: Faber & Faber, 1997).

Murphy, Peter T., 'Climbing Parnassus, & Falling Off', in *At the Limits of Romanticism: Essays in Cultural, Feminist and Materialist Criticism*, ed. Mary A. Favret and Nicola J. Watson (Bloomington: University of Indiana Press, 1994), pp. 40–58.

Newlyn, Lucy, *Reading, Writing and Romanticism: The Anxiety of Reception* (Oxford: Oxford University Press, 2000).

Norman, Sylvia, *The Flight of the Skylark: the Development of Shelley's Reputation* (Norman, OK: University of Oklahoma Press, 1954).

North, Julian, *The Domestication of Genius: Biography and the Romantic Poet* (Oxford: Oxford University Press, 2009).

Ogden, James, *Isaac D'Israeli* (Oxford: Clarendon Press, 1969).

Oxford English Dictionary (Oxford: Oxford University Press, 1884–), www.oed.com.

Oxford Dictionary of National Biography (Oxford: Oxford University Press, 2004–), www.oxforddnb.com.

Parker, Mark, *Literary Magazines and British Romanticism* (Cambridge: Cambridge University Press, 2000).

Pearson, Jacqueline, *Women's Reading in Britain 1750–1835: A Dangerous Recreation* (Cambridge: Cambridge University Press, 1999).

Peterson, Linda H., 'Nineteenth-Century Women Poets and Periodical Spaces: Letitia Landon and Felicia Hemans', *Victorian Periodicals Review*, 9:3 (Fall 2016), 396–414.

Pfau, Thomas, *Wordsworth's Professionalism: Form, Class and the Logic of Early Romantic Cultural Production* (Stanford: Stanford University Press, 1997).

Poovey, Mary, *Genres of the Credit Economy: Mediating Value in Eighteenth- and Nineteenth-Century Britain* (Chicago: University of Chicago Press, 2008).

Pratt, Lynda, 'Family Misfortunes?: The Posthumous Editing of Robert Southey', in *Robert Southey and the Contexts of English Romanticism*, ed. Lynda Pratt (Aldershot: Ashgate, 2006), pp. 219–38.

Punter, David, *The Literature of Terror* (London: Longman, 1980).

Raven, James, *The Business of Books: Booksellers and the English Book Trade* (New Haven: Yale University Press, 2007).

Rigney, Ann, *The Afterlives of Walter Scott: Memory on the Move* (Oxford: Oxford University Press, 2012).

Robertson, Fiona, *Legitimate Histories: Scott, Gothic, and the Authorities of Fiction* (Oxford: Clarendon Press, 1994).

Robinson, Jeffrey C., *Reception and Poetics in Keats: "My Ended Poet"* (New York: St. Martin's Press, 1998).

Roe, Nicholas, *Fiery Heart: The First Life of Leigh Hunt* (London: Pimlico, 2005).

Rogers, Deborah D., *Ann Radcliffe: A Bio-Bibliography* (Westport, CT: Greenwood Press, 1996).

Roper, Derek, *Reviewing before the 'Edinburgh': 1788–1802* (London: Methuen & Co, 1978).

Rose, Mark, *Authors and Owners: The Invention of Copyright* (Cambridge, MA: Harvard University Press, 1993).

Ross, Marlon B., *The Contours of Masculine Desire: Romanticism and the Rise of Women's Poetry* (Oxford: Oxford University Press, 1989).

Russell, Gillian and Clara Tuite, 'Introducing Romantic Sociability', in *Romantic Sociability: Social Networks and Literary Culture in Britain, 1770–1840*, ed. Gillian Russell and Clara Tuite (Cambridge: Cambridge University Press, 2002), pp. 1–23.

Rutherford, Andrew (ed.), *Byron: Augustan and Romantic* (London: Macmillan, 1990).

Saglia, Diego, '"Freedom's Charter'd Air": The Voices of Liberalism in Felicia Hemans's *The Vespers of Palermo*', *Nineteenth-Century Literature*, 58:3 (2003), 326–67.

Sangster, Matthew, 'British Institutions, Literary Production and National Glory in the Romantic Period', *POETICA*, 82 (2014), 39–57.

Sangster, Matthew, '"You have not advertised out of it": Samuel Taylor Coleridge and Francis Jeffrey on Authorship, Networks and Personalities', *Romanticism and Victorianism on the Net*, 61 (April 2012), https://doi.org/10.7202/1018602ar.

Saunders, J.W., *The Profession of English Letters* (London: Routledge and Kegan Paul, 1964).

Scott, Grant F., 'Felicia Hemans and Romantic Ekphrasis', in *Felicia Hemans: Reimagining Poetry in the Nineteenth Century*, ed. Nanora Sweet and Julie Melnyk (Basingstoke: Palgrave, 2001), pp. 36–54.

Schellenberg, Betty A., *The Professionalization of Women Writers in Eighteenth-Century Britain* (Cambridge: Cambridge University Press, 2005).

Schoenfield, Mark, *British Periodicals and Romantic Identity: The "Literary Lower Empire"* (New York: Palgrave Macmillan, 2009).

Sharafuddin, Mohammed, *Islam and Romantic Orientalism* (London: I.B. Tauris, 1994).

Siskin, Clifford, *The Historicity of Romantic Discourse* (Oxford: Oxford University Press, 1988).

Siskin, Clifford, *The Work of Writing: Literature and Social Change in Britain 1700–1830* (Baltimore: Johns Hopkins University Press, 1998).

Sisman, Adam, *The Friendship: Wordsworth and Coleridge* (New York: Viking, 2007).

Speck, W.A., *Robert Southey: Entire Man of Letters* (New Haven: Yale University Press, 2006).

St Clair, William, *The Godwins and the Shelleys: A Portrait of a Family* (London: Faber and Faber, 1989).

St Clair, William, *The Reading Nation in the Romantic Period* (Cambridge, Cambridge University Press, 2004).

Stauffer, Andrew, 'Hemans by the Book', *European Romantic Review*, 22:3 (2011), 373–80.

Stewart, David, *Romantic Magazines and Metropolitan Literary Culture* (Basingstoke: Palgrave Macmillan, 2011).

Stillinger, Jack, 'The "Story" of Keats', in *The Cambridge Companion to Keats*, ed. Susan J. Wolfson (Cambridge: Cambridge University Press, 2001), pp. 246–60.

Storey, Mark, "Bob Southey! – Poet Laureate': Public and Private in Southey's Poems of 1816', in *Robert Southey and the Contexts of English Romanticism*, ed. Lynda Pratt (Aldershot: Ashgate, 2006), pp. 87–100.

Stott, Anne, *Hannah More: The First Victorian* (Oxford: Oxford University Press, 2003).

Suarez, Michael F. and Michael L. Turner (eds.), *The Cambridge History of the Book in Britain Volume 5: 1695–1830* (Cambridge: Cambridge University Press, 2009).

Suarez, Michael F., 'Towards a Bibliometric Analysis of the Surviving Record', in *The Cambridge History of the Book in Britain Volume 5: 1695–1830*, ed. Michael F. Suarez and Michael L. Turner (Cambridge: Cambridge University Press, 2009), pp. 39–65.

Sutherland, John, 'The British Book Trade and the Crash of 1826', *The Library*, 6th Series, 9 (June 1987), 148–61.

Sutherland, John, *The Life of Walter Scott: A Critical Biography* (Oxford: Blackwell, 1995).

Sutherland, Kathryn, 'Fictional Economies: Adam Smith, Walter Scott and the Nineteenth-Century Novel', *ELH: English Literary History*, 54 (Spring 1987), 97–127.

Sweet, Nanora and Julie Melnyk, 'Introduction' to *Felicia Hemans: Reimagining Poetry in the Nineteenth Century* (Basingstoke: Palgrave, 2001), pp. 1–15.

Taylor, Barbara D., '*Felicia Hemans and *The Domestic Affections, and Other Poems*, or Mrs Browne's Publishing Project', *Women's Writing*, 21:1 (2014), 9–24.

Taylor, Barbara D., 'The Search for a Space: A Note on Felicia Hemans and the Royal Society', in *Felicia Hemans: Reimagining Poetry in the Nineteenth Century*, ed. Nanora Sweet and Julie Melnyk (Basingstoke: Palgrave, 2001), pp. 115–23.

Tenger, Zeynep and Paul Trolander, 'Genius versus Capital: Eighteenth-Century Theories of Genius and Adam Smith's Wealth of Nations', *Modern Language Quarterly*, 55 (June 1994), 169–89.

Tessone, Natasha, 'Displaying Ireland: Sydney Owenson and the Politics of Spectacular Antiquarianism', *Éire-Ireland*, 37 (Fall/Winter 2002), 169–86.

Throsby, Corin, 'Flirting with Fame: Byron's Anonymous Female Fans', *The Byron Journal*, 32:2 (2004), 115–23.

Tonra, Justin, 'Masks of Refinement: Pseudonym, Paratext, and Authorship in the Early Poetry of Thomas Moore', *European Romantic Review*, 25:5 (2014), 551–73.

Turner, Cheryl, *Living by the Pen: Women Writers in the Eighteenth Century* (London: Routledge, 1992).

Towsey, Mark and Kyle Roberts (eds.), *Before the Public Library: Reading, Community, and Identity in the Atlantic World, 1650–1850* (Leiden and Boston: Brill, 2017).

Valenza, Robin, *Literature, Language, and the Rise of the Intellectual Disciplines in Britain, 1680–1820* (Cambridge: Cambridge University Press, 2009).

Walpole, Hugh, *Reading: An Essay* (New York and London: Harper & Brothers, 1926).

Walter Scott Digital Archive, Edinburgh University Library, http://www.walter-scott.lib.ed.ac.uk.

Wellesley Index to Victorian Periodicals, 1824–1900, http://wellesley.chadwyck.com.

Wheatley, Kim (ed.), *Romantic Periodicals and Print Culture* (London: Frank Cass, 2003).

Wheatley, Kim, *Shelley and his Readers: Beyond Paranoid Politics* (Columbia, MO: University of Missouri Press, 1999).

White, Newman Ivey, *Shelley*, 2 vols (New York: Alfred A. Knopf, 1940).

White, Simon J., *Robert Bloomfield, Romanticism and the Poetry of Community* (Aldershot: Ashgate, 2007).

White, Simon, John Goodridge and Bridget Keegan (eds.), *Robert Bloomfield: Lyric, Class and the Romantic Canon* (Lewisburg: Bucknell University Press, 2006).

Williams, David, 'The Missions of David Williams and James Tilly Matthews to England', *English Historical Review*, 53 (October 1938), 651–68.

Williams, Raymond, *Culture and Society 1780–1950* (London: Penguin, 1961).

Wimsatt, William K. and Monroe C. Beardsley, 'The Intentional Fallacy', *Sewanee Review*, 54 (Summer 1946), 468–88.

Woolf, Virginia, *A Room of One's Own*, in *A Room of One's Own and Three Guineas*, ed. Anna Snaith (Oxford: Oxford University Press, 2015), pp. 1–86.

Wolfson, Susan J., *Romantic Interactions: Social Being and the Turns of Literary Action* (Baltimore: Johns Hopkins University Press, 2010).

Wu, Duncan, *William Hazlitt: The First Modern Man* (Oxford: Oxford University Press, 2008).

INDEX[1]

A

Abrams, M.H., 191
Addison, Joseph, 23, 240
Aikin, Lucy, 119, 262
Altick, Richard, 51, 56n17, 238n14, 289
Anacreon, 141–144, 146, 161
Analytical Review, 96–97, 99, 243
Andrews, Kerri, 283
Andrews, Sir Joseph, 186
Annesley, Robert Matthew, 203
Annuals, 53, 118, 155, 158, 160, 173
Anti-Jacobin, 31, 43, 44, 87, 101, 235, 240–248, 271
   influence of style, 259
   'The Jacobin,' 244–246
   'New Morality,' 43, 247
   rationale for style, 246
Anti-Jacobin Review, 98–101, 118, 195, 221, 237, 244, 248
   on Capel Lofft, 221
   on Mary Cockle, 118

   on *Memoirs of Modern Philosophers*, 98–101
Antonius, Marcus, 109
Athenaeum (1807–9), 262
Athenaeum (1828–1921), 239
Atkinson, Joseph, 141
Austen, Jane, 37, 62, 102–103, 205, 215, 304, 308
Authorship
   connection between lives and works, 3–6, 14–20, 326–330
   death of the author, 4, 332
   denigration of authorial labour, 27–33, 190, 247, 321
   difficulty of living by the pen, 6, 20–22, 35–36, 53, 57, 179, 194, 231
   and exclusion, 11, 39–41, 101, 155, 198, 212, 215, 217, 247, 251, 333
   modes of success, 28–29, 33–35, 121, 273, 315

---

[1] Note: Page numbers followed by 'n' refer to notes.

© The Author(s) 2021   355
M. Sangster, *Living as an Author in the Romantic Period*, Palgrave
Studies in the Enlightenment, Romanticism and Cultures of Print,
https://doi.org/10.1007/978-3-030-37047-3

Authorship (*cont.*)
  outline of changes during the
      Romantic period, 41–46
  and professional status, 1–2, 5, 14,
      21–26, 81, 90, 117, 123, 137,
      158, 201, 208, 229, 231,
      233–234, 248–250, 296, 308,
      309, 315, 321, 323
  reasons for considering,
      8–11, 332–334
  Romantic ideal, 2, 18, 36–37,
      39–41, 129, 136, 313, 315,
      318, 320, 329–332
  and sociability, 7, 8, 14, 84, 93, 102,
      111, 120, 139, 140, 146, 148,
      166–167, 172, 278, 281, 295
  See also author name entries for
      specific case studies

B
Baillie, Joanna, 173, 175
Ballantyne, James, 77, 81n86,
      298–301, 305–307
Ballantyne, John, 81n86, 298,
      300–302, 305
Banks, Joseph, 182
Barbauld, Anna Laetitia, 33, 39, 112,
      155, 163
  Eighteen Hundred and Eleven, 33
  reviewing Felicia Hemans, 163
Barrell, John, 42n91
Barrett, Eaton Stannard, 267–269
Barthes, Roland, 4, 5, 332
Barton, Bernard, 36, 175
Batchelor, Jennie, 192, 208, 211
Beardsley, Monroe C., 14n1
Beaumont, Francis, 301
Bebbington, D.W., 291
Beckford, William, 241
Bedford, Grosvenor Charles, 130,
      134, 137
Behrendt, Stephen C., 41, 111, 168

Beilby, Ralph, 291
Benatti, Francesca, 139n56
Benger, Elizabeth, 101
Bennett, Andrew, 5, 38, 39, 321, 325
Bentley, Richard, 46, 330
Bentley, Thomas, 181
Betham, Matilda, 94, 111–118
  'Fancy fettered,' 113–115
  The Lay of Marie, 115–118
  relationship with Charles Lamb,
      112–113, 116–118
  relationship with George
      Dyer, 111–116
  relationship with Robert Southey,
      115–116, 118
Big Six, 36, 39, 311, 332
Black Dwarf, 239
Blacklock, Thomas, 86, 198, 199
Blackwood, William, 68, 75–76, 169,
      170, 305
Blackwood's Edinburgh Magazine, 5,
      19, 32, 45, 75, 86, 88–90, 96,
      102, 151, 169, 170, 178, 237,
      239, 267, 269, 325–326
  absolutely coining money, 178
  approbation of Walter Scott, 86
  attack on William Hazlitt, 32
  attacks on Leigh Hunt and his
      circle, 19, 88–90
  generosity to Percy Shelley, 88–90
  on genius, 90, 326
  George Croly on Percy Shelley, 269
  on Thomas Moore's *Lalla Rookh*, 151
  venue for Felicia Hemans'
      poetry, 169
Blair, Alexander, 183
Blair, Hugh, 86, 198
Blake, William, 5n6, 15–16, 29, 36,
      37, 39, 217
  annotations in Joshua Reynolds'
      Works, 15–16
  patronage from William Hayley, 217
Blakey, Dorothy, 207, 213

Bland Burges, James, 186, 193
Bloom, Harold, 319
Bloomfield, B.C., 219n133, 222, 228
Bloomfield, George, 219, 228
Bloomfield, Hannah, 226
Bloomfield, Robert, 48, 74, 215–229,
    319, 320
  appropriations of identity, 222, 227
  defence of conduct, 227
  denigrated after death, 228
  difficulty of reinvention, 224
  efforts to support, 225–226
  launch, 219
  patronage, 217, 219, 220, 222,
    224–226, 228
  situation in the 1800s, 222
  situation in the 1810s, 223
  success of *The Farmer's Boy*,
    219, 222
  suspicions regarding character
    of, 226–227
  tensions with Capel Lofft, 220
Bluestocking Circle, 27, 32, 278,
    279, 286
Borges, Jorge Luis, 3–5
Boscawen, Frances, 278–280,
    285, 286
Boscawen, William, 187, 193
Bourdieu, Pierre, 7, 9, 10
Bowles, Caroline, 137n52
Bowyer, William, 184
Bradley, Andrea, 256
Brant, Clare, 94
Briggs, Asa, 76n74
Bristed, John, 248
British Critic, 112, 165, 213,
    237, 241
Brontë, Charlotte, 123, 137n52
Brooke, Edward, 184
Brooks, Maria Gowen, 137n52
Brougham, Henry, 196–197,
    248, 251

Brunton, Mary, 14
Bryant, William Curran, 175
Brydges, Samuel Egerton, 225
Bunyan, John, 135
Burke, Edmund, 182, 193, 237,
    238n14, 276, 277
Burney, Frances, 24, 215, 287
Burns, Robert, 162, 195,
    198, 199–200, 319, 327
Butler, Marilyn, 241–243
Butler, Samuel, 188
Byron, George Gordon, 5n6, 9, 19,
    25, 27–29, 31, 36, 37, 39, 45,
    46, 57, 59, 63, 64, 66, 70, 74,
    76, 79, 81, 82, 89, 101, 105,
    117, 119, 122, 134, 146, 150,
    152, 154, 158, 175, 187, 189,
    197, 218, 219, 251, 264,
    266–268, 271–275, 293–295,
    301, 302, 308–315, 318, 327,
    329, 330
  on all-author authorship, 27–28
  Beppo, 27
  change of tack in 1816, 313–314
  the character of the poet, 315
  debate on fate of memoirs, 81–82
  effects of wealth and status, 312,
    313, 315, 319
  English Bards and Scotch Reviewers,
    27, 57, 187, 218, 251
  highly-rated poets, 28, 61
  on James Montgomery, 70
  on John Murray, 134
  on the Moore-Jeffrey duel, 146
  payments for early Murray
    poems, 63, 313
  power of self-presentation, 312
  relationship with Leigh Hunt,
    105, 117
  on Robert Southey, 122
  scorned by Mary Cockle, 119
  site of fascination, 311

C

Cadell, Robert, 46, 307, 330
Cadell, Thomas, the elder, 284
Cadell and Davies, 161, 299
Cadogan, William, 285
Campbell, Thomas, 28, 68, 74, 158, 164, 254–256, 308, 319
Canning, George, 43, 235, 244
Carlyle, Thomas, 240
Carpenter, Charlotte, 297
Carpenter, James, 144, 148–150
Carswell, Catherine, 200
Castlereagh, Lord (Robert Stewart), 150
Chalmers, Alexander, 68
Chambers, Frances, 35
Chambers, Robert, 196, 199–201, 203, 204, 304
Chambers's Edinburgh Journal, 200, 201, 239
Champion, 93
Chandler, James, 41, 138, 144, 146
Chapone, Hester, 285
Chateaubriand, François-René, 152, 187
Chatterton, Thomas, 127, 187
Chaucer, Geoffrey, 88
Cheap Repository Tracts, 288–292
Chorley, Henry Fothergill, 156–157, 167, 171–174
Christensen, Jerome, 28n43, 311, 313
Christie, William, 250n50, 253
Circulating libraries, 54, 60, 192, 207
Claims of Literature, 187–193, 215
Clare, John, 117
Clarkson, Thomas, 17
Clery, E.J., 33, 205n82
Clive, John, 272
Cobbett, William, 227, 239, 274–275
Cochran, Peter, 313
Cockburn, Henry, 233–234
Cockle, Mary, 118–120

Cockney School, 86–90, 265, 267, 269
Colburn, Henry, 34, 330
Coleridge, John Taylor, 103–104, 167–168, 264–265, 268–270
    on Eaton Stannard Barrett, 269
    on Felicia Hemans, 167–168
    on Henry Hart Milman, 270
    on Leigh Hunt, 104
    on Percy Shelley, 103–104, 264–265
Coleridge, Samuel Taylor, 5, 15, 17–19, 24, 26, 29, 36–38, 43, 46, 55, 69, 86, 102, 112, 115, 124, 126, 129, 137, 145, 158, 165, 170, 175, 187, 217–219, 247, 264, 288, 312, 315, 317–319, 321, 322, 324, 326–329
    Biographia Literaria, 24, 326
    as depicted by William Hazlitt, 328–329
    early relationship with Robert Southey, 86, 124
    on labouring-class writers, 218
    letters to Francis Jeffrey, 17–19
    marginalia, 15
    on Matilda Betham, 112
    privilege, 319
    scorning Matthew Lewis and Thomas Moore, 145
    Wedgwood annuity, 29, 55, 217
Coleridge, Sara, 118
Collins, A.S., 237
Connell, Philip, 135
Constable, Archibald, 76, 77, 299–302, 305–307, 330
Cooke, Mary, 103
Cookesley, William, 30
Cooper, James Fenimore, 175
Copeland, Edward, 55, 56
Corfield, Penelope, 23, 231, 249, 321

Cottle, Joseph, 125, 127
Cowper, William, 135, 217
Cox, Jeffrey, 8, 86–88
Crabbe, George, 238, 272, 317
Craig, David, 131
Critical Review, 99, 112, 125, 212, 220, 237, 241, 243, 249
Croker, John Wilson, 33–34, 266, 269
  on Anna Laetitia Barbauld, 33
  on George Croly, 269
  on John Keats, 266
  on Sydney Owenson, Lady Morgan, 33–34
Croly, George, 269, 272
Cronin, Richard, 19, 32, 81n89, 146, 331
Crosby, Benjamin, 223
Cross, Nigel, 207, 215
Curran, Stuart, 259
Currie, Janette, 317

D
Dale, Thomas, 183, 206, 209, 210
Dallas, Robert Charles, 63, 64
Dart, Gregory, 14, 89
Darwin, Erasmus, 269
Davenport, Selina, 207
Davis, Leith, 139n56
Davis, Lockyer, 184
Dawson, Richard, 181
Day, Thomas, 181
de Castro, Guillen, 104
de Genlis, Félicité, 120
De Quincey, Thomas, 240, 327, 329
de Staël, Germaine, 112, 162, 165
de Vega Carpio, Lope, 104
Della Cruscan poetry, 27, 30, 31, 270
Demers, Patricia, 281, 293
Denney, Peter, 224, 227
Dickens, Charles, 308
Disraeli, Benjamin, 329

D'Israeli, Isaac, 21–23, 27, 66–69, 136, 180, 187, 188, 194, 200, 201, 203, 204, 229
  on authors by profession, 22
  Calamities of Authors, 21, 66–68
  on genius, 21
  reviewed by Robert Southey, 136–137, 229–231
  on Robert Heron, 194, 200, 204
Donaldson v. Beckett, 78
Donegall, Barbara, 146, 147
Downey, Edmund, 291
Downman Hugh, 183
Dryden, John, 188, 299
Du Mitand, Louis, 203
Duncan, Ian, 154, 296
Dundas, Robert, 297
Dybikowski, James, 180, 189, 193
Dyer, George, 68, 111–113, 115, 116

E
Edgar, Chad, 160n116
Edgeworth, Maria, 39, 215
Edinburgh Annual Register, 115, 164, 301
Edinburgh Monthly Magazine, 75
Edinburgh Monthly Review, 169
Edinburgh Review, 17–18, 31, 44–45, 48, 57, 66, 70, 72, 76, 80, 129, 135, 145, 150, 155–156, 197, 233–235, 237–239, 246, 248–264, 272, 300, 302, 326, 331
  assertions of authority, 234, 248, 251, 256, 259, 272
  character of, 44, 234, 235, 249, 254
  coverage, 251
  decline of, 331
  distribution arrangements, 76, 80
  on Felicia Hemans, 155–156
  on James Montgomery, 44, 70, 260–264

Edinburgh Review (*cont.*)
　on the Lake School, 18, 256–257
　rates of payment, 249
　on Robert Southey,
　　252–253, 256–257
　Robert Southey's rejection of,
　　129, 262
　sales of, 237
　on Thomas Campbell, 255–256
　on Thomas Moore, 31, 145,
　　150–151, 257–260
　on Walter Scott, 300, 302
　on William Herbert, 66
Edwards, Elizabeth, 171n151
Eger, Elizabeth, 32, 286
Eisner, Eric, 327
Eliot, T.S., 2, 5
　'Tradition and the Individual
　　Talent,' 2
Elmsley, Peter, 126
Enfield, William, 212
English PEN, 1
English, James F., 10n14
English Review, 213, 242, 243
Erickson, Lee, 69, 331
Examiner, 45, 88, 104, 109, 110,
　149, 239
Ezell, Margaret, 87

F
Fairer, David, 132
Feldman, Paula R., 112, 116, 117,
　157, 158, 164, 165n134, 168,
　169n142, 174
Ferris, Ina, 34n66, 184n23, 251, 302
Finn, Margot, 55, 201, 202
FitzGerald, Pamela, 119
Fitzgerald, William Thomas,
　187–189, 226
Fitzroy, Augustus Henry, 219,
　221–225, 227

Fletcher, John, 301
Forster, Edward, 299
Foucault, Michel, 8, 40
Fox, Charles James, 182, 256
Franklin, Benjamin, 181
Fraser's Magazine, 239
Frederick the Great, 182
French Revolution, 26, 32, 42, 49,
　181, 275
Frend, William, 100
Fulford, Tim, 122n1, 222, 224

G
Gales, Joseph, 69
Gamer, Michael, 37, 65n43,
　122–123, 126, 128–129,
　205n82, 205n83
Garrick, David, 283–285
Garside, Peter, 14n3, 74n70, 206, 302
Gentleman's Magazine, 66, 165,
　184, 242
Gifford, William, 27, 30–31, 82, 101,
　117, 130, 131, 133, 236, 244,
　246–247, 249, 300
　attacked by William Hazlitt, 31
　The Baviad and early career, 30
　editor of *Anti-Jacobin*, 30, 246, 247
　editor of *Quarterly Review*, 31, 130,
　　236, 300
　invoked in debate on Byron's
　　memoirs, 82
Gillies, Mary Ann, 305n91
Gillray, James, 43
Gilmartin, Kevin, 288
Godwin, William, 42–43, 62, 97–101,
　247, 265
Goldberg, Brian, 25, 123
Goldgar, Anne, 83
Gosse, Edmund, 139, 140
Grafton, Duke of, *see* Fitzroy,
　Augustus Henry

Great Britain Philatelic
  Society, 109n73
Griffin, Dustin, 21n23, 25,
  81n86, 216
Groom, Nick, 127n15
Grosvenor, Richard, 30
Guest, Harriet, 44
Gwatkin, Ann, 284

H

Hall, William Henry, 35
Hamilton, Charles, 96
Hamilton, Elizabeth, 93–102
  betrayed by Mary Hays, 94–95
  revenge in *Memoirs of Modern
    Philosophers*, 98–101
  reviewed by Mary Hays, 96–98
  self-fashioning, 95, 97, 98
Hammond, Brean, 54
Hamsun, Knut, 9
Harris, John, 77
Hastings, Warren, 96
Hawkins, Ann R., 212n106
Haydon, Benjamin Robert, 85,
  90–93, 225
Hayley, William, 29, 217
Hays, Mary, 93–102
  Memoirs of Emma Courtney, 98
  mocked in the *Anti-Jacobin
    Review*, 98–101
  review of Elizabeth
    Hamilton, 96–98
  traduced in *Memoirs of Modern
    Philosophers*, 98–101
Haywood, Ian, 224
Hazlitt, William, 31–32, 91, 140,
  234, 235, 236, 240, 248,
  293–295, 298, 304, 310,
  312, 327–329
  on the *Edinburgh Review*, 234, 248
  on Lord Byron, 293, 310, 312

on the *Quarterly Review*, 236
on Samuel Taylor
  Coleridge, 328–329
on Thomas Moore, 140
on Walter Scott, 293–295, 298, 304
on William Gifford, 31
Heber, Reginald, 164, 171, 271
  on Henry Hart Milman, 271
Heidegger, Martin, 190
Helme, Elizabeth, 207
Hemans, Felicia, 39, 48, 121,
  154–175, 259, 275, 281,
  297, 317
  annual verse, 160
  association with John Murray,
    164–167, 169, 171
  association with William
    Blackwood, 169–170
  connections with female
    authors, 172–173
  considered by Francis
    Jeffrey, 155–156
  cosmopolitanism, 161–162, 175
  Dartmoor, 170–171
  early correspondents, 163–164
  early life and education, 160–163
  'Epitaph on Mr. W—, a Celebrated
    Mineralogist,' 166–167
  financial gains from career, 157–159
  generous paratexts, 175
  patronage, 161, 163
  Poems (1808), 161–163
  reception of early work, 163
  reviews of 1810s works,
    164–165, 167–169
  social performance,
    158–159, 174–175
  theatrical work (*The Vespers of
    Palermo*), 171–174
  *Wallace's Invocation to
    Bruce*, 169–170
Henley, Samuel, 241, 242

Herbert, William, 57–66, 71, 251
  Helga, 58–59, 65–66
Heron, Robert, 48, 86, 194–204,
    209, 216, 225, 226, 229–231
  death, 204
  early life and education, 197–198
  incarceration, 203
  letter to the Literary Fund, 194–196
  literary profits, 202
  moral character, 200–201
  and Robert Burns, 199–200
  social performance, 201–202
  St Kilda in Edinburgh, 196, 198
Higgins, David, 5n7, 46, 325–327
Hill, Herbert, 124, 126, 130
The Hive, 239
Hobhouse, John Cam, 82, 269
Hoeveler, Diane Long, 213
Hogg, James, 317
Holcroft, Frances, 112
Holcroft, Thomas, 43, 247
Hole, Robert, 278, 283
Holland, Lord, *see* Vassall-Fox,
    Henry Richard
Holmes, Richard, 55, 56
Home, William, 297
Homer, 81n86, 270
Hone, William, 42
Hood, Thomas (publisher), 221, 223
Hookham, Edward, 35
Hookham, Thomas, 206, 213
Horne, Richard Henry, 139
Horne Tooke, John, 245
Horner, Francis, 248
Howard Payne, John, 267
Hunt, Leigh, 19, 42, 45, 86–89, 91,
    92, 94, 101–111, 117, 139, 163,
    240, 266, 319, 329
  correspondence with Lord
    Holland, 104–106
  correspondence with the
    Shelleys, 106–111

  on grief and art, 107–108
  on imaginative flight, 106–107
  on Mary Shelley's
    handwriting, 108–109
  practices of association, 87,
    104, 109
  praised by John Keats, 92
  on promotion and
    publishing, 109–110
  traduced by John Gibson Lockhart,
    19, 88–89
  on unworldliness, 111
Hunt, Marianne, 139, 267
Hunter, Alexander, 300
Hunter, Maria, 207
Hurst, Robinson & Co., 77, 306

I
Immortal Dinner, 85, 90–91
Inchbald, Elizabeth, 215, 329n28
Institutions, 2, 7–11, 19, 20, 24, 26,
    37, 39, 42, 48, 54, 88, 122, 170,
    181, 184, 191–192, 216, 227,
    234, 250, 255, 272, 274, 279,
    320, 325, 328
  See also Literary Fund; Royal Society
    of Literature
Irving, Washington, 79

J
Jackson, H.J., 5n6, 15–16, 137
Jackson, J.R. de J., 118
Jacobus, Mary, 322n13
Jeffrey, Francis, 17–18, 25, 31, 32, 44,
    57, 129, 145–147, 150, 151,
    155–156, 233, 235–238, 246,
    248, 251–253, 255–264, 272,
    302, 303, 319, 326
  addressed by Samuel Taylor
    Coleridge, 17–18

on the attitudes of the Lake
poets, 256–257
on the character of the *Edinburgh
Review*, 235, 272
on the circulation of ideas, 259–260
duel with Thomas Moore, 146
earnings from *Edinburgh
Review*, 249
on Felicia Hemans, 155–156
final gift to William Hazlitt, 32
on James Montgomery, 44,
70, 260–264
on Robert Southey,
252–253, 256–257
on Thomas Campbell, 255–256
on Thomas Moore, 31, 145,
150–151, 257–260
on Walter Scott, 302
on women, 155–156, 258–259
Jerdan, William, 36, 56, 86, 170
Jerningham, Charlotte, Lady
Bedingfield, 118
Jewsbury, Maria Jane, 156, 157, 162,
173, 175
Johnson, Alexander, 183
Johnson, Joseph, 243
Johnson, Samuel, 21, 24, 78–79,
216, 287
Jones, M.G., 276, 281
Jones, William, 170
Juvenal, 30

K
Keach, William, 33
Kearney, John, 143
Keats, John, 5n6, 20, 36–38, 46, 69,
85, 86, 88–93, 264–268, 310,
319, 324
attacked by John Wilson
Croker, 266–267

defended by Percy Shelley, 267–268
at the Immortal Dinner, 90–91
sonnets addressed to Benjamin
Robert Haydon, 91–93
Keen, Paul, 26, 180, 243, 318n5
Kelly, Gary, 95, 289, 290
Kelly, Linda, 144
Kelly, Ronan, 139
Kingston, John, 85
Kinnaird, Douglas, 313, 314
Klancher, Jon, 237–239, 242, 250
Knight, Charles, 238
Koenig, Charles, 235
Koenig, Friedrich, 52

L
Lafontaine, August, 207
Lake School, 18, 86–87, 121,
129, 138, 202, 252, 257,
264, 315
Lamb, Caroline, 101
Lamb, Charles, 36, 43, 85, 90–91,
112, 113, 116–118, 205, 240,
247, 317, 318
correspondence with Matilda
Betham, 116–118
at the Immortal Dinner, 90–91
Lamb, Mary, 112, 118
Landon, Letitia Elizabeth, 39, 86,
155, 175, 294, 295, 298, 329
on her own reputation, 329
on Walter Scott, 294, 295,
298, 309
Lane, William, 205–208
Lansdowne, Marquess of, *see*
Petty-Fitzmaurice, Henry
Lee, Debbie, 222
Lennox, Charlotte, 35, 187
Lévi-Strauss, Claude, 41
Lewis, Matthew, 145, 319

Literary Fund, 20, 24, 35–36, 48, 81, 111, 112n83, 140, 159, 179–194, 197, 203, 206–208, 210, 214–216, 226, 229–231, 247
   Anniversary Dinners, 186–187
   character of committee and subscribers, 24, 183, 193
   David Williams' ambitions for, 81, 179, 189, 191, 193
   initial challenges, 181–184
   production of *Claims of Literature*, 187
   Robert Southey's negative view, 230–231
   scale of applications, 35, 230
Literary Gazette, 36, 170
Literary Journal, 212
Lloyd, Charles, 95
Lloyd Baker, Thomas, 226–227
Lockhart, John Gibson, 19, 88, 89–90, 102, 134, 267, 296n64, 301
Lofft, Capel, 218–221, 224
London Magazine, 239, 326
Longman & Co., 47, 62–63, 72–74, 76–80, 128, 131n29, 132, 150, 152, 153, 206, 299, 305
   copyright divisions, 77–79
   entanglements with Hurst, Robinson & Co., 77
   half-profits payments, 62–63
   James Montgomery's *The World before the Flood*, 72–74
   publishing Eliza Parsons, 206
   publishing Robert Southey, 62–63, 128
   publishing Walter Scott, 299
   relationship with John Murray, 79–80
   relationship with Thomas Moore, 150, 152, 153
   William Godwin's *Lives of Edward and John Phillips*, 62
Longman, Thomas Norton, 80, 119, 150
Lonsdale, Lord, *see* Lowther, William
Low, Dennis, 137n52
Lowther, William, 217, 227
Lyrical Ballads, 5, 70, 86, 205, 288, 321

M
Macaulay, Thomas Babbington, 135
Macqueen, Robert, Lord Braxfield, 297
Maginn, William, 325
Malthus, Thomas Robert, 170
Mandell, Laura, 160
Marat, John-Paul, 245
Marcet, Jane, 119
Marks, Cato, 278
Martin, James, 183
Matoff, Susan, 56
Mayer, Robert, 295
McGann, Jerome J., 38, 320
McGurl, Mark, 10n14
McKitterick, David, 53
Mee, Jon, 30, 43, 104
Mellor, Anne K., 39–40, 281
Melnyk, Julie, 159
Merry, Robert, 30
Miles, Robert, 205n82, 256
Milman, Henry Hart, 171–172, 175, 267, 268, 270–272
Milton, John, 62, 70, 72, 79, 88, 90, 270, 271
Minerva Press, 205–207, 241
Mirror of Literature, Amusement, and Instruction, 239
Mitchell, Robert, 183
Mitford, Mary Russell, 172–173
Moira, Earl of, *see* Rawdon, Francis

Mole, Tom, 28n43, 311, 313
Monkhouse, Thomas, 85
Montagu, Elizabeth, 216, 279, 280, 285, 286
Montgomery, James, 44, 69–75, 158, 260–264, 319
  origins and career, 69–70
  profits from *The World before the Flood*, 72–74
  savaged by the *Edinburgh*, 44, 70, 260–264
  The World before the Flood, 70–75
Montgomery, Robert, 102
Monthly Magazine, 195, 198, 228, 237
Monthly Review, 62, 99, 112, 132, 163, 165, 172, 212, 213, 241, 243, 249, 252–253, 265, 288
  on Eliza Parsons, 212, 213
  on Felicia Hemans, 163, 165, 172
  on Mary Hays' *Emma Courtney*, 99
  on Matilda Betham, 112
  on Robert Southey, 252–253
Moore, Jane, 139n56
Moore, Thomas, 19, 22n25, 27, 28, 31, 48, 56, 74, 79, 81, 82, 121, 131n29, 138–155, 157, 158, 161, 202, 237, 257–260, 281, 297, 304, 308, 312, 319, 329
  admired by Byron, 27
  attacked by Francis Jeffrey, 31, 145, 257–260
  attacks on his morality, 145
  Bermuda post, 144, 152
  character of, 139–140
  Corruption and *Intolerance*, 147
  costs of renting property, 56
  debate on Byron's memoirs, 81–82
  duel with Francis Jeffrey, 146
  early life and education, 140–141
  1810s satires, 149
  government pension, 154
  Irish Melodies annuity, 149, 153
  Lalla Rookh, 150–152
  at Leigh Hunt's, 139
  letter to Lady Barbara Donegall, 146–148
  as 'mediocre hero,' 138
  Odes of Anacreon, 141–143
  patronage, 141, 144, 147, 151, 153
  reputation-building and finances, 143–144
  writing biographies, 152
More, Hannah, 112, 119, 273–294, 296
  The Bas Bleu, 286–287
  Cheap Repository Tracts, 288–292
  early years and education, 282
  evoked by Jane Porter, 119
  friends and networks, 279, 281, 283
  legacies, 275, 293
  perceived authority, 275, 281
  refashioning popular forms, 278–279, 288–289
  Slavery, 287–288
  social fluency, 281
  success of *Percy*, 284–286
  Turner annuity, 282
  Village Politics, 276–280
  writing for theatre, 283–286
More, Patty, 282, 283
Morgan, Lady, *see* Owenson, Sydney, Lady Morgan
Morning Chronicle, 149, 150, 186, 247
Morning Post, 80, 125, 126, 172, 195, 247
Morris, Thomas, 181, 186
Morris, William, 308
Morton, Karen, 210n98
Moxon, Edward, 331
Murphy, Peter T., 37, 61n32
Murray, Alexander, 197

Murray, John, 47, 57, 59, 61–68,
    75–77, 79–82, 121, 129–130,
    132–134, 136, 150, 152,
    164–167, 169, 170, 172, 175,
    229, 235, 248, 262, 270, 272,
    300, 305, 311–314
  book trade politics, 68, 76–77
  debate on Byron's memoirs, 81–82
  estimate for *Calamities of
      Authors*, 66–68
  flattery, 66, 133
  publication proposals for William
      Herbert, 59
  publishing the *Quarterly Review*,
      129, 134, 235, 248, 300
  relationship with Byron, 63, 134,
      312, 314
  relationship with Felicia Hemans,
      164–167, 169, 170, 172
  relationship with Longman &
      Co., 79–80
  relationship with Robert Southey,
      64, 129, 132, 133
  relationship with Thomas Moore,
      81–82, 152–153
  relationship with Walter Scott,
      300, 305
  relationship with William
      Blackwood, 75–77
Murray, Lindley, 78
Myers, Mitzi, 291

N
National Union of Journalists, 1
Nelson, Horatio, Admiral, 64, 132,
    133, 162
Newlyn, Lucy, 38–39, 87, 172,
    319, 321
New Monthly Magazine, 162, 170,
    205n83, 239, 326
Newton, Isaac, 91
Nichols, John, 68, 184, 186

Nicholson, Matthew, 161, 163–164
Norman, Eliza, 207
North, Christopher, 178
North, Julian, 6n8, 327–328
North, Lady Anne, 285

O
Ogilvie, John, 143
Opie, Amelia, 119
Opie, John, 112
Otway, Thomas, 187, 188
Owenson, Sydney, Lady Morgan,
    33–36, 39, 269

P
Paine, Thomas, 43, 247
Paley, William, 280
Parker, Mark, 240n21
Parry, John, 171
Parsons, Eliza, 48, 205–216, 225,
    226, 229, 231, 241
  The Castle of Wolfenbach, 211–212
  claims for works, 210
  consequences of writing for
      profit, 213–216
  in debtors' prison, 209
  first Literary Fund application, 208
  life story, 206
  reviewers' opinions of her work,
      212–213, 241
  writing for the Minerva
      Press, 206–207
Patronage, 23, 25, 170, 330
  Blake, William, 217
  Bloomfield, Robert, 217, 219, 220,
      222, 224–226, 228
  Coleridge, Samuel Taylor,
      29, 55, 217
  Gifford, William, 30
  Hamilton, Charles, 96
  Hemans, Felicia, 161, 163

Heron, Robert, 199, 216
  Literary Fund, 184, 229, 231
  Moore, Thomas, 141, 144, 147,
      148, 152, 154
  More, Hannah, 283
  Parsons, Eliza, 216
  Scott, Walter, 28, 297
  Southey, Robert, 127, 130, 137
  Wordsworth, William, 29, 217
Peacock, Thomas Love, 35,
    102, 329
Pearson, Jacqueline, 120
Peel, Robert, 136, 158
Penny Magazine, 238, 239
Pepys, Sir William Weller, 287
Perry, James, 68, 150
Peterson, Linda H., 171
Petty-Fitzmaurice, Henry, 152, 154
Pfau, Thomas, 26
Pindemonte, Ippolito, 175
Pitt, William, the younger, 42, 182
Plumptre, John, 103
Poetical Register, 163, 221
Polidori, John William, 101
Political Register, 239
Polwhele, Richard, 101
Poovey, Mary, 38–39
Pope, Alexander, 21, 27, 81n86
Porter, Jane, 94, 118–120, 164
  letter to Mary Cockle, 119–120
Porteus, Beilby, Bishop of
    London, 279
Power, James, 149, 153
Pratt, Lynda, 122n1, 137
Priestley, Joseph, 247
Prince of Wales (later George IV),
    141, 144, 161, 194, 216
Prout, Samuel, 60
Publishing
  at author's expense, 59–61
  book trade co-operation, 75–81
  copyright divisions, 77–79

costs of paper and printing,
    52–53, 66–67
  developments during 1820s,
      52–53, 330
  Fourdrinier papermaking
      machine, 46, 53
  half-profits arrangements, 61–63
  limited potential profits, 20, 22, 25,
      29, 53–57, 67–69, 191
  ongoing sales, 72, 128
  prevailing model around 1800, 52
  printing press, 46, 52
  printing press, steam-driven, 52, 238
  relative cost of books, 55–57
  sale of copyright, 63–65
  stereotyping, 46, 52, 238
  by subscription, 65
  See also authors' and publishers'
      names for specific cases
Puddicombe, John Newell, 288
Punter, David, 205n82
Pye, Anne, 226
Pye, Henry James, 187
Pye, Walter, 226

Q
Quarterly Review, 31, 33–34, 44–45,
    48, 62, 64, 70, 87, 89, 129–132,
    134, 135, 157, 162, 165, 167,
    229, 233, 235–239, 244, 248–251,
    254–255, 262–272, 300, 326, 331
  on Anna Laetitia Barbauld, 33
  on *Calamities of Authors* and the
      Literary Fund, 229–230
  decline of, 331
  on Eaton Stannard Barrett, 268–269
  on Felicia Hemans, 162, 167
  on George Croly, 269
  on Henry Hart Milman, 269–271
  on James Montgomery, 262–263
  on John Keats, 266–267

Quarterly Review (*cont.*)
  origins, 235
  on Percy Shelley, 89, 264, 271
  processes of affiliation, 87, 271
  on Robert Southey, 130, 135
  Robert Southey's association with,
    129, 132, 133, 250
  sales of, 237
  on Sydney Owenson, Lady
    Morgan, 33–34
  on Thomas Campbell, 254–255
  Walter Scott's association with, 129,
    236, 249, 254–255, 300

R
Radcliffe, Ann, 39, 205, 213–215
Raven, James, 47, 52, 68
Rawdon, Francis, 141, 144, 152
Rees, Owen, 150
Reeve, Clara, 205
Reform Bill, 49
Reiman, Donald, 268
Republic of Letters, 83, 180, 194
Reynolds, John Hamilton, 102
Reynolds, Joshua, 15–16, 164
Rigaud, John Francis, 183
Rigney, Ann, 298, 309
Ring, John, 234
Ritchie, John, 85
Roberts, Kyle, 184n23
Roberts, William, 275–276, 279
Robertson, Fiona, 303
Robinson, Jeffrey C., 266n105
Robinson, Mary, 329n28
Roche, Regina Maria, 207
Rogers, Samuel, 25, 27–28, 60–61,
  74, 147, 148, 158, 175,
  197, 217, 225, 227, 308,
  319, 320
  admired by Byron, 27, 61
  assisting Robert Bloomfield, 225

  assisting William Wordsworth, 217
  invoked by Thomas Moore,
    147, 148
  personal wealth, 28
  publishing on his own
    account, 60–61
Roper, Derek, 247, 254
Roscoe, William, 161–162, 164, 170
Rose, Mark, 78n80
Ross, Marlon, 40
Rousseau, Jean-Jacques, 182
Royal Literary Fund, *see* Literary Fund
Royal Society of Literature,
  1, 170–171
Russell, Gillian, 84–85, 87, 91
Russell, John, 22n25, 154, 196
Ryder, Sean, 139n56

S
Saglia, Diego, 162
Samuel, Richard, 286
Saunders, Julia, 292
Schellenberg, Betty, 23–25
Schiller, Friedrich, 175
Schoenfield, Mark, 236, 248
Scott, Grant F., 169n143
Scott, Henry, Duke of Buccleuch, 28,
  297, 301
Scott, Walter, 25, 27–28, 36,
  45–46, 56, 59, 61, 66,
  74–77, 81n86, 86, 128–130,
  150, 154, 158, 164, 173, 175,
  201, 218, 236, 249–251, 254,
  255, 262, 268, 272–275,
  293–310, 312, 313, 315,
  317–320, 327
  admired by Byron, 27, 61
  association with the *Quarterly
    Review*, 129, 236, 249,
    254–255, 300
  Author of *Waverley*, 302–305

book trade entanglements, 298–301, 305–307
on the character of a good Review, 236
early years and education, 296–297
on the *Edinburgh Review*, 249, 255
and history, 298, 302, 307, 309
master of networking, 295–296
price of novels, 56
professional paradigm, 308–309
receipt of patronage, 28, 297
relationship with Felicia Hemans, 164, 173
scale of influence, 201, 294, 296, 303, 304, 308
on Thomas Campbell, 254–255
unmasking and debts, 306–307
Scott, Walter, the elder, 297
Secret History of the Court and Cabinet of St. Cloud, 80
Seward, Anna, 301
Shakespeare, William, 9, 112, 162
Sharafuddin, Mohammed, 139n56
Shelley, Mary, 39, 106–111
correspondence with Leigh Hunt, 106–111
Shelley, Percy, 5n6, 36–38, 46, 60, 61, 88–90, 102, 103, 106–111, 154, 235, 264, 265, 267–272, 314, 319–321, 323, 324, 327
attacked in the *Quarterly Review*, 264, 271
attacking the *Quarterly Review*, 235, 267–268
bird poems, 106
on Byron, 314
correspondence with Leigh Hunt, 106–111
gift to Leigh Hunt, 110
'Hymn to Intellectual Beauty,' 107
on the importance of poets, 321, 323
on John Keats, 267–268
praised in *Blackwood's*, 88–90
publishing on own account, 60, 61
titled privilege, 319
Shelley, William, 107–108
Shepherd, William, 131n29
Sheridan, Richard Brinsley, 152
Shiprut, Esther, 22
Sinclair, Sir John, 196
Siskin, Clifford, 26, 38, 242, 250, 320
Sisman, Adam, 322n11
Sismondi, Jean Charles Léonard de, 162
Smith, Adam, 79, 182, 190, 303
Smith, Charlotte, 29, 39, 65, 155, 178, 212n106, 319
Smith, James and Horace, 101, 187
Smith, Sydney, 248
Society of Authors, 1, 81
Solander, Daniel, 181
Southey, Edith, 118, 124
Southey, Herbert, 137
Southey, Robert, 16–17, 28, 43, 48, 63, 64, 70, 72, 73n68, 74, 86, 112, 115, 116, 118, 121–138, 140, 141, 144, 152–155, 157, 165, 220, 225, 229–231, 244, 246, 247, 249, 250, 252–253, 256, 257, 262–264, 271, 272, 281, 297, 300, 312, 330
association with the *Quarterly Review*, 129, 132, 133, 250
on authorship as a career, 123, 136–137
on *Calamities of Authors*, 136–137, 229–230
choosing own reviewers, 130

Southey, Robert (*cont.*)
  discomfort with John
      Murray, 133–134
  early life and education, 124–125
  editing the *Remains of Henry Kirke
      White*, 16–17, 127
  establishment at Keswick, 126
  government pension, 28, 128, 136
  held up as inspiration in the
      Quarterly Review, 272
  on James Montgomery, 262–263
  later prose, 135–136, 330
  Life of Nelson, 64, 132
  on the Literary Fund, 229–231
  parodied in the *Anti-
      Jacobin*, 244–246
  pragmatic approach, 128–129
  and professionalism, 123, 137
  profits from *Roderick, the Last of the
      Goths*, 63
  puffing, 102
  relationship with Matilda Betham,
      115–116, 118
  returns from *Madoc*, 127
  reviewed by Francis Jeffrey,
      252–253, 256–257
  on Robert Bloomfield, 220
  Wynn annuity and early periodical
      writing, 125–126
Speck, W.A., 125, 128
Spectator, 240
Spenser, Edmund, 88
Standard Novels, 46, 330
Stanier Clarke, James, 132
Stauffer, Andrew, 160
St Clair, William, 29, 47, 55,
      56, 61, 62, 74, 220, 237, 295
Steele, Richard, 240
Sterne, Laurence, 79, 199
Stevenson, Sir John, 149, 153
Stewart, David, 239, 240n21
Stockdale, John Joseph, 60, 141
Storey, Mark, 131

Stothard, Thomas, 60
Stott, Anne, 275, 277, 282, 287, 290
Street, Thomas George, 288
Stuart, Daniel, 125
Stuart, James, 181
Suarez, Michael F., 54n11
Subscription, 65
  Bloomfield, Robert, 225
  Burns, Robert, 195
  Charlotte Smith's *Elegiac
      Sonnets*, 178
  Cheap Repository Tracts, 291
  Eliza Parsons' *History of Miss
      Meredith*, 206, 216
  Felicia Hemans' *Poems* (1808), 161
  internal book trade lists, 65
  Isaac D'Israeli's *Calamities of
      Authors*, 68
  Literary Fund, 184, 194
  Sydenham, Floyer, 183
  Thomas Moore's *Anacreon*, 141
Sutherland, John, 77, 297, 300
Sutherland, Kathryn, 303, 305, 308
Swainson, Isaac, 183
Sweet, Nanora, 159
Swift, Jonathan, 198–199, 299
Sydenham, Floyer, 183

T
Tait's Edinburgh Magazine, 330–331
Talfourd, Thomas Noon, 214
Talleyrand-Périgord, Charles
      Maurice de, 80
Tasso, Torquato, 175
Taylor, Barbara D., 163, 170
Taylor, John, 117
Taylor, William, 127
Tegg, Thomas, 79, 80n84
Tenger, Zeynep, 190
Tessone, Natasha, 33n65
Thelwall, John, 245, 247
Thomson, James, 79, 198

Thrale, Hester, 287
Throsby, Corin, 311
Timperley, Charles Henry, 238
Tonra, Justin, 139n56, 143
Topham, Edward, 184
Towsey, Mark, 184n23
Trelawney, Edward John, 329
Trolander, Paul, 190
Tuite, Clara, 84–85, 87, 91
Turner, Cheryl, 54
Turner, J.M.W., 60
Turner, William, 282
Ty, Eleanor, 100
Tyler, Elizabeth, 124

V
Valenza, Robin, 26
Varma, Devendra, 213
Vassall-Fox, Henry Richard, 104–106,
    162, 227
Vernor and Hood, 74n70, 219, 223
Vesey, Elizabeth, 286
Virgil, 270
Voltaire, 91, 182, 241

W
Wagner, Richard, 9
Wakefield, Gilbert, 245, 247
Walpole, Horace, 205, 216, 276, 287
Walpole, Hugh, 309–310
Webb, Cornelius, 88
Wedgwood, Josiah, 29, 55, 181,
    217, 219
Wedgwood, Tom, 29, 55, 217, 219
Westall, Richard, 151
Westminster Review, 239, 326
Wheatley, Kim, 108–109, 259–260
White, Edmund Henry, 203
White, Henry Kirke, 16–17, 127

White, Newman Ivey, 88
White, Simon J., 219n131, 220, 222
Whitehurst, John, 181
Whittaker, George, 77
Wilkes, John, 184
Williams, David, 20, 24, 48, 81, 140,
    178–194, 201, 208, 215, 216,
    229–231, 247, 303
  attempts to interest patrons in the
    Literary Fund, 182–183
  on authors' value,
    179–180, 189–191
  belief in intellectual liberty, 180
  Claims of Literature, 189–193
  and the Club of Thirteen, 181
  on institutions, 192–193
  on patronage, 215–216
  reasons for establishing the Literary
    Fund, 24, 81, 179, 189
Williams, Raymond, 136
Wilton, Charles Pleydell
    Neale, 166–167
Wimsatt, William K., 14n1
Windham, William, 211,
    214n120, 227
Wollstonecraft, Mary, 40, 98
Wooler, Thomas, 239
Woolf, Virginia, 282
Wordsworth, William, 5, 19, 22, 26,
    29, 36–38, 46, 63, 69, 72, 85,
    90–93, 107, 129, 139–140,
    157–159, 197, 205, 217, 225,
    256, 257, 264, 288, 315,
    317–322, 324, 326, 327, 329
  awkwardness at parties,
    85, 139–140
  considered by the
    Edinburgh, 256–257
  considered by the Quarterly, 264
  Distributor of Stamps, 29, 85, 217
  'Essay, Supplementary' (1815), 22

Wordsworth, William (*cont.*)
    'Extempore Effusion Upon the
        Death of James Hogg,'
        157, 317–318
    on Felicia Hemans, 157, 159
    'High is our calling, Friend!,' 93
    at the Immortal Dinner, 90–91
    patronage, 29, 217
    payment for *The Excursion*, 63
    'Preface' to *Lyrical Ballads*, 5, 205,
        256, 288, 321, 323

privileged background, 319
on Robert Bloomfield, 225
shifts during the 1820s and 1830s,
    318, 325
Wu, Duncan, 267
Wynn, Charles Watkin Williams, 125,
    128, 158

Y
Yearsley, Ann, 288

Printed by Printforce, the Netherlands